Tonight She Was Finally Joel Shand's Wife!

He was more adept than she with the buttons, pausing to kiss her once, so deeply that Jessie began to slide into a euphoric haze, and then, more eager than ever, Joel drew a ragged breath and finished off the buttons.

The dress slid off her shoulders, and she shivered in the night air, until Joel ran his hands over her, slipping undergarments out of the way, caressing her breasts and slim waist and kissing her again until she was breathless.

He murmured endearments as he explored, with mouth and hands, the curves and valleys of her body. This was not the first time that they had lain together, but it was the first time they had come together without guilt or shame . . .

And when it was over, when they had reached the explosive peak and begun to subside into blissful drowsiness, Joel whispered, "If we wake up early enough in the morning, we could do this again before we cook breakfast. Or we could just forget about breakfast . . ."

DAYS
OF VALOR

A NOVEL BY

Willo Davis Roberts

WARNER BOOKS

A Warner Communications Company

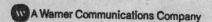

1

The adventure was under way.

Like everyone else in the wagon train on that April 12, 1857, Jessica Campbell Ryan had begun the day in a state of excitement and anticipation. And now, as she slid gratefully down from the hard wooden seat, surreptitiously rubbing at her aching bottom, Jessie finally felt the reality of it, that they were at last moving toward California. Her brown eyes, contrasting sharply with her pale, fine hair, were alight with her newfound joy.

Behind her, Annie Ryan grunted as she lowered her considerable bulk, then sighed with relief. "Won't be much left of me by the time we get there," she observed, "if it's all as rough as this. Maybe we could spare another blanket for padding to sit on."

Alongside them, ahead and straggling in their wake, other wagons rolled creakily to a welcome halt. Dogs, newly invigorated by this change in movement of their owners, barked and wagged their tails; the children—twenty-four of them in the entire company—were reviving as well, and running about so that mothers cried out to them in warning or with orders. Already, far ahead where the wagonmaster had drawn up the first of the eighty-two wagons, there rose a curl of smoke.

"Somebody's got supper going," Annie said. She was a heavy woman in her middle years, her hair going gray though her blue eyes were still bright. The lines in her face had deepened in the past two days, Jessie noted. Ever since the death of her only son, who had been buried beneath the Missouri soil only yesterday, never to see the western places for which they had all yearned.

Poor Ben. He probably would not have been any happier in California than he had been anywhere else, Jessie thought,

5

stretching her cramped limbs. And then, guilty reflection, *but at least I'm free of him now.*

She didn't want to think about Ben. "I'll look for some wood for a fire," she offered, and didn't hear Annie's response. In truth, though she was hungry and would welcome food, she didn't care if she ate cold biscuits and simply staggered into bed, she was that tired.

Once she began to walk around, however, she discovered that she was working the cramps out of her legs and that her energy, like that of the dogs and the children, was renewed.

Two other girls, perhaps sixteen and seventeen—from the wagon behind Annie's—were also exercising muscles too long inactive, and they looked at her expectantly as Jessie approached.

"We're supposed to find wood for the fire, but there doesn't seem to be anything but grass," the older one said in greeting. She was a pretty girl with glossy chestnut hair and a sprinkling of freckles across her nose; though she could not have been more than two years Jessie's junior, she seemed far removed from Jessie's nineteen years of experience. "I'm Mamie Groves, and this is my sister Alice."

"Jessie Campbell," Jessie said, and then remembered that, legally, she was the widow of Ben Ryan. The marriage had never been consummated, and Jessie had not felt in the least married to the bearlike young man who had never wanted to be married to her, either. "Ryan," she now added belatedly, and thought the girls looked at her with curiosity, as why would they not? "I think," she said, turning the subject, "that there might be wood over there, along the creek."

There were trees along that bank, sturdy cottonwoods for the most part, just putting on their leaves. The girls fell into step with one another, heading toward the small stream. Others were doing the same, eager to get supper going so that it could be eaten before dark.

Alice Groves was a younger replica of her sister Mamie; almost the only thing to distinguish one from the other was a crooked tooth which did nothing to diminish Alice's attractiveness.

"We saw you earlier," Alice said now, lifting her long skirts so as to keep them above the dusty grass. "You have such lovely hair, the kind I've always wanted instead of plain old brown. It's almost the color of ripening wheat, such a pale gold. And up close I see that you have brown eyes instead of blue like most blondes. It makes a striking combination."

6

Before Jessie could respond to this, Mamie chided, "You talk too much, Alice. There's a twig, you'd better take it."

Obediently, Alice stooped to pick it up, her expression rueful. "It's hardly big enough to bother with. We won't get much of a fire out of twigs."

"Everybody else is looking, too. We can't pass up anything. There, there's a whole limb. We should have brought an ax."

Indeed, a sizable branch had come down, and they looked at it, speculating on whether or not the three of them could drag it back to camp. There were smaller bits of debris, but this one limb alone was enough to assure a real campfire.

"Perhaps," Jessie suggested, "we could share it. Or even cook over the same fire."

"Do let's," Mamie agreed. "If you and I take this end of it, Alice can keep the other end from dragging too heavily. And then we'll come back for some water. It looks to be clean and fresh."

The Kansas River, which they had crossed shortly after dawn, had been muddy with spring runoff, hardly suited to drinking. This small stream, however, was still clear because its banks were grassy and clean. Livestock was being driven to drink below camp by a group of men and small boys so the women could fill their containers from here without contamination.

"I noticed you were traveling with an older woman," Alice said as they began to make their way back across the expanse of grass with the big limb. "Is she your mother?"

Briefly, Jessie thought of her own mother, dead now and buried on distant Beaver Island off the coast of Michigan. She swallowed. "No. Annie Ryan is—was—my mother-in-law." She hesitated, then added enough more so that she hoped Alice would give up the inquisition. "Her son, Ben—my husband—died in Missouri." She didn't mention that he had been shot to death, nor that he had not really been her husband at all, except in the eyes of the law. A marriage of convenience, it had been, and had proved no convenience to anyone.

"Oh, I'm sorry." Alice's gray eyes turned on her with sympathy. "You're so young to be a widow. And you have a baby, too, haven't you?"

Jessie stumbled and nearly went down with her portion of the cottonwood limb. This was what she had anticipated, the questions of her fellow travelers, their censure if they knew the truth. She had been over and over it in her mind,

7

indeed had scarcely slept for thinking of it. Whatever she said now would set the pattern, and she desperately wanted the friendship and the respect of the other women.

She withdrew her foot from the rabbit hole, or whatever it was, and regripped the branch to resume tugging it along. "I lost my own baby. She was born too soon, and she died." She heard their murmurs of sympathy and concentrated on telling as much of the truth as she had to, and not leaving any bad impressions unnecessarily. To be a good liar one had to have an excellent memory, Mama had always said. Better to tell the truth in the first place. Only sometimes that didn't seem wise, either.

"How sad," Mamie commiserated. "But there is a baby . . . ?"

There was a baby, of course. How to explain Lauren, without exposing too much?

"Annie and I—she was my husband's mother—have agreed to take care of him. He was born only two days ago, and his mother died in childbirth. His father was killed shortly before that, and there was no one to take him."

Her legs were trembling, whether with the effort of moving the heavy limb toward camp or because of her inner turmoil was uncertain. How to explain Lauren? No, dear God, it was too much to ask of her, to explain it all. She felt as if she spoke through a mouthful of fluff off the cottonwoods.

"I don't know much about babies; my own didn't live long enough for me to learn from her. But Annie knows about babies, and all manner of things about healing. Mrs. Allen, in the wagon ahead of ours, has a month-old child and milk aplenty for the both of them, so we're most fortunate. She will feed him for us."

"But what a chore to take on, two women by themselves!" Alice's gray eyes were big and round. "To rear a stranger's child alone!"

"No doubt Mrs. Ryan will marry again," Mamie speculated. "Heaven knows there are plenty of single men on this train to choose from." She giggled. "Ma says she's going to keep a close eye on us, because the farther we get from Missouri, the better we'll look to lonely men."

"As pretty as you both are, I'm sure they're looking already," Jessie said, and was relieved that they had reached the wagons where Mrs. Groves came forward with an ax to chop the wood they had brought.

The questions Jessie had feared had risen, their first day

out. And there would be more; there was no relaxing her guard because she'd hurdled the first of them.

Resentment churned inside her, for all that she'd agreed to take the child of another woman. Had it not been for the infant, she might have taken her place as simply another of the women headed west, recently deprived of a husband, free to fall in love again.

As it was, she'd been coerced into accepting young Lauren, and there were people in the company who knew at least some of the details of his birth, though not all of them. Jessie suppressed a shudder, and tried to remember that when they reached California they would all separate, going their own ways to different places. Whatever people knew, or suspected, would go with them.

Yet she did not think she could ever look upon Suzanne Merriam's child as her own, and she felt it unfair that the infant had been thrust upon her. If only, she thought now, turning toward the wagon as a thin wail rose from the cradle where Lauren had been sleeping, her own tiny daughter had survived, her own Joella Viola. How different she would feel if the child were her own!

She lifted him, of necessity cradling the small body against her breast as she climbed for the second time down from the seat. He had stopped crying the moment she picked him up, and Jessie peeled back the blanket in which he was wrapped, staring down at the tiny red face.

He was not, she thought, as beautiful as Joella had been. But he was sturdy, healthy, and had a will to live. He turned toward her, rooting for a nipple, and Jessie felt a strange sort of pain run through her, from groin to breast.

And then young Mrs. Allen—Virginia, she had asked to be called—was beside her, laughing, holding out her arms.

"I heard him crying, and I've only just fed my own Charlie, but there's plenty for this one, too."

Jessie handed him over to his surrogate mother, watching as the young woman opened her bodice and allowed the child to suck. Jessie would have been uncomfortable nursing a baby without retreating to the privacy of a wagon, but Virginia, a slender washed-out blonde with eyes as faded as her hair, seemed unaware of the bustle around her, of wagons being unloaded of cooking supplies, of livestock being herded to water, of the ring of ax on firewood.

Virginia also had a daughter, Nellie, who was two. The child came to where her mother sat on the wagon tongue (for

Annie had freed the animals that drew it, and pegged them out a short distance away) and stared first at the baby, then at Jessie.

Nellie was a pretty child; her hair was a sunny gold and lay in ringlets, and her thick-lashed eyes were a vivid blue. Had Virginia looked like that, at the same age? Jessie guessed that Virginia Allen was no more than twenty now, but deprivation and hard work had aged her beyond that.

Was this her own fate, to look thirty by the time she was twenty? No, Jessie thought, no. It was true, she had during the past year come through some dreadful times, but they were behind her. Her future was bright, and ahead lay romance and adventure and happiness. Even the child suckling so noisily in Virginia Allen's arms would not jeopardize that happiness, because she would not allow that to happen.

Virginia met her eyes and laughed. "Little pig, isn't he? He'll soon catch up to my Charlie if he eats so much! He's really a lovely baby, isn't he?"

Annie Ryan, coaxing life into a reluctant campfire a few yards away, replied before Jessie's silence became noticeable. "He's a bonny one, he is. And we're lucky to have found you, ma'am. I've known of babes fed on other than mother's milk, but they didn't thrive. This one, you've saved his life."

Down the line of wagons, halted for the night, some sort of ruckus was struck up. They all turned their heads toward the shouting voices, the barking dogs, but it was too far away to make out, and after a moment the noise subsided. Jessie saw Joel Shand, mounted on the sturdy Indian pony he had chosen over the more beautiful white man's horses, smack in the middle of whatever was happening. Even from this distance she could see the breadth of chest and shoulders, the lean waist and thighs, the thick dark cap of hair with a tendency to wave.

She couldn't see his eyes, but she didn't need to. They were a dark hazel that looked sometimes green, sometimes brown, and were capable of penetrating to her very soul. Disconcerting, and not quite the same eyes as those of the boy she had fallen in love with, all those miles and years from where they were now. At least the man behind them was not the same.

Well, for that matter, she was not the same either, was she? Jessie poked with a foot at a burning twig, sending it back into the center of the fire, scarcely aware of what she did. No, she, too, had changed.

But they hadn't changed so much they'd lost their love for each other, Jessie thought fiercely. No matter that they were having to get acquainted all over again after months of separation. She still loved him, she was certain of that.

Virginia Allen had followed her gaze. "I didn't learn very much except that I was needed to nurse the baby. You're engaged to marry Mr. Shand, are you, ma'am?"

The questions again. A wave of something near despair swept over Jessie. There was so much that could not be explained, not so that this woman or the others would really understand how she had come to be in her present circumstances. Yet she was incapable of lying about it, even if the odds were good that she would get away with it. Which, of course, she couldn't count on at all. At least a few of her fellow travelers were aware of some of the events surrounding Lauren's birth just before the wagon train left Missouri, and of Ben's death.

None of these things were what she wanted to talk about to strangers, but Annie had warned her to marshal her thoughts. "Curious," Annie had said. "They'll all be dying of curiosity. Best think what you're to say."

Engaged to marry Joel Shand, when her own legal husband was no more than cold in the grave? Jessie didn't want to say that outright.

"Joel and I knew each other very well, a long time ago," she said at last. "We planned to be married. And then . . . things happened. I thought he'd been killed in a boiler explosion on a ship, and he thought I was dead, too. We had given up looking for each other. And I married Ben Ryan, because I was . . . alone."

That was the truth, as far as it went. No need to add that she had been pregnant with Joel's child and desperate enough to be persuaded into something that had been wrong and foolish, for Ben as well as for herself. She hadn't been able to save Ben from his own folly, and the marriage had done no more for her than to provide a roof over her head. It hadn't been enough. It hadn't even saved her child, for whose sake Jessie had given in to Annie Ryan's urging to marry her son.

And now that child was gone, and Jessie had a chance to start over again, to make up for some of her past mistakes. To take her place as a respectable member of the community of the wagon train, if they did not condemn her on the basis of the things she had had to do.

If only she could put it all behind her, and be accepted by

these people for what she was now. How much easier it would be if she had not agreed to take Lauren, another woman's child, a woman whose image was burned eternally into Jessie's memory. Yet what else could she have done? She loved Joel, and he had put it to her in such a way that she could hardly refuse to rear his son, and Suzanne Merriam's.

Virginia sighed. "A woman needs a man, no mistake about that. Don't know what I'd do if I lost my man. And Mr. Shand is a very attractive one; you're lucky." Her smile flashed as she watched the commanding figure on horseback a few hundred yards away. "So is that young fellow traveling with him. A cousin, is he? That blond fellow with the curly hair?"

"Collin Aubin," Jessie supplied, her mouth again going dry. For Collie was another of the things she couldn't explain, not fully. Collie, who was not Joel's cousin but his half brother, something not even Collie himself knew. "He's from Chicago. His father is a prosperous merchant there."

"I never been to Chicago. Nor much of anywhere else," Virginia said. "Did you ever go there? To Chicago?"

"Yes. I was there for a short time." The memories rose in a choking cloud, and even now, knowing that Joel was not dead at all, the pain of those days knifed through her.

"Did you like it? The city?" Virginia's pale blue eyes were alert with interest, and she put out a hand to touch the curly head of Nellie, who leaned against her knee, sucking a thumb. "Was it exciting?"

Exciting? No, Jessie thought wryly, that wasn't the word she would use. "Frightening, I'd say. I was alone, and hadn't much money." And had just learned she was pregnant, and that the father of her child had presumably been killed in an accident. "It was very big, and full of people and horses and buggies and wagons, and no, I didn't especially find it exciting. I wanted to go home, only . . . only there was no home left to go to."

Homesickness swept over her even now, long after she'd thought herself recovered from it. Homesickness for the beautiful island in Lake Michigan, for the family that was no longer there. Grief for her mother and sister, both buried in the sandy shore, and longing for the other sister who had been driven off the island after King Strang's assassination. Zadia, the only one of her family left alive, whom she would probably never see again.

Virginia's gaze broke from hers momentarily, as she raised the baby to her shoulder to pat him. Then, even as she spoke, that gaze swept over Jessie's skirt with its band of plain brown material around the hem, the same material that had been used to lengthen all her dresses.

"I couldn't help noticing the way you let down your clothes. Mrs. Hale said you was most likely a Mormon, come from some island up north, where that man was killed."

It wasn't a question, yet it was. That, too, might well be held against her, that she'd been a member of King Strang's band. Mormons were not held in high repute anywhere, it seemed, except perhaps in Salt Lake City. And it was too much to hope that all the people she met would mind their own business. There were few newspapers available, and little in the way of entertainment except for what people made up themselves. Learning about their neighbors—every detail—fed that need for mental sustenance.

"My mother married one of King Strang's followers," Jessie said reluctantly, yet knowing it was as well to tell it now and be done with it. Maybe once they'd chewed the gossip over for a few days, they would forget it and treat her as the individual she was. "Or rather, she married Mr. Ritter, and then he joined the Mormons on Beaver Island. And, of course, my sisters and I went with them."

Virginia had forgotten the baby against her shoulder, which didn't matter too much because he'd fallen asleep now that his belly was filled. Her lips parted in anticipation, she demanded, "Is it true the men had more than one wife at the same time?"

Jessie hesitated, and saw that Annie was watching her with sympathy across the black cooking pot she'd just hung over the fire. Jessie hoped she wasn't going to have to go through this with every person she met, on the entire train. "Some of them did," she admitted finally. "Not very many of them. A man had to be able to afford two wives and families, and not many of them could."

Virginia's tongue snaked over her lips as avidly as if she had been afforded a glimpse into a Mormon bedroom. "Do they sleep with both wives at the same time?"

Jessie caught herself on the verge of saying sharply, *Of course not.* "No. Each wife has her own room, her own bed. Aside from the few men who were polygamous, the Strangites were little different from anyone else. They were hard-working and God-fearing people."

"But they shot him, didn't they? His own people, they

13

killed him, that man who said he was a king." Virginia waited almost breathless for whatever Jessie had to tell.

Jessie, who had actually witnessed the shooting, who had stood in frozen horror as James Strang's blood ran out on the unpainted boards of the dock, who had observed his shocked and agonized face, took no relish in the telling, though she had not liked the man nor believed in many of his teachings.

Annie was cutting chunks of potato into the pot, and from an apron pocket produced a sprinkling of the herbs that livened up her cooking. She nodded almost imperceptibly; *Go on, tell her, and she'll leave you alone after this*, was the unspoken message.

Jessie didn't know whether that would be true or not, yet there seemed no alternative other than blunt rudeness against the onslaught of questions from strangers, and that would only make matters worse. Besides being critical of her background and experiences, they would dislike her personally, and she couldn't afford that.

"The assassins had been his followers," Jessie said flatly, trying not to remember how Thomas Bedford and Alexander Wentworth had attacked the unarmed and unsuspecting Mormon leader with a horse pistol and a revolver, and how as he lay mortally wounded Bedford had beaten the man about the head and shoulders with the former weapon, as if to reduce a once proud man to a bloody jelly. "They were the ones who actually killed him, though they'd been led in that direction by other men, enemies of Mr. Strang."

"They said he had five wives. Four of 'em young enough to be his daughters, and all those pregnant."

Jessie felt a twist in her stomach, a sense of revulsion, but who was to say that she, too, would not be curious about such a man, had she not known him and seen him die? King Strang had created a legend with his own life. "That's true enough," she conceded.

Clearly the other woman was fascinated by the idea of one man having four pregnant wives at the same time. "I heard about it. Oliver—that's my husband, Oliver—he told me. There was talk, back in Illinois where we lived then, about the people on that island. They was all driven off, after their king died."

Jessie's throat closed. Yes, they had all been driven off, except for those who were buried there. The Gentiles who had swarmed over Beaver Island had forced out with no more than the clothes on their backs over twenty-five hundred people, and somehow—she would never know how—her sister Audra had died, and been buried there beside the house where Jessie had lived. Audra had died, the others had scattered, and Zadie with her husband Dennis and her new baby and Dennis's brothers and sisters, where were they? Zadie had written to Aunt Winnie in Independence to say that they would be heading west by the end of March, seeking a better life elsewhere, but she didn't know Jessie was also traveling in the same direction.

Zadie and Dennis could be ahead of them now, out there on the prairie, or coming along behind somewhere, and Jessie might never know, never find them again. For a moment she almost hated Virginia Allen for reminding her so vividly of all that she'd lost.

And then Virginia nodded, and remembered the baby, and returned him to Jessie to be placed in the cradle.

"I reckon everybody in this train is going west to try to escape something," Virginia said. "As much as to find something better. I buried two babies, as well as my ma and pa, back in Illinois. And then when our cabin burnt to the ground, and everything in it, we didn't have the heart to rebuild and start over. Oliver said we didn't have enough land to ever do any more than keep us just from starving. He said let's go west, maybe there'll be some of that gold left by the time we get there." Her smile was rueful. "You reckon that's right? They might still have some of it on the ground, for us to pick up? Even if they don't, Oliver says he heard there's farmland, more of it and better than in Illinois, though I think he's just saying it's better to make it easier for me to leave my home. Oliver's a good man. And I reckon he deserves some supper, now that I got both the younguns fed."

This time she laughed in an open and friendly way. "I'll hear your little one cry and I'll be back, three-four hours or so. He's so big and healthy it don't seem to hurt him to go that long between feedings. It's been nice talking to you, ma'am. I'm glad we got good people to neighbor with on the way west."

Jessie, holding Lauren against her, feeling the warmth of the small body, watched her go. Virginia's own infant slept in a wooden crate beside the Allens' wagon, and Nellie, still sucking her thumb, trailed after her mother.

Two infants buried, besides her mother and father. Well,

15

Jessie thought, had she believed she was the only one who grieved, who'd suffered personal losses?

She turned and met Annie's gaze. "Guess I'm going to wear out my throat, telling everybody what it was like to be a Mormon," Jessie said wryly.

Annie reached for the sleeping infant. "I shouldn't wonder the word will get around. She'll tell a few, and they'll tell some more, and the whole train will know it all without you telling each and every one of them," she predicted. "She's right, everybody's running away from something. Poverty, or grief, or a noose, some of 'em. At least we ain't got anybody chasing us, which is more than some of 'em can claim."

No, Jessie thought. Nobody chasing us, no law seeking us out. But she felt the tremor in her limbs, the perspiration that had come out on her skin during Virginia's probing. She had felt weak and sick, worrying about the questions to come, and how she would answer them truthfully without setting everybody against her.

She didn't know whether she'd come through her first test successfully or not.

And then she heard him coming, on the sturdy, ugly Indian pony, and Jessie turned with a lightening of her spirits toward Joel Shand.

2

The first time she'd met Joel, he'd been poaching rabbits on her stepfather's land, and he'd rescued her from a half-wit who'd attempted to rape her. She'd begun to fall in love with him right then, she supposed, though she hadn't admitted it even to herself for a long time. She had been only thirteen.

Joel had rescued her from a number of things, and he'd loved her as no one else had ever done. She would retain to her dying day a sense of guilt when she remembered that she'd allowed him to make love to her, and that the lovemaking had resulted in Joella. Joel brushed such matters aside as of no consequence, for they'd intended to be married, but it was different, for a woman. She couldn't quite convince herself that it was all right because they had been so deeply in love, and he was going away, and they'd felt a desperate need for one another. Sometimes she thought it must be easier to be a man, for the male viewpoint skimmed over details like marriage lines and got on to the important things, like being together.

Her guilt extended to Ben Ryan and his death, too. She had long since forgiven Annie for throwing her and Ben together, for urging marriage upon them. It had been wrong, and it had not worked, but Annie had genuinely cared about them both and hoped that her son could come to love a woman in a natural way.

Poor Ben. He couldn't help what he was, and he hadn't deserved to die, though even Annie admitted that it was probably for the best. Annie hadn't talked much about Ben since it happened, but she had finally admitted that there was nothing anyone could have done to make her son a normal man. Had he not been killed—with a shot meant for Jessie—his problems would only have gone on and on, until eventually he'd have been murdered in his own right, by irate men who considered him a deviate, an abomination, because of the urges over which Ben had no control.

Jessie thought, with her rational mind, that perhaps Ben would have preferred it this way. But that didn't ease her own guilt, in being the instrument of his death, even though what they'd been trying to do was to save Suzanne Merriam from her husband's brutal rage.

She guessed that there would always be something to feel guilty about. Like the child she had just put back into his cradle. He was, she knew, a beautiful baby. Had he been her own, she would have cherished him as she'd cherished tiny Joella in the three days the child had lived. Yet she couldn't help remembering that Joel had fathered this child, with another woman, and even the fact that he had at the time believed Jessie to be dead didn't alleviate the pain that caused.

Joel slid out of the saddle and allowed his mount to graze. He came toward her, grin widening on his face, and would have kissed her right there in public had not Jessie stepped hastily away from him.

"Joel, we're involved in enough scandal already. Don't let's give them anything else to talk about."

"Why not? Who cares what they think?" Joel said, but he stopped beside the fire. "How are you holding up, Annie?"

"As well as any old woman," Annie said, smiling at him. "Without all this padding, though, I'd need a crutch to walk after that ride. Two thousand miles of this is going to be a long way. Maybe it'll shake off some of my fat."

"If it works that way," Joel suggested, "this girl is going to be skin and bones. And she's too thin already."

Jessie changed the subject. "How far did we come today, do you think?"

"About twelve miles, Captain Horn thinks." "Captain" was an honorary title for the wagonmaster, since he'd never captained anything else, as far as Jessie knew. She had seen him, a man of small yet commanding stature, brown as an Indian, with a scraggly graying mustache over tobacco-stained teeth.

Jessie sucked in a breath of dismay. "Twelve miles! And we have more than two thousand to go?"

"We'll do better when we settle into a routine. There were all kinds of problems that slowed us down today, but we'll smooth out by tomorrow. In fact, the last hour or so nothing bad happened to anybody." The grin flashed again, and once more Jessie was disconcerted because she could not read what lay behind the hazel eyes. During the months they had been apart, Joel Shand had learned to school his face to hide his inner feelings, and at moments like this she felt as if he were a stranger rather than the man she planned to marry.

"Twelve miles," Jessie repeated, trying to calculate in her head. At ten miles a day, it would take two hundred days to reach California!

"Cap Horn says there'll be plenty of days when we do twenty miles." He didn't say there would be days when they'd do less than twelve, but Jessie guessed that. "Don't worry, we're leaving early enough so we'll make it before the snow falls in the mountains. That shouldn't be before late October."

"There's no telling when the snow will fall, is there? I mean, those poor people in the Donner party, some years back. They got caught in an early snow."

The ill-fated Donner party had resorted to cannibalism to survive, and the memory of it was enough to chill the blood of many of the travelers, particularly the women.

"We'll get across into California long before there's snow.

18

Jessie, unless Ma Ryan needs you here to cook, take a walk with me. I need to move around off that horse for a while."

"Go along," Annie said, waving a hand. "The stew will tend itself, and I'll watch the baby."

Jessie had forgotten the baby. She did, when he wasn't fussing; was it because she didn't really want to think about him? But no, as Annie said, he was only a baby; she could harbor no malice against an innocent infant.

"How's he doing?" Joel asked as Jessie fell into step beside him. There were still people foraging for firewood along the creek bank, so they turned in the other direction, across the open prairie which spring had carpeted in pale green.

"He's healthy and sturdy," Jessie said, subdued. "And Mrs. Allen seems to have plenty of milk for him and her own babe, too."

"Did it tire you badly today? Riding that wagon since dawn?"

"No more than it tired anyone else, I'm sure. We moved so slowly much of the time, I wondered if it might not be easier to get down and walk. I think I could walk faster than the oxen moved, at least on this sort of terrain."

"Why don't you try it, tomorrow? I wouldn't mind walking part of the time myself, only Cap Horn appointed me to ride up and down and keep track of what's going on behind him. Collie will drive one of our wagons, and Jim Hastings's oldest boy the other, so I'll be free to move around."

Jessie hadn't seen much of Collin Aubin, the young man who thought he was Joel's distant cousin. To admit that they were half brothers would mean to acknowledge as well Joel's illegitimacy. Whether that would matter to Collie or not, Jessie didn't know. He seemed a pleasant young man, very young at eighteen compared to Joel's mature twenty-three, with his fair curls and naive blue eyes. Collie had a ready smile and better manners than most, which was no more than expected of the only son of a wealthy Chicago family.

Yet it was Joel, for all that he'd had none of the benefits of Collie's upbringing, who sent the heat surging through her by his nearness, as she felt it now. He didn't have to touch her to make it begin, and indeed, she was almost afraid to submit to that touch, however casual it might be.

He shortened his stride to more nearly match her own, and Jessie lifted her skirt with the brown band at the bottom, to keep it from brushing the grass.

"They're talking about us already," she said, panting a

19

little, for she had to hurry to keep up even when he slowed down. "Virginia Allen asked if I were a Mormon. Because of the way I'd lengthened my skirts. Does everyone know we wore short skirts that exposed our pantalettes?"

"Probably. It isn't just us they're talking about, Jessie; everybody talks about everybody. It's only to be expected, I suppose, when a hundred and thirty-six people start out together on a journey that's going to take months. There won't be much else to think about, except keeping ourselves fed and moving, so we'll all talk about each other. I'm glad I'm not riding the wagon with Collie; all he can talk about is Patrice Hammond, and he's crushed that the Hammonds didn't come on with the train. In fact, I wasn't sure I was going to talk him into coming, either, if Patrice stayed behind."

Jessie could make no comment upon that. For herself, she was glad Patrice Hammond and her parents were not in the same train. For Patrice was almost the mirror image of her dead sister Suzanne, a constant reminder of the woman who had borne Joel's child while married to another man. It would have been painful in the extreme.

"Perhaps the Hammonds will eventually catch up with us," Jessie said halfheartedly.

"I doubt they want to, except for Patrice. She seemed taken with Collie as much as he was with her. But her parents don't want to think about Suzanne or the baby; they wouldn't have given him up if they'd cared about him instead of their own disgrace. No, I don't think they'll come anywhere near us if they can help it. And there are plenty of other girls."

"Not too many in our train, young and single ones. Are there?"

Jessie put out a hand to his sleeve to slow his pace, for she was beginning to gasp for breath. She knew at once that the touch was dangerous, and she drew back her hand as if she'd touched fire.

"Jessie, for God's sake, how long are we going to pretend we're strangers?"

"We're not," Jessie protested, but she took a step backward when he lifted a hand toward her. "I...I told Virginia Allen the truth, as far as I could. That we'd been engaged to be married while we were on Beaver Island, and that each of us thought the other had been killed. It's nobody's business how long ago that was, or how long Ben's been dead, but she knows he only died recently. And it's not seemly that we display

20

affection in public, especially when we can't be married for a long time."

"Why not? I mean, why can't we be married for a long time? If it had been up to me, I'd have hauled out a preacher in the middle of the night before we left Missouri, and had him tie the knot. What are we waiting for? Propriety? Propriety is stupid, in most cases. Propriety turned everybody against my mother, though she was worth any dozen of them. You're a woman alone, we have a baby to consider, and I'm damned sick of sleeping by myself."

Warmth crept up her throat and into her cheeks. "There's no one to legally marry us, in any case."

"There will be. There will be settlements out there, a few, anyway. Army posts, if nothing else. Sometimes, this past couple of days, I've wondered if you've changed your mind about marrying me."

"No." Her voice was soft, pleading. "I only need a little time, Joel. I thought you were dead. I married Ben, and then I found you again and it's all so . . . confusing. Sometimes—" she hesitated, then confessed in a spurt of candor—"sometimes I feel I don't know you any more, and I need time to learn who you are, who you've become."

"I'm the same man I always was," Joel said roughly, reaching for her hand, and this time he didn't allow her to draw away. The touch sent a tremor through her, the same and yet different.

"No, you aren't. A great many things happened to you while we were apart. You found your father, after wondering about him all your life before, and you met Suzanne, and she had your child . . ."

"Is that what you're upset about? Suzanne? I told you, I thought you were dead, and I never intended anything serious between me and Suzanne, I never loved her. In fact, by the time she told me she was going to have a child, I didn't even like her very much. All her beauty was outside; there was none like yours, all the way through. I didn't believe the child was even mine; God knows she saw enough other men and lured them out to that damned summerhouse of hers. It wasn't until she swore it when she was dying that I believed her. He *is* mine, Jessie, I'm convinced of that now. And he's bothering you, too, isn't he? Lauren? You don't want to be saddled with Suzanne's son."

Jessie opened her mouth to protest, though most of what he said was true. He didn't give her a chance to utter a word.

"Well, he's my son, too. And I won't do to my son what Richard Aubin did to me. I won't call him my father, he never was and never will be; my birth was just an accident to him. He was engaged to somebody else and never intended to marry Ma, and the money he sent through the years was only a sop to his conscience, not any real concern for Ma and me. He abandoned me, and my life was hell because of it, and so was Ma's, and I won't have that on *my* conscience. I won't do that to a child. Why can't you love him, Jessie? I know there's so much love in you, and I want it . . . for me and for my son."

He was looking down at her from his towering height; even though Jessie herself was tall she had to tilt her head to look into his eyes when they stood so close together. And they were too close together; he had captured both her hands, now, and the sensation this touch provoked was making her hot and cold at the same time, and weak in the knees.

He was older than she'd remembered, more than the few months they'd been apart; he had filled out through the chest and shoulders, and there was a crisp curling of dark hair showing at the neck of his opened shirt that had not been there before. He had always worked with his hands, and they'd always been callused and toughened; that was the same. And so was her response to him, the physical response that had nothing to do with what her mind told her.

Her gaze slid past him, toward the wagons they had left behind, and she saw women around their campfires, and men working with the animals and wagons. Whether anyone was watching them or not she couldn't determine, but one thing she *was* set upon: there would be no further scandal.

Jessie withdrew her hands, forcefully, because that was the only way Joel would let her go. He stared down at her in exasperation. "Damn it, Jessie, we're betrothed! Aren't we?"

The dark hazel eyes were penetrating, almost frighteningly so. Unconsciously Jessie rubbed at her hands where his grip had bruised them.

"Yes, of course. Only I think it's best to . . . to allow a little time to pass, first. There are people in the train who were nearby when . . . when Ben was killed. Some of them know I . . . shot the man who killed him, and that . . ."

Joel's face softened. "All right. All right, Jessie. I don't want to talk about any of that, I just want to forget it. But if you can't forget it yet, I guess I can wait a little longer." Amusement suddenly touched the wide, mobile mouth. "You

22

want to be courted all over again, is that it? I thought I'd done that once, and won you, but if we're these different people you think we are, I suppose we have to do it all over again."

He was making fun of her, she knew, yet Jessie grasped at the idea. Because it would give her time, and give the strangers time to forget the violence that had taken place those last few days in Missouri, and with that passage of time she would grow comfortable with Joel again, the way she had once been.

He laughed openly, now, good humor restored. "All right. May I call upon you after supper, ma'am?"

"Yes, that would be nice," Jessie said demurely, and then her own lips twitched. "Annie will no doubt provide chaperonage."

"No doubt," Joel echoed, his voice dry, but he turned her about toward the wagons and began to walk back, and Jessie gave a small sigh of relief.

It was true that she was concerned about acceptance by the strangers who would be their neighbors for the duration of this journey; but it was mostly herself that Jessie thought of, and the need to become reacquainted with this man who had once seemed almost a part of herself, and now was, at times, another of the strangers.

3

Jessie slept fitfully that first night, her pallet laid atop various packing crates in the rear of the covered wagon. Many of the families slept out on the ground, probably more comfortably than she, but she could not leave Lauren entirely to Annie Ryan to care for, and Annie said it would be best to keep the baby inside.

"Besides," Annie said wearily as they prepared for sleep, "this time of year, we could get a good rain before morning.

Drying out wet bedding is a chore I don't look forward to." She didn't add "at my age," and truthfully Annie did not slacken any efforts to do her share and more of the work to be done, but she was past fifty, Jessie thought. It was only reasonable that the younger woman accept a major part of the responsibilities, especially for the infant.

Twice during the night she rose when the baby cried; she changed him and made sure he was clean and dry when she took him to Virginia Allen to nurse, stumbling through the darkness with only the faint glow from dying campfires to guide her way. She sat, bone-weary and numb with the night chill, waiting until it was time to take the child back.

They didn't talk much during those feedings; both Jessie and Virginia were too tired to make conversation. And it seemed to Jessie that she had no more than crawled back under her blanket, her feet no more than warmed again, when it was time to rise for the day.

Yet once she was up and had sipped coffee from a tin cup, taking care not to burn her mouth, Jessie's spirits began to climb. For it was April on the prairie, and she was headed for California, and she had found Joel again. Everything else would, in time, take care of itself.

The wagons rolled out that second morning with little confusion. Joel rode by, pausing only to make sure they had no problems, and was gone; it gave Jessie an inner warmth to know that he was there, in the same wagon train.

Females alone were not welcome on the trail. The hardships were too great, and Captain Horn was adamant about the matter; a woman couldn't be expected to know about such things as handling mules and oxen and repairing wagon wheels and tongues, nor could they be expected to manage by themselves under the adverse circumstances they would certainly meet as they crossed the continent.

Ben's death would have ruled out any chance that Annie could go on to California if Jessie hadn't fought for her. Briefly but fiercely, she informed Joel that a way must be found for Annie to go, because Jessie would not leave her behind. He himself, of course, would take the responsibility for Jessie, since they were to be married.

Joel had arranged for Andrew Satler, a gangly fifteen-year-old who looked as if he'd never had enough to eat, to drive Annie Ryan's wagon. He'd started out with it, that first morning, and Jessie privately thought that he was no more an expert with oxen than she herself. Indeed, Annie knew considerably more, and by noon she'd suggested that the boy might be of value to his parents.

"Been handling critters since I was knee-high to a grasshopper," Annie observed, settling her bulk onto the seat and taking the reins. "I reckon we'll make out by ourselves all right, and if that captain comes along, we can tell him our driver is coming right back."

That was fine with Jessie. It wasn't that she disliked the boy, but with him there on the seat the conversation between herself and Annie was necessarily constrained. The things on both their minds were not matters they cared to discuss before a stranger.

Not that they discussed them much, at first. But by the second day, as the sun rose behind them and the fragrance of the new grass and the spring flowers rose along with the rich aroma of the oxen, the thoughts became too much to contain in silence.

Annie began to speak first, not looking at her companion, staring ahead as intently as if she could already see the mountains they must cross to reach the mythical California. She didn't mention the violent death of her son, instead recalling Ben as a child.

"Always a good boy, he was. Never got into trouble, or hardly ever. Sean didn't whip him but once or twice, the whole time he was growing up. He was always big for his age, and strong. And he was always good to his ma, Ben was."

Jessie searched for something to say that would revive the good memories, not the bad ones. She had long since forgiven Annie for manipulating her into a marriage with Ben, for all that the results of it had been disastrous. Like Jessie, Annie had done what she felt was for the best.

"After my girls died of the smallpox—Lillie was eight and Sarah was ten—Ben was all I had left. He was a good-looking boy. I had such high hopes for him." Annie sighed and her massive bosom heaved. "I mind the time he brought home a baby rabbit," she said, and was off on a tale of childish adventures that Jessie found difficult to reconcile with the Ben she had known.

"I reckon it was terrible, what I done to you and Ben," Annie said at last, when she'd run out of stories of the good old days. "I never meant to hurt you, girl. I hope you know that."

"Of course I know it, Annie," Jessie said softly.

"When I saw you was going to have a baby, and you hadn't told anybody so I guessed you wasn't married to that young man of yours, but was going to marry him if he hadn't died, why, I could see you needed somebody more than that old aunt of yours. A husband. I thought maybe Ben would be a husband to you."

She sighed again, audible over the sounds of the creaking wheels and the plodding oxen feet.

Jessie moistened her lips and wondered if they were going to crack if she had to continue to breathe this dusty air and be exposed all day to the sun and the wind. "I guess Ben couldn't help the way he was, Annie."

"No. I reckon he couldn't. For a long time I didn't want to believe it, that my son wasn't a real man, like. He was a fine person, Ben was, except . . . in that one way. And I thought maybe he just never knew the right girl, you know, someone pretty and young, like you. I thought maybe he'd learn . . ." She trailed off, distracted by a bee that hovered around her, shooing it off.

Learn to love a girl, Jessie thought, finishing Annie's sentence silently. "Ben couldn't help the way he was, Annie."

The older woman nodded. "I know that now. I guess maybe I always knew it, somewhere deep inside, but I didn't want it to be true, so I tried to think different." Her voice altered perceptibly. "Maybe that's why Ben had to die the way he did, to punish me for trying to play God with you and him. Because if that Cass Merriam hadn't shot him, you'd still be married to Ben, a man that couldn't ever really be a man. I could see how terrible it was, what I done, after you found your own young man again. How terrible, if you was legally tied to Ben and couldn't ever marry Joel Shand. He's a fine man, Joel is; reminds me of my own Sean, God rest his soul."

There was nothing to look at but the blue bowl of sky overhead and the endlessly undulating grass-covered hills. Those and the wagon train ahead and behind them. Jessie saw nothing of these external things, however, her thoughts turned inward.

"I felt the same when my mother died, that it was a punishment for my own shortcomings," Jessie said. "And again when Joella only lived for three short days—it was a punishment, because I wasn't supposed to have had a baby, when I wasn't yet married to Joel. But Joel told me that was foolish, to think that way. That if I really believed in God I couldn't believe He'd punish *me* by letting someone else die."

She hesitated, then, warmth flooding her face, she rushed on, before her own shame should overpower the need to ease Annie's suffering. "Joel said if God really punished people for their sins, he would do something to *them*. Not to innocent loved ones. He was talking about my sister Zadie, and you mustn't misunderstand, because she's really a lovely person, but she was...was tempted beyond her ability to resist."

Jessie risked a glance at Annie's face and found nothing worse than curiosity and interest there. "She was forced into a marriage with a man much older than she was—one of the Mormon elders—and he was cruel to her. I saw the bruises once. And she told me she...she prayed for his death. She said she'd rather die herself than share his bed again, after he'd nearly died from a heart seizure. She fell in love with his son, Dennis, and they..." Jessie's cheeks flamed brighter, and she could not put the rest of that into words, but she didn't need to. Annie was uneducated, as far as book learning went, but she was a perceptive and intelligent woman.

"And she's the one who escaped from that island, when all the trouble took place," Annie supplied. "She wasn't the sister who was killed."

"No, she wasn't. She and Dennis are fine, and they'll be heading west, the same as we are, and nothing bad has happened to them at all. Her letter sounded very happy. Of course I suppose something still could happen, but..."

Annie slapped the reins against the broad rumps of the oxen, urging them to a slightly increased speed. "Your Joel is a wise man, for such a young one. He's right. God don't punish the rest of us for our sins by striking the innocent. Bad things happen to all of us—like my little girls, what could their deaths have been punishment for? Young as they were, they never did much of anything wrong. And my Sean—well, God knows he did aplenty over the years afore he was taken, but if he was being punished for that, why wait forty-two years? No, I guess I really know Ben's death wasn't a punishment, only I keep going over it in my head, thinking if I'd done this or that, or not done it, maybe he'd still be alive. Though I reckon deep in my heart I know it's for the best, that he's gone."

A tear trickled down her cheek, and she made no move to wipe it away. "Seems to me just the ordinary things of living are punishment enough for anybody, no matter what they done."

"Joel said," Jessie managed around the ache in her throat,

27

"that the Bible says death is a reward, that we go on to something better than this life. So it's stupid to think of death as a punishment for anything."

"You're lucky to have found an educated, God-fearing man. I hope you know that, girl."

Jessie's mouth twisted ruefully. "I know I'm lucky, and I *do* love him. But he's not a Christian, Annie, for all that he knows the Bible so well. He learned to read from it, is why, but he never accepted what it teaches. That's why they wouldn't let me marry him, on Beaver Island, because he wouldn't become a Mormon or even a Christian. He was so angry about what happened to his mother, who was so devout and who never did anything wrong that I ever heard of, except to fall in love with Joel's father and then found out too late he didn't intend to marry her. And he hated his father so badly; all he ever talked about was finding him, and sometimes I wondered if he only wanted to find him so he could...could kill him."

She shot another look at Annie, guiding the oxen without conscious thought, and saw no shock there at such a statement. Annie had lived for over half a century, and she'd seen and experienced a good many things. Annie was not quick to condemn anyone for anything.

"Well, being born to a woman not married to your father is hard on a person," Annie conceded. "But it ain't the end of the world. He's all right now, a man in his own right."

It certainly seemed that this was so. Joel obviously enjoyed his role as assistant to the wagonmaster, taking charge, giving orders. Still, Jessie did not lose her uneasiness about him. That inner hardness, the compulsion to overcome illegitimacy and to succeed, was so strong that it came near to frightening her.

He had agreed to court her for the second time, and though she knew he considered this an absurd charade, he cared enough to do it for her sake. Jessie herself felt it was imperative. She could not yet bridge the gap of their separation to become his wife and assume the responsibilities of mothering Joel's son without some measure of emotional preparation. And though she thrilled to his touch as much as she had ever done, she was not ready to go to bed with him, even though she had willingly made love with him all those months ago on Beaver Island.

There were moments when she wondered if she would ever want to make love again, with anyone, even Joel. She remembered that terrible night when Cass Merriam had dragged her into his rented room and thrown her across the bed, when he had used her so brutally in spite of her advanced pregnancy, so that a short time later Joella had been born three months early.

Yet she had known, even at the time, that rape was not the same as an act of love. Joel would never hurt her in that way, and she remembered the joy of lying in his arms. She dreamed about it, and woke feeling the need of that closeness again. When she was with Joel, though, the desire had a disconcerting way of ebbing and flowing, so that she was almost as apprehensive as she was anticipatory.

Part of that stemmed from the change in Joel, and in spite of his protestations to the contrary, she knew that he had changed a great deal. When she mentioned this to Annie, the older woman only nodded.

"Men grow up. They got to toughen up, or they wouldn't survive," Annie said. "He's a strong man, like my Sean."

Strength was fine, Jessie thought. Papa had been strong, and she had adored him. Her stepfather, Tully Ritter, had been strong in his own way, had taken a path of blind stubbornness not totally free of stupidity; convinced of his own righteousness, Tully had been unable to see anyone else's side of things, with the result that he had trampled over all their feelings and their rights—his wife's, and those of his three stepdaughters.

Was that what she feared? That Joel would turn into a tyrant like Tully? How could he, when Tully was everything that Joel hated?

There was another area of her life that tormented Jessie with wildly conflicting emotions, too. Tiny Lauren, a handsome child by anyone's standards, was in her care. Yet she turned over most of that responsibility to Annie, guiltily ignoring his cries for the few extra seconds that it took for the older woman to reach into the cradle for him.

Jessie had not wanted to take the baby. Lauren was Suzanne Hammond's child—Suzanne Merriam when she died— and a constant reminder that Joel had made love to the infant's mother. His protestations that he had not loved Suzanne, that he had, indeed, been seduced by her in an attempt to get him to marry her, were undoubtedly true. But Jessie didn't really understand why Joel had succumbed to that seduction.

Oh, she knew that men had physical needs that must be

satisfied, much stronger urges than most women (guiltily she thought of her sister Zadie, whose urges had certainly been powerful enough), but she could not imagine herself going to bed with anyone other than the man she really loved. How could it be so different for Joel, if he had really not cared at all for Suzanne?

And then Jessie looked at Annie, and was reminded of Ben, and she remembered that for a short span of time she, too, had had her needs. It still made her face hot to remember how she had contemplated approaching her husband to consummate their marriage, and had only been saved from the total humiliation of rebuff by the arrival of the men looking for Ben with the idea of stringing him up.

She had, of course, been married to Ben at the time. She'd thought she would be married to him for the rest of her life, and while she had not loved him, Jessie had reasoned that she could not forever subdue the physical ache that built within her unless she truly became Ben's wife. So maybe it wasn't so different, what she had felt, from what Joel had experienced, though it *seemed* different. Joel had *not* been married, nor anticipated marriage to Suzanne.

Jessie wished she'd never seen Suzanne, had not known what a beautiful young woman she was, had not seen her son. Had not been persuaded to take that son to raise as her own.

Had the child been anyone's other than Joel's, Jessie knew she would have been drawn to it as she'd always been drawn to babies. She would have fondled it and cooed over it, and, she was certain, have grown to love it.

She was not at all certain that she could ever love this child.

It was a shocking admission, even to herself, and one that made Jessie ashamed, yet it was the way she felt. She didn't have any urge to pick the baby up, to comfort him, to fuss over him as she had done over her sisters' babies.

If she had refused Joel's request—no, his demand—that they take the child after Suzanne's death, would he have chosen Lauren over herself?

No, Jessie thought. He loved her, he'd always loved her.

Yet she wasn't as certain of that, either, as she'd have liked to be, that if he'd had to make a choice, he would have chosen her.

4

The days grew longer and warmer. Jessie often walked alongside the wagon rather than riding with Annie, and though at first she tired quickly, within a week her legs were stronger and she began to enjoy the exercise. By evening, though, she welcomed the halt, and began to enjoy, as well, the friendship of those traveling in the nearest wagons.

Because of Lauren, she saw a good deal of Virginia Allen. Her husband called her Ginny, and she asked Jessie to call her that, too.

"She don't mean any harm with her questions," Annie said. "She's just lonely and needs someone to talk to about women's things."

"That would be fine," Jessie observed dryly, "if that didn't include how *we* happened to be the ones to take Suzanne's baby, and what it was like to be a Mormon."

"Can't blame anybody for wondering about the Mormons," Annie insisted. "Especially after that king feller got himself assassinated. That's different from just being shot, the way that happens to a lot of people. And having all those wives, it'd make anybody curious."

"Well, if there was any way I could have kept them from knowing I was one of King Strang's band, I'd have done it. I'm tired of talking about what it was like."

"It ain't as if you're the only one they're curious about, you know. Did you hear about the Ridbacks? That couple two wagons up from the Allens?"

"No, what about them?"

Annie looked her full in the face and grinned. "You're just as curious as everybody else, girl. Only it's different when the gossip is turned in another direction, eh?"

Jessie had to laugh, for it was true. "All right, what about the Ridbacks?"

"There's those that think they're both married..."

Jessie waited with a quizzical expression.

"...but not to each other. They say she run away from an old man that's her husband, and *he* deserted a wife with two little ones."

Jessie's amusement faded. "There was a time when I might have condemned them, the same as everybody else. Now I can't. I saw what happens when a woman has to marry a man she can't love, a man who isn't good to her. And I'm not really anybody to talk, am I? I couldn't marry Joel, but I guess if I'd been forced into a marriage with a man I hated, the way my sister Zadie was, maybe I'd have run off from him, too."

"You wouldn't've left your younguns."

"No. Probably not," Jessie agreed, and thought again of Lauren.

"When you going to start taking an interest in that one?" Annie inclined her head toward the cradle set down beside the wagon.

Warmth crept up Jessie's throat and flooded her face. "He's taken care of, isn't he?"

"Fed and washed and changed," Annie conceded. "But you're not mothering him, girl. A baby needs that, being held and cuddled."

"You do it," Jessie said, sounding defensive. "He's not unhappy, is he? He doesn't cry except when he's hungry or wet."

"I don't mind doing for him," Annie said mildly, "but I'm not the one Joel Shand expects to mother him. He wants you to raise that child, and you said you'd do it. But you never touch him unless you have to."

Jessie bit her lip, unable to think of a response that would not add to her guilt in this regard.

Annie's weathered face softened. "Ah, Jessie! Don't think about the babe belonging to *her,* think that he's a helpless little thing that needs love as much as any other! Think," she added slyly, "how you'd want someone to do, if it was you who died, and the baby was Joella."

Annie was right. Jessie knew that. She resolved to make an effort, because common sense told her that she must, yet it would not be easy.

What was easy was responding to Joel's courtship, the moments he had time for between the things that must be done. His task each day was to ride up and down the column of wagons, offering advice, heading off trouble, settling disputes.

Disputes there were.

"Damned fools," Joel said, handing over a tiny bouquet of buttercups gathered along a creek bank. "Nobody wants to ride in anybody else's dust, but with all these wagons, how're we going to manage that? And this morning Mrs. Atherton and Mrs. Von Wald got into a tussle over some firewood, and Mrs. Von Wald was shoved so close to the fire her skirt went up; lucky there was a bucket of water nearby and she was wearing the full complement of petticoats, or she might have been badly burned. Never occurred to either of them that they could share the fire, since they were both making mush. Walk out with me, Jessie, and tell me how your day went."

Jessie touched the flowers to her lips, unaware of the picture she made, her pale hair drawn back into a matronly knot that was not enough to make her look older than she was, her eyes brown velvet as she looked up at Joel through dark lashes. "I walked twelve miles, or however far we went. It's easier, now that my legs are getting used to it, than sitting all day on a hard seat. I don't know how long my shoes will last, though, if I walk every day." She looked down ruefully at her dusty feet. "Let's walk over by the creek, and I'll bring back a bucket of water to do the dishes later."

"I'll see if I can get you some moccasins, the first Indians we meet," Joel offered.

Jessie felt a small prickle along her spine. "Will we be meeting Indians soon, do you think?"

"Cap says not to worry about them. They're mostly friendly, especially if you have something to trade them. Collie and I brought stuff for that, beads and things, bright cloth. They like bright colors. Listen, after supper, when it's dark, let's take a private walk. When everyone else isn't hauling water or firewood, and watching us. Even in a beginning courtship, we should be able to talk without being overheard, shouldn't we?"

Jessie gave him a demure smile from behind the buttercups. "By the time supper's over, the baby will wake up and I'll have to take him to Ginny to be fed."

He regarded her with mingled humor and frustration. "You're going to use Lauren to make things as difficult for me as possible, aren't you?"

"No, why should I? But a baby does need attention, Joel. I think," she added in a burst of candor, "that having a baby about on one's honeymoon, when that time comes, will not be the most convenient of arrangements."

His humor was unruffled. "Maybe not. All I care about is that we get to that honeymooning pretty soon. Like, maybe, tomorrow."

"Tomorrow!" She forgot the flowers, and the baby. "How can we begin a honeymoon tomorrow?" The idea, however farfetched, was both beguiling and unnerving.

"By getting married tomorrow. The wagon train won't go through Topeka, but Cap says there's a preacher there. If Collie rides ahead and can talk him into it, he could meet us at Rossville when we cross the Kansas again. We could be married right away, which makes a lot more sense than taking a chance on finding someone else to do it farther out west."

He stopped walking and reached for her free hand, oblivious of the little girls a short distance away who were filling their aprons with twigs for kindling. "Jessie, I love you. I want to be married to you, the way we always planned. If the preacher will come, will you do it? Right away?"

A suffocating sensation rose through her chest, and her blood seemed to thicken so that she felt light-headed, as well, as if she would swoon. Only she'd never done anything so silly in her life, and wouldn't now.

"Say yes, Jessie," Joel urged.

The fragile buttercups were crushed between them as she went into his arms, the fire spreading from their lips through their veins, and all of a sudden Jessie knew that he was right. It was pointless to wait, when all she'd really wanted in life for years now was to be Joel's wife.

Her own mother had remarried within a few weeks of Papa's death, of economic necessity. Why, then, should not Jessie marry for an even better reason, for love?

The heat enveloped her, tingling through chest and belly and loins, and she forgot the children watching, forgot everything except Joel.

The wedding took place the evening they camped on the banks of the muddy Kansas, the last time they would encounter that river on their journey. Missouri with its civilized towns, its rolling grassy hills and familiar stands of maple, hickory, elm, and pine, was well behind them. Kansas Territory was an alien place, a vast expanse of grassland providing feed for cattle and horses but little in the way of

34

reminders of home for the travelers. Alice Groves found it frightening, she confessed, all that blue sky and empty space, with no houses, no people but those of their own train, and the only trees a few cottonwoods straggling along the creekbanks, almost hidden in shallow gullies.

It was not frightening to Jessie, though it was awesomely different from the wooded island she had left behind. Except for a few forts scattered across the prairies, there were few settlements beyond their present location until they would cross over the great mountains and go down the other side.

The train halted for the night on the riverbank, and in honor of the occasion Annie stewed a chicken Collie had brought back from Rossville, and added to the rich broth her own tender dumplings. Jessie scarcely knew what she ate. It was impossible to think about food, when Joel sat across the fire from her, seemingly immune to her own flutterings, forking the stew into his mouth. When he looked up and grinned, the sensations intensified.

Soon now, in a matter of an hour or so, she would be Joel's wife.

It had been a warm and sunny day, though with considerable wind—no wonder it blew the way it did, Annie had observed, with nothing whatever to stop the sweep of it—and with approaching dusk, the air grew chill.

Nothing could chill her inner warmth, however; Jessie felt it spreading, tingling through her, as it had done ever since Joel had sent Collie ahead for the preacher. She had scarcely slept last night, thinking ahead to *this* night. Yet she wasn't tired from that lack of rest; indeed, she'd never felt more alive, more vital and energetic.

The entire encampment was livelier than usual. This was their first excuse for a celebration, and they intended to make the most of it. True, they had not yet passed the bounds of civilization, but they felt as if they had. The women, especially, not as strongly drawn toward the wonders of California, were already missing homes and friends and families. They were only beginning to make new friends among their fellow travelers, and what better way to hurry the process along, and forget their loneliness, then to participate in a wedding and an evening of music and dancing?

A circle of campfires was built against the encroaching darkness, and as soon as their few simple dishes were rinsed off and dried, Annie and Jessie retired to the privacy of their wagon to prepare for the nuptials.

"I wish I had a real wedding dress," Jessie said, examining her choices by candlelight. "Something that didn't have a brown band around the hem of it. I dreamed of this for so long, of being beautiful for Joel on our wedding day, and look at me! Dusty shoes that are so thin on the bottoms that the stones hurt my feet, and a dress I've been wearing once or twice a week for the past year and a half!"

Annie regarded her with a smile. "It won't matter. With that shine in your eyes, nobody's going to be looking at your dress or your shoes. You're a beautiful young woman, Jessie, and I couldn't be more proud if you was my own."

For a moment the tears pricked in her eyes, because her own mother could not be here to share this moment, nor her sisters, and then Jessie blinked and reached for Annie's hand. "Thank you, Annie. I hope Joel thinks I'm pretty."

"I can tell you the truth of that. I watched him, at supper, watching you. Like you was one of them fancy candies—what do they call 'em, bon bons?—that he couldn't wait to take a bite out of."

Jessie laughed, a low, happy sound. "I think the blue check is the prettiest, don't you? And somewhere there's a bit of blue velvet ribbon that I can tie around my neck, and maybe enough to hold back my hair . . ."

She rummaged through the contents of the opened trunk and came up with the ribbon. "Maybe in the dark no one will see that the brown stuff doesn't match the rest of the dress."

She unbuttoned the bodice of the dust-stained garment she had worn all day and laid it aside. Annie had brought in the remains of the water heated for dishes; it was only tepid, but she was getting used to that. Jessie thought of Joel, off somewhere performing his own ablutions, and the warmth increased all through her.

"Oh!"

Annie turned questioningly, from where she had been repacking the trunk. "What's the matter? It's not time for your monthlies, is it?"

"No, no!" Jessie laughed a bit nervously, then sobered. "But I forgot to give him the ring. The one we're to be married with!"

It had been his mother's wedding ring, and Joel had given it to her as a pledge of his love, the first night they had lain together. She had tried to convince herself that they were as good as married, then, though she had known all along that it wasn't true. Certainly no one else would have thought so.

36

She had worn it, for a time, while she was pregnant with Joella. And she had not had a ring—nor wanted to wear Joel's on her finger—while she was married to Ben. So it had gone onto a string around her neck, where it lay now in the hollow between her breasts, a thin band of gold that gleamed in the candlelight.

"Don't worry. I'll slip it to him before the time comes," Annie offered, and accepted the ring, still warm from the touch of Jessie's body. "Go on, get into that dress, and I'll help with the buttons. I remember what a state I was in, the day I married my Sean! All thumbs, couldn't do a button to save my soul." She saw Jessie's face, revealing mingled emotions, and added gently, "You ain't the only one ever jumped the gun on the wedding lines, child. Reckon lots of people who do that don't admit it, 'less the child shows up too soon and gives them away. And it's no reason not to take full pleasure in your wedding night."

Jessie said a brief, silent prayer that Annie was right, and examined herself in the small hand mirror after her hair had been brushed smooth and secured with the bit of ribbon. She was pretty, wasn't she? All brides, they said, were beautiful. Joel deserved no less.

In the cradle, Lauren set up a thin wail, and Annie scooped him up to soothe him. "Ah, there, now, that's all he wanted, a little attention. Don't worry about this one tonight, girl, I'll see to him. You deserve one honeymoon night before you take on a baby."

One honeymoon night. Well, that was better than a lot of people had, Jessie told herself, and turned to peek out between the canvas flaps.

"It looks as if everyone in the train is here. And Joel...is it time to go out, Annie?"

It was Collie who handed her down from the wagon, though Jessie was scarcely aware of it. Her attention was all for Joel, who stood tall and strong and incredibly attractive, waiting for her. He'd washed and put on a clean shirt, and his dark wavy hair blew in the Kansas wind.

The preacher was a dried-up little man by the name of Hayforth, who, being as susceptible as anyone else to the temperature of the wind, cut short the sermon in which he might otherwise have indulged and got down to the wedding lines at once. Jessie stood before him, seeing the blur of a hundred faces around her in the light of the campfires, aware only of her own rapidly beating heart and the tall figure

37

beside her. She remembered that once before Joel had told her that he, too, had butterflies in his stomach, and how it had calmed her to be told that. Did he have those butterflies now, or was he as controlled as he appeared to be?

And then she felt Joel's hand close around hers, nearly crushing it, and she knew that he was no more blasé than she was.

It was over. They had been pronounced man and wife, and Jessie lifted her face for the gentle kiss that only hinted at withheld passion; the crowd milled around them, offering best wishes and kisses for the bride.

There were gifts brought to the newlyweds: small things, yet meaningful because they were wedding gifts. A china thimble with rosebuds painted on it, a pillow, a sheet, a cup and saucer with forget-me-nots in a border pattern, a quarter from this one, a dime from that one.

The Groves sisters moved forward and took charge of the gifts after Jessie had thanked the givers, both of them nearly as radiant as the bride.

"She's so lovely," Mamie said wistfully. "I wish I looked like that."

Beside her, Collie Aubin glanced down at the girl and smiled. "You're pretty enough to suit anybody," he said, and was rewarded with a flushed smile.

"When you get through with all that stuff," Collie suggested, "why don't we have some of that spiced cider Mrs. Ryan is stirring up over there?"

Alice was left to organize and deliver to the wagon the rest of the gifts, including a live chicken and a loaf of fresh-baked bread. There was no shortage of partners, however, when she turned back to the circle of dancers, for there were far more men on the train than women.

Music was provided by a fiddle, a harmonica, and a flute, all played with more enthusiasm than expertise, which did nothing to diminish the pleasure of the dancers.

Jessie was an excellent dancer. Dancing had been one of the primary diversions of the Mormons on Beaver Island, and it was she who had taught Joel the intricacies of the steps. She moved easily into his arms now as her new husband smiled down at her.

"Let's show them how it's done, teacher," he said, and suddenly her nervous bemusement was ended, and she was with her old friend Joel, which he had been before they became lovers.

His touch and the music worked a spell. It didn't matter that the dance floor was a grassy meadow, that the only illumination for the scene was a circle of leaping fires, that the evening breeze was cold. They kept themselves warm enough, stomping and swaying to the rhythm, sipping the hot spicy cider between sets, and their own excitement generated the most heat of all.

Jessie would have preferred dancing only with Joel, but that, of course, was impossible. She was whirled around by complete strangers with their winter beards still covering unfamiliar faces, and by others whom she knew by sight, like Oliver Allen and Collie Aubin and the wagonmaster, Captain Horn, who spat tobacco juice into the fire when they pranced near enough to it.

And then, because of course they would all be stirring at dawn, for not even a wedding could cause them an hour's delay in their journey, it was time to allow the fires to die, the merriment to subside, and the newlyweds to retire to Joel's wagon.

There was good-natured and only mildly ribald humor as goodnights were said. And finally Jessie was alone with Joel, fingers suddenly inept over her buttons in the darkness—to have lighted a candle would have meant they would have been silhouetted inside the canvas top to any viewer outside—and the time was here. Now, tonight, she was finally Joel Shand's wife.

"Jessie," Joel said, and she knew from the tone of his voice that he, too, felt the wonder of it, for the longing was there, the love, the joy of which they had both been deprived for so long.

She made a faint, strangled sound. "The buttons . . ."

She heard his chuckle, then felt his fingers close over hers. "Let me do it. I've always wanted to undress you. I'm going to want to do it every night forever. Oh, Lord, Jessie, we've waited so long for this. . . ."

He was more adept than she with the buttons, pausing to kiss her once, so deeply that Jessie began to slide into a euphoric haze; and then, more eager than ever, Joel drew a ragged breath and finished off the buttons.

The dress slid off her shoulders, and she shivered in the night air, until Joel ran his hands over her, slipping undergarments out of the way, caressing her breasts and slim waist and kissing her again until she was breathless.

Quickly, Joel divested himself of his remaining garments,

and drew her down on the lumpy pallet that was his bed. He buried his face in her hair, pulling it loose from its pins and the velvet ribbon, murmuring her name, over and over.

Lying awake the previous night, thinking forward to this moment, Jessie had feared that it would be spoiled by the memory of Cass Merriam's brutal rape. It was not. She never thought of Merriam at all, for there was no similarity between Cass's attack and Joel's performance now.

He murmured endearments as he explored, with mouth and hands, the curves and valleys of her body. This was not the first time that had lain together, but it was the first time they had come together without guilt or shame. In no way did Joel reveal that there had been those other times; he was gentle, tender, restraining his own passion until hers mounted to meet it, sweeping her along on a flood of sensation and emotion that surpassed anything Jessie had ever imagined to be possible.

And when it was over, when they had reached the explosive peak and begun to subside into blissful drowsiness, Joel did not release her, but drew her into his arms, against the hard-muscled length of him.

His whisper could not have carried beyond her own ears. "If we wake up early enough in the morning, we could do this again before we cook breakfast. Or we could just forget about breakfast..."

His breath was warm on her neck, his hand a comfortable weight on her bare breast. Somewhere, she thought hazily, there was a nightgown she had intended to put on, but it hardly seemed to matter. In the morning, in the daylight, she might be shy about rising naked before him. For the moment, however, she was content to remain where she was, reveling in the masculine strength and warmth of him.

"Goodnight, sweetheart," Joel murmured, and a moment later the slow even breathing of sleep overtook him.

Jessie, in a delicious lethargy, did not doze off quite so quickly. She had been concerned that she would not meet Joel's expectations, that she would be disappointed in the intimate relations, but neither of those things had happened.

She loved Joel Shand, and she truly felt that she had come to him as a bride. She listened to the Kansas wind as it whipped a loose flap of canvas, and she curled more closely against Joel and thanked God (with a flash of insight into what Zadie must have experienced) that she and Joel had found each other again.

5

In the wagon behind Joel's, Collie Aubin found it difficult to fall asleep. In his mind's eye he pictured the lovemaking taking place, something he had yet to experience but imagined in some detail.

Collie was not as naive as everyone thought he was. True, he was not yet nineteen years old, and because of the protectiveness of his parents he had been prevented from some of the experiences of living which might otherwise have been his lot. He looked younger than he was, with his butter-colored curls and his blue eyes, and he had an unfortunate tendency to blush, though he thought since they'd joined the wagon train he was beginning to bring that under control. After all, one is not easily embarrassed by things that are said so often.

Even Joel, with whom he had become good friends since Joel had turned up at the business establishment owned by Richard Aubin almost a year earlier, did not know that Collie was aware of their true relationship.

The son of a distant cousin, Richard had said when he brought Joel home to dinner. And, on the surface, the family had seemed to accept that statement as fact. Yet even if Collie hadn't observed the tightened mouth and the dangerous spark in his mother's eyes, he would have realized the truth.

For the love of God, Collie thought, anybody could see that Joel was the spitting image of Richard Aubin. His father had been wise—if he was to keep Joel around at all—to admit to a blood kinship, since anyone would have to be blind not to see it plainly in the strong faces, the crisp dark hair, the height and breadth of shoulder.

Collie had never heard anyone question the business of being cousins, though he thought surely some must have suspected the truth, but he himself had had no illusions about

41

it. Joel was his half brother, son of some woman his father had not married, a son Richard Aubin would rather never have encountered in this life.

Collie wasn't certain why his father had accepted his illegitimate son as a supposed "cousin" and actually introduced him into the family. Joel might have blackmailed his father in some way, though Collie didn't know that; he only felt that Joel was capable of using pressure, and that his father—*their* father—was not necessarily strong enough to resist such pressure. Collie had, after all, observed his parents all his life, and knew that Mabel Aubin kept a tight rein on her husband in many ways.

Whatever his parents thought about Joel Shand, Collie liked him. When Joel talked of heading for California gold fields—tales varied as to whether or not there were any riches left out there—Collie had been fired with the desire to join him. In vain Mabel pleaded that he had a marvelous future right there in Chicago: he would fall heir to Halvorsen Mercantile, which had come into the hands of Richard Aubin through his wife's family, and his social status was as assured as his economic one.

His mother's pleadings fell on deaf ears. Collie admired Joel—he recognized that the difference in maturity between them was more than the five actual years could account for—and he longed for adventure that would never be his if he stayed safely in Chicago.

Besides, there was Patrice.

He'd been in love with Patrice Hammond for as long as he could remember. Their families moved in the same social circles, and Patrice was a pretty little thing, with dark hair and big dark eyes, and a figure that made him ache to look at her.

If it hadn't been for that mess with her sister Suzanne, Patrice and her parents would have accompanied this wagon train; she would be here now, within his sight if not his touch. He couldn't help thinking about Patrice, knowing that Joel and Jessie were locked in an embrace of the most intimate nature, only a few yards away.

His loins ached now, and gradually the memory of Patrice faded, supplanted by a picture of the chestnut-haired Mamie Groves, which didn't do anything to alleviate his discomfort. Still, Mamie was here, a few wagons away, while Patrice had probably not yet left Westport.

That was something, Collie thought. The next time there

was a dance, he'd try to do more than bring Mamie a glass of cider. After a while the ache subsided, and Collie slept.

Farther along the line of wagons someone else was wakeful.

The stories that were whispered about Clara and Virgil Ridback would have been expanded considerably if the truth had been known. Clara introduced herself as Mrs. Ridback, when she was in fact still Mrs. Eben Snyden. She had been, before that, Mrs. Carl Maxon.

Clara was nearing thirty, though she confessed (coyly) to no more than twenty-three. Her hair was a rich, burnished auburn, which was the color nature had provided, and lush red lips which were assisted by the surreptitious use of cosmetics, as was the permanent flush in her cheeks.

Not that she cared, really, if they suspected she used artificial aids to increase her beauty. Poor, drab little creatures, she thought most of them. Except for that Jessie Ryan, who seemed too stupid even to know how pretty she was. With that hair, Clara felt she could have done something quite spectacular, rather than to pin it back in a bun.

The "marriage" to Virgil Ridback had occurred when she joined him in Independence, a month after he'd left her in Ohio. Eben Snyden had a big house in Ohio, and two hundred acres of prime land, and a dozen servants so that Clara didn't have to soil her hands on anything if she didn't want to. Eben was also sixty-two years old.

She'd been dazzled by Eben's wealth and possessions. When Carl Maxon took his pretty wife to live in one of the cabins on Eben's land, he'd thought she was as much in love with him as he was with her.

Clara herself had thought she was in love. Carl was a virile and handsome young man, though he hadn't a cent to his name, and the first year they were married his lovemaking had made up for the things they didn't have.

It was only after she saw what a great house could be like—saw that a woman could have jewels and pretty clothes and other people to wait upon her—that Clara began to hanker after more than a poor young husband who made a meager living working someone else's land.

When she saw that Eben Snyden was observing her, Clara was flattered. She coaxed Carl into the money for a new dress, and made it up herself with a neckline more suited to a belle in a southern mansion than an Ohio farmer's wife. It was

43

worth it, though, because when Carl wasn't around she paraded past the big house without the fichu that her husband would have insisted should cover her creamy breasts and throat, and Eben saw her.

Saw her, and decided he wanted her.

For a time, Clara was content with teasing him. It excited her, so that her sexual juices flowed more prodigiously, and Carl was delighted that his bride of a year could still be so passionate.

Eben Snyden was not content to be teased, however. He made it clear, in educated tones though rather vulgar language, that he wanted Clara in his bed. She was intelligent enough to know that what she gave away would be considered of little value, and pointed out to him, somewhat archly, that she was a married woman.

"I have a husband who would be most upset if I were . . . indiscreet," Clara pointed out.

Eben regarded her coldly, though that was not the sensation that tortured him every time he thought about her. "That can be taken care of," he assured her.

She never knew with any degree of certainty whether the accident a week later really *was* an accident, or whether Eben had arranged it. All she knew was that while Carl was working with an unbroken stallion there had been a ruckus that ended with the horse being shot, and leaving Carl Maxon trampled and broken.

They brought him home on a door unhinged from the nearest cabin for the purpose, where Clara nursed him for the three days that he continued to live.

Suspicion and guilt plagued her, and she was sincerely appalled at what had happened to Carl. But after he had died and been buried, and she was free to turn her interests where she liked, she did not long delay falling into Eben Synden's arms.

She had, Clara congratulated herself, been very clever. She had convinced everyone in the county of her grief over Carl, and had won the sympathy of most of them at her plight as a penniless widow. She had resisted Eben Snyden's efforts to entice her into his bed, or to allow him into hers—he was not at all particular about which bed it was—until she had led him with utmost cunning to propose marriage.

It didn't matter that much to Eben whether he married her or not. His own wife of thirty years had passed on several years earlier, and their children were scattered and gone.

There was no one to say him nay, no matter what he did. His bones were growing old, and one thing he thought would warm them was a beautiful young wife.

Unfortunately, the honeymoon period was rather brief. True, Eben had pressed upon her every material thing that any woman could ask for, but his physical agility in bed did not last out the first year.

Clara found that clothes and jewels did not make up for the lack of a husband able to perform his marital duties. Her hungers grew to intolerable proportions, to the point where she began a cautious movement toward the young man who had been hired to take over Carl's job.

Virgil Ridback was as virile as Carl had been, and as penniless. He had a wife and two children, of whom he was moderately fond, but he was not proof against a beautiful redhead who "accidentally" exposed her ankles and her bosom whenever he was about. He had never been near a woman who smelled the way Clara did, nor one who aroused him to such heights simply by smiling in his direction.

It did not take Clara long to figure out a way to escape an impotent old husband in favor of a young man able to satisfy her needs. She did not consider committing murder, or arranging a fatal accident; Eben was failing healthwise, now, and she guessed that he would not pursue her if she left. She had, however, no intention of leaving with only what she had brought into the marriage.

She took not only her jewelry and all the clothes she could pack into the wagon Virgil acquired for that purpose, she stole every cent of Eben's money she could put her hands on, and since it was just after harvest time when she left, that amount was considerable.

She gave no thought to the slender girl Virgil was leaving behind, nor to his sons. One could not, after all, take on the burdens of the entire world; a woman had to look out for herself.

The trouble was, they'd spent most of the winter holed up in a lodging house in Independence, with little for either of them to do, and Clara and Virgil found that the only thing they had in common was an insatiable appetite for sex. It was enough, for a while, but by spring, both of them were short of temper. Virgil was not as innovative as she'd hoped he would be; he had definite ideas about what was proper and what was not, in the marital relationship, and his ideas did not match his supposed wife's.

Clara might have looked for another protector, except for the fact that she'd made the mistake, in the first blush of romance, of allowing Virgil control of the money. She had looked all over the wagon before they left Missouri, and she still didn't know where the devil he'd hidden it. His increasing jealousy and superior attitude were driving her wild; what did he have to be superior about, when it was *her* money that had made it possible for them to flee Ohio?

She saw Joel Shand the first day they were at the campground outside of Westport. He came striding past their wagons, tall and muscular and incredibly masculine—younger than she, of course, but so *beautiful*.

She knew, when his gaze swept over her, that he found her attractive, too. That look restored a little of the good humor she'd lost when Virgil had shouted at her over burning his oatmeal, though how she was expected to cook over an open fire in the rain was beyond her. Naturally she didn't stand there, getting soaking wet, to stir it constantly.

Clara had smiled tentatively, and Joel smiled back.

She spent the rest of the day hunting feverishly for the box with the cash in it, the cash that was rightfully hers. She didn't find it.

It had been a major disappointment to learn that Joel Shand was engaged to marry that Ryan chit. *That* one wasn't wasting any time; Clara hadn't been in camp more than a few hours before she heard some of the details of how Jessie Ryan had become a widow only the day before. Become a widow when she'd shot and killed a man who was beating his wife to death even as she was in labor, and in his last action the fellow had fired at Jessie, as well, and killed Ben Ryan by mistake. At least, that was the story. Who knew what the truth was?

Clara wasn't entirely discouraged by Joel's interest in Jessie. She continued to bring herself to Joel's attention, and she could see that he admired her.

And now, tonight, he was bedding the girl. Well, it wasn't as if Jessie was a virgin; she'd been married to Ben Ryan, but it was rather stimulating to think about, anyway. No doubting what *they* were doing, there in the darkness a few wagons away.

Just thinking about it made Clara eager herself. Virgil Ridback was perfectly willing to match her ardor, and when he fell back in satisfied relaxation, he told her, "You're a real hot woman, Clara. The best I ever had, even if you are close to thirty."

That spoiled it for her. She jerked away from him, annoyed and sharp. "I've told you, I'm only twenty-three!"

Virgil laughed. "Sure you are, babe. Hell, it don't matter to me, not when you can tumble a man in bed that way."

Whatever pleasure she'd taken in their union was gone. Damn him, anyway! She'd find that money, and when she did, she'd make up her mind whether she was going to stay with Virgil or not. Quite possibly not, if someone better came along.

Joel Shand had married that prissy little Mormon piece, but that didn't mean he had to stay with her, or stop looking at any other females.

It was a long way to California, Clara thought. Who knew what could happen before they got there?

At least two other people lay awake longer than usual that night of Jessie and Joel's wedding.

It was inevitable, Mamie Groves reflected, that when one *knew* what a couple were doing on their wedding night, one would think about the matter of making love.

The closest she'd ever come to it was allowing Jimmy Welch to kiss her, after a church social back home; it had been very pleasant, up to the point where her father had come around the corner of the church and caught them. After that, she didn't care to remember.

Alice squirmed beside her on the straw tick—thrown under the wagon on a piece of canvas to keep it clean and dry, as there wasn't room for the entire family to sleep in the wagon—and Mamie whispered, "Are you thinking about them, too?"

Alice waited a few seconds to see if the faint voice had carried through the wagon bed to her parents over their heads. When there was no reprimand to indicate that Adrian Groves had overheard them, she replied in an equally low tone.

"I guess nobody can help thinking about them. I wish it was me, married to a good-looking man like that."

"I wonder if she likes it?" Mamie speculated. "I mean, I know she was one of those Mormons, but she's a lady. You can tell by the way she talks."

"We'll be able to tell by the way she looks in the morning," Alice said. "Don't you think?"

"Probably. Alice, I'm going to get me a man before we get to California. Somebody on this train, maybe that Collin Aubin. I know he's awfully young, but he's nice."

"Yes, but I'd rather have someone knows a little more. Collie's young and he's spoiled, sort of. Grew up in a rich family, with a big house and servants and all. Likely he didn't learn how to do much of anything a man needs to be able to do. He can't hardly swing an ax without chopping off a toe. Well, he skinned his boot, anyway."

"He'll learn," Mamie said hopefully. "And there's not a mean bone in his body. Not like Pa."

"No, not like Pa."

Overhead, something fell in the wagonbed and a male voice cursed. The girls curled more closely together for warmth, for the wind whistled beneath the wagon as well as over it, and the blankets were worn thin.

They knew better than to talk when their father was awake and might be disturbed. A moment later they realized that he, too, had been aroused by the wedding, though neither of them gave Adrian credit for enough imagination to be visualizing the newlyweds as they were doing themselves.

The sounds above them went on for some ten minutes or so, and then there was silence. Mamie waited until she heard the first snore before she whispered again.

"I wonder if Ma likes it? She never says anything, one way or the other."

"It wouldn't make any difference, anyway," Alice pointed out. "Whatever Pa wants, that's what he's going to do. I hope I can find me a better man than that, one that'll at least ask me once in a while what I want."

"Me, too," Mamie agreed. They didn't talk any more after that, but they both went to sleep with the same thoughts in their minds, each wishing it had been she who had joined Joel Shand tonight in the wagon a few places back.

6

Jessie woke feeling strangely comfortable and happy. The hand resting on her bare hip slid upward, cupping a breast, and it was only then that her eyes flew open as she remembered.

"Good morning, Mrs. Shand." Joel nuzzled her neck, then rose on an elbow so that he could kiss her. It was immediately apparent that he didn't intend to stop there.

"No, Joel!" The exclamation was muffled, for if anyone was stirring in the chilly dawn there was nothing to prevent being heard through the canvas walls. "What time is it?"

"Cap hasn't signaled yet, so we have time." Insistently, he pulled her deeper under the quilts. "You liked it last night, and if we don't do it again now, we'll have to wait another whole day...."

To Jessie's relief, she heard the cry echoing down the line, "Rise and shine! Rise and shine!"

"There isn't time. Besides, it seems...sinful, to make love in broad daylight."

"Why? Your precious Bible doesn't say anything about a man loving his wife only in the dark. All right, I'll give in this time, because they'll be giving me looks and remarks aplenty anyway, without me showing up late. But be prepared to go to bed immediately after supper tonight. This time I'll be the teacher, all right?"

He slid out of bed and stood in the narrow space between the carefully packed crates and boxes of supplies. Jessie caught and held her breath at the sight of him. Totally unself-conscious, Joel pulled on his trousers, muscles rippling over his biceps and back, then bent to kiss her before reaching for a shirt. "Come on, get up, you lazy female! Or I'll change my mind and risk whatever the hell they have to say about it, and come back to bed with you."

Jessie lifted a hand to the dark mat of his chest, liking the crisp curling hair there. She kissed him back, nearly undoing her resolution not to invite another amorous advance, then pushed against him with her fingertips. "Go! Let me dress and get a fire going, so we can have coffee before we start."

Joel stood as erect as it was possible to do in the confined space. "I'll go, but only after you get up. I want to see you, all of you, in the daylight. The way I saw you that first time, remember? When I surprised you swimming in the cove?"

She clutched the quilt under her chin, but Joel was having no false modesty. He jerked it away, grinning, so that she had to get up at once as the goose bumps rose all over her flesh.

"God, how beautiful you are! I love you, woman," Joel told her, and with another quick kiss he was gone.

She dressed quickly, shivering, but the chill was only on the outside. Inside, she felt warm and cozy and safe, as she had never done before in her entire life.

Annie, bless her, already had a small fire going; Jessie smelled the bubbling coffee, and she moved forward to help with the rest of the breakfast. Besides the chickens, Collie had brought back fresh eggs from town, and this morning there would be a special breakfast of fried eggs and bacon, a wedding gift from Joel's "cousin."

"Good morning," Mamie Groves chirped, and Jessie swung about to see the younger girl heading toward the river for water. Something in her face made Jessie flush, in the way that brides have always done.

"Good morning," Jessie echoed, and was glad that Mamie did not linger to talk.

A moment later the words were repeated when Clara Ridback strolled past on some errand. She, too, allowed her gaze to rest speculatively on Jessie's face, and this time Jessie felt anger rising with the embarrassment.

She turned to follow the other woman's progress, saw her stop to speak to Joel, pulling a thin wool shawl tightly across her full bosom so that it was displayed to advantage.

Jessie spoke almost savagely to Annie, who had just taken Laurie up from his cradle. "I don't think I like her, whether she's married to Virgil Ridback or not. She looked at me as if...as if she'd *watched* us last night, Joel and I."

Annie nodded. "No use to worry about it. Folks can't help thinking about it, with newlyweds about. I did, myself—re-

50

member my first night with Sean, I mean, for all it was years and years ago. Pay them no mind; they'll forget about you soon enough, and come up with something else to think about."

"I hope so," Jessie said sincerely. She felt as if her whole body was afire, as if all their neighbors had been voyeurs last night.

Having spoken to Joel, Clara Ridback was returning, and this time she didn't speak, only smiled in a sly way that made Jessie want to scratch her face.

When Joel showed up for breakfast, sniffing appreciatively over the tin plate Jessie handed him, she asked, "What did she want? That woman who calls herself Mrs. Ridback?"

Joel caught the animosity in her tone and grinned. "Mostly I think she wanted to speak to the bridegroom. If she was a cat, I'd say she was in heat."

Even from a husband, that was a statement that again made the color scorch her face. One didn't discuss such things between the sexes. She had an uneasy conviction, however, that Joel wasn't going to be one of those men who carefully censored his conversation for the benefit of his wife, the way Tully Ritter had.

"I don't like the way she looked at me," Jessie muttered, breaking eggs into the hot grease for her own breakfast.

Joel was still grinning. "If she's looking at you, it's because she's jealous. Of your age, and your beauty, and of the fact that you just married me."

Jessie forgot the eggs, glaring at him in astonishment.

"Well, you don't think much of yourself, do you!"

"I think I'm the luckiest man alive," he told her, the amusement softening to tenderness, "to have a woman like you. Don't let her bother you, honey. You're everything she's never been and never will be, and if you think about her at all, feel sorry for her."

He devoted his attention to the meal and Jessie ate her own in silence; the uneasiness remained.

An hour later, the train rolled on, heading toward the distant and invisible mountains.

7

Life on the trail was not easy, yet for Jessie those first few weeks as Mrs. Joel Shand were sheer bliss. She was toughening up so that she could walk for miles every day, and she had always enjoyed being out of doors. She wore a bonnet to keep the worst of the sun off her face; even so, her skin took on an apricot tone that was most becoming with her brown eyes and pale hair.

She spoke with Annie and Virginia Allen and the other women of domestic matters, the problems of cooking over open fires and drying clothes when they could not stop long enough to drape them over the bushes, and commiserated with the Groves sisters about how fast their shoes wore out and the impossibility of replacing garments put to much stress by their present circumstances.

Mostly, though, Jessie found herself watching for Joel as he rode up and down the straggling column of wagons, delighting in his smile and his touch when he came near, and contemplating the nights when they would be together. In daylight Joel might be authoritative and different from the man she remembered; in the dark, he was loving and giving, banishing any doubts she had had along the way.

Even the baby was not as much a trial as she had feared he would be. Lauren thrived on Ginny's milk, and when Annie acquired a goat from a discouraged traveler whose woes led him to head back toward the settlements of Missouri, they no longer had to depend on Virginia Allen to feed the child. Jessie found milking a goat little different from milking a cow, which she had learned to do that summer she lived on her stepfather's farm in Michigan.

Annie observed approvingly as Jessie fed Lauren this new milk, for it meant the girl had to hold the child and cajole him into accepting an improvised rag-and-bread teat instead of the breast nipple he'd grown accustomed to. The first feedings were difficult, and Annie knew that Jessie would gladly have handed the child over to her as an expert, but the older woman made it a point to be busy elsewhere when the baby was fed. The physical contact between Lauren and Jessie was essential.

It wasn't long before Jessie was smiling at her success, and when the baby smiled back at her, she felt a beginning twinge of maternal response. The first time she called him Laurie, Annie turned her back to hide her own smile of satisfaction.

Joel, too, was gratified that this relationship was taking a turn for the better. He knew perfectly well that Jessie would not have accepted the baby if he hadn't insisted upon it, and to some degree he understood her reluctance to take on Suzanne's son. Since he had been quite truthful, however, when he told Jessie that he had had no love for Suzanne at all, he assumed that she would forget the matter. It should not provide any impediment to Jessie's ability to mother the child.

Though Joel was concerned for Laurie's welfare, he was too busy to contribute much to it beyond a perfunctory query from time to time. Caring for an infant was woman's work, and he had plenty of chores of his own.

Cap Horn's wisdom in allowing only parties headed by adult males to join the train was soon evident.

"Even that isn't enough to avoid trouble," Joel reported. "I never knew there were so many damned fools running around loose."

It bothered Jessie a little when he made derogatory statements about anyone, but if she attempted to voice a small protest, Joel had a way of silencing her with a kiss. Which usually led to more than a kiss, if he could get her inside the wagon.

Every hour's travel took Jessie farther away from everything—except Joel—that had ever meant anything to her. Her home was home no longer, of course. Mama was dead and buried, so was Audra—though Audra had left several children—and Zadia and Dennis were somewhere either ahead or behind her—and from now on home would be wherever Joel was. She hoped that already a child was growing within her, the physical manifestation of their love for each other, a child of their own.

She felt a twinge of guilt, realizing how that had been

53

worded in her mind. A child of their own. Not Suzanne's son, but hers.

She did not, of course, say any of this to Joel.

The wagon train was a moving community, and gradually Jessie became acquainted with her new neighbors. She hadn't realized, until she'd lost them forever, how much the neighbors among the Saints had meant to her. Her girlhood friend Laura, and Laura's brother John Wesley and his wife Caroline, who had conspired with her to protect her relationship with Joel when seeing him had been strictly forbidden. Where were they now? Would she ever make friends like that again?

The Groves sisters were eager to be friendly. They were rather like puppies, young and awkward and exuberant, sometimes walking with Jessie beside the wagons, more frequently showing up as soon as the dust had settled when they halted for the night.

They were insatiably curious about life with the Mormons, yet there was no malice in their probings, and Jessie answered as freely as she could bring herself to do.

The business of polygamous marriage was uppermost in every mind when anyone said "Mormon." And King Strang himself—what had he looked like? Had she known his five wives? How had her mother reacted when her husband took a second wife? If Strang had not been murdered, would Jessie eventually have been one of the plural wives?

"No," Jessie said firmly. "I was always in love with Joel, and he wasn't a Mormon. I would never have married anyone else." She had learned to be adroit at turning the subject. "Would one of you like to feed Laurie? While I help Annie with supper?"

They adored Laurie. They were worth cultivating if only for that reason, for feeding a child with a rag dipped in goat's milk was a time-consuming process, and there were many other chores connected with a baby as well. It wasn't long before Jessie figured out that Mamie had another reason for cultivating a friendship, too.

"Your husband's cousin is such a handsome man," Mamie enthused. "Will he be eating with you folks every night?"

"No, I shouldn't think so. Last night he brought in three rabbits, and he asked Annie to cook them. But we aren't planning on having him here tonight."

"Oh," Mamie murmured, plainly disappointed. Collie had brought her a glass of cider the night of the wedding;

then he'd only smiled and nodded in passing. "I suppose...he's engaged to someone back home."

It was a transparent effort, but Jessie obliged. "No, not engaged. He's only eighteen, after all. There was a girl he liked a great deal...Patrice Hammond. If they'd come along on this train, as planned, I suspect he might eventually have proposed to her. But they may never make connections with us again; Mrs. Hammond was ill, and they may be weeks behind us."

"There are plenty of single men in this train," Alice said quietly. "They're always so busy, though. They scarcely have time to pause to visit, and Pa is so particular who we talk to...."

Her sister made a snorting sound. "Like as not we'll never get married, with Pa doing the picking. Unless it's some older man, a rich man. Not that there's anybody like that in the train, far as I know. I was almost engaged to a boy back home, only Pa didn't approve. Ma would like to see us both married, and I'd like to...to have a man of my own. And a darling baby, like Laurie." She bent over his cradle, making cooing sounds, and the infant bared naked gums in a display of delight.

It wasn't long before Jessie learned one of the reasons why the Groves sisters were so anxious to find men of their own, aside from the ordinary reasons why every girl so hoped.

Adrian Groves was a constant thorn in Joel's side, and his name came up with increasing frequency. Groves was a complainer and a whiner. His equipment was badly cared for and constantly broke down, and he had to borrow most of the tools he needed to fix things. He was inept as a repairman, and usually sought out the owner of the tools to do the actual work.

Though he didn't look anything like Tully Ritter, he reminded Jessie of her stepfather. He had a way of expressing an opinion as if no one could possibly refute it, though most of the time he displayed no particular insight or intelligence. He was a small man with a reddish mustache stained with tobacco juice, and the palest blue eyes Jessie had ever seen.

By the third day on the trail, he had a feud going with the man traveling behind him, a beanpole of a young man named Harry Kelly. Kelly traveled too close, or too far away, or scared Groves' heifers, or stared at Alice too boldly.

Groves was not a man to admit to making a mistake, but by the time they'd crossed into Nebraska, Groves was afraid.

He was used to forests, and this vast expanse of grassland intimidated him. The wind never stopped blowing, and the undulating sea of grass held no beauty for a man used to the security of trees. You could burn trees, and build houses of them, and fashion a new yoke for the oxen or an axle for the wagon. All the grass was good for was fodder for the animals.

So far they'd had plenty of water, but the talk of plains ahead, where water would be at a premium, sent currents of alarm through Adrian Groves. Sometimes already he felt an overwhelming thirst, and he would rush to the barrel secured at the rear of the wagon to quench it, and think about what it would be like if there were nothing in the barrel.

It didn't matter that hundreds of people had crossed the continent before him, that most of them had reached their destinations in Oregon or California. He didn't care about the others; he worried about himself. Plenty of travelers had died in the attempt to reach the golden land, and his terror grew that he would be one of them.

If his wagon broke down, and he couldn't fix it, would they leave him behind? Under a scorching sun, without water?

If they had encountered a returning train, Groves would have turned around and gone back to Missouri, even though there was nothing for him there, either. He'd never have left Indiana if he'd been able to keep body and soul together there. It had been all he could do to outfit a wagon for the journey, and the farther they went, the more he suspected that his preparations had been inadequate. He hadn't brought an extra wagon tongue, and there sure as hell was no hickory out here to fashion another one. The damned cottonwood would scarcely make a fire to boil a pot of beans, and was no use at all for repairing any part of a wagon.

While he recognized that the wild tales of Indian atrocities told around the campfires were either exaggerated or related of a bygone time, Groves was afraid of Indians, too. Savages who scalped and tortured, lurking out there below the horizon. He suspected that his fellow travelers, most of whom knew no more than he, delighted in tormenting him, seeing his discomfort when they spoke of hazards still to come. Yet there was a grain of truth there, too, and the more distance they traveled away from Missouri, the more tense Adrian Groves became.

Never of particularly good disposition, he grew more and more short-tempered. And he took out his frustrations on those closest to him, his wife and daughters.

56

Most of the time his abuse was verbal. Occasionally, the temper erupted into blows, and Jessie noted, and pointed out to Joel, the fact that Mamie had visible bruises the day after they'd heard Adrian's voice raised in anger from the Groveses' campsite.

"I know," Joel said grimly. "He's a mean one. There's not much anybody can do about how he treats his family, though. Not unless he kills somebody."

No wonder Alice and Mamie longed for husbands of their own. Cruel as Tully Ritter had been in many ways, he had never physically harmed her, Jessie thought in belated gratitude. She liked the Groves sisters and wished she could help them, yet a man had a right to rule his family in his own way.

Sarah Groves was a wispy, faded woman, with only traces of the beauty her daughters had inherited. She seldom spoke much, though she clearly enjoyed the company of other women and liked listening to their gossip. She never disputed her husband, and as far as Jessie could see didn't stand up for her daughters, either.

It was amusing to watch Mamie's inexpert yet charming attempts to capture Collie's attention. Whenever he came over to the fire Annie and the newlyweds shared, Mamie was sure to show up within a few minutes, on the slimmest of pretexts, so that Collie couldn't help acknowledging her presence. What his real reaction was to this, Jessie couldn't tell, though he was always pleasant and polite.

When she tried to probe the question with Joel, he made a snorting sound. "Collie can do better than those girls, I should think."

"What do you mean by that? Mamie's a lovely person!"

"Pretty, yes. But those Groveses are trash, Jessie. Uneducated, dirt-poor, and shiftless to boot."

Her mouth firmed in a way that Joel was beginning to recognize as ominous, though since they usually reconciled after a minor spat by making love with renewed fervor, he didn't really try too hard to placate her at once.

"Mamie's father is shiftless, I'll grant you. That doesn't extend to the rest of the family, as far as I can see. And since when has it been so terrible to be poor and uneducated?"

His grin was intended to be disarming. "Because we've all of us been poor and uneducated, you mean? Well, there's something about people that makes you know what they're like. And Adrian Groves is not the kind of man I'd have included in this wagon train, if it'd been up to me. He won't pull his own weight, he can't control his own family except with brutality, and he's a troublemaker. Getting involved with his womenfolk is asking for trouble, right there, because there's no getting them away from him. He isn't going to approve of anybody who comes sniffing around those girls, even if the man's intentions are honorable."

"And you don't think Collie's would be, if he liked Mamie?"

Joel shrugged. "Who knows? He's certainly not mature enough to marry the girl, in my opinion. And what other course is honorable?"

"You would have married me, at that age," Jessie reminded, "if they'd allowed us to do it."

"I'd been earning my living, and Ma's, since I was half-grown. I knew how to do it, to work like a man, by the time I was twelve. Collie never earned a penny except in that store his father owns, and what he doesn't know about females would fill a book."

"And you, of course," Jessie said, the sweetness of her voice tinged with something sharp, "know all about females."

Joel laughed. "I'm learning. Like, right now my wife is getting angry with me, and the best way to get that pout off her lips is to kiss them."

She put up her hands to hold him off, turning her face aside when he would have followed through on his statement, still annoyed with him. "I'm serious, Joel. I like Mamie and Alice, and I'd like to help them."

For a moment he seemed to consider overpowering her physically, then decided against it and let her go. "Well, I don't say you can't talk to them. But you'd be wise not to get too deeply involved, Jessie. That old man of theirs is poison."

She knew that was true, yet it only made her more determined to befriend the sisters. She remembered how much it had meant to her, when she had been befriended by those who sincerely tried to help. And it bothered her that Joel made the sort of judgments that he did, lumping Alice and Mamie with their father.

Still, for the most part she was deliriously happy with Joel. And as the country grew more threatening, she was glad to be under his protection and not that of someone like Adrian Groves.

They had passed a few graves beside the trail before they were even out of Kansas. They passed others, most of them marked with no more than a cross of twigs or a board torn from a wagon, many of them without names or dates. Those that were marked told poignant stories of death from cholera or accident. Several of them were infant graves, and they brought tears to Jessie's eyes as she remembered Joella.

They had crossed the Big Blue River, where the mosquitoes were huge and left most of the travelers a mass of itching lumps, and they saw dead animals, riding past them silently, each praying that his own would not meet such a fate. At Alcove Spring, which gushed clear and cold from a ledge of rock forming the stream, they paused long enough for the women to do the laundry, while every possible container was filled with the sweet water.

From this point on they began to climb, and those whose wagons were overloaded began to discard items that could be done without, in order that the bullocks could pull the slopes. The wild plum trees were in bloom, and the women looked at them, regretful that by the time the fruit could be picked they would be far beyond this area.

Their diets were supplemented by wild game, mostly rabbits and a few antelope, the latter small-boned creatures that tasted much like the venison Jessie had known at home; they longed for fruit and vegetables, however, carrying with them mostly potatoes and turnips from last year's crops. One evening Jessie and Mamie discovered some leeks, which were gathered to add variety to soups and stews for a few days.

On the 17th of May they met their first Indians.

"Pawnees," Joel reported. "Cap says they're harmless."

The band, only a dozen strong, walked into camp and stood about until Cap suggested that they be offered merchandise in trade. Feeling a trifle apprehensive in spite of Captain Horn's assurances, Jessie walked a step behind Joel as he carried his Indian trading goods to where they stood.

They were a bedraggled group, stolid and evincing no curiosity in the white men except for the items to be bartered. Their garments were of deerskin, Jessie judged, so rank that she could smell them from a distance of six or eight yards.

Their heads had been shaved except for scalp locks, stiffened with grease so as to stand up like the horns of some strange beasts. No one except the wagonmaster could understand a word of their language, and even he communicated as much by gestures as by speech.

True, these particular Indians did not appear dangerous, yet Jessie had heard the tales of Pawnee warriors, who often took whites prisoner and made them slaves. The thought of being made slave, or worse, squaw, of one of these creatures was enough to make the hair prickle on the back of her neck.

They were well satisfied with the trinkets Joel and a few of the others offered; Joel was elated with his own first foray into bartering, for he had two pair of moccasins—one for himself and one for Jessie—and a brooch.

It was not an Indian brooch. Jessie stared at it almost with revulsion as it was laid on her palm, moistening her lips. "Where did he get it? Did he take it off some white woman he scalped?"

It was intricately wrought in gold filigree, set with tiny red stones that she assumed were garnets. It *was* beautiful, but if some unfortunate female had lost her life over it, Jessie wanted no part of it.

Joel and Cap Horn entered into some sort of palaver with the brave, and Joel finally turned back to her with reassurance. "He says he found it beside the trail. He swears he has never drawn white blood."

Jessie studied the Pawnee, brave the insolent eyes that might show derision for the sensibilities of the white squaw, who said something to Cap.

"It's probably true," Cap told her. "Lot of people jettisoning things along here, stuff they don't absolutely have to have. There's a dresser over there, see? Belonged to somebody's grandma, more'n likely, but they carry it this far before they see their wagonmaster was right about how much they could haul. The trains pass through here regular, and nobody's having any trouble with this tribe. You can wear the pin with no guilt, Mrs. Shand."

She didn't really want it, but it was easy to see that Joel was delighted to be able to give her a gift, so she only murmured her thanks.

"It's pretty, isn't it? Just garnets, I guess, but one of these days I'll buy you diamonds, Jessie. Like my grandmother wore."

"I don't need diamonds." She twisted her mouth in wry humor. "Can you see me with a diamond necklace and my dusty gingham dress and walking boots?"

"You won't always wear dusty gingham. I'll buy you silks and velvets, the kind of clothes a lady wears. You're a lady, and you deserve the best, and I'll get it for you."

Though she didn't argue with him, she was sincere about not wanting diamonds. She dropped the brooch into her apron pocket, knowing that she'd enjoy wearing it if she could be sure about its former owner, knowing as well that would never be possible.

She turned away, then hesitated when Clara Ridback moved through the handful of women who had been brave enough to approach for a close examination of the Pawnees.

"Mr. Shand," Clara said, and Jessie's fingers curled into small fists before she could stop them. "Ask him if he'll sell me that necklace he's wearing. Those teeth, or whatever they are."

Why did she put her demand to Joel, instead of to Cap Horn, who could communicate with the savages? Jessie held her ground, unwilling to leave while this woman was here, resenting the way Clara moved to Joel's side, as if she belonged there.

It was, of course, the wagonmaster who conveyed Clara's request, and turned back to her with the Pawnee's reply. "He says the necklace is valuable to him. He cannot part with it."

Clara rested a hand on Joel's arm and looked up at him through thick lashes. "Ask him if he'd trade it for my earrings." She tugged at one of them, extending a palm with the delicate little hoop on it, toward the impassive brave.

The Pawnee's gaze slid toward the crate Joel had set at his feet. His words were dignified and without emotion.

"He says, you can have his necklace for the earrings— both of them—and one of those glass-beaded necklaces," Cap translated.

Clara flashed Joel a smile of such warmth that Jessie felt burned by it. She almost took a step toward the two of them before she realized that several of the other women were watching her; Jessie forced herself to keep her feelings out of her face and stayed where she was.

"Will you give him the necklace? Please?"

The transaction was done, and the trading ended. The Pawnees mounted their horses and rode away, and the crowd dispersed to their cooking pots.

Jessie waited until they were out of earshot of the others before asking in a voice that was almost too controlled, "Why did you have to pay for her necklace?"

"With a string of glass beads that hardly cost me anything? What difference did it make? It was easier than having her make a fuss about it; it's the kind of woman she is."

"I don't care for the kind of woman she is," Jessie said, watching where she put her feet so as to avoid the cow pies and the gopher holes, or prairie-dog holes, or whatever they were. "Everyone was watching us, you and me, when she put her hand on your arm that way." That *intimate* way, she meant.

Joel shrugged the business aside. "And what did they see? A woman who makes a fool of herself all the time, a poor pathetic thing that has to paint her face to make it look good, or so she thinks. And you and I are in love with each other, so we shut everybody else out; she can't do anything to spoil what we have, because we won't let her."

To Joel, the incident was insignificant, quickly forgotten.

Yet the resentment smoldered in Jessie's breast, and not all of it was directed at Clara Ridback.

8

They toiled up the valley of the Little Blue River, fighting mosquitoes and increasing daytime heat, seeing an occasional small band of Pawnees who didn't approach close enough to do any more trading. Jessie wore the Indian moccasins and found them wonderfully comfortable for walking; they didn't slip the way that leather soles did, and she was thankful to discard her regular shoes.

Sometimes, when Laurie was fussy, she carried him on her back in a sort of sling Joel had improvised for the purpose; he seemed more content there, a small warm spot between her shoulders. He was growing chubby and thriving on the goat milk; both Jessie and Annie fashioned garments for him out of some of the flannel Joel had brought for trading purposes. Diapers were a chore, because the places really handy for washing them were few and far between, and it wasn't always easy to get them dry. Jessie said nothing of this to anyone, and rubbed goose grease into her hands after she'd done the laundry in cold water, without soap, hoping that they wouldn't get any more chapped and ugly than they already were.

"You won't have to do that when we get to California," Joel promised, holding her hands in both of his to kiss her palms. "I'll get you a laundress, and a nursemaid, and a cook..."

"Joel, don't be silly!" She pulled back her hands, laughing. "We're never going to have a houseful of servants. I don't even want them!"

"Yes, we will," Joel said, and there was unexpected intensity in the words. "I'm going to give you a big house and everything a lady should have. The things my ma grew up with, and then never had all those years after I was born. The things you deserve, Jessie."

It was a romantic notion, and what harm did it do, for Joel to dream of riches? She'd heard it before, Joel's description of that huge, elegant house in Toledo where his mother had grown up, and she listened again to the details about crystal chandeliers and soft carpets and polished floors and stair railings.

It was, in Jessie's mind, a mirage, one of those mystical pictures she'd heard about that shimmer in the distance out on the desert they were approaching, pictures that wavered and disappeared as one approached. Let him dream, she thought.

As they approached the Platte River, they encountered areas of odd white patches of crystallized salt which the animals licked avidly; they stopped overnight near Fort Kearny, where there were no supplies to be obtained but the travelers could trade off some of what they themselves carried for cash money from the soldiers. There was also a doctor there whom several people consulted about their medical problems. Jessie would have loved having the man diagnose her suspected pregnancy, but if she was indeed carrying Joel's child, there were as yet no signs strong enough to confirm it. Besides, Annie, who saw the doctor, said that he was a drunkard and did not look trustworthy.

The Platte was a wandering, sprawling river, with many channels that meandered miles apart across the treeless expanse of prairie; it would be their lifeline for a long way and many days. In most places it was not very deep—only a few inches—but was hazardous because there were occasional holes where a man might plunge in to the depth of his neck, and besides that, there were patches of quicksand. Earlier travelers had, in kindness to their followers, put up makeshift signs of warning at some of the worst places, but they could not count on all others being safe. One of the Von Wald's cows was lost in the sinking sands, completely swallowed up before the younger boy could run for help from the men of the train. It was a sobering experience, and mothers were careful to warn their children and to watch them closely.

"Too thick to drink, too thin to plow," an observer had stated some years earlier, and this was so true that it was repeated, over and over, among the immigrants. It was water, and muddy or no, it would keep their stock alive, and with the stock, themselves.

The trees were virtually nonexistent, and the travelers were introduced to buffalo chips for their evening fires. These were the large flat dried droppings of the buffalo herds that roamed the area, and while they did send up a rather pungent aroma, they burned well enough. At first the girls were fastidious about carrying them, but necessity soon wore them down, and they filled their aprons and their buckets as if the fuel were the usual twigs.

The first time Cap Horn and a trio of hunters brought in one of the great shaggy beasts to be roasted over their fires, there was not a single dissenting voice about the value of the buffalo: the meat was delicious, far superior to anything they'd eaten since the beef they'd brought from Missouri had run out. It gave some of them new heart about the strangeness of the land in which they traveled.

They needed all the heartening they could get.

Joel's task was to keep everyone out of trouble, and to get them out of it when his first efforts failed. Along the Platte, the wagons sank to their axles in sand; wagon tongues, axle trees, and oxbows splintered and broke, and time must be taken to replace them.

After the third day in a row when he'd had to assist Adrian Groves out of one situation or another, Joel came to supper weary and sweat-soaked and grumbling.

"Cap never should have let him join us. He's not equipped, and he's slowing everybody down. Sometimes I feel like I'm just a nursemaid for Adrian Groves, and the man doesn't even have the gratitude to thank me for it."

"Why don't you get Collie to help you more?" Jessie suggested, thinking of Mamie.

A basin of water had been allowed to sit on the back of the wagon so that the silt would settle. Joel plunged his face into it and came up splashing water around his neck and ears, then reached for a towel. "Collie's more trouble than he's worth. He's got hands softer than yours." And then, seeing her face, he reached for her. "Honey, that wasn't meant to be cruel—everybody's hands are chapped! I just meant Collie's never done anything with his hands. He's a tenderfoot in every sense of the word. I can't even teach him to handle an ax without endangering everybody within shouting distance. And he knows even less about fixing wagons. He's building up muscle but still isn't a lot of help when he puts his shoulder to the back of a wagon to heave it out of a sinkhole. Christ, I'll be glad when we get through this rotten country!"

Jessie made a silent plea for forgiveness for the blasphemy. "It won't be like this when we get to California, will it? I couldn't bear it if I had to live in a place like this the rest of my life!" She looked around the barren landscape, where even the grass had given up the fight to stay green, though it still provided sustenance to the stock. "I need trees, and water..."

"There's the Platte," Joel said dryly, "three miles wide, and knee-deep. It better be true, what they say about California. God, I'm starved. Is supper ready?"

Joel was busy doing things all day, Jessie reflected. He didn't spend as much time as she did, looking at the scenery. It depressed her and frightened her, a little, though everyone said it would be better once they crossed the mountains.

Would they ever reach them, the mountains that kept them from their goal? Some days she looked across the empty land and doubted.

They ate in silence more weary than comfortable; they had traveled, Joel estimated, twenty-three miles that day. They listened to a tirade against his family by Adrian Groves, delivered in a voice that made Jessie cringe. When Collie wandered over to share coffee with them, after his own solitary supper of cold beans, Jessie said pointedly, "I'd hate to belong to that family. I feel so sorry for poor Mamie and Alice."

"He's miserable, all right," Collie agreed, accepting the tin cup Joel offered. "I think you've got trouble brewing there, Joe. Groves and Harry Kelly had words over that least bullock of Kelly's, trampled over Mrs. Groves's laundry or something, and Groves threatened to shoot it."

Joel swore. "He's a bully, and most bullies bluster a lot. I hope that's the case now, because if Kelly loses an ox he's likely to do some shooting of his own. We've still got a hell of a long way to go, and one bullock might mean the difference between getting Kelly's wagon through and having to leave it behind. You're friendly with Kelly. Why don't you calm him down, and be sure if anything does happen, he comes to Cap or me instead of taking matters into his own hands."

"Sure, I'll talk to Harry. Just don't expect me to get near Adrian Groves." Collie sipped cautiously, for it was easy to burn one's mouth on the tinware. "I hear we're going to have a dance when we get to the forks of the Platte. Celebrate, sort of, that we've got that far. I was just thinking, Joe, if you're the one figures out the watches that night, give me an early shift, will you?"

"And miss the dance?" Jessie asked. "You're such a good dancer, the girls will surely be disappointed, Collie!"

"I think I'll be safer watching for Indians than getting mixed up with those females." Collie confessed. "I wasn't aiming to get me a wife before I got to California and figured out how to take care of one, but those girls sure got marriage on their minds."

"Maybe you ought to think about it," Joel advised. "It's not bad, if you pick a pretty, spirited one."

"If they were all orphans, it would help," Collie said, and though he didn't mention Mamie by name, Jessie wondered if it was Adrian Groves who was making him uneasy, rather than Mamie.

Joel stood up and threw the dregs of his coffee out across the dry grass. "Well, guess I'll walk along and check on things before I turn in. I'll only be gone a few minutes, Jessie."

Because Collie was there, he didn't suggest that she undress and wait for him in bed, but she was afraid that Collie knew what he meant, anyway. She was glad Collie didn't look at her. She had already fed Laurie and tucked him in for the night, and after the men had gone she wandered ahead to speak to Annie. They talked for a few minutes and Jessie had just turned to go back to her own wagon when they heard the altercation, in raised, angry voices.

"Now what?" Annie muttered. "Seems like folks are getting edgy, kick up a fuss over nothing."

"It's this country," Jessie said, straining to see what was happening around the dying campfire a few hundred yards away. Joel was there, surely that was Joel, and who else?

She drew in a breath when she recognized Clara Ridback, unmistakable in a rose silk dress. Nobody else on the train had a gown that color, just as no one else wore silk. Her hesitation was brief; Jessie began to move briskly toward the small group and heard Virgil Ridback's voice, slightly slurred as if he'd taken a few nips from the bottle everyone knew he kept in his wagon.

"Why don't you watch where you're going? A man's got a right to sit by his own fire without some oaf tripping over his feet."

She couldn't make out her husband's rejoinder, but she saw Ridback stand up, his complexion ruddy in the firelight. His mouth was ugly.

"I'll tell you what, Shand. I can do without your advice. Who made you second in command of this outfit, anyway? I don't take no orders from a kid ain't even dry behind the ears yet. And while we're on the subject of things I don't like about you, mister, I don't like you buying presents for my wife."

Jessie nearly tripped over some unseen obstruction, then hurried on past the Athertons, who stood beside their wagon, also caught up in whatever was unfolding in this small drama.

"Oh, Virgil, it wasn't anything but an Indian necklace," Clara protested in an amused tone. "Just to prove, when we reach civilization, that I actually got within touching distance of the savages."

Joel's back was toward her, and Jessie had almost reached him when she twisted her ankle in a hole and paused, gasping against the sudden pain.

"I didn't exactly buy your wife a present, Ridback," Joel said, holding his temper with obvious effort. "She paid with her own earrings, which were far more valuable than anything I had to offer, and the brave wanted a few glass beads thrown in. Ask anybody who was there."

Ridback's lips drew back to reveal his teeth. "Get this straight right now, Shand. Keep away from my wife, you bastard."

If the man had been content with everything except his final two words, Joel would probably have turned around and walked away from him.

As it was, being called a bastard, that term that had so often been applied to him throughout his life, was too much for a temper already frayed by a difficult day.

Jessie reached for his sleeve and felt the material slip through her fingers as Joel lunged toward his antagonist.

Virgil went sprawling, his head hitting the side of his wagonbed with an audible *thunk*, surprise etched on his face as he then slid to the ground.

This time Jessie managed to get a hand on Joel's arm, feeling the bunched muscles that bespoke his intention of another blow if the man got up. Virgil didn't, only lifting a hand to his mouth, saying nothing.

Clara did not rush to her husband's defense. Indeed, she didn't even look at him. Instead she was watching Joel, a faint smile playing around her full rouged lips, a smile that made Jessie's fingers tighten convulsively.

"No, Joel! Leave him alone," she said urgently, softly, and knew that she really meant *leave her alone*.

For a matter of seconds, Joel resisted her pressure. And then she felt some of the rigidity go out of him; he turned his back on the couple and strode off at such a pace that Jessie was hard put to keep up with him.

At their own fireside, Jessie offered to put a strip of soft cloth over his bloody knuckles, but Joel brushed her aside. "It'll heal. It's not the first time I've split skin on somebody's teeth. If he ever calls me a bastard again I'll do worse than that."

"He didn't even know about...about your background," Jessie told him quietly. "He was drunk, and angry because he thought you'd paid some attention to his wife. You wouldn't like it, either, if some man brought a gift to *me*." She resisted putting into words how she had felt about his contribution toward the Indian necklace Clara wanted. "Forget it. He didn't mean anything about you personally, and you'll only make matters worse if you carry a grudge."

Joel kicked dirt over the last of the fire to put it out and said flatly, "Nobody is going to call me a bastard and walk away from it. I'm not going to let anybody throw dirt in my face any more, Jessie. Ever. I'm going to be somebody; people are going to respect me."

She understood his feelings, for his childhood had been one of not only material deprivation but of torment over something he couldn't help—the fact that his father had never married his mother. She didn't think it likely that knocking out the teeth of anyone who reminded him of that, however innocently, would help him win his goal. Yet while a part of her ached for him, another part recognized that striking out in this way would do nothing to help him achieve what he wanted.

Joel glanced back to where the Ridbacks' glowing coals were the only ones left as far as he could see. He drew her firmly against him, bending to brush his lips against her hair.

"Come on, teacher, let's go to bed," he suggested.

For the first time, his lovemaking had an urgent, rough quality to it that she knew came from the hurt he suffered at being relegated from assistant wagonmaster to bastard, a step back into the past he struggled to escape. He did not actually hurt her, but there was not the tender touch she had come to revel in, and when his hands slid over her hips and breasts there was a demand in them, a demand that she heal his wounds.

Jessie did it in the only way open to her, with her lips and her body, and prayed that it would be enough, that this would not set the pattern for their future, because she would rather hurt herself than see Joel suffering.

In the morning no one mentioned the episode, but she had no doubt that every man, woman, and child in the outfit knew what had happened. No one had time to dwell upon it, however, for there was plenty of other excitement to think about.

They were moving steadily forward across the almost featureless terrain when the cry went up from somewhere in the rear of the caravan. "Buffalo! Buffalo!"

Jessie, walking beside the wagon driven by young Andrew Satler, stopped and looked back, shading her eyes against the sun, which was as yet only halfway up the blue bowl of sky. At first she could see nothing, and then she felt it: the trembling in the ground beneath her feet, the vibrations caused by hundreds of running animals.

Within minutes she could see them, off to the north, and they were coming fast, at an angle suggesting they would cross the trail behind the wagon train. She looked up at young Satler and smiled. "Fresh meat, maybe?"

"I hope so," Andrew agreed, grinning in response.

Their anticipation was short-lived, however, for Cap Horn rode toward them, shouting orders. "Get your stock together! Hold your bullocks! The herd won't cross behind us; they never do. They'll swerve and try to cross ahead of us, and they may stampede our animals! Get the women and children into the wagons!"

He was gone, repeating his message, and Jessie hastily scrambled up onto the back of the wagon where she could stand to watch. From this distance off the ground she could see much better, and the herd of running animals was huge.

Hundreds of them, maybe thousands, she thought, numbed. Great hairy shaggy beasts much larger than the cattle or the bullocks that drew most of the wagons, with horns that could toss a man or gore a horse unwary enough to get too close.

Only too clearly she saw the truth of Cap Horn's prediction. The leaders of the herd, hooves thundering in a rhythm she could feel even through the wagon wheels, veered away from the drifting of dust that rose in the wake of the train, and a moment later the first of them raced alongside the caravan. Jessie almost forgot to breathe.

The buffalo were immense. Their wild red eyes were almost as intimidating as those curved horns and the sheer bulk that was surely sufficient to overturn a wagon and crush it to splinters, and its riders with it.

As if in response to Jessie's thought, the wagon swerved sharply and for a perilous moment she clung quite literally for her life. To be thrown off meant to be trampled by the oncoming wagon behind even if the stampeding herd missed her.

Splinters tore into her hands, but she dared not let go, and then she regained her balance and swung herself between the canvas flaps, into the wagon. Her palms stung, though she scarcely noticed it.

Jessie made her way forward in the wildly careening conveyance, falling several times against the edges of boxes that would leave bruises, and she didn't feel that either.

Young Andrew fought frantically to slow the pace of his bullocks, but crazed by the smell and noise and speed of the buffalo, the draft animals went wild. There was no holding them; the best they could hope for, Jessie saw, was to keep the wagon upright until the buffalo had passed and their own animals could be calmed.

The whole thing could have lasted no more than five minutes, yet it felt like years. The sound was incredible; the air reverberated with it, and Jessie reached the front of the wagon and clung to the seat, kneeling behind it, gasping an incoherent prayer.

Ahead, she saw a bucket fly off the side of Annie's wagon and disappear under the pounding hooves, flattened almost before it struck the ground. Dust rose in choking clouds, obscuring her vision, and she wondered where Joel was. Not caught in the midst of that murderous herd, please God!

And then the thundering diminished, and there was left only the battle to calm their own animals. That was task enough, and when at last he pulled the bullocks to a halt, trembling and sweating, Andrew sat white-faced and limp, every muscle aching, his shoulders feeling as if they'd been pulled from their sockets.

One of the bullocks went down on its knees, and Jessie, dragging herself up onto the seat, looked at it in dismay. "It's hurt," she said, finding it difficult to summon enough breath for speech.

"It's a miracle if they ain't all broke all their legs," Andrew said, showing the same lack of breath. A wagon careened around them—Adrian Groves's wagon—and they saw a wheel detach itself and roll slowly out across the prairie for some yards before the wagon pitched to one side and plowed a furrow through the dry ground. The driver was catapulted over the footboard and onto his stumbling animals, disappearing between them.

All around them, now that the buffalo had surged ahead of and beyond the train, they heard men's shouting voices, children's cries, a woman's shrill scream. Not everyone had stopped as quickly as Andrew, and not all had escaped damage.

Jessie and Andrew jumped down as soon as they thought their shaky limbs would hold them. Andrew stood at the bullocks' heads, speaking to them, soothing them. "Can't see nothing wrong with this one," he said, "but he don't want to get up."

The animals were rolling their eyes in fright, flanks heaving and dark with sweat. Jessie didn't think they'd take off again. They were clearly exhausted.

"Stay here with them," she instructed. "I'll see if Mr. Groves is hurt."

By the time she reached that wagon, Mamie and Alice were helping their mother to her feet, trying to soothe her near-hysterics. Mamie looked at her, white face streaked with dust, and left her mother to Alice's attentions.

"Pa's hurt, I think," she said, and moved with Jessie to the tangle of harness and oxen and driver.

One of the bullocks had broken its neck; Jessie swallowed and diverted her ministrations to the man pinned beneath the great body.

Adrian Groves was not unconscious, though he wished that he were. His legs were crushed. He knew it, and he could not move. So far there was little pain, only the terrible sensation of weight, but he knew the pain would come. His wide eyes stared up pleadingly at the two girls.

"Get help. Get the thing off from me."

Clearly there was nothing they could do themselves. "Stay with him," Jessie said, seeing Mamie's terror, "and I'll find someone to help."

That was easier said than done.

The wagon train had splintered off in a dozen directions. Animals were down, wagons overturned, and every man had his hands full trying to see to his own family. She met Collie, pale but otherwise looking normal; his wagon was intact, and his animals would be all right once they calmed down, he thought.

"It's Mr. Groves. He's pinned beneath a dead ox."

Collie, for the first time since she'd met him, swore and failed to apologize for it. "I can't move an ox by myself. I'll see if I can find Joel."

"You haven't seen him?"

Collie shook his head. "No, but if I know Joel, he was out there trying to head off that damned herd. God, did you ever hear such a noise in your life? I thought we'd all be killed."

"See if you can find him. Hurry, Collie!"

Collie strode off through the dust that was beginning to settle, exposing a nightmare scene. Panic had by no means ended because the buffalo herd had passed them; rather, the damage was only now being realistically assessed, and the fact that no one appeared to have been killed did not entirely mitigate the extent of the disaster.

Jessie hurried past the Von Walds, wandering among their possessions, which were strewn over a considerable area; Mrs. Von Wald, a plump middle-aged woman, stood in the midst of her brood looking at the remains of her grandmother's china, the shards with hand-painted roses incongruous against the dusty earth.

The Allen wagon remained upright, and the heaving bullocks stood quivering as Oliver evaluated the situation. Nellie, tears streaking her dirty face, tugged at his trousers for a reassurance he didn't have time to give her; she turned when Jessie approached to put up her small arms.

Jessie scooped her up, disregarding the dirt and the fact that the child had wet herself. "Is Virginia all right?"

"She's got a knot on her head the size of a goose egg, but other than that she's all right," Oliver said distractedly. He was a tall, thin young man, as washed-out as his wife, and with almost identical coloring. He ran a hand through his fair hair, glancing toward the wagon. "Threw Charlie out of his box, though, and he was screaming his head off. Guess that's a good sign, that he can still cry. She's got him quiet now."

"Mr. Groves is pinned under a dead ox," Jessie said. "Collie's looking for Joel, to try to get him out. A wheel came off their wagon and threw him out. Can you help?"

For a moment he only stared at her as if her words did not penetrate. Then he nodded, and raised his voice. "Ginny? You all right? I got to go help somebody."

Virginia's head appeared between the canvas flaps. "Go ahead. Charlie ain't hurt much, just scared. Lucky he fell on those quilts. You all right, Jessie?"

It was the question repeated up and down the line, if the scattered forces could be so termed. "You hurt? You all right?"

There were plenty of injuries, but as far as Jessie could see, most of them were minor. Annie had suffered a wrenched shoulder, but she didn't think it was out of place. Grimacing in pain, she moved toward Jessie through the confusion. "Where's the baby? Did he get hurt?"

Dear God. She hadn't even thought of Laurie, and he hadn't made a sound. Jessie's eyes went wide; she thrust Nellie into her father's arms and ran back toward the wagon, scanning the scene for Joel. He would have been on horseback; he ought to be visible, but he wasn't.

She didn't hear Andrew's question: "Is Mr. Groves killed, ma'am?" She clambered up the spokes of the wheel and virtually fell into the wagon, an ache in her chest, a panic over what she'd tell Joel if the baby had been killed. And she hadn't even thought about him!

The cradle was canted slightly to one side, resting against the edge of the tick where Joel and Jessie slept. The baby lay asleep, one chubby fist in his mouth, and even as she reached for him to make sure that he breathed, Laurie made sucking noises.

Her knees went weak with relief. She stayed her hands, resisting the impulse to hold him against her. No, better let him stay asleep as long as he might; there were plenty of other things to do.

She saw Joel coming as she leaped back to the ground, and this time the relief was overwhelming, enough so that it made her feel, for a moment, physically sick. He slid off the horse and caught her in a quick embrace, then released her before she was ready to let him go.

"Laurie?"

Her laughter was unsteady. "Slept through the entire thing! Joel, Mr. Groves..."

"I know, Collie told me. It'll take more than the two of us to get that bullock off from him."

"Oliver Allen is there, and Andrew could help now..."

She moved with them, sure she would hear the baby when he woke. She stood by, listening to Mrs. Groves's quiet weeping as the men struggled to lift the dead animal off her husband. They did it by bringing a couple of spare yokes from neighboring wagons, rolling the bullock until they could get the yokes under it, and then lifting them enough so that two other volunteers could pull the injured man free.

By this time Adrian Groves was in agony. Joel, sweat dripping off the end of his nose until he wiped it with a sleeve, stared down at the man with a muttered curse. "Both legs crushed, by the look of it. Be lucky if he ever walks again."

Sarah Groves stared at him pathetically, whether in concern for her husband or for herself and her daughters uncertain in Jessie's mind. "What will we do?" she asked.

"We're only a little way from Fort McPherson," Joel said slowly. "It may be there's a doctor there."

No one said anything. They all knew that many of the army outposts were without medical personnel, and that among the so-called physicians in those that were supplied there were drunks and incompetents. Still, they had little in the way of choices.

Jessie spoke uncertainly. "Annie knows a bit about healing."

"Fetch her," Joel said, and Jessie ran to do his bidding.

9

"Shouldn't wonder," Annie reported, "if those legs oughtn't to come off. Pretty well smashed, they are. I can set a broken leg, but not when it's been crushed that way."

Adrian had been carried, moaning, to the shade of Annie's wagon. His own could be repaired, Joel said, but it was not the highest priority on his list. Going on today was impossible; there were too many injuries to care for and too many wagons to repair.

Several wagons were damaged past the point of being salvaged. It was part of Joel's responsibility to attempt to make other arrangements for those families who could not proceed in their own conveyances, and he left Jessie and Annie to do the best they could with the injuries.

Laurie woke and had to be fed, which turned out to be a problem because his milk from the morning had been spilled during the stampede, and the goat was nowhere to be found. In the end, Jessie delivered the child to Ginny Allen, knowing she could trust her to see to him until Jessie herself returned.

All of the remaining injuries were far less serious than Adrian's crushed limbs. There were plenty of bumps and scrapes, and a few gashes that would leave nasty scars but were not life-threatening so long as they did not become putrefied. And there was Virgil Ridback.

Jessie was bent over a small boy with what Annie diagnosed as a fractured wrist, though the bones were not far out of place. It should heal with only a slight deformity, Annie thought, if they immobilized it for a few weeks.

"Younguns heal fast," she said, and went to search for something to use as splints. She returned with a pair of wooden spoons, and bound these along the thin forearm with strips from a pillowcase while Jessie kept the child quiet and still.

"Mrs. Shand."

Jessie straightened as Annie put the last knot into the strips of cloth, and looked into the blue eyes of Clara Ridback. It was the first time she'd ever seen the woman in less than a well-dressed-and-coiffed state, yet strangely enough having her auburn hair falling loose from its pins, and dirt smearing one artificially tinted cheek, did nothing to detract from Clara's beauty. That she was pale was obvious, however, for the rouge stood out in too-bright spots.

"Yes?" Jessie said, maintaining her reserve.

"I'm looking for Mr. Shand."

"He's busy up ahead somewhere with the damaged wagons, I think. I don't know exactly where."

Clara swallowed. "My husband is hurt. I need help with him."

For a moment Jessie felt a twinge of compassion, for she could see that it cost this woman something to have to make this request of her, rather than of Joel. And then she hardened her heart and her voice, keeping to a noncommittal tone.

"Mrs. Ryan and I are doing what we can for the injured. We'll be along as soon as we've finished here."

Clara's tongue snaked over dry lips, and then she nodded. "Thank you. He's in considerable pain, and I don't know what to do for him."

Annie stared after Clara's retreating back. "Only thing we got on this train for pain, that I know of, is whiskey. And Virgil Ridback's got his own supply of that."

They left the mother soothing the little boy, and picked their way through the chickens that had been turned loose from their crates and were now being pursued by the younger Von Walds.

"Keep an eye out for Nanny," Jessie suggested. "I don't know where she got to. I hope she wasn't trampled by the buffalo."

The temperature was rising under a cloudless sky, and the dust rose in choking clouds around their feet. Jessie looked at the river and longed for a cool, clean stream rather than this shallow, muddy mockery of the creeks she had known at home. A bath—a quiet cove with a sandy beach—would go a long way to restore her spirits.

But there was only the turgid Platte, which was almost thick enough to walk on, and the fresh water must be retained for drinking and cooking purposes.

Virtually every family had its share of injuries and damages. Much of the latter was to sentimental items, such as treasured china which was now smashed beyond repair. An occasional woman stood weeping over her lost possessions, but most of them moved with stoicism among the wreckage, salvaging what they could and saving their tears until they could be shed in private.

By the time they reached the Ridback wagon, Clara had washed her face and combed her hair. Without the rouge, which she had not had time to reapply, she looked younger and prettier, and the auburn hair was a shimmering cloud around her face. Jessie noted that at the same time she saw Joel coming from the opposite direction.

"He's hurting pretty bad," Clara said. "I got him a pillow, but I didn't think I ought to move him. His leg's broke."

It was, indeed. It didn't take an expert to determine that, since a splinter of bone protruded through his trousers. He was white under his beard, and when Jessie dropped beside him to touch his arm, Virgil was cold and clammy despite the heat.

Annie made clucking sounds. "Going to be a problem to set that one," she said. "But if it ain't smashed like Mr. Groves's . . . well, we'll have to cut those britches off'n him."

"Not my leg," Virgil pleaded, moisture standing on his brow. "Don't take my leg."

Joel brought out a knife and slit the pant leg so that the injured member could be examined. Behind him, Jessie winced at the sight of the wound, though she stifled her audible dismay.

"You ain't gonna cut it off," Virgil said through his teeth. "Not my damned leg, you ain't!"

"You're right," Joel told him. "I don't know enough to do it. What do you think, Annie? Can we set it? If I pull on his shoulder and we get Collie to pull on his ankle, can you get a splint on it? Will it heal, with an open wound that way?"

"Be better if it was cold weather," Annie said. "But no help for that, is there? Jessie, you fetch Collie, and I'll see what I can find for splints. Wooden spoons won't be enough for this one."

"Gimme a drink," Virgil said. "Clara, get my bottle from under the seat."

A few seconds later Clara reported, "It's broke. It's all run out."

Virgil swore. "Get another one, then. They can't all be broke! In the box at the very back of the wagon."

Five minutes later, Clara emerged with a full bottle which had been carefully packed and had remained intact. Had her husband been in any shape to observe her closely, he would have realized that she had found, as well as the whiskey, something even more valuable. The coins he had packed beneath his whiskey bottles had trickled out the broken corner of the same packing crate, and she had taken time to scoop them up and re-hide them before she brought the whiskey. Not that it mattered, for Virgil wasn't going to be in control of things for some time to come.

The whiskey had not yet done its work when the procedure was begun. Jessie was instructed to stand at Annie's side to provide whatever assistance she needed, while the men pulled from both directions.

Virgil uttered one high piercing scream and went mercifully limp. The bone slide back into place, and while Collie and Joel strained to hold it there, Annie worked quickly to pad the oozing wound with clean sheeting. Then, with Jessie's help, she secured the entire thing with two boards (ripped off the side of one of the wrecked wagons) on either side of the leg, and looped a strip of cloth about his ankle to put as much tension as possible on the leg when the cloth was tied over a block beneath the foot.

"Better cover him up with a blanket," Joel advised.

Clara had watched without flinching, and now moved to obey. "Do you think it'll get better?"

Joel shrugged. "Like Annie says, it'd be better if it was cold weather. Not so likely to get maggots in it when it festers. On the other hand, sometimes the maggots clean it out, and that seems to help, too. If you're religious, say a prayer."

Clara summoned a smile, though she was clearly shaken. "Thank you. All of you. We appreciate it. Only now I don't know what to do next. I can't drive that wagon, and Virgil isn't going to, either."

"I'll see if I can find someone else to do it. We've got a couple of families without wagons of their own to drive, now."

"What about him?" Clara looked down at her unconscious husband. "How am I going to move him?"

"Is there a place for him, a straw tick or something inside? Maybe we better lift him in there now, Collie, before he comes to. Get a couple of those boards and we'll make a stretcher."

"Is it going to hurt something awful, to be jogged along in that wagon?" Clara asked.

"Keep giving him sips of that whiskey when he wakes up," Joel advised. "It'll do as much good as anything we've got."

Again the smile flickered. "Thank you. I don't know what I'd do without you."

Inside Jessie, something tightened. Now the woman would have all the excuse she needed to call upon Joel for assistance, to seek him out for any little thing. And Joel would go, no doubt.

"I'd better see to Laurie," she said, and didn't know if Joel even heard her. He was still standing there, talking to Clara Ridback, when she walked away.

They were a sorry lot that straggled into Fort McPherson the following day. An unscheduled day's rest, however, put them into better spirits to continue their journey. Clothing and bedding, spilled out onto the ground during the stampede caused by the buffalo herd, were washed and mended. Some of their stock had been killed; some had been injured so that they had to be destroyed. Most of the animals that had strayed, like Nanny, were eventually rounded up, little the worse for wear.

The two wagons damaged beyond repair were cannibalized for parts, and the couple and young single man who had lost their vehicles teamed up with others; while this meant leaving a few things behind, they could at least voice their gratitude that they left no graves in the dry Nebraska earth.

Almost every day now they had passed graves, silent reminders of what might lie ahead for themselves. Yet they had come this far safely, and most of them felt they would be among those spared to complete the journey.

The army doctor commended Annie and Jessie for their efforts among the injured. "Very neat work, ma'am," he said, addressing Annie as the senior member of the team. "A pity about Groves and Ridback, though. There's nothing to be done with Groves's legs, I'm afraid." He was a thin, dry man, as sere as the countryside in which he lived. He tugged at a faded cinnamon-colored mustache. "His wife don't want to say what to do, but I've told her the truth. If she takes him on with her, don't let me amputate, he ain't got a prayer. He's never going to walk on those legs again, and if he tries to keep them, they're going to kill him."

His words chilled Jessie. No doubt he saw many such things, and had made many such verdicts, but his matter-of-fact tone was quietly horrifying, even though she'd expected such a reaction from him.

Annie, too, was stolid. "What about the other one? That Virgil Ridback?"

"If it was my leg, I'd take it off. He says no. And his wife says it's up to him. I can't operate if somebody don't say so. My guess is that if he keeps the leg now, you'll bury him somewhere going across the desert."

The two families had until morning to make up their minds. Then the train would be moving on.

Mrs. Groves came to the physician that evening, her face white and her eyes puffy from crying. "He says to take 'em off," she reported. "He can't stand the pain."

The doctor regarded her with unspoken compassion. "Amputation ain't going to stop the pain, ma'am. Leastways, not right away. What it's going to do is save his life, if he wants it saved. Some men don't in these circumstances. What did he do, back home? For a living?"

"He was a farmer," Sarah Groves said.

"I don't reckon he's going to farm no more. But maybe he can do something else useful." He didn't suggest what. "If we're going to do it, the quicker the better, ma'am. I'll have the men bring him over to the surgery."

There was no one on the post who didn't know the amputations were taking place. Including Virgil Ridback. He writhed on his own bed of pain, grasping Clara's wrist as she tried to walk past him in the narrow confines of the wagon, hurting her.

"Don't you let them take my leg, you understand? I'll kill you, if you let some goddamned sawbones make a cripple out of me."

"I won't be the one to say it," Clara told him. "He thinks you'll die of that leg, though."

"I won't. Not if you take care of me proper like. You hear, I won't die! And let me tell you something else, woman. Just because I'm trapped in here don't mean I won't know what's going on outside."

She stared at him, into the whiskey-blurred eyes. "What's that supposed to mean?"

"It means you don't go messing around that Joel Shand, you hear? You stay away from him!"

Her mouth twisted. "What am I supposed to do? I can't handle this wagon, nor you, by myself."

"Get somebody else to help, then. Not Joel Shand."

Clara pulled free then and left him without replying. A woman had a right to look out for herself, and now that she had the money, she wasn't tied to Virgil any more. Not unless she wanted to be. She was sorry for him, sorry he was hurting, but she had her own welfare to think about, too.

That Joel Shand, he was only a boy, really; yet he exuded a masculinity that drew her like a bee to a magnolia blossom. He was wasted on that insipid little Mormon girl. Newlywed or not, she guessed that he had more virility than he could dissipate on Jessie. Under cover of the darkness, blocking out the sounds from the surgery across the way and the drunken maunderings behind her, Clara sat on the wagon seat and smiled softly to herself.

10

Having decided upon the amputation as the doctor recommended, the Groves family was then faced with a second, equally momentous, decision. Either they could all stay at Fort McPherson until someone came along who'd take on the task of getting them back to Indiana, or Sarah and the girls could go on to California without him.

Neither choice seemed possible. There was nothing left for them in Indiana, or they'd never have gone from it in the first place. And what could three females do, alone, in the distant land? They could not take up farming on their own, and they had almost nothing in the way of resources except what they carried in their wagon.

"We'll take him on with us," Sarah decided.

The doctor looked at her slack-jawed. "Woman, you don't know what you're proposin' to do! I just amputated both the man's legs! He's going to be in the torment of hell for weeks! And jarring around in the back of a wagon is likely to break open the stubs, and you got no doctor with you to do for him."

"We got Annie Ryan. She done real well with the injured."

"Well, yes, she did, for a woman with no training, but she's not a doctor. She going to stop the bleeding when it starts? Sew him back up if anything breaks open? Keep him from screaming his throat out with the pain?"

Sarah was quietly stubborn. "He don't want to wait to go back home. We already talked about that. Besides, it might be months before anybody comes along that would get us there; everybody's going west, not east."

"It'll be months before he's fit to travel," the doctor told her, tugging at the brushy mustache.

"What can you do for him, about the pain, that Annie Ryan can't do? Give her some of that laudanum like you used to quiet him."

"I haven't got enough to give her what you'd need. He's going to hurt for weeks, months! Can't you understand that?"

"Give us what you got," Sarah insisted. "We was heading for California and there's more waiting for us there than if we go back. I got two daughters to think about, and they'll have a better chance of marrying well if we go on west. There wasn't nobody for them at home; all the young men headed for California the last few years."

He argued with her, but in the end, he gave in. He gave the laudanum to Annie and explained how it was to be used. He instructed her in the other foreseeable emergencies, as well, though he didn't expect much. "It's a damned fool notion, taking a man's just lost both his legs out over that country you got ahead of you. There'll be times when that wagon will be stood on end, getting over a mountain, and full of water, crossing a river. He's in no shape to stand that kind of treatment, let alone riding for twenty miles a day being jolted all day long."

"It's what he wants, his wife says."

The man threw up his hands in disgust. "All right! Take him and go! He ain't army, I got no control over him!"

They rolled again at dawn. The planned dance at the forks of the Platte was not mentioned; they had lost a day of traveling, and they were not exactly in a celebrating frame of mind.

They crossed the South Platte at Lower California Crossing, a grim undertaking that did nothing to lighten the general mood. The river was swollen from a recent rain that had soaked their bedding and drenched their spirits as well, and though the water was in most places no more than three feet deep, the current was swift enough to sweep the unwary off their feet, and the quicksand was everywhere.

By the time they gained the far side everyone was sweat-soaked and exhausted, and they plodded along toward the North Platte with many thoughts of the lands they had left behind them. Would anything in California, Jessie wondered, make up for this?

It made tears come to her eyes, to think about cool pine forests when there was nothing to be seen but low desolate hills devoid of anything resembling the vegetation she had once taken for granted.

When she spoke of her longings to Joel, he wrapped her in a firm hug. "Wait until we get to California," he told her. "Everybody says it's wonderful there."

They passed the places named by earlier travelers, milestones of their progress, and wondered at the red rock formations called Court House Rock and Chimney Rock. As they neared Scott's Bluff, the dust that had accumulated on every surface was washed away in a near cloudburst that terrified animals and humans alike with spectacular thunder and lightning.

The water sluiced over the wagons, finding its way in to resoak the bedding they had only just dried out, trickling into trunks and boxes. The earth turned to mud that sucked at the wheels almost as vigorously as the quicksand had done. Cap Horn called a halt to their movements to wait out the storm, which was the worst Jessie could remember.

Laurie, frightened by the celestial racket, screamed from his cradle, so that Jessie held him on her shoulder, trying to soothe him with her pats and words that were often drowned out by thunder. Although it was no more than midafternoon, the sky was as dark as dusk except when the lightning crackled around the horizon, and then, for a matter of seconds, it was light enough to read a newspaper, if they'd had one.

Joel grinned at her, resting one hand on her shoulder. "Didn't know it was going to be this much fun, did we?"

"Fun!" Indignation exploded out of her, so that the baby cried out in protest again. "I hate it, I hate everything about this dreadful place! We must have been crazy to think we could get all the way . . ."

Words failed her, and tears stung her eyes.

Joel bent to kiss her on the mouth, maneuvering Laurie's head to one side in order to do so. "Honey, this will be over in half an hour, and the sun will come out again. Thousands of people have made it all the way to California, and we will too. And when we get there, we won't be a renegade Mormon and an illegitimate no-account; we'll become people of property, and I'll get you those diamonds and a fine house—"

She allowed herself the comfort of his tender kiss for only a moment. "I don't want diamonds and a fine house, I just want to be off this dreadful prairie and have a little house with some *green* grass and some trees around, and a place for a garden..."

"They grow everything in California. Pumpkins this big"—he gestured to indicate an impossible size—"and potatoes big enough to feed a whole family, one potato! And oranges, they grow oranges there, Jessie, and more wheat to an acre than anybody in Michigan ever heard of—"

She had always been skeptical of the claims for California, and now she was downright disbelieving. Here on the Nebraska plains, being soaked by a cold rain that came through the canvas and flinching from the lightning that blinded her as the thunder momentarily deafened, she could not believe that there was anything good ahead for any of them.

"Mr. Shand!" The voice was female, raised over the noise of the storm, and Jessie's teeth clenched as she recognized it. "Mr. Shand, can you help me, please? Virgil's bed is getting soaked. I can't move him by myself, and he's so hot with fever!"

"I'm coming," Joel said, and gave Jessie another light kiss, this time on the forehead. "Don't worry, sweetheart. I won't let anything happen to you."

He brushed past her in the narrow space, walking bent over as he had to do beneath the canvas top, and disappeared between the rear flaps. Jessie stared after him in frustration and rage. She needed him here, with her and Laurie, yet he was off to that dreadful Clara Ridback, who used every pretext she could to lure Joel to her side. Damn the woman, Jessie thought savagely, and then realized she'd said it aloud when Laurie squirmed and cried.

Joel was right about one thing. The storm quickly passed, and the sun came out hotter than ever, so that steam rose from everything. There was to be no halt to dry clothing and beds, however; the order came to push on, even though progress was slow because of the mud.

The two injured men were kept as comfortable and as quiet as whiskey and laudanum could make them, which was not saying very much. Virgil Ridback was feverish, and to give her credit, Clara spent a good bit of her time beside him, bathing him with a cloth that could be kept only a little cooler than his skin.

Whenever Adrian Groves began to come out of his stupor, his wife dosed him again from the brown bottle the army doctor had given her, though Mamie cautioned her about it.

"There isn't that much of it, Ma. What will we do when it runs out?"

Sarah Groves regarded her husband with eyes that threatened to overflow. "I can't let him hurt that way."

"But it'll be worse than it is now, when the medicine runs out!"

"I don't think it will matter," Sarah said, and turned away.

Mamie stared after her. What did she mean by that? That Adrian was going to die anyway, no matter what they did?

She wasn't sure how she felt about that. The idea of death frightened her, no matter whose it was, and though there were no firm bonds of affection between them, her father's death would be devastating, simply because he was the one who had always seen to them, provided the food and the clothes and the shelter they needed. Who would do that, if Adrian died?

"Well, who will do it if he lives?" Alice asked practically when Mamie voiced that thought. "Pa isn't going to work again, ever. We're taking care of him as if he was a baby, right now, and it's never going to be any better, Mamie."

"Maybe with wooden legs, like old Mr. Stokes..."

Alice stared at her with pity. Mamie was an intelligent girl, but she was clutching at straws. "Mr. Stokes still had one good leg, and he had enough spunk to learn to use a wooden leg. Pa's got both legs off just above the knees, and he's not the kind of man with the gumption to tackle something as hard as learning to walk on two wooden pegs."

This was so obviously true that Mamie didn't bother to admit it. "We're going to have to shift for ourselves," she said, jumping to the next logical step in the thought process. "Sometimes I think Collie Aubin likes me, and then he mentions that other girl, that Patrice Hammond."

"If Collie doesn't ask you to marry him, there'll be somebody else," Alice said kindly. "California has lots more men than women, everybody says so."

Mamie's mouth took a bitter twist that sat uncomfortably on the soft, full lips. "Nobody else on this train has any more than looked at me except Rich Fuller and Aaron Douglas.

85

Rich isn't right in the head and Aaron wouldn't wash if there was a bathtub full of clean water in the back of his wagon. Oh, I suppose I could count Clifford Simonson; he looks at me and speaks, but he's a mean man. I've seen the way he treats his animals. I don't reckon he'd treat a woman any better. I'd just as soon starve to death as be married to someone like that."

They didn't know exactly when they crossed over into Wyoming Territory; there was little change in the dreary landscape. Fort Laramie was no more than a milepost on the trail, for although some supplies were available there, they were at exorbitant prices, and few of the immigrants had any cash to spare. Indeed, because the going had become more difficult, the way was littered with items that had been cast off by those unwilling, or unable, to transport them any farther. Anything not tied securely might well fall out on its own, and for the most part the irate drivers refused to halt to retrieve anything.

Clara Ridback found what seemed to Jessie constant reasons to call upon Joel for assistance. Jessie recognized that the woman did truly have problems, for the boy driving their wagon was far from an expert, and Virgil was of no use for anything, not even advice; he had sunk into a stupor induced by equal parts of whiskey and fever.

Jessie didn't like what was happening to her. Her resentment grew until she wanted to scream with it. At first she only complained to Annie or Mamie—she wished Joel were not the second man in command, so that he had to attend to everyone else's problems while the ones at home were left entirely to her—but one evening, after an especially trying day, her control broke.

The heat had been intense, leaving her sticky and itchy. She longed to be able to wash her hair (the Platte was useless for this purpose) and bathe, and simply breathing the dusty air made her feel as if her lungs were singed. Laurie felt it too, and that was no doubt why he was so fussy, crying much more than usual. She stripped off most of his clothes, down to a diaper and a little shirt and belly band, but then the dust settled on him in a soft grit, which did nothing for his comfort.

When she went to feed him she discovered that the milk had curdled and she had to round up Nanny (while Laurie screamed his frustration in the rolling wagon) and obtain enough milk for his feeding. Even with his stomach full, however, Laurie did not want to go back to sleep as he ordinarily did, and she was forced either to walk, carrying him, or to sit inside the lurching wagon trying to calm him.

Joel scarcely came near her all day. A wagon broke a tongue and he fell behind to help repair that. A small band of Indians rode out from the arid hills, and while they were not threatening, they did ask for tribute. They proved easily satisfied with beads and colored cloth and a watch that no longer ticked, but during the period that the train was halted for the necessary palaver, the women waited uneasily for the catastrophe that might occur if the talk were not successful.

In late afternoon the sky took on an unpleasant tinge, and Jessie watched it warily, wondering if they were in for another of those horrid storms. When she mentioned it to Annie, who had decided to walk with her for a distance, Annie grinned. "At least it would cool us off. We could bring out the soap and wash the clothes we have on, anyway."

"And then walk around in them wet until we catch our deaths," Jessie said crossly. Laurie had at last fallen into an exhausted sleep, and she longed for a rest herself, but knew that would be impossible in a jolting wagon, and it would be hours before they stopped for the night. They were crossing the Black Hills, and though Cap Horn had promised a good watering spot this evening, it was hard to believe there would be anything worthwhile in this desolation. Tears stung her eyes. "I'm so tired, Annie. So tired of this whole trip. We should have gone back to Michigan, somewhere we wouldn't have been taken for Mormons, and built us a cabin in the woods, and put in a garden. We could have lived that way, with a garden and venison and fish to eat."

Annie, trudging beside her, murmured in sympathy.

"Why is it," Jessie demanded, "that men always have to go off somewhere else? They can't be satisfied with the place where they are?"

"It's the way men are, I reckon. My Sean was the same. They got to see the far side of the hill."

"The far side of this hill"—Jessie reached out to the projecting corner of the wagon to assist her up the incline—"is just like this side. Bare and dry and ugly." To her chagrin, she felt the tears spilling over, and she wiped at them angrily with her free hand. "If only I weren't so *tired!*"

Annie swiveled her head for a closer inspection of her companion. "You had your monthlies lately?" she asked.

Jessie loosened her hold on the wagon and nearly fell.

"What? Oh, Annie! What day is it? I haven't calculated the days..."

"I did, this morning. It's the eighth of June, if I've remembered to figure it out every day."

Jessie's breath caught in her chest as she did some rapid figuring. "Annie, do you think...?"

For a moment a wild, sweet joy overcame her fatigue and physical discomfort. "Could I be...?"

Annie laughed. "You been married a month and a week, now, haven't you? How you been feeling first thing in the morning?"

"I haven't felt any worse than usual—the heat and the dirt and these awful hills are so depressing—oh, Annie, if I *am* carrying Joel's child, it won't hurt it, will it? What we're going through now, and until we get to California?"

"Babies are sturdy," Annie assured her. "Long as you don't fall bad or something like that, chances are you'll carry it all the way."

She didn't add *this time*, but Jessie did, silently. She'd lost Joella because she'd been raped by the man who was married to Laurie's mother. This time she had Joel, and he'd never let anything like that happen to her again. Yet there was still a formidable trek ahead of them, and she feared this country now, as she had not done at first. It was a brutal country, sucking the life out of those who attempted to tame it by crossing its barren hills.

A child. A child of her own. Long after Annie had left her, unable to continue the difficult climb on foot, Jessie plodded beside the wagon, hugging the hope to her. It was too soon, Annie agreed, to know for certain, but the possibility was there, that new life grew within her.

That was the only good part of the day. When an unexpected halt was called late in the afternoon they were still a few miles from the "good watering spot" and Jessie lifted the fussy baby and climbed down to see what the problem was. She took it for granted that it was a problem; why else would they delay their progress when it was so essential that they cross those distant mountains before the snow fell?

It was difficult to imagine the snow now, but the threat was there, always hanging over them. Reach the mountains in plenty of time to cross them before winter, or risk perishing as the Donner party had done, except for those who resorted to cannibalism to survive.

The word came down the line: "Rattlesnake bite!"

"Who?" Jessie asked, throat suddenly even more dry. It shouldn't be Joel, because he usually rode rather than walked, but there was always that chance.

"Clara Ridback," Oliver Allen told her. "Dropped something and went to pick it up and practically stuck her hand on the critter, laying there between the rocks."

Jessie paused, wondering if it was safe to walk any farther, though the ground was bare of any hazard she could see. Were there many rattlers around?

Others were moving, though, welcoming this opportunity to stretch their legs and relieve arms aching with the strain of guiding reluctant animals hour after hour. Jessie decided to chance it and moved forward, drawn reluctantly but with a compelling curiosity toward the Ridback wagon.

It was Clara, all right, and as usual it was Joel who'd been called to assist her. This time it was a legitimate reason, not a hastily invented excuse; there was no doubting that.

Clara was pale and sweating, her eyes wide with terror, her lips trembling visibly. She was seated on a box someone had handed down, and Joel knelt before her, his mouth pressed to the back of her hand as he sucked and spat, sucked and spat, getting rid of the poison. Jessie knew what he was doing, knew that someone had to do it. Yet his position and actions were a grotesque parody of a lover kissing his beloved's hand, and something twisted in Jessie's midsection.

She stood silently with the others in the semicircle. When at last Joel stood and reached for the dipper on the water cask secured to the side of the wagon, she felt a flicker of fear that he would have ingested some of the poison himself.

Joel rinsed his mouth and spat again, several times, before he was satisfied.

"Am I going to die?" Clara asked, her voice coming from far off.

"Lots of people get bit by rattlers and get over it," Joel said in a gentle tone that Jessie had previously thought reserved only for herself. "I think this one just barely flicked you, and he's a little one, too. The little ones don't have as much venom."

"Give her a shot of whiskey," someone said, and a murmur of agreement ran around the circle of onlookers. Jessie stood silent, patting the baby on her shoulder to keep him quiet; she was ashamed of her animosity toward Clara, even while it smoldered undiluted by sympathy for the woman's predicament. Annie came forward with a medicinal bottle, and

89

Clara choked down a swig or two of its contents. Then a rag was soaked in whiskey to be tied over the wound.

"You'll be wanting to lie down," Joel suggested, drawing Clara to her feet. The boy who was driving the wagon looked down with a scared face as Clara, gray and oozing perspiration, turned to one side to vomit into the sagebrush.

It took two men to lift her back into the wagon, where Clara collapsed on the pallet beside her husband, who was in too much of a stupor to realize she was there. There would be pain and more nausea and extreme weakness, and then she would either get better, or she would die.

No one had yet died on this journey, though the string of graves they had passed bore mute witness of the perils of traveling to California. Jessie turned away, jiggling Laurie to quiet him, and made her way back to her own wagon. She remembered how her sister Zadia had prayed for the death of her husband, so that she would be free, and for the first time Jessie felt a flicker of understanding of that prayer.

Not that she would pray for any such wicked thing, of course. It was Jessie, not Clara, whom Joel had married. He would have been kind and helpful to anyone in Clara's situation; it had nothing to do with finding her attractive.

Yet as the day wore on, the heat plastering her garments to her in a smelly second skin, the dust working into her hair and down her neck and forming a grit between her teeth, Jessie found it harder and harder to speak softly to Laurie when he cried, harder to keep from crying herself in sheer fatigue and discomfort.

When at last they reached the promised campground at Warm Springs, not even that place raised her spirits, for Joel did not turn up to help her down with the baby. He had, Collie reported, a problem with replacing a wagon tongue and would be along later.

Jessie stood behind the wagon seat, looking out at one of the nicest places they'd camped in many days. The springs gushed out of a rocky wall, water she knew to be clear and sweet after the muddy turbulence of the Platte, and the bath she had been wanting was now a possibility, yet she didn't feel any better.

Where was Joel? Whose wagon needed repairs? Would he stop and see how Clara was doing before he thought to come and see about *her?*

A clump of cottonwoods provided shade, and though there was no graze here for the animals, the human beings were delighted with both trees and clean water. Annie approached, grinning broadly, to stand beside the wagon wheel. "The men are going downstream after supper, and we'll have the pool here to ourselves for our baths. And Collie says Cap Horn's agreed to lay over for a day so we can wash our clothes in clean water."

Ordinarily Jessie would have been as jubilant as the rest of the women over this. A day of work, scrubbing and wringing and hanging to dry virtually every garment one owned, was a rest compared to spending a day on the trail. To be truly clean again, even briefly, was something much to be desired.

Jessie didn't smile, however. She shifted Laurie to her other shoulder and spoke flatly. "He hasn't stopped crying for the past two hours. I don't know what's the matter with him. It's too much to ask, Annie, for me to take care of a baby this way! I don't know anything about babies."

Annie's eyes narrowed slightly, though she maintained her good humor. "Most people don't, till they've had 'em. And your sisters both had babies, didn't they? Anyway," she added before Jessie could reply to that mild reproof, "he's probably just as uncomfortable as the rest of us. Let me take him. I'll wash him off in the spring—the water's warm, they say, and maybe that's all he needs. Just cooling off."

She reached up for the baby, and Jessie gladly handed him over before she descended to the ground. "I hope something helps. If he cries like that all night, I don't know what I'll do." Her tone implied that it would be something drastic.

She did not, however, feel any better when Annie had taken the fussy infant away. She wasn't hungry, but she knew Joel would certainly be starved, and she wondered what she could feed him that would not require building a fire. The cottonwoods had already been picked clean by earlier travelers, so there was little to burn, and besides it was too hot and she was too tired to care.

She found some cold biscuits and spooned out a dish of yesterday's beans and sat eating them without gratification, resentment building as no one came near her. Even when Annie returned with Laurie, clean now and no longer protesting when he was laid in his cradle, Jessie's spirits didn't rise. Dry biscuits, without the butter she'd grown used to when Tully Ritter kept a cow or two, were not inspiring.

It was nearly dusk when Joel finally turned up. He did not immediately notice that Jessie was oddly silent and unwelcoming; he helped himself to biscuits and beans without comment, squatting on the ground to eat.

He glanced over at her with a grin. "Too bad we can't have the spring to ourselves, just you and me. They're making the men go downstream, and the women will use the pool. Still, there'll be afterward, when we're all cool and clean in our own bed."

Jessie didn't rise to the bait of intimacies to come. At the moment, it was the last thing that interested her. "Whose wagons needed repairs?" she asked.

"Moyer's, and then Crabtree's." Joel swallowed half a biscuit and sighed. "I guess just about everybody's could use something. Greasing, at least. Allen's dropped a wheel in a hole and cracked an axle we'll have to replace. And one of Ridbacks' bullocks has gone lame. Maybe if we lay over for a day, the animals will be in better shape, except that there's nothing much here to feed them. Cap says maybe we'll send some of the younger men on ahead with as much of the stock as we can spare, and they can wait for us. The trouble is there'll be a shortage of good water for a few days, only those damned alkali lakes that are worse than nothing."

They'd already learned a little about alkali, which had the power to eat through their shoes and poison any creature that tried to drink water containing it. At the moment, however, Jessie's mind was on something else.

"You stopped by Ridback's wagon, then, on the way here?"

"Yeah." Joel missed the tense edge to her voice and forked more beans. "I don't like the look of Virgil; he's burning hot. We're going to try to get him over to the spring after the women have bathed, see if that will help a little. Adrian Groves looks bad, too. We should have left him at Fort Laramie, no matter what he wanted."

"Did you see *her*? Clara?"

"She doesn't look good, either. I asked Annie to take a look at her. Except for giving her whiskey for the pain, though, I don't know what we can do for her. Either the poison will work itself out of her system or it won't. Annie thinks she'll probably get better, though. Says she's seen people with rattler bites who swelled up worse and they got over it. Be careful, Jess, when you're walking. Those damned things are everywhere."

"You stopped to see Clara, but you couldn't bother to come and see how *I* was," Jessie said. She heard her own voice, petulant and disagreeable, yet she couldn't seem to care. "It never occurred to you that *I* might need something."

He looked at her in surprise. "Did you? I thought you were all right, and I sent Collie to tell you I'd be a while, repairing that damned wagon."

"Laurie cried all day. He hardly stopped for a minute."

Joel scraped up the last of the beans and set his plate aside. "I suppose he's miserable with the heat and the dirt, like all the rest of us. Will Annie watch him while we bathe, do you think? So we can get to bed and enjoy making love while we're both clean, for a change?"

She gave him a stony stare. "That's all you think about, making love. As if that makes everything right."

At long last Joel really looked at his bride, saw her trembling lips, her dark eyes swimming with tears. He reached for her hand, covering it with his own, hard and warm.

"Well, it helps a lot," he said quietly. "It's what keeps me going, some of the bad days, Jessie. Knowing I can hold you in my arms that night."

Quite of their own volition, two tears spilled over and trickled down her cheeks. "I wish we'd never started for California. I wish we'd stayed in Michigan, or Illinois, or Missouri. I hate this heat and all this red rock, and no clean water—"

"The water's clean tonight."

"—and having a crying baby, and feeling sick—"

"Sick? Are you feeling sick?"

Even Jessie, wallowing in this totally foreign self-pity, could not have missed the concern in his voice. He moved toward where she sat on a large rock and slipped an arm around her waist to draw her close. "What's the matter, honey?"

"I don't know. I just hate it, all of this, and I wish I could go home—"

The longing, the weariness, overwhelmed her. When Joel drew her into his arms, stroking her hair, murmuring, she gave in to it. "We're going home, Jess. You'll like it in California, you'll see. It won't be like this. Now come on, go take your bath, and I'll get one, too, and you'll feel better. You know you will."

And she'd probably succumb to his caresses, too, she thought ruefully, not fully realizing why she felt the need to resist what she had always previously enjoyed. Already his hand rested on her breast, his thumb moving so that the nipple rose against its stimulation, and the liquid warmth spread through her.

Jessie did not give in to it, though; she rose and stepped away from him. "I'm going to wash my hair," she said, and headed for the wagon for soap and a towel, leaving Joel to wonder what in hell was the matter with her.

11

Jessie remembered the bathing at Warm Springs for a long time, because it was the last good place for several weeks. She was not yet certain enough of pregnancy to make an announcement to Joel, but the signs were there in her increasing moodiness and a tendency toward tears. Joel was patient and loving—sometimes almost too loving, she thought on the night when she had again coped with a screaming baby for most of the day, and had for the first time flatly refused his advances.

Joel was astonished. "But you like it as much as I do!" he insisted, running a callused hand over her bare belly so that she jerked away from him.

"Joel, I'm tired! I don't feel like it tonight!"

"How can you not feel like doing something that will make you feel so good? It'll relax you, help you to sleep."

"I'm tired enough to sleep this second, if you'd leave me alone," Jessie said crossly. And then was made a liar when Joel withdrew to fall into immediate slumber, while she twisted and turned and allowed tears to dampen her pillow, tears she couldn't explain even to herself.

"It's the baby coming," Annie said complacently when Jessie had expressed some of this inexplicable moodiness to the older woman. "I was crotchety with Ben and the girls, all three. It does something to a woman besides making her belly swell up. You'll get over it shortly, girl; don't worry about it."

Knowing that there was a physical reason for her wild

swings of mood did help a little to temper her suddenly acid tongue, but not to make her any happier. Of course, if she were expecting Joel's child she was happy about *that*. Yet as the difficult and dreary miles fell behind them, it still seemed an incomprehensible distance to the end of the journey, and feeling queasy and extraordinarily tired were added burdens.

On June 16, the day they passed by Independence Rock, Adrian Groves died.

Nothing dramatic had happened. He had not raved in fever, like Virgil Ridback. He had seldom even complained, although it was obvious to his family that he was in great pain, and he kept them awake at night with his involuntary moaning unless the laudanum was liberally dispensed before they turned in.

The company could see the great whale-shaped rock for hours before they reached it; some planned to climb it, as earlier travelers had done, to add their names to those already written there. When they paused for a nooning there, Sarah Groves discovered her husband was no longer breathing.

It was their first death, and it sobered them. A grave was quickly dug, a few words read from the Bible over it, and the caravan went on.

Mamie and Alice endured their mother's sobbing as best they could, wondering if she grieved for her husband or feared for herself. The future of three females with virtually no money and no skills at providing for themselves seemed grim enough to make Mamie want to sob herself. But she did not truly regret her father's passing except insofar as it meant they must shift for themselves. Adrian had not made himself a beloved father with his concern for them. It would have taken a heart of stone not to have felt compassion for the man's suffering after the amputation of his legs, and Mamie thought that he was probably better off dead than alive, since he would never have walked again, and perhaps never have passed the point where the suffering ended. He had cried about the pain in his feet long after they were gone.

Clara Ridback spent several miserable days fearing that she would die before the next dawn of the rattlesnake poison; when she finally woke one day feeling somewhat better except for incredible weakness, she realized that death did not stare her in the face after all, at least not immediately.

She rose from her bed and tottered forth making a silent resolution. If she ever got off this godforsaken prairie, she was going to have all the things she'd ever dreamed of in life, no matter what she had to do to get them.

Virgil's parched lips blistered with the fever, and she continued to allow him enough of the whiskey to keep him inactive; the stench of his injured leg finally drove her outside to sleep under the wagon instead of in it, and she wondered if he, too, would need a leg amputated, and if so, who could be found to do it.

They plodded onward, and then began their climb into the Rockies. No longer did they estimate their travel at twenty to twenty-five miles per day; some days it was no more than three or four miles, for the climb was steep.

The air was cooler as they climbed, though, and Jessie felt better for it. On the 24th of June, after a forty-four-mile drive from the Big Sandy to the Green River with no water in between, across an arid area with no feed for the animals, the night was so cold that there was a skim of ice on the water buckets when they rose. Jessie shivered and drew her woolen shawl around her and reveled in the change of temperature.

Laurie seemed to thrive better in the cooler air, too. He sucked contentedly at the goat's-milk-and-bread teat, or his small fingers, whichever he could get, and smiled up at anyone who bent over his cradle and spoke to him.

Jessie was certain now. A child was developing in her own belly, and after the first few weeks when she felt confused and depressed and irritable, those sensations gave way to one of well-being. She would have Joel's son, and she looked forward to it with increasing joy.

She broke the news to Joel as she lay in his arms after an ardent session of making love, and was gratified when he raised himself on an elbow to peer down at her face, dimly visible in the filtered moonlight.

"Jessie! Honey, that's wonderful! Listen, have you talked to Annie? Do you know the right things to do? To take care of yourself?"

She laughed. "Annie says everything's fine."

"Maybe you ought not to walk any more. You'd better ride in the wagon."

"I'm safer walking. I'm strong and healthy, and walking's good for me. Better than being jounced around in a wagon that's apt to be overturned if a wheel drops in a hole. You want the baby, don't you, Joel?"

"I want the baby more than I've ever wanted anything,"

he said, nuzzling into her neck so that his words were muffled. "Except you, Jessie. You're what I want the most of all."

It seemed, for a while, that Joel was not seeing very much of Clara Ridback. He was more attentive to Jessie, more concerned with her welfare, making it a point to check on her before he took on the other chores that being Cap Horn's helper entailed. Clara was getting better, though as Mrs. Von Wald remarked to Annie, the woman was milking every possible drop of sympathy from every male in the company, from Cap Horn to the young boy who drove her wagon.

Jessie didn't care what Clara did to attract masculine attention as long as she left Joel alone.

Except for Annie, who had guessed, they told no one about the coming child, hugging the secret to themselves; it renewed the love between them, intensified it, so that they made love passionately, then slept in each other's arms in an aftermath of euphoric bliss.

If only, Jessie thought, the days could be as wonderful as the nights. In the dark she could pretend that they were at home on Beaver Island, surrounded by the clean cold waters of Lake Michigan, or even that they had reached the mythical shores of California, which would be far different from the terrain where they now traveled. Please, God, she prayed, let us reach California safely!

But California was still a long way off. They toiled up the sides of the great mountains, seeing fir trees for the first time in many weeks, and the air was tangy with the scent of them. And then, without knowing quite when it happened, they had crossed the Continental Divide, where the waters now rushed toward the Pacific instead of to the east, one more momentous step toward their goal.

They could not pause to enjoy the milestone, however. It was the 21st of June, and they had many miles to go. To the south and southwest they saw snow on the peaks, snow to remind them that there was yet another range of mountains to be crossed before the new snows fell. To the north lay the bleak and barren Wind River Mountains, offering no refuge, and so they plunged down the western slopes. Jessie imagined she could smell the first hint of autumn, though Joel laughed at her and held her tenderly.

"Don't worry. We've plenty of time. We'll get there long before winter."

Going down the mountains was almost worse than climbing up them, for it was difficult to hold back the wagons on precipitous inclines, and more than once a wagon got away and was smashed to bits on the rocky walls.

One of those wagons belonged to the Ridbacks.

Joel blamed himself to some extent, because he ought to have remembered that the young boy driving it in Virgil's place was too inexperienced to handle the almost vertical descent.

"You had plenty of other things to worry about," Jessie protested. "Everybody was having trouble with that descent. I thought Laurie and I were both going to be thrown out and run over, and Andrew managed it; he's the same age as the Curtis boy, and there weren't enough men to go around."

It was a disaster, all right. Virgil Ridback was thrown free and landed on jagged rocks; his screams raised the hair off Jessie's head. She was one of the first on the scene, while the wagon wheels that were off the ground still spun in the dusty sunlight.

She took one look at the blood oozing through the bandaging on his injured leg and gagged, turning away. Annie, where was Annie? She knew her wagon had come down safely, but where was it?

"Help me," a feminine voice pleaded, and Jessie, trying to calm the crying child in her arms (she later discovered that in her terror over the descent she had squeezed the baby so hard she left bruises on his flesh), moved toward the overturned wagon.

It was beyond repair, splintered and smashed, the Ridbacks' goods spilled out and scattered, looking as if an entire herd of buffalo had stampeded over it. In the midst of the wreckage, Clara sat, beginning to weep.

Ahead of them on the trail, men struggled and swore at their animals, trying to calm the terrified beasts and to assess their own damages. Behind them, another wagon came too fast, the driver white-faced and yelling obscenities, so that Jessie jumped aside to avoid being trampled. She didn't know where Joel was, or Annie, or anyone else who had time to help.

She looked back at Clara. As far as Jessie could see, the other woman wasn't seriously hurt. "Can you get out of there?" Jessie called. "Before another wagon runs into you?"

Clara swiveled to look up the trail and pushed aside debris, scrambling to her feet, wincing on a sprained ankle as she made her way to Jessie's side. "Is Virgil dead? He's stopped screaming."

"More likely he's passed out from the pain," Jessie told her. "Maybe we should try to get him over beyond those rocks, out of the path of the rest of the wagons. I think we can move him if we each take an arm."

Clara's face was smudged and pathetic. "His whiskey's gone. All of it, I think, every bottle broke. It's all over everything."

Jessie placed the baby in a mossy hollow at the base of a small fir and ignored his protests as she and Clara dragged the unconscious Virgil to safety. Joel, where was Joel? she wondered, and wished someone else had been here to deal with the Ridbacks.

No one came, however, for some time. The remainder of the wagons continued to come down the face of the mountain, every driver fearing each moment would be his last, the bullocks bellowing in fear as the heavy conveyances pushed them from behind. Joel searched her out, concern easing when she stood up with the baby now quiet against her breast, and Jessie moved into his arms for a quick moment of reassurance. There was no time for more.

He swore at the sight of the Ridback wagon. "How bad is he hurt? We can't take him on in that. Mrs. Ridback—" He had raised his voice, and Clara turned from contemplation of her husband. "You'd better sort out the most valuable of your belongings. I'll try to find someone to carry as much as they can of them, but you'll have to leave everything heavy and bulky behind. Take a few clothes, and we'll try to salvage the best of your foodstuffs. We'll have to leave everything else."

"Everything?" Clara's voice rose, wavering out of control. "But I have a trunk of dresses, and my mother's wedding silver, and—"

"You'll have to leave those. Just a few changes of clothes," Joel specified. "My wife will help you, if she can find someone to keep the baby. How bad is your husband hurt?"

"His leg's broken open. It's bleeding," Clara said dully. "I can't leave my mother's silver; it's too valuable."

"It's also heavy, and you no longer have a wagon. I'll send Annie back to you, Jess, for Laurie and to look at Virgil. I'll see if I can find space in a wagon for the Ridbacks and their bundle."

He strode off into the confusion, leaving Clara to look angrily at Jessie, as if she'd issued the orders. "I won't leave my mother's silver," she said.

Jessie had no intention of fighting with her about it. She switched Laurie from one arm to the other and began to sift through the rubbish, shifting things with the toe of one moccasin. Silken undergarments, now soiled yet still beautiful with lacy trim, a blue velvet gown that had been torn beyond repair, a smashed china lamp that crunched under her feet. "Maybe we could find a sheet and lay it out," she suggested, "and pile the things on it you're going to keep."

"I'm going to keep all my clothes, and the silver."

Jessie refused to respond to the defiant words. She stifled a stirring of sympathy, for though she had never had possessions such as these, she knew that she, too, would be reluctant to leave them here.

In the end, though Clara first demanded and then pleaded, most of her belongings were abandoned. Rich Fuller had been persuaded to take a bundle or two, but he was unwilling to pitch out any of his own supplies to do it. He was less than enthusiastic about hauling Virgil and agreed only after Joel swore at him and promised that Clara would tend the injured man herself.

Jessie saw Clara's face as the precious silverware was thrown out. There were genuine tears in the other woman's eyes, though whether they were from sentiment or greed was impossible to judge. "Someone else could carry that, if Mr. Fuller has no room," Clara tried one last time.

"Nobody has any extra room for anything heavy," Joel decreed, and Cap Horn backed him up.

"Be plenty of people throwing away more than that afore we get there," Cap said dryly, and walked off.

They mended what they could, abandoned what was damaged beyond repair, and moved on. When Virgil regained consciousness there was nothing to give him for the pain, and he stared with bloodshot eyes in an unshaven face at the woman he had married.

"Get me something," he begged. "Whiskey, anything."

"I asked," Clara said. "If there's a bottle of spirits of any kind that didn't get broken when we came down that damnable mountain, nobody's admitting it. There isn't anything, Virgil."

"Then get me a pistol," Virgil said.

For a moment she stared into the tortured face. "I don't even have that. It was one of the things they made me leave behind."

"Then get somebody else's. I'm going to die anyway, ain't

I? Let me do it easy. Not like this, laying in my own stink, hurting so bad I can't even think straight—get me a gun, Clara."

She moistened chapped lips. "I don't know anyplace to get one. Nobody leaves guns lying around." Her gaze slid reluctantly toward the stained rags holding his leg in the splint. "You probably should have let the doctor take the leg off. It would've healed clean then, maybe."

"And what the hell good is a man with one leg?" Virgil demanded. "You going to stay with me, if I only got one leg, Clara?"

She could force no response to that, though he read the answer in her mute face. He threw himself away from her, covering his face with an arm until she finally moved away.

After a while, Virgil stirred and began to grope among the few belongings that had been carried along with him. He was very pale, and sweat soaked his body and his face beneath the beard; he ignored the pain through sheer willpower, knowing that it was the only way to end his own suffering.

When his fingers, grown incredibly weak, finally closed around the object he sought, Virgil allowed himself to rest a few moments. Then he drew the knife out of its sheath, the knife he'd used for butchering hogs and later deer or antelope, and most recently to help dress out a young buffalo.

He could see his wife's back as she sat beside Rich Fuller on the wagon seat, saw her profile as she turned to respond to something the other man had said.

Bitch, he thought. She'd found the money, he knew she had, or she'd have demanded to know where he'd hidden it when they were allowed to transfer their belongings to his wagon. She hadn't mentioned it to him, which meant only one thing. When they got to civilization, she intended to leave him, take the money and go. With some other man, he thought. Clara'd never have any trouble finding another man, not with her looks. Beautiful, she was, only inside she was a selfish bitch.

A bundle was there beside his pallet, a sheet in which she had wrapped the clothes taken from the trunk they had refused to allow her to carry. He tested the blade, which cut through the sheet with ease, revealing blue velvet and rose-colored silk.

"Bitch," he said thickly, and then, before he had to fall back in exhaustion, he carefully stretched out his left wrist over the bundle of Clara's clothes.

The knife bit into the flesh easily, as easily as it would have sliced through the throat of a yearling pig, and he scarcely felt it. The pain in his leg was far worse than this.

Virgil gasped for breath and slid backward onto the pillow, too depleted of energy to watch the viscous red fluid that pumped out of his wrist onto the bundle of gowns. It didn't hurt, though he was aware of a faint throbbing sensation.

Gradually his vision dimmed, and the pain receded, and he sank gratefully into oblivion.

12

It was a fitting place to bury a man, Jessie thought bleakly. Dreary, dry, treeless. How many more of their company would be laid to rest before they reached California?

The mountains had provided only a brief respite, with the stands of pines, from the landscape she had come to hate. Not only because it was so alien to anything she'd known before, but because it threatened the child she carried. In only a short time, she had become fiercely possessive of the child.

She was not the only woman in the train who was pregnant. Belle Snow, the wife of a man fifteen years her senior, carried her third child in a belly bulging to a point that suggested the birth was not far off. Jessie did not know the woman well, but had seen her speaking with Annie and guessed that Belle had asked for help when the time came.

There had been two miscarriages since their departure from Missouri; Jessie prayed earnestly that she would not add to that statistic. She did not feel that God would be that cruel, to take a second child from her, leaving her only another woman's child to rear, but she could not be quite certain of that. In spite of Joel's assurances that God did not punish people for their sins by allowing the death of those they loved, Jessie carried the guilt of her own shortcomings. Although she had fired Ben Ryan's gun in defense of another woman's life, as well as her own, she had broken the Sixth Commandment. She had killed Cass Merriam. How could she know that God had wanted her to do that?

And she had broken the Seventh Commandment as well. Though the love she shared with Joel now had the sanction of God's teachings, of the church to which she had once belonged, she had not waited for marriage to consummate that love. Joel laughingly insisted that since neither of them had been married to anyone else at the time, it was not adultery, but since they had not been married to each other, either, Jessie couldn't take that view. Neither would anyone else.

She knew that some of the other women still looked at her askance, constantly reminded by her lengthened skirts that she had once been a Mormon. Jessie had not made many close friends among them, except for Virginia Allen and the Groves sisters.

Once, when she made an innocent statement about the Allens making good neighbors and hoping they'd settle within visiting distance of each other, Joel's reaction was unsettling.

"Oliver Allen's a decent enough man, but he'll never be any more than a small dirt farmer."

Jessie stared at him in surprise. "What's wrong with that? We're going to be farmers too, aren't we?"

"Maybe. But not small, not insignificant. We're not going to live in any sod house, not for long, anyway. You'll find better people to be friends with, Jessie. Can you picture inviting Ginny Allen to a party, wearing a silk dress?"

Her voice was tart. "I can't even imagine *me* at a party wearing a silk dress. And Ginny would be welcome in my house wearing whatever she happened to have."

As usual, Joel's response to her crossness was a hug and a kiss. "You'll wear silk, I promise you. The best that money can buy. We left all the bad things behind when we left Beaver Island, and all the good things are still ahead of us. You'll see, Jess."

Well, Jessie reflected, it was hard to imagine things like silk dresses and parties now. She was more concerned that there be sufficient feed for their stock, to get them across this great expanse of desert, and that Nanny keep producing the necessary milk for Lauren. And when they reached California she'd settle for water and trees; to the devil with fancy trappings.

Unconsciously, she had taken to resting her hands on her

still-flat abdomen, trying to detect some sign of the new life within, and she planned for her baby. A good life needn't mean a rich one, with money and social position that made one too good for old friends.

Since their father was gone, Alice and Mamie were pathetic in their attempts to win husbands before the wagon train disbanded. They were pretty girls and average in their accomplishments of housewifely things, and it seemed to Jessie most unlikely that they would be left to wither away as old maids. Yet she understood their fears of that, and of the matter of simply providing food for themselves and their widowed mother.

Sarah Groves was undoubtedly a liability. Several of the young men would not have been averse to courting either of the sisters had not the mother dampened their enthusiasm. For one thing, Sarah mourned her husband audibly, nearly every minute of the day. She sighed often and allowed stray tears to fill her eyes or trickle down her cheeks.

And she insisted on chaperoning her daughters to protect their reputations, all that they had left of value. Courting a girl under her mother's moist and dismal eye was more than most men were willing to do.

Alice fared the better of the two, since her interest was caught by Harry Kelly. Harry was a tall thin young man with nondescript features and coloring, but he had a ready smile and a quiet good humor. Though he had not liked Adrian Groves, he found Adrian's younger daughter pleasing, except for the difficulty in speaking to her away from her mother.

He had considered proposing, because he was lonely and would have welcomed Alice in his bed. There was, however, one problem; he suspected that if he took Alice, he'd also have to take Sarah Groves, and he didn't want her. The idea of supporting the woman, having her in his own household for the rest of her life, was a strong counterbalance to his physical needs.

Alice was astute enough to realize that her mother was a major stumbling block to the path of romance.

"They say," she told Harry on one of the few occasions she had for a relatively private conversation, "that men far outnumber the women in California. Perhaps Mama will meet someone and marry again."

Harry grunted a noncommittal response. He doubted that anyone was likely to look twice at Sarah Groves until she'd stopped her infernal sniveling. It wasn't as if the man had been a good and loving husband to her; she *couldn't* be genuinely grieving this way for the bastard, Harry thought. Much more likely she was worried about herself, what was to become of her. Well, Harry didn't intend to take on that responsibility. He didn't stop trying to get Alice away from her, though in a country like the one they traveled through that wasn't easy. If a man talked a girl into walking out with him, there was nothing to screen them from public view unless they strolled behind one of the massive rocks that were strewn about as if by a giant hand; and in that case, not being visible only made matters worse as everyone was well aware of the disappearance and speculated upon it to the detriment of any girl's reputation.

Mamie might have had her pick between Rich Fuller and Aaron Douglas, although now that Rich had taken Clara Ridback into his wagon he was less attentive to Mamie. He wasn't overly bright, and besides that he was probably among the most poorly equipped of the travelers, which was one reason he'd had room to take some of the Ridbacks' belongings into his wagon after their own was destroyed.

Aaron was brighter, with a sharp wit that was sometimes entertaining, but he didn't bother to bathe even when it was convenient to do so. One tended to shift around to an upwind position when talking to the man. Mamie tried to imagine going to bed with him and shuddered in disgust before discarding the idea.

It was Collie Aubin she wanted. Joel's cousin from Chicago.

Collie, with his golden curls and his blue eyes and his refined manner. Collie, she knew instinctively, would *be somebody*. And when she thought about going to bed with *him,* her cheeks grew rosy so that Alice asked solicitously if she weren't getting too much sun.

"If only Mama would leave us alone once in a while," Mamie complained to her sister. "He does talk to me when she's not around, only as soon as she shows up you'd think somebody'd sewed his mouth shut. I know he still thinks about that other girl, that Patrice Hammond. But God knows where she is; it's unlikely he'll ever see her again. And if I could just talk to Collie by myself, walk out with him..."

"Maybe," Alice suggested, "I could think of something to divert Mama's attention. I mean, when we get to Soda Springs, and we're stopped long enough to wash, maybe I could keep her busy with me and you...you could say you're helping Jessie with the baby, because she'll have to scrub clothes, too. It would give you a chance to talk to Collie alone."

Mamie considered that, her dark-fringed hazel eyes thoughtful. "I'd have the baby, of course. I don't think Collie would be nervous about that." A smile began to form around her mouth. "It might even occur to him that I'm not only pretty, too—maybe not as lovely as that Patrice, but certainly I'm not *ugly*—but that I'm quite domestic and will make a good mother for his children someday."

Alice reserved an opinion about that, since she suspected that most men would be thinking more of their own immediate gratification than of future offspring. Still, if she could draw her mother's fire long enough to allow Collie and Mamie to reach a point where he could propose, her own chances would be better. If Harry knew that marrying Alice wouldn't mean bringing Sarah along with her, he would be much more likely to take the plunge. And if Mamie married first, it was only logical that Sarah would go with *her*.

And so they planned, and schemed, and worried about what would happen at the end of their journey. The sun was hotter than any of them had ever encountered before, and one of the older men dropped in his tracks when the heat became too much for him in addition to the exertions of getting his wagon through the sand. They buried him, and Cap Horn decided that his goods were common property, and that Clara and the Groves females could share his wagon for their goods, thus relieving those who had taken them in.

It was not a happy decision for Mamie and Alice and their mother, for none of them cared much for Clara. She had, it seemed to them, wept more tears over the garments ruined by her husband's blood than over the man himself. She had knelt, tears streaming down her face, on the banks of a muddy stream, trying to soak them clean, and had only given up the task as hopeless when she saw the velvets after their immersion.

Now that she had only the calico and dimity that were standard apparel for the rest of the women, it was harder for her to put on airs. Yet she managed to do it, in her words and her manner; she made it clear that she was used to better things, even though she did not currently have them.

Still, they all welcomed the opportunity to travel again with some control over their possessions. They had a young boy handling the bullocks, though Mamie was learning. She

106

had an unpleasant premonition about the future and decided she'd better learn as much as she could about the things that her father had always done, in case they were still on their own after they'd reached California.

"If Mrs. Ridback whines one more time about the silver she had to leave back there," Mamie told Jessie between her teeth, "I do believe I'll smack her."

And Jessie, on impulse and without thinking about it, added quickly, "If she doesn't stay away from my husband, I'll join you."

She bit her tongue at once, for though Mamie's eyes widened the other girl was not surprised by Jessie's feelings.

"She does seem to call upon him overmuch," Mamie agreed, and left Jessie feeling worse than before because it seemed that she was not the only one to have noticed Clara's proprietary attitude toward Joel.

The fact that Clara and Sarah Groves were both recent widows did nothing to draw them together. They were distantly courteous to each other, recognizing that it was inappropriate for Clara to continue to travel with an unmarried man since Virgil's death, yet each resenting the other's presence in the newly acquired wagon that must be their home.

"I can't say I like Mrs. Ridback any more than Mama does," Mamie confessed. "Yet in a way it's not been all bad, to have to share quarters with her. She distracts Mama's attention from Alice and me, a little bit."

Jessie had been only too glad to hand Laurie over to Mamie while she herself attended to other chores. If it helped Mamie to spend some time with Collie, so much the better.

Joel made no protest over their arrangement, for he knew that Mamie truly felt affection for the baby and would care for him conscientiously. He shook his head in tolerant amusement about the purpose of Mamie's mothering exhibition for Collie's benefit.

"What is there about females," he asked, "that makes them all want to see every man married?"

"Don't you think a man is happier when he's married?" Jessie demanded.

"Well, it depends on the woman, of course. *I'm* happier married." He reached for her, and Jessie adroitly maneuvered out of reach, for once he'd touched her all conversation was likely to come to an end. "Collie's so young. He's learned a lot since he left Chicago, but he's still only a boy. He's not ready to marry."

"I think you're wrong about that. I've seen him watching Mamie from time to time."

"That's not a need to get married, it's a need to relieve himself. If he were still in Chicago..."

"Mamie's ready to get married," Jessie said hastily, not wanting to hear the end of her husband's speculation. "And she and Collie are well suited. They would be better off together than apart."

"Ho, there's the meat of it. Mamie's your friend, and you want to get her married off. She's young and pretty and she won't have any trouble getting married, when the time comes. There are hundreds of men to every female in California. If you have to be concerned about a lone female, why do you ignore Clara Ridback? She's less able to look after herself than Mamie, and hasn't a mother and sister to keep her company."

Jessie tensed. "She strikes me as well able to look after herself. She's considerably older than Mamie, and more experienced. She's had two husbands, or is it three? No doubt she can find herself another among all those desperate males."

Joel heard the edge of antagonism. "Is it because she rouges her face? She's really a decent woman, Jessie, and she's afraid of what's going to happen to her."

"Everybody's afraid," Jessie pointed out woodenly. "There are so many of us to be concerned about, why do you choose Clara Ridback?"

He stared at her in exasperation. "I don't *choose* her. I just feel sorry for her. She's lost her husband, she's lost her clothes and most of her valuables—"

"Now she has to dress like the rest of us," Jessie interrupted.

"I'm not saying she's any more deserving of friendship and sympathy than anyone else, only that she's a human being and needs those things as much as Mamie Groves."

"I *like* Mamie Groves."

"And you don't like Clara Ridback."

"No," Jessie said coolly, "I don't."

"None of the women seem to like her."

Jessie said nothing to that, feeling that his observation only proved her own unstated point.

Mamie arrived then to take Laurie into custody while Jessie hauled her soiled clothes to the spring for laundering. Joel shrugged and went off to make certain that necessary repairs were being made to various bits of harness, which did not hold up well in this climate. He did not understand in the slightest why Jessie, usually so sweet, should be so disagreeable about anything connected with Clara.

Clara was not washing her garments along with the other women that evening. She had lost all the prettiest ones, for the blood soaked into them from Virgil's slashed wrist had proved impossible to remove. Still, she had had plenty of other, more ordinary gowns. And while there were things she could have washed, she had no intention of subjecting herself to an hour or two of the inhospitable company of the other women. They did not include her in their conversations, for the most part, and spoke only when she spoke to them first. To the devil with them, then; she'd use the spring after the others had finished, or wait until they came to the next spring.

She was, therefore, at loose ends while the rest of the women were gathered out of sight beyond the circle of wagons. She wandered along the line, careful of where she put her feet, for the memory of the effects of snakebite was strong, and saw Collie working over something near his wagon, and that Mamie Groves, cradling the Shand baby in her arms, standing talking to him with some animation.

For a moment Clara felt a twinge of regret that she was thirty and not nineteen, and then she lifted her chin. She didn't, after all, *look* thirty. And Joel Shand was moving in her direction, though he hadn't seen her yet. She altered her direction so that their paths would cross, and arranged a smile on her features.

13

On the Fourth of July they passed through the divide between the Great Salt Lake drainage and the Snake River. There was a fine stream and that evening they celebrated the holiday with music and dancing.

Jessie danced with the others, though less vigorously than usual, because of the baby she carried. She was pleased to see that Collie spent most of his time with Mamie, though he also danced with Alice and even with Clara Ridback. One had to admit, however reluctantly, that the woman was stunning even though she wore only a flowered calico gown; her rich auburn hair managed to come loose from its ribbons during the festivities and provided an entrancing frame for her lovely face; Clara was, in fact, one of the most popular partners, though many of the women regarded her with distaste and disapproval. In a day when widows often remarried of necessity within days of the time their husbands were buried, as Jessie's mother had had to do, there was still note taken of the fact that her period of grieving had been brief.

The one Jessie really wanted to dance with was Joel; he was attentive and handled her, as a watching Annie remarked, as if she were made of glass. When Jessie murmured that she thought she'd better rest for a few dances, Joel looked down at her teasingly.

"You want me to rest with you?" There was double entendre there, so that warmth swept up the column of her throat and into her face. Jessie laughed, glad that he found her so desirable that he seemed unable to stay for long away from the subject of making love.

"No, thank you. You may dance, but only with the old women," she told him in mock seriousness.

In the smoky dusk behind her, a figure moved, became Clara Ridback, and the light clear voice carried over the other voices. Intruding, dampening what had been between Jessie and Joel.

"Do I qualify, Mrs. Shand? May I dance with your husband?"

For a moment Jessie couldn't credit the audacity of the woman. Beyond Clara she caught a glimpse of Mamie and Collie, laughing together, and she was glad for her friend. But mostly she was aware of Clara, lips redder than nature had provided, a bosom fairly bursting out of the flowered calico, waiting for her reply.

Clearly Clara did not expect to be relegated to the "older woman" status, but she didn't expect Jessie to flatly refuse her, either. Her smile broadened in anticipation of the little Mormon's gauche reponse, Jessie's inability to refuse gracefully.

She would have been warned had she been able to detect the quickening of Jessie's pulses. Indeed, the anger rose in Jessie in an overwhelming wave, though the smile remained fixed on her lips, for all that it was a stiff one.

"I think there are many single men being deprived of your company, ma'am," Jessie said. "It would be more appropriate that you dance with them, rather than a man who is yet a bridegroom. Besides, my husband is going to walk me back to our wagon; we do enjoy our little time together, by ourselves." She swiveled to fix the too-bright smile on Joel. "Shall we tell Annie we're ready to go?"

Joel had intended to engage in the celebration until it ended, surely an hour or two on down the line. He didn't care one way or the other about dancing with Clara—Jessie was the best dancer in the entire lot, and the prettiest, as well. Yet he detected that note in her voice that warned him to tread warily.

He murmured his goodnight and left Clara without a partner as the fiddle swung into a lively air, her smile completely erased.

"You really tired, honey?" Joel asked, sliding an arm around his wife's still slender waist. Annie saw them and rose from her seat on a wagon tongue, cradling the sleeping baby, and fell into step behind them. "Not too tired to end this Fourth of July the right way, I hope?"

Had he resisted her efforts to keep him away from Clara, her temper might well have flared; she knew that she had grown moderately unreasonable of late but in this instance felt that she was right. Since he came with her at once, however, with no objections, Jessie's good humor resurfaced.

"And what way would that be, sir?"

"I'll be happy to show you," Joel assured her, tightening the embrace, and Jessie decided she had not deprived him of a well-earned celebration, after all.

Later, lying in his arms as his hands explored the body that clearly delighted him, as his mouth closed over hers in a kiss that left her breathless, Jessie had a moment of lucid thought: Clara Ridback had not been removed from the field, she'd only been set back a trifle. And then as Joel's lips burned a trail down her throat to her breast, she forgot everything except that she and Joel were finally together and that she loved him more than life itself. She didn't even notice when the music ceased and the voices called goodnights; she sank deeper into ecstasy, and then into contented sleep.

Cap Horn had chosen to take the northern route into Idaho by way of Fort Hall rather than to travel through Utah and the land of the Mormons led by Brigham Young. It was not that Young's followers were hostile or inhospitable: indeed, the Mormons were happy to sell, for scandalous prices, anything the travelers might need. They were, however, a feisty lot, with an abundance of rules and regulations easily broken by those not of their faith. And they didn't care for Gentile men who showed an interest in their women, for all that they seemingly had more than enough to go around since Brigham Young had a different wife for nearly every day of the month.

Jessie was disappointed that they would avoid the settlement at the Great Salt Lake. She didn't think it likely that Zadie and Dennis had come ahead of their own train, but there was always such a possibility. And if her sister and her husband were coming on behind, they might pick up a message here.

"They won't join Brigham Young's band," Joel protested. "For one thing, Young won't take kindly to James Strang's leftovers, I wouldn't think—after all, they excommunicated Strang. And besides that, I wonder if Dennis and Zadie will want to stay with the Mormons any more than we did."

"Dennis was a Mormon. His whole family belonged to the church," Jessie reminded him. She stared south at the naked hills, as if she could penetrate the distance that way and see whether the people she sought were there.

"And Dennis seduced his father's wife and took her in

adultery," Joel said flatly. "Maybe he's now legally married to her, since his father died, but it seems to me they'd feel uncomfortable, staying in the old man's church."

There was some logic in this. Jessie was not certain that Joel's assessment was a correct one; she suspected her sister had been willingly seduced, and since King Strang was one of those who had forced her into an unwanted marriage, Zadie had no reason to love or respect the Mormons.

"Still, what if they are there, Joel? What if they just pass through? Cap says lots of wagon trains go that way."

"What do you want to do? Go by way of Fort Bridger by ourselves? Cross the Great Salt Desert alone? I've heard tales of that place, miles and miles of dead land. No water that's drinkable, no grass. If they reach California, we'll find them eventually. They'll write to your Aunt Winnie in Independence, and you'll write to her, too, and then you'll each find out where the other one is."

"If Aunt Winnie doesn't die of old age before all that's accomplished."

"It's not like you to be such a pessimist," Joel accused, with some justification.

Jessie knew that, yet felt compelled to defend her position. "Well, she's an old lady, and she's all alone now. And how can you expect any woman to stay cheerful, after months of this dreadful country, with the mosquitoes and the snakes and maggots in the meat and weevils in the flour and..."

To her horror, Jessie began to cry.

Joel was at once contrite; he gathered her into his arms to soothe her. He was not feeling the same stress that she did, and though the wild strange country was not to his liking as a place to live, he had enjoyed seeing it, even with all the hardships that traveling through it entailed. The great red rock formations, looking like castles and fortresses against the sky, were fascinating. The streaks of multicolored stone— red, mauve, pink, and green—were like nothing he'd ever seen before.

He wouldn't be seeing them again, either. Once he got over those tantalizing mountains still out of sight to the west, he'd stay there. In the meantime, however, while he struggled to keep the wagons moving and the people from dying, why not make the best of everything else?

"Don't you think the country is beautiful, in its own way?" he demanded later of Annie Ryan. And Annie, glancing toward the cradle where Laurie slept in contentment, spoke in a voice that would not carry to Jessie inside the wagon.

"It's a man's country, not a woman's. It's too—too harsh, too cruel. A woman dries out, withers away, in a place like this. Her skin gets so rough she's ashamed to have anyone see it, or touch it. And there's danger every step of the way. Women are afraid. Besides, boy, your wife is expecting, and that does peculiar things to a woman. More than swelling her belly. It makes her weepy even when she's living in a sound house in a safe place, with a good man. It makes her tireder than usual, and in need of more loving."

"Is that what it is? Because she's breeding?"

"More'n likely," Annie assured him. "Don't be too hard on her, boy; she's a special person, and she's made of good stuff, but this is hard on her, harder than it is on you."

He was busy, every day, all day, with more chores than the average man in the train because he took on the responsibility for the rest of them as well as for himself, and he had little time to indulge an unreasonable wife. Yet he tried.

He did not understand why it did not seem to cheer her when he spoke of the big house he would build for her, the rich clothes she would someday own, the diamond he would put on her finger. Jessie extended a hand toward him, displaying the brown and roughened skin.

"I'm as dark as those savages, and I'd look as absurd with a diamond as they do with all those horrid bones and teeth around their necks."

Nothing he said seemed to have the desired effect. In the dark, however, naked bodies entwined, Joel brought back the Jessie he loved. He made her smile, and even laugh, and brought her to passionate climax after climax, her urgency as great as his own. And when it was over, she slept in his arms. Joel was content.

The journey had been long and hard, and this nearly final lap of it was the hardest of all. In the full heat of summer they moved through the desert lands where often what little water there was could sicken and kill the stock. Feed was sparse, game even scarcer, and Jessie felt as sick as if she'd drunk of the poison water because she knew there was more of the same, and worse, still to come.

Yet for all that, she began to feel better, physically and mentally. When the queasiness of early pregnancy subsided, she underwent a spurt of extreme well-being. She continued to walk most of the time, rather than endure the jolting of the wagon, and the walking did not tire her as badly as it had for a few weeks.

One night when they were camped along the Humboldt River Jessie was awakened by Annie's voice, calling her. "It's Belle Snow, she's in labor. She says she's always had her babies easy, but I'd be obliged to have you standing by, in case I need help."

"I'll be right there," Jessie replied; she scrambled out of bed and groped for her clothes. She bent over Joel, who had scarcely awakened, and touched his shoulder. "Joel, if Laurie cries, you'll have to tend him. I'll be at the Snow wagon."

Joel grunted agreement and sank back into slumber before she had climbed to the ground.

Jessie had attended various birthings before, and she took a moment for a silent prayer before she joined Annie in the crowded wagon. Ernie Snow had done his best to make a passageway where they could stand, and Annie had set him to heating water to bathe mother and babe when the ordeal was done. The two older children slept only yards away from where their mother labored, rousing slightly when Belle cried out, only to sleep again as soon as the sound had ceased.

A baby girl was born at dawn. Annie handed the tiny creature over to Jessie and devoted her own attention to the new mother, leaving Jessie to her own devices.

Jessie accepted the basin of warm water brought by the relieved husband and father, working atop a crate at the back of the wagon, as sunrise spread a pink glow over the world around her. A baby girl, perfectly formed, the tiny delicate fingers so beautiful that Jessie felt tears in her eyes. It had been eight months since her own little daughter had been born, and died, a child that might have been as healthy as this one if Cass Merriam had not raped Jessie and precipitated an early birth.

That wouldn't happen this time. Cass Merriam was dead, and Joel was here to protect her from anyone else. Her baby would be born in February, months away, but he would be as perfect and as precious as this one.

She wrapped the infant in the blanket Belle had made ready, and carried her back to the exhausted but exhilarated mother. Belle smiled up at her, then craned her neck to see the child in the crook of her arm. "My, ain't she a beauty, though!"

They had to agree that she was. Annie grinned at her

115

helper. "I don't need you any more, child. Why don't you go on home, now that it's time to get up anyway?"

"All right. I'll look in on you before we start," Jessie told Belle, and again climbed down from the wagon.

The morning air was cool and fresh, with a sweet smell to it, perhaps from the sage. Cap had not yet sounded reveille, and the encampment slept around her as she padded quietly back to her own wagon. Though she was tired, it was a good kind of fatigue; she had participated once more in the miracle of birth, and her own turn would be coming, her own baby, a baby that would live as Belle's lived.

Joel was still asleep, as was Laurie. She stood staring down at Joel, putting out a hand to his shoulder to wake him, and then stopping. A warmth spread through her, an excitement, a joy that would not be denied.

Instead of waking Joel, Jessie quickly unbuttoned her dress and dropped it and her shift around her ankles, heedless of wrinkles. The air was cold on her skin, but that only lasted for a moment, and then she slid naked into the comfort of the bed.

For the first time ever, Jessie initiated the lovemaking, rousing Joel from sleep with hands and lips, her slender body pressed against his with an ardor that brought his dark hazel eyes open in astonished delight.

"Jessie?"

"It'd better be Jessie," she said, giggling, and then found the laughter cut off as he came fully awake, passion soaring to meet hers, and neither of them heard reveille when it came, nor cared.

14

Jessie always remembered Nevada as a vast wasteland, so hot that at times she felt she could not breathe the air. Joel insisted that she give up walking, for the sun was too much for her, and indeed the earth was too hot; it burned through the soles of her moccasins.

And then, praise God! They reached the eastern border of California. There was still a mountain range to cross, the Sierra Nevada, but they were almost there, and well within the time limit set by nature, for they would surely reach their destination before the snow fell.

Sierra, Cap Horn told them, meant "mountains," so there was no need to say "Sierras" when they spoke of this final obstacle to their goal. That it was a major obstacle they knew; the mountains were steep and as dangerous as anything they had yet survived. But when they had conquered the Sierra, it would all be over. They would be home.

Home. The word had a foreign taste on their tongues. For all their lives, they would refer to "back home" meaning Indiana, or Michigan, or Ohio, or Missouri, wherever they had come from. Yet now they were close to the place that would be, from now on, home.

"It's hard to imagine living in a house again," Jessie said, turning to look back over the blue-hazed valley and the hills beyond, through which they had just come; the scene was far less terrible, seen from the slopes of the last range of mountains, than it had been to travel through. "After all these months with nothing but canvas around us, and wheels beneath us...just think, Annie! We'll have solid walls, and glass windows, with curtains, and a fireplace to cook in, or even a stove—and we can light a candle without being afraid to burn the roof from over our heads!"

"Clean water," Mamie Groves added dreamily. "Clean,

cold water for a parched throat, clean enough so it won't leave stains in your clothes and a mess in your hair—and enough of it to bathe in, all over!"

The other women chimed in with the things they had been dreaming of, the things they had not dared to think about too much until they finally came close to the realities.

A garden patch, a place to launder clothes, chairs to sit in, goose feathers to refill their ticks, churches, schools.

They had only to cross the Sierra.

They did not have to follow the footsteps of the ill-fated Donner party, many of whom had perished while others had resorted to cannibalism. Jessie was glad of that, for it would have brought that horror too close, to know the trail was the same.

Instead, Cap would lead them over Carson Pass to the south, a route opened some years ago by Mormons returning from California to Salt Lake City. It was mildly unsettling to think that some of the travelers who had preceded them had not chosen to stay in the promised land.

It made Jessie tremble inside. "How can they think about going back across that awful desert? Oh, Joel, what if it's all lies? What if there is nothing for us in California? What if it's only a pretty fairy tale that will vanish like the mirage along the Humboldt when we draw near to it?"

"They were Mormons," Joel pointed out. "I reckon the Mormons weren't any more popular in California than they've been anywhere else. It's not the country itself they're leaving; it's the gentiles they can't abide, or who can't abide them. They're going to join Brigham Young and be with their own kind. Jessie, don't worry about it. Once we're over those peaks, it will be all downhill, and California will be everything they said it would be. The land of milk and honey, just like in the Bible."

It was almost a miracle in itself that the closer they got to it, the more possible it seemed. Although the trail was steep and strewn with granite boulders of incredible size, the streams were clear and cold. The growth changed from sagebrush and scrubby pines to tall ponderosa and juniper and sugar pine, which scented the air with a fragrance that brought back memories of Beaver Island.

The day that she stood on the shore of the lake called Tahoe, a glowing blue-green gem more beautiful even than her beloved Lake Michigan had been, inhaling sweetness of the surrounding pines, resting her gaze on the fresh greens and blues of nature that she had missed for so long, Jessie cried with joy. Emotion swept through her in a scalding wave.

"It's true," she said, her voice quavering. "Sometimes, crossing that god-awful desert, I didn't think we'd ever find anything beautiful again. And this is...is almost like heaven."

"I told you. Everything we heard about California couldn't have been lies. We're going to have everything we've ever wanted, Jessie. Everything."

On impulse, she hugged him, in full view of the other awestruck pioneers around them. "Oh, Joel, can't we just stay here? I can't imagine a more beautiful place to live!"

"There's no farmland here," Joel told her gently, for he, too, was stirred by Tahoe. "Even if you cut down all the trees, there would be mostly stone underneath—all that granite is miles deep. Down the other side of the mountain Cap says there's a valley bigger than any valley we ever saw— hundreds of miles long, more than fifty miles wide. And a climate where a man can grow anything anybody can grow on the face of this earth, almost. Don't cry, honey, if we leave here. What we find at the end will only be better."

That was hard to believe, that anything could be better than this. But it was true about the soil and the granite beneath it. In places the rock was covered only with a skim of moss that could be peeled off with a fingernail.

"I'm only crying because I'm happy," she assured him, "happy that the worst is over, and that it's as wonderful as this."

That night in his arms, her happiness was complete. Long after Joel had fallen asleep, the tears continued to trickle from under her eyelids, and Jessie simply let them come. They had survived the desert and the Rocky Mountains, and they would survive the High Sierra, and their son would be born in the wondrous valley next spring. Even as the moisture lay on her cheeks, Jessie's lips curved in a smile.

Jessie went back to walking because it was safer than riding. She and Mamie and Alice plodded along together, being careful to position themselves so that if a wagon rolled backward they would not be crushed by it. Two more wagons were lost during the ascent, but this time it was not regarded as quite so disastrous as the earlier losses. The end was near.

At nine thousand feet elevation, the sweet air was thin, and they labored for breath and tired quickly. Though the route was as precipitous as anything they'd yet encountered, and the men and beasts strained and sweated in their efforts to lift wagons up nearly vertical walls, Jessie's spirits stayed high, as did those of most of the rest of the travelers.

Progress was slow, for the most part. The peaks of these mountains rose to more than fourteen thousand feet, and even in late August they found occasional patches of snow in the sheltered areas, snow that was quickly translated into dessert with the addition of sugar flavored with their precious vanilla beans.

"I know a woman who went to Europe, to Austria and Switzerland," Clara Ridback said, and for once they listened with interest. "This is just the way she described the country, the Alps—that's what they call the mountains there. And the Alpine meadows are like these, with an icy stream running through them, and filled with tiny flowers."

The meadows were sheer delight. The walking was easy, and the grass so deep and green even this late in the year that the stock could graze to their fill. Around them great boulders, bigger than the houses they remembered back home, surrounded the meadows, drawing children and adults alike to climb them for the pure adventure of it.

"As if we needed any more adventure," Annie said, puffing, as she achieved the top of one particularly imposing monolith and gazed down its far side on an idyllic scene of rock-strewn stream and lush grasses.

Jessie soaked in the beauty of it, the cool sweet air, the clear water so different from that of the muddy rivers that had sustained them over much of the continent, the life-giving grasses, the plentiful firewood. Please, God, she prayed, let it be like this, where we are going. Let us live in such surroundings forever.

Mamie interrupted her musings, hurrying along on her worn-out shoes to match the pace of her friend. "Jessie, have you heard?"

"Heard what?" Jessie asked, pausing to allow Mamie to catch her breath. Ahead of them a waterfall cascaded down the side of the canyon, catching the morning sunshine so that a rainbow arched across its spray. "Look, Mamie! Oh, Lord, I wish we could stay in this spot forever!"

"Tomorrow, or maybe the next day, we're going to split up," Mamie said. Her face was pink with the exertion of running. "Part of the train is going down the South Fork of the American River, into Sacramento. The rest, just a few I think, are going to head for the North Fork of the Stanislaus, through a place called Big Trees. Do you know which way you'll go?"

She meant, of course, which way would Collie go, for Collin and Joel would take the same route. And since Collie had made no declaration of any sort, Mamie wanted desperately to stay with the party in which he traveled.

"I don't know. I didn't know we weren't all going to continue together, though I suppose since we're so close to the end of the journey . . . I'll ask Joel."

Mamie brushed back a lock of chestnut hair which had escaped its ribbon. "Oh, Jessie, what am I going to do if Collie doesn't offer for me? Mama is so weepy we can hardly bear to be around her, though we understand her fears. She keeps asking what's to become of us, once we're over the mountains. What will we do to keep ourselves? It will soon be winter, and we have very little cash money left, and not much in the way of foodstuffs, either. If only Mama would make herself appealing, either to Collie or to Harry—Alice says it's because of her that neither of them will propose, and I don't doubt she's right. I can't blame them, really, but if they go off and leave us, then we'll have to start all over again with someone new, in a strange place." Mamie's eyes filled with tears. "I love him, Jessie. I really do."

"Well, you haven't parted yet. Don't give up. Oh, there's the baby, I'll have to feed him. But walk here, Mamie, ahead of Collie's wagon, where he can see you. Maybe if he thinks about you, and how soon you'll be parting if he doesn't do something about it . . ."

When her friend had gone, Mamie continued to make her way beside the wagon, far enough to the side of the main trail to assure her visibility to the drivers behind her. Now that they were out of the blistering sun she had discarded her sunbonnet, so her hair was displayed. It was probably her best feature, since her skin had darkened from too much exposure to the sun; her hands looked like raw meat even though she rubbed them with any kind of fat she could get to combat the effects of the elements. She'd been pretty when she left Missouri, but no woman could truly retain beauty through what they'd all been through.

Collie had come to talk with her in a friendly, open way. He often asked her advice about such domestic matters as how to cook or repair something, and he was always grateful when she brought him a fresh batch of biscuits or a dried-apple pie. Yet he'd never touched her, except when they were

121

dancing; then his blue eyes were bright, his grin wide, and he chose her as a partner more often than anyone else.

The wagons slowed as they approached another of the small streams that meandered through the meadow. Apparently this one was deep enough so that they had to use some care in fording it, for the train had come to a complete halt. Mamie saw that several of the men had climbed down from their wagons to discuss the matter, Joel among them though still on horseback, and then he, too, dismounted.

There would be a delay, then. Mamie turned her head and looked at Collie.

He lifted an arm, indicating that he was aware of the situation, and a moment later he'd secured the reins of his standing bullocks and joined Mamie on the ground.

"Looks like they're going to make a slow crossing. There are plenty of them now, they don't need me. Want to walk over there, in the shade, for a few minutes?"

"Yes, of course. It's warm, isn't it?" Mamie tried to smooth her hair, then remembered that doing so exposed her hands, which looked like no lady's hands should ever have looked.

They walked across the carpet of spring green, reveling in its softness after all the dust and rock. Mamie suddenly giggled. "I have a wild fancy to take off my shoes—they're worn through, anyway—and cool my feet. Maybe," she said daringly, "even in the water."

The creek curved here, behind a rock, so that within a few yards they were out of sight of the rest of the wagon train. Collie stepped onto an outcropping and dropped to his stomach, scooping up a handful of water to drink.

"It's like ice," he said, grinning. "You want some?"

Her hesitation was brief. "Yes, though I don't think I can reach it that way."

"I'll get it for you."

She knelt beside him, and it gave her a peculiar sensation that was so overpowering she scarcely tasted the water, to drink from his hand. It was not the hand of a gently raised boy who had only worked in his father's Chicago store; it was a man's hand, broadened and tanned and with calluses on the palm upturned to cup the water.

She could not drink without touching her lips to his hand, and that touch set up a trembling that she was afraid was visible to him. Mamie stood and looked upstream, covering the reaction.

"There's a place up there where I think I could walk right

to the water. Put my feet in it, even. You wouldn't tell any-body if I did, would you?"

"I'll join you," Collie said, and they made their way along the bank of the stream that gurgled over stones, around boulders, in its quest for a defile that would eventually lead to the sea.

They sat on a large flat rock to remove their shoes. Mamie moved quickly, knowing that her mother would disapprove, that she might lose her own nerve if she hesitated, unable to look at Collie to judge his reaction to what was clearly an unladylike action. But, she thought with a sudden reckless-ness that was uncharacteristic of her, this might be her last day in Collie's company, and what did she have to lose?

The rock was sun-warmed under her feet, though it retained a chill where it lay in shadow. She walked out toward the creek, enjoying the freedom of bare feet and the rough texture beneath them. She heard Collie behind her, and spoke without turning her head.

"Look, there's almost a bridge of stepping-stones. I wonder if we could cross . . ."

"Be careful, it's deep there," Collie cautioned. "Look, there's a fish! A trout, I think!"

Mamie turned her head to watch the silvery shining crea-ture, and was therefore unprepared when the second rock she stepped upon shifted beneath her. The choked cry caught in her chest as Collie's arm came around her, strong and hard about her torso, the hand that she had only moments ago touched with her mouth now cupping one breast as he drew her back against himself.

For a moment they balanced precariously there; Mamie felt the wet of her dress against her ankles, but that was only with a distant corner of her mind. In the forefront was the sensation of that male hand on her breast, the male body behind her in an unplanned embrace.

And then, after a moment during which Collie steadied them both on the more secure rock closer to shore, the parody became real. Mamie's heart hammered both in her chest and in her throat; the gurgle of the stream joined with a thunderous pounding of blood in her ears as Collie turned her around, still within the circle of his arms.

He wasn't smiling now. A pulse jumped visibly in the V of his open shirt, and his eyes were wide. "Mamie," he said, in a tone different from any she had previously heard.

She couldn't move. She didn't want to move. Her breasts

were drawn against his chest, her face uplifted, and Mamie closed her eyes as their lips came together.

It was a gentle kiss, a chaste one, yet it ignited a fire that flowed through every inch of her. Though he no longer touched her bosom, the fire was especially intense there, in the breast that had been covered by his hand. And it was most intense in the place he did not touch at all.

It was a shattering experience, far more compelling than she had anticipated. How could it be, that he could so arouse her inner sensations in areas so removed from where he caressed her?

"Collie! Where the hell are you?"

The shout brought them both back to sanity. They stepped guiltily apart, so abruptly that Collie then had to reach out once more to keep her from toppling off the stepping-stone into the water.

"I'm coming, Joel!" Collie looked down into the upturned face, unmistakably rosy with intense emotion, and this time when he moved away from her Mamie stood on her own.

"We need some help," Joel called, and to Mamie's vast relief he did not come the rest of the way to where they stood, so that she remained screened by the great boulder.

Collie paused for only a few seconds, to look at this girl who was not Patrice Hammond but those flesh had been softly yielding to his touch, whose kiss had awakened an ache in his loins that would be some time dissipating. "Later," he breathed, and was gone from sight.

Mamie made her own way back to shore, moving carefully so as not to slip into the water. She felt numb, yet at the same time something had come vitally to life inside her, something yearned for and now miraculously present.

No one paid any attention when she emerged into the meadow. The wagons were being hauled across the creek, made dangerously by sharply sloping banks with their jumbled large and small rocks, so that it was all the men could do to keep each conveyance from tipping over sideways. Mamie felt as if she drifted across the grass, as if music played around her, as if she were enveloped in a protective cloud.

Later, Collie had said.

Now that things were at last moving in what seemed the desired direction, she didn't in the least mind waiting until later.

15

Once they climbed into the Sierra, game became plentiful. There were rabbits and squirrels in great numbers, and most gratifying of all, there were deer. Joel was one of a dozen men who brought down game on a regular basis, for he had always hunted for his meat.

Jessie, who had eaten more venison than beef during her lifetime, roasted a haunch over a real wood fire, and they ate until they were all uncomfortably full. The red meat gave them strength for the remainder of their journey, and promised plenty after months of so little.

There was still the downward side of the Sierra to cover, and their experience had been that going down a mountain was often more difficult than going up. Yet the nearness of their goal, the plentitude of meat and grass and water, buoyed their spirits. There was music around the campfire that night, and the smoke of burning pine was a perfume as well as an insect repellent against the clouds of hovering mosquitoes.

"Which way will we go, when the trains divide?" Jessie asked as she cleared away the supper things.

Joel, overfull and growing drowsy, leaned back against a rock and picked his teeth with a straw. "Cap Horn is heading for Sacramento, because that's where most of the people want to go. But that's a city, and I'm not looking for a city. We've talked it over, and about a dozen wagons will go with us, over the Big Trees Route. That will take us down a river called the Stanislaus, and into the valley where there's farmland. Once there, we should be able to make it through the winter without any trouble, Cap says."

"How will we know the way, without Cap Horn or someone who's been over the trail before?"

"It's well marked, well used. And it's not as steep as some of the places we've gone down. We're almost there, Jess." He grinned at her, teeth gleaming in the twilight. "There were a few times when I wondered if we'd make it, but it's a sure thing, now. And we're together as a family—you and Laurie and me, a family. With a daughter on the way, too."

"A son," Jessie corrected.

"A son? Well, I've no objection to sons, but we already have one of those. Let's have a girl, a pretty one exactly like you—with big brown eyes and those thick lashes, and hair the color of ripening wheat, and skin like—"

She clamped a hand over his mouth. "Don't say what the skin is like, not till I've had a chance to get it back to normal."

He laughed, easily wrestling her hand away. "Skin like silk. There are still parts of you like that, like silk."

She wondered if she'd ever get over blushing at some of the things he said to her. She made no reply, though her thoughts remained stubbornly fixed on a boy. Jessie would have a son of her own.

Mamie, too, ate venison for supper. None of her family had shot it, of course, but Joel had generously shared his game with the wagonload of women. As usual, Clara had done little to assist in its preparation, though she ate of it readily enough.

After supper they sat around their small fire, tired yet unwilling to go to bed. Mamie was acutely aware of the lone figure two fires back, eating his own pan-fried venison liver, smothered in wild onions gathered along a creek bank. Later, Collie had said, but he had made no move toward her, and Mamie didn't know how to make the first overture without attracting unwanted attention.

Sarah Groves wiped the last plate and resettled it in its crate. "This is such a pretty place. If only your pa had lived to see it."

They could hear the tears in her voice, though it was dark enough to hide the ones in her eyes. Mamie stood up restlessly, unable to endure another spate of sentimentality over a man she had really not liked very much.

"I'm going to walk over and talk to Jessie for a few minutes before I turn in," she said, and hoped her voice didn't convey her real intentions. "You want to come, Alice?"

Her sister rose with alacrity. She, too, had a low tolerance for Sarah's plaintive voice, and besides, Harry was probably alone at his fireside, beyond her mother's view. "Wait, I'll get a shawl. It's getting chilly."

It was, though Mamie hadn't noticed. Her own inner fires, so long banked, were smoldering enough to warm her all the way through. She reached for her own shawl, for at this elevation the nights grew downright cold as soon as the sun dropped behind the trees.

Sarah frowned, watching her daughters. "I don't know as it's safe to wander around at night. Belle Snow spotted a black bear this afternoon."

"No bear is going to come close to all these campfires," Mamie predicted. "And we'll be together, so don't worry about us. There are sentries posted, as there always are."

"Don't stay late, then," Sarah admonished, and poked another stick into her fire.

The girls did not remain together longer than it took them to get out of their mother's sight. Both were wild to know whether or not their own wagon would be going with Cap Horn's band or Joel Shand's, and while Mamie knew that Collie would be accompanying his supposed cousin, Alice had no such information regarding Harry Kelly's plans, and neither of them knew where the wagon in which they rode would go. The men who would make the decision might well feel that since the women knew no one at either end of the trail, it wouldn't matter which road they took.

Mamie left her sister at Harry's campfire, accepting a cup of coffee she didn't want in order to have an excuse for pausing there. Mamie's pulses raced in anticipation, for as she approached his wagon Collie rose and ambled off toward the edge of the forest.

He had seen her, she was sure of that. And he wasn't trying to get away from her, he was only moving to a less lighted area where they could speak in privacy.

Just remembering his touch sent the sensations through her again, the frightening yet wondrous prickle of excitement along all her nerves; her own body was new and strange and promised something she could not describe but which she longed to experience.

She did not risk attracting attention by glancing around to see if she were observed. She moved, not quickly but with purpose, in the direction Collie had taken, though she could no longer see him. He had vanished into the darkness of huge trees.

"Mamie!" The voice was low, scarcely heard above the chuckle of the brook over stones only a short distance away.

"Here," Collie said, and she turned and felt her hands captured by his. "I hoped you'd come," he told her.

Now that she was here, she didn't know what to do or say.

"Are you cold?" Collie asked, for she was trembling, though it was not with chill.

"A little," Mamie confessed untruthfully. "Shall—shall we walk, or is that dangerous? Will we risk falling over a cliff?"

"No, no, it's perfectly safe. See, after you get used to it you can make out the trees." He released her hands, then immediately put an arm around her waist to guide her. His hand rested just above her waist, so close to the breast he had touched earlier, and Mamie felt giddy. She stumbled over an unseen root and was immediately supported and drawn into an embrace.

"You're so pretty," Collie said into the hair over her ear. "And so soft..."

His hands searched out the softness, in hip and waist and breast, and then his mouth covered hers, gently, tentatively.

Like every female, Mamie had dreamed about being kissed. It had been almost as good as this, the dream, but not quite. She relaxed into it, feeling as if her bones were melting, mingling with the blood that carried the warm languor to every part of her.

She only came to her senses when she realized that Collie—or her own weight, gone limp—was carrying her toward the ground. Mamie gulped air and whispered urgently, "No! No, please—I—I must go back, Mama will be looking for me—"

He released her at once, except for a steadying hand on her elbow.

"I'm sorry. I shouldn't have taken advantage of—" He broke off, when Alice's voice carried to them across the intervening shadows.

"Mamie, I'm going home now."

"I'll have to go, too. Oh, Collin, when the train splits up tomorrow I may have to take the other route from the one you're taking—"

"No," Collie said quickly. "There's no reason for that, not if you want to go with us. I'll speak to Joel; it doesn't matter to him, and if Mrs. Ridback wants to go to Sacramento, why, she can finish the ride with someone else."

"But the boy who's driving the wagon—"

"Someone else can drive it, so he can join his folks. The

128

Von Walds are going with us, maybe their Henry will do it. Don't worry."

She didn't. He kissed her quickly on the lips, and then Mamie hurried toward her sister.

"Harry says—" Alice began, at the same time that Mamie said, "Collin says—"

They both laughed, small, happy laughs. "Harry's going with the Shands," Alice finished. "And Collie, too?"

"Yes." Mamie sobered. "If only there was some way to be rid of Mama, or at least to make her stop sniveling so much. I think he might marry me, if he knew he didn't have to take Mama, too."

Alice had no solution for that, their shared problem. For the moment, though, it was enough to be traveling with the part of the train in which Harry Kelly and Collie Aubin would go.

In the meantime, they would both pray earnestly and trust to the good Lord to see to their futures.

The last lap down the western flank of the mountains was not an easy one, yet it was so beautiful that even Jessie did not worry overmuch. With the others, she stared incredulously at the trees for which this trail was named. "Big Trees" was an inadequate description of the forest giants, the Sequoias. They rose two hundred feet and more in the crisp thin air, and were so thick through that a stump would have provided more floor space than many of the cabins they had left behind. For the fun of it, Harry Kelly and Henry Von Wald measured the base of one of the massive trunks and pronounced it well over one hundred feet in circumference.

"We could hold a square dance on its stump, if anybody could cut it down without getting killed," Collie observed, and when his smile rested on Mamie she felt warm all over.

There were more important things to be considered than dancing on stumps, of course. The trail was precipitous in many places, and the entire company, now reduced to only twelve wagons, struggled to descend the remaining eight or ten thousand feet to the valley floor.

They passed by several small lakes, and reveled in the crystal waterfalls that were everywhere, providing an ample supply of that commodity that had been, for so long, so scarce. They worked their way across meadows still bearing what appeared to be spring flowers, tiny blossoms like those in the real Alpine settings, and past bushes loaded with blackberries so large and sweet that every woman in the group would have voted to stop and gather them, had they been given a vote. As it was, they brought out pans and buckets and picked as many as they could without falling too far behind the wagons.

They met a group of prospectors coming up the trail, a dirty, hardbitten lot with discouraged faces. Joel called a halt long enough to converse with them.

"Is there still gold?" Collie asked eagerly, bounding forward.

One of them wiped sweat from his brow and rested a hand on his mule's flank. "If there is, we sure ain't findin' any of it," he said. "They say a feller brought new color out of there"—he gestured to the north—"along the middle fork of the Mokelumne. But he ain't tellin' just where, naturally, and Bud, here, he went lookin' and didn't find nothin' more'n we been turning up along the Stanislaus."

They did not look prosperous. Still, the travelers had heard for years about the golden treasures of California, and were not easily discouraged.

"You ever find any?" Collie persisted.

"Oh, sure, a few years ago anybody wanted to walk outside his back door could find a nugget or two. Or at least," the man amended more truthfully, "a little dust, did he want to work for it. There's still mines going, but you try to move in on any of 'em and you'll get your ears shot off."

"What about farmland?" Joel asked, quietly but with no less intensity than Collie had shown in regard to the gold.

"Farmland?" The man stared at him blankly. "You want to farm, there's the whole goddamned valley, thousands of acres of it. I guess you can plow it up if you want to, though there ain't no way to get water on most of it less'n you stay along the river bottoms. Me, I have to go back to farming, I'll go back to Illinois where it rains once in a while."

Jessie, listening from the wagon seat with Laurie in her arms, ventured a question that, propriety or not, must be answered. "Doesn't it rain in California?"

The man's eyes narrowed, and she could see that he disapproved of forward females, though after he'd gazed at her for a few seconds she saw admiration creep into his expression, as well. He spat tobacco juice into the grass at his feet. "Rains aplenty in the winter, when you don't need it. In the summer ain't even a cloud floats over that valley to dump a drop or two—it's the hottest, bluest sky you ever seen, ma'am.

130

And the dryest country this side o' hell." He spat again. "Well, we'd best be movin' on. Want to get over this next stretch afore dark, maybe get us a young buck for supper. You seen many deer?"

Within a few minutes the travelers, from east and west, had moved on, each in their own direction. No one else seemed bothered, but Jessie was. No rain? Dryest country this side of hell? Was the man serious, or only teasing her? It was hard to tell with men, sometimes; their humor often took a turn inexplicable to the female mind.

Now that he was no longer riding herd on an entire wagon train, Joel had taken over the driving of his own wagon again, his horse trailing behind. Jessie liked having him beside her, liked being able to talk to him, though his conversation was not always satisfactory.

"Do you suppose it's true? That it's so dry, that there's no rain? How can you farm if there's no rain?"

Joel slapped the reins lightly over the broad rumps of the bullocks. "Jessie, I promise you. We'll farm. Why do you waste all that energy worrying about things that probably won't ever come to pass? Why can't you trust me?"

"I do trust you. Only there are things you have no control over, like the rain."

"Well, worrying about it won't make a single drop fall that I know of. I'll see you're fed, and have a roof over your head. And someday I'll see that—"

She interrupted him. "Don't tell me about the fancy house and the clothes and the jewels. Please, don't."

"Why not? I want those things for you. I'll get them."

She bit her lip and remained silent. She could not make him understand how little value she put on those things. She did not really think that acquiring fancy trappings was going to be within his power, and she felt saddened if that was going to detract from Joel's feelings about himself. He had grown up in poverty, abandoned by a father who had not cared enough about Joel's mother to marry her; he had been an outcast in the village where he lived, except for the friendship of an old man, the town drunk; he had felt rejected and looked down upon, even by the Mormons among whom he had lived for a time; although none of them had been deliberately cruel to him, they had never ceased to make him aware that, as a gentile, he was not good enough to marry one of their daughters.

She had hoped that his illegitimacy was something that

could be forgotten, left behind in the midwest, but she feared that Joel carried it with him, a festering sore seen only by himself, a wound that could only be healed when he achieved the respect and the wealth that his mother's family had had, the respect he thought he had earned. If only he hadn't gone to Toledo, she thought. If only he hadn't seen that aristocratic and cold grandmother, with her fine clothes and grand house, he might have been content with a log cabin built on the shore of Lake Michigan, instead of having to cross the entire continent in search of what he considered greater things.

Well, they'd crossed the mountains and the desert, and they had nearly reached the part of California to which he aspired, and no doubt it would all work out, as things generally had a way of doing.

"Still," she said wistfully, "it would be wonderful if we could stop right here, and build a cabin in one of these meadows, and live here forever."

Joel gave her an indulgently exasperated glance, shaking his head at the folly of the female mind. "In the winter there's snow twenty feet deep in most of these canyons."

"We're used to snow. I like snow."

"We couldn't farm here, Jessie. It's no better for that here than it was back there around Lake Tahoe. The ground is made of granite, with just enough sod to support a layer of grass."

"It supports those huge trees, and the ferns..."

"The trees can put down powerful roots into the cracks between the rocks. You couldn't grow corn here, or wheat, or oats. Look, there's a doe and a fawn, there in the shadow beside that boulder."

The subject was turned, as it always was when Jessie brought up a viewpoint he didn't share. Joel would listen, seemingly patient, until she'd expressed herself. And then, if he could not persuade her with his own words to an opposite view, he would distract her attention by something entirely different.

It was disquieting, yet in truth she *did* trust Joel, did trust his judgment and his ability to care for her and their coming child, and Laurie. She nearly forgot Laurie, and added him onto the end of her thoughts. It was only, as she had said, that there were many things Joel could not control.

As if he read her thoughts, he grinned at her now. "If you can't let me do the worrying about things, Jess, say your prayers. If you really have faith, let God take care of everything."

"I pray all the time," Jessie responded. But secretly, deep down inside, she remembered that God had allowed her mother to die young, and Audra even younger, and that God had not interfered on that dreadful day now more than a year ago when assassins' bullets had cut down James Jesse Strang at the peak of his self-proclaimed ministry. Praying was not quite enough to eliminate her fears.

16

The places they came to and heard about had an odd intermingling of names. Jessie rolled the Indian words on her tongue, liking the sound of them: Tuolumne, Yosemite, Mokelumne. And there were those with Spanish origins: Mariposa, Sonora, Montezuma, and Hornitos were equally melodious.

And then there were the names the miners had bestowed upon their surroundings, names that made her vaguely uneasy. Places like Moccasin Hill, Rattlesnake Creek, the Garrote Trail, Poverty Hill, Chinese Camp, Six Bit Gulch (the amount of gold taken out of it?), and Bloody Canyon. The town of Placerville was, they were told, more commonly referred to as Hangtown, for obvious reasons.

"Soon hang you as look at you," one traveler informed them. "Can't say as most of the ones they strung up didn't need it—but they're so damned eager they make mistakes once in a while."

Upon seeing his wife's face, Joel laughed. "That's in a mining camp, honey. The men are always a rough lot in a place like that. We won't be living in a mining camp."

Not that Collie and some of the others weren't thinking about the mining camps. They were told by virtually everyone that the peak of the gold mining was over, yet there were enough reports—most unsubstantiated by their informants—that there was still gold in the hills to whet the imagination and the excitement.

"Lot easier to pick up gold nuggets off the ground than to plant something and wait for it to grow and then harvest it," Collie said, laughing. Collie knew nothing about farming, and he carried merchandise from Richard Aubin's store that he hoped to peddle to the Californians; beyond that, he didn't know what he would do, but he seemed uncommonly unconcerned about the matter.

Whenever they stopped beside a stream for the night, or to prepare and eat a meal, the men would swarm over the gravel-bottomed creek, looking for the yellow glint of gold. Several times they found what they thought might be the valuable ore, but none of them could be sure it was not fool's gold, which was worth nothing at all. Still, they carried all the little flecks with them, just in case.

They came down out of the hills in early September.

The great valley spread out before them, nearly four hundred miles long through the heart of California, the combined Sacramento and San Joaquin valleys which were in reality only one.

Jessie's heart sank as they drew nearer to it. It was true that in the fall one couldn't expect the land to be in a state of eternal spring, as the Sierra had seemed to be. But the land that spread out before her was one of dry, rolling hills, as denuded of vegetation as much of the desert behind her had been, with scrub oaks along the rivers and ravines so dark a green as to appear, from this distance, to be black.

There was grass, but it wasn't green. And up close the trees had not even the beauty of the cottonwoods; the leaves were small and prickly and covered with the dust of the travelers' passage. Occasionally there was a large oak that offered considerable shade, but the temperature had risen sharply as they descended toward the valley floor, and there was not nearly shade enough for comfort.

Sweat moistened their faces and soaked their garments. Clouds of grasshoppers rose around them, great nasty things that occasioned panic when they slid down the fronts of dresses or caught in the women's hair. It didn't help Jessie's sense of humor to be told that the Indians sometimes ate them, considering them a delicacy.

The Stanislaus River was still there beside the trail; it had dropped into a deep canyon so that most of the time there was no access to it. One could stand on an overhanging bluff and see it, turbulent white water over the rocks, 150 or 200 feet below.

The only game they saw now was jackrabbits, scrawny long-eared creatures that proved to have little meat when captured for the pot. "It doesn't matter," Joel said. "There are plenty of deer in the hills, and they're not that far away."

Jessie looked back toward the Sierra, taking on a blue haze behind them, promising coolness and beauty with trees and streams, then out over the valley.

This, then, was the magical California, and she knew a moment of sick apprehension. For this they had left Beaver Island, and even Missouri? Dear God, she thought, don't let Joel decide to stay here.

But stay he did.

Their small caravan came down a steep hill to the river, and waited their turn to cross on the bargelike vessel to the town of Knight's Ferry. Upstream, the Stanislaus squeezed through the opening in the rocky canyon walls, then plunged, pale green and white froth, over the rapids. The crossing took only a few minutes, and each of the wagoneers was two dollars lighter in the purse by the time it was accomplished.

There was less grumbling over this than there might have been, because, after all those months on the trail, they had finally reached civilization.

Knight's Ferry boasted a community of some eight hundred people. There was a sawmill and a flour mill powered by those powerfully rushing waters; and as they rolled into the village they saw that there were plenty of other things that they'd all missed so much.

Some of the buildings along Main Street were frame; some were made from locally produced brick or stone. All had roofs and windows and doors and amenities the travelers had grown unaccustomed to.

"Look!" Jessie exclaimed as they jounced along the dusty thoroughfare paralleling the river. "Are those oranges? Growing on a tree?"

"I told you it would be worthwhile," Joel said, grinning broadly. He lifted a hand to indicate a shingle hanging over a doorway. "They got a lawyer. And there's a hotel, several hotels, and a general store. I bet they have a school, too, seeing how many little ones are running around. They must have a post office, too, maybe in the general store, so you can send a letter to Zadie, at your Aunt Winnie's. All the refinements anybody could want," he proclaimed.

It wasn't Chicago, but it was better by far than an army post in the middle of a grassless, treeless plain. There were a few window boxes with bright flowers in them, and curtains in the windows. Fruit trees had been planted to supplement the native oaks, and they gazed in wonder at their first palm trees. Women lived in this place, Jessie thought. Women like herself had made homes and were rearing families here; it was not the savage frontier she had dreaded. It made her feel better, for everything she'd heard about the mining camps had been appalling, even though she thought that some of the stories *must* have been exaggerated.

"There's a house that's mighty fine," Joel pointed out, and Jessie obediently turned her head to look at it. It was two stories high, on a foundation that lifted it at least four feet off the ground level, and there was a veranda across the front with chairs where its occupants could sit and watch the traffic and the river.

No one sat there now, yet it had a solid, homey air that promised security to the newcomers, too. They could stay here, they could live in such places as this.

"It's nowhere near as grand as the one *she* lived in," Joel said. He never referred to his maternal grandmother by name, but Jessie knew by his vocal inflection who he meant. "And won't hold a candle to the one we'll have, someday."

That someday was rather far in the future, Jessie thought. Yet it didn't matter to her. No longer would they spend day after day jolting over rocky trails or sinking axle-deep in quicksand or mud. No longer would she cower under the canvas cover during a storm; instead, she would soon have a roof over her head, and solid walls around her. They would put down roots here, roots of their own sort.

"We'll stop over there at the blacksmith's," Joel decided, "and get some information. Want to get down and stretch your legs?"

Jessie did so with alacrity, carrying Laurie with her, to join the other women in the following wagons. Annie came forward, looking ruefully down at a shoe sole that flapped loose, then beaming around at her fellow travelers.

"My, this is a fine town. Look, they sell wallpaper, of all things, and there's a boot shop. I wonder what they'd ask to make me a pair of decent shoes?"

The other wagons rolled to a halt behind Joel's wagon, and

136

the newcomers all dismounted and stared around them in varying degrees of gratification. Already Clara was moving across the street to peer into the windows of the general store, shading her eyes so as to better penetrate the gloom within. Jessie, who had felt a similar urge, stifled it.

"This is the official end of the trail," Joel said. "From here on, everybody's on his own."

"Not you, Annie," Jessie said quickly, glancing at her husband for his reaction. "You'll come with us, of course."

Joel must have heard, but he was turning away toward the open smithy, neither seconding her invitation nor rejecting it.

The older woman shook her head. "You won't want an old woman around, young newlyweds like you. Looks like there might be something I could do to earn my way in a place like this." Her eyes rested speculatively on the hotel. "I've cooked my way before; I can do it again. I wonder would they be put off if I asked about it, this fool shoe falling off my foot the way it is?"

She gave Jessie a smile and headed toward the hotel, a bulky woman of middle years who had lost husband, daughters, and son, yet could carry her head high and end a two-thousand-mile journey by announcing her intention of hiring out at a job that would tax the strength of a much younger person.

Jessie watched her go with mingled feelings. She had grown to love Annie like a second mother, though she was very different from Viola Campbell Ritter. No doubt it was best if Annie did make her own way, but it would be hard to give her up, both as a friend and as a helper with Laurie. Jessie had grown to depend heavily on the other woman. What would she have done without Annie, after Laurie had been thrust upon her? And what would she do when her own infant came?

As if knowing she'd thought of him, the child in her arms began to whimper. The small knot of travelers was dissolving, as each of the men headed for the information post of the smithy, and the women drifted off toward whatever drew them most in the row of shops that faced the river. Jessie decided she would save that pleasure until later, savoring the treat to come as she had saved the icing on her cake when she was a little girl. She'd enjoy the general store more if she didn't have to share it with Clara Ridback.

The Groves family had no such qualms; they were all three

moving in that direction, though since Collie alone of the men had turned toward the store that was not surprising. Mamie did not intend that Collie should forget her, even for a few minutes, poor dear.

Jessie felt the heat rise with the dust from the road, bringing out moisture on her body under her clothes. The orange tree offered a few yards of shade, and she left the wagon to take advantage of that, cradling Laurie against her shoulder.

Oranges, growing on a tree the way that apples did back home. She stared at them in wonder. Would they be able to have orange trees, too? When they had a place of their own?

An elderly man came out of the house beyond the tree and saw her there. He came down the steps, and Jessie offered a tentative smile. "I hope you don't mind if I admire your oranges? I've never seen them growing before."

"Purty, ain't they?" the old man agreed, hitching at his suspenders. "They ain't real sweet, like the ones they raise down near Los Angeles, I reckon, but they're fairly tasty. Have yourself one, ma'am. They're good for a woman that's nursing a youngun."

Jessie blushed but did not tell him that she wasn't nursing Laurie. She reached for the nearest fruit and smelled the pungent aroma as her thumbnail tore away the peeling to make a hole so that she could suck the juice.

He was right, it wasn't terribly sweet, but the flavor was marvelous to someone so long deprived of fresh produce. She thanked her benefactor and then, since he seemed disposed to linger, lifted her gaze to his dwelling.

"Is there a reason why all the buildings are up so high off the ground?" A trickle of juice escaped onto her chin, and she wiped at it awkwardly, juggling the baby.

"River," the old man said succinctly. And then, seeing her confusion, added, "Comes up like a devil during the rainy season, washes away anything ain't nailed down. So we put our houses on stone, get 'em well above the reach of the water. First house I built went downstream, and my wife with it, and everything else I owned. Did a better job with this one."

Jessie's eyes had grown wide. She swiveled slowly and stared across the street, where the Stanislaus was out of sight below the bluff except upstream, where she could hear it as well as see it, thundering through the canyon.

It did not seem possible that the waters could rise this high, yet there was nothing in her informant's face to suggest that he was teasing her.

"Did...did your wife...was she all right?"

"Drowned." He plucked one of his own oranges and began to peel it with fingers so brown she wondered if he had Indian blood, though there was no Indian look to his features. He reached up to push his hat back, exposing a line of pale skin just below a wisp of white hair. His eyes were very blue and alert.

"Been a widower since eighteen and fifty-two," he said. Unexpectedly, he chuckled, revealing gaps in his teeth. "Silas Wofford's my name. I own the hotel, over there. Don't live in it. Too damned noisy. I like my sleep at night. Heard your bunch ride in, and I come out to see who you were."

"I'm Jessica Shand," she told him. "That's my husband over there, the tall, dark one."

Silas examined Joel in silence for a moment, then spoke in his dry way. "Gold's pretty much gone by now, if that's what you come for."

"Joel wants to farm."

The old man grunted. "Plenty of land, though it ain't all free no more. Grow anything. Wheat, oranges, any damned thing. Grapes. My grapes ain't ripe yet, but you come back when they are, missus, and I'll give you some."

Warmth swelled inside her, a liking for this old fellow who was so friendly to a stranger. "Thank you. I'll remember that, Mr. Wofford."

"Oh, hell, everybody in Knight's Ferry calls me Si. We ain't too formal in these parts. I got a garden, too. Too damned hot to go pick anything now, but you come back in the morning and I'll give you a bunch of carrots and some lettuce. Too late for peas and such. Got a peach tree, but it's too late for peaches, too. You ever eat a nectarine?"

Jessie shook her head, still sucking on the orange. She was getting used to the tartness.

"Best thing you ever ate. Better'n an orange or even a peach. Next summer, you remember to come and see me, and I'll pick you a basketful."

Jessie stopped sucking for a moment. "Do you give your fruit and vegetables away to everyone?"

He chuckled again. "Nope. Just the pretty ones. Too bad you got that strapping big feller looking after you. Silas Wofford may not be much to look at, but he's a man of substance in Knight's Ferry. And I don't make no bones about it, I'm lonesome, missus. That's why I come out and look over the

139

newcomers. You got any spinsters or widow ladies in your train?"

One of the widow ladies emerged from the general store at that very moment, and Jessie turned to watch her cross toward the wagons. "That lady is recently widowed. Her name is Clara Ridback. She's very pretty, don't you think?"

Silas contemplated Clara's rich auburn hair and full-breasted figure. "Right handsome," he agreed.

Behind her, Sarah Groves and her daughters also descended the steps to the street. "And that's Mrs. Groves—her husband died on the trail, too—with her daughters."

"They spoken for?"

"Mamie and Alice? Well," Jessie temporized, "they're sort of...courting. There haven't been any proposals yet. At least that I know of."

"Pretty little things, ain't they?" The blue eyes revealed merriment. "Wouldn't look at an old man like me, but it don't hurt me to look at them, does it?"

The females were all animated, excited at having come to the end of their travels, at having been able to buy a few of the things they'd been missing for months. Even Sarah Groves was smiling, the pinched look gone from around her mouth.

They had been facing away from the hotel, but they both turned when Annie spoke behind them. "They already got a cook," she said to Jessie. "Reckon I'll have to find something else."

Silas Wofford openly surveyed this newest member of the train. "I'd be obliged if you'd introduce me, missus."

Jessie did so, noting that Joel had apparently finished his conversation with the blacksmith and was heading back to the wagon. "Mr. Wofford owns the hotel," she told Annie. "Maybe he could suggest something."

Silas pursed his lips and tossed his orange peeling into the road. "Got me a good Chinee cook. Works for practically nothing, and my patrons ain't particular, as long as they get their bellies full. The Chinamen work at the laundry, too, and really, that ain't no job for a woman. You wouldn't believe the stinking clothes them miners bring in here to be washed."

"I thought you said the gold was gone?"

Silas shrugged. "'Tis. But that don't stop all them fools from hunting it. Oh, somebody finds a nugget once in a while, and they keep finding enough dust to coat the end of your finger. They'd get rich faster if they went to hauling mail or raising a garden, but they all want to strike it rich."

Annie regarded him with interest. "Do you know anybody who ever did strike it rich?"

"Oh, hell yes! Did myself! That's how I got the money to build the hotel! But I didn't keep on digging after that, it's too hard work for an old man. And there's too many claim jumpers ready to slit your throat for whatever you found. I'm no match for them fellers any more, though if it was twenty years ago I'd have give as good as I got."

His eyes narrowed as he wiped moisture off his brow with a soiled handerchief. "Say, missus, you know anything about birthing a baby?"

"I've birthed a few," Annie said modestly. "Somebody here-abouts needing a midwife?"

"That there is. We got a midwife, old lady Bowers, but she's half blind and she always smells like a still, so the local ladies don't cotton to her much. Right now she's tending a poor little thing having her first, been in labor four days. I kept hearing her hollering for a couple of days, and she ain't had the baby yet, but she don't yell any more. Leastways, not loud enough so you can hear her in the street."

"If the other midwife is there, she won't welcome me, no matter how bad the mother is," Annie pointed out with con-siderable logic. Yet her expression revealed her concern for the unfortunate young woman.

"Tell you what," Silas said, hitching up his trousers and wiping orange juice on them. "I'll take you over there, and see what her husband has to say. Nice young feller, works for me once in a while when he ain't out in the hills looking for gold."

Annie nodded. "You tell Joel to take care of my wagon, Jessie. And if I don't get back here before he's ready to move on, he can come back after me later."

Jessie watched them go, stirring up dust in the road, her sympathies rising for the young woman who had been in labor for four days. If anyone could help her, Annie could.

Jessie hadn't had any trouble when her own Joella Viola was born, but of course the baby was three months early and tiny, and she'd died in a matter of hours. This time it would be different, for the baby grew safely inside her, and Joel was there to protect her until the time came for the birth. Jessie suppressed a tremor of apprehension at the idea of being in labor for four days, attended only by a drunken midwife.

Laurie, snuggled hotly into her shoulder, whimpered in his sleep, and Jessie imagined the small creature growing within her, the baby who would be her own and perfect in every way, and she was smiling as she walked to meet her husband across the street of Knight's Ferry, California.

17

They spent their first night in the town, all but Clara Ridback remaining in their wagons rather than pay out any of their precious dollars for accommodations at the hotel. The women spent the evening walking through the streets, admiring the houses and the vegetation—the palm trees excited a great deal of admiration—and talking among themselves and with the friendly women who came out to greet them.

The men, all of them, spent the evening drinking and absorbing information at a saloon.

Because of their sleeping infants, Jessie and Ginny returned earlier than the others to the wagons parked on a grassy verge overlooking the river. They had ventured down to the water to bathe their feet at dusk, and then carried buckets back to their wagons for all-over sponging when it was dark enough to provide the necessary privacy.

Jessie had just finished her ablutions and was feeling quite restored to her own standards of cleanliness when she heard Annie's voice.

"Jessie? You in there?"

"Yes, Annie. Come on up. Or shall I come down?"

"Come outside," Annie requested. "I hope I'm at the end of having to climb in and out of those confounded things; I'm getting too old and too fat for that kind of exercise. Ah." She grinned in the faint illumination from the surrounding shops, all of them still wide open for business though it was nearly nine o'clock. "You've had a bath. I don't suppose you have any water left for an old woman who needs a wash-up in the worst way."

"There's half a bucket," Jessie offered. "It was very cold when we brought it up, but I think it's better now. Joel can go down for another pailful for himself." She glanced toward the saloon, from which issued a burst of male laughter. "If he comes home before dawn, that is."

"It can't be too cold to suit me," Annie said, easing down onto the wagon tongue, the seat to which they'd all become accustomed. "Ah, that little bit of a breeze feels good, don't it?"

"I wonder if it's always this hot in September," Jessie murmured, positioning herself so as to catch all of the breeze there was. "Laurie has heat rash, I guess. I put him to bed in only a diaper. I was afraid to bathe him in that water until it warmed a little." And then, remembering where Annie had been, "Did you get the baby born?"

"That I did, after the husband threw that old witch out of the place. She couldn't stand up, she was so drunk, and too stupid to see the baby was turned wrong, poor tyke. I delivered one before that was turned that way, worked like the very devil himself to get it turned right. I couldn't turn this one, but we finally got it butt first. Mercifully the mother fainted with the pain, and the child looks as if we'd dropped it, it's so bruised. But it cried and before I left it was beginning to suck, so I reckon it'll be all right."

Annie sighed in fatigue and gazed at the traffic that continued to flow onto the street from the ferry landing. "Busy place, ain't it? You know, Jessie, I think maybe I could earn my way here delivering babies and nursing the sick. They got no doctor, for all their fancy wallpaper store and their lawyer. The problem would be to find a place to live that wouldn't cost the earth." Her voice turned rueful. "I don't have much cash money left, and just enough goods to set up housekeeping if I'm careful. This time of year, I can't even plant a garden to keep myself fed through the winter, so I got to bring in something. I don't relish eating nothing but the rest of my beans and mush and rice."

"Annie, I meant what I said, about you coming with us. At least for the winter."

"I know you did, child. And your man probably wouldn't say no to it; he's a good man. But you're hardly wed, and never had a roof over your heads to yourself, and whatever he builds for you to live in is going to start out small, no

143

doubt. He'll want privacy, and it ain't like you'd need me through the winter. That youngun won't be along much before early February, will it?"

They both turned toward the saloon as a series of shots rang out, then relaxed as this was followed by another burst of laughter. Two riders drew up before the building and hurried inside, as if eager to join the fun.

"I hope we're not going to stay in town long," Jessie observed. "I mean, it's been marvelous to see stores again, and other people, but I don't think I could sleep through this racket, if they go on this way all night."

"They say it's not as wild a town as it used to be, when all the mines were going steady. And it's nothing to Sacramento or San Francisco. But there's plenty of people passing through here, besides the eight hundred or so that live here. They got a school, Jessie. It's a town where people plan on raising families. So tomorrow I'll set about trying to find a place to live. A room somewhere, maybe, if anybody's got a spare one."

"How about the hotel?" Jessie glanced in that direction, where it appeared that all the patrons were still wakeful if one could judge by the lights and the activity viewed through an open front door.

Annie grunted. "That old Silas Wofford won't give any discounts to somebody stays there all winter, I'd wager. It's eight dollars a week, room and board. He's interested in making a dollar in everything he does, or he don't do it."

"He gave me an orange," Jessie said. "And he told you about the young woman having the baby. He didn't have any stake in that."

Annie grunted again, shifting her weight on the wagon tongue and swatting at a mosquito. "Wanted free medical advice for himself, on the way over there."

"Oh?" Jessie waited, and then when it was obvious that Annie was not going to divulge what the medical problem was, she asked in amusement, "Did you give it to him? Free?"

"Oh, I gave it to him. Didn't cost me anything, really. And he knows everybody in town. He says there's nobody knows much about broken bones or babies or fevers. But I don't aim to pay regular rates in his hotel, even if I had the money. What's happening with everybody else, Jessie? Are any of the others staying on here?"

"I guess that's what most of them are deciding, over there in the saloon. At least it's the excuse they've given for drinking half the night. Mrs. Groves and Mamie and Alice would like to stay here in town. I don't blame them, women without a man to protect them. But they don't know a blessed thing about earning their own livings. The girls hoped Harry and Collie would propose by now, but so far they haven't."

They sat for another hour, talking in a desultory, contented fashion, before they parted to retire. Jessie was tired, though not especially sleepy. She kept hoping Joel would return and make love to her, but he didn't come. She lay thinking about California, and how different this was from what she'd expected. In the mountains, in those Alpine meadows of crystal streams and gigantic trees, she would have been content to spend the rest of her days. She was more dubious about these rolling dry hills and the smothering blanket of heat that lay over them.

Yet she was happy that they had come to the end of their journey, and that she and Joel were together. Whatever happened, she would never be alone again, please God.

She said her prayers, sleepily now, and drifted into a slumber only occasionally disturbed by raucous laughter or gunshots. It did not appear that the shots were fired in anger, only in high spirits.

When at last the group in the saloon gave up for the night, they poured into the street in a noisy explosion of activity. Jessie roused enough to hear one feminine voice among the masculine ones—Clara Ridback's—and her husband's response to whatever Clara had said; and then the wagon rocked as he climbed the wheel and entered its interior. He barked his shin on a box, swore softly, and stood in the narrow aisle to strip off his clothes. She could smell the whiskey on him even before he crawled into the bed beside her.

"Joel?" she murmured, and he groaned in response.

"Sorry I woke you up, honey," he said, and then he was snoring before she could reply to that.

It was another half hour before the street sounds subsided, and Jessie went back to sleep.

Harry Kelly took a job at the sawmill. He would live in his wagon until he had time to throw up a shack on the edge of town. His decision made it easier for Alice Groves to stand firm on the issue of remaining in Knight's Ferry.

"You and Mamie can go on somewhere else if you like, but I'm going to stay right here," she said in a tone that brooked no argument.

Sarah twisted her hands in an unconscious gesture of un-

145

certainty. "But what will we do here? How will we earn a living?"

"How will we earn a living anywhere? There's no bakery, Mama. There's a flour mill, and everybody for miles around comes here to use the ferry, so there's plenty of traffic. There are more men than women in this country, and men don't cook for themselves much. If we can get a little house with a stove in it, an oven, we can open a bakery. We can bake bread, and maybe pies. There are blackberries growing wild all over those hills behind town. You and Mamie can pick berries, and I'll make the pies."

Mamie, knowing that Collie Aubin would remain in the vicinity where Joel Shand chose to settle, agreed. "There's an empty shop at the far end of town from the ferry. It's filthy, but we could clean it up. All we'd need would be the stove."

"Buying a stove would take practically all the money we have," Sarah said fearfully.

Her daughters stared at her in exasperation. "The money wouldn't any more than get us through the winter, and then what? Then it would be too late to invest in any kind of business. Let's go look at the store building," Alice said. She had never been a particularly assertive girl, but desperation lent her strength.

The shop was small and it was more than dirty. It had stood empty for six months because a fire had damaged it, although the roof was still intact and there was only a small area of the floor that needed replacing. A job, Alice thought, for Harry, in his spare time.

The clincher was that behind the shop itself was a tiny two-room apartment that opened into a hard-packed yard that was, Alice decided, adequate for a garden plot if they hauled water from the river to soften it. They could live there, in the two rooms barely large enough to allow for their beds and the dresser Sarah had managed to salvage of her belongings; as Alice pointed out, they would spend most of their time in the bakery itself.

Oliver Allen found land back toward the mountains, fed by a small stream; his aspirations were modest compared to Joel's, and within a week he was hauling logs down from the forest for a cabin.

"One room for now," Ginny reported cheerfully, "with a loft for sleeping. By spring maybe we'll add a lean-to kitchen. You come and visit us when we get settled, Jessie. I'm going to miss having you for a close neighbor."

The Von Walds said their goodbyes and continued on toward the south. The others scattered too, except for Clara. She alone of the group had plenty of money, and she began at once to spend it on clothes to replace those ruined when Virgil had killed himself. She was ensconced in a two-room suite at the hotel, and immediately had it furnished to her own taste with new rugs and window hangings and furniture sent out from San Francisco. She did not make the mistake of being too forward, too bold, in this town. There were plenty of unattached men, and Clara intended to feather her nest as best she could; she could afford to take her time about doing this, and she intended to be comfortable while she waited for opportunity to present itself.

Joel and Collie rode out to inspect the various possibilities and chose a building site on the south bank of the Stanislaus. A small creek that would furnish water for their household joined the river there, and there was plenty of land suitable for farming.

"Collie doesn't really want to farm, but he's willing to pool our resources to get started. It's wheat land, or grazing land, if I can get together some stock besides what Mrs. Groves sold me. Fellow owns the adjoining land, name of John Curtis, will sell us a few more bred heifers to get started. Beef isn't bringing the price it did during the height of the gold rush, though, so I'm thinking of planting to wheat. There was a family on this spot, all died of smallpox about three months ago; we'll burn down the shack they lived in and put up our own. You'll like it, Jessie. Lots of wide-open space, and nobody pressing in on us. We'll start with a cabin, but it won't be long before we can put up a real house, like the ones here."

"Smallpox? Joel, we have a baby; and we're expecting another one." Disquieted, Jessie voiced her thoughts.

"I told you. We don't touch anything of theirs. We'll burn it, and start fresh."

"Is Collie going to live with us, then?" That was disquieting, too. She had, after all, left Annie in a rented room in town, and she'd much rather have had Annie than Collie living with them, if they had to have anyone at all.

Joel laughed. "Well, maybe part of the time. I think he's going to want to stay in Knight's Ferry mostly, though. The bright lights of the city, even a little one like this. He's young and fancy-free, after all."

And Mamie was in Knight's Ferry. Jessie hoped that was

partly it, but hesitated to mention Mamie, for fear Joel would convey her words to Collie.

It wasn't until they'd been in California for two weeks that Joel finally removed his family and wagon to the new homestead. He had brought hardware and tools and other goods to sell, and he'd been able to unload most of them right in Knight's Ferry; with the cash, he had enough to get started on his own place. Jessie wondered if it bothered him that his goods to sell had been provided by the father who had never acknowledged him; she didn't ask, and Joel didn't talk about it. It had been a bribe, really, she thought, a way to get this embarrassing son away from Chicago. How appalled the Aubins must have been when Collie had elected to go with his supposed cousin, so that the heir as well as the illegitimate son was removed from their lives.

Well, Richard Aubin had owed Joel something, and Jessie felt no qualms about the use of the man's money. It made it possible for them to buy lumber at Locke's mill instead of cutting and splitting logs himself, and to put real glass in the windows, right from the start.

Joel was so proud and pleased with his choice that Jessie didn't have the heart to voice her own misgivings. The river was beautiful as it surged around assorted boulders in a miniature rapids below the bluff. But the land itself was barren except for a few scrub oaks along the defile cut by the creek, and the hills stretched endlessly in all directions, devoid of vegetation except for the dry grass.

"We'll put the house over there," Joel said, gesturing. "We'll start small, of course, but by spring we'll try to enlarge it. It'll be more snug during winter if it's small, anyway. And over there"—he gestured again—"we'll put the barn, and a chicken house. A fellow in town has a few hens he's willing to part with, to get us started. I figured over there would be the best place for a garden, come spring. Easiest place to get water to, from the creek. I'll see if I can't set up a waterwheel to lift it, so you won't have to carry it in buckets. And over there . . ."

He went on, explaining what he planned to do, and Jessie's mind slid away from the words. The charred remains of a small house were a poignant reminder that another family had tried to live here, and had instead died.

Her eyes blurred, and for a moment she imagined she could see Beaver Island. There would be towering pine forests—the trees not as big as those they had seen in the Sierra, but fragrant and beautiful nonetheless—and miles of sandy beach, beyond which Lake Michigan would stretch to distant shores, all green-blue and sparkling in the sunshine.

Jessie blinked, and it was all gone. Around her lay barren hills; heat rose shimmering from the hard-packed earth, a heat intense enough to make her queasy with it.

"We'll have it all, Jess," Joel said. "Everything we've ever dreamed of—the big house, and the crops and the fields, and nobody will ever look down on us again."

The ache in her chest and throat grew, suffocating her, and Jessie could not reply.

18

The house was small and compact and sturdy, not of logs like the one Oliver Allen built, but of lumber newly planed and aromatic. Jessie watched it grow, and she tended Laurie and cooked for the men and hauled water from the creek— for Joel had not yet kept his promise about the waterwheel— to do the endless heaps of laundry.

Only on Sundays did she see anyone other than Joel and Collie; then, though he could not be persuaded to ride to Knight's Ferry for church services, Joel would condescend to visit with his neighbors, or invite them to visit at his own homestead. Collie went into town several nights a week, returning only long after Jessie and Joel had fallen asleep. It gave them a few hours to themselves, and it also brought Jessie a feeling of being in touch with the rest of the world when he told her what was happening with other people, even those she didn't know.

Mamie and Alice had their bakery, and their bread and pies found immediate acceptance. Baking was an uncomfortable chore in the heat, but by early October the high temperatures were waning, and the fact that they were ac-

149

tually keeping themselves so relieved and delighted them that the Groves family made little complaint.

Hearing about them was not as satisfying as visiting with the other women, however, and Jessie was adamant about a visit with someone over the Sabbath. Mamie and Alice took the place of the sisters she had lost or left behind, and even Ginny Allen was welcomed with open arms when she and Oliver came by, for all that Joel spoke of them with condescension. Jessie had wandered the surrounding area and sought out the blackberries growing along the creek; she made her own pies, and dried berries for the winter, and offered what hospitality she could to any who passed by.

She had been on the land for over a month before she met their nearest neighbors, John and Eva Curtis. They came to visit, apologizing for having taken so long. Eva had been confined for the birth of their fifth child.

Jessie liked them on sight. John was tall and thin, Eva was short and still rounded from her recent pregnancy. Both were rather homely. After the first few minutes, Jessie never thought of that again, for they were friendly and Eva was talkative and lively, a fountain of information about the country and the people who lived in it.

Over a cup of tea, Jessie marveled that Eva was able to stay so well informed when she was tied down at home with five small children.

Eva laughed. Her hair was mouse-brown and tied in a rather untidy bun, but when she laughed her whole face lit up and Jessie was reminded of the Mormon women who had been so open and so helpful to a newcomer, back home on Beaver.

"Everybody knows our place. They stop, going up river or down, for a cup of tea and a slice of my pie. The price of food is news, and I pass it all along. Can't get a newspaper regular in this place."

"How long have you been here?" Jessie asked, relaxing into a comfortable relationship with this woman who had only minutes ago been a stranger.

"Two and a half years. You're lucky, coming in the fall the way you did, dear. You'll have a chance to get used to the climate gradually, instead of the way we did it. We reached the mountains too late and had to stay at Tahoe over the winter, and then we came over the pass in early spring and were here when summer struck. Lordy, I thought I'd die, that first year! I was carrying Arabella, and I said the reason she came so easy was I was sweating so it just greased her way into the world!"

Jessie moistened her lips uneasily. "It was very hot when we got here, to Knight's Ferry."

"Oh, it'll be a lot hotter than that, in full summer. You learn not to pick up a tin cup that's been out in the sun; my Herman burned himself bad on a cup last summer. And you can't hardly stand to wear enough clothes to be decent. I tell you," and here Eva leaned forward and lowered her voice, though the men were outside and beyond hearing, "there's those that think I don't teach my younguns to be modest, but I let 'em go in the river even if it does plaster the clothes right against 'em like a second skin. Even the girls. Girls get just as hot as boys, don't they? I thank God for that river. I think I'd just purely die if there wasn't someplace I could go to get cooled off once in a while. I make Herman, he's eight, stand on the bluff when I go in the water myself, to be sure nobody comes along and sees me. You might think that's awful, but I told John, if he expects me to live in this god-forsaken place, he better figure I'm going to cool off the best I can."

Jessie had listened with horrified fascination. "It gets even hotter than when we came, then?"

"Oh, Lord, yes! There's a thermometer at the general store in Knight's Ferry, and summer before last it got up to one hundred and twenty degrees one time when I saw it. You don't need a frying pan to cook your eggs; just leave the pan in the sun a few minutes, then crack the eggs in and let it stand a bit. I wanted one of those thermometers myself, but John says it'll just make me more miserable, knowing how many degrees it is."

"Do you ever get used to it?" Jessie asked faintly. "Even a little?"

"A little," Eva conceded. "And it helps if you're not in the family way."

Jessie hesitated, then confided, "Our baby will be born in February. What's it usually like then?"

"Oh, February, that's a marvelous time to have a baby! It's mostly beautiful in February, especially toward the last part of it. I had Arabella in August, and I liked to died the last two months. My feet swelled up so I couldn't get my shoes on—not that a body really wants shoes in that heat, anyway, but so many people stop at our place and it's embarrassing if they catch you barefooted—and my wedding ring nearly cut my finger off, it got so tight. Oh, you're lucky, Jessie—do you mind if I call you Jessie?—to be having your baby before the heat sets in."

After the Curtises had gone, Jessie mulled over Eva's description of living in the great valley in the summer. Would Joel ever agree to leave it, if the heat caused so much discomfort? Right now he thought everything about the place was so wonderful that she couldn't talk to him about any of the disadvantages she saw.

She was heartened, though, by having Eva Curtis as a neighbor. She was only six miles away, and while that was a bit far for frequent visiting back and forth, Joel had assured her that eventually they would have horses and maybe a buggy to get around in. Six miles was nothing with a horse and buggy.

She saw little of Annie, and she missed her. Annie was filling a need in the community of Knight's Ferry and the surrounding area, and every time Collie or Joel returned from town they reported that Annie was tending this one or that, delivering babies, setting broken bones, dispensing her herbal remedies for aches and fevers. Annie had indeed found her niche and would manage nicely on her own.

One person the men seldom mentioned was Clara Ridback. Jessie knew she was still in town, and that she'd purchased a small shop similar to the one in which the Groves family had set up their bakery; it too had living quarters connected with it, and she was transforming that second-floor apartment into a very comfortable place. She had set herself up as a milliner, and sold as well elegant items such as gloves and purses and evening slippers, things the ladies of Knight's Ferry were delighted to find so readily available.

"She comes in about twice a week and buys bread," Mamie reported. "She seems to have plenty of money, and we heard she paid out cash for the shop, and did all the painting and fixing up herself. It's real pretty," she admitted. "Alice and I went in there once, just to see what she had. When we get our stove paid for, maybe we'll each get us a bonnet—she has one there, with green ribbons..."

For the most part Jessie was kept too busy to get really lonely, though she sometimes longed for the female companionship she'd had on the trail as she scrubbed and hung out line after line of diapers. The tasks had been easier with someone to talk to to make the time pass more quickly.

And at night, there was always Joel.

He was exuberant about what he was doing, optimistic about the future, and joyfully loving when he came to bed. That loving colored her entire life, and stilled (at least temporarily) many of her fears.

There was one set of neighbors they did not meet for some time, though they heard about them immediately. Indeed, since the Rancho Sañudo was one of the few remaining Spanish land grants in this part of the valley, and the envy of the smaller ranchers whose property adjoined it, Joel heard about it the first day he was in town.

The Sañudos were a proud Spanish family, and the land had been theirs for over a hundred years. "Twenty-two thousand acres," Joel reported. "God, I'd give my soul for that much land!"

Statements like that tended to make Jessie uneasy; she had learned to pray *God forgive him* when he uttered these blasphemous thoughts, though she seldom voiced her sentiments.

"It's not as big as El Rancho del Rio Estanislaus across the river—that's over thirty-six thousand acres—but it's a fair spread." Already he was absorbing the western phrases, many of them of Spanish derivation, and Jessie consciously tried to make them her own as well. She liked the names, liked the melodious flow of the language. "The Sañudos live off to themselves, don't mingle much with the Americans. They say in town that since the old man died their fortunes are dwindling, but so far they haven't offered to sell off any of their land." Joel licked his lips, almost as if he were tasting the acquisition of some of the Sañudo acres. "If they ever do, I hope to God I can come up with the money to buy some of it. Imagine, Jess, having more than twenty thousand acres!"

"I wonder if they have trees around their house," Jessie said wistfully, though Joel did not notice.

"John Curtis says the house is a damned palace. They have more cattle than they can count. That's what they use it for, grazing. Never have planted an acre of wheat, John says, and that's probably why they aren't as rich as they used to be. The money's in wheat these days, not beef any more."

"Eva never mentioned them. Is there a family left, now that the old man has died?"

"A widow and a son and daughter. John didn't say how old they are, but grown, I think. The Spaniards and Mexicans keep their women to themselves, so probably Eva never met the women, even if they've lived only a dozen miles apart for several years. You want to go into town with me on Saturday night, Jess? We could spend the night with Annie, Collie says. You could even," in a burst of generosity, "go to church services on Sunday morning, with Mamie and Alice, before we start back."

The prospect of an outing absorbed her complete attention, and she gave no further thought to the unknown and unseen neighbors, the Sañudos.

It was a fine Sunday in early December when Jessie remedied that situation, though not at all in the way she could have anticipated. Joel and Collie were both at home, resting after a strenuous week; they wanted neither to visit nor be visited, but to sit in the sun and soak up its warmth.

The climate of California continued to amaze them. There had been not a drop of rain until late October, and when it came it was gentle yet steady, so that the creek and the river rose perceptibly, and the hills began at once to take on a green tint through the dead grasses.

On this particular day, however, the sky was as blue as it had been in September, and as innocent of clouds, and the temperature was such that Jessie longed to be outside; she would need only a light shawl for comfort.

She approached the men dozing in the sunlight outside the front door, rousing Joel with a touch on his shoulder. He opened his eyes, shaded beneath one of the broad-brimmed hats everyone wore here, and smiled at her.

"Hello, teacher. Want a lesson in kissing this afternoon?"

Jessie slapped at him and glanced in embarrassment at Collie, who prudently pretended to be asleep. "No," she said, but allowed herself to be drawn down so that their lips met. She withdrew quickly, however, before his invitation could be extended to something more outrageous. "Joel, Laurie's sleeping. I just put him down. Will you listen for him, so I can take a walk for an hour or so?"

"Long as you don't expect me to feed him," Joel agreed. "Where are you going?"

"Oh, I don't know. Along the river bluff, I guess. I like to watch the water. And then maybe up the arroyo where the creek comes down. I've never been very far in that direction." *Arroyo* was one of the new Spanish words, and it felt good on her tongue.

Collie stirred and opened his eyes. "Maybe you better carry a pistol with you, Jessie, up the arroyo. I saw a rattler sunning

154

himself up there yesterday. Day like this, they come out sometimes even this late in the year."

"Rattlers?" Jessie froze, remembering how Clara Ridback
had reacted to snakebite. "I won't go there, then."

"Honey, they could be anyplace, even along the river where
all the rocks are. Collie's right, maybe you better take the
pistol. Just in case."

"I don't want to take a pistol," Jessie said. Already the
proposed outing was being spoiled, and she hadn't left the
yard.

"You don't have to shoot it, necessarily. But if you have
it, you can if you need to," Joel said gently. He knew her
aversion to firearms stemmed from the last time she'd handled one, when she'd had to kill Cass Merriam. "Shooting a
rattler isn't like shooting a man, honey. Here, I'll get it and
you can tighten up that holster of Collie's to carry it, so it
won't bother you."

She almost wished they hadn't mentioned snakes, because
the first half mile or so she kept watching for one of the nasty
things. She'd never been afraid of ordinary snakes, but rattlers were deadly. Even if they didn't kill you, their venom
was highly poisonous and could make you sicker than a dog.
And she had no idea how being bitten might affect her unborn
child.

She was about seven months along now, and showing quite
plainly. She tried to disguise her condition with loose-fitting
garments and voluminous aprons, though Joel teased that
anyone could see what she'd been up to, as he put it. Why
did men take such delight in making a woman's face turn
red?

There was a rutted road along the edge of the bluff, for
there was enough traffic to beat down the grass and transform
the earth into mud or hard-packed ruts which would cause
an unwary walker to break an ankle. Jessie walked well to
the bluff side of the trail, both to avoid having to watch every
step and to allow herself to see the river.

What was it about water that was so endlessly fascinating?
This was nothing like her beloved Lake Michigan, but it had
a wild beauty of its own as it hurled itself, frothing white
over the green of its depths, around rocks and through narrowed canyons. The water was higher than usual today; she
thought about Silas Wofford's tale of floods in Knight's Ferry
and was glad her own home was well above its reach.

She walked for some time, reveling in the peace and quiet.

She seldom got away from Laurie. Laurie was nine months old now, an engagingly attractive child with dark hair beginning to curl and huge dark eyes like Joel's. His smile was disconcertingly like Suzanne's, and at times Jessie felt a pang of renewed pain that the man she loved had made love to this child's mother, no matter what his rationalizations. Laurie could sit alone, and was getting ready to crawl, yet by the time Jessie's own babe was born, he would still be no more than eleven months old. She scarcely had time to breathe now; what would it be like when she had a new baby in addition to Laurie?

Jessie sighed and paused to look down over the frothing water, lost in her own thoughts until brought back to the present by a sound that was startling in an area where she thought herself alone.

A gunshot, a rifle, Jessie noted. Someone after a rabbit, maybe?

The water's thunder drowned out any accompanying sounds, but the person who fired the shot must be somewhere fairly close by. Jessie began to walk along the bluff again, and approached a place where the ground sloped more gradually down to the river so that it was possible to descend without risking one's neck. A small stand of scrub oak had provided a screen for the figures below her, and for a moment Jessie stared, uncomprehending.

There were four men on the riverbank, none of them paying any attention to the girl watching from above. It was immediately apparent that three of them were aggressors against the fourth, who stood slightly apart from the others in a stance suggesting that the man knew his danger.

A horse nickered, and Jessie's attention was momentarily distracted; yes, there were three horses tied behind the trees. There was no sign of a fourth horse.

Her gaze swung back to the men. The trio with their backs to her wore flannel shirts and jean trousers; all were armed, two with pistols and one with the rifle she had heard fired. Her heartbeats quickened; surely they had not been shooting at the fourth man?

If his position on a rocky outcropping only a yard above the swirling water had not set him apart, his clothing would have. It was hard to judge height, looking down on him this way; the man was slender except for his shoulders, and he wore black broadcloth with a white shirt and a dark cravat, and boots polished so that she could detect the shine from

156

where she stood, the boots of a horseman, with pointed toes that would slide easily into stirrups.

He had worn a hat, too, with some sort of band that glinted with silvery embroidery; it had been knocked off and rolled a few feet away from him.

One of the men said something, gesturing with the rifle; Jessie didn't make out the words, but the intimidation was plain enough. The cornered victim spoke back, apparently calm, yet with force.

Dear God, Jessie thought numbly. What were they trying to do? Force him off the boulder into the river? It was in flood, and the current would throw a man against the rocks with incredible violence; even as she watched, a tree limb ten feet long hurtled past, smashing against granite boulders first on one side, then on the other, and was gone, submerged in the boiling froth.

The three each took a measured step toward the figure poised as if to fight, except that he alone was unarmed. There now remained no more than half a dozen yards between them, and again the bearer of the rifle gestured with it, taunting in words that Jessie could not make out.

The man in black replied this time without words. He spat.

Jessie was scarcely aware that she edged closer to the men, who were completely unaware of her presence. The menace of the trio was unmistakable; she was convinced they meant to kill the other man, perhaps by shooting him if they couldn't force him into the river.

Earth gave way beneath her foot, sending a small trickle of stones down the embankment, but the noise of it was covered by the sounds of the water. Though the man in black faced her and must surely see her, now that she was actually descending the pathway, he gave no sign. His attention remained fixed on his antagonists.

Jessie crept toward them, the pistol ready in her hand. For a moment she was nearly overcome by nausea as memory rose like vomit; Cass Merriam's face as he had aimed his own weapon at her, confident that he could kill her, and then her own finger squeezing the trigger of Ben's pistol, and the expression of surprise that wiped away Merriam's confidence. Wiped out his life.

There had been no doubt that Cass had to be killed. He had beaten his wife so badly that she subsequently died; he intended to kill her would-be rescuers, and only Jessie's instinctive action had kept him from accomplishing just that.

She did not know any of these men, but the intent of the three to murder the one told her enough. She could not allow that to happen.

The nausea passed, and though a tremor ran through her entire body her finger on the trigger was steady enough for her purpose. She had achieved a position directly behind the assailants, close enough so that she could at last make out their words.

"Give up, Sañudo! Take the easy way out, and back off that rock, before we have to shoot you off it!"

Sañudo. The name registered with Jessie, the man who owned the big ranch that Joel so coveted, the neighbor she had not yet met. Her mouth was dry, there was perspiration on her body beneath the gingham dress and the wool shawl, yet she eased closer—though not too close. It would not do to be within their reach when she finally made them turn around.

Perhaps Sañudo took courage from the hope that rescue was at hand; or perhaps, as Jessie later decided, the man would have spoken in the same way in any case, because he was a man of courage.

"Truth will come to light," he said. "Murder cannot be hid long."

It had the suggestion of a quotation, though Jessie did not know its source. The men facing Sañudo took it for bravado.

"It'll be hid, all right. We'll put a bullet right through your heart, and you'll go over into the water. When they find what's left of you, nobody'll ever know you didn't die in the water and rocks, just like your horse."

"It was a good horse," Sañudo replied. "And you will one day pay for his life, señores."

The middle man in the facing trio laughed. "Not likely, señor," he said, giving the form of address a mocking note. "Go on, back off that rock."

Jessie dared wait no longer. They took, in unison, another of the forward steps that brought them closer than ever to their prey. She tried to speak, failed, and forced out the command at last in a voice that carried over the sounds of the river.

"Drop your weapons!"

They had not known there was anyone else within miles of them. They froze, though only for an instant, and then two of them whirled to face her while the rifleman continued to cover Señor Sañudo.

"Why, it's a little lady, and in no shape to be running around by the river," one of them said.

Jessie almost took a step backward, as three pairs of eyes looked her over. Two of the men smiled; the third laughed aloud at this girl with her wavering weapon.

"Drop your guns," Jessie ordered. Her heart was beating so loudly that it almost drowned out the river in her hearing.

She saw the speaker's nearly imperceptible movement, and she steadied the pistol in both hands and fired.

19

She could not, at the last moment, bring herself to kill him outright. Not that she was certain she could have put the bullet where she wanted it, anyway. But instead of aiming for his midsection, Jessie lowered the pistol enough to strike something less vital but no less painful.

The man howled in agonized surprise, and the pistol he'd been holding slid across the rocky surface at his feet. His companion made a move to swing his own weapon in her direction, and Jessie squeezed the trigger again.

The men stared at her, one holding a hand that dripped blood over his dropped pistol, the second doubled over a shattered thigh, and the rifleman stood trying to watch both Sañudo and this lady in an advanced stage of pregnancy.

That the lady was prepared to kill someone if necessary was plain to all of them, in spite of her youth and pallor. The wind whipped wisps of fair hair about her face; she would have liked brushing them aside but feared that if she didn't use both hands on the pistol she would drop it, and the crisis was by no means over.

Up to now she had acted instinctively, as she had done to attempt to protect the life of Suzanne Merriam. She did not know why the three men wanted to kill the fourth man, only that she could not allow a presumably innocent human being to be murdered.

Now, facing those unreadable eyes, Jessie was suddenly overcome with the fear engendered by the reality. True, she had a pistol trained on them; one of the men was no longer armed, and a second, though his weapon was still at hand, was engrossed in the injury where Jessie's shot had torn through his thigh.

The third still held the rifle, aimed, at the moment, halfway between Jessie and Señor Sañudo. And all three were still deadly, dangerously so. They had intended to kill Sañudo; they were unlikely to be squeamish about eliminating, as well, an unknown female.

For a moment her eyes blurred and the pistol wobbled, but before the rifleman could take advantage of that, Jessie had recovered. Within her the child kicked.

Her child. Joel's child. A child whose life depended upon what she did now.

She steadied the weapon in both hands, breathed a silent *Please, God,* and fired again.

Joel, who had taught her to shoot, would have been proud of her. She hit the rifle barrel and tore the gun away, sending it skidding into the river.

Señor Sañudo sprang forward before the rifleman could regain his balance, snatching up the dropped pistol, and the crisis was over.

Vaguely Jessie was aware of the strength and the grace of Sañudo, who was, she now saw, the smallest of the four men, though there was nothing small about his presence of mind.

Now in control, Sañudo flashed her a tight-lipped smile as he stepped back to a safe distance from his enemies.

"Very good shooting, señora," he congratulated her. The smile disappeared. "Now I think, señores, you will march back up the hill and we will seek the law in Knight's Ferry. Perhaps the señora would be good enough to follow with the horses."

"The hell we'll march anyplace with you, you damned Mexican," the rifleman said, and went for the sidearm Jessie had not noticed that he wore.

Sañudo's confiscated weapon exploded in deafening sound, and the rifleman reeled back, having taken the shot full in the chest. Jessie forgot to breathe as he staggered, slid, and went over the edge of the rock into the turbulent water.

Within seconds, he was gone, swept downstream by the relentless current. Jessie did not even see his head resurface.

The man with the bloody hand released a stream of vituperation that ceased only when Sañudo swung the pistol in his direction.

"One does not speak in this fashion before a lady, señor," Sañudo informed him, and the man fell silent, nursing his hand. His remaining partner looked up with a face beaded with moisture, twisted in agony.

"You can see I ain't walking noplace," he said in a voice made ragged by pain. "The bitch ruined my leg."

This time Sañudo did not resort to shooting. He walked to the fallen man and slapped him, hard, across the face with his free hand.

"I told you, señor, one does not use such words before a lady. Señora," he said over his shoulder without turning, "would you be good enough to bring a horse, so that his friend can lift this man onto it. They killed my mount, and we are still short a mount, but we must convey our prisoners to the authorities, so that they can be hanged."

Jessie was shaking so that she was not certain that she could comply, but she gasped out a few words, and moved toward the horses. One of them reared at her approach, until she stepped to one side and spoke quietly to calm the animals enough to allow her to untie one of them.

Sañudo gave orders as if he were used to it. He had a melodious voice, yet with a crisp edge now. "Get your friend up there, and mount behind him. And do not do anything else that is foolish, señor, or you will not live long enough to greet the hangman."

Jessie heard her own voice, a stranger's voice. "I don't need a horse, sir. I can walk home; it isn't far."

"I wouldn't dream of allowing a lady who has just saved my life to put her own at further risk," Sañudo told her, the smile touching his lips. He was, Jessie realized, a very handsome man. Dark hair and eyes, with a thin line of mustache across a finely modeled upper lip, he was as different from his attackers as he could possibly have been.

Now that she was close to him, Jessie saw that there were red flecks on his white shirtfront, and she cried out softly. "You are injured, too, sir!"

He lifted a hand and she realized that it was bloody, but his smile widened slightly. "Only a trifling thing, señora. They chose to shoot the pistol out of my hand when I came upon them running off my cattle. Cattle rustling is not tolerated in this part of the country, by your countrymen any more than by mine. I must thank you, señora, for your courage in coming to my aid. And"—the smile broke into a full laugh—"I commend you as well for your shooting ability. In any future battles, I would be most grateful to have you on my side."

The unborn baby kicked again, and without thinking she put a hand on her belly over the spot. "I couldn't stand by and let the three of them kill you."

"The odds were not in my favor," Sañudo conceded. "Ah, do we have more company?"

The pistol, in a steady if bloody hand, swung toward the bluff, and Jessie cried out in relief. "Joel! Joel, I'm all right!"

The tension went out of the hand holding the weapon. "Your husband, señora? Very good, then I need not worry about your safety."

Joel and Collie came down the bluff at breakneck speed, reining in amidst a trickle of rock and earth that followed them down. "Jessie, what the hell's going on? We heard shooting and we thought—" Joel was off the horse, gathering her into his arms in a hard embrace before he turned toward the elegantly garbed Spaniard.

"You'd be Sañudo?" he hazarded a guess.

"That is correct, señor. Luis Sañudo. And you are my new neighbor to the west?"

"Joel Shand. This is my—cousin, Collie Aubin. What the hell happened here?"

"Your lovely señora saved my life from those who would have taken it. I came upon them rustling my cattle, and attempted to protect my own property. Unfortunately, I was outnumbered and outshot, and they killed my horse beneath me and sent it over the bluff into the river. They did not quite manage to send me over with it, but were about to remedy that oversight when your *esposa* came along. She has my eternal gratitude, and that of the family who depend on me."

Jessie, still within the circle of Joel's arms, felt the pounding of his heart, or was it the pounding of her own? How welcome his arms were, the warm strong arms she had come to depend on, the man she loved. Now that he was here, she could afford to shake all she liked. Joel took the pistol out of her limp hand, and had he not been holding her upright, she thought she might have sunk to her knees.

"You need any help getting the two of them to town?" Joel

asked. His gaze swept over the horses. "Three horses? Was there another man?"

"I had to shoot him," Sañudo said calmly. "One less fee for the hangman, but then he has work aplenty anyway, does he not?" He swung himself into the saddle of the unfamiliar animal, which reared, then steadied under his expert hand. "Thank you, Señor Shand, but the odds are distinctly better now than they were a few minutes ago. I do not believe I will have any difficulty in delivering my prisoners to the proper authorities. *Adiós! Adiós, señora!*"

A few minutes, Jessie thought. Was that all it had been since the men had killed his horse and tried to force Señor Sañudo into the river after it? It felt like a lifetime.

"I think I'll tag along with Sañudo, just to make sure," Collie said, and wheeled his mount to follow the trio climbing the embankment. "Don't wait supper for me, Jessie! I may stay in town tonight!"

Joel didn't look after the departing figures. His attention turned to his wife.

"My God, honey, how did you get mixed up in it?"

She told him as they rode home, she encircled by his protecting arms. And later, when they lay naked upon their bed in the aftermath of lovemaking, Joel rested his hand upon her swollen belly to feel the baby kick, and told her tenderly, "You're the most beautiful, bravest woman in the world, Jess."

Jessie laughed, looking down at the protruding mound that sheltered the coming child. "Beautiful? When I look as if I've swallowed a seed of the world's largest pumpkin?"

"You get more beautiful to me every day," Joel said. And she smiled, knowing that he meant it.

Jessie went into labor on the 14th of February.

She woke with a backache, which was not particularly unusual, and went about her customary chores—setting the bread to rise, dressing and feeding a demanding Laurie, tidying the house before the men came in to breakfast. She had served them and decided that she felt a bit odd, not at all hungry, and was halfway between table and front door to fetch another bucket of water when she realized that her abdomen was distended and hard, almost in a cramp.

Jessie stopped, awareness sweeping over her. To make sure, she stood until the cramp had receded, then came again, before she was certain.

"Jess?" Joel saw the expression on her face and stood up, overturning his chair in his haste. "Jessie? Is it starting?"

She laughed, uncertain. "I think so, maybe. There, it's coming again." She reached for the back of a chair and clung to it, gasping, while Joel covered one of her hands with his.

"Collie," Joel said without looking at the younger man, "you better ride in and bring Annie back. We've got time to get her, haven't we, honey?"

"I understand it often takes a good many hours," Jessie said. "Maybe even days."

"Did it just start?"

"Well, I just noticed it. But I guess I was having twinges last night. I kept waking up because my back hurt. Yes, Collie, please. Fetch Annie."

Only upon her assurance that there would surely not be anything important happening for a long time did Jessie persuade Joel to go on about his chores after Collie had saddled up and ridden off to town. Even then, he stayed fairly close to the house, coming in periodically to make sure she was all right.

Laurie seemed to sense that something was amiss, for he was into everything. He had been walking for several weeks, an accomplishment that delighted his father, while dismaying Jessie. Nothing was safe from Laurie's attention, including the open fire on the hearth, and several times Jessie had rescued him within seconds of overturning a kettle of boiling liquids upon himself.

Today the little boy outdid himself. He made a puddle on one of the hooked rugs placed to remove the mud from the feet of those entering the house, and then, when Jessie took it outside to dry, Laurie got into the bread she had rising on the table and emptied a pan of it onto the floor. He was happily squeezing it between tiny fingers when she returned.

"Laurie! You naughty boy!" Jessie said, and snatched the dough away from him only to survey it in resignation; it was too dirty to eat now, and she pitched it out the door for the benefit of whatever wild creature might take a liking to it. She was cleaning off the child's hands and face when a sharper pain struck her, so that she gasped and eased Laurie to the floor before she dropped him.

He stared at her with a cherubic smile, the dark curls and the greenish-gray eyes so much like Joel's that she felt a stab, as well, of the lingering pain that he was not her own.

"Here," she said, when the contraction had subsided a moment later, "let Aunt Jessie wash your hands."

Joel had been disturbed at first at her reluctance, verging on downright refusal, to teach the little boy to call her mama.

"You're going to be his mother, so why not?" he'd asked, exasperated, when Jessie referred to herself as Aunt Jessie.

"Because he was born before we were married," Jessie said evenly, though knowing full well that wasn't the only, or even primary, reason. "And eventually he's going to hear us mention how long we've been married, and figure out something worse than the truth. He shouldn't even know he's your son, Joel. It will make him feel the way you did, to know you were illegitimate."

"No it won't," Joel refuted her logic with his own. "My father denied me in every way. I'm acknowledging Laurie. I'm going to raise him, the way I wish I'd been raised."

"Joel, think about it. If we say that we simply took him in, adopted him as our own, it won't matter when he was born, or when we were married. If we say he's our own, they'll think *I* gave birth to him before we were married." Her face grew warm at the thought.

"Why should they? You can admit he's my son, without saying he's yours."

"How do I do that? Make an announcement to everyone we meet? Besides, I couldn't have given birth to him when my own child died only a few months before he was born. Do I announce who his mother was, or what? It's all so confusing! It will be so much simpler to tell the truth: that he was born to Suzanne and Cass Merriam, and that there was no one to take him, so we did."

"He's going to look just like me." Joel stated the obvious. "The same as I looked like my father."

"Then we'll say his mother was your cousin, or something," Jessie insisted stubbornly. "That would make us aunt and uncle, and that would be better for all concerned, including Laurie. It will raise fewer questions all around."

She didn't say to him that she could not, physically could not, refer to herself, with the child, as Mama. She was not Laurie's mother, and though she cared for him, rocked him when he was sleepy or cutting teeth, and stitched endless small garments for him, she could not give Joel this thing he asked for. She could not pretend to be Laurie's mother.

It didn't make any difference to Laurie, she thought. He was cared for and treated with affection, and in every way behaved as if the entire household revolved around him and surrounded him with love. She *did* love him, she told herself, as she would love any child, but that was not the same as what she would feel for her own blood children.

Today it was hard to remember that she was Laurie's beloved Aunt Jessie. He went from one thing to another, touching, spilling, breaking, eating inappropriate materials, and all the while her contractions grew harder and closer together.

She paused during one calm moment to say a prayer for the child she would soon deliver. A son, a healthy son, she begged. For herself it wouldn't matter if the baby was a daughter, but men wanted sons of their own. This child must be the equal of Laurie in Joel's eyes, and therefore had to be a son.

She had punched down the bread and allowed it to rise for the final time when Joel returned to the house for lunch. He lifted Laurie to his shoulder and carried the little boy around the room that served as both kitchen and bedroom, unaware that he left a trail of mud from his boots as he walked.

"I wish you could go out to the top of the hill and see it, Jessie. Green, acres of it, the wheat coming up. If we'd had time to work up more land, or could afford to hire help, we'd have the entire place producing this spring. Next year it'll be better; we'll have it all under the plow."

Jessie scarcely heard him. If Joel wanted acres and acres of wheat turning green, she was happy for him, but at the moment her attention was fixed on something far more important. She glanced at the clock Joel had bought her in Knight's Ferry and saw its hand standing at nearly noon.

"Shouldn't Collie be back soon? With Annie?"

"The pains getting hard?" Joel asked, swinging Laurie back to the floor and reaching for her. "You want to lie down, honey?"

"No, what good would that do? I feel as if I need to double over forward, when they come. And the bread is nearly ready to bake—if I can't do it, Joel, don't forget to bake the bread."

He drew her into his arms and kissed her. "Don't worry about anything, Jess. Just have this baby safely, and keep on being my wife."

She was calm enough on the surface. She set water to boil, so that Annie could wash her hands and have warm water to bathe the baby. She laid out fresh linens for the bed, and one nightgown for now and another to change into after the baby had been delivered. She drew up the cradle Joel had made during the winter near the bed in the corner of the room. In it she put the garments in which the new baby would be dressed.

Though there was a box of tiny shirts and bands and gowns that had been Laurie's, Jessie had made everything new for this baby. Maybe eventually he would wear his half brother's hand-me-downs, but not to begin with. This baby would have his own things, as he deserved.

"They're here!" Joel said suddenly, and walked to the front door to throw it open. "Annie, and Mamie's with her, too!"

"Mamie! I haven't seen her in months! Oh, come in, come in!" Jessie cried, hugging both women in her joy and relief that they had arrived. Joel was very good at a great many things, but he'd never delivered a baby, and now he wouldn't have to learn.

"I thought I'd come, too, and stay for a while to help you after the baby comes," Mamie said, peeling off her shawl, which gave out an odor of damp wool. "Mama and Alice can manage for a week or two without me."

"Oh, I'm so glad you came!" Jessie exclaimed, and then drew in a sharp breath as the next contraction began. It was the strongest one yet, and by the time it was over Annie was easing her toward the bed. Mamie had taken over young Laurie, and the men were shooed outside for the duration of the birthing process.

The baby was born in late afternoon, a lusty, squalling little boy. Exhausted and smiling, Jessie examined him to ascertain that he had all the necessary parts, then surrendered him to Mamie to be cleaned and wrapped in soft flannel blankets and laid in the crib. By the time Joel reentered the house, Annie had combed Jessie's hair and gotten her into the fresh nightgown; he sank to the bed beside her and bent to place a kiss on her lips before he looked into the cradle.

"A boy," Jessie told him. "I knew it would be a boy."

Joel covered her hand with his while peering at his new offspring. "Where's his hair? He hasn't got any hair."

"He does, but it's too fair to show up much. I'm afraid he's going to have my coloring, rather than yours."

"What difference does it make? We'll have one dark and one light, just like ourselves." He brought his attention back to her. "Well done, Jessie. Are you all right, too? Not...torn, or anything?"

"Annie says I'm fine," Jessie told him. "Only I'm terribly tired. I think I could sleep for days."

Joel kissed her again, and sat beside her, holding her hand, until she fell asleep.

Annie stayed for three days, just to make certain everything was all right. The household revolved around the needs of a new baby, but Tristan Joel, as they named him, was an extremely good infant. He sucked enthusiastically, and slept the rest of the time, even when he was wet. Laurie was fascinated by the newcomer and had to be restrained from poking the baby's eyes and mouth, but there was at first no jealousy because there were plenty of people around to cater to him as well as the infant.

Becoming a father again—and this time he had anticipated the birth and not been unprepared for fatherhood—made Joel exuberant with both his sons. Since the weather had turned fair, he carried Laurie with him to do his outside chores, and that in turn made it easier on the women in the house, though Jessie felt moments of panic at the thought of eventually being left with both children to see to by herself.

Mostly, however, she rested from her ordeal, and visited endlessly with her old friends. Mamie, though genuinely concerned and certainly a great help in the household, had come primarily to be closer to Collie, Jessie thought. Collie and Joel had moved into the barn for the time being, while Annie and Mamie made up pallets on the floor, a minor inconvenience for all concerned.

Jessie, propped in bed to nurse Tristan, felt as if her heart was swollen to bursting with happiness. She teased gently. "Is Collie any nearer to proposing, Mamie? He's nineteen now. That's old enough to take a wife. And he could build a house on this land, so we'd be close neighbors."

Mamie's face was prettily flushed from the fire. "I think he's closer, Jessie. But he needs to feel he has some means; he's spent most of what his father gave him before he left Chicago. When the wheat is harvested and he has his share of that, I think he may be braver about setting up his own household." She grinned, revealing dimples. "I think he's had such a good example, watching you and Joel, that the idea appeals to him."

"I hope so. Tell me, what's happening in Knight's Ferry? Do you see anyone I know?"

"I see Virginia Allen once a month or so. She's expecting

again, you know. I think she's due in early September. I don't envy her, going through the summer in the family way, from what people say about the heat in this country. Though I don't know if it will bother us as much as most; we've gotten used to baking all day, so the shop is usually very hot."

"Silas Wofford sent along some grape jam, as a gift for the new baby," Annie stated unexpectedly. "With his best wishes, of course."

"Really? How thoughtful of him. Did he make the jam himself?"

"No, no, *I* made the jam," Annie admitted. "But they were his grapes. He said if I'd put up the jam, we'd share it."

Was there something in Annie's tone? Jessie glanced at her old friend speculatively. "Are you seeing quite a bit of Mr. Wofford, then?"

"In a town the size of Knight's Ferry, how can I not?" Annie asked, not really answering the question. "He's a wily old man, generous one minute, pinching for pennies the next. We have something in common, so we visit from time to time. On the street," she amended, so that Jessie wouldn't misinterpret the statement.

"Oh? What do you have in common?"

"Age," Annie said drily.

Jessie laughed. "He must be twenty years older than you are!"

"Fifteen, closer to it." Annie corrected. "But that's older than most of the rest of the inhabitants. There's mostly young folks, come out here to make their fortunes. Most of 'em ain't made it, at least not with gold, but the farmers are fortunate enough to be able to afford all kinds of things, so the shops stay in business. Speaking of shops, another of your old acquaintances just added another shop to her millinery business."

Jessie's mouth quirked wryly. "You're speaking of Clara Ridback, I assume."

"The same. I have to say this for her, Jessie. She knows how to invest her money so it produces more. She has a dress shop now. Hires two women to sew, besides selling things already made up, in San Francisco. And ladies' shoes. You want a pair of fancy slippers, Clara's the one to sell them to you."

"I doubt if I'll be dancing for a while. Or going to entertainments. My entertainment will all be right here at home," Jessie said, in a tone leaving the impression that nothing could be more entertaining than caring for a husband, two babies, and a cousin.

"I'm surprised Clara hasn't found another man," Mamie commented. "No, no, Laurie, don't touch the mending basket! The way she was always flirting with some man while we were on the trail, I thought the first thing she'd do when we reached civilization and she could replace her pretty dresses would be to find another man. A rich one," she amended unnecessarily.

"Oh, she has her male friends," Annie contributed.

"Oh? Who?" Mamie demanded.

"Any number of them, from what I hear. Nothing indiscreet—she has a maid, now, lives in with her, to chaperon. The girl swears nothing takes place that shouldn't—the gentlemen come and visit and she serves them brandy, and drinks tea, herself. No doubt when one comes along that's rich enough, she'll latch on to him."

"I thought Silas Wofford might let his eye rove in that direction." The baby had finished nursing, and Jessie raised him to her shoulder and patted gently. "He said he was lonesome, looking for another wife."

Annie laughed. "Silas is too smart to fall for the likes of Clara Ridback. He might take a woman like her into his bed, but he wouldn't marry her. Silas has a sharpness about business matters, and he won't chance any of his money falling into the hands of someone like her. Is that the men riding off somewhere, just when it's almost time to put supper on?"

It was not riders leaving, however, but a single rider coming in. Mamie went to the door when Joel called out a greeting, and Jessie turned to face the visitor who entered a moment later, glad she was in her best nightgown for all that she covered it with the quilt.

She had not seen him in nearly three months, but she had thought about him many times. Señor Luis Sañudo, whose life she had saved, stood in her doorway with his hat in his hands, and Jessie was very pleased to see him.

20

"Señora Shand," he said, moving forward, smiling. "Forgive me for disturbing your rest; your husband tells me you are only recently delivered of a son."

"Yes. We've named him Tristan. Come and see," she invited, rocking the cradle to one side so that her sleeping child was displayed.

Sañudo looked into the cradle with apparently genuine interest. "A very handsome child. Yet how could he not be, with so lovely a mother? And he will have his mother's coloring, the blond hair that has no gold in it, but is the palest of pale browns, no? And eyes like his mama's, too?"

"It's too early to tell. Right now they are very dark blue, but I hope they'll be like Joel's." Jessie beamed.

She had thought she remembered him quite vividly, but his attractive dark looks struck her anew. This time, of course, he had not just been through a physical assault and an intimidation by three armed men, and his dress was immaculate and elegant. He was, Jessie realized, older than she had first thought—thirty, or thirty-five. Except for Joel, he was quite the most handsome man she'd ever met.

"My congratulations, señora. And again, my apologies for disturbing you. But I see you have two ladies here to assist you, and I hope that will make it possible for you to grant my request."

He wasn't smiling now, and Jessie looked up at him, puzzled. "Yes, sir?"

"I was told in town that the medicine lady was here, at your house. I have need of her services. My mother is very ill, and my sister, Bonifasia, has no skills as a nurse. If the Señora Ryan is not urgently needed here, I would be most grateful if she would accompany me to examine my mother."

Jessie turned to Annie. "Yes, of course, you'll go, won't you, Annie? This is Señor Sañudo, our neighbor to the east."

The expressions on both women's faces revealed their recognition of Luis Sañudo's name. He had dispatched one rustler by shooting him and delivered two more to town, where they were brought to a brief and perfunctory trial. It had not been necessary to take a corroborating statement directly from Jessie, the magistrate ruled; hearsay on her testimony, relayed by Collie Aubin, was sufficient. The rustlers had been summarily hanged for their offenses.

"Give me a few minutes to put my belongings together," Annie said at once. "Then I'll be glad to do what I can, if your mother's illness is one I can deal with."

"She is an old woman, but one does not allow one's mother to die any earlier than must be. She has much pain, and has taken to her bed. Should it be that all you can do is make her suffering less in the time left to her, we will be grateful for that, señora."

Annie stood for a moment at Jessie's bedside, looking down at the sleeping baby. "Well, you won't be needing me here any more, anyway, with Mamie to help. The babe is as beautiful as any I've ever seen. All you need, Jessie, is a few weeks of rest before you take on all your chores again. So I won't come back here, after I've seen to Mr. Sañudo's mother."

Jessie reached for the older woman's hand. "Thank you, Annie. For everything."

Joel carried Laurie into the yard to watch the departure. Mamie stood for a moment in the doorway, then came back to the rocker beside Jessie's bed, sinking down with a sigh.

"My, that one's a handful, isn't he? Jessie, why didn't you tell me about this Luis Sañudo? He's the most beautiful man I've ever laid eyes on! And he's rich, too! It's a wonder Clara Ridback hasn't sought him out!"

"I should think he could do much better than Clara," Jessie said at once, then wondered why she should be so vehement about it. As long as Clara stayed away from Joel, who cared who she took up with?

"Of course, Collie's very handsome, too," Mamie mused. "And my chances are probably better with him, wouldn't you say?" Again she showed her dimples, and they laughed together, planning Mamie's strategy in leading Collie to the altar. He was, Jessie agreed, weakening fast. They might even plan for an early-summer wedding.

* * *

Spring came in late February. The valley was transformed into a place of beauty by the greening hills and fields, blossoms appeared overnight, wildflowers grew in profusion, and the Stanislaus ran cold and fast within its banks.

Joel and Collie had worked themselves half to death, planting wheat through the winter and until the end of March; but if Jessie had expected that when that planting was done they would rest for a time, she was disappointed. Land must continue to be worked, a laborious process with their horse-drawn plows, the unturned sod resistant to the steel blades, for the planting of corn and other crops that would feed them the following year.

Jessie's garden plot was worked up so that she could plant it by mid-March, and hoeing and watering were added to her daily chores. She didn't particularly mind; she quickly recovered her strength after Tristan's birth, and she took such joy in her son that she sang as she worked, whether indoors or out. The baby was fat and contented, gazing up at her with eyes that gradually became brown like her own; he smiled readily, especially when Laurie hung over the edge of the cradle.

By mid-May, she became aware of the threat of full summer.

Temperatures climbed. She had no thermometer, but Collie would report, on his return from town, that the instrument outside the general store had stood at ninety-five or a hundred degrees. Jessie swallowed her dismay, and tried not to think what it would be like during July and August.

The increasing heat did not seem to bother Joel. He drank vast quantities of water, carried to the edge of each field in a bucket where within half an hour it would be a comfortable temperature for bathing, and within an hour would, he declared, boil an egg. His clothes would darken with sweat, which in turn evaporated, providing a sort of cooling system.

Jessie did not perspire in the same way, and Annie told her that was why the heat bothered her so much more. It turned the poisons inward, often making her feel sick. Indeed, she went through a period of several weeks when she thought she might be pregnant again, for she was queasy and light-headed when she went out to work in the garden after breakfast; when her monthly show proved that theory wrong, she decided it was simply the heat. If she could stay cooler, she did not feel sick at all.

The little house was like an oven, and there was no shade

except for the scrub oaks along the creek. Jessie would take a blanket to spread on the creek bank in that meager shade, and leave the baby lying there naked except for a diaper, while she and Laurie sat in the creek itself. It was undignified, it was scarcely proper, yet it was the only way to survive. She was glad Eva Curtis had admitted to her own dunkings in the river, so that it did not seem quite so outrageous.

Jessie would gladly have gone to the river, for it was wider, deeper, and colder. Yet she did not feel up to managing an infant and a small boy to go that far, or to keep watch over both of them while she cooled herself in the waters that were so much more dangerous. The creek was shallow enough so that Laurie would have had to lie face down in it to do himself any damage.

Jessie learned to be cautious about touching anything that had sat in the sun. Not only tin cups and pails, but nails or rakes or a chunk of firewood with pitch oozing from it, pitch that would be hot enough to hurt when it stuck to one's flesh. She could not bear to wear shoes, yet the wooden floor in the house and the hard-packed earth between her rows of beans and cabbages were uncomfortable to the soles of her bare feet. Shifts and stays went the way of shoes: she wore a loose dress with a single petticoat beneath it, sometimes sitting down in the creek to soak all the garments and wearing them that way for the brief period it took for them to dry on her, cooling as they did.

With two children in diapers, she washed every day. Joel had put up a long clothesline to hang the diapers out, and by the time she got to the end of the line she could go back to the beginning and take down dry diapers, except for a tiny patch under the corners where the clothespins had been, a patch that dried before she'd carried the clothes to the house.

There was no dew on the grass, and even at night the earth did not entirely lose its warmth to the touch. Some nights they carried their ticks out under the stars to catch the faintest breath of moving air, because the house was too stifling even for Joel to sleep. On those nights Jessie lay beside him, praying for the coolness of dawn, and tears leaked onto her cheeks as she remembered the home she had left behind for this place. Up there, to the east, the Sierra Nevada promised cold streams and cool meadows and tall trees. But Joel did not go up into the Sierra.

"You can practically stand here and watch things grow,"

Joel enthused. "I swear, Jessie, the corn's up an inch from yesterday! My God, what we could do in this country if we could get water all over it during the summer!"

Jessie had not credited the statement that it did not rain during the summer here; now she found it was the literal truth. The last rainfall soaked the earth in mid-May. It did not rain again, not so much as a drop, until October.

The sky was hot and blue and cloudless. Water became a precious commodity, for all that the river ran below their house; it was a long way to haul water, and the men were busy with other things. Crops were to be planted, and then to be harvested. Hauling water was women's work, and Jessie had to be contented with what she could lift with the water-wheel from the creek until, in August, that small stream dried up completely. Then the men had to help her, hauling water casks from the river in the wagon.

There were insects that thrived in the heat.

One night Jessie, who slept restlessly without a covering sheet and wished she dared remove her nightgown as well, woke to Tristan's fretful crying. She reached out a hand to rock the cradle, thinking that her son, too, was uncomfortable because of the heat.

The crying turned to piercing screams, and Jessie sat up, groggy, tired, confused. He had given up night feeding some time ago; what was the matter with him now?

It was not until she had lighted a candle that she perceived the problem. She choked on a cry, reaching for the child in horror. For the tiny body was covered with an army of ants, the red marks of their bites visible even in the diluted light.

"Joel! Joel, wake up! Tristan's covered with ants, they're eating him alive!"

Joel came awake, bounding out of bed and running for the water bucket beside the door. "Here, hold him out, I'll wash them off with this! God almighty, there must be a thousand of them!"

It took them half an hour to rid the baby of the ants and calm him. She knew nothing to do for the bites except to put soda and water on them, and in the end Tristan fell asleep more from exhaustion than because he was no longer in distress.

Jessie was so angry and upset that she was incoherent. Joel tried to soothe her by pointing out that the ants had apparently been searching for water, and they had been drawn to a wet washcloth she'd laid over the edge of the

175

cradle after wiping Tristan down with it to cool him before he went to sleep.

"We just won't have anything with water near him again. I'll put coal oil into something and set the ends of the cradle in it so they won't pass it. It won't happen again, honey."

Jessie stared at him in unabated fury. "It happened this time, didn't it? I've never seen such ants in my life! Look at him, he's a solid mass of bites! I hate this country! I wish I'd never come here! I hate the heat and the dust and the insects and the snakes! I hate you for bringing me to this godforsaken place!"

She heard her own words, saw something change in Joel's face, and would have bitten off her own tongue to have unsaid the words.

Yet they had been said; they hung in an ugly cloud between them.

Joel drew a long, painful breath. "I'm sorry, Jessie. I didn't know you hated...everything...so much."

It had always been Joel who came to her, before, when there was any disagreement or misunderstanding, when she was in need of comforting. This time he simply stood there, arms at his sides, unable to hide his own hurt, let alone do anything about hers.

For long moments they faced each other in the candlelight. A terrible ache rose in Jessie's chest and throat, and her vision blurred. And then she moved, reaching out to him, hugging him convulsively, burying her face against his bare chest.

"I didn't mean it, Joel! Not about you! I could never hate you, I love you too much! But I hate this *place,* the heat and the ants..."

She dissolved in tears, and Joel's arms came around her in the familiar embrace. "I know it isn't much yet, Jess, but we won't be in this little shack forever. When the wheat is harvested there should be some money, and we'll build on. It shouldn't be more than a few years before we can build the big house we want...."

It wasn't the house, Jessie thought, wondering how on God's earth to get through to him. She didn't care if she lived in a small house with few luxuries. A big fancy house would still be in this merciless heat, away from the woods and the water she so loved.

She didn't try to explain it further. She allowed her tears to be wiped away, and she went back to bed, though for a time she could not sleep; she imagined ants crawling over her, and every time the baby made the smallest sound she reached out to touch him, to make certain there were no more ants in the cradle.

21

Collie brought her willow twigs to be planted along the bank of the creek, so that eventually they would provide some shade for the house during the worst of the afternoon heat.

"They grow faster than just about anything else," he told her. "And I got you a little orange tree, too. It won't grow so fast, but someday you'll have your own oranges, right in the front yard."

Jessie planted the twigs and rejoiced when they put forth roots and tiny slender leaves. Unlike the dark scrub oaks, they were a tender green in a world of sunbaked brown. Her garden flourished, producing incredible quantities of peas and beans and potatoes and cabbages. She liked working in the garden, though it was hard and must be tended in the cool of morning or evening; she dared not take the babies outside in the middle of the day, except to the shaded area of the creek where they all soaked themselves as long as there was any water left to do it.

Collie spent less and less time with Joel, and more and more in town. Jessie was all in favor of his courtship of Mamie, especially now that Harry Kelly had finally proposed to her sister Alice. On the assumption that Sarah Groves would continue, with Mamie, to operate the bakery, he felt safe in taking Alice into the cabin that could not possibly have provided living space for his mother-in-law.

The wedding took place on a Saturday night, so as to allow for the effect of it to wear off before the guests and the bride-groom all returned to work on Monday. Jessie had a new dress for the occasion, her first since leaving Michigan that didn't have that telltale band of brown around the hem to lengthen it. It was green-sprigged white dimity, as cool as anything could have been in this climate, and she had a new green ribbon for her hair, as well. Her figure had regained its slimness after Tristan's birth, and she was eager to show off her son, who was a most appealing infant.

Jessie felt a twinge of something like apprehension when Joel, clucking approvingly over his newest son, said, "Hurry up and grow, Tris. I need you in the fields."

"What if he doesn't want to be a farmer?" she asked, keeping her tone light as Joel handed her up into the wagon that had still not been replaced by the desired buggy. "What if he wants to be something else? A lawyer, or a teacher?"

Joel grinned. "If he's anything like his mother, he'll be whatever he damned well wants to be. Here, Laurie, you sit right there in the middle by Aunt Jessie, and don't poke the baby in the eyes, all right?" Then he smiled up at his wife. "You'll be the prettiest girl there, prettier even than the bride."

She felt pretty. Her hair, which reached to below her waist and was usually done in a great knot at the back of her head, had been washed and brushed until it shone. Sometimes she wished it were the golden blond that her sister Audra's hair had been, but Joel thought it more striking, and more unusual, than that, and it was pretty. For this occasion she'd braided it and wore it in a coronet atop her head, with a few tendrils carefully curled at each temple, crimped there with a curling iron only that morning and protected by a wide-brimmed bonnet.

Jessie seldom got to Knight's Ferry, and the trip was always a treat. There were stores to explore, small items to buy, and best of all, the company of other females.

Mamie and Alice had made friends among the established Knight's Ferry families, and among them were enough young girls eager to play with the babies so that Jessie was for the first time freed from the restrictions of motherhood, at least for a few hours. She joined in the laughter and the talk, admired the pretty clothes, and enjoyed the compliments on her hair and her dress, as women had done down through the ages.

The wedding was lovely, with Alice in a dress she had made herself. It was held in the shaded yard behind the bakery because that was the coolest place they could find. Harry Kelly had purchased two kegs of beer, which had been chilled in the river until needed; the men worked up a sweat wrestling the kegs up the bank and wasted no time in refreshing themselves at once when they'd reached their destination.

The ladies and children drank lemonade, and everyone shared in the cake Alice and her mother had made the day before, an elegant three-tiered delicacy decorated in pale pink rosebuds. It was the finest wedding cake anyone in Knight's Ferry had ever seen, and had already, Mamie confided, resulted in orders for two more of similar design.

Jessie marveled at the perfection of the rosebuds. "How did you learn to make them?" she asked, allowing Laurie to eat one off the end of her finger before he was carried away by his youthful keepers.

"We had the very devil of a time with them at first," Mamie admitted, laughing. "Our first attempts were terrible. We ate them all ourselves, until I had to let out my skirts, and we decided we could sell them to the children six for a penny, even if they didn't look right. We didn't put any on the cakes until we'd learned to do them properly."

Jessie studied her friend as she munched cake. "You're looking very lovely, Mamie. As pretty as Alice, even if she is the bride. Very happy. Are you happy?"

"Yes." Mamie's smile deepened. "Collie is really courting me now, you know. He asked Mama's permission. And he can't help being impressed by all this, now can he?"

They looked around the yard, at the fruit trees decorated with pink and white crepe paper streamers and wires from which hung lanterns that would be lighted at dusk. Everyone was in his best clothes, and the children ran and played and the women caught up on the latest gossip, while the men drank and talked farming and mining.

"I predict," Jessie said, licking frosting off her fingers, "that Collie will propose by the end of summer."

Mamie did not reply to that. She didn't have to; her own expectations were clear in her face. She'd already sought out a place for them to live when the time came, for the old lady there now was leaving in September, to go to her daughter's in San Francisco. It was a tiny house but a charming one, halfway up the hill behind Main Street, built of adobe and covered with climbing vines and rose bushes, with its own garden and peach and apricot trees. The old lady wanted to sell it, for her husband had died, and she would take a very small sum, one that Collie should easily be able to come up with once he'd collected for his share of the harvested wheat.

She hadn't mentioned it to Collie yet, but she would soon. Maybe tonight, Mamie thought, if the wedding put him into a romantic mood as it had done for her.

It was not of romance that Collie spoke when they finally were alone together. He brought her lemonade and sipped at his own beer, now warming, and leaned against the giant fig tree. Usually he was good-natured and smiling. He became suddenly serious, however, and Mamie's heartbeat quickened.

"I need to talk to you, Mamie."

"Yes, of course." She glanced over her shoulder and saw that Alice was dancing with her new husband; everyone was busy elsewhere, paying no attention to the pair near the fig tree. "It's a beautiful wedding, isn't it, Collie?"

"Sure," Collie said, though as if he were not thinking about the wedding at all. "Listen, Mamie...I don't know how to say this."

"Just say it straight out—we're friends, aren't we?" she encouraged. "We can say anything to each other, can't we?"

"I hope so." Still he hesitated, draining the glass of beer before he went on, while Mamie waited, hands tightening in a clasp at her waist. She was wearing pink, in keeping with the color theme of the wedding, and her rich chestnut hair was carefully curled around her face; she knew that she had never looked prettier than she did right now.

What he said, however, was not what she'd prepared herself to hear.

"Mamie—damn, why is this so hard to do? Mamie, I'm going to make a change in my life, a big change. I'll have to stick around until the wheat is all harvested, a few more weeks—Joel will kill me if I try to pull out before that's done, because then he'd have to hire more help, and he doesn't want to spend the money that way. It's a big crop; everybody says we've got as good a stand as anybody in San Joaquin County, or maybe in the whole valley. There'll be some money coming then, a decent amount for our first year, even when we put part of it back into the land. But the money's the least of it, in a way...."

He stared at her as if willing her to understand, while Mamie fought rising uneasiness. He didn't sound like a man about to propose to a girl he loved.

"Damn it, I'm not cut out to be a farmer," Collie blurted. "Joel likes it, plowing the ground, walking behind a horse all day, cutting the wheat—everything about it. He gets excited

180

watching things grow—an inch a day, the corn comes up, but who cares? I need something more in my life than wheat and corn and working all alone every day and falling into bed at night so tired I can't sleep—"

This did not sound promising at all. Mamie's smile had congealed, though she tried to maintain a semblance of it. "Farming is very hard work," she agreed. "What do you want to do instead? Open a business in town, like your father had?"

"My father inherited a business that had already made several men rich. He had more customers in a day than any shopkeeper in Knight's Ferry has in a week. And I didn't like it all that much, either. I sure didn't come to California to sell canned goods and tinware or walk behind a plow, either. Do you understand, Mamie?"

She understood that he was not about to offer her marriage, and nothing else mattered. She pressed her lips together to keep them from trembling and vowed that no matter what he said she would not disgrace herself by crying.

At least her voice didn't quaver; it came out sounding flat and matter-of-fact. "What do you want, Collie? Adventure? Excitement?"

His blue eyes brightened, and he reached for her hands, not noticing that they were limp and unresponsive. "You do understand! You're a girl in a million! Most women don't think in terms of adventure."

Mamie didn't either, though it was impossible to admit that at the moment. It didn't seem to matter that she did not reply, for now he spoke eagerly, with enthusiasm. "I wasn't quite ten years old when the news came about the gold strike in California. Everybody who came in the store talked about it, even my parents did. Not that my father wanted to join in the gold rush, but it was partly because of it that his fortunes increased as they did. He sold all the things they needed to head west, except for their oxen and the wagons themselves. The men came in and ordered supplies, getting ready to go in the spring of '49, and I listened to them all. Heard how they were going to get rich in California."

Mamie's lips moved of their own volition. "You were already rich."

"But I didn't do anything to get that way! My father, my grandfather, already had done it, and that made it different. There was no adventure there, just growing up enough to take my place beside my father, measuring out yard goods, counting out cans, weighing sugar and flour and telling a man what kind of plow he needed to work Illinois land, and what would be best for California, all without ever trying any of it myself."

He dropped her hands now, reaching to pluck one of the gigantic fig leaves that hung around them, absently shredding it between his fingers.

"I'm a greenhorn, I admit it. Or I was when I got here, anyway. But it's been almost a year, and I've learned a lot. I've listened to the men who've found the gold. Practically everybody's found dust, and some of them have picked up nuggets that are so big a man can hardly hold one in his hand."

"And you want to look for gold," Mamie said, still sounding flat and stilted. "The gold rush is over. Everybody says so."

"The big part of it, maybe. But people are coming in here to the assay office every week with new finds. There's no way of knowing how much is still out there in the hills, or along the rivers. It washes down in the water from the mountains, you know, and it could be anywhere."

"Big companies control most of the mines now," Mamie said. She, too, listened to the talk in the town.

"That doesn't mean there are no veins of ore left. There are hundreds of creeks and gullies in the Sierra, and there could be gold in any of them."

"Men have been all over the mountains for the past ten years. They've looked in all those places."

"But the streambeds change, Mamie. In the flood season the water rolls away rocks, uncovering new places to look. Sometimes the channel changes, cutting a new place, through virgin territory. And the gold could be anywhere, just buried under the ground. I've got to go look, Mamie. Maybe in my old age I can settle down to a town job—not as a farmer, though—but not yet. I owe Joel the help through this first harvest season, because he brought me along knowing I'd be more of a hindrance than an asset, and I owe him something. Not past this next month or so, though. Then I'm going looking for the gold. I owe myself a year, anyway, to see what I can find."

A year, Mamie thought, and struggled with the sting of tears. A year! And she was already nearly nineteen years old.

"If I strike it rich, and I've got as good a chance as anyone else, I can do whatever I like for the rest of my life," Collie told her, earnestly unaware of the pain he caused her. "Build a big house here in Knight's Ferry, up on the hill so we get the breeze and can look down over the river. Maybe a store of some kind, I don't know. There's plenty of time to think about that."

We get the breeze, he'd said. Did he mean her, as well as himself? It was a long way from a proposal, and she couldn't help the moisture that formed in her hazel eyes.

"I'll miss you," she said, striving for an unemotional response, not totally successful.

"And I'll miss you." His voice grew tender, and he reached for her hands again. "I'll be back to town from time to time, though. For supplies and everything. Some of your blackberry pie." He grinned happily. "It'll only be for a year or so, unless I strike it rich before then."

Her throat ached with the effort of appearing normal, unconcerned. It wouldn't do to let him know he was breaking her heart, not when he hadn't actually asked her to marry him. "Have you told Joel yet?"

Some of his exuberance faded. "No. I'll tell him soon, though. So he won't be counting on me to help with the fall planting. As soon as he gets this year's crop harvested he'll be working up the land again, putting in more wheat, but he'll have the cash money from this crop, so he can hire someone else to help him. Plenty of men around needing jobs."

Men who had come west for the gold and not found it, Mamie thought. Yet she could not say this, could not crush the excitement in him, even though she did not share it.

She drained her lemonade, which had grown tepid, and turned back toward the wedding party, unable to endure any more. She wished she could go inside and fling herself on the bed she had shared with her sister and bawl her eyes out, but she knew she couldn't do that. Not until the wedding was over, and everyone had gone home, Alice to the little cabin with Harry.

A year, she thought in despair. A year was such a long time.

22

Joel was more annoyed than surprised at Collie's defection, though he suspected that anyone he found to take his half-brother's place on their acreage would work with more zeal than Collie had shown.

Jessie knew there were men available for hire; her concern was for Mamie, Mamie for whom she had predicted a fall wedding.

"There are plenty of single men around Knight's Ferry," she said darkly, "and Mamie might not be waiting for him when he comes back."

"If she loves him, she will be," Joel said, unconcerned with that aspect of the problem. "Oh, I met Luis Sañudo this morning, and he asked after you and young Tristan."

Pleasure surged through her. "Did he? How nice. Did you ask after his mother?"

"Yes. My mother brought me up well, you know, and my wife has continued to train me in good manners," Joel teased. "The old lady is much better after Annie brought her some kind of herb or something. Says she doesn't have the chest pain and shortness of breath as bad as she did." He turned away, then paused in the open doorway. "Oh, he invited us to visit them. He would like you to meet his mother and his sister; sounds like they don't go anywhere much, and they don't entertain very often, either, since so many of the Mexicans and Spaniards have moved on."

"Been run off, do you mean? That's happening, isn't it, Joel? Some of them are being deprived of their lands?"

He lingered a moment longer. "Those Spanish land grants aren't legal, a lot of them. The descriptions are so vague nobody can say what they mean, so how can they hold up in court? 'Two miles due east from the large rock on the bank of the river' or 'a league and a half from the skull on the top of the hill' or 'bounded by the three oaks at the bend of the river' and more of that ilk. What large rock? Which skull, which may no longer even be there? And the same with the trees. More have grown up so there are a dozen instead of three, or they've been cut down for firewood, or burned in a grassfire. So their papers are dismissed when the matter's taken to court."

"American courts," Jessie said uncomfortably. "American judges, ruling in favor of Americans who've moved in and taken over lands that have belonged to the Mexicans and the Spaniards for years."

"It doesn't happen to all of them, not the ones smart enough to make sure their legal descriptions will hold up. Or the ones who'll defend their lands with guns if they have to. Sañudo has a legal grant, it's already been tested. So now all he has to do is keep the rustlers off his spread."

"Is he having trouble that way again?"

"Seems so. He figures they drove off about a dozen head two days ago; he tracked them to the river, where they were driven across. A dozen head isn't much, but it whittles away his stock, and it infuriates him. I feel sorry for the rustlers if he catches them in the act; I doubt he'll haul the next batch before a magistrate and wait for a legal hanging."

Jessie stood, after Joel had gone, staring out into the fall sunshine, remembering. When threatened, Luis Sañudo had not hesitated for a moment to shoot to kill. Yet had not she herself fired when she felt it necessary? It still made her sick to think of it, but she knew that under similar circumstances she would do the same thing again.

She went about her morning tasks, spirits brightening at the thought of a visit to the Rancho Sañudo. She would wear her prettiest dress, the dimity she had worn to Alice's wedding, though it was a bit light for this time of year. Or, she thought, growing more daring as she considered it, why not a new dress altogether? There was money, now, from the sale of the wheat; surely Joel would want her to appear at her best in meeting these aristocrats, and a new dress would be in order. She could look for the material the next time they went to town.

When Joel came in for the midday meal, he heard her singing—the voice that had soared with a Mormon choir now lifted in a hymn for the benefit of two small children—and he smiled. He'd gotten a gem when he married Jessie.

They rode to Rancho Sañudo in style, in the buggy Joel had promised when the money was available to pay for it. It was roomy enough for the four of them, and light enough for the single horse to pull it; a fringed top kept off the heat of the day. They had been invited to spend the night so that they need not rush their visit.

Jessie had again done her fair hair in the coronet of braids with the curling tendrils at each temple; though Joel had not said anything, she saw by his eyes that he found her beautiful, and it was not all because of the new dress.

The material was a fine merino wool, dark brown in color, and she had crocheted collar and cuffs of a softer cream color. With it she wore the garnet and gold filigree pin Joel had acquired from the Pawnees, her sole piece of jewelry, having at last made the effort to overcome an aversion to a brooch that might have been taken from its owner by force.

Tristan slept in her lap, a sweet-faced angel with a halo of sunlit hair. Laurie stood between them on the seat, one hand on Joel's shoulder, the other on Jessie's, delighted at the buggy ride.

The hills had not yet taken on the green of winter, and after they'd passed by the wheat stubble of their own fields they followed the trail between slopes burned by the summer just past. They had left home early in the morning, yet even so the day grew warm before they saw the tops of trees in the opening between the hills, the trees that signaled their approach to the main house, or hacienda, as the Mexicans called it.

Excitement trickled in Jessie's veins as she leaned forward for her first look at it. She was not disappointed.

There were dozens of outbuildings, including cottages where the Mexicans who served the Sañudos lived. Dominating the scene, however, was the main house, gleaming white in the noon sunlight. It was huge, the biggest house Jessie had ever seen, including those on the streets of Chicago, with red-tiled roofs and chimneys, shaded by enormous trees that must have been growing for generations to have achieved such proportions. Twin fig trees partially protected the western facade from the force of the afternoon sun.

Neither of them had ever before seen the graceful Spanish architecture with its iron-grilled windows and doorways, glistening whitewash, colorful tiles. This, Jessie knew instinctively, was the right kind of house for this climate—thick adobe walls to hold the heat at bay and, glimpsed through a wrought-iron gate opening onto a tiled corridor that led into the interior of the massive rectangle, a garden.

A real garden, not the hard-worked rows of vegetables such as she kept at home, but a garden of flowers and bearing fruit trees and beauty such as she had not ever seen before.

Luis came out to greet them himself, attended by various servants dressed in bright clean costumes, colorfully embroidered, the women's skirts revealing slender ankles unencumbered by the pantalettes the Mormon women had worn.

A smiling elderly woman took the sleeping Tris; a younger one assisted Laurie down, while Luis raised his arms to lift Jessie to the ground as if she weighed nothing at all.

There was a curious sensation within her at his touch, for she had never been touched by any man other than Joel, except for her father and, on a few affectionate occasions, her stepfather. Luis was not as tall as Joel, nor as huskily built, yet there was the strength of tempered steel in his lean muscles.

He was, in fact, only a few inches taller than Jessie; he smiled a greeting as he let her go, then looked beyond her to Joel. "Welcome to Casa Sañudo, *señor y señora!* Come, it is very warm here in the sun for November, is it not? My sister has ordered a meal set out for our visitors, and Mamacita is eager to meet you. She has very few visitors these days, and today she is feeling exceptionally well, no doubt due to her anticipation of the pleasure of your company."

He led them into the house through the tiled corridor, turning aside, before they reached the tantalizing garden, into a huge long room where the coolness enveloped them and protected them from the glare of the sun. It was, by American standards, a bare room, for the tiled floors were not carpeted except for one area before an empty fireplace where two settees faced each other over a colorful rug; the walls were several feet thick and as white as if they'd been painted only that morning. A painting of Christ hung on one wall; opposite it, twenty feet away, was a painting of a bowl of flowers, meticulously rendered; over the fireplace, dominating the room, was a life-size portrait of a man Jessie immediately took to be the elder Señor Sañudo, painted when he was little more than his son's present age. He was a handsome and imposing figure in a dark but by no means somber costume, for jacket and the hat held in one hand were elaborately and lavishly embroidered in gold threads. The dark eyes stared directly into Jessie's, as if probing her reasons for being here.

It was almost a relief to turn away when Luis introduced his family. Mamacita, the Señora Teresa Sañudo, was a tiny woman with the same black eyes as Luis and snow-white hair held high with a Spanish comb; she wore black unrelieved by either color or jewelry, except that there was a diamond ring on one finger. She welcomed the newcomers with a smile, and waved forward her daughter to be introduced as well.

Bonifasia was considerably younger than her brother; Jessie guessed her age at twenty-four or twenty-five. She was small and slim and very pretty in a shy way; her brown eyes revealed delight in the company of another young female. She wore a full-skirted gown of deep blue silk with a neckline cut low enough to show the beginning swell of her breasts; as if the beauty of her throat and bosom were not enough in themselves, attention was drawn there by a pendant that must surely be a sapphire, for it sparkled and gave off blue flames when Bonifasia turned so that the gem caught the light.

Her voice was soft and pleasant. "Welcome, señora. We are most happy to have you as our guests."

She spoke English less well than Luis, but there was no difficulty in understanding her. The old lady's speech was well laced with Spanish words, for which she would apologize and then look to her son for the correct word in English. They all spoke together for a few minutes, and then Bonifasia suggested that Jessie might like to freshen up before the noon meal was served.

Jessie soaked up every detail of the house as they moved through it. Dear heaven, how different this would be, in the hundred-degree heat, from her own frame cabin! Surely the heat would take a long time to penetrate the thick adobe walls, and the tile would remain cool to walk upon. In the winter perhaps she would choose to put down rugs to make the rooms warmer, but in the summer . . . yes, heavenly coolness. She could hardly wait to exclaim upon it to Joel, for when they built the big house he was always talking of.

Bonifasia led her up a broad curving stairway to the second floor, opening onto a gallery that ran around the entire inner rectangle of the house, and Jessie gave an involuntary cry of pleasure. She paused to look over the intricately wrought railing into the garden which filled the center of the house.

"How beautiful! And how cool and lovely it must be with the fountain and the trees in the summer!"

"Yes, we spend much time in the *patio*," Bonifasia conceded. "There is a stairway there"—she indicated a corner of the house—"and there, so that you may descend without going through the rest of the house. We have given you this room, señora; I hope it pleases you. The children will have the room beyond, which is our old nursery and therefore equipped with cradle and crib. Do not concern yourself with your children; Manuela will care for them as she did for me, when I was an infant."

The room into which Jessie was ushered was larger than their entire house at home. It, too, was spartanly furnished, for the Spaniards recognized that clutter meant heat. The bed was high and huge, with deeply carved oak headboard and foot posts, covered with a crocheted white spread. A great matching chest and an armoire, a small sofa in rose brocade, a pair of matching chairs, and a chaise longue completed the furnishings.

"There is warm water for washing," Bonifasia said, indicating the pitcher and bowl, and then, with a faint blush, opened the door of the commode to reveal the third piece of china. "I will leave you for now, and return in, say, half an hour?"

Jessie thanked her, and no sooner was the girl out of the room than she tried out the chaise longue; she had heard of them, but never seen one before. Yes, very comfortable it would be for curling up on an afternoon with a book, if she had a book. Perhaps Joel's ideas about a fancy house were not so farfetched after all. Something like this would be very nice.

She washed and stretched out on the high bed, luxuriating in its softness. Luxuriating, as well, in the knowledge that her children were being cared for, that for a moment she might close her eyes without worrying what Laurie was getting into.

She was too excited to rest, however. After a few moments her eyes opened, and she stared up at the ceiling, which was far overhead so that the hot air could rise well above the level which the inhabitants had to breathe. Lord, what a glorious house! And that garden—would they mind if she went down and walked in the garden? But of course not, for Bonifasia had told her about the stairs.

A moment later, she was descending into that marvel in

this land of sunburned grass and black-green oaks, and to her increased pleasure, she found Luis Sañudo there before her.

He turned at the sound of her heels on the tiled walkway that encircled the *patio* on the ground floor. "Ah, you would like to see our garden? Allow me to walk with you, for your husband has gone to attend his horse. I assured him that Pedro would take good care of it, but he says it is a new horse, rather skittish, and he'd feel better handling it himself."

Jessie smiled at him, then put out a hand to touch a late-blooming rose. "I can't believe the beauty of this place. What did your sister call it? The *patio*?"

"This country would be too harsh without a place like the *patio*," Luis assured her. "It stays much cooler than the world outside, because of the growing things, and the fountain. Would you like to see the fountain?"

They strolled along the tiled pathway, with her host naming the various flowers and trees that she did not recognize, enjoying her amazement that some could still bloom this late in the year. The fountain, in the center of the space surrounded on all four sides by the hacienda itself, was a thing of beauty, and would undoubtedly help to cool the *patio* in the summer.

"How does it work? Where does the water come from?"

"There is a spring in the hills behind the hacienda, which provides water both for the fountain and for the kitchen. It falls far enough so that the fall creates pressure to take the water where we want it. It also flows into the laundry, in a building off that way. Do you like the flowers, señora?"

"I love them, but I haven't raised any yet. I've been too busy with beans and potatoes and things we'll eat through the winter." She turned from the fountain to survey the trees, now mostly denuded of foliage. "Fruit trees of all kinds, aren't they?"

"Oranges, lemons, apricots, peaches, plums, nectarines, and cherries. We tried to grow apples but the climate is not really cold enough for them; they do not do well, though a few miles up the mountains they can be grown. Would you like cuttings of the fruit trees for your own orchard?"

Jessie lifted her face, revealing extreme pleasure. "Could I? Oh, I'd love to have cuttings of everything—anything," she amended quickly, and saw Luis Sañudo break into a laugh.

"You shall have cuttings of anything you like, señora," he

assured her. "And that bell indicates that our meal is waiting
for us."

The dining room was as vast as the living room, or *sala,*
had been; they ate at a table that could easily have seated
two dozen people. Since they were only five, they sat at one
end of the polished oaken board, and ate from fine china and
crystal that Jessie was almost afraid to touch.

Across the table, Joel grinned at her, and she smiled back,
getting his message clearly enough: someday we'll have
things like this, too. They were served by two young women
in the brightly embroidered skirts and blouses, who moved
silently on sandaled feet. They ate a salad of vegetables from
the Sañudo gardens—not the *patio,* but a more ordinary one
outside the immediate grounds—and salmon caught in the
Stanislaus and baked to perfection under a garnish of onion
and lemon slices. Jessie could have made an entire meal on
the salmon alone. The meal ended with delicately flavored
melon, eaten with special small silver forks.

During the meal they talked of inconsequential things;
the Sañudos put themselves out to be hospitable and gracious,
and since Señora Teresa had to have many words translated,
there was considerable laughter as well as good talk.

After the meal, the women retired to a smaller *sala* where
Tristan was brought to Jessie for nursing. Bonifasia and her
mother both asked permission to watch, then peered with
obvious delight at the small child as he sucked, smiling approval.

"Beautiful baby," Señora Teresa said, enunciating carefully so that Jessie would understand. Her following words
were in her native tongue, which Bonifasia translated.

"Mamacita begs that you will forgive her. She must retire
to rest. She has enjoyed meeting you, and she hopes to join
us all at dinner, but for the rest of the afternoon, she must
lie down."

When the old lady had gone, Bonifasia fell silent, content
to observe the nursing child. When he had finished and fallen
asleep, the smiling Manuela came to carry him away.

Jessie laughed softly. "I never thought I wanted servants,
but I can see that there are advantages. Especially in the
middle of the night, when one wants to sleep."

Bonifasia nodded. "It is very helpful to have servants.
Spanish women of our class expect to have servants to care
for their children and keep their houses. Our men expect us
to keep ourselves beautiful for them." She made a small,

rather endearing face. "Of course, I have no man of my own. I am a . . . how do you say it in English? A spinster?"

"You are still young and beautiful," Jessie assured her. "Someone will come along for you, I'm sure."

Bonifasia's smile was sad. "I do not think so, señora. I am four and twenty, and that is quite old to become a bride. There was a time when I thought I would marry a neighbor, but he was . . . was killed. And there are no suitable neighbors any more, for a Spanish girl to marry. There are only gringos now, Americanos, who do not want Spanish women. We have not been raised for the sort of life they offer, nor trained to serve them as they require." She lifted soft white hands, beautifully shaped and cared for. "These are useless for the tasks common to Americanas. And my . . . my health is fragile. I could not, I think, do the things that you do, to keep the garden and the house and have the babies, all by myself."

"You're a woman like any other, only more beautiful," Jessie said truthfully. "And if you loved a man, you'd learn to do what needs to be done."

"Do you think so?" She considered that with some seriousness. "Ah, well, that is not likely to happen, señora. I do not meet any eligible men. We have no visitors here any more, and I have not left Rancho Sañudo in over three years."

"Three years! You don't even go to Knight's Ferry?"

Bonifasia shrugged slim shoulders so that the blue silk outlined provocative curves even more snugly. "It is not suitable for a Spanish woman to go to such places. Only men do so."

"But your brother . . . surely he sees the problem? That you are a normal woman, needing love and companionship?"

Bonifasia's lips curved in a rueful smile. "You do not understand our ways, señora. In Spain it is better that a woman remained unmarried, unfulfilled, than that she marry beneath her own class. And since the coming of the Americanos, there are virtually none of my class left. At least, that is how Luis sees it. He is head of the family now, and I cannot marry anyone without his permission."

"But you aren't in Spain! You're in America! Practically in the United States; California will become a state soon."

"On the rancho, I remain a maiden of Spain. And I do not leave this place," Bonifasia told her. "But come, I make you to be not happy, and that is very rude of me. Would you like to tour the *casa*, to see how we live?"

And so Jessie spent a marvelous afternoon exploring the

most beautiful house she'd ever been in. It was somewhat bare for her tastes, and she imagined filling it with colorful rugs and pictures, and with roaring fires in the many fireplaces. Since all the firewood must be hauled down from the mountains, it must be a steady task for several men to provide a winter's supply, but judging by the number of people Jessie saw engaged in either household or ranch chores, there was no shortage of hired help.

She noted one very handsome young Mexican working near the corrals and wondered if Bonifasia took no notice of him or his fellows simply because they were not of the proper class. In three years of unbroken isolation, she thought, she'd have made friends with *someone,* and class be damned. And then she was ashamed of the profanity that had come unbidden into her mind.

Dinner was again served in the massive dining hall. By then it was chilly enough so that there was a roaring fire in each of the two great fireplaces. Señora Teresa rejoined them, still in her widow's black; Bonifasia had changed into another of the full-skirted, low-necked gowns of whispering silk, this one in a deep rose that lent color to her rather pale cheeks. Aging or not, Bonifasia was a beautiful woman, Jessie thought, and caught Joel's admiring gaze upon her, too.

The meal was as elegant and as lavish as anyone could have hoped for. Besides the beef one might expect on a cattle ranch—crisply browned on the outside and pinkly tender on the inside—there was a haunch of venison, a roast of pork, and a chicken dish with squash and peppers and other ingredients Jessie didn't recognize—hot to the tongue, but delicious.

"I must warn you that some of the seasonings are warm," Luis said in considerable understatement, and Jessie noted that the serving women refilled both water and wine glasses as soon as anyone sipped from them.

For the first time Jessie ate tortillas, the flat, unleavened corn cakes that served the Mexicans as bread. And there were fruits and vegetables beyond counting, many of them in sauces that completely changed their texture and taste from the boiled variety the Americans were accustomed to. The most interesting of the new foods was the avocado, a buttery sort of fruit (or was it a vegetable?) that blended well with an assortment of other things, and which Luis was proud of raising in his own gardens, as it was not commonly produced in this area.

When they rose at last from the table, after a meal that had continued for more than two hours of leisurely courses and much refilling of wineglasses, Jessie felt happy and vaguely lightheaded. No wonder they wanted servants, she thought, surveying the array of serving dishes and the food still on the table. It would take one woman a week to clear away a single dinner table.

They retired this time, not to the grand *sala* nor the smaller one where the women had gone earlier, but to the library. This was a room Bonifasia had not shown her, because the men were talking there and men, Bonifasia gave her to understand, were never disturbed when they were speaking between themselves.

It was, Jessie decided immediately, her favorite room of the entire house.

Here, too, a fire had been kindled, and they all gravitated toward it, for the evening was late and grew cold. Windows looked out over the *patio*, though little could be seen now, and on the inner wall were hundreds of books, books that drew Jessie irresistibly.

"So many!" she exclaimed, and Luis moved to her side, brandy glass in hand, as he left Joel to his mother and sister before the fire.

"My father was a great reader," he told her. "And I—well, I follow in his footsteps in many things. Including the love of books. Are you a reader, señora?"

He was very close to her, and Jessie caught some unknown but tantalizing scent. The mustache was fascinating—good grief, she thought, had she drunk too much of the wine, despite her careful sippings? How could she feel this magnetic pull to an attractive man, when she was wildly in love with her own husband? Yet feel it she did, and she wondered uncomfortably if Luis was aware of it.

"I've had little opportunity to read much other than the Bible and the newspapers, when I was at home," she said, moving a trifle apart from him. And then, because she felt the need to say something to keep the conversation on an impersonal basis, "You said something that day, by the river, when the men would have killed you. It sounded like a . . . a quotation perhaps. Something about—murder will not be hid?"

He left the breathing space between them, sipped from his glass, then reached up to take down a heavy volume from a shelf over his head. "I do not quite remember what I said,

194

señora, but it might have been 'Truth will come to light; murder cannot be hid long.' Though I fear that had they succeeded in forcing me into the river, in my case it might have been hid sufficiently for their purposes. Would that be the quotation?"

"Yes, that was it. You *were* quoting!" She was amazed that any mind could come up with such a thing, at such a time.

"It is from the writing of an Englishman, William Shakespeare. Are you familiar with any of his work?"

He was close to her again, the book open in his hands, and Jessie tried to focus on the written words that swam alarmingly, just beyond her grasp.

"Yes, here it is. From *The Merchant of Venice:* 'Truth will come to light; murder cannot be hid long.' I might have said something quite different, also from Mr. Shakespeare." He flipped pages and read aloud, "'If I must die, I will encounter darkness as a bride, and hug it in mine arms.' That was not my feeling at the time, however, and I was most grateful that I did not have to die that day, señora. To quote again, 'Death is a fearful thing, for we know not into what darkness or fire we go,' is it not so? And there are many pleasures still to be explored here on earth, as well as responsibilities to those around us."

The smile he turned on her made Jessie's legs suddenly weak. Did he include her in those pleasures? She blinked, and withdrew perceptibly, aware of Joel across the room, speaking to Señora Teresa, and of Bonifasia standing before the fire, watching them.

The wine, Jessie thought. It had been a mistake to drink the wine, when she wasn't used to it. The others had all drunk far more, and none of them seemed affected by it at all, yet her head was swimming and she felt overly warm, on the far side of the room from the hearth.

"I have never read Mr. Shakespeare, though I've heard of him," Jessie murmured. "How marvelous it must be, to have access to all these books."

She took a few steps from him, running a finger over the backs of some of the volumes, seeing that many of them were in Spanish. Yet the book in his hand was in English.

"My father read only Spanish," Luis offered, reading her mind. "And most of the books are in my native language. I also read English, however; it seemed necessary to learn to do so, when the Americanos began to come into what I regarded as my own country. One can ignore a few foreigners;

to ignore them when they come in hordes is to play the fool. One must learn to deal with what one cannot prevent."

"And does it help you, knowing how to speak and read English?" She began to move back toward the others, feeling the need to reach Joel, to feel his solid presence. Luis fell into step beside her, the book still in his hand, forgotten.

His reply was moody. "It has not solved the problems, yet it has, perhaps, prevented additional problems that would have come had I not been familiar with the language. For instance, I had to go into an American court to defend my right to my own land; I would have been at a distinct disadvantage there, speaking no English."

"But you proved your right to it," Jessie said. "Your land grant was upheld."

"For the time," Luis said. "Yet it is a valuable property, and the Americanos—forgive me if I say this bluntly, señora—seem determined to gain not only the gold of California but the land. My fight to retain what is mine is not over, I fear."

They rejoined the others, and Señora Teresa looked up with a smile at the two of them. Whatever she said made Bonifasia blush becomingly.

"Mamacita suggests that our guests might enjoy hearing Bonifasia play the piano. She plays very well," Luis said, coming out of his black mood, smiling, putting his empty glass on the mantel. "And I have heard that you sing most prettily, señora. Would you care to join my sister in a musical performance?"

The rest of the evening passed very pleasantly. Bonifasia was, indeed, an accomplished pianist, and after a little floundering around to find something to which Jessie knew the words, they joined piano and voice in a repertoire of selections that brought applause from the audience.

When Señora Teresa announced that she must once more retire, the party broke up. Jessie was still exhilarated, feeling the effect of the wine and, perhaps, the company and the surroundings. She climbed the stairs on Joel's arm, leading him to the huge bedroom that had been allotted to them.

"Imagine, living like this all the time!" she said, pausing just inside the doorway to see that here, too, a fire had been lighted against the chill, as candles had been provided to drive away the shadows. The bed was turned down, and the nightdress Jessie had brought with her was laid out across it.

"We will, someday," Joel promised. "Like a museum, this place. The library was all right, but the rest of it isn't to my taste. We'll make it homier, when we build our own. Where are Laurie and Tristan?"

"Through that door. With Manuela, who knows all about babies. I scarcely thought about them all day, except when they brought Tristan to be nursed." She turned her back so that Joel could undo her buttons. "I feel sorry for Bonifasia. She doesn't think she'll ever meet anyone she'll be allowed to marry. I wonder what she does to keep herself busy, when the servants do all the work?"

"Judging by her skill on the piano, I'd say she practices six or eight hours a day," Joel said. He finished the buttons, his breath warm on the back of her neck, then slid the brown merino down over her shoulders and kissed one of them. "Well, it's been interesting, but I'll be glad to leave for home, after lunch tomorrow. He hasn't gotten around to business yet, but he has me curious, I'll admit."

Jessie twisted around to face him. "Business? But I thought this was a visit to get acquainted with his mother and his sister."

"Oh, that too. But it's all for a purpose. The Sañudos have held themselves apart from the gringos, as they call us. There is no love for the Americans, and we're Americans, too. Luis wants something. I can hardly wait to find out what it is."

Her mouth sagged in astonishment. "Wants something from us? But he's wealthy, he has this enormous ranch and this beautiful house, and we . . . we're just beginning, on such a small scale, by comparison. What could he want of us?"

"I don't know, but he does," Joel said with conviction. Then he began to unfasten his own garments, grinning. "Let's see if it's any more fun to make love in that fancy bed than in our own at home, shall we?"

23

"He's afraid," Joel said as the buggy rolled down the hill away from Casa Sañudo. "That's why he invited us here, why he wants to be friends with one of the gringos. Quite apart from the fact that he's taken with my beautiful wife."

So Joel had been observing when she thought him engrossed in a conversation with Bonifasia and Señora Teresa. Clear-headed this morning after a good sleep, Jessie considered his words, disquieted. "Why should he be afraid? Of what?"

"Of losing his land. Twenty-two hundred acres of prime land, and buildings worth a small fortune. A prize worth taking, to anybody with guts enough to do it."

The buggy wheel hit a rocky obstruction and jounced the passengers, so that Tristan protested; Jessie held him against her, patting him, and stared at her husband past the squirming Laurie. "But how can anybody take anything from him? You said he'd been to court, that his land grant title had been upheld."

"True. Once. That doesn't mean nobody can challenge it again. And they're trying. Oh, yes, Señor Luis Sañudo is fighting for his life in a society quite different from what it was before the gold rush began, before California was flooded with Americans. He hates their guts, but there isn't much he can do about them except try to work under their laws, and those tend to favor us, not the Spanish and the Mexicans."

"He said he'd had to learn to speak and read English, to protect himself," Jessie said slowly. "But I don't understand how he can still be threatened if the court declared his title valid."

Joel grimaced, flapping the reins over the horse's rump and sticking out an elbow to push Laurie back onto the seat. "Not everybody is as honest as you are, Jess."

"What's that's supposed to mean?"

"I mean judges are open to bribery, for one thing. Sañudo is scared. He's afraid someone is going to come up with enough cash to persuade another judge that the first ruling was in error; that Rancho Sañudo is fair game, ripe for the picking. Besides that, there's plenty of riffraff running around now, not even trying legal means to get control of his land. Running off his cattle, trying to ambush him—what chance do you think that beautiful but timid little sister of his would have against men like those you stopped from murdering him? Hell, if they put a bullet in Sañudo's back, they'll sweep over that place like a new broom. Those Mexicans working for him won't have a chance against anybody with guns; they're peasants, farmers, not fighters. They'll cut and run at the first sign of danger, leaving Bonifasia and the old lady to fend for themselves."

Horror sent a chill through her, though the sun was warm and the day as glorious as May would have been at home. "Surely the law wouldn't uphold anyone who took over his place by force, especially if they killed Luis to do it!"

"With enough money in the right places, the law will do damned near anything anybody will pay for. If those men had forced him into the river that day you came along, do you think anybody could ever have proved it was murder, or who did it? Even if they'd shot him, by the time anybody found his body downstream, who'd know there was a bullet in it, after it'd been smashed to pieces on those rocks? What proof would there be who did it? And without Luis, who would defend the place, or the women?"

Jessie could not believe it would be that simple. "But the ranch is well known, it's valuable, surely the authorities wouldn't just allow anyone to walk in and take it over? Even if something happened to Luis?"

"You think not? Jessie, the place we're on was just taken over. The family that was on it died, and we came along and stepped in before anybody else got around to it. I couldn't have paid for that much land. Two dollars an acre, and it takes a lot of acres to get rich in this country, even if it will grow damned near anything. It'd be beyond belief if you could get water on it. The entire valley and miles up into the hills could be the same kind of garden Luis has in that *patio* of his, with enough water to irrigate it."

They crested a hill, giving them a view out over the vast valley, and Joel gestured with one hand. "Look at it! Collie

199

wants to find gold in the hills, but the gold is right here, in the valley. Someday they'll find a way to water it during the dry season, and everybody who owns a thousand acres will be a millionaire. Maybe anybody who owns five hundred acres. And I aim to be one of them, honey. I'll get you a diamond that will make that one of Señora Sañudo's look like a gnat compared to a fly. And a blue silk dress, like that one Bonifasia was wearing. You'd be real pretty in that color blue."

Jessie wasn't thinking about luxury items. She was remembering Luis standing before the three men who would have killed him, a man who could spit his contempt at their boots, a man who defied them against impossible odds, even before he had the hope that she would come to his rescue.

"Luis is not a coward," she said now.

"I never said he was. I said he was afraid. That's not the same thing at all. Bravery is doing what needs to be done even if you're so scared you can hardly breathe. If he was a coward, he'd do what so many of his fellow countrymen have done; he'd give up, run for Mexico and save lives even if he couldn't save his property. Luis won't run. He'll hang on until the last drop of blood is soaked into his land. The land is everything to him, and I understand that. I admire him for it, because it's the way I'd feel, in his place. But he knows he can't do it alone."

"How does he think you can help?" Jessie cursed the fact that she hadn't been privy to the conversation that led Joel to these conclusions, the "men's talk" from which women in the Spanish culture were always excluded. "You haven't either wealth or influence."

"I'm a gringo. That puts me a step ahead of him right there, with any legal battle. And I've taken up land adjoining his. He didn't come right out and suggest an alliance between us, but I think he's leading up to it. He did ask me to be aware of strangers encroaching on his property—some of it's a lot closer to us than to his hacienda. And he gave me the authority to challenge anybody I see on his land. His own men will be carrying written authorizations for being there. A man without that authorization is trespassing."

"I don't like the sound of that. You getting into a fight over his land. What if they tried to do to you what they tried to do to Luis?"

"It's always a possibility," Joel admitted, not sounding overly concerned. "It's less likely with me, though. Mine is not a Mexican land grant, and I've filed all the right papers to make mine a legal title." He looked at her suddenly and laughed. "I had an idea that if I hadn't been married already, he might have offered me his sister."

Jessie was not amused. "What a horrid idea! To sell off his sister, whether she wanted you or not, in order to protect his land?"

"It's done all the time. Marrying off women of good family to families of means, to increase the means. Especially among royalty. They did it in the Bible, don't you remember? No, don't think Luis would hesitate for a minute to marry off his sister to someone who might be valuable to him. Pity I'm not single, isn't it?"

She knew he was teasing, yet she could not resist asking, "Would you take him up on the offer, if you were single?"

"I'd consider it pretty carefully. Twenty-two thousand acres is a lot of land, and Bonifasia wouldn't be hard to take. More docile than the wife I've got, I suspect. Used to taking orders without question. You should pay attention, Jess, and see how well disciplined the Spanish women are."

Jessie made a snorting sound. "If that means having nothing to do except play the piano and dress up with no one to see me, and having no say about anything that happens in my life, no thank you."

"I didn't think you'd go along with that," Joel said, grinning. "And I'm not sure I could enjoy living with a woman who wouldn't put me in my place once in a while."

They fell silent after that, and several times Jessie noticed his expression and wondered uneasily what he was thinking about whatever Luis Sañudo had said to him.

The letter came two days after Collie had loaded up his wagon and left for the hills.

Oliver Allen brought it by on his way downriver, having picked it up from the post office in Knight's Ferry. Virginia was with him, carrying the new baby and with Nellie and young Charles peering around her from the back of their wagon.

Jessie had not seen the Allens for months, and she was eager to visit with them. She held the baby, a boy named Richard Oliver, and exclaimed over him, while Virginia had to pick up first Laurie and then Tristan; little Nellie, only slightly less chubby at three and a half than she'd been at two, had to be lifted to see the baby, as well.

Oliver tolerated this female foolishness for several minutes, then drew something out of his shirtfront and handed it over. "Picked this up when I stopped into town. Looks like it's traveled a far piece, to catch up with you; postmaster said he got it in San Francisco a week ago. A miracle it ever found its way to the right place."

Jessie took it wonderingly, then cried out as she recognized the handwriting. "Zadie! It's from my sister Zadie!"

It had been sent to Independence, in care of Aunt Winnie, and someone had written "Died" after the old lady's name. Tears pricked Jessie's eyes, though she had known that Winnie was old and infirm. And after her own name, an unfamiliar hand had scrawled, "Married Joel Shand, went to Californy."

"We can't stay," Ginny told her, seeing that emotion threatened to overflow. "Oliver wouldn't have let me stop at all except that we had the letter. Maybe on the way back, when he's not in such a hurry to go look at some cattle that's for sale."

Jessie saw them to the door, scarcely aware when they drove away. A letter from Zadie, after all this time! Was it a reply to her own letter, or simply Zadie's own attempt to make contact?

Her fingers trembled as she opened the missive, and then her eyes were so filled with tears that she could at first not make out the writing inside.

It had been written nearly a year ago. Not an answer to Jessie's letter, but the answer to Jessie's prayers.

They were all well, Zadie wrote, except for Caleb, Dennis's younger brother, who had succumbed to cholera while they were on the trail; he had been buried, at age fourteen, on the open prairie, along with a dozen others in their wagon train who had been stricken.

The rest of the family, including their own infant son, had survived and were hale and hearty. They had come over the Oregon Trail and down the great Columbia River, where they spent a few weeks at The Dalles regrouping, replenishing their supplies, and resting up for the remainder of the journey downstream to where the Columbia met the Willamette.

"Dennis has taken up two hundred acres of prime forest land above the valley," Zadie wrote. "As well as about twenty acres in the valley itself, where we are building our cabin. Several other families from our wagon train have taken land in the same area, and all work together putting up barns and cabins, so the building goes quickly. We are so grateful to God for seeing us safely across that terrible wasteland, except for poor Caleb, of course. There is much work to be done, for the land must be cleared before it can be farmed. But it is a beautiful country, Jessie, and I pray that you, too, will find your way here. There are vast stands of evergreens, and water aplenty, and the soil is rich and deep. Dennis says it puts our pathetic little farm on Beaver Island to shame, for it will produce enough for us and our children's children for a hundred years.

"Oh, Jessie, how I do pray that this will find you! I have heard nothing of the rest of the family except that Audra died, miscarrying her child when the Gentiles came to drive out all our people from the island. I do not know where her children are now, though I assume that her Kenneth and Betty have them. Of Tully Ritter and Sylvia I have heard nothing, which we can only hope means that they escaped with their lives after Strang's assassination. Jessie, if this reaches you, write to me here in Oregon Territory, so that we may rejoice that we are both safe and well. Let me know what has happened to you, and how you go along now."

There was more, which Jessie had to wait to read until she could stop her tears. Joel found her at the table, face streaming, and picked up the letter to see what had set her off.

"You're dripping all over it," he commented, "and you'll never be able to make it out if you don't stop. Why are you crying? It's clear enough they're fine, except the boy who died, and you scarcely knew him."

Jessie swallowed and wiped at her eyes with her hands. "I thought I'd never hear from her again. Oh, Joel, listen to what she says about the place where they are—vast stands of evergreens, and plenty of water, and deep, rich soil—"

He placed the letter on the table, out of reach of her still watering eyes, and hugged her. "Honey, the soil here is rich and deep, too. And there will be water, eventually, and we can grow anything. Almost year round, here, which is more than they can do in Oregon. We never saw a single snowflake all last winter, not like it snows there."

"I like the snow," Jessie said. "I loved it. I loved the seasons, and the beauty of the land. Oregon is beautiful, too."

"So can this place be. We'll work to make it what we want. Honey, I've got to go into town and see if I can't hire another man or two. Damn Collie, running off and leaving me this

203

way. I'm going to see if I can't borrow against next year's crops, to start building our own house. Not this little one; we'll use this for hired help, and start over for the big house. The other side of the creek, I think. I looked at that water system of Sañudo's and I think we have enough fall to do something like that here. Get the water piped right into the house. What do you think about that?"

He had succeeded in distracting her attention from the lure of Oregon Territory, though not in the way he intended. "What do you mean, borrow money to build? I thought we weren't going into debt, Joel. There's nothing wrong with this place; we can certainly spend another year in it, until the money comes in from next year's crop."

He bent to kiss her forehead, which was the only dry spot available. "Let me take care of the business, will you, Jess? Borrowing's no crime; everybody out here does it, rather than wait forever to raise the money for what they need. And there's no risk involved. Our wheat is nearly in; it'll only take another week or two if I can get two more men right away, and another horse. The crop is money in the bank, as sure as if it was gold nuggets lying beside the creek."

He left her there, one child trying to climb into her lap to see what was the matter with Aunt Jessie that she cried, and the other angrily demanding from his bed to be fed, and after a time she dried her eyes and went back to her tasks, hoping that Joel knew what he was doing.

He had thought it a simple matter, to walk into the bank in Knight's Ferry and ask for a loan to cover the cost of building the house he'd been planning in his head for years, now. To discover that he was mistaken, that a loan was not readily available to a relative newcomer as it was to those more firmly established, left him both shaken and angry.

"I've got nearly two hundred acres planted in wheat," Joel told the banker forcefully. "We'll begin to harvest in June, and you know what I made on last year's crop. The money went through your bank."

The man spread his hands in a gesture of helplessness. "I'm sorry, Mr. Shand. The money we have to lend belongs to our investors, of course. And it is limited. We don't have enough to finance every project that anyone in the community undertakes. Naturally, we finance those that promise the most security, the least risk. I'm afraid, sir, that the loan you ask for is simply not possible at this time."

Mr. Babcock was a short, stout man of middle years, with a fringe of graying hair around a balding dome that ranged from pale pink to a full blush when he became emotional. The tint deepened as he saw the scowl distorting Joel Shand's features.

"What the hell risk are you talking about?" Joel demanded. "I told you, the wheat's planted. It's only a matter of waiting until it's harvested. It's going to be sold, you know that."

"You are a relative newcomer to San Joaquin County, Mr. Shand." Babcock spoke placatingly, but to Joel it seemed patronizing. "Having a crop in the ground is no guarantee that it will eventually produce an income. A flood could well wipe out—"

"A flood! For crissake, my place is hills! Hundreds of feet above the river!"

"—the entire crop," Babcock said, growing pinker. He was unused to being spoken to in that tone of voice. "A fire—a fire can wipe out thousands of acres of grain in a matter of hours. And a drought can do the same thing, given a bit more time. You have lived here how long, a little over a year? You have not yet suffered through a drought, but I assure you, it is a very real possibility, one we must consider."

There was a certain logic to what the man said, though Joel was too upset to admit it. "The house itself," he insisted, "should be plenty of collateral. It'll be worth more than what we put into it, in lumber and nails. A fine house, not some squatter's shack."

"A fine house, to be sure. I am certain that is your intent, and that it will be as grand as anything in Knight's Ferry. However, what we have to consider, sir, is that a house is only as valuable as the amount it will bring at a forced sale. A five-thousand-dollar dwelling in a community where there are no citizens willing or able to pay more than a thousand dollars for a house is a liability, Mr. Shand. It is not my money at stake in such a transaction, it is money belonging to our investors. I cannot risk it on such a matter at this time. Of course I value your patronage of this bank, and I hope to be able to serve you in the future, but at the present time I simply cannot—"

Joel pushed back his chair with a harsh scraping sound, rising to tower over the diminutive banker. "All right. You've made it clear enough. I think, though, that when I need any banking done in the future I'll find another bank."

Babcock came to his feet also, his plump hands fluttering. His assessment of Joel's situation was accurate, he felt, yet there was something about the man that suggested he might be a formidable antagonist at some future date; when he had learned his business and the country that must support it, say.

"I am truly sorry to have had to deny this loan, Mr. Shand. May I suggest that there are private individuals in town who might be willing to loan the money you need. At a higher interest rate than the bank, no doubt, but—"

Joel turned his back and walked out, leaving the banker still talking behind him. Damn the man to hell, anyway. He'd been so sure he could just walk in and get the money he needed to build that house! He'd dreamed of the house for so long, and then after seeing that goddamned palace that Luis Sañudo lived in, seeing Jessie against that setting, comparing her to the Sañudo women in their silks and jewels —he didn't want to wait another year to build the house. He wanted to build it now.

It was raining and the street was a sea of mud that squished up around his boots. Joel was unaware of either the mud or the rain. He slogged across the street toward the saloon, feeling a strong need for a drink of something to warm his belly, and the companionship of other men. Real men, who worked for a living, not like Babcock sitting on his fat behind in the bank.

In midafternoon, there were a dozen men drinking, all of them known to Joel at least by sight, though the only one he knew well was John Curtis. John lifted a hand, and Joel pulled out a chair at his table and sat down.

"Joe, you know Ernst Groblock? And Peter Van Liew?"

Joel acknowledged the introductions and ordered a whiskey, the same as the others were drinking. If John had been alone, Joel might have told him of his fruitless attempts to borrow money; as it was, he didn't care to expose his private business to these near-strangers. He sat with them for ten minutes, drained his glass and had another one, then rose to his feet. "Guess I better get on toward home. Jessie'll have supper on before long."

The rain had increased to a sluicing downpour that ran off the brim of his hat and down the back of his neck, but he was so used to working in bad weather that he scarcely noticed. He left his wagon—brought instead of the buggy because he'd anticipated hauling home the first batch of lumber for the foundation of his house—at the far end of the street, and he strode toward it, feelings little calmed by the whiskey.

The bolt of material in the shop window caught his attention through his own depression and chagrin. Was it true, everything the banker said, or was it only Joel Shand who would have been denied the loan? he wondered. Would Babcock have made out the papers to sign if it had been one of those men he'd just drunk with who'd wanted it? Jessie said he thought too much about his illegitimacy, that no one here knew or cared about that, but it continued to rankle; it was quite possible that someone from the wagon train knew, or guessed, his background.

Jessie. Everything he wanted, he wanted for her. He stared into the shop window at the green silk. Not blue, like Bonifasia's dress, but a shimmering deep green. He pictured Jessie in it, stunning, every bit as stunning as the Spanish girl.

The bolt stood on end, with a swath of material draped around the bolt and then spread out toward the front of the display area. Across it lay a pair of white gloves. Simple, understated, elegant.

Joel knew nothing of fashion, but he recognized elegance.

What the hell, he thought. He couldn't buy Jessie her house, yet, but he wasn't broke. He could take her home the material for a new dress.

He didn't even realize it was Clara Ridback's shop until he'd walked through the front door.

24

Clara came forward with a smile. Her rich auburn hair was elaborately dressed, held high on her head with combs like those the Sañudo women had worn. She was well corseted, so that the slimness of her waist was emphasized under the deep blue worsted, as was the magnificent swell of her breasts.

He had forgotten how pretty she was.

Her smile widened when she recognized him. "Why, Joel Shand! As I live and breathe! It's about time you crossed my threshold. I was thinking about closing up for the day, as it's nearly five, and my ladies don't usually shop after that time. They're home cooking supper. How are you?"

Joel's mouth twisted in a revealing way, though he said, "Tolerable. Looks like you've got yourself a nice little shop here."

He stared around at the assorted female accouterments, tastefully displayed. It was, even to his ignorant male eye, a shop with class. As Clara herself was a woman of distinction. For the first time he had a glimmering of understanding of her grief at the loss of her clothes while they were on the trail; dressed like this, she was head and shoulders above any other female on the train, except for Jessie.

"I like it," Clara said. She had learned to modulate her voice, so that it was low, seductive. "And it earns me a living. Well, part of a living. It's enabled me to invest in various other things as well. Did you come in for something in particular, or just to visit an old friend?"

He didn't admit he hadn't even known it was her shop. "I saw the stuff in the window—that green silk."

"Ah, yes! Beautiful piece of goods, isn't it? Were you thinking of a gown for Mrs. Shand?"

"Expensive, is it?"

"Moderately," Clara admitted. "But worth every penny. It would be perfect on Mrs. Shand, marvelous with her coloring. Shall I bring it back here under the lamps where you can see it better?"

She carried the bolt from the window to a table where she spread it out, then lifted an end of the material to drape it across her own bosom. "Isn't it lovely?"

For a matter of seconds he was distracted by the breasts outlined beneath the silk. "Lovely," he agreed, and reached out a tentative finger to touch the fabric on the bolt, well away from the danger zone. "Give me enough of it for a dress, then."

"And thread," Clara purred. "She'll want matching thread."

He watched her cut through the silk, admired the white, graceful hands. There was a modest diamond on her left hand, one she hadn't worn when he'd known her. Even a shopkeeper could have a diamond, he thought, and pictured it on Jessie.

And knew, growing uncomfortable, that it wouldn't look right on the hand of a woman who washed her own dishes and diapers and worked in the garden. Jessie's hand was brown from the summer sun and often chapped from the washing.

Well, it wouldn't be that way for much longer. Maybe he'd have to wait another year for the house, and when he got it he'd have to hire help for her, because it would be too big a place for Jessie to manage alone. And then her hands would be soft and white again, too.

"Will there be anything else?" Clara asked, carefully folding the silk. "Gloves? How about gloves to complete her costume? Of course, a hat would be very nice, too, but perhaps she'd prefer to choose that herself, after the dress is made. But gloves?"

She brought them for him to see, standing rather close so that she wafted scent toward him. He wondered if Jessie would like that perfume, if he took her some of that, but he didn't know if Clara sold it, or only wore it.

"All right. A pair of those, too," Joel agreed. He was beginning to relax. He even felt slightly drunk, though that wasn't likely on two whiskeys. "Can you wrap them up good, so they won't get wet on the way home?"

"Of course." Clara consulted a tiny watch pinned to her bosom. "It *is* time to close. I'm having dinner with a friend, but not for two hours; right now I think I'll have a cup of tea, to tide me over until then. Why don't you join me, Joel Shand? A nice hot drink before you go out for that long, wet ride?"

He knew he ought to head for home. Jessie would be expecting him. Yes, he thought with a resurgence of bitterness, expecting him with a load of lumber to start building her a house. And he wouldn't have the lumber.

He opened his mouth to say he'd better get on home, and heard his own voice saying instead, "That'd be real nice, ma'am."

He followed her up the narrow stairway at the back of the shop to her apartment above. Though there was not much light, he caught an occasional glimpse of well-turned, silk-clad ankles, and, probably because of the whiskey, imagined the calves above them and felt more warmth than the whiskey had engendered.

Though Clara's living quarters were not spacious, they were very attractive. No rag rugs here; there was a fancy carpet with an oriental-looking border of stylized flowers, and before a small fireplace were matching sofa and loveseat done

209

in a dark green velvet that provided a perfect background for a female with auburn hair.

The furniture hadn't been made in Knight's Ferry, Joel observed. She'd had stuff brought in from San Francisco, maybe even shipped around the Horn. Furnishings like those his grandmother had had in her fancy Toledo house, the house in which his mother's name had not been spoken for twenty years, the house in which he had not been welcomed.

He was welcomed here.

Clara urged him onto the loveseat and took time to put another log on the fire before she set about making the tea. The water was already hot in a kettle that swung out from over the open fire, and they had only to wait until the beverage steeped.

From a tiny kitchen, she produced as well small cakes on a hand-painted china plate; she smiled as she seated herself on the sofa opposite him and poured out tea into matching cups.

Joel sipped at it, feeling awkward with the delicate china cup in his large hand. A downward glance showed that mud had fallen off his boots onto the fancy carpet, and he swore softly and reached for it.

"Don't worry about it," Clara said. "When it's dry I'll pick it up, and no damage done. One can't expect to entertain a gentleman in such weather without a bit of mud once in a while. Have a cake. Your friends the Groves ladies made them, and they're very good."

He felt himself relaxing in the heat from the fire, and the inner warmth of the tea and the whiskey. The cake was good, too.

Clara leaned her head against the green velvet, smiling at him. "I'm sure Jessie will love the silk; you have excellent taste, Joel."

He scarcely noticed the transition from formal to informal address. "This is a real comfortable place you have here. Very nice."

"Yes. I like it. Eventually I may buy a house, perhaps up on the hill, but for now this is quite convenient. There is an outside stairway as well as the inner one, which is handy for visitors who come after the shop is closed."

After dark, did she mean? Gentlemen friends?

For a moment Joel stared at her speculatively, but she took the matter no further. She sipped at her tea, hair gleaming with an inner fire in the candlelight. She didn't make him feel that he had to talk, and for some reason that made him want to do it.

"I guess a dress isn't as good as what I wanted to take her, but it's better than nothing."

Clara waited, eyebrows slightly raised.

"Well, I didn't exactly want to take her the house, but I thought I'd be able to take the materials to start building it. Only Babcock turned down my request for a loan."

It must be the whiskey, though he hadn't actually drunk all that much. Why was he telling Clara this? But he was, the words sort of leaked out of him, and Clara listened intently, as if what he said mattered to her as well as to him.

"So I guess we'll have to wait until the wheat's in, next summer. Only right now, through until March, I'd have time to work on it more. By summer I'll be too busy with harvesting and working up the land again."

"Babcock's a fool," Clara said.

Joel laughed without amusement. "That he is, but he's the one who controls the money."

"Not all of it," Clara said.

Something in her tone brought his head up. "I've heard his wife is a big spender," he said, though he was fairly certain that wasn't what she'd meant at all.

"Oh, yes, she's one of my best customers. She has been of considerable help in making me a moderately wealthy woman. Of course, I had a small amount of cash when I got here, and I've invested it wisely." Clara didn't mention the fact that she also had friends with more money than discretion, who saw fit to take care of many of her expenses because they delighted in the pleasure it gave her, and the gratitude she showed. "As it happens, I do have at the moment a sum I was considering investing in a mill to be built on the upper Stanislaus. However, nothing has been agreed to yet. I mean, the money is not committed."

For a few seconds that didn't register. Then it did, and Joel remembered Mr. Babcock's suggestion of a private party to finance his house. He put down the cup and saucer very carefully.

"The house I have in mind to build will be a fine one," he said, keeping his tone controlled. "Collateral in itself, I should think. Lending money to build it wouldn't be much of a risk."

Clara sipped at her own tea. "Oh, there's always some risk in lending money. Things happen that a person doesn't foresee. So, a prudent lender takes precautions. For instance, a mortgage on the land as well as the house to be constructed would make such a transaction safer to a lender."

For a matter of seconds rebellion, even anger, surged through him. Clara was smiling, and though her mouth was soft, her eyes were not.

"Speak out plain, ma'am," Joel said. "You suggesting you'd finance my house if I put the land up as well against the loan?"

Clara laughed. "Ah, no fencing around for you! Well, yes, that's what I'm offering you, Joel Shand. The money to build the house you want. I'm well aware you've no intention of losing your land; it will only make you more conscientious about repaying the loan, won't it? And as long as you do that, with the agreed-upon interest, why, there's little risk to either house or land. It's of no great importance to me where I invest my money, only that I draw a good rate of interest on it. And when you've paid me back, after next year's harvest, why, I'll reinvest somewhere else."

Joel moistened his lips. "What interest do you want?"

Jessie was thrilled with the green silk. She held it against her, trying to see herself in the tiny mirror that was all the cabin boasted. "Oh, Joel, it's gorgeous! I can't wait to make it up! And there's enough for a very full skirt, and I'll cover matching buttons...and gloves, too!"

He watched her, grinning his pleasure in her delight. "Next time we get invited over to Rancho Sañudo, you'll put them all in the shade. And when we invite them to our house, we'll see who has the most class."

Jessie laughed, refolding the silk with reverent fingers. "I can just see us entertaining the Sañudos here. Señora Teresa can sit there, and Luis there—and the rest of us will sit on the bed or the floor. And I'll feed them a bowl of beans with corn bread, and—"

He caught her and swung her around, into his arms. "Not this house. The one I'm going to start building tomorrow."

For a moment she forgot to breathe. "Oh, Joel! Did the bank loan you the money?"

"I brought home the first load of lumber. As soon as I've used that up, I'll go back for the next batch. We'll be living in our new house by next summer," Joel said, and kissed her, hard.

He had no intention of telling her, ever, where the money had come from, to build her house.

25

The *Knight's Ferry Bee* of August 12, 1859, carried the
story, complete with a sketch by a local artist, of the new
home of Mr. and Mrs. Joel Shand. Nearly a hundred people
signed the guest book at their open house, where a lavish
table was set for the visitors, many of whom were able to
travel for the first time over the new bridge across the Stanislaus which had at last put the ferry out of business.

Jessie had watched the house grow with mixed feelings.

Joel consulted her on very little to do with it, except for
the decorating which came at the very last. There she was
given virtually a free hand, since he admitted to knowing
nothing about colors and fabrics and fancy furnishings.

Jessie had spent two summers in the heat of the San Joaquin Valley. She had visited, in July, Casa Sañudo, and found
it twenty degrees cooler in the hacienda than in her own
small house, by reason of those thick adobe walls which in-
sulated it against the California sun.

Adobe, Joel said, was for Mexicans. What he wanted was
a traditional American house, like the finest of those he'd seen
in Chicago. He didn't mention his mother's family home
in Toledo, yet Jessie knew his compulsive needs could be
traced back to that. When she tried to point out that the
adobe was so much more protection against the enervating
temperatures, he only laughed.

"Honey, this is going to be a real house! Two and a half
stories high, so the heat will stay mainly in the attic, not like
in this little place where we're right under the roof ourselves!
There'll be big windows that catch the breeze, and high ceil-
ings. Sure, that adobe is cool in the summer, but it's *cold* in
the winter! You saw what that house is like, a fireplace in
every room, and it takes two men and a boy to keep the wood.

213

cut to feed them! Don't worry about it. This house will be everything you ever dreamed of."

It *was* a beautiful house. Jessie wondered uneasily if it was not too big, too elaborate, too elegant for the likes of themselves.

David Tulloch himself supervised the materials that went into it, from Tulloch's mill. None but the finest woods were used. It faced the river, with an imposing veranda opening into a spacious entryway with French wallpaper, all white and gold above the wainscoting. By the time Laurie and Tris were big enough to reach above that three-foot paneling, they'd be old enough to know better than to touch the paper, Joel said when Jessie questioned the practicality of it.

It was the most beautiful wallpaper she'd ever seen. There was more of it in the twin parlors that opened to the right of the entryway, and up the stairs to the second floor.

The dining room, while not as large as the one at Casa Sañudo, was more to both their tastes. There was a cut-glass chandelier, made in Hungary and shipped to San Francisco around the southern tip of South America; when filled with lighted candles, it was enough to dazzle the eyes of the most blasé visitor. Beneath it sat a table of richly polished mahogany, surrounded by ten chairs upholstered in a deep green that matched the deeper tones in the wallpaper. This was Jessie's favorite of all the papers in the house, though not of the elegance of the white and gold of the other downstairs rooms; here, she could pretend she was at home again, in a climate more to her liking, for the walls were covered in a massive mural of a woodland scene, complete with foliage in varying shades of green, and a tiny trickling waterfall repeated twice on each wall.

Joel had had a lavish hand in filling the great sideboard, too, for he said they could not set their cracked old china on such a table; he ordered through Clara Ridback complete service for twenty-four people in a delicate, hand-painted china, and heavy, ornate silverware to accompany it.

It was too much, too soon. Jessie knew it, and tried to temper Joel's buying; he would not hear of taking second-best, nor shorting themselves of anything that went with a house of these proportions and pretensions.

Behind the dining room lay the kitchen and pantries, with both fireplace and great iron stove upon which one could heat two tubs of water at the same time. True to Joel's promise, water was piped in to eliminate any further need for hauling water—except during the dryest part of summer, when the creek did not always provide enough for their needs.

Across from the dining room was a smaller room which would serve as music room (they did not yet have a piano, but Joel said by next year they would buy one) and library. They had few books, yet the cases were there, glass-fronted for protection of the volumes that would eventually fill them.

Upstairs, on the second floor, there were five bedrooms, all of them big and airy, looking out over either the river or the surrounding hills. Jessie preferred the river view, while Joel wanted a view over his fields; they compromised with a corner bedroom that gave them both.

The furnishings were not complete when the housewarming was held, of course. Even Joel had to draw the line somewhere on the spending, and only their own room was fully furnished abovestairs, with the nursery minimally equipped for the two little boys who raced up and down stairs, shrieking their pleasure at their expanded world.

Joel was like a small child at Christmas, Jessie thought, showing each set of visitors over the entire house, pointing out its best features, basking in their admiration.

If only they had earned the money to pay for it first, rather than borrowing, Jessie would have been more likely to do the same. Still, what female would not have celebrated moving into such a fine house? Joel was so proud of it, and of being able to give it to her, and since he wasn't worried about paying for it, why should she be?

The Sañudos did not come to the open house; Señora Teresa was ailing, and Bonifasia had never attended such a gathering in her life. Luis came, several weeks after they'd moved in, and allowed himself to be taken on a tour. He properly admired everything, though Jessie privately wondered what he thought of the gringo house, so different from his own.

He brought her a house-warming gift, handing over a red-leather-covered book, which Jessie accepted with a smile.

Selected Works of William Shakespeare, read the title in gold letters.

"Thank you! How thoughtful! As you can see, our library doesn't rival yours yet!" She brushed her fingers over the cover, and put the book behind one of the glass doors. "So the children don't touch it. I'll look forward to reading it, after they've been put to bed."

Luis was courteous, pleasant, as he always was. Yet it was

215

clearly Joel he had come to see, not herself or the house. The men vanished into the front parlor and, to Jessie's astonishment, closed the door behind them.

What on earth? She knew that in the Sañudo household women were excluded from any discussion of business, but she had not thought Joel would make such a point of it.

Cries and thumpings brought Jessie out of her speculations about the reason for Luis's visit. Laurie and Tristan were squabbling over something, and she had to separate them physically. At a year and a half, Tris was a sturdy child, but he was no match for Laurie, who was eleven months older; he sobbed his frustration and showed a bluish lump rising on one temple where Laurie had struck him with the object of their disagreement, a hammer left behind by the carpenters.

Jessie snatched the hammer away, administered a sharp swat on Laurie's behind, and swept up her son to comfort him, alarmed by the rapid swelling and immediate discoloration.

The parlor door opened and Joel looked out with a scowl. "What the devil's going on?"

"Laurie hit Tris with the hammer," Jessie said, raising her voice to be heard over the bellowing of both children. "In the head."

Joel glared at the three of them. "You baby Tris too much, Jess. Boys will fight over things. Let them sort it out between themselves."

"But look at his head!" Jessie protested. "He's too little to stand up to Laurie and a hammer!"

Joel made no reply, withdrawing and closing the door. No doubt he was embarrassed that his neighbor should see the household in such a state of sound and confusion, but resentment smoldered within her. She didn't baby Tris, she only tried to protect him when it was necessary because Laurie was bigger and stronger and more aggressive.

It took her several minutes to calm both children; Laurie was made to sit in a chair, while she rocked Tristan until his sobs subsided. The older child glared at her, unrepentant, and Jessie wondered uneasily what she ought to be doing about Laurie. He was very rough, and while Joel thought it was only childish play—what else could it be, at less than two and a half?—Laurie disturbed her sometimes. When he became angry, he didn't care what he picked up to strike the younger child.

Joel had promised her household help, and the couple who would move into the little house they had vacated had not yet arrived. Joel had not met the wife, only the husband, whose name was Clifford Murray; Clifford would work for wages, taking Collie's place in addition to the seasonal help hired, and his wife Fanny would assist in the house. Jessie wished the woman were here now, to deal with Laurie while she put Tristan into his crib for his afternoon nap.

"You stay in the chair until I come back," Jessie told the little boy, who stared at her stolidly from dark, enigmatic eyes.

She didn't know whether or not he would do it, but she had to put Tris down. And then she wanted to be on hand as soon as Luis left to learn what he'd come for.

She was flabbergasted when Joel didn't tell her. "Just business," he said, and put on his hat and went outside.

Business? What business?

For a moment she was annoyed, and then she forgot Luis. While she had been gone, Laurie had gotten down from the chair, toddled into the room across the hall, and was pounding a cup into the consistency of sand with the hammer she had been foolish enough to leave lying on the table, within reach if he stretched to his full height.

Jessie stared at the smashed remains of the china, rage filling her to the point where it took all her self-restraint to keep from shaking the child's head loose from his shoulders.

"Laurie, you naughty boy! What will your Uncle Joel say that you've been so wicked?"

The china had not even been used yet, and the cabinet in which it was kept had seemed secure against small fingers; it was a set, and she did not think they could replace the cup. Her fingers cut into the child's arm so that he cried out, and kicked at her, and she swatted him again, only by the greatest willpower refraining from beating him bloody.

He took his punishment in the same way he always did, staring at her tearlessly with those dark eyes so like his mother's, sitting down in a corner of the room to play with his blocks when she had done with him.

She hoped to God he hadn't done Tris any serious injury with the hammer. She wished Annie were here to look at her son and reassure her, but Annie was seldom a visitor; they lived too far out of town.

That night in bed she waited until Joel was in a post-lovemaking lethargy before she brought up the subject of Luis again. "Is something wrong at Rancho Sañudo, darling?"

"No. No more than usual, anyway. Rustlers, he's always having trouble with cattle rustlers. The ones who don't make it in the mines feel they have a right to eat anybody's beef, so they take it. It would save everybody a lot of trouble if they'd just go up in the hills and hunt down wild game, but that's too much effort, I guess." He put an arm around her and drew her close. "Goodnight, honey."

There was more to it than that, Jessie thought. They wouldn't have closed the door just to discuss cattle rustling. She sighed. She supposed that eventually Joel would tell her, whatever it was.

Collie came home just after Christmas.

He was very thin, but he looked fit enough, tanned and with his curly hair bleached even blonder than it had been before. His voice was deeper, a man's voice, Jessie thought as she and Fanny Murray set out food for him on the kitchen table.

Joel saw him ride in and came to the house, leaving Clifford Murray to continue with the last of the planting. He stood in the doorway, grinning, surveying his supposed cousin.

"Well, did you come back rich?"

Collie bit into a heavily buttered slice of bread and chewed with obvious relish before he replied. "Not yet, though I brought in a little dust. I stopped in Knight's Ferry to have it assayed and put in the bank. But it's still out there, Joe. Hell, an army of thousands couldn't cover every little wash and gully in those mountains. They're bound to have missed some of it."

He helped himself to cold roast beef and a hastily heated bowl of potatoes and carrots, left over from the previous night's supper. "I nearly forgot what good cooking is, Jessie. I sure got tired of beans and mush, and picking weevils out of the mush. If it hadn't been I took a day off once in a while to run down a deer, I'd be skinnier than I am."

"You going to stick around awhile?" Joel asked. Jessie looked at him sharply, for there was something in his voice, a subtle nuance that she recognized as out of the ordinary, though she did not understand what it was.

"Until some of the snow melts. God almighty, Joe, you ought to see the snow in that Tuolumne Meadows. Remember where we came through it on the way over the pass? Fourteen feet deep, and that's not even drifts. Fellow by the name of Henderson has a cabin there, and all that was sticking out of the snow was the chimney. A man can't hunt gold under all that, let alone keep warm."

Snow, fourteen feet deep, Jessie thought, cutting apple pie to place before him. How she missed the snow, the cold, crisp weather of Michigan! True, they had always longed for spring weeks before the snow was gone, but there was something exciting about the snow when it began to fall, and it was beautiful beyond description. There was little of beauty about this constant drizzle, except that it washed away the ravages of the summer heat and turned the hills green again.

"Well, glad you're back and nobody shot you for your poke," Joel said, and went back outside.

Fanny Murray was a scrawny little thing of about twenty; she and her husband both looked as if they'd been underfed most of their lives. She had faded red hair and freckles, and though she obviously adored her lanky Clifford, she gazed in slack-jawed admiration at Collie Aubin. She hurried to refill his coffee cup, brought an extra dollop of butter, and offered blackberry jam for his bread.

Jessie allowed him to eat his fill before she asked, "Did you see Mamie while you were in town?"

Collie pushed back his chair with a sigh of repletion. "No. She wasn't there. She was out to Alice's. Did you know Alice is expecting?"

"Yes, of course. Not for another month, though. Is she having trouble?"

Collie raised eyebrows that glinted with the same gold as his hair. "You think Mrs. Groves would fill me in on any such details? I don't think she was even very pleased that I went into the bakery, for some reason. She was very cool."

"She probably thinks you've hurt Mamie, abandoned her," Jessie said. "You *did* tell her you wanted to court Mamie, didn't you?"

He had the grace to look uncomfortable. "Well, yes, but Mamie understands about what I need to do."

Did she? Jessie thought, but did not say it. Instead, she busied herself with the pies she was making. Joel liked fresh pie, and said that Jessie's crust was so much better than Fanny's that she always made it herself.

Collie stood up and stretched. "You think Joel will kill me if I get a few hours' rest before I pitch in and help with the

219

planting? He must be nearly finished with it by now, anyway, isn't he?"

"Not quite. We're planting some of Luis Sañudo's land, too, where it adjoins ours. Joel persuaded Luis that there is more cash money to be made in wheat than in just beef stock; the price of beef has fallen very low."

"And Joel's working Sañudo's land? For nothing?" Collie asked, surprised.

"They have some sort of reciprocal agreement. I don't know what it is." Jessie made a face. "They talk business like the Spanish men, behind closed doors. Little boys playing at secrets, I think."

Collie grinned. "I'll listen in, and report back to you," he offered. "Hey, what's the racket? You got company coming?"

"I wasn't expecting anyone," Jessie said, reaching for a towel to wipe her hands. "It does sound like horses and wagons, though. Here, Fanny, you can put the berries into these crusts. I'll go see who's coming."

She hurried through to the front of the house, complacent about it now after having lived in this luxury for four months. It was a huge house and took considerable upkeep; she'd never have managed it without Fanny's help, and sometimes wished she had a whole retinue of servants, like the Sañudos. It was easy to see now why they had so many.

Her front yard was full of men, horses, and wagons. She saw Joel coming in from the nearer hills to investigate, and stepped out onto the veranda to recognize some of the Mexican workers from Rancho Sañudo.

The foreman, Pedro, came forward smiling a greeting. "*Buenas tardes, señora!* I have come with the promised trees from Señor Luis! He says I am to consult with you at every step, but that you are to defer to my judgment in matters of planting when the soil or the moisture is of importance."

"Trees?" Jessie stared beyond him at the four wagons. Four! she thought, dazed. "They're all full of trees?"

"Fig, apricot, peach, nectarine, cherry, plum, quince, orange, pomegranate, persimmon, filbert—have I forgotten any? Also grapes, gooseberries, raspberries. This is not the proper season to transplant strawberry plants, but those will come in due time."

Overwhelmed, Jessie saw the men climbing down, taking out shovels, preparing to work.

"Señor Luis has made us a plan to follow," Pedro told her, drawing a folded sheet out of his shirtfront and extending it to her. "Unless you request many changes, we should be able to complete the work within three to four days."

Jessie took the sheet, feeling as if it were Christmas all over again. The willows she had planted along the creek (which were beginning to shade the little house, but did nothing for the new one except to provide a bit of greenery to ease the uniform drabness of the landscape) were reaching a respectable fifteen feet or so in height, but she had planted nothing around the big house itself.

She handed the sheet back to him after noting that the house and grounds had been drawn out to scale, with indications of where each of an incredible number of trees were to be placed. "How many men do you have with you, Pedro?"

"A dozen, señora. We will sleep in our wagons once we've unloaded the trees, and we will do our own cooking. You have no need to be concerned with our welfare."

Trust Luis to have considered all these things. Jessie paused a moment longer. "How is Señora Teresa?"

Pedro shrugged. "She is an old lady, señora. And these things that happen, they frighten her."

Jessie's eyes narrowed. "What things? What frightens her?"

Something shifted in the man's face. Again he shrugged. "Ah, old women, they are disturbed by many things, no? *Por favor,* señora, I will speak to Señor Shand and seek his approval before we begin to turn the earth, no?"

He left her quickly, so quickly that Jessie's suspicion increased. What things did he speak of? He had obviously thought she knew of them, then when she had revealed her ignorance had sought to cover up his error.

She stood for a few minutes more, watching as he and Joel consulted over the drawings, before she went back into the house. Joel was keeping something from her, and that in itself disturbed her. She could only hope that it was nothing really serious, nothing that would affect her own family.

The trees went in as if planned by a master gardener, which perhaps Pedro was. He was the only man in the crew who spoke much English, and it seemed to Jessie that, though he was smiling and courteous, he avoided her. There was always something he needed to supervise in a different area when she came out to inspect their work.

Jessie anticipated that Collie would make a ride back to Knight's Ferry to see Mamie; he did not. He joined Joel and

221

Clifford in the fields, and in the evening he and Joel sat talking in the parlor while she bathed the children and put them to bed. They did not close the door, but they spoke in low voices, so that their words did not carry into the hallway. When Jessie joined them, they spoke at once of the planting going on, of the generosity of Luis in providing such an assortment of plants, and she knew they had changed the subject by unspoken consent.

So Collie was being made aware of the mysterious concerns, whatever they were, and he did not seek her out later to explain anything, as he had promised to do.

Jessie's disquietude grew.

26

By mid-January, Jessie knew that she was pregnant again. Her delight was tempered by the knowledge that Alice had delivered a stillborn son only a few weeks earlier, yet there was no reason to think that her own pregnancy would end in such a way.

Collie had gone to town once, returning with that news. He did not volunteer anything about Mamie, and when she asked, he told her that Mamie was well, and very busy in the bakery. Sarah Groves was ailing with some unspecified complaint, and Mamie was doing the work of both of them.

Jessie could not tell how he felt about any of this, except that his mouth tended to go flat when he mentioned Sarah. She longed to visit with Mamie, but a trip to town was difficult to manage. There was so much to do at home, and the children were such a handful. She and Fanny both ran after them all day and still didn't always quite keep up with them.

One day was especially trying. It had rained for three days, which meant that the children had been cooped up inside. Laurie, the natural leader, was quite inventive at thinking up things to do.

He had, by noon, emptied bluing over the sheets Fanny was washing so that they had to be rinsed several additional times to take out the coloring; he had reached up over the edge of the table where a trio of pumpkin pies were cooling and not only gouged the heart out of one pie but burned his fingers so that Jessie had to hold his hand immersed in cold water until he stopped crying; and he had managed to pinch Tristan's fingers in a door so that they turned purple and necessitated a half-hour session of rocking to calm the younger child down.

Laurie capped his performance, just as his father entered the house for a change from his soaked clothes, by pulling over a cup of tea onto Jessie's lap as she sat for a brief rest before putting the midday meal on the table.

Fortunately the tea had cooled enough so that she was not actually scalded, though she jumped to her feet with a cry and pulled the wet garments away from her body.

"Laurie, how many times have I told you—!"

Joel scooped Laurie up just in time to save him from his third smacking of the day. "Here, young man, let's get you out of trouble's way." The boy perched on Joel's shoulder, smiling down on them all. "Jess, you'll have to keep your teacup out of his reach."

"And how do I do that?" Jessie demanded. "He climbed on the chair to reach it. I can't watch him every minute, Fanny and I together can't watch him every minute, and he's destroying the entire house!"

"Well," Joel said amiably, "I think maybe it's time, my boy, that you learned to do what the men do. If Aunt Jessie will dish us up some of that soup, we'll get back to work. You can come along and learn to ride a horse."

"He's not even three years old," Jessie protested, though in truth there was considerable promise in the idea of having Laurie out from under her feet for even a part of each day.

"That's old enough to start learning what it's like to be a man," Joel decreed.

And from that time on, Laurie spent a great many hours with Joel, riding before him on one of the big farm horses, or walking beside him on legs that quickly lost their chubbiness, cultivating the rows of corn. He did not even seem to mind getting cold or wet, though sometimes his lips would be blue when Joel brought him to the house; then Jessie would warm him with a rough towel, and put him in dry clothes, and find him less difficult to deal with because the edge had been taken off his energy.

Tristan, eleven months younger, sometimes stood at the window and watched the pair ride off. "Me, too, Papa," he said once, but Joel only laughed and ruffled his fair hair.

"When you're bigger, Tris. Right now you can take care of Mama."

Life was certainly easier with only Tristan in the house most of the time. He played quietly with his toys, and he loved to have Jessie sing to him or tell him stories. She even read to him out of the Shakespeare book, for all that he didn't understand any of it.

> Take, O take those lips away,
> That so sweetly were for sworn;
> And those eyes, the break of day
> Lights that do mislead the morn;
> But my kisses bring again, bring again;
> Seals of love, but seal'd in vain, seal'd in vain.

Jessie didn't understand it all either, but she loved the rhythm and the beauty of the words; Tris would lie contentedly against her breast, his breath warm on her throat, the softness of his hair against her cheek bringing an overwhelming love and contentment to her.

By late January the rains ceased.

At first none of them realized there was any cause for concern. The temperatures were at a comfortable level, so that Jessie could take the children outside to play, watching them closely so that they did not damage any of the new young trees nor wander too close to the creek or the river. Some of the trees were already putting out tender green shoots and buds, and the wheat on the hills created a rolling carpet of even paler green.

It rained only once during the month of February, and Joel began to scan the sky, looking for clouds that were not there. His temper grew shorter, even with Laurie, though never for long, but Jessie knew he was beginning to worry.

"The wheat needs moisture," he said. "If only there was some way to get the goddamned river water up in the hills!"

When he encountered Clara Ridback in town, she made no mention of the outstanding loan between them, nor did Joel, but it loomed larger and darker in his mind all the time. The house had cost more than he'd originally planned, and

224

then he'd sort of gotten carried away, furnishing at least the main rooms. Without the rugs and sofas and chairs, the place would have been as bare as the Sañudo hacienda seemed to him. People had to look up to a man who had a house the likes of his, Joel thought, but as the days went by and there was little or no rain, and the wheat did not grow as rapidly as had the previous crop, his pleasure in the house decreased.

Always, in the back of his mind, was the knowledge that he had mortgaged his land as well as the house.

Jessie woke in darkness, feeling the warm, hard length of her husband beside her. Joel slept deeply, as a man does after a day of physical labor. The house was cold and she was reluctant to get out of bed, but something had wakened her.

It came again, a small cry. "Mama!"

Tristan. He'd begun to have bad dreams at night, disturbing her sleep as well as his own. She suspected that Laurie contributed to the nocturnal disturbances with his lively tales of monsters in the shadows, of Indians creeping up to scalp them, of unnamed creatures with sharp teeth waiting to pounce from the grass as the children passed.

"Where does he get such ideas?" Jessie had demanded, and Joel only laughed.

"He has an imagination. Tris does, too. He told me a frog had bitten off his toe and showed it to me, as if it was a bloody stump, and said, 'See, Papa?' What a pair they are."

"Well, please don't encourage the things that give Tris nightmares," Jessie requested. Yet, with or without encouragement from anyone, the bad dreams continued. Jessie lay for another moment or two, hoping the dream would run its course and Tris would go back to sleep, until the cry came again.

"No, don't, Laurie, don't!"

Jessie slid out of bed without disturbing Joel and, shivering, pulled a warm robe about her. She didn't bother to light a candle; she knew her way about the house now without illumination.

The floor chilled her bare feet as she padded across the hall and into the nursery. She found her son's bed by feel and sank onto the edge of it, reaching for the little boy.

"Tris! Wake up, darling, you're dreaming! No one is hurting you."

She drew him against her and felt his small heart hammering; his hands clutched at her as he buried his face in her breast, until at last he came awake and realized she was there.

She sat holding him until he fell asleep once more, then tucked him under the covers and stood up. Her feet were like ice. She decided to ask Joel to bring her a pair of warm slippers the next time he went to Knight's Ferry. She always had to get up at night when she was pregnant, and there were several cold months left before she wouldn't need slippers. A smile curled the corners of her mouth. She'd go back to bed and put her icy feet on Joel's to warm them, to prove her need of the slippers.

Only she didn't go back to bed, after all.

As she turned away from Tris' bed, she was drawn to the window that looked out over the hills. Something—

She pressed her hand against the frigid glass as she drew aside the curtain, an uneasiness growing within her even before she understood the significance of the faint glow in the eastern sky.

It was too early for dawn, for only minutes earlier it had been pitch-black, and the glow was too low to be the rising sun; she'd seen that often enough to know where it would be. Higher, much higher than this, for the Sierra stood between her and the horizon.

The glow deepened, brightened, and at last she understood. Fire.

She forgot the chill, though the flesh stood up in goosebumps all over her.

She caught a little toe on a doorframe, passing through it, and the pain scarcely registered. She fell against the edge of the bed, calling Joel's name, and he came awake at once, reaching for her.

"Jessie? What's the matter?"

"Fire! Something's on fire! Beyond the hills, it must be at Rancho Sañudo!"

He was out of bed, striding naked down the hall to look out the same window she'd observed it through; she heard him hit something, swear, then come back on a run. Jessie curled on the bed, clutching the injured toe, momentarily crippled by the pain.

Joel was grabbing for trousers, shrugging into a shirt. "It's got to be a big one, to show up that plain from behind the hills. Call Collie. Tell him to saddle up three horses. I'll get Clifford."

He jammed his feet into boots without benefit of socks and

she heard him running down the stairs. Jessie forced herself to forget the pain, enough to hobble toward the room where Collie slept on a pallet because the room was as yet unfurnished.

He was already wakened by Joel's racket, calling out to know what was the matter.

"A fire, at Sañudo's," Jessie gasped, and heard Collie rolling off the pallet onto the floor. "He said to saddle three horses."

She moved back, shaking with more than chill, to the nursery window. Was the pink glow redder now, or was that only her imagination?

She went back to her own bedroom and lighted a pair of candles, then dressed quickly. She could not force a shoe over the swelling toe, so settled for two pairs of stockings, then ran downstairs.

Joel came through the back door as she reached the kitchen. "Where's Collie?"

"He's coming. Joel, will the fire come this way? Will it burn the wheat, green as it is?"

"It'll burn anything in its path, dry as everything's got," Joel muttered. "Wind's from the southeast, which may be a little in our favor, though not much. Everything's too damned dry." He looked beyond her to Collie, who came on the run through the swinging door still stuffing shirttails into his trousers. "Let's go! Clifford's meeting us at the corral."

He turned briefly to Jessie. "Keep watch on it. If the fire crests the far hill, so you can actually see the flames, take the kids and go down to the river. Wade out in it if you have to. Fanny'll be here to help you in a minute."

And with that he was gone.

Jessie forgot both the cold and the painful toe. Her chest ached with the difficulty of breathing, and the fear was an enveloping, suffocating cloud.

What about the house? Everything they had was here, within these walls, and two women with two small children couldn't save much. Couldn't save anything, if she was realistic about it, she thought.

When Fanny came through the door, her freckles looking large and dark in the candlelight, they hugged briefly, then went back up the stairs to the nursery window.

They huddled there together, praying both aloud and silently, while the little boys slept, watching the glow in the nighttime sky.

27

They saw the blazing barn as they topped the last of the hills, saw the scurrying dark figures rushing helplessly around it. Joel recognized Luis in his white shirt and dark trousers, directing the wetting down of the nearer outbuildings; there was nothing they could do about the barn itself, and the hundred tons or so of hay it had contained.

The hacienda had taken on a pinkish cast, but so far was untouched. Bonifasia and several serving women stood inside the opened ironwork gates in their nightclothes covered by dressing gowns, proof enough of the terror they felt. Joel spared no more than a glance at them; they were safe enough where they were for the time being, and if the old lady was sufficiently terrified to suffer a fatal heart seizure, there was nothing anyone could do about that. Señora Teresa was slightly deaf; maybe, with luck, she'd sleep through the entire disturbance; Joel hadn't seen her among the spectators.

If she wasn't up, watching or trying to prevent the spread of the fire, she was the only such person on the ranch.

No attempt was being made to save the burning barn and its contents; there was nothing anyone could do about that. Instead, Sañudo's men scurried about with buckets wetting down the nearest buildings; even women and young children beat at the grass with wet blankets when stray sparks were carried toward the house or the line of adobe huts where the workers lived.

"Come on," Joel urged, and the trio plunged their horses down over the crest of the hill, into the inferno scene.

A shift in wind would be all that was needed to send that fire racing through the range grass toward his own wheatfields, his own house. The house he had not paid for, and for which he had also mortgaged his land.

Luis heard them coming and turned, with an uplifted arm.

And then there were shouts from some of his own men, who ran back into the firelight, herding four men before them, men who staggered and fell and were prodded roughly to their feet.

Joel never knew for certain whether or not he'd have stopped Luis if he'd realized his intentions in time. For Luis waved his men aside and shot the intruders where they stood. The first two were taken by surprise; they had expected to be hauled back to Knight's Ferry for trial. But there was to be no trial.

The second two arsonists turned in panic, to flee anywhere but toward this man who extracted his own justice, and were shot in the back.

Joel slid out of the saddle, appalled yet feeling that this *was* justice. There was no time to contend with the fallen men; there was still the fire to subdue, to contain.

Luis wasted no time in thanking them for coming. "Maybe we can keep it on that side of the creek if we start a backfire," he said. His voice was hoarse from shouting orders. "Any of you know anything about backfires?"

Both Joel and Clifford muttered acquiescence; only city-bred Collie had no practical knowledge of such things, though he recognized the principle.

Only the fact that the stream which watered Rancho Sañudo divided the estate, and that the blazing barn was on the opposite side of the creek from the house, saved Luis from losing everything.

They lighted their small backfires along the eastern edge of the defile, careful that none grew to the proportions necessary to leap the water to the other side. By the time the main fire reached out to them, there was a sufficient expanse of already burned grass so that the flames had nothing upon which to feed; like some voracious monster, the fire fell back and contented itself with consuming the outbuildings and the corrals still within its reach.

They had done all they could do. They stood and watched the buildings burn.

The horses had been turned loose to run screaming their terror into the night; Luis wasn't concerned about them, as his men would round them up by daylight. At least the fire had been discovered before it trapped the animals and destroyed them.

There was precious little else, except for the hacienda itself and about half of the workers' quarters, that remained at dawn when the barn stood in smoking ruins.

The wind and the backfires had prevented extensive damage to the grasslands that fed Luis's cattle. He had lost all his hay, however, the hay that had been expected to carry his stock through the remaining two or three months of winter before the new grass would be sufficient to feed them.

Luis stood over the men he had shot, flipping one of them over with the toe of his foot to gaze down impassively at the intruder. "Does anyone know this man?" he asked.

There was no reply.

The second man was one Collie had seen in the saloon in town, though he didn't know his name. The third was totally unknown, like the first. The last man, one of those who had tried to run and been shot in the back, drew a long breath from Joel.

"You know him?" Luis asked sharply.

"Name's Callahan. His father's a judge up in Stockton."

A murmur, no more than a sigh, ran around the circle of listening Mexicans. They knew what the Americano justices thought of Mexican land-grant holders who shot gringos, no matter what they were caught doing. The Americano courts insisted on dispensing the justice in California these days.

Luis sought out his foreman. "Put them in a wagon. We will take them to town when it is full daylight."

"There is no wagon, señor. All were lost in the fire."

Luis was tight-lipped. "All right. Then round up enough horses to carry them." He glanced then at the trio who had come to his rescue. "If it would not be too much trouble, *amigos,* to accompany us? To testify to the magistrate that they were caught running from the scene of a fire intended to destroy everything I own?"

"Sure. We'll go in with you. Where are their own horses? They walked in so they wouldn't be heard, but they must have left horses somewhere between here and town."

Luis swung again toward his men. "Find their horses." And then, to Joel, "Come inside. I believe we all need a drink."

The women were nowhere in sight; no doubt they had withdrawn from the tiled passageway when it was clear that the house was no longer in danger.

Luis led the way into the library, where a more welcome blaze greeted them against the morning cold, and lighted several candles to add to its illumination. He poured brandy for them, brandy that burned down their throats and spread outward from their bellies.

Luis dropped into a chair and gestured them to do the same. Clifford sank awkwardly onto the elegant chair, conscious of his sooty clothes and his dirty boots; Collie and Joel gave no thought to such things. They were of little moment in such a situation.

"So," Luis said when he had drained his glass and reached for the bottle to refill it. "It happens again. Not a nuisance, this time, like the running off or killing of my cattle, the ambush and intimidation of my men, the small fires that we find and put out before any damage is done. This time, the damage is great. The lives of my mother and sister were threatened, the homes and lives of all my people."

His eyes burned with a fanatic glaze, so that Clifford and Collie both felt chilled by it.

"You can rebuild a barn and outbuildings," Joel said. "Nobody died, except the ones who deserved to die."

"There are things we must discuss, my friend. Serious things." Luis glanced at Clifford and Collie. "I think perhaps your men might like something to eat, after such a night's work. I will have the women serve you something, señores, if you will follow me."

He did not ask Joel to accompany him; when he returned, he filled the glasses for the third time and looked Joel straight in the eye.

"If this continues, *amigo,* I cannot hold out against the Americano bandits forever. No doubt I will be in trouble this time, for shooting four gringos, including the son of a magistrate. It is even possible..." He hesitated, then finished in a flat tone, "...that the magistrate himself is one of the conspirators who would own Rancho Sañudo, despite the legality of my title to this land which has belonged to my father and to my grandfather before him. Not matter that I shoot only to protect what is clearly mine; they will not let me go on killing gringos."

This was all so true that Joel saw no point in commenting. Frontier justice was swift and final, but the authorities took a different view when the justice was administered by a Spaniard than if dispensed by one of their own.

"An idea has been growing in my head for some time," Luis said, and Joel saw beads of perspiration on the man's forehead that were out of keeping with the temperature of the room. "An idea that I did not really want to contemplate seriously—but which I now must put to you. As a neighbor, as a friend. As one of the gringos, but as a man I believe I can trust."

Joel waited, tired but alert and wound up, because in saving Sañudo's place they might have saved his own as well. His mortgaged house and his mortgaged land. He felt almost sick with relief, knowing how close he'd come to disaster. He waited for the proposal that Luis Sañudo would put before him, and even before Luis spoke Joel knew that it would be to his own advantage as well as Luis's, whatever the proposal was.

Jessie and Fanny crouched at the window, unable to take their eyes off the pinkish glow of the eastern sky. Behind them the children slept unaware, undisturbed by the women's whispers.

Should they not carry out their most precious belongings? Fanny wondered, whose most valued treasure was a china teapot her grandmother had carried across the plains in a covered wagon.

Jessie glanced around her, as if she could see her own possessions in the darkened bedroom. "We couldn't carry enough to be of any use. Get your clothes, if you like. If we have to run, we'll each have to carry one of the boys, so we won't be able to manage much of anything else. But you could take whatever you want to save down to the river now, put it well out on the rocks, and it would probably be safe."

Fanny shivered. "And you would stay here with the babies?"

"I don't want to take them out until I have to. There'll be no way to keep them warm, once we leave the house. There's nothing to be afraid of, Fanny. Just take your things and go down to the river, then come back."

"No," Fanny said, almost inaudible. "I'll stay here, until you go, too."

The room was incredibly cold; Fanny finally got up and brought quilts from Jessie and Joel's room, and they wrapped themselves in them and kept their vigil. Jessie's limbs grew cramped and her toe ached so badly that she knew she'd broken it. Fine shape she was going to be in if she had to make her way in the dark down to the river, unable to get a shoe onto that foot without excruciating pain.

She must have dozed against the windowsill, for she jerked upright when Fanny said, "Look! Isn't it dying down?"

She forgot that she was stiff and cold. It was, surely the glow had diminished!

They watched and waited, and eventually were certain, for the rosy tint faded and above the mountains the sky took on the gray of dawn.

Neither of them suggested going to bed. Neither would sleep until the men returned.

They rose only when they heard the horses coming, and were sure that all three were there.

"They'll be wanting hot coffee, and food," Jessie said, and limped toward the stairs, and the kitchen.

Joel did not speak to Collie until Clifford had gone home with Fanny, until they'd eaten their cold meat and bread and drunk their fill of Jessie's coffee. Until Jessie had gone upstairs, expecting him to follow.

Though Collie was ready for a few hours' sleep himself, he paused obediently when Joel called him back.

"I need to talk to you. In the parlor, where we can close the door, in case Jessie comes back downstairs," he said.

"In the parlor? Hell, Joe, there's no fire in there," Collie protested. "I'm cold clear through my bones now."

There was no yielding in Joel's expression or stance. "I don't want Jessie to hear us."

Collie swore, poured himself another cup of coffee, not to drink but to warm his hands upon, and followed Joel into the parlor.

It was indeed cold in the room. It was a gray day, though there was no rain, the rain they needed so badly. Joel pulled the door closed behind them and faced his half brother in the light that filtered reluctantly through the curtains.

"Luis is in bad trouble," Joel said.

Collie stared at him, eyes aching with the need to rest. "Well, I'm not a complete fool, Joe. I figured that out for myself."

"Tonight wasn't the first thing they've done to him, to try to get his place. It's been going on for months—hell, a couple of years! Only he's running out of options. With our testimony that those men came onto his land for the express purpose of burning his barn, and anything else that would catch fire, they probably won't hang him for shooting them, even if one of them was the son of a judge. There's just a chance he's right, that Judge Callahan had a hand in it, putting them up to it. Because if they can hang Luis for murder, that ranch

233

will fall like a ripe plum into whatever hand is there first to catch it. The old lady and the girl can't do anything to hold it, not without him."

Collie nodded. "I can see that. But why are we talking about all this like it was some deep, dark secret? Jessie's a sensible woman. It won't hurt her to know what's going on."

Joel grimaced and rubbed at his chin so that the whiskers rasped. "She's not going to like what Luis has proposed."

"Oh?" Collie wondered if he was so tired his brain wasn't working at all any more. Nothing Joel was saying seemed relevant to *him*. Why didn't he get it over with, whatever the hell it was, so they could both go to bed?

There was something in the way that Joel was looking at him that made Collie feel as if he should take a step backward, though he resisted the impulse.

"Luis has had an idea for some time now. He didn't want to do it, I don't reckon he wants to now, because that land means everything to him. But he knows he's not going to save it unless he does something drastic. It's only a matter of time before he loses everything...unless he gives up the title, or part of it, to one of the gringos, as he calls them."

"Well, maybe that's the sensible thing to do," Collie said. He sipped at the coffee, after all. "Sell out, take the money, and go to Mexico. Much as that place is worth, even with the outbuildings burned down, he ought to be able to do all right in his own country."

"Mexico's not his own country. His ancestors came from Spain, but he was born right up there, in that big house, and so was his father. He thinks of *this* as his country. He thinks of the ranch as his heritage, and he's not going to walk away from it, even if he could find an American rich enough to pay him for it."

"So what's he going to do?" Collie sipped again.

"He wants to find a trustworthy gringo to marry his sister, and put the title to the land in the American's name. Nobody will mess with an American title, not if the transfer is made while his own title is still holding up in court. Naturally, Luis will continue to live there, to run the place. And it's right next to us, unless you look for the markers you can't even tell where his fields end and ours begin."

"What good does that do anybody? You planning to kill off Jessie?" Collie asked, amused, and then yelped and slopped coffee over his hand and swore. "Damn you, Joe, don't go setting me up for anything! I'll pick my own wife, thank you!"

He did not believe, at first, that Joel really meant this thing. But the expression in Joel's eyes, as much as his words, was convincing.

"Collie, just hear me out. Don't start arguing till you've heard me."

"You can't be serious. You can't expect me to marry some girl I never even met."

"Meet her, then. There's time for that, I should think. Bonifasia is a beautiful young woman, Collie. Black hair, dark eyes with lashes so thick you could sweep the floor with them. A complexion like . . . like a rose petal dropped into a bowl of cream. Delicate, like."

"You're crazy," Collie said, and wondered why the words sounded so hollow.

"No. But I want that extra land joined onto mine. Luis can keep control over the cattle end of the business, but I've already got him thinking about farming part of that land instead of grazing it. Twenty-two hundred acres added to ours, man! We'd wind up with one of the biggest spreads in California."

"It'd still be Sañudo's, far as I can see. On paper the title might be American, but I don't picture Luis Sañudo as the type to just hand over his ranch to anybody else. Besides, I don't want to be a damned farmer. You know that."

"You don't have to be. Let Luis run it; all you have to do is take a share of the profits."

"And marry his sister."

"It won't be a hardship, I promise you. Go up there when you're cleaned up and respectable-looking and see her."

"And what's she going to say to this great idea of her brother's? Marrying a man she doesn't even know?"

Joel's mouth flattened, and there was no humor in it at all. "She's a Spanish woman, born and bred to obey orders. She'll do as she's told."

"And that's supposed to make me happy?" Collie set his coffee mug down on one of Jessie's tables so hard that its contents slopped over onto a crocheted doily; he didn't notice. "Why the hell should I tie myself for life to a woman I don't even know, when I got a girl I've half promised to marry, right over in Knight's Ferry? You picked your wife. Leave me the privilege of picking mine."

"You in love with Mamie?" Joel asked. "Or have you just got used to her? You never proposed to her, did you?"

"Not yet, but I was planning to. When I find that gold, get

235

me a good start so I don't have to be a dirt farmer. No. No, Joe, you and Luis get together and think of something else to save his rancho. Count me out."

"You're not in love with Mamie, and you haven't even met Bonifasia. What can it hurt to meet her? I'd marry her myself, in a minute, if it wasn't for Jessie." Joel grinned, then glanced at the door as if his wife might have overheard. "All I'm asking, Collie, is that you think about it, and meet the girl. If you'd fallen in love with Mamie, you'd have asked her before this. And you wouldn't be willing to go off and leave her for months at a time, searching for gold. She's just a pretty little girl you met and liked, but you didn't fall in love with her. You don't even know what love is, yet. When you do, why, this will seem like calf love to you."

"Joel! Aren't you coming up to bed?"

Jessie's voice drifted down the staircase and through the closed door. Joel called back, "In a minute, honey!" And then, more quietly to Collie, "Think about it. Think about the advantages."

Joel slapped the younger man on the shoulder and moved out into the hall, heading for bed and a few hours' sleep to finish out the night.

Collie stared after him, for the first time angry at this half brother he had virtually idolized, whom he had followed all the way across the country in the search of a more exciting life.

Who the hell was Joel, to try to pressure him into marrying a woman he didn't know, in an alliance to give Joel the land and the wealth he yearned for?

Collie followed the other man up the stairs, heard their voices in the privacy of their room. He wasn't in love with Jessie, but he envied what Joel had with her. The love, the understanding, the companionship. It was what he wanted for himself.

Still, he thought a few minutes later as he shucked his clothes and crawled into bed, he wondered what this Bonifasia Sañudo was like. It wouldn't hurt to take a look at the girl.

28

This pregnancy was not going well. Jessie consulted with Annie after several episodes of spotting and more of cramping.

"I can't bend over and pick up anything off the floor without starting to cramp," she told her old friend. And then, flushing, "I can't even...make love, without causing it."

"Well, you got that Fanny there to help you. I think you'd better stop doing the things that cause the cramping. Let Fanny pick up, and run after the boys. And tell Joel he'll have to restrain himself for a few weeks, see if it makes a difference."

That was easier said than done. Joel needed her loving now—as much as she needed his—especially since he was so worried about the wheat. It needed rain. This was nearing the end of the normal rainy season, and the skies stayed bright blue and devoid of clouds. The wheat didn't grow, and while it was not yet a total loss, she knew Joel was worried sick about it.

Still, if she wanted a baby—and she did, and so did he— it seemed wise to follow Annie's advice.

Joel took the suggestion better than she'd thought he might, though it was hardly something he could accept with enthusiasm. He continued to be affectionate, holding her and kissing her before they went to sleep; it was difficult not to take the release they both craved, but on the few occasions they succumbed to overwhelming temptation, Jessie was frightened by the resulting contractions.

It did help to let Fanny do more of the work, and to spend an hour or two resting during the afternoons, though Jessie felt guilty about that. Laurie and Tristan were too much for Fanny, in addition to preparing meals and doing the laundry. If they'd had the money, they would have tried to find another hired girl, because without Jessie's active participation in keeping it clean, the house began to show the results of neglect. It simply wasn't possible to keep up with cleaning and dusting such a large house, and there were times when Jessie wished that she, rather than Fanny, lived in the little house across the creek.

Ginny Allen came to see her, and so did Eva Curtis, though Eva had to bring her entire brood with her and when her five were added to Jessie's two, poor Fanny nearly went out of her mind trying to keep them out of trouble.

Still, Jessie appreciated their support. Eva advised staying in bed altogether if the new routine didn't solve the problem, though she realized that this would put a dreadful burden on Fanny.

"Lucky *she's* not pregnant," Eva said cheerfully, and pulled her youngest away from one of Jessie's hand-painted lamps before it was overturned. "I guess you heard that old lady Sañudo is very sick, didn't you?"

"No," Jessie said. "I hadn't. She's been in poor health for so long, though, and then I suppose that fire they had was very upsetting. For a while it looked as if there would be charges brought against Luis, for taking the law into his own hands. If Joel and Collie and Clifford hadn't testified on his behalf, they might even have considered him a murderer."

"Well, murderers is what *they* all were, if you ask me." Eva reached out to wipe Arabella's runny nose. "Nothing but the grace of God the house didn't go, too, along with the barn. The Sañudos never was sociable with the rest of us, always kept to themselves, but they never caused any trouble, either. I wouldn't wish them anything but well. Tell me again, Jessie, about that house of theirs, what it was like."

Two days later Jessie was delighted to find Annie on her doorstep, an unexpected visitor.

"Just been over to Rancho Sañudo," Annie said, shedding her heavy shawl and following Jessie into the kitchen, where Fanny produced tea. "Señora Teresa is sinking. Her heart, and there's not much I can do for her. She has trouble breathing, and she coughs all the time; it takes more strength than she has, poor soul. I feel sorry for that Bonifasia; her mother is all she has for company, and she knows she's going to lose her soon. They wanted me to stay on there until the end, but I told 'em I couldn't do that. Bertha Sovereign's third is due any day, and they'd never get me in time, from all the way out at Sañudo's. I have to go back to town, but I wanted to stop by and see how you're doing." Her scrutiny was keen, and Jessie pushed at her hair, which was coming loose from its pins.

"It's better, when I don't do much. But it's so hard on Fanny. If only Laurie would take a nap when Tris does, so she could sit down and put her feet up every afternoon! But Laurie's decided naps are for babies. He's almost three. I suppose he's only normal for that age, from what Ginny and Eva say, but he has so much energy, and he's into everything. Yesterday Fanny heard them giggling in the pantry and went to see what they were up to, and Laurie had painted Tris all over, from head to foot, with blackberry jam. Tris thought it was great fun, and was sucking it off as fast as he could, and trying to rub some of it on Laurie. It took both of us to clean them up, and then Joel came in and laughed. I'm afraid I didn't think it was very funny, and I yelled at him ... I suppose it's because I'm expecting again. Why do we have to be this way, at a time when we should be the most loving we ever are, with our husbands?"

Annie shook her head. "Men wouldn't think things like that was so funny, either, if they was the ones had to clean up the messes. You still showing blood, Jessie?"

"No. Not for three weeks now. And the cramps don't happen unless I bend over or exert myself too much."

"Well, I got all the patients I can handle for right now, so be careful. I'd better get on. Señora Teresa asked about you, bless her heart. I think she'd like you to visit, and I know Bonifasia would, but I told them you weren't feeling too perky."

After Annie was gone, Jessie felt a surge of guilt, that she had so submerged herself in her own difficulties that she had not given much thought to her neighbors. Tomorrow, she decided, she would try to make up some of her pies—Joel said she had the lightest hand with a pie crust he'd ever seen—and send them over with a little note. If she couldn't go herself, she could at least let them know she was thinking of them.

"Good idea," Joel said when he heard of the project. "Let Collie take them; I want to send a message to Luis, anyway, and I don't have time to go myself. I'm trying to finish that little dam on the creek; it won't provide water for more than a few acres, but I feel like I have to do something. I can't just sit here and watch my crops dry up and blow away. John Curtis thinks we may have a really bad summer; he just came down from the hills and there isn't much snow in the mountains to run off come spring. He says a few years ago our creek went bone dry by the end of July. I hope to God that doesn't happen this year."

Jessie stared at him in alarm. "The river won't go dry, too, will it?"

"The Stanislaus? Nobody ever heard of it going clear dry. But it's a hell of a long haul to get water from there for the house and stock. If it's a drought year, I'll get rid of everything but the horses we have to have to work the land, and one cow to keep milk for the boys. Make an extra pie for us, too, will you, Jess?"

"Yes, of course," Jessie said, and while she rolled out the crusts and prepared the dried apples for filling, she prayed more earnestly than ever that God would save them from this impending disaster.

Collie knew that the message to be delivered to Luis Sañudo was an excuse to send him over the hills to the neighbor's, to meet Bonifasia. He was torn between irritation and an odd sort of excitement, overlaid with guilt.

Was it true, what Joel said about not loving Mamie? Just liking her? Well, he liked her all right. He liked being with her, he could talk to her about all kinds of things he never discussed with anyone else. And he liked kissing her.

Joel had laughed when Collie said that.

"You always like kissing girls, no matter who they are. That doesn't mean you're in love with them."

Collie wasn't sure about that. He hadn't kissed very many. Patrice Hammond, far back in the distant past; he'd kissed her, and she'd excited him a great deal. He'd lost Patrice, and then Mamie had come along, and while she had not Patrice's beauty and refinement, Mamie was a pretty little thing, and kissing her had stirred the sensations he longed to give free rein.

He missed Mamie when she wasn't around, and he'd thought of her a lot, especially during the nights alone when he was up in the Sierra for months at a stretch.

He didn't know, now, whether he really wanted to meet this Bonifasia or not. He'd almost rebelled at Joel's request to deliver a note (written and sealed) and Jessie's pies with a verbal message of support to the ailing old woman and the daughter who would soon lose her.

Nobody could make him marry anybody he didn't want to

marry, Collie thought. He was a grown man. Not nearly as naive and inexperienced as he'd been when they'd left Chicago nearly three years earlier.

He'd do what he damned well pleased, Collie told himself, and rode on toward Rancho Sañudo.

Bonifasia was everything Joel had said she was.

Her black hair was done in an elaborate upswept style, held with large combs. She was exquisitely beautiful, with her high cheekbones and great dark eyes with the thick black lashes, a perfect complexion, lips pink and well shaped, and a figure that made Collie realize there was at least some truth to Joel's allegations. That tiny waist, the swelling breasts not quite concealed by her dark blue watered-silk gown, were enough to send interesting sensations through any man.

Did she know her brother had offered her to Collin Aubin?

There was nothing to indicate, one way or the other. Bonifasia acknowledged the introduction in a soft, sweet voice; her smile was shy, yet pleased; she thanked him for Jessie's pies and good wishes, and penned a brief note for him to take back to her.

Other than that Bonifasia did not speak to him, except to say goodbye when he left; she sat, engrossed in needlepoint, while Collie and Luis discussed weather and crops, after Luis had scanned the note from Joel without commenting on it to either of them.

"She's older than I am," Collie said. "I asked Jessie, and she said Bonifasia's twenty-six. More than four years older than I am."

Joel grinned, "Can you look at her and say it matters? She couldn't be any prettier if she was sixteen. Did she stir your juices? Just a little bit?"

Color flooded Collie's face, and finally he had to smile, too. "A little," he admitted. And he didn't realize that from that point on, Joel considered himself to be part owner of Rancho Sañudo.

The wedding was set for the 10th of May. What Bonifasia's feelings were on the matter no one knew; no one asked. The arrangements were all made by Luis and Joel, with Collie's somewhat, though not totally, reluctant acquiescence.

"You're going to have to tell Jessie," Collie said.

"Naturally. Wait a few days. Maybe she'll be feeling better. You ride in and tell Mamie, too."

Collie moistened his lips. "I haven't seen Mamie in a month or more. She must have guessed by this time that things have cooled between us. Might be better if the news didn't come straight from me—if, say, I left the word out to Harry Kelly, and he told Alice. Alice could let Mamie down easy, better than I could, probably."

Joel's eyes narrowed, and he turned away before Collie saw that. It was a cowardly decision, in Joel's opinion, but it confirmed what he had thought about the relationship between Collie and Mamie. If Collie really loved that little dirt farmer's daughter, he wouldn't have been swayed by anyone else's needs.

Still, Joel thought it safer that Collie didn't confront Mamie directly before the ceremony; there was still the chance that he'd break down, if *she* did, and renege on the betrothal to Bonifasia. He'd be fine, once he was married to the girl, once he'd been to bed with her.

He realized, with amusement, that Collie was as much a virgin as the Sañudo girl. He'd be so entertained with being initiated into the pleasures of the marriage bed that he'd soon forget about Mamie Groves.

And there would be no boundary lines between the Sañudo ranch and his own. Already the papers were being drawn up, for a three-way partnership between Luis and Collie and Joel. The new title would ensure that the Sañudos could live out their days on the land of their fathers. And that Joel and Collie would not be dependent upon their comparatively few acres and the whims of bankers like Arthur Babcock.

Finding a time when Jessie felt well proved impossible. As the time drew near for the wedding, Joel's apprehensions about relaying the news to his wife mounted, until he was almost as nervous as Collie.

Jessie spent her mornings throwing up, her afternoons lying flat in a darkened room with a cold cloth over her eyes. She tried to direct her household from that position, and Fanny gave up trying to keep the house scrubbed and polished and concentrated on the absolute necessities. The one good thing about the lack of rain was that she could turn the little boys outside to play, and there was less outside than inside that they could get into, though they still managed to produce a crisis or two each day.

Joel chose a time when Jessie had been resting for several hours and had risen feeling somewhat better, as she often did late in the day.

She sat before her dressing table and brushed out her hair, and then, too tired to redo it in the coronet of braids or even into a bun on the back of her neck, had turned back to him, leaving it flowing loose over her shoulders and down her back. She was twenty-two years old, and though there were dusky smudges under her eyes, he thought she was even more beautiful than she'd been when he'd married her nearly three years ago.

He'd planned out, in his mind, how he would say this. Many times, many different words, all of them difficult. It was even worse than he'd feared it might be.

"We're invited to a wedding on Saturday, Jess," he told her, and felt a surge of guilt at the delight that came into her face. He went on quickly, before she could put any false hope into words of her own, words that would only make the situation more difficult. "It'll be small, just family, because Señora Teresa is obviously dying. But she's anxious to see Bonifasia wed before that happens."

Pleasure became bewilderment. "Bonifasia?"

Jessie put down the hair brush and waited, lips parted.

"Bonifasia is marrying Collie. On Saturday."

For a moment he thought she was taking it very well; and then he realized that the color—what little she'd had—was draining from her face, leaving it chalky.

Her lips formed the word, so softly that he scarcely heard it. "No."

"He met her the day he took the pies over. It was love at first sight, I guess, for both of them." He tried to sound jocular, and wound up sounding defensive.

Her head moved very slowly at first, from side to side. "No. No, they didn't. Joel, what have you done?"

He was taken aback by that question. "Why do you think *I've* done anything, for God's sake?"

"Collie's been in love with Mamie for years."

"The hell he has! If a man loves a woman he doesn't wait years to marry her! He could have married Mamie anytime he wanted to. Certainly when he got his share of the first year's wheat money; he was as well off as most men are when they get married. As well off as *we* were. Any man who can swing an ax can build himself a cabin, and in this place if he

243

can shoot or fish he can keep a family fed. He could have married Mamie anytime, if he'd wanted to."

"What have you done?" Jessie insisted. She was cold, cold all the way through, and her shawl lay on the bed a few yards away; she felt so sick she didn't think she could walk over and pick it up. "What is in this marriage for you, Joel?"

"Jessie! I thought you'd be glad that Collie and Bonifasia are getting married."

She pressed her lips together to keep the tremor from increasing, surveying this man she'd loved for as far back as she could remember, from the moment she'd first seen him. It wasn't the way he'd said. She knew with an instinct as deep and as strong as that love that Joel had, somehow, manipulated Collie.

"It's the land, isn't it? Collie isn't marrying Bonifasia, he's acquiring the land. And Luis—" Joel didn't volunteer the information, so she puzzled it out, slowly, painfully. "He's going along with it, marrying his sister off to an American, to protect his land. Both of you, you and Luis, scheming over the land. That's it, isn't it?"

Exasperation made him spread his hands in a gesture of helplessness and take a step toward her. "Jessie, all Collie had to do was see the girl—"

"Girl! She's years older than he is, and he intended to marry Mamie. You talked him out of it, somehow. I know you never wanted him to marry her, but this is awful, Joel. This is wicked, to think up something like this, for your own benefit."

"I didn't! It wasn't my idea at all, it was Luis's suggestion, and he wouldn't have done it if he hadn't thought it was for his sister's benefit as much as his own! You said she felt bad that there was no one suitable for her to marry. Well, Collie's suitable, and he wants to marry her—good God, what do you think I did, held a gun to his head? And if it benefits all of us—Collie and Luis and us, you and me—why, what's wrong with that?"

Jessie's hands knotted into fists in her lap, fists that wanted to make claws, to strike out at him in a way that had never occurred to her before. He looked the same, the same height and breadth and attractiveness she'd known and loved, but she felt fully what she said. It was a wicked thing he had done to Collie and Bonifasia and Mamie, especially Mamie.

"I'll never forgive you for this, Joel," she said now, in a

voice so low, so controlled, that some of the iciness she felt was transmitted to him. "Never, so long as I live."

It was because she was pregnant that she was taking it this way, Joel thought. But there was something in her face, in the set of her small chin and the compressed lips, in the brown velvet of her eyes, that made him almost afraid.

29

Jessie did not go to the wedding.

Joel did, riding off, dressed in his best, with Collie shortly after dawn on Saturday morning.

He had come to the door of their room and spoken softly. "Jessie? It's time to go now. How are you feeling?"

Jessie did not answer. He stood there in the dimness for nearly a minute, waiting; it was only when she turned her face away from him, toward the wall, that he withdrew and went away without her.

Until last night he had continued to sleep with her in the big bed they had shared ever since moving into this house. After he had told her of the wedding, when he had attempted to touch her, to talk to her, Jessie had lain stiff and silent, until he gave up. During the daytime she spoke to him in as normal a manner as she could manage, in regard to meals and necessary things. At night she did not turn to him, did not respond to his tentative hand on her belly or breast, nor to the plea in his voice.

Last night, when he had come into the room and begun to undress, Jessie had spoken flatly. "I'm feeling very unwell, Joel. The slightest movement makes it worse. I think it would be best if you slept somewhere else tonight."

Joel went rigid with shock. He knew she was upset—he'd expected she would be—but he'd figured she'd get over it within a few days. His immediate reaction was to want to tear off his clothes, and hers, and make love to her. Violently, if necessary, until she succumbed to her own passion and admitted that she needed him as much as he needed her.

He didn't dare, however. Annie had sought him out to warn him, in case Jessie had minimized the dangers; if she were to carry this child safely to term, he must do nothing to bring on a premature labor. To do so might cost not only the child's life, but Jessie's.

He did not dare touch her at all, not even to cover one of the limp hands with his own. He swallowed his rage and his fear, and withdrew from the room. Jessie did not ask where he slept, and if she cried herself to sleep, she did not tell him that, either.

"I don't believe it," Mamie said when Alice told her. She went very pale, and nearly tore her handkerchief between her fingers. "He wouldn't marry anyone else. Not without telling me, himself, that he no longer loves me."

Alice was torn with pity. "Do you think I'd carry such a tale to you without being certain it was true? Collie told Harry himself. He knew I'd tell you."

"How could he? How could he do it, when we...we've talked of marriage, when he'd found his gold..." Tears filled her hazel eyes and slid down her cheeks, unchecked. "Is that it? That Sañudo woman is rich? Is that why?"

"I don't know. I don't know," Alice said helplessly, and held her sister while Mamie cried.

His conscious intention was to buy something for Jessie, a gift to placate her, to make her understand that he loved her, that he couldn't bear this rift between them.

Subconsciously, Joel needed to delay returning home. He dreaded trying to relay to his wife the details of the wedding, dreaded even more not communicating with her at all, and wondered if it would help to get so drunk that he couldn't go home until the following day. Maybe if he didn't return by nightfall, Jessie would become concerned about him.

On the other hand, how terrible it would be if she did not.

He'd had several drinks, but he was far from inebriated when he walked through the door of Clara's shop. There was a customer—he had to think a minute who she was—and he stood to one side, waiting.

Oh, yes, Louise Babcock. The banker's wife. He didn't know her, except by sight. She was a buxom woman, taller

246

and heavier than her husband. Elegantly gowned and shod, she was trying to choose between two hats.

"I like this one," she said, peering into the hand mirror that Clara held for her. "Except for those feathers—I *adore* those purple feathers!"

"I have some more like them," Clara told her. "I could remove the green ribbons from this one and replace them with the feathers, if you like." She glanced past her customer to Joel and raised her voice slightly. "I'll be with you in a moment, Mr. Shand."

Louise Babcock swiveled her head to look at him. "Oh, yes, Mr. Shand," she murmured, and Joel wondered if her husband had gone home and told her that Joel had wanted to borrow money, and Babcock had turned him down. "You're the one who married one of those Mormon women," she said.

"My wife's a Christian, ma'am," he said, feeling the whiskey working in him. "But she's not a Mormon. Her ma married a man who became one, but Jessie never did."

The woman had bulging eyes, rather like a bulldog Joel had once seen. They were fixed upon him. "I understand that she was there, when that man—what's his name? Strang?—when he was shot and killed. I don't know how a woman of sensitivity could bear to go through such an experience."

"Women of sensitivity go through all kinds of things, seems to me," Joel said. Was she suggesting that Jessie was not a decent sort of woman? "Like birthing babies," he said. "They mostly all do it, though it can be a bloody sort of business." And then, as her face became mottled, he added, "Not to mention what they do to get in the family way in the first place."

Blood suffused her face fully at that; the woman turned hastily away from this uncouth lout who had obviously stopped off in a saloon on his way here. She stripped off the hat on her head and handed both bonnets to the proprietress. "I'll take them both. You may deliver them later. Good day, Mrs. Ridback."

She did not glance in Joel's direction as she swept past him on the mingled scents of perfume and perspiration. The back of her neck was still red when the door closed behind her.

"Old cow," Joel muttered, and Clara laughed.

"Yes, she is. But she's one of my best customers. She has the money to buy anything she likes. Did you have to insult her?"

"Seems to me I was just defending my wife."

"I'm not sure your wife would approve your method of defending her," Clara chided gently. "Mrs. Babcock is one of the society leaders in Knight's Ferry, you know. A very influential lady."

He already knew he'd said the wrong thing, that he'd deliberately antagonized the woman, and that incurring her dislike was foolish, no matter what he thought of her privately. He changed the subject.

"I want to buy my wife a present."

"Certainly. That's what I'm here for. Did you have anything special in mind?"

"I don't know. Something to cheer her up." He hesitated, then decided to be frank. Clara was no priss like Louise Babcock. "She's expecting again, and she's not been feeling well."

"Ah! Perhaps she'd like something like this." Clara turned and lifted before him a gossamer garment such as he had never seen, in a pale blue gauzy stuff that showed her hands right through two thicknesses of it. "And over it the lady wears this," she said, and reached for another garment of the same color in a thin silk, with lace at throat and cuffs. "I believe I also have a pair of slippers to match—ah, yes, here they are. The entire ensemble would make a beautiful gift."

He imagined Jessie in the gauzy gown, knowing that her nipples would show through the transparent fabric, as would the triangle of hair below. He felt his sexual desire, long suppressed, rise uncontrollably; Joel shifted his hat in his hand, hoping to cover the external evidence from this woman.

"I could wrap it for you," Clara offered, "if you'd like to take it with you."

He heard his voice, hoarse over the sound of blood pounding in his ears. "Yes. Thank you."

He hadn't even asked the price, but it didn't matter. He might not be able to make love to his wife until the baby was delivered in September, but he had to be able to *talk* to her, to *touch* her. He had to break through the wall of bitterness and anger Jessie had erected about herself.

Clara turned away and began to fold the garments in layers of tissue paper. She stood in such a way that he was acutely aware of her as a woman; her breasts were full and high under the dark green fabric of her gown, and her auburn hair was glorious. One curl dangled, carelessly he thought, over the smooth white skin of her bosom rising out of the tight bodice of the dress.

The things went into a white box and were tied with a string, securely so that he could carry it all on horseback. Clara didn't hand it to him, however, but placed it on the counter. She turned toward the door and locked it, pulling down a shade through which he could read, backwards, the word CLOSED.

"How is your wheat crop, Joel Shand?" she asked then, coming back toward him. "They tell me it won't be a good year for wheat."

He was suddenly cold. "No, it doesn't seem to be. Not unless we get a lot of rain yet, in the next couple of weeks. Even then, it probably won't be enough." His mouth was very dry, and he swallowed painfully. "I don't know if I'll be able to pay you the entire thing, the loan you made me, all at once. Not and have enough to keep my family until the next harvest. Not unless I borrow some of it."

Luis would probably loan it to him, but he hated like hell to ask. Not so soon after the marriage, so soon after the partnership papers had been signed.

Clara smiled. Her lips were redder than Jessie's, and he wondered if she put something on them to make them that way. He couldn't tell for sure, even close up this way.

"I'm not worried about it. If you don't pay it all this year, you can do it next year. Of course, I'll expect interest on the unpaid balance—"

"Of course," Joel agreed quickly, relief sending spasms through him; or was it relief? She was so near, now, near enough so that he had only to bend his head to kiss her—

Jesus, what was he thinking!

"Just before Mrs. Babcock came in, I ran upstairs and put the kettle on for my evening tea. And I've been in these shoes all day." She lifted her skirts and stuck out a foot, sideways, so he could see the trim ankle above the soft kid boot. "I need to get out of them, off my feet. Why don't you come up and sit with me for a cup of tea, and tell me how my investment is doing, exactly?"

It was dangerous, going behind her up those narrow stairs. He knew it, yet he went. His blood was like clotted cream in his ears, so thick he felt deaf except for the sound of the pulses there. Scent wafted out behind her, and woman-smell, tantalizing.

He'd joked with Collie about Bonifasia stirring his juices. Well, by God, this woman was certainly stirring his own! How long had it been since he'd had any release? Weeks, since Jessie and Annie told him he mustn't endanger the baby by making love to his own wife.

They emerged into Clara's apartment, and she waved him toward the same loveseat where he'd sat before. "Excuse me, let me get out of my shoes, and this corset—"

He didn't sit down. His mouth was dryer than ever; what he needed was another whiskey, not a cup of tea.

What he needed was to get out of here. Take his package with the gifts for Jessie, and get the hell out of this apartment.

He didn't go. He knew he couldn't. He had put his box down and stood waiting, and when Clara walked out of the bedroom beyond the velvet curtain that covered the doorway, she was wearing one of those thin things like what he'd bought for Jessie.

It was green, and it wasn't totally transparent, but he could see the outline of erect nipples, which were barely covered as the neckline plunged nearly to her . . .

Joel felt sweat breaking out on his body, heard his own breathing.

"You take yours without sugar, don't you?" Clara asked, and bent to reach for the teapot. The garment fell forward, loose around her, and he saw that she'd not only taken off her corset and her shoes, she'd taken off everything else as well. Her flesh was creamy white, unblemished; one thigh flashed before she drew the cord tighter around her waist and straightened up.

She didn't pick up the teacup, however. He no longer held his hat in front of him; he'd dropped it onto a chair when he walked into the room, and there was no hiding his need. His desire.

Clara came right up to him, so that he felt her breath on his face, still smiling. He didn't remember who reached for who, but suddenly they were entwined, arms around each other, her soft flesh pressing against him, her mouth open beneath his, tongue probing, at first delicately and then with a rising passion.

He wasn't drunk, at least not on whiskey. He would excuse himself, later, with the fact that he hadn't touched his own wife in weeks, and couldn't for months more. A man could only stand so much of doing without what he'd come to have so much of, what he needed as much as he needed the land and the food he ate.

He carried her into the bedroom, shouldering the velvet

250

curtain aside; there was a velvet coverlet on the bed, but it had been turned down to reveal clean white linen sheets.

The only light came from the other room, but he could see enough of her, all right; magnificent breasts and belly and thighs, and that glorious auburn hair spread out on the pillow, free of its pins.

No man could resist her, Joel thought, and in a burst of anger, no man should have to, after what he'd been through.

Clara offered him her body, and he took it.

30

By the time he reached home it was full dark. He'd had time to think, to be ashamed, to realize that Jessie would kill him if she knew. Well, there was no reason why she had to know. No one had seen him leaving Clara's place, and they had no reason to suspect the truth even if they had. He carried a box of things he'd bought for his wife, after all.

God knew he felt better physically. All those nights of wanting Jessie, not daring to touch her, and then standing at that wedding ceremony this morning and seeing Collie and Bonifasia married, imagining their first night together— hell, what man wouldn't have been driven to do what he'd done, when the opportunity offered?

It wasn't quite enough of an argument to assuage his guilt, but it came close.

There were lights in the kitchen, and also in his and Jessie's room upstairs. Joel was surprised to find Fanny in the kitchen, turning with a basin of steaming water as he entered from the back.

"You still here? Is something wrong?"

Fanny rested the basin on the table. "The missus has been poorly all day. I didn't want to go home and leave her alone, not with her having those cramps for the past few hours. Ever since the middle of the afternoon. I wasn't sure if I should send Clifford for Mrs. Ryan or not; the missus said no, that you'd be home any time. She's better now, I think, but I was going to sponge her off some and get her into a clean gown, so she'd sleep better. If you're hungry, there's still stew in the kettle."

"No, I'm not hungry. Was she up this afternoon when the pains started? Did she do something besides rest, the way she's supposed to?"

"She got up and came down to help me when she heard all the yelling." Fanny grimaced apologetically. "I couldn't manage all by myself. Those little devils—" She paused, remembering that they were Joel's children. "I mean, that Laurie, he climbed up and opened the top part of the china cabinet, when I was busy out here, and started throwing down those crystal glasses for Tris to play with. Tris thought it was very entertaining until the first one smashed, and he cut his hand, and then Laurie fell off into the broken glass, too, and it was the worst mess I ever saw. I cut my own feet, right through my slippers, when I went running in there to see what was going on. They both was scared when they saw the blood all over themselves, and started screaming bloody murder, and *she* heard 'em and came running downstairs—"

Fanny paused for breath. Her freckles stood out starkly on her normally pale face. Joel had never understood what Clifford saw in her; she was the homeliest, scrawny little thing, but she worked like a trooper, Jessie said.

"I didn't know which to do first, get her back to bed, or tend the little ones. They wasn't cut so bad, when we got 'em washed up; we just tied rags over the worst places. I was more worried about the missus; she couldn't hardly get back up the stairs into bed, and it was hours before she finally dozed off to sleep again. She really wants to carry that baby bad, Mr. Shand, but I don't know if she's going to be able to do it. Not with four more months to go, and her getting like this every time she moves, practically."

He wanted the baby, too, but he wanted Jessie more. He bounded up the stairs ahead of Fanny and let himself into their bedroom.

Jessie stirred and turned her head, and for an instant Joel saw another figure superimposed on her image: auburn hair rather than pale blond, a fuller figure, an open, eager mouth. And then it was Jessie, his beloved Jessie, looking pale and frightened.

"Honey," he said, moving quickly to the bed, "I'm sorry

252

I'm so late getting back. I went into town—I brought you something."

He rested the white box on the edge of the bed, but she didn't look at it.

"Did he do it? Marry Bonifasia?"

"Yes. I swear to God, Jessie, Collie wanted to marry her! I didn't have anything to do with it."

She stared at him, and he felt as if she probed inside his mind, seeing the truth of all things there. The idea was preposterous, of course, but it made him feel afraid.

She put her hands on her rounded belly under the sheet, and he could tell by her breathing that she was suffering another of the contractions that tightened the abdominal muscles in that grotesque imitation of labor. An imitation that could, at any time, become real, he supposed, and expel the child too early. It couldn't possibly live if that happened now.

"I thought you'd come hours ago, or I'd have sent Clifford for Annie," she said. There was no censure in her voice, only a statement of fact, and Joel felt the first flickering of understanding of what his burden of guilt would be like. Tears squeezed from beneath her closed eyelids. "I don't want to lose this child, Joel. I lost one, and that was enough. I want this one to be safe."

"It will be," Joel said, covering one of her hands and pressing it reassuringly. "Just stay quiet, and don't go running downstairs no matter what happens. I'll see if I can find someone to come out and help Fanny for the next few months. Maybe even Annie would come."

"No. She won't come. She's needed by too many other people."

Fanny stood in the doorway with the warm water. "You want I should sponge you off now, missus?"

"I'll do it," Joel said quickly, but Jessie rolled her head from side to side, not opening her eyes.

"No. Let Fanny do it. I'm so tired, Joel. Please go away and let me sleep."

And so he went away, bitterness building his justification for what he had done earlier in the evening. And Jessie's tears oozed silently in the dark for a long time before she slid into slumber.

Eva Curtis had told her that summer was a terrible time to be pregnant. This pregnancy proved it.

The last rainfall dampened the ground on the 17th of May. It wasn't enough moisture to change anything. The crops were stunted, though not totally destroyed; the wheat produced half the bushels per acre of the previous year, and though the drought raised the prices of everything, it was not by enough to compensate for the reduced crops.

Joel made a payment to Clara, plus an interest payment on the outstanding balance. He began then, doggedly, to rework the land for the next crop. He had a year's grace, but another such year, without sufficient rain, would probably cost him his house. Even Luis could only help him so far; Luis had suffered this year, too, like every other farmer in the valley.

The white box sat on the dressing table for four days before Jessie opened it. She lifted the gossamer gown and felt her jaw sag; she'd never imagined anything so sheer, and blushed at the thought of wearing it, even before Joel.

Before Joel. Well, she hadn't been to bed with Joel for some time now. He'd made up a bed in one the back bedrooms, and at least she didn't have to fight with him about that.

There was no way to keep it a secret from Fanny, who must make the beds because Jessie couldn't bend over enough to do it. She told the girl that they'd decided to sleep apart for now, since the slightest movement disturbed her, and Joel must be up so early. She didn't know if Fanny believed her or not.

Jessie examined the gift articles, her eyes blurred, and then she refolded them and put the box aside. The gown and the robe that went over it were for lovers, and she no longer felt as if she and Joel were lovers.

Truly, even if she hadn't been so hurt and angry over Joel's manipulations of Collie and Bonifasia and Luis—she was convinced that he *had* manipulated them all, for the land— she was not feeling very lover-like.

There was virtually nothing she could do, save lie in bed, that didn't bring on the dreaded contractions. The pain was not severe, it was more discomfort than actual pain, but every time the contractions began she feared a premature birth. Just such as had happened when she was raped by Cass Merriam back in Missouri, when Joella Viola had been born too early and had soon died. That could not happen again, she prayed. Please, God, spare this child, and I won't ask for another one. Just this one more, a normal, healthy son.

During the harvest season Joel would rise before dawn,

as he had done when the crop was a good one; it took just as long to cut the stunted wheat as it had taken for the good crops before. Only the yield was less. He would be gone from the house before Jessie and the children stirred in their beds, to take advantage of the cool morning hours. The heat did not bother him the way it did Jessie, but there were few men, even the Mexicans, who could work in the afternoons.

The new alliance meant that Luis sent his men to help with the harvest; when the crew moved to Luis's lands, Joel and Clifford would go with them. Joel was persuaded to the Mexican custom of *siesta,* sleeping during the heat of the day, then returning to work again in the evening.

Jessie seldom saw him, and she made no move to invite him back into her bed. She grieved for Joel as if she had lost him forever, as indeed she wondered if she had. He said no more about where he slept, in fact spent so little time in the house that he didn't say much about anything. He didn't even ask why her eyes were so often puffy and reddened from the tears that leaked out in spite of her efforts to prevent them.

Joel did find another woman to come out from Knight's Ferry to help with the house and the children. Her name was Sally Arminter. She was past thirty and looked forty, mostly because she was overweight. She grunted when she climbed stairs or bent over to pick things up from the floor, but she was a good cook, and she had a way with the little boys that both Jessie and Fanny admired. She liked them, fed them treats, and paddled them impartially when they got out of line.

Sally's husband was a miner, and he'd kept them very well with the gold he found until a few months earlier when he'd been waylaid by claim jumpers and beaten senseless. He was recovering now, and Sally needed to earn their keep until Fred was able to go back to the gold fields; she agreed to come only if Fred could come, too.

The Arminters slept in a shed behind the house and ate in the kitchen. Knowing they would not stay long, Jessie was grateful for the help while it was available. She no longer had to feel guilty about what poor Fanny tried to do alone.

Summer burned through the valley with a vengeance, scorching everything in its path. Sally had brought a thermometer with her, which was nailed to the side of the house, and on days when Jessie looked at it at seven o'clock in the morning and saw it standing at over a hundred degrees, she knew the day would be dreadful. It was not actually that hot yet. The mercury rose because the sun shone directly on the thermometer early in the morning, but one could gauge by that early reading what the temperatures would be before the day was over.

Sally didn't seem to mind the heat particularly; she perspired profusely, and though she would sometimes wet down a towel or an apron to wind around her head, she was not slowed down because of the heat. "I just like to know how much I'm suffering," she'd say, after checking and reporting a temperature of 112 degrees.

Jessie's suffering was genuine. She felt weak and sick whenever it got hotter than about ninety degrees, a sickness which passed when evening came and the temperatures dropped again. Annie, who came out at least once a week to see her, said that she felt the heat worse than other people because she didn't perspire enough.

"It's a cooling system," Annie explained. "If you was like that Sally, water running out of her like a spring freshet, it wouldn't bother you so much. I guess the Lord intended you to stay in a different climate from this one."

Jessie thought wistfully of the Oregon country Zadie described in her letters, but after a time or two she didn't mention Oregon to Joel. He made it clear he would never consider moving there.

They practiced the local cooling system, for what it was worth. At the crack of dawn, before the sun actually touched the eastern side of the house, they would draw all the blinds on that side, and close all the windows, to keep in whatever coolness they'd managed by having everything wide open at night. As the sun moved, Fanny would move just ahead of its path, shutting windows and drawing shades, until in midafternoon they could bear it no longer and must open the windows on the shaded side of the house to let in whatever breeze could be caught. By suppertime the house would again be wide open on all sides, allowing them vagrant breaths of air.

Jessie grew to hate looking at herself in the mirror. Her belly bulged with the approaching birth, and her skin had grown sallow; inside the shaded house, it looked yellow and unhealthy, yet she could not bear to go outside where the sun might have given her back some of the color of which her pregnancy had robbed her.

Except for her stomach, she was thin. Annie, Sally, and Fanny all urged her to eat, at least for the child's sake, and she tried. But the food seldom tasted good, except for the melons and fruit that Luis sent over from Rancho Sañudo, and old Silas Wofford sent out from Knight's Ferry by way of Annie.

She would have died, Jessie thought, except for those fruits. Great luscious peaches and nectarines, sweet and juicy; apricots the color her cheeks had once been; chewy figs that must be eaten in moderation if they were not to bring on a premature birth, Annie warned; raspberries and strawberries that Fanny served with thick cream. And avocados—she loved avocados.

Jessie went nowhere; travel either by horseback or by buggy was strictly forbidden, both by Annie and by Joel. (He did pay that much attention to her, Jessie thought, though he mostly gave his orders through one of the serving women, rather than directly to her.)

Annie insisted that she get some exercise, though it must be of the sort which didn't bring on any alarming symptoms; otherwise, she pointed out, Jessie would have no strength, no muscles in shape to deliver her child.

The only exercise that didn't precipitate immediate difficulties was walking, and she tried to do that inside the house during the day, out among the trees Luis's men had planted for her in the evenings. Many of the trees had not lived, because they hadn't had a good enough start before the rains ceased. Had she been able, Jessie would have carried water in buckets from the dwindling stream for them; it was hard to watch them die. It seemed almost a premonition of what was to come, of the death of her child. She tried not to allow herself to think about that, but the loss of her precious trees was deeply disturbing.

The great and beautiful house looked better, now that Sally was there to help keep it dusted and polished. But the wood felt warm under her hands when Jessie touched a wall or a window sill. The floors were heated beneath bare feet.

If only Joel had listened to her, had built of adobe and tile! She remembered the smooth coolness of the tile at Casa Sañudo, and wished she were able to go and visit there, to escape, even briefly, the temperatures that were leaching the life out of her.

John and Eva Curtis came to visit occasionally, and Ginny and Oliver Allen less often, since they were farther away. Several times Mamie rode out with Annie, but since she and Jessie could not contrive to be alone for more than a few minutes at a time, they did not talk of the things uppermost in their minds.

Once Mamie asked, with tears heavy in her thick-lashed hazel eyes, "Is he happy with her, do you think?"

And Jessie, heart aching for her friend, replied, "I don't know, Mamie. I haven't seen either of them since the wedding." She might have added, Joel goes over there, and he must know, but he doesn't tell me. He seldom speaks to me at all. That, however, she kept to herself.

If she thought her own unhappiness was a secret, Jessie was mistaken. Anyone who had known her, seeing her now, would recognize that more than a difficult pregnancy troubled her. They all guessed rightly that things were amiss between Jessie and Joel, yet each held her own counsel and asked no questions.

By late August Jessie wondered if her personal misery would affect her unborn child. Where had it gone, all the happiness she had known with Joel?

Was it worth it, to continue to blame him for something that was over and done, which nothing could take back, to continue this course of unforgiveness?

It wasn't, of course. Yet she didn't know what to do about it, how even to begin to chip away at the wall between them. She saw so little of Joel that the opportunities were scant for so much as a friendly word in a friendly tone of voice.

It was a Saturday and Sally and her recovering Fred had gone into town for the day, to visit friends and attend to their own business. Fred was nearly ready to strike out again for a few months of gold seeking, though Sally had promised to stay until Jessie was on her feet after the childbirth.

Fanny had baked the morning's bread and laid out cold meat and fruit for the noon meal, then left with Clifford for a swim in the river. Fanny seldom took any time off at all, and when she'd asked, somewhat timidly, if Jessie thought she could manage with the boys during the afternoon, Jessie had urged her to go. The thought of the cool green and frothy waters of the Stanislaus was almost more than she could bear. She hadn't seen the river in months, and though she knew it was now very low, and that it was muddy instead of clean, she pictured it as she loved it. Had it not been for the Stanislaus, there would have been no beauty in this land at all.

Tristan was put down for a nap on a pallet in the dining room so that Jessie wouldn't have to go upstairs to attend him, and she thought she could keep track of Laurie for a few hours.

For once the child played quietly in a corner of the room where she sat with her book of Shakespeare open on her lap. She tried to read—this book, along with the Bible, had been her primary source of comfort during the months she had been made almost an invalid—but she couldn't keep her mind on the words.

She longed for a different sort of comfort, for her husband's arms around her, his lean hard body against hers, his murmured endearments. Tears blurred her vision, tears of self-pity, and she was ashamed of them before they fell, yet she could not stop them.

The situation was at least partly of her own making, Jessie thought. And to end it would probably depend entirely upon herself. How, then, did she go about it? How did she take the first step toward healing the breach?

Engrossed in her own thoughts, she forgot about Laurie. She did not notice that he dragged a chair a few yards toward a window, did not see as his small fingers tugged at the heavy braided cord that held back the draperies when they were opened.

They were not opened now, for they helped keep out the heat, and the cord hung in a loop that could be unfastened easily, even by a three-year-old. One had only to lift the end of it off the hook that held it, and then refasten it the same way, to secure the length of green velvet to one side.

Laurie was intrigued by the noose formed when the drapery was closed. He had seen that shape before a week or so earlier, when Joel had taken him to town in the buggy to bring back supplies. That one had not been a braided velvet cord, but a rope, and it dangled from the limb of a gigantic oak tree outside of town.

"What's that?" Laurie had demanded, and Joel, as usual, had taken the child's question seriously and answered it truthfully.

"It's a hanging tree. It's what they do with bad men, who kill other men or steal horses or cattle. They put the rope around their necks and hang them."

Laurie squirmed on the seat to look backward as they drove on past the hanging tree, watching the noose as long as it could be seen. And now here was a similar noose in his own home.

He could reach it if he stood on the chair. Aunt Jessie

didn't like him to stand on chairs. He slid a glance her way, to see if she were watching. She paid no attention to him, and so he moved the chair carefully to where he wanted it; it slid easily on the waxed boards, with almost no sound.

He had to reach high to unhook the end of the cord, and then it was too short to put about his own neck. Laurie considered for a moment, and then, with another glance at Aunt Jessie to make sure she was still inattentive, he stepped upon the chair's arm.

He teetered there, steadied himself, and brought the loop around his neck. Now, to complete the noose, he had only to reach up and put the end of the cord back over the hook there, and be the bad man being hanged.

It was a game. If it was fun, he'd play it again, later, when Tris woke up. Tris always liked his games except when he got hurt. Tris was a crybaby.

Had the distance been another half an inch, he couldn't have done it. As it was, Laurie secured the noose around his own neck, and then, thrown off balance by the effort of stretching to his utmost limit, he pitched sideways.

The chair slid out from under him, skidding on the waxed floor. His legs flailed, and his arms, and the noose tightened around his neck so that he could not breathe, could not cry out.

Jessie heard the chair. At first she did not credit what she saw, the little figure dangling, struggling, three feet off the floor.

She gave a strangled cry and sprang out of her chair, reaching for him, lifting him, easing the pressure on his neck. The cramps cut through her body at the effort, yet she dared not slacken her efforts. His face was so close to hers, turning blue, the dark eyes wide and frightened, and she had to lift him enough to loosen the noose...

Dear God, please, please give me strength!

She tried so hard, and felt she was winning the battle, for Laurie gave a choked cry that moments earlier had been impossible. Using both arms, she lifted him as high as she could, ignoring the knifing pains in her own abdomen. Yes, the child's face was red now, not blue; he was getting at least a little air, but he was so heavy, such a sturdy, husky little boy.

Her arms ached with the effort of holding him. If she could get his feet on a chair, then she could use one hand to release the cord from its hook. Only the chair had slid beyond her reach. She balanced on one foot, reaching out with the other in the hope of hooking a toe around a chair leg to draw it close enough.

It was beyond her. She couldn't do it. It took all her strength, using both arms, to keep Laurie high enough so that the cord did not strangle him.

He struggled, making it harder for her to hold him, crying out now in his terror at this game that had gone wrong.

His knees struck her belly, hard enough to make her cry out in turn; she tried to reason with him, to beg him to hold still, but he was too frightened to hear or obey.

"Fanny! Fanny, help me!" she screamed, and knew her cries would not carry to the little house across the creek, nor to the river. "Oh, God, Joel, somebody! Help me!" Jessie screamed.

Laurie fought Jessie, fought the velvet rope, and Jessie concentrated entirely on keeping the child high enough so that the noose would not kill him.

She was totally unaware of praying, over and over, Please, God. Please, God. Please, God.

31

She never knew how long she fought for Laurie's life, and perhaps for her own and that of the unborn child.

After a time she became aware of wetness between her legs. The pain in her belly and in her chest was unrelenting now, and her arms felt as if they were torn from their sockets. When she tried to hold the child with one arm, to hitch him upward far enough to loosen the cord, the noose would tighten so that she had to give up and use both arms to keep him high enough.

Laurie was hysterical; had she been able to soothe him into quieting down she might have managed to do *something*. As it was, she had to fight both the little boy and the noose;

she forced herself to ignore what was happening to her own body.

She felt the warm trickle, saw the blood on the floor beneath her feet. And then she heard a sound from the kitchen.

At once her flagging strength was reborn. She inhaled deeply and screamed with all her might. "Fanny! Fanny, help me! Help me!"

It was not Fanny. Joel stood in the doorway, then practically dove across the room, one arm encircling her as he lifted Laurie easily and tore the velvet rope loose from the confining hook.

Jessie sank onto her knees, heedless of her skirts in the blood there, sobbing for breath, doubled over until the pain eased in her chest.

Laurie was crying, clinging to Joel.

"My God, Jess, what happened?"

It took her a few minutes to tell him. She was exhausted; her breath came in agonizing gulps.

"Oh, Joel, I prayed you'd come! I don't know how much longer I could have held him, and I couldn't reach the chair . . ."

"It's all right now. Nobody making this much noise could be hurt very bad," Joel said, putting the child on his knee as he knelt beside her, reaching for her. "Is it starting? Are you having the baby?"

"I don't know, I suppose so, but it's too early! I'm bleeding, and it hurts, Joel! It hurt so much to try to hold him up, but if I didn't, he would strangle, and I was afraid nobody would come!"

She leaned into him, weeping, and even in her fear knew the comfort, the joy, of renewed closeness with Joel.

His arm tightened briefly, then released her. "I'll send Clifford for Annie, and then I'll carry you upstairs. Don't try to move until I get back here with Fanny. Laurie, listen to me. You have to stop crying and be a big boy and take care of Aunt Jessie until I get back, all right? Laurie? Can you be a big boy?"

Laurie drew a final hiccoughing breath, considering the matter. "My neck hurts," he said, putting his hands to the marks where the cord had bitten into his flesh.

"Yes, I know it hurts, but Aunt Jessie saved you, and now you're all right. But Aunt Jessie is sick, and you must take care of her for a few minutes."

He was on his feet, running; she heard the back door slam

behind him, heard his shout long before he was close enough for Clifford to hear him.

Jessie crouched there on her knees, feeling the spreading wetness, gasping for breath when the contractions eased, praying that it was not too soon for this child. Only a few weeks early; many children lived when they were born a few weeks early.

If it didn't, it would be Laurie's fault.

The thought came into her mind as she stared at the small face with the tousled dark curls. Laurie leaned toward her, putting a small warm hand on her knee. "You hurting?" he asked earnestly.

He was only a child. He might well have killed himself, playing some childish game. But he hadn't done it on purpose, he bore her no malice, and she was swept with shame at the fleeting bitterness she had felt.

"Yes, Laurie," she said softly. "Aunt Jessie is hurting. Hold my hand, will you, until Uncle Joel comes back?"

He crept against her, into what lap remained, and they were clinging together, when Joel and Fanny returned, consoling each other.

Joel carried her upstairs, and Fanny brought towels to make a pad beneath her. It was Joel who undressed her, murmuring things that made her feel better even though nothing had changed her physical condition. It had been stupid, wicked, to waste so many of the days they might have had together. What if she died now? What if she bled to death, giving birth to Joel's child? What if there were no more days together, after this one?

His hand closed over hers, and Jessie turned her own, so that she could squeeze his. "Joel..."

"I'm here, honey. Clifford's gone for Annie, and Fanny and I will stay here with you."

"I love you, Joel," she said.

He bent to brush his lips across hers. "I love you, too, sweetheart. Lie still now, and rest."

"Don't leave Laurie alone," she reminded. "See that he has his supper, Fanny. And listen for Tristan when he wakes from his nap."

"I'll see to 'em, missus," Fanny said. She looked scared and very young. "If the mister will stay with you here, I'll see to the younguns, and put on something for supper."

"It doesn't matter what," Joel said, not looking at her.

"Anything cold will do. I'll sit here until Clifford and Annie get back."

The contractions seemed to be slowing. Joel kept one hand on the mounded belly under the sheet, gauging the intensity and roughly timing them. After a while he realized that she had fallen asleep, and he stared at her, an ache in his throat. He'd never prayed for anything in his life, and he'd often made fun of Jessie because she prayed for everything from nice weather for a picnic to having the peach tree live and her hair turning out nicely when they were going to a party or a celebration.

He closed his eyes. If there was a God, a God who listened, who cared, as Jessie insisted He did, then what harm could it do to call upon Him, as his mother, too, had always done? He'd never seen that it helped his mother much, but Jessie often got what she'd asked for.

Please, God, don't let her die, nor the baby, either.

If, as he'd always suspected, there was no one up there listening at all, why, he hadn't made things any worse, Joel thought, by pleading with no one.

Rosalie Leona (the middle name for Joel's mother) was born at dawn on the 2nd of September, 1860.

She was not as pretty a baby as either Laurie or Tristan had been, but she was alive, and she howled lustily and sucked readily after she got the idea of how her stomach could be filled.

She was dark and smaller than either of the boys had been. Jessie had been in labor for four days, and she was so exhausted that she was scarcely aware of anything; she wanted only to sink into the bliss of sleep, but she knew the baby was a girl. She smiled drowsily when Annie placed the tiny bundle in the crook of her arm. Bigger than Joella Viola had been, and so different. Surely this one would live.

Joel barely glanced at the baby. "How's Jessie?" he demanded of Annie.

The older woman pursed her lips. "Well, she wasn't in as good a shape to have a baby as she ought to've been. Trouble the whole time, and this heat's enough to kill a girl like her. And she's lost a lot of blood. Matter of fact, she's still bleeding, some, but I don't think it's a hemorrhage, now. I'll stay on until she's out of danger, though there's not much I can do if she keeps bleeding, to tell the truth. There's something else, Joel. I'm no doctor, but I've delivered a lot of babies over the years. And the way she's tore, I doubt if Jessie will have any more. I've seen a few cases like this, where the womb was damaged, so it won't hold a baby past the first couple of months. Makes a woman miscarry time after time, if she gets pregnant."

Joel met her gaze squarely, though inwardly he was quaking the way he had when he'd known he was going to make love to Jessie for the first time. "You saying I can't ever have Jessie for a wife again, without killing her?" Was this to be his punishment for that episode with Clara? But he didn't believe in divine retribution, did he?

"No. No, I ain't saying that. Whatever you two do after she recovers from this is up to you. And most women don't die from a miscarriage; they just bleed for a few days. Could be a woman would feel it was worth that, from time to time, to be able to love a man the way she wants to love him. When she's better, you can find a doctor that knows more about it than I do. Maybe he'll think different. Anyway," Annie broke into a smile, "you got yourself a fine daughter."

The "fine daughter" wanted to eat every couple of hours, and demanded the nipple in a voice that made them all laugh. She might be little, but she certainly sounded healthy enough.

Jessie scarcely knew when they brought the baby to her for the first twenty-four hours. After that, her own strength began to return, slowly, slowly, and her heart was full of thanksgiving. Not only for a living, healthy child, but for having made up with Joel.

32

Collie and Bonifasia came to visit when Rosalie was three weeks old. Bonifasia wore black, including a veil of lace to cover her face, for Señora Teresa had died the day after Rosalie's birth.

"Very quietly, in her sleep, *gracias de Dios,*" Bonifasia said, taking the chair beside the bed where Jessie still had to spend most of her time. "It was a mercy, for she had suffered much."

"I'm very sorry," Jessie said. And then, reaching for the cradle beside her, "Would you like to hold her?"

Bonifasia put back the veil and bent over the cradle, smiling. Up close, Jessie saw that she looked older than she had on the last occasion when they'd been together. Her delight in the baby was apparent, as she lifted Rosalie and crowed over her, cuddling close, settling into the rocker again. "How beautiful she is! How perfect her tiny fingers! What a marvel, to have a baby, no?"

"This one is certainly a miracle," Jessie agreed. "Considering how close I came to losing her, so many times, before she was finally born."

"They told me you were very ill," Bonifasia said. "But I am pleased to find you looking much better, surely? There is color in your face, and you smile. A baby is something to smile about, no?"

"Yes," Jessie agreed, smiling more broadly.

Faint pink tinged Bonifasia's cheeks. "I would have come to see you sooner, but Collin thought it better that I did not try to ride out until the morning sickness was ended, for riding made it worse. I, too, am to have a child."

Jessie exclaimed over the news, genuinely glad, and amused by the way the young woman pronounced her husband's name. It came out sounding more like Coleen than Collin. "And what will you pray for? A boy or a girl?"

Bonifasia became serious. "A healthy child is all I will ask, after all these years of thinking I would never have a child of my own. And Collin does not care, either, he says, though Luis insists the first child must be a boy. It is important to carry on the family, even if it will not be the family name of Sañudo."

Jessie hesitated, then asked the question that had been uppermost in her mind. "Are you happy, Bonifasia?"

For a moment something flickered in the girl's face, something Jessie could not interpret. And then a sweet smile curved the delicately shaped lips.

"I am very happy," Bonifasia said in a quiet voice. "I have Collin, and I will have a child, and I am able to visit a friend, from Casa Sañudo, to see your beautiful daughter. What more could a woman ask?"

She bent over Rosalie, her face alight, but Jessie wondered if Bonifasia had left something out of her recital of blessings.

The heat of the year finally subsided, and the rains came as they were supposed to in October, and again the fields were planted. Jessie grew rapidly stronger, and Joel decided that he could afford to keep on two women to help in the house. After Sally had gone off with her recovered husband, deciding to live with him on his claim until it was too deeply covered with snow to make it workable, Joel found another woman from Knight's Ferry, a widow by the name of Gretchen Van Liew.

Gretchen was nearly forty, a sturdy, comfortable woman well able to deal with domestic crises and energetic small boys. She had no family, and was greatly pleased to be taken into the household of the young Shands. Having her there made Jessie's duties very light, so that she could devote herself mostly to the children.

Rosalie grew chubby and good-natured; her dark hair came in thicker, and her eyes were going to remain brown, they decided. By the time she was four months old, she was decidedly pretty; she won over the entire household with her smiles and gurgles.

Bonifasia had her baby, a girl she named Teresa Dolores, on the 8th of March, after an uncomplicated labor. Collie rode over to tell them the news, and he seemed pleased, but Jessie sensed that he'd come to relay more than the news of his daughter.

She didn't find out until Joel had seen him off, to return to the house with a mildly troubled expression.

"What's the matter? Isn't Bonifasia all right?"

"Oh, she's fine."

"The baby . . . ?"

"The baby is perfect. He's pleased about the baby. Thinks she's prettier than Rosalie." Amusement at this absurdity touched his lips briefly. "No, it's Collie. He's heading off up into the Sierra again. Looking for gold."

"But what for?" Jessie asked, bewildered. "He doesn't need it now, does he? I mean, he's a partner in the combined ranches, and he gets a share of everything they earn, doesn't he?"

"Same as Luis and I will be getting at harvest time. Only he doesn't feel as if he's earning it. He wants to do something

267

on his own. He wants to go up in the hills. He's leaving day after tomorrow."

"Right after the baby was born? With Bonifasia not even out of bed yet?"

"So it seems. Well, he's a grown man. I guess he can decide for himself what he wants to do," Joel said, and turned the subject to something else.

Jessie remembered Bonifasia's hesitation, slight though it had been, when asked about her happiness. It hadn't been Collie's idea to marry her, she thought uneasily, no matter what Joel said. It was true that Joel couldn't have forced his half brother into a marriage he didn't want, but he could have persuaded him into it. Bonifasia was such a pretty thing that any man would have admired her, but would Collie ever have married her had not Joel urged him to it?

It bothered her, thinking about it, though she said nothing more to Joel. She didn't always like the things he did, the attitudes he took about other people, but she loved him. And that was the important thing to remember. She mustn't ever let them grow apart again; life wasn't worth living unless there was love between them.

Mamie sat over the ledger, entering the figures in neat columns, the credits and the debts. They were making a living, though little more than that. Not enough so they could save anything, she thought drearily.

Was this the way her life was to go on forever? Up every morning at four, baking bread so that it would be ready for everyone to have fresh by early afternoon? Decorating cakes for other people's birthdays and anniversaries and weddings? Going to bed every night so tired she could not always fall asleep? Listening to her mother's unconscious sighing, having nothing of her own except this little shop with the small rooms behind it?

Her mother was in the bedroom back there now, already asleep. She'd protested at Mamie's working on the books so late. Come on to bed, she said, and do that in the morning.

But in the morning was the Sabbath, and Mamie didn't want to spoil her one day of freedom by having to add figures. She had stayed in the front of the shop, and now she yawned and stretched as she stood up.

And jumped, smothering a small cry. For there was a man looking in the front windows.

After staring into the face with the curly golden beard for

a matter of seconds, Mamie stifled another sound, then moved swiftly to the door to turn the key. Instead of allowing the man into the shop, however, she stepped out into the summer night.

"Collie! What are you doing here?"

She thought she controlled her voice rather well, making it sound as if he were only a customer, a casual friend, instead of the man she still dreamed about and longed for.

"Mamie, I hoped I'd get to talk to you. How are you?"

She was trembling so that she put out a hand to the jutting bay beside the door, to steady herself. "I'm fine. I thought you were hunting for gold, up in the mountains."

"I was. I have been. Mamie . . ." His teeth glinted in the light from the shop window, and the beard showed up in golden highlights as he smiled. "I found it. I found gold. A real strike, I think, not one of those that'll peter out in a week or two."

"Congratulations. You're luckier than most."

"There's still gold up there, for them that want to work for it. The mines around Big Oak Flat are taking out shipments regularly, every month. Mine won't be that productive, but I've brought in enough to be sure it's gold. I just left the assay office, and I carried in over two thousand dollars' worth of it."

"It's nearly ten o'clock. The assay office closes at six."

"Well, I went on over to the saloon and had a bite to eat, and a drink," Collie admitted.

"Several drinks, more like," Mamie said. "You're too late to buy bread. We sold every last loaf we baked today."

"I didn't come to buy bread. I came to talk to you."

Mamie swallowed hard, fighting the anger and the frustration that rose and threatened to choke her. "You're late. I expected you almost a year ago. Before you married . . . her."

Collie shifted from one foot to the other. "I talked to Harry Kelly. I knew Alice would tell you."

"Do you think that was enough? That my sister told me the man I'd thought was going to marry me was going to marry somebody else? Would it have been enough for you if I'd sent word through Jessie that I'd changed my mind and was marrying someone else?"

She saw him swallow in turn. "No. It was the cowardly way out. I've been sorry ever since, Mamie."

"Well, I guess an apology is better late than never," she told him, and made a move to reopen the door behind her.

"Ma's in bed. She'll be wondering why I haven't turned in, as well. I'm glad about the gold, Collie. I hope it makes you very happy."

He caught her wrist and held it, must surely feel the accelerated pulse pounding beneath his fingers. "Mamie, wait. I have to talk to you."

"I should think if you just came in out of the hills, you ought to go home and talk to your wife." She tugged against him, but his fingers were like steel.

"Mamie, for God's sake, don't do this to me. To us. It was a mistake, marrying Bonifasia. Joel wanted it so bad, wanted to tie his ranch—our ranch—in with Sañudo's, and he said I wasn't in love with you, I only wanted a woman, and that I could be just as happy with . . . her. Mamie, I do love you. I didn't know it for sure myself, then, but I know it now."

She was shaking, unable to free herself from him, on the verge of tears. Why was he telling her this now, when it was too late? "You should have thought of that a year ago! What use is it now? Let me go, Collie. I don't want to talk to you, I don't want to hear anything about . . ."

"Yes, you do. You love me, too, I know you do." He swung her around, into his arms, crushing her against his chest, bruising her mouth with a kiss so violent that she felt, at first, as if she were being violated.

And then the kiss softened; he murmured her name, brokenly, into her hair. And while his embrace was still passionate, it was tender, too. "Mamie, Mamie, don't deny me!"

She felt herself yielding, for was this not, after all, what she had craved, dreamed of, for such a long time? And yet there was something else in her, too, something disconnected from the body that would have given in to him totally. Mamie drew back at last and held him away.

"No. Stop, Collie. I mean it. Stop."

"But you love me, you couldn't have kissed me that way if you didn't love me—"

Someone was coming along the street, and Mamie had no intention of being caught kissing anyone, let alone Collin Aubin, and stirring up talk throughout the town. She hadn't much of her own, but she had respectability, her own good name.

Collie saw the approaching drunk, too, and reached for her wrist again, to pull her into the shadows of the oleander bushes at the corner of the building. They stood there, trying to control their noisy breathing, until the man had passed.

"There can't be anything between us," Mamie said dully; the moment had given her a chance to regain her composure, to recover her common sense. "You're married, you have a child. You have responsibilities."

She could barely see his face now, and it was changed because of the beard, but she knew what he looked like. She had long since memorized this particular face.

"It was a terrible mistake, marrying her. I didn't love her, being beautiful isn't enough to make a woman loved by a man. Joel kept making jokes, telling me how she would be in bed, and I was young enough, fool enough, to believe him. Don't, Mamie, don't pull away, listen to me! Bonifasia isn't a woman at all, she's an exquisite doll who plays at everything she does. She can't talk to a man, she has no understanding of what I think or feel, she's used to someone else doing everything that needs to be done, waiting on her, catering to her, yet keeping her in a cage, like a pet bird. That's what Luis has done for years, kept her as a pet! And she doesn't even want out of the cage, not really. She doesn't know what to do with freedom if she has it. She'd have died on that trek from Missouri. She's like a rose petal that begins to wilt the minute it's detached from the rose. She has no substance of her own, none."

Someone else was leaving the saloon, and again they waited, so close together in the dark, for the trio of laughing men to pass. Mamie prayed that her mother was sound asleep, that she wouldn't come seeking the daughter who was late to bed. She could smell the scent of orange blossoms and the summer air stirred the hair on the back of her neck, and Collie's fingers maintained their iron grip on her wrist.

"You're married to her," Mamie said at last, when the men had gone. "She's the mother of your child."

"She slept with me," Collie said, and there was acid in his voice, corrosive, painful. "She did everything I wanted her to do. She never questioned a thing I asked of her. It was as if she was one of those French toys, the kind you wind up with a key to make them perform. If she felt anything, she never said so. My sister had a music box, once, when she was about twelve. She would wind it up, and the ballerina would twirl in time to the music; and that's how Bonifasia was. A mechanical doll, moving to the tinkling music. Artificial, incapable of being a real woman, a real wife."

He was breathing harshly in his agitation, his need to

convince her. He was hurting her wrist, but Mamie said nothing, had ceased to struggle.

"I can't go back there and live that way, Mamie," Collie said, and there was conviction in his words. "I've got to have something more than that in my life, in all the years there are left. I need you, I want you."

His words tore at her heart, yet she came back to the undeniable. "You're married to her. You have a responsibility to her, and to the child."

"She has Luis; she doesn't need me. I was just a means of making a legal tie between us—Joel and me—and the Sañudo family. They used me as if I were a herd bull," he said, and there was a savagery there she had never before heard from Collie. "Breeding stock, both of us. It's not her fault. She didn't plan any of it, or ask for it, and she couldn't do anything about it. It was Luis and Joel who cooked it up between them, and it's great for them both, but it doesn't give me anything I want. Nothing. If I were to die tomorrow, it wouldn't make an iota of difference to any of them. Life will go on at Rancho Sañudo, and Bonifasia will live the way she's always lived, surrounded by luxury and servants to do everything she wants—except to let her come alive, to live. And she'll raise the child the same way she was raised. There wouldn't be much I could do about that, either, even if I stayed. Luis is master of that house, not me."

Mamie felt tears gathering in her eyes. She recognized that though he made excuses, though he had been cowardly in allowing the things to happen that had happened, much of what he said was valid. Yet what was to be done? There was such a thing as divorce, but it was not for ordinary people, and certainly not for Catholics such as the Sañudos. Luis would never allow such a thing to happen to his sister; he'd kill her husband and make her a widow, first.

Collie's tone softened. "Come with me, Mamie. Come away with me. We'll go back up into the hills—it's so beautiful up there, not like this godforsaken place—and nobody will know us, nobody will care about us. She'll never miss me, and Joel and Luis will still have what they care about, their damned land, and we . . ." He choked with emotion; she could not doubt that it was genuine. "We'll have each other."

The temperature had not dropped, yet Mamie felt icy. "And live together in sin?"

"Where's the sin in loving someone? I'll admit I should have been stronger, less stupid. I shouldn't have listened to

272

Joel. But it's too late to consider that; it's done. Now I have to find a way out, and if you'll come with me, we can leave it all behind. Everything. We'll be together, the way we should have been if Joel had left us alone."

The temptation was there. She felt it, a powerful sensation surging through her veins. To go with him, to love him, to be loved by him, it was all she had ever asked of life.

Yet her head was not completely softened. This time when she attempted to withdraw from his grasp, he let her go, and she drew a long, unsteady breath.

"Let me think about it, Collie," she said, for she knew that if she refused him at this moment he would not accept it, would not allow her to go inside. And go inside she must, and soon, before it was too late, before that rushing blood betrayed her. "Let me sleep on it."

He thought he'd won. He pulled her close for another quick kiss, a kiss that burned her like the branding irons used to mark the cattle on the open range. There was enough light filtering through the leaves from the bakery windows so that she could see the white of his teeth as he grinned.

"I'll be back tomorrow," he said. "Tomorrow evening, just at dusk. Bring whatever you want to take with you. I have two horses. We'll just leave, quietly, without talking to anybody. I have a little cabin up there—it's not fancy, just a shack, but when I get the rest of the gold we'll move on, somewhere we can have a place of our own. Away from here, where nobody will ever find us."

Mamie pulled free, heedless now of anyone who might be watching. She had to go into the bakery and put out the lights there, and she thanked God that Collie did not try to hold her any longer. She could not have borne it, another moment of his touch and his presence.

She moved through the darkness of the shop and into the tiny living room–kitchen behind it. From the adjoining room Sarah called out sleepily, "Mamie? Haven't you come to bed yet?"

She never knew how she kept her voice steady. "It's so warm, I'm going to sit in the backyard for a few minutes, Ma. Go back to sleep."

She made it outside before the tears came, before the sobs were audible. She moved as far from her mother's open window as she could get, leaning against the fig tree that still retained some of the day's heat in its sturdy trunk and limbs,

273

and bit her lip until she tasted blood, trying not to make sound enough for anyone to hear her.

Oh, God, oh, God, she thought, why hadn't he come to her before, as he'd promised to do? Why had he allowed Joel and Luis Sañudo to draw him into a loveless marriage, a marriage that was nevertheless legal and binding, a marriage he would never escape as long as he lived?

For she knew she could not go with him. She could not pretend to be his wife when she was not. She could not have his children—illegitimate children—she could not do that to any child. And she could not hurt her mother and her sister that way, either, leaving them with the shame of what she had done.

Her mother complained and was not much fun to be around, but she was a decent, God-fearing woman. She had nothing except the little bakery, which she couldn't run by herself, even if people would continue to patronize an establishment run by the mother of an adulteress.

Adulteress. It was a word that had struck fear into her heart even before she fully understood what it meant. And the stigma would attach itself not only to the perpetrator but to everyone connected with her.

Alice and Harry, they were expecting another child; they were making a living, and they had made a place for themselves in this community. They had made friends, and enjoyed a small measure of social life. They didn't want Sarah with them. God knew she'd probably destroy what happiness they had, if she had to give up the bakery and move in with them. Mamie didn't think Harry could put up with living in the same house with Sarah, not for long.

And even if it were only for herself, Mamie thought, exhausted from crying yet with the terrible ache still wracking her chest and tearing at her throat and making her head hurt, too, she couldn't do it. It went against everything she'd ever been taught, everything she believed was right.

She couldn't go with Collie. Her body throbbed with the anguish of her need for him, but she couldn't go with him.

At last the night air grew cool enough to be uncomfortable, and Mamie rose, stiffly, and walked back into the house.

No one else even knew Collie had been there. It was several weeks later before Joel went to town, and the men who had seen Collie in the saloon assumed that his "cousin" had seen him, and made no mention of the younger man's presence.

Mamie explained her swollen, reddened eyes by saying she'd gotten dust in them; since the street rose up and shifted itself around every time the wind blew, that was feasible. If there were those who didn't believe it, why, none of them said so.

She knew Collie wouldn't go without her simply because she didn't show up at dusk, as scheduled. He would think she'd been detained, and he might even come inside, asking for her.

Better by far that no one even knew he'd been there, Mamie thought. She wrote him a letter while the bread was baking, letting Sarah think that she still labored over the ledger. It was perhaps the most painful thing she had ever done, and she put in all the reasons, all the other people who would be hurt, if she did as he asked.

She didn't know if he'd accept her reasoning and go on alone, but she prayed most earnestly that he would. She did not know if she could bear to see him again, to look into his eyes and kill all his dreams, as he had killed hers a year earlier.

When it was time to close the shop, she went outside and, with a quickening heartbeat, placed the letter, pierced by a twig, on the oleander bush. He'd expect her to be there, and it would show up plainly enough at dusk.

There was nowhere she could hide to make sure it was Collie who found it. At this time of evening, most of the children who wandered the streets of Knight's Ferry would be home, having their suppers. Some of the older ones would be back out, playing games until dark, but she could only trust to an Infinite Mercy that none of them would see her letter and read it. She had not addressed it to him by name, and had signed it only with her initial; still, any adult who came across it would be able to figure out who the principals were. Yet she knew nothing else to do.

When, just before her mother went to bed, Mamie said she wanted a little air, Sarah made no comment. Mamie's heart was beating so hard that she pressed her hand over it, as if to keep it inside her rib cage, as she let herself out of the front door of the bakery.

There was no light behind her this time, and the only people on the street were a group of men before the saloon, laughing and talking loudly, paying her no attention.

She moved toward the bush and parted the branches, revealing the one where she had placed her note.

The leaves were skinned off the branch, and the note was gone. On the ground at her feet, Mamie picked up the small pouch, feeling within it the grittiness of small stones, though she knew before she looked that they were nuggets, not rocks.

Collie had found her message, and had left one of his own, though she wasn't sure what it was, nor how she could ever act upon it. She hid the little pouch in the hollow between her breasts, and went back into the house.

33

In the east, President Lincoln issued a call for troops after Fort Sumter was fired upon. Joel read the headlines and said gravely, "It's war. They're going to fight."

Jessie scarcely noted his concern. It was all so far away, too far away to cast much of a shadow over her own life. She had a full household to manage and three young children, and Rosalie was learning to creep and so required constant supervision. Their lives went on much as usual.

The wheat crop was good that year and the price remained high. Joel paid off the balance of his loan to Clara Ridback, though he did not take the money to her directly. This time, he had no intention of being enticed into her sweet-smelling apartment, let alone into her bed.

Clara was amused, and moderately disappointed, that he chose to send his hired man, Clifford Murray, with the money and a request for a receipt for it. She wrote out the receipt in a businesslike way, and wondered what Murray thought of the transaction.

There was enough money to furnish the rest of the house, and Joel ordered bedroom suites from San Francisco, and a set of twin rose-brocaded sofas for the front parlor, the one reserved for company. There was a piano, too, of rosewood, which was installed in the library/music room, and new books. They were an odd assortment, since Joel had not picked them by title, only specifying that they have colorful leather covers, yet Jessie found much to her liking among them.

Carpets were bought to cover the polished wooden floors in the two parlors, and one for their own bedroom. Laurie and Tristan were settled into separate rooms on the second floor; only Rosalie remained in the nursery, which took on a feminine air.

The final importation from San Francisco was a young woman by the name of Miss Caroline Smythe. She would teach Jessie, and eventually Rosalie, to play the magnificent new piano. She would also serve as a governess for all three children, since they were clearly too much for Jessie to manage on her own.

Jessie had regained her health completely, and had without difficulty persuaded Luis to provide her with more fruit trees to replace those that had died in the drought. She loved working outside, when it was not too hot, and she felt up to taking the buggy by herself and driving over to visit Bonifasia and little Teresa Dolores, or into Knight's Ferry to shop or visit Mamie and Alice and Annie.

It was time, she decided, to have a social life beyond that of their own home. Her first dinner party, with John and Eva Curtis as guests, was a great success, and Jessie felt encouraged to try something on a larger scale.

This time her guests included Alice and Harry Kelly, the Tullochs, and three other couples from Knight's Ferry. Jessie was not sufficiently accomplished as yet to play the piano for them, but Caroline Smythe did. She was a rather plain, brown-haired young woman, with a smile as sweet as it was rare, and she was, Jessie thought, an angel at the piano.

Everyone enthused over the evening, and the Shands were invited back to other homes in the following weeks as the year of 1861 drew to a close. There were new garments for everyone in the family, evening dresses for Jessie, purchased at Clara's shop, that displayed her bosom and the string of pearls Joel had given her as an early Christmas present.

There was one small blemish on their contentment. Jessie brushed it aside as inconsequential, although she sympathized with Joel's feelings. Louise Babcock, wife of the banker, who had not been invited to any of Jessie's doings, made a slighting remark about upstarts who married Mormon women, and word got back to them.

"What do we care?" Jessie asked. "She's no particular friend of ours, nor do we want her to be."

277

Yet Louise Babcock was unquestionably one of the social leaders of Knight's Ferry. And since the boundaries of the adjoining San Joaquin and Stanislaus counties had been shifted so as to place Knight's Ferry in the county of Stanislaus, and the town had been made the county seat, this was where everything of any importance took place. Stockton was far away, with a society of its own; there was developing in Knight's Ferry a definite class structure, and Louise Babcock intended to be at the top of it. Anyone who was not invited to her sociables was excluded from the cream of the county society.

"We have our own friends," Jessie pointed out. "Ginny and Oliver and John and Eva, and Mamie and Alice and Harry—and the Tullochs are very nice, don't you think?"

"John and Eva Curtis were invited to the Babcocks' for dinner the week after they were here," Joel said, rankled by this discrimination. "I don't know how she found out about me, my background, but she knows. That Louise Babcock. She made a remark in my hearing, about who my father was. Suggesting I didn't know. At Tim Riley's wedding, of all places, just stirring up trouble."

Jessie felt a spurt of anger of her own, against the woman who would hurt Joel so over a matter that was none of his doing, but she kept her tone level. "She cannot possibly *know* anything. You are building your own reputation, Joel, and it's a good one, for an honest, hardworking man. Why torment yourself over the opinion of an odious woman we both despise?"

Yet she knew that it ate at him, that his resentment fermented and soured him. His answer was to become bigger and better, to shower Jessie with gifts of elegant garments, to fill his household with luxury items that sometimes stretched his income a bit too tight for Jessie's comfort.

With the recovery of her health after Rosalie's birth, they had become enthusiastic lovers again. Annie had warned Jessie of the damage caused by that birthing; Jessie took the news calmly. "I asked God for one more healthy child, and He gave her to me. If it is His will that there be no more babies, why, I have a lovely family now."

"I didn't say you couldn't get pregnant again, only that you probably couldn't carry a baby to full term," Annie told her.

Jessie hid her disquietude with a seemingly serene smile. "Then we will be happy with what we have. I will not withhold

278

myself from my husband." Though she didn't add *I won't drive him elsewhere for what he must have,* Annie understood. No more was said of the matter.

In mid-December, Collie returned home.

Not to Casa Sañudo, at least not at once, but to Joel and Jessie's house. He showed up one evening as they sat together in the music room, Joel perusing a month-old copy of the *Sacramento Union* while Jessie practiced one of the simple tunes she was learning on the piano. Clifford's hounds began barking, and Joel rose to see what was setting them off.

Jessie paused in her playing, then stood in delight when she heard Collie's voice. She had suspected that something had happened between Collie and Mamie, for Mamie had not been herself when they visited together, but she had not probed a tender area when Mamie did not volunteer any information. If Bonifasia was unhappy or humiliated because of her husband's absence, she had never revealed such emotions to Jessie. She seemed content with her lovely little daughter, perhaps more content than she had been while Collie was there.

Now Jessie moved to meet him, lifting her face for his brotherly kiss. He was bearded and there were lines of weariness in his face, but his smile was bright.

"Lord, it's a nasty night! What a hell of a place this is, one winter without enough rain to keep the wheat from shriveling up, and now the rivers're so damned full it's worth your life to try to ford one. Even that little creek of yours is spilling over its banks." He looked around in the candlelight at the warm, attractive room. "Lord, you're really fixing the place up. And you look beautiful, Jessie."

"Thank you. Are you hungry? Thirsty?"

"Both. I don't need anything heated up, though, just some bread and cold meat, if you have it. And maybe a glass of whiskey, or brandy. This looks like a room where a good brandy would be available."

They sat and talked while he ate. He had come down out of the hills because everything was so wet he couldn't bear it any longer. "There's mold on everything I own—my bread, my underwear. Only the gold didn't turn green." He grinned at them. "I brought quite a bit of it with me. Enough so I wouldn't really have to go back up there, if I chose not to. I didn't get it all, though, so maybe come spring..." He drained the brandy glass with an appreciative sigh. "Something to be said for money, can buy liquor like that."

Joel obediently refilled the glass, and Collie asked at last, "Have you seen Bonifasia? And the baby?"

"She's hardly a baby any more," Jessie told him. "She's almost nine months old, and she's creeping. She's a lovely little thing, Collie; you've missed a great deal, not watching her grow up."

Collie sobered. "I know. But I had to go. She's healthy, then, and everything is all right?"

"With Bonifasia, how does one know?" Jessie asked. "She doesn't tell us anything personal, of how she feels. She's rightfully proud of Teresa Dolores. She doesn't talk much of anything else."

He regarded them gravely. "It was a mistake, my marrying Bonifasia. I wasn't what she wanted, except for fathering her child. And she's not what I need, either."

Jessie had known that, yet his admission was shocking. "What will you do now?"

"I don't know. I don't think she wants me back, any more than I want to go back. I can't live in that house. It'll never be home to me, not if I lived there a hundred years. It's Luis Sañudo's house, and it always will be."

"Take Bonifasia and live somewhere else, then," Joel said roughly, angered that Collie had brought this up with Jessie. "You can afford a house in town, if that's what you want. I have your share of the wheat money in the safe, right over there."

Collie shook his head. "No. It might be better in a different house, but Bonifasia still wouldn't be the wife I need. I should have stood up to you, Joel. I should have married Mamie."

Jessie felt as if a knife had twisted in her chest. She looked at Joel and, though he struggled for composure, saw the truth written there. He had coerced Collie into the marriage, as she had known he had, and he'd ruined at least three lives because of his own greed for the land. She felt sick, and wished that Collie had simply stayed away, had not come back into their lives to make them face painful facts better left unacknowledged.

Collie stood abruptly. "I haven't had a real bath in weeks. Is there any chance I could get some hot water and some soap? And take over my old sleeping pallet for a day or two, while I decide what I'm going to do next?"

"Your old room is filled. We have a governess, a Miss Smythe," Jessie said, striving for a normal tone. "You can have the other bed in Laurie's room, if you like. It's the one on the left at the top of the stairs. He's asleep, of course, but nothing wakens him. And there's water heating in the kitchen, as always. Joel can bring the tub for you."

Did Mamie know? she wondered, getting down fresh towels to be carried to the kitchen a few minutes later. How cruel, how wicked! Even the fact that Collie had been a man grown, a man who had only to assert himself, did not take away from Joel's part in the tragedy.

She wished with all her heart that Collie had not come west with them, or that Joel had been content with his own acres. Poor Mamie, and poor Bonifasia.

She laid the towels across the back of a chair and went upstairs, hoping she would be asleep before Joel and Collie finished talking, before Joel came to bed.

34

The rains came as if they would never stop. Day after day of continuing rain, until the natives became uneasy, and began to worry about another flood like the one in 1852, which had swept away some of their houses, and some of their families.

Jessie went to town in the buggy to consult with Annie over a cough that Rosalie had contracted; Miss Smythe and the boys went with her for the outing, though it was such a miserable day that they were all damp and cold by the time they reached the bridge.

It was an awesome experience, driving over it after they'd paid the toll. Jessie almost wished she hadn't come, for the water was wild and high, swirling closer to the planking than she'd ever seen it. The horse was skittish, and it took all her strength and skill to hold him in the center of the bridge.

Laurie and Tristan were fascinated, leaning out over the edge of the buggy and from beneath its canopy so that Miss Smythe spoke sharply to them and pulled them back.

Annie lived by now in a comfortable small place of her own, on the hill behind the bakery. Jessie wanted to see Mamie, yet at the same time did not want to see her, because she would have to admit that Collie had returned, and she did not want to talk to Mamie about Collie, especially not in front of anyone else. There were customers in the bakery, she saw as she drove past, and she did not stop, but turned the corner and urged the horse up the hill.

Annie greeted them with pleasure, kissing them all around, except for Miss Smythe. Rosalie was her particular favorite, as she was everybody's. She had, after an unpromising start, turned into a charmer in every way, with her huge dark eyes and soft black curls.

"Cookie," she begged, and Annie obligingly produced a cookie, and one for each of the little boys as well.

"Come in, sit by the fire, and dry out. What a winter this is! I feel as if I haven't seen the sun in months, and everybody in town is sick of one thing or another. Bonifasia was in to see me this morning." Annie shot a look at the governess, who was divesting the children of their damp garments, and lowered her voice so that it wouldn't carry to Miss Smythe. "She said she came for one of my herbal remedies for a female complaint. What she really wanted, though," and Annie lowered her voice even further so that Jessie leaned forward to hear, "was to know if it was true Collie had come back, that he was at your place. She'd heard a rumor that he'd been seen in town."

Annoyance twisted Jessie's features. Why did Collie put them in this position? If he didn't want to live with Bonifasia, why, she supposed that was his right. But the least he could do was to see the woman himself and let her know how matters stood. Bonifasia seemed quite content without him, so delighted with her small daughter that she didn't need anyone else, but why must she be humiliated by hearing rumors about her husband and having to beg strangers for information?

"He's there," Jessie said shortly. "If he comes again, you can tell her that, I guess. Though I hope he'll go and see her himself."

Annie nodded. "I thought so. I've a notion Mamie Groves saw him." She lifted a hand to shush Jessie's exclamation. "Not that I saw Mamie, you understand. But Sarah Groves was here, wanted something to help the girl sleep. Said she's been having nightmares, crying out in her sleep, and not been herself for several days. I sort of put two and two together, you know."

Poor Mamie. If he couldn't marry her, he should at least have the decency to stay away from her, Jessie thought crossly. Men are so stupid and so selfish, sometimes; they don't think how much they're hurting a woman.

Rosalie began to cough, and Jessie's attention was turned toward her daughter. "Listen to her! I've been afraid to put her to sleep in her own room at night, and she's kept us both awake for two nights now. Can you do anything about the cough?"

Annie took the child on her lap, resting an ear against the small chest to listen, while Rosalie giggled at this silly game, then obediently opened her mouth so that Annie could look at her throat.

"I think her lungs are involved. I'll get you some of my herbal syrup. She won't like the taste of it, so put a little honey with it, so she'll swallow it. The boys have it, too?"

"Not yet. But I suppose they might get it, as they're all together so much. Give me a big bottle, please, Annie."

Jessie would have liked to stay and visit. She felt uneasy, though, remembering the way the water had boiled through the gorge just above town and swept under the bridge. "I guess I'd better get back. I don't want to be trapped on this side of the river if it continues to rise. What do they think, here in town? Silas Wofford, he told me about his wife drowning when his house was swept away in '52. Does he think it will happen like that again?"

"Could be. Of course this time his house is built much higher, so he thinks it will hold. There's a few people on the lowlands have stowed everything they could in their attics and come into town until the water goes down, which may not be for several weeks. December and January are the most likely months for floods, Silas says."

Did Jessie detect something in the way Annie said the man's name? "Are you seeing Silas regularly?" she asked.

"He's always underfoot. How could I help seeing him? Besides, he has more aches and pains than any one man could rightly claim, and he likes my specifics for his rheumatism."

Jessie's mouth softened in a teasing grin. "Are you still treating him for nothing?"

"Oh, he pays for the liniment and the potions. He gets a lot of advice for free. On the other hand," and here Annie's own grin emerged, "he has one of the best gardens in Knight's Ferry, and I haven't had to plant one of my own."

"He'd be a catch, wouldn't he? One of the richest citizens in town?"

Annie snorted. "Oh, I'm too old for that kind of foolishness, and so is Silas. Well, you go on, get your younguns home, girl, and give my best to your husband. And to Collie, if he's still there, though my message to him ought to be to get his life straightened out before he hurts people any worse."

They had several errands to run, and Jessie took care of them as quickly as she could. There was a letter from Zadie, which gave her a brief lift of spirit. If only Joel could be persuaded to go to Oregon to visit her sister!

"Someday," he'd say when Jessie brought up the subject. "When they have roads you can get a buggy over." She knew it would be a difficult journey on horseback, especially with the children, though she would gladly have attempted it in good weather. Only getting Joel away from his land during planting or harvesting season was impossible, and there wasn't time enough between them for such an extended trip. Jessie sighed and tucked the precious letter into her reticule.

It was not late, but the sky was very dark, and she didn't want to be on the road after dusk. This time of year, dusk came early even when it wasn't raining.

The wheels made a racket on the wooden bridge, and again the little boys leaned over to see the rushing water, so that Miss Smythe had to admonish them to sit still. Surely the water was higher, Jessie thought, almost to the bottom of the bridge; thank heaven she had not delayed any longer. When she stopped to pay the toll, the man stared up at her from under a dripping hat brim, and she asked impulsively, "Do you think the bridge will hold?"

"Has so far," the man replied, pocketing her coins. "I wouldn't waste any time on the road, though, ma'am. The river's nearly as high as I ever see it get, and there's places where the road is close to the top of that bank. Could get dangerous if this keeps up, wash out a bit of road where the river undercuts the bank."

"I'm going straight home," Jessie assured him. "I'll be there before dark, so I'll be able to see if there's anything amiss with the road."

It made her nervous, though, for the rain came down in a steady sheet that made it hard to see very well. Not that she needed to see much, unless the road had washed out since she'd been over it, for the track was easy to follow and the horse knew it well.

Several times, when the road came close to the top of the bluff, she could see the river far below. See it and hear it, for it made a terrific racket as it boiled over the rocks. It carried debris with it, logs and small trees, and once she thought she recognized a chicken coop.

Laurie leaned over and whispered to Tristan, and the younger boy tugged at her sleeve. "Mama, can we stop and watch the river?"

"No," Jessie told him, "we're going straight home. Maybe Papa will take you to the bluff below the house tomorrow, and you can see it then, but right now we must get Rosie home before she takes a chill and gets any sicker."

Both boys had always been fascinated by water, any water. They waded in it, played in it, swam in it, wherever and whenever they encountered it. She didn't blame them; in a country where the summers were so hot it was a pleasant way to cool off.

Nobody needed cooling today, however, nor could anyone swim in that current. Both Jessie and Miss Smythe sighed in audible relief when they finally saw the lights of home, golden beacons welcoming them out of the rain and the falling darkness.

Fanny met them at the back door, while Clifford took the buggy to unhitch it and stable the horse and rub him down. The traveling party burst into the warm kitchen, rich with the odors of baking bread and the beans and ham that would be their supper. The boys tugged at Fanny's skirts, telling her about the river, small voices piping with enthusiasm.

Rosalie was coughing, and Jessie got out the herbal concoction to dose her, then handed the child over to Miss Smythe. "I think she'd better have a bath and get into bed. She can have her supper there instead of with the family. I think she's too tired, and she feels hot, too."

"I'll see to it. Perhaps I could have my supper with her," Miss Smythe suggested, and took the little girl to carry her away upstairs.

Fanny shot Jessie a look when the boys had run off to wash up for the evening meal. "Clifford says the river's really on a rampage. Does it look dangerous, ma'am?"

Jessie was shrugging out of her woolen garments, draping them to dry on the hooks behind the door. "Yes, I'd say it looks dangerous. It was nearly to the bottom of the bridge when we crossed it. I guess we'll stay home from now on until the water starts to go down. Thank God we built on high ground."

Joel came in the back door at that moment, almost squashing her into the wall of coats. "Sorry, love. You just get here? I came over the hills and nearly mired down in the creekbed. I guess we don't have to worry about the drought taking our wheat this year. Is that ham I smell?"

The cold and the damp had given them all an appetite; they ate heartily, and the little boys chattered with great excitement about passing over the flooding river. "Can we go see it, Uncle Joel? Can we go down close and look at it?"

"In the morning," Joel told them. "We'll go and look at it."

Jessie served up buttered carrots, placing some on each of their plates. "Collie didn't come in to supper?"

"He rode over to Casa Sañudo. I expect he'll be back, though. He didn't take any of his things." Joel slathered butter on a thick slice of bread, which he dipped into his beans. "He wasn't anxious to go, to talk to either Luis or Bonifasia, but I told him he ought to. They'll have heard he's back in Stanislaus County by now, and they'll wonder."

"Yes. They do know; Bonifasia visited Annie this morning, and asked. I hope . . ."

She didn't finish that, and Joel didn't ask what it was that she hoped.

Jessie was up several times during the night when Rosalie coughed and had to be given the medicine. It seemed to soothe her throat, and then she would fall back into sleep. Jessie stared down at the tiny face in the candlelight, a warm feeling of maternal love sweeping over her. Such a beautiful child, Rosie was. As she returned to her own room, she thanked God for his mercy in sparing this little one she had come so close to losing, and prayed that the present cough was only a passing illness.

She heard the rain, steady and unrelenting, as she snuggled against Joel and went back to sleep.

In the morning, dressed in their warmest and exultant because the rain had slowed to a drizzle, festive as if they were going to a party, the entire household set out for the bluff to view the river.

Jessie was busy with the little ones, trying to keep them

from plunging into puddles over their boot tops, and Joel's exclamation brought her head up with a snap.

"Jesus Christ! That can't all be the Stanislaus!"

He knew she didn't like him to swear that way, taking the Lord's name in vain, and he tried to remember not to curse in front of the children; Laurie, especially, loved to try out any new words he heard, and he always remembered them.

Today, however, Jessie did not even think, *Forgive him, Lord,* as she usually did. Because when she raised her eyes she saw water stretching a mile wide, and almost to the top of the near bank.

She sucked in a deep breath. It hadn't reached the top of this bank even in the flood of '52.

Instinctively, she reached for Joel's arm. "It won't come all the way over the bank, will it?"

"It'd have to be practically the whole Pacific Ocean to fill up the entire valley," he said, but there was a note of doubt in his voice.

It was cold, and Jessie shivered. She looked behind her, to where Miss Smythe came carrying Rosalie, well bundled against the chill. It probably hadn't been wise to bring the child out, but Rosie had begged to go wherever the rest of them were going, and they'd given in.

Laurie and Tristan broke into a run, and Joel plunged after them, yelling, "Come back here! Stop this minute, or I'll blister your backsides, you hear me?"

Jessie ran, too, though he stopped them well back from the edge. "You don't go a step unless you're hanging onto my hands, you understand?"

They nodded, not subdued, not frightened at the prospect of sliding off that muddy bank into a river that had grown to an ocean, overnight. They urged Joel as close as he would go; since they didn't have to look down to see water, he decided that they did not need to be at the very edge as they would have liked.

Laurie stooped and picked up a fallen branch and flung it into the river. The current tossed it, tore it away from the edge and out into midstream, where it quickly vanished. He looked up at Joel in elation. "I made a boat, Uncle Joel! Will it go to the sea?"

"It'll go to the sea, all right," Joel told him. "You want to throw one, too, Tris?"

The smaller boy pounced upon another twig, so tiny that Jessie could hardly see it in his hand, and Joel let him take the necessary steps forward so that his "throw" would carry it into the water. Tris crowed his delight, and Jessie watched them, one child clasping each of Joel's hands, the dark head and the fair one, faces upturned and laughing.

There was something exciting, compelling, about the turbulent water, muddy though it now was, without its normal beauty. The power of it was awesome, and Jessie was repelled as much as fascinated. Thank God, she thought again, that we built well back up from the banks, where we're safe.

Rosalie coughed, and Jessie turned, contrite, toward the governess and the little girl. "She'd better go back inside," Jessie decided, and called to tell Joel.

"All right. I'll stay out here with the boys a little while and watch it," Joel said over his shoulder, not looking at her. He was as enthralled at the spectacle of the swollen river as the children were, she thought.

By evening it was possible to see the water from the second floor of the house, something they had never done before. Normally, the river was far down between rocky bluffs, but it had filled the gorge and spread over the lowlands, and now approached the tops of the banks, more than a hundred feet above its normal level.

Jessie stared out at it, wondering what it was doing in Knight's Ferry. How much higher were they here than in the town? Mamie's shop was on Main Street, as was Silas Wofford's house, and most of the other businesses. Many had rebuilt, after the disastrous flood ten years ago, on higher elevations, with foundations to lift the buildings above the level of those waters; would they be high enough now? Were the waters deeper, this time, than they had been in '52?

The little boys pressed their faces against the cold glass, unwilling to be dragged away from the entertainment provided by nature for so ordinary a matter as eating their supper.

"If we had a boat," Laurie said, "we could go on it, Tris. We could ride in a boat."

"No, you couldn't," Jessie said, more sharply than she'd intended. "The river is out of control now; there's too much water. No one could manage a boat. It would tip over, and you would drown."

"I can swim," Laurie proclaimed, twisting his head to look at her.

"No one could swim in such a current as that is now," Jessie assured him. "It is too fast, too strong. Not even your

288

Uncle Joel could swim in it. Come along, Fanny says that supper is waiting, and we must go down and eat it while it's hot."

Collie showed up when they were halfway through the meal. Fanny brought him a plate and he loaded it with venison and potatoes and onions, and some of Jessie's light, fluffy dumplings. "There was water coming over the bridge when I left town," he said through a mouthful of dumpling. "They're afraid it'll go out if this keeps on much longer. Or even if a big enough log or stump comes downriver tonight. Nobody at the bank had ever seen the water get this high, and there were three fellows there who remember the big flood. I'm glad I got my business taken care of when I did, or I'd have stayed in town, probably, rather than risk getting back here in the dark."

Joel and Jessie exchanged glances. He had gone to see Bonifasia, presumably, the previous day. And then he had had business in town. What business? Joel cut off a great chunk of butter to let it melt atop his dumplings.

"Business at the bank?" he asked.

"I put the gold into an account there. Stupid to carry it around. If I'd fallen in the river today, with that in my poke, I'd have wound up in San Francisco Bay, I shouldn't wonder."

"You did get over to Rancho Sañudo yesterday?" Joel asked, putting the question that Jessie had not dared.

"I talked to Luis, and to Bonifasia, too." His face shifted behind the curly golden beard, softened. "And Teresa Dolores. She's going to be a real beauty when she grows up, isn't she?"

They could all agree with that. The little boys sat side by side, making mountains and rivers of their potatoes and gravy, giggling quietly to themselves. They did not appear to be listening to the adult conversation at all, and would not likely have understood the nuances anyway, Jessie decided.

"Did she come to you?" Jessie asked. How terrible, she thought, to have a child who did not recognize you as a parent, as was the case with little Teresa, whose father had gone away to search for gold when she was only a few days old.

"Not at first, but I gave her a bauble, and she opened up like a flower after that. Climbed on my knee and pulled my beard." He sobered and shot Joel a telling glance. "I talked to Luis. Plainly. And we agreed that if I wasn't going to stay here, or rather there, there were matters that needed to be taken care of."

So, Luis had not flown into a fit of anger and shot him.

Jessie wouldn't have been terribly surprised if that had been Luis's reaction to what he might well consider the desertion of his sister and her child. She wondered how Bonifasia had taken it, how she felt about a husband who did not want to live with her, and guessed that as long as Bonifasia had Teresa Dolores, she didn't need a husband who didn't love her.

"And they're all taken care of, then?" Joel asked. He reached out a hand to grip Laurie's wrist, as the child was about to add milk to his plate to make a more satisfactory lake for the bit of crust he intended to float upon it. Though Laurie's face registered disappointment as the glass was set firmly on the table, he made no protest.

"Yes." Collie ate as if he'd missed the last few meals. "I made out a will, dividing any property and funds that I have between Bonifasia and you, Joel. And if there's ever a matter to come to a vote, about the ranch or the business, and I'm not available to cast mine, I'll go along with whatever you want."

Joel's eyebrows rose. "And Luis agreed to that?"

"Yes. Unless I'm proved dead. Then the votes will be split between you and Luis." Collie grinned and lifted the napkin to wipe gravy from the beard around his mouth. "You'll have to fight it out with him the best you can, in that case."

"So you're going back up in the hills, then, for the rest of the gold."

"As soon as this winter's over and the river goes back down. It might have opened up more of my claim, all this water moving the rocks around. Looks like all the snow in the Sierra coming down the Stanislaus, though I guess the San Joaquin and the Sacramento are probably as bad. I want to talk to you about that after supper, Joe. I talked to the lawyer in town; he made up the will and also a quit-claim deed to my diggings. I'll draw you a map, in case you want to get up there. There's more gold, I know there is."

"And what will you do until the water goes down and the rest of the snow melts? You plan to stay on here, with us?"

Collie shook his head. "No. I thought I'd go over to San Francisco for a month or so, see the bright lights, kick up my heels a little. It might even be where I'll want to live, eventually. I guess it's not the same as Chicago, but it's a city, and a city was what I was used to, before you came along."

There was something in the way that Collie stared at Joel across the table that made Jessie's breath catch in her chest.

He knows, she thought. He knows Joel's his half brother, not his cousin.

Her gaze slid to Joel, and she saw the recognition of it there, too. Yet neither man said a word. Only after Fanny had served the rhubarb cobbler, and Miss Smythe came to take the little boys away to bed, the men went into the study, and she heard them talking for a long time while Jessie and Fanny cleared away the table and washed up the dishes.

A mine, she thought. Gold, lying in nuggets on the bottom of a stream, or beneath an overturned rock. Please God, it wouldn't tempt Joel. It wouldn't draw him away.

But of course not, she told herself. He was obsessed by the land, the land he had here. The land he'd have even more control over now, because Collie had told Luis he would throw in his lot with whatever Joel wanted to do. She felt a twinge of uncertainty about how Luis would take that, if Joel wanted something involving Luis's land that Luis himself did not approve. But that was foolish, too. Joel wouldn't try to do anything to usurp Luis's control over his own lands. The written agreement was a legal technicality to protect the land, nothing more.

"Goodnight, Miss Jessie," Fanny said, hanging up her apron and opening the back door. "I'm almost afraid to go out in the dark, for fear the water'll have got clear up here. I hope Clifford has a light in the window for me."

"He has, I can see it," Jessie said, pulling aside the curtain to peer out into the night. "Goodnight, Fanny. I'll see you in the morning."

Joel and Collie were still deep in conversation. Jessie paused at the doorway—at least this time they hadn't closed the door to keep her out—and saw that they bent over a table, and that Collie was drawing something, explaining.

"You go up that little gully, and when it divides, you take the westernmost one. You'll know it's the right one because there's a big dead oak there, maybe forty feet high. Right here."

Joel didn't notice her there in the doorway, and Jessie went on along the corridor and up the front stairs. On the landing she paused to push aside another set of curtains; this time she could see nothing, for there were no lights at the front of the place. Even when she pressed her face against the pane and held her hands to both sides of her head to shut out the light behind her, she could not make out anything at all.

Well, Collie had come in little more than an hour before. The river couldn't have risen much in an hour, and it had still been between the bluffs then. That sounded rational to her, yet Jessie was uneasy as she moved down the upper hallway, carrying the candle Miss Smythe had left at the head of the stairs for her.

She lighted a candle in her own room, then returned to the hall. There was a faint glow under the door of the governess's room; Miss Smythe liked to read in bed after she'd retired. Jessie moved quietly, opening first Laurie's door, then Tristan's, making sure they were asleep and covered. Tris slept with a big rag doll she'd made him when he was only a year old, his arm thrown protectively across it. Jessie smiled and bent to kiss his cheek.

Rosalie was asleep in her own crib tonight; the herbal cough remedy Annie had given her had helped enough so she thought she could entrust her to Miss Smythe again, though of course if she heard the child coughing more than a time or two, Jessie would get up and go to her. She had a governess for the children and ought to be able to leave such things to her, Joel said, but Jessie argued that as she wakened anyway when she heard one of them, she might as well reassure herself by checking on them, too.

She had laid a fire in the room earlier, and Miss Smythe had been kind enough to light it, so that the room was now a pleasant temperature. She didn't really need the candle, Jessie thought, though she didn't put it out. On a night like this, it gave an added illusion of warmth.

She undressed and washed in cold water, shivering. When she opened the drawer for a nightgown, her groping hand encountered something other than the flannel she had intended to wear.

The lovely blue gauzy gown Joel had brought her before Rosie was born. What was it doing on top? She'd folded it and put it underneath all the others, such a long time ago. Once she'd put it on, when she was alone in the house in broad daylight, and blushed to see how much of her showed through it.

Joel had never asked her why she didn't wear it, though she knew he must have wondered. She took it out now, and on impulse pulled it over her head. In the mirror, in the firelight, it was most revealing.

Jessie felt warm at the thought of being observed in such a garment, even by her husband. Yet Joel was her husband.

He wouldn't have bought this for her if he hadn't expected her to wear it. And even though she was nearly twenty-four years old, and had borne three children, she still had the figure of a girl. Slim, with high, firm breasts and smoothly curving hips and thighs.

She turned toward the bed, smiling, and hoped that Joel would not be long in coming up to join her.

Jessie woke to the clatter of small feet in the hall outside her door, and then Miss Smythe's shushing voice, "Be still, you'll wake your mama!"

Jessie grinned. She turned her head and saw that Joel had already gone; she'd slept so soundly that she hadn't heard him leave. She sat up and realized, as soon as the quilts slid down, that she was naked, and that the beautiful nightgown lay in a heap on the floor.

She stood up, picked up the gown and folded it over a chair, and dressed quickly. How could a country so intolerably hot in summer be so damp and cold in the winter? The chill seemed as severe as any she remembered from her girlhood in Michigan where temperatures had often plunged below zero, though here it seldom even reached freezing.

She emerged into the upper hallway, glancing toward Rosalie's room, where she heard the governess talking to the child, singing her a little song in French. French, Jessie thought. I wonder if I'm too old to learn another language. Bonifasia would teach me Spanish, and it is as melodious as French, perhaps more so.

As she reached the head of the stairs she could not resist looking out at the flooded river. It was somewhat like trying to resist putting one's tongue into a hole in one's tooth, even if the expectations were negative ones.

Somewhere below a door clicked shut, and she called out, "Joel?" There was no answer, and she returned her attention to the river. Dear God, it didn't seem possible that it could have risen any more, but surely she could detect swirling froth at the very level of the top of the bluff? Yes, there went an uprooted tree, one that would make the boys want to ride on it if they were to see it, it was so large.

This house was set well up off the ground on a sturdy foundation, yet she wondered if she should tell Fanny and Clifford to move their bed over to the kitchen tonight, for the little house across the creek was set practically on the ground.

It didn't seem possible that the river could ever reach this far, but if it did . . .

The smell of bacon rose up the stairway, and she was suddenly ravenous. No doubt Joel had gone out to do chores, and would be in ready for breakfast any moment; she ran down the stairs as if she were a girl, eager to meet the day in spite of its being another sullen, gray one.

Collie had just come in the back door, wiping water off the nimbus of yellow hair. "Whew! Looks like it's never going to quit. Joel says put breakfast on the table, he'll be in in a minute. That heifer is about to calve, and he may have to pull it—it doesn't look as if it's coming easy."

Fanny turned from the stove with a platter of eggs. "It's all ready, right now. Did the boys come down with you, Miss Jessie?"

"Why, no, they came down before I was even out of bed. . . ."

Jessie stopped, alarm spreading through her even before any conscious thought gave it meaning. "I heard them on the stairs, as I was getting up."

Fanny stared at her. "They never came back to the kitchen, ma'am."

The door. She'd heard a door close. It hadn't occurred to her at the moment, but it could have been the front door.

The blood drained from her face. The water, they were so entranced with the water, and they'd talked about taking a boat out.

Jessie snatched at the first outer garment that came to hand, a heavy jacket of Joel's. She had nothing over her head, but she didn't wait to look for anything. She turned and ran through the house, yelling back over her shoulder. "Get Joel! The boys may have gone out to look at the river again!"

She heard Collie swear, then his feet pounding on the polished floor behind her, and Fanny's cry. Collie reached the door at the same time she did, and they nearly knocked each other down getting out the doorway, and down the front steps.

Jessie squinted through the rain and the fear flowed through her, as powerful as the runaway Stanislaus. For the little boys were there, standing on the very edge of the bank which ought to have been thirty or forty yards above the river, and instead was at the very brink of it.

She could make them out clearly enough: the taller one with a windblown thatch of dark curls, the smaller one with fair hair plastered to his head. Tris threw something, tottered, and caught his balance, causing Jessie to strangle a cry of horror.

"Laurie! Tris! Come back here!" Collie bellowed, and plunged toward the children.

It was impossible to tell if the boys heard. They were still so far away, and the water created its own voices, voices that seemed to Jessie a terrifying lure to two small children who gave no thought to its hazards.

Collie yelled again, and this time both heads turned toward him. Tris took an uncertain step, then stopped, still well within the danger zone.

It was Laurie who did not move, except to look over his shoulder. And as Collie ran and Jessie watched, the earth gave way beneath the boy's feet, and Laurie flailed his arms—oh, so briefly!—and slid backward into the roiling water.

35

Jessie's throat seemed to tear with her screams. She gathered her skirts in both hands and raced toward the spot where Laurie had vanished over the bank.

Oh, God, no, no! Please, God, no!

She stumbled, went to her knees on the soggy ground, and regained her footing. Tris took a few bewildered steps toward her, beginning to realize what had happened, his pale face puckering.

Collie had cut off downstream the moment Laurie fell. From behind Jessie heard Joel's shouts, and Fanny's, and Clifford's. They were all coming, but it was too late—too late—

She reached out for Tristan and pulled him away from the water, the ugly, deadly, muddy water, her breath coming in sobs. She caught him up and hugged him tight, felt his heart hammering against her own as she clutched him, until he cried out with the force of it.

"Mama, Mama, Laurie fell! Laurie fell in the water!"

She turned, then, in time to see Collie go into the river, so far downstream. How had he run so far, so fast? Her chest ached, her legs were trembling, yet she made herself move.

Miss Smythe had come out onto the front porch and stood there, her face unreadable from this distance but surely reflecting the dismay that Jessie felt; she was holding Rosalie, wrapped in a quilt against the weather.

Jessie could hardly speak, yet she must. "Run to Miss Smythe," she told her son, and gave him a push in that direction, waiting only to see that he obeyed before she began to run again, along the top of what had once been the bluff.

She didn't stay too close to the edge for fear more of the bank would be washed away, but she was close enough to see the malevolence of the river, the devastation of which it was capable only too evident as bits and pieces of someone's cabin were swept by at incredible speed. Dear God, it would take a horse at full gallop to keep up with that, she thought in despair. She didn't look at the cabin roof, she kept her eyes on those figures ahead, those running, futile would-be rescuers.

Please, God, please, God, she begged, and didn't know whether she spoke the words aloud or not. There was a stitch in her side, yet she had to keep running, could not stop, even if it was too late...

Joel shouted something she couldn't make out, and Clifford reached him a moment later; and then, miracle of miracles, Jessie saw their heads. Bobbing like the wild bits of debris, the dark gold head and the smaller black one. Joel was hanging onto Clifford, who lay flat on the ground, and wading out into that maelstrom—

Oh, God, please, please don't punish me for my sins in this way, not Joel, too, oh please...

The litany pulsated through her mind, the stitch in her side was excruciating, yet still she ran.

Joel stretched out his hand, chest-deep in the water, the cords standing out on his neck, his face etched in anguish. Stretched out toward the two heads moving toward him, propelled by the brutal force of the water.

Only Jessie saw the tree coming behind the heads. A huge oak, complete with a root system that had been torn loose from some embankment upstream, hurtling toward them like a missile shot from a gigantic canon. She screamed a warning, but there was nothing anyone could do; Joel made a convulsive grab, nearly pulling Clifford off the bank into the river, and his fingers closed over the dark, wet hair.

The plunging tree caught Collie alongside the head with a violence that threw him well out of Joel's reach, even had Joel been able to reach for him. He could not, of course, and he scrambled back to shore with the limp small figure.

Jessie stood, now all need to run was past; the sickness spread through her so that she thought she would vomit. Her eyes were still fixed on where she had last seen Collie's face, white behind the beard, his eyes and mouth wide open, running muddy water. Had she seen his hand curl around one of those great roots, could he possibly have survived both the river and the blow?

The tree swept on, turning, plunging, bucking like a horse in some eccentricity of the current, and there was no one clinging to it now. No bobbing head in midstream, nothing but the shingles off someone's roof, and the labored breathing of all of them, there beside the river gone mad.

Jessie fell to her knees beside Laurie as Joel worked over him, trying to force life back into the small body. Laurie's eyes were closed, and his lips and fingernails—such little fingernails—were blue.

Jessie looked up and saw Fanny's face, the freckles like bright bits of paint spattered there, the sympathy naked in her eyes.

"He's not dead," Jessie said, and heard her voice as if it came from the bottom of a mine shaft, tremulous, unrecognizable. "Collie kept his head above water, he tried so hard..."

Joel had rolled the child over and pushed on his back, his ribs; water gushed out of Laurie's mouth. And then, oh, God, would there ever be a sweeter sound? Laurie choked and gagged and threw up.

It was impossible to distinguish tears from the rain on their faces. But there was no time for joy.

Joel rose, carrying his older son; Laurie's arms went around his neck but that was the most the boy could do; he sagged in exhaustion and continued to retch.

Joel's chest was heaving, his face haggard. "There's a chance Collie will make it to shore. Get the horses, Clifford—Fanny, roll up a blanket, something to wrap him in if we find

297

him. If he wasn't knocked out when that damned tree hit him, he might have managed to hang onto it—"

The effort of speaking was too much for him; he continued slogging toward the house, hugging Laurie to him. The others tried to keep up with his long strides, Clifford breaking into a loping run as they neared the buildings, heading for the barn.

No one said anything. Joel laid Laurie down on the brocade sofa in the parlor, then headed out the back door without a word.

Jessie stripped the sopping garments off the child while Fanny hurried to bring towels to rub him dry, and Miss Smythe built up the fire in the room. Tristan, his dark eyes wide and troubled, stood to one side, watching, gaze fixed on his mother's face, the barometer which ruled his life.

Once she looked over and saw him, tried to smile reassurance, yet tears were so close that it couldn't have helped much. It might well have been Tristan who went into the river, she thought. Tristan and Laurie, both. They might easily have drowned. I can swim, and I would have gone in after them if Collie hadn't been there, but I'd have been too late, and I'm not strong enough. We would all have drowned, instead of only Collie.

She was certain Collie was dead. She cried inwardly for Collie, for Joel in his blind hope of finding his brother alive, yet there was no time for tears. She had all she could do right here, to keep this little one alive.

Laurie was so icy, so pale, and the bluish color was all over his sturdy young body. They rubbed at him briskly, trying to turn the blue to pink. Fanny brought hot milk, and when Laurie could sit they held the cup for him, so that he could sip. His teeth were chattering now, his entire body shook, and finally Jessie wrapped him in a blanket and sat with him in the rocker drawn close to the fire, holding him tightly against her, until at last he fell asleep.

A refrain ran through her mind: Thank you, God, for this one's life. And please, help Joel to find Collie, whatever's happened, so that we'll know.

Tristan came to lean against her knee, and she put out a hand to draw him near, her eyes brimming. How close she had come today to losing nearly everyone who meant anything to her. How close to the end of all her dreams.

And still there was Collie; when she closed her eyes she saw his face, his blond hair dark and wet, the eyes wide, the mouth gasping for breath. It would not go away, no matter what she did.

It was nearly dusk when the men returned. The women heard them coming, and no one moved. They all waited, bracing themselves for the worst, knowing even before they were told that the quest had been fruitless.

Joel's shoulders sagged, and his eyes had sunk into his head. Clifford, who usually spent very little time in the house and never before had ventured past the kitchen, came into the parlor, where they all stiffened, awaiting the blow.

Miss Smythe sat holding a sleeping Rosalie. Laurie slept, too, his open mouth now pink in color, on the damask sofa; he had been afraid to be put to bed in his own room, and Jessie did not want to let any of them out of her sight. Tristan clung to her knees; she drew him close against her, feeling the welcome warmth of him, the small bones, the precious flesh of her flesh.

Only Fanny rose when the men came in, waiting.

Joel's eyes met Jessie's across the room, the beautiful room they had made together, which now meant so little except that their children were safe in it.

He shook his head and moved toward the fire, holding out his hands. "We couldn't find any sign of him. We found the tree, the one that hit him. We're both pretty sure it was the same one; it had lodged crossways of some big rocks about ten miles downstream, where the riverbed widens out and the water's not so deep. There was nothing on it, no sign of Collie. If we ever find him, it'll have to be after the water goes down."

For long moments no one said anything. Then Jessie forced starch into her legs, pushed herself out of the chair.

"You'll both be starved, and you're drenched. Get into some dry clothes, and Fanny and I will get you something to eat."

They hadn't cooked a meal that day; except for Tristan and Rosalie, no one had eaten anything. They were not hungry now, either, but Fanny moved obediently toward the kitchen, where she began silently to prepare the food that nobody wanted, that would choke them all to eat it.

Eating seemed so pointless now, yet it was what they always did at this time of day, and so they did it.

The flood of 1861–62 was the worst in history.

In Knight's Ferry the waters rose twelve feet above any previous recorded level; they were powerful enough to carry

299

away houses, millstones, and huge boulders that had remained in the streambed for centuries.

Half the town was swept away: the mills, the bridge, the shops and houses along Main Street. The general store remained, though the water had reached to the height of its counter inside, and much of the merchandise was gone or damaged beyond salvaging. A safe had been carried away, filled with gold, and for weeks after the flood receded, there were those who hunted for it, along the river bottom, among the rocks.

The devastation along the San Joaquin and Tuolumne rivers was great, but that along the Stanislaus was far greater, for there were more settlements along its banks.

The day after Collie had been swept away, Joel and Clifford rode off early in the morning to see what had happened elsewhere, to do what they could to help.

John and Eva Curtis had been in their house when it was jolted off its foundations; Mr. Tulloch, who owned one of the mills that had been destroyed at Knight's Ferry, was of the opinion that they could right the house, once things dried out a bit.

"Jack it up, somehow," Eva related from the safety of the Shand home, where they had fled for refuge after a night spent in their tilted home, expecting momentarily to be carried on downstream. "I don't know how they'll manage that, but if Mr. Tulloch says so...I was never so scared in my life, Jessie. The little ones clung to me and begged to be assured we weren't all going to die any minute, and what could I say?"

Ginny and Oliver Allen, well back up a canyon from the Stanislaus, had thought they were safe enough, until Ginny got up at night when Nellie had a nightmare, and stepped into four inches of water.

"I woke up Oliver right quick," Ginny said, "and we got the younguns up, didn't even take time to get 'em dressed. The barn's on higher ground, we thought we'd be safe *there*, but we hadn't counted on the little creek adding to what was rising from the river. We was cut off, in the barn, for two days. We didn't have nothing to eat but some chicken feed, and the little ones was too young to chew that. I told them to chew on the alfalfa; it would keep a cow alive, seemed like it might do for human beings, too, for a short while." She shivered, even sitting in Jessie's cozy parlor before a roaring fire. "That water kept getting closer and closer to the barn

300

door, and then finally it came inside, and Oliver said maybe we better make us a raft or something, before it was too late. He and Charlie started tearing boards off the barn, so the wind came in something fierce, and said if the water reached the loft we'd tie ourselves to the raft and pray to God to deliver us. I never prayed so long and so hard in my whole life, not even coming across that terrible desert. Funny, ain't it, don't know which is worse, not enough water, or too much of it."

They had not had to take to the raft after all, which was a good thing. None of them thought the flimsy thing would have survived in the rampaging waters for long. Their barn had shifted position during the last few hours, reviving their terror, but then Charlie noted that the high-water mark inside its walls was dropping. And sure enough, the river had begun to go down.

Their house and all its contents vanished into the flood. They were left with their barn, a chicken house and a dozen chickens, and most of their livestock.

"And the clothes on our backs," Ginny said. "I reckon we're amoṇg the lucky ones. There's plenty dead down river, besides poor Collie."

It was true. Dozens of people were drowned, along with hundreds of head of cattle and sheep, chickens and pigs, dogs and horses.

With the bridge out, it was difficult to make contact with the inhabitants of Knight's Ferry, yet the word got around somehow. Annie was fine; her little house was perched far enough up the hill so that it had escaped all damage. The Groveses' bakery, below her, had not fared nearly as well.

They had had plenty of warning, as far as that went, for half the village had stood and watched the river rise around the bridge and carried the latest news back to those who did not choose to stand in wind and rain anticipating doom.

Mamie finally went to see for herself, half believing that the tale-carriers were exaggerating, and came back with her hair blown half off her head and her mouth set in a firm line.

"We'd better get out, Mama. Pack up everything we can carry, and move to higher ground."

Sarah Groves gaped at the daughter who was almost a stranger, for all that they worked side by side in the bakery every day. Mamie had grown withdrawn, was not the smiling girl she remembered, the good-natured, the thoughtful. She was quiet, introspective, and given to easy tears for the most absurd reasons. Now the girl was telling her, in the middle of the afternoon, to pack up and get out of the only home she had.

"Where will we go?" Sarah asked weakly. "How can we leave our belongings here?"

"We'll take our clothes, that's about all we can carry, and go to Alice's," Mamie decided, already putting her intention into action without even bothering to take off her wet cloak.

"To Alice's! Walk three miles, for heaven's sake? I can't walk that far, not in this weather!"

Mamie straightened from the bundle she was making of her own garments to give her mother a look devoid of sympathy. "Well, I certainly can't carry you. You can go up the hill to Annie Ryan's, if you want to, though if this turns out to be as bad as it seems likely to be, Annie'll have more than a houseful. Better go to Alice's, where there won't be anybody but family." She looked at a skirt, decided it wasn't worth carrying three miles, and tossed it aside. "There're those who think most of the town will go. Certainly all of Main Street. This old building here, why, it isn't even on a decent foundation. It'll probably be one of the first to let loose, when the water gets here. I think we'd better go up the hill and across, not try to walk down the street toward the bridge. If the dam goes out we'll get a lot more water in a hurry, and I don't intend to be in it if I can help it."

She threw a few more things into the bundle and tied up the sheet around it, while Sarah watched her uncertainly. "Well? Are you going to take anything, or just go in the clothes you have on? Alice's won't fit you, nor mine, so you'd better have at least a change of your own."

Reluctant, yet nudged by her daughter's words, Sarah made a halfhearted effort. After a moment, Mamie began to do the selecting for her, quickly, no wasted motion, as if the water even now were creeping in their front door. The sensation was so strong that Sarah paused to look, just to be sure it wasn't happening.

"Alice hasn't got room for us," she said once, and Mamie didn't look at her.

"She's got a kitchen floor, and that's more than we're going to have here in a few hours. You want that shawl, or shall I leave it?"

"What will we do about the shop? The stove, the baking pans, all our supplies? We just bought a hundred pounds of flour..."

Mamie made a face and a sound that wasn't quite a laugh. "You want to try to carry that flour up the hill? Maybe, if we're lucky, the stove won't go with everything else, though I wouldn't count on it. If the water can move boulders as big as a house, it can move one old iron stove. There, is there anything else you want to take? No? Then let's go."

Sarah hesitated, then picked up her own bundle as Mamie led the way out through the shop and into the street. "Mamie, aren't you going to lock the door? Someone will come in and help themselves, with no one here to tend anything . . ."

"Let them salvage anything they can," Mamie said indifferently. "We can't take any more." She led the way down the street, away from the bridge, and began the climb up the hill.

As she saw others, hunched against the rain, carrying their belongings, Sarah became truly afraid. They, too, were fleeing the storm, the flood. Maybe it wouldn't even be safe at Alice's, and there was already a houseful there, with three younguns and Alice in the family way again.

Dear God, she thought, lifting her eyes to the wet sky, what was to become of them?

They were passed by Louise Babcock, handling her own buggy piled high with trunks and bundles. The woman gave them not a look or a word, urging her horse on up the hill. They saw Silas Wofford on his front porch; he waved and didn't move, his attention on the activity at the other end of town, nearer the river.

Sarah was afraid to look back, as if, like Lot's wife, she might see something so evil that she would be stricken deaf and dumb on the spot, be turned to a pillar of salt that would disintegrate in the rain that appeared to be going to go on falling forever. Over a month, now, since it had stopped for more than a few minutes, as if it were God's punishment inflicted upon them for their sins.

The lawyer, James Hartley, caught up with them and walked beside Mamie for a few minutes, carrying a large box. He was moving his records, he told her, as he'd been warned by Arthur Babcock at the bank that the expectation now was that all of Main Street would be gone by morning.

At the top of the hill they turned at the sound of wagon wheels, and Sarah gave a cry of relief. Harry Kelly jumped down and helped them up, tossing their bundles into the wagon behind the seat.

"Alice sent me," he said succinctly, and that was the extent

303

of the conversation until they reached the little house placed high and safe above the town.

The newspaper came out later in the week, printed on brown paper, in half-sheets, because that was all that was available. Luis brought a copy, a Luis looking older and tireder. "I would have come sooner, but I was assured that though Collin had been lost, you were otherwise all safe here."

"And at Casa Sañudo?" Jessie asked, though since that was situated up a broad canyon far from the Stanislaus, she had not been worried about it.

"All is as well as it can be, under these circumstances. Teresita does not know she has lost her father, and Bonifasia—" He paused, and then decided not to say anything about his sister. "I had thought to ride downstream, farther than Joel and Clifford went on the day it happened. Perhaps, somehow, Collin was carried a long way; someone may have news of him. I will stop by on the way back to tell you what I have learned, even if it is nothing," he said with a weary smile.

That evening they read the paper at the supper table, eaten in the kitchen because that room was easier to keep warm than the parlors. Joel ran a finger down the list of losses—a flour mill, valued at thirty-thousand dollars; houses, shops, the hotel that belonged to Silas Wofford—"It doesn't say anything about his house, so maybe that didn't go."

He stopped, and Jessie leaned forward to read the fine print. "What is it? What's the matter?"

"The dead," Joel said heavily.

Jessie's throat closed and then she made herself speak. "Is Collie listed?"

"No. This is only the bodies they've recovered. There's another list, over here, of those presumed dead."

"Who, then?" She waited, not daring to speculate.

"Clara Ridback. She wasn't drowned, she was killed when the building came down and something struck her on the head. Someone saw her and pulled her out of the water. It appears she had gone to bed and to sleep. The shop simply collapsed, with her in the middle of it."

Clara Ridback. Jessie sighed in relief that it had not been someone she cared about. "Maybe nobody warned her. She wasn't close to very many people, was she?"

Joel spoke slowly, remembering. "I don't know. She did a

good business, but I never heard that she had many close friends." Except the men who had sometimes climbed the stairs in the dark to her second-floor apartment; he'd heard about a few of them. Rich men, all of them. Men who'd had more important things to do, with the river about to wipe out the town, than take a chance on being seen going into Clara's place in daylight. "And Mr. Sully. Remember, the old man who made the saddle for Laurie's birthday? He was a grouchy old fellow, but I sort of liked him. He made beautiful saddles."

He'd had to add someone's name, he couldn't show shock at Clara's death alone, not the way Jessie'd always felt about her.

Jessie pushed her plate aside and scooted her chair around so that she could read along with him. "They're going to start building a new bridge at once. It'll take them months, though, won't it? We won't be able to drive to town before spring."

The destruction was appalling. Homes, stores, bridges, dams, and ditches, or flumes, that brought water to the remaining mines. Jessie read aloud, " 'Table Mountain ditch has sustained a loss of nearly a mile of flume at the upper end of the ditch, which probably cannot be replaced much short of twelve-thousand dollars. The San Joaquin ditch is nearly all washed away for nearly a mile, and though the dam is injured in some degree, the continuing high water makes an estimate of damages difficult, though it is felt to be in the vicinity of twelve-hundred dollars.' " She lifted her face to Joel's. "How in heaven's name will all those things be replaced? So much money! And yet the money's the least of it, isn't it?"

She reached into her apron pocket and brought out a sheet of paper, which she smoothed on the table. "I found this today, in Collie's room. He was writing to his mother."

Joel stared at it, making no attempt to read what it said. "I suppose we'll have to send it on to her. I'll have to . . . tell her what happened to him."

"Tell her how brave he was," Jessie urged softly. "Tell her that both Laurie and Tristan might well have drowned, had it not been for him. I couldn't have reached them in time, and they didn't even hear me when I called to them. If they hadn't turned when they did, Tris would have been on the edge when the bank crumbled, too, and Collie couldn't have saved them both—"

Joel hugged her, shutting off her words. He didn't need to be told again how close it had been. His brother, and both his sons. He had gone along with Jessie's insistence upon representing himself as Laurie's uncle, but within himself he never thought of the child as anything but his beloved son.

"You know," he said, "I used to think about writing to her about Collie's death. When we were crossing the mountains and the deserts. Several times things happened to people, and I thought, what if it was Collie, instead of Adrian Groves, who got his legs crushed? Or what if the buffalo had stampeded over him? I didn't want anything to happen to Collie, you understand, it was just that sometimes I thought about the things that *could* happen to him. He was so young, such a greenhorn, such an innocent. And I hated his mother."

"Did you want to hurt her? To tell her he was dead?"

"I don't know if I wanted to, exactly. Only she was so opposed to him coming with me, it's the main reason I agreed to bring him. Because it would pay her back, a little, for what she did to me."

"She knew you were Richard Aubin's son," Jessie said softly. "How else could she feel about you, Joel? She was engaged to marry him, and while he was away on a trip he seduced your mother. You were the proof that he had been unfaithful to her, and then you went there, to Chicago, and threatened everything that made up her life. How could she have welcomed you?"

She felt the rigidity of the arm around her and put it down to his emotion about Collie, not to the reference to infidelity. It was a relief to him, in a way, that Clara was dead. Sometimes he'd had the odd notion that Clara might have found it amusing to let Jessie know about that night he'd taken Clara to bed. Now Jessie needn't ever know, needn't ever be hurt by it.

"I suppose she couldn't," he admitted now. "Yet I disliked her then, and I'll never like her. Did he tell her anything about Bonifasia, and Teresa Dolores? Or should I tell her?"

"I didn't see anything about them. He was only beginning the letter," Jessie said. "Maybe it would be kinder not to mention them. Not to let them know they have a granddaughter they'll never see or know. Or would it ease their grief to realize that something of Collie lives on, in a beautiful little girl? I don't know which, Joel."

He didn't know, either. He didn't show her the letter to Mr. and Mrs. Richard Aubin, of Chicago, Illinois, when he had finished it, so she didn't know what he decided.

She imagined what it would feel like to lose a son; she

would not inflict that pain upon anyone, not even the woman who had hurt Joel so badly in protecting her own family. Under similar circumstances, Jessie thought she'd probably have had to reject the illegitimate son, too, to protect the other children.

Whatever it was Joel had written, Jessie hoped that it was done in an attitude of pity, not of cruelty. She didn't ask.

36

As if nature wreaked her vengeance upon the sinful settlers, the great flood was followed by drought. So soon after the waters had all but wiped out the communities along the Stanislaus, the heat came again. The sky was unfailingly a brilliant, cloudless blue; the fields grew scorched and brown.

Jessie miscarried in June, and again in September. When Joel sat at her bedside, helpless as men were always helpless against such things, she squeezed his hand.

"It's nothing. I'll be up and around in a day or two," she assured him. "I prayed for Rosalie's safe birth, and swore I wouldn't pray for any more if she was spared."

What kind of God extracted that sort of promise from a woman? Joel thought savagely, but he didn't put his doubts into words in front of Jessie. "If I didn't make love to you—" he began, and she lifted her fingers to lay them across his lips.

"If you didn't make love to me, I would shrivel and die," Jessie said softly, and he did not have to finish the sentence, at least not aloud. If he didn't make her pregnant, she would not bleed this way, would not have to retire to her bed for a week or two at a time. Guilt assailed him, but his need was too great. He could not have a celibate future.

News from the east continued to be bad. Jessie would have spared herself the ordeal of reading about battles, casualties, and defeats, having plenty of problems to deal with at home.

Joel, however, read aloud to her and the names became familiar. Shiloh, New Orleans, Bull Run. Lee, Jackson, McClellan. But the conflict remained too distant to touch more than the periphery of Jessie's awareness.

That fall Jessie's merciful God allowed yet another tragedy to stalk the already stricken land. Smallpox spread rapidly from one settlement, one isolated farmhouse, to another, so that all were afraid to visit, afraid to risk contracting it.

Fanny, who almost never went off the place, succumbed to it only a few weeks after Jessie had risen from her second miscarriage. Jessie was torn between the compulsion to nurse the girl and the fear that she would bring the contagion home to her children.

Joel settled the matter by refusing to allow Jessie near the little house where Fanny lay dying. It would not be fair to her own family, he insisted. He left it to Clifford to nurse his young wife; Joel carried cooked food and other supplies to them, leaving them on the doorstep rather than handing them over in person. He bought new sheets rather than risk anyone's handling the contaminated ones, which Clifford was instructed to burn.

By the end of October, Fanny and Clifford were both dead, as were more than a dozen of the Mexican workers at Rancho Sañudo. Teresa Dolores had it, and Bonifasia, and both recovered, though they were scarred. Luckily the child's face was spared, for the mother's was not.

Two weeks after the double funeral, there was a wedding in Knight's Ferry to which they were invited, but they did not go. Joel was adamant that the children not be exposed to any disease, though it seemed that the smallpox was waning. He refused to take chances.

So Jessie sent her love and good wishes to Annie Ryan and Silas Wofford, who had decided, after all this time, to marry and live together. Silas was not as wealthy a man as he had been; he had lost his hotel and various other properties in the flood, and he said he was too old to rebuild or start over on any enterprise. That was for younger men.

His bones grew cold, however, and he was lonesome. He'd injured a leg during the flood, trying to salvage as many of his belongings as he could. He had managed to save his house, at the cost of a fracture that would leave him with a permanent limp; walking would never again be easy for him, and he didn't want to live alone.

Annie, in her turn, though she intended to continue ministering to the sick, was lonely, too. Jessie was the closest family tie she had; Jessie's youngsters were the grandchildren she would never have, but they lived too far away in the country. She needed someone of her own. Though she suspected that Silas wanted a nurse and cook as much as a companion, she took only a few days to decide to accept his proposal. She rented out her little house on the hill, reserving the right to return to it if she should ever feel that she wanted her privacy again, and moved into Silas Wofford's house on Main Street. It gave her a sense of well-being to be addressed now as Mrs. Wofford, and she found that Silas was not as selfish as she'd feared he might be. When she came home at odd hours, after delivering a baby or binding up a wound suffered in some accident, Silas would often have a pot of soup ready for her, and he would sit across the table as she recounted the details of her day. When she wanted to talk, he was a good listener. When she chose to remain silent, the old man would patter around the kitchen in his slippered feet, bringing her tea, slicing her bread, and Annie grew comfortable in the relationship, even to sharing Silas's bed. There were worse things, she told him, than two elderly people keeping each other warm, and Silas cackled in amusement.

In December, they had an unexpected visit from James Hartley, the lawyer from Knight's Ferry.

He had come to see Joel, who was at that time up on the hill behind the house attempting to enlarge the small dam he had constructed across the tiny creek, to conserve every drop of water that he could so that none should fall needlessly into the Stanislaus and go unused. Jessie sent Laurie up to fetch him, ushering the gentleman into the front parlor and offering him a cup of tea and a plate of cakes. She knew of no business that Joel had with the man, and curiosity hammered at her.

He was a man of forty, and he wore a business suit, something not often seen in Stanislaus County outside of church services. He ate a small cake, helped himself to a second one, and looked around the parlor. "Lovely home you have here, Mrs. Shand. Very nice. I'd heard it was most elegant. You were fortunate that you lost nothing in the flood." And then he reddened, embarrassed at his *faux pas*. "Of your property, I mean, of course. So many houses washed away, though few of them were as nice as this one. Of course, if one loses one's home, it doesn't matter how fine it was, does it? I offered my condolences to your husband on the loss of his . . . cousin, Mr. Aubin, of course."

There was a hesitation at his mention of Collie which Jessie could interpret in only one way. Did he doubt that Collie had been Joel's cousin? Was he aware that they had been half brothers, and that Joel was the illegitimate one?

And if the lawyer knew it, was it common knowledge?

As far as she knew, no one had ever looked down upon her for marrying a man who did not have a legitimate name, and she didn't think she'd care if they did, though of course she kept his secret. She loved Joel for what he was, not for what his parents had or had not done. Still, this was disturbing, because she knew that it would bother Joel.

"There were many losses," Jessie said. "All of them very sad."

"Yes, yes, of course. Fifty inches of rain in one winter! Who would ever expect such a thing! Still, they know the floods go in ten-year cycles, and we'd best prepare for the next one in '72 or thereabouts, I suppose. The river was forty feet deep at the town, had you heard that?"

"Yes," Jessie said, "I had."

"I hope it doesn't distress you to talk of it? It's a little easier now that they've put a footbridge over the river, but we're back to the ferry for horses and buggies until they finish the new bridge. This one is to be a covered one, did you know? And will be much stronger and higher, so that it can never be washed out again, eight feet above the level of the old one. It will be a great blessing to have a good bridge again."

"Yes," Jessie agreed. She sprang up in relief when she heard the horse outside. "Here, I think this is my husband now."

She hoped they would not conduct their business, whatever it was, behind closed doors. That hope was dashed when Mr. Hartley expressed the need to convey some confidential information, and Joel nodded.

"Jessie, I could use some of that tea. And a couple of cakes, if there are any more."

She brought them back quickly, disappointed to find that the lawyer was going on with the same sort of chit-chat he had employed with her. It was not until the door had closed behind her that his tone took on a professional note, and Jessie stopped shamelessly outside that door to listen. If men insisted on being so secretive about things that were just as

310

important to the women as to them, then they asked for eavesdropping.

"I do not know if this will come as a surprise to you, Mr. Shand, but I pray you will pardon the length of time it has taken for me to come to you. There was so much to do, after the flood, you know. So many things to attend to. I knew about Mrs. Ridback's will, of course, as I drew it up, but since she was not present, like the rest of my clients, to badger me about it, I'm afraid it slipped my mind until recently."

Jessie froze, and Joel made a peculiar sound. "Mrs. Ridback? Clara Ridback? What does her will have to do with me?"

The lawyer cleared his throat. "Quite a bit, sir. I gather that Mrs. Ridback had no family, no family at all. She laughed when I suggested while I was handling some of her business transactions that she should make out a will. Since she had no one to leave her money to, and she was a young woman, she asked what difference it would make. I explained to her that dying intestate could create all sorts of complications for those appointed to settle her estate, and that—" He paused to cough. "I told her that her assets might fall into hands other than those she would have chosen. Actually, since so much of the property on which she held mortgages was washed away in the flood, the estate is much diminished from what it would otherwise have been. Still, what remains is of substantial value, and when I prevailed upon Mrs. Ridback to name an heir, she named...you, Mr. Shand."

Incredulous, Jessie heard the words. Why would Clara have left anything to Joel? And what would the community think when they heard about it, as they surely would?

Joel sounded as astounded as she felt. "Me? But why? She must have said why."

"I didn't press her as to *why*, Mr. Shand. That was, after all, none of my business. I was satisfied that she had made proper arrangements for the handling of her estate, which she did. Now, I have brought along with me a description of the various properties involved, and the titles will be made over to you in due time. I'm afraid the cash involved is a relatively minor sum—I've already instructed Arthur Babcock that the money she had in the bank will be credited to your account—but there is, as you see, a list of other properties—"

There were footsteps and childish laughter from the front

hallway, and Jessie straightened and moved away from the door.

Clara Ridback, of all people. What an extraordinary thing to have done, left all her property to Joel.

It troubled her as she went about her work. She had not yet found a replacement for Fanny, and Miss Smythe only took care of the children; she did not participate in the housekeeping, so Jessie had plenty to do. Yet her mind was not upon her tasks. She could see, in imagination, the eyebrows rising as people heard the news. Why would Clara Ridback have left her fortune, whatever it amounted to, to Joel Shand?

Jessie wasted no time in talking to Joel as soon as the lawyer had left. "What did he want?" she asked, point-blank, and knew a strange inner sense of relief when he told her the truth about it. Why, had she expected him to deny what the lawyer had said, to lie about it?

"Why on earth would she have done such a thing?" Jessie demanded.

Joel shrugged. "How the hell do I know?"

"But she must have had a reason! People are going to think she had a reason—" Jessie stopped, because she didn't want to put into words what she thought people were going to think.

"Hartley said she laughed when she told him to put my name in there as heir. She thought it was a joke, to begin with. She was a young woman, for God's sake. She didn't expect to die! Didn't expect anybody to see the will except Hartley." He grimaced and reached for one of the cookies Jessie had just taken out of the oven. "She never thought I'd ever get any of it, but she thought it was funny to put my name in there. Probably because she knew it would stir up a hornet's nest of speculation, make everybody wonder." He stood, chewing thoughtfully, his gaze on his wife's face. "She knew you didn't like her, Jess. Maybe she hoped that if, by some small chance, she *did* die and anybody ever heard of that will, she'd stir up all kinds of trouble. For you, and for me. That it would make people think what you're thinking now."

She felt the heat in her face. "I'm not thinking anything, I'm only wondering."

"Wondering what I'd done to earn any part of her estate?" Joel asked dryly, gathering up a few more cookies to stick into his pocket before he went back outside. "She was a troublemaker, and she made eyes at me often enough on the trail so it was pretty plain she'd have welcomed my attentions if I'd offered them. She was older than you, Jess, and not as pretty; she was jealous of what you were and what you had. And she was spiteful enough to play this mean little trick, to drive a wedge between us, if she could. To hurt you, to hurt me, for not being what she wanted me to be. Are we going to let her do it? Spoil everything good we have, with suspicion?"

"Do you really think she was capable of doing something like that?" Jessie asked faintly. "It seems so . . . so evil."

"I don't know if she was evil. I think she was mostly selfish, and jealous, and this was her idea of a joke. A private joke, maybe, because she didn't expect to die, not at her age, she didn't."

"What . . . what are we going to tell people? If they wonder about it?"

"Not a damned thing," Joel said flatly, and walked out of the house.

Which, Jessie decided, was the only thing they could do that wouldn't make matters worse. Still, it made her very uncomfortable, and she wished Clara Ridback had named someone else in her will.

The amount of money involved was not large, as Hartley had said, but it was cash money, something few farmers ever saw much of, or held onto for long. Joel reinvested it, as Clara had been doing all along, part of it in a new bakery for Mamie and Sarah, part of it in a tin shop and a shoe shop.

No doubt there were those who wondered, but no one came right out and asked. Joel had such an arrogant air that it would have taken a brave man to put a question about the legacy, or to make a joke about it. Jessie was not as adept as he at handling the umcomfortable situation; she did feel compelled to make the explanation they had arrived at, to her close friends. She made no bones about her resentment that the woman could have deliberately chosen such a way to humiliate her, and wished she could take the matter in stride, as Joel did.

Her trees were spared by the flood, even nurtured by the wet winter, which enabled the trees to establish good root systems; most of them survived the subsequent drought when Jessie set the children to hauling water by the bucket for them. They turned the house and grounds into a showplace.

Had it not been for Clara's charity, or whatever it had been, they might have had a far more difficult time of those following years when the crops again were stunted for lack of rain.

Payments were slow in coming in on the mortaged lands, because of course the drought affected them all; without crops, a farmer cannot pay his debts. Jessie became uneasily aware that Joel was not as generous as he might have been in making arrangements for new payment schedules. One unfortunate fellow who came to beg for an extended term of payment left the house nearly in tears over the prospect of losing his land, and Jessie, who had overheard the last part of their conversation, could not refrain from comment.

"You aren't really going to take his land if he can't satisfy the demand by fall, are you, Joel?"

Her husband gave her a level glance. "Why wouldn't I? That's the terms he made. Payment, plus interest, by a given date, which I've already extended for him twice. He put the land up for security. That's how business works, sweetheart. There's risk involved on both sides, and if a man can't pay as agreed, he loses his collateral."

"But you didn't put up anything, you ran no risk—it was Clara Ridback's investment, not yours. And the man has a family to care for."

"Jessie, every man has a family to care for. You can't go soft because of that, or nobody'd ever collect anything. Stay out of the business end of things, honey. You don't know anything about it, and your heart is too soft."

She understood the necessity for lines being drawn in a business deal, but she felt there was room for some leeway in matters of this kind. A shiftless man, a shirker, was one thing; but a farmer couldn't help the fact that it didn't rain for years at a time, couldn't help a plague of grasshoppers that devoured his crops just before harvest time. As long as it wasn't actually taking food out of their own mouths, couldn't they afford to let the man take a little longer to pay his debt?

There *was* a monetary worry, even with the inheritance from Clara, which Joel hadn't anticipated because he thought Luis would handle his own end of it, and that turned out not to be the case.

Luis seldom came to the house except on business, though the way he looked at Jessie made her think he might have liked to. He often brought her books for her growing library—

invariably chosen to please her, unlike the volumes Joel had ordered at random to fill the empty shelves—and sometimes he talked to her about them after she'd read them.

On this occasion, beyond a perfunctory smile and greeting, Luis paid no attention to her at all. Eavesdropping was impossible, since Jessie was training a new housekeeper and could not have listened in undetected. Mrs. Sullivan was a willing woman, recently widowed and unused to working for anyone else; she'd never been in such a fancy house before. So Jessie, well-schooled by Bonifasia, stayed in the dining room, explaining how she handled the china, where each piece went, and how the table was to be set for a forthcoming dinner party for twelve. Mrs. Sullivan, poor soul, was overwhelmed by the array of silver and crystal, and Jessie wound up drawing her a diagram of each place setting.

Uncharacteristically, Luis left the house without pausing to wish her *adiós*, or *hasta luego*. Curious, Jessie left Mrs. Sullivan studying the drawing she had made and crossed the hall to where Joel stood staring out the window after the departing horseman.

"Is something wrong, Joel?" She had carried with her one of the silver spoons, and she polished it absently on her apron. The way Luis rode, you'd think the devil was after him.

Joel spun around and smashed one fist into the other palm. "Wrong! Yes, I guess you'd say that. Would you believe Luis is behind on his taxes, and didn't think it was important enough to worry about? The Mexicans did not have those taxes, and he finds them unreasonable, so his attitude was to ignore them. And he only bothers to tell me about the matter when a legal paper is served on him, demanding payment within thirty days or forfeiture of his ranch."

Jessie's jaw sagged. This was far worse than anything she could have anticipated. "And he doesn't have the money? But Luis is one of the richest men in the valley."

"He has one of the largest landholdings, but that doesn't mean he has the cash. You should have heard him, explaining to me how many families he supports, what his expenses are, how everything is tied up in the land. The damned fool, he actually thought that because the title to the land is now in gringo names, they wouldn't go this far, wouldn't take his land! I disabused him of that notion in a hurry," Joel said, though with little satisfaction.

"He has never understood American ways," Jessie said. "It is all so different from what they did under the Mexican

315

government. Even with his learning English to protect himself, the whole concept is strange to him. How much money does he need?"

"A lot," Joel said, not trying to conceal his bitterness. "Do you know there's enough silver in that saddle of his to have paid for this house when it was built? He has plenty of things like that, those diamonds his mother wore, and Bonifasia now has—do you think he'll consider selling them, to raise the money? He looked me square in the face and said it was unthinkable! The family jewels, he said, as if they were the children! He's a child himself, in many ways!"

Jessie waited, wondering how bad it really was. She knew little of how much money there was for anything; Joel always seemed to find a sufficient amount for whatever they needed or wanted.

"They all lived that way, those Mexican land-grant holders, for years, all their lives," Joel conceded. "This was the land of milk and honey; for generations they had more than they knew what to do with—silver saddle trappings and elegant clothes and jewels for their women, and big houses with dozens of servants. He's got far more people on that place than he needs, now that the cattle market is so depressed. But do you think he'll let any of them go? They're 'his people' and he's responsible for them! All those mouths to feed, and they're of no use to him. They don't bring him any return."

"What do you want him to do? They were born on that land, the same as he was. They won't know anything else."

"Well, they won't know even that if he doesn't come up with the money for the goddamned taxes. If *I* don't come up with it," he amended savagely. "God, I thought we'd talked about business often enough so he had some idea—but he's a child, an innocent, about so many things!"

There was no sound from the dining room behind her, and Jessie wondered if Mrs. Sullivan was taking this all in, and if she'd mention it the next time she was at her son's in Knight's Ferry. She didn't get along with her daughter-in-law, so she didn't want to live with her son, but she'd requested two days off a month so she could see her grandchildren. If she talked about Shand business there, would it immediately be known all over San Joaquin and Stanislaus counties?

"Will we need to mortgage this house?" Jessie asked. She liked the house, she was used to it, but she didn't put it before people. She fully understood Luis's refusal to turn out any of his Mexican laborers; they had nowhere to go, no way to fend for themselves after a lifetime of existence under the almost feudal *patrón* system.

Joel glared at her as if she'd expressed some blasphemy. "I'll never mortgage this house. Not for any such damn fool thing as Luis Sañudo's taxes, anyway."

"What, then?"

"The gold," Joel said finally. "I'll have to use Collie's gold. After all, his widow and daughter will benefit as much as anybody. Only, by God, this had better be a lesson to Luis. He'll have to change his style of living enough to allow for such things as gringo taxes, no matter how much he resents them, and learn that even having my name on his deed won't save his lands. And he'll have to cut his losses on the cattle that're dying because of the drought and consider agriculture. All right, there's a flood every ten years or so, and a couple of those ten years are likely to be dry ones, but there's still more money in grain than there is in cattle, if I can only get that through his head. 'My father always raised cattle,' he says, as if that makes one damned bit of difference to what is happening *now*."

She understood Joel's logic. Yet she felt for Luis, too, on his great ranch that was like a small kingdom, a kingdom he had always known and could not bear to lose or change.

Across the continent, the rumblings of war continued. Jessie thanked God that California was so far away from the battlegrounds, doubly thanked Him that Joel did not have to fight in a civil war that divided the country into two factions: one for, one against slavery.

He read the reports avidly, for all that they were published days or even weeks after the events took place, although the new telegraph lines linking east to west eventually shortened those times considerably. Joel subscribed to Sacramento and San Francisco papers, as well as the local weekly, comparing viewpoints and expounding his own theories to Jessie and the wide-eyed children.

"The railroad's crossed the Mississippi," he told them, "and it's possible to ride a stagecoach from San Francisco to St. Louis. The country's drawing together. Someday there will be trains all the way across the entire United States. People won't have to travel in covered wagons any more. They'll probably come all the way in a couple of weeks, maybe less."

Weeks, instead of months. Jessie thought of that long,

punishing journey, of the sufferings and deprivation, and marveled at the picture Joel's words evoked. Would there someday be as well trains to Oregon, so that she could visit Zadie and her family? If they were able to cross the Rockies and the Sierra with trains, why not the Trinities and the Siskiyous to the north?

"Can we ride on a train?" Laurie asked, his eyes bright with interest.

"Why not? One day we'll be shipping our grain to eastern markets, and maybe our cattle, too. You can go along to bring back the money," Joel told the child, grinning, momentarily diverted from the newspaper stories.

There was no forgetting for long, though, because every week the papers came. While the primary concern of the Californians was the drought that sucked the juices from men and beasts as well as from the land, they were aware as well of the horrors of that war. They read the reports of casualties, and prisoners taken, and men missing in action, and Jessie guiltily thanked God that Joel was not among them, that he was here, safe and well.

Men came to the house now to talk to Joel. It was no longer unusual for them to be closeted for hours behind closed doors; she knew they talked of politics, of power and influence in the state of California. Sometimes they came to dinner, with or without their wives. When it was only the men, the children must not disturb their elders. When the wives came, the men restrained their conversation of importance until the women had withdrawn to the parlor; then they drank their whiskey and smoked their cigars in the library, so that Jessie despaired of ever getting the stink of tobacco out of the draperies and the carpets.

Jessie heard enough to know that Joel was contributing money to election campaigns. He backed those who thought as he did about the importance of irrigation, the necessity of using tax funds to further such major projects. She was too busy with household and family matters to worry about it.

Some of the visitors she liked, and some she didn't. The wives were all stylishly dressed. Many of them wore jewelry, and Jessie had the uneasy conviction that most of them would have had nothing to do with her if they hadn't wanted her husband to make contributions to their husbands' causes.

She thought them superficial and shallow, not women she could talk to easily and freely, the way she'd always done with Mamie and Eva Curtis and Ginny Allen. She missed

Mamie, for all that she hadn't seen a lot of her in recent years; she'd known Mamie was there, a few miles away, if she needed her. The Curtises still came to dine occasionally, but Joel was so unenthusiastic about the Allens that Jessie had stopped including them in any of her formal dinner plans. She wasn't willing to give them up altogether, however, and made it a point to take the buggy to visit them at least once a month, and to invite Ginny over for an afternoon of talk between her own excursions.

The war in the east was drawing to a close. Everyone said the South could not withstand much more. The Union forces had drawn upon Californian grain, and the price was up; for a few years they had neither drought nor flood, and the crops were abundant. The Shands, along with their neighbors, flourished and expanded their holdings, and Joel bought Jessie a diamond ring.

It felt too heavy on her hand, which Joel said was ridiculous; she refused to wear it except for the formal dinners with the men who pulled the strings behind the world of elected officials. The other women's eyes brightened at the sight of the stone that sparkled so in the lamplight, and Jessie liked the women even less than she had before.

She came home from Knight's Ferry one day, after a satisfying visit with Annie and Silas, with the news that Arthur Babcock was running for mayor. Joel gave her a look that startled her in its intensity, and said, "Don't worry. He won't make it."

Jessie paused with one glove half off her hand. "How can you say that?"

"Because I know who's going to win, and it won't be that son of a bitch Babcock."

Slowly, Jessie removed the glove and dropped it onto a table. "How can you possibly be certain of that?"

Joel laughed. "Honey, don't worry about such things. Just take my word for it. There are plenty of people, including me, who don't want Babcock in office, even a minor one. The man with the money behind him will win, and that's not Babcock."

His amusement was tinged with a bitterness she didn't understand. "I know you've never liked the man very well, but I didn't know you actively *disliked* him. What did he ever do to you?"

"His wife insulted you, once, and I set her straight. And Babcock himself turned me down for a loan. I wasn't good enough to borrow his goddamned money. Well, now he isn't

319

good enough to be mayor of my town, and I won't let him be. I'm meeting John Curtis this afternoon. I have to go. I'll be home in plenty of time for supper."

Disquietude rose within her. Turned down for a loan? When had that been? She didn't remember Joel ever mentioning borrowing money, except that one time, to build the house. And he'd gotten the money that time, he'd brought home the lumber. Of course he didn't tell her everything to do with the business end of running a ranch; he knew she was less than enthralled with it.

So he could have applied for a loan at some other time, though she didn't remember when. Still, it didn't seem sufficent reason to keep a man from running for mayor, from winning an election, just because he hadn't approved a business loan.

It bothered her that it was possible to do that; it didn't seem right. Yet Joel only laughed and assured her that it was perfectly legal. His stock reply was, "Don't worry about things you don't understand, honey. Let me take care of it."

She didn't mention it again, but Arthur Babcock lost the election. None of the men who came to talk to Joel seemed at all surprised. They laughed and drank Joel's whiskey, and one of them said, "Now, let's get us a representative in Sacramento." And everybody laughed again.

Jessie didn't make any attempt to listen in on their conversations. She was afraid that maybe she didn't want to know what they said, or what they planned, and knew that was cowardly. Joel didn't take her opinions seriously, and without consciously making such a decision, she rejected any sort of confrontation that might lead to a rift between them.

She remembered that other time, when she and Joel had not talked or slept together, before Rosalie was born. She couldn't risk another such separation. She kept her mouth shut, and did the things Joel wanted her to do about entertaining, and wore the diamond at the dinners. And prayed, for she knew not what.

37

Laurie was eleven when he figured it out, that Joel was his father.

He examined his own features in the huge gilt-framed mirror in the front hallway, and then he studied Joel's face. Then he looked at Tristan, as tall as Lauren but slimmer, and back into the mirror.

Laurie awaited a time when Jessie was busy at the kitchen table, when Mrs. Sullivan was not about, and put his question. "Aunt Jessie, did you know my mother and father?"

Jessie cut another slice through the rolled-up noodle dough before she answered. "Yes, of course, Laurie. I've told you about your mother."

"Tell me again. "

"Her name was Suzanne, and she was very beautiful. She had dark hair and eyes, just like yours. I didn't know her well, but I thought she was a good, kind person."

"And my father?" Laurie pressed, leaning into the edge of the table so that some of the flour got onto his shirtfront. "What was he like?"

He had mentioned his father before, and he'd noticed that Aunt Jessie always acted strange when he did it. Her mouth went flat and rather tight, and her voice altered, too. "I only saw him a few times. He was tall and dark. That's all I know about him."

If that was all she knew, why did she dislike his father? And if his father was a man named Cass Merriam, why did Laurie look so much like Joel Shand?

It made Aunt Jessie uncomfortable when he asked questions about his beginnings, though she was willing enough to talk about anything else he wanted to know.

"Is Uncle Joel really my uncle?"

Jessie kept on cutting noodles and spreading them out to

dry on the big floured table. "I've told you, Laurie. It—it's a courtesy title. The relationship wasn't really as close as that. After your parents both died, we took you to raise."

"But my name isn't really Shand."

"No. It was Merriam, but we thought it would be easier all around if we gave you our name. You don't mind, do you?"

"No," Laurie said. But he wondered why, if they'd given him their name, they made him call them Uncle Joel and Aunt Jessie, instead of Mama and Pa, the way Tristan and Rosalie did. He couldn't quite bring himself to ask her about that.

He had looked in the big Bible that stood on its own table in the library, on the page where such things were written. His own name was there, in Aunt Jessie's neat, easily read hand: Lauren Joel Merriam Shand, and his birthday: April 10, 1857. Across the page was the date of Joel and Jessie's wedding: May 2, 1857. So he'd been born just a few weeks before they were married. And his middle name was Joel. Surely that was significant?

Under his own name and date of birth were those of Tristan and Rosalie. He supposed that what was written there must be true—would God strike you dead, if you wrote a lie in His Book?

Yet there was the way that Aunt Jessie almost squirmed when the subject of his parents came up, and the fact that he could see that he looked a lot like Uncle Joel.

Understanding came to him gradually, and it was a mixed blessing. He adored Joel, and he wanted to be his son instead of the son of some nameless man whose mention made Aunt Jessie's lips go flat. Yet if he was Joel's son, why did they say he was not?

There was only one reason that he could think of. He was illegitimate. When his mother had died, Joel had 'done the right thing' by him and taken him to raise. He didn't know where the man who was supposedly his father came in, but Laurie's instinct was strong: Cass Merriam could not be his father.

Laurie had no doubts about Joel's affection for him; he knew Joel favored him over Tristan, as Aunt Jessie favored Tris over him. Yet he'd have liked to call Joel Pa, the way Tris did, and he couldn't.

He put his conclusions into words one day when he and Tris were sitting in a haystack, eating ripe peaches they'd snitched off one of Aunt Jessie's prized trees. They were huge, juicy peaches, and the juice ran down their chins and made their fingers sticky; they wiped them on the hay and let the sun dry the rest of it.

"Uncle Joel's not my uncle, at all," Laurie said, watching a cloud overhead that was shaped like a ship, one of those Spanish galleons such as he'd seen pictured in one of Aunt Jessie's books. "He's my father."

Tristan, who had lain back and rested his head on his hands, sat bolt upright. "He is not!"

"Yes, he is. Look at us. We have the same color hair, and our noses and our mouths are just the same, except mine are smaller."

"Your eyes are different. Your eyes are dark brown, and Pa's are sort of greenish brown," Tris argued.

"That doesn't matter. You don't have to get all your looks from one parent. My eyes are like my mother's. But everything else is like my pa's, and they're just like Uncle Joel's"

Tris regarded him uncertainly. It was a new idea, that Laurie might be Pa's son, too. "You can't be," he said, "because your ma wasn't ever married to Pa."

Laurie laughed scornfully. "He didn't have to be, stupid. If your pa isn't married to your ma, you're illegitimate. A bastard." They were words he had heard only recently, in a conversation between two of Joel's more careless visitors. He'd asked one of the hired hands about the expressions later. The man had given him an odd look, but he'd explained the matter. It gave Laurie a peculiar sense of power to use the words now, knowing as he did none of the grown-ups would approve.

"But Pa was married to Mama. He couldn't be your father."

"Yes, he could, Tris. You don't have to be *married* to somebody to give them a baby. You just have to *do* it with them."

Tris snapped a straw in half and then broke each half into a dozen pieces. His thin face was serious. "Do what?" he asked, though he halfway knew already. He wanted Laurie to put it into words, so he'd be sure.

"You know. Like old Lucifer does with the cows, so they'll have calves. People do it, too."

"They don't, either," Tris said, half repelled, half fascinated.

"Yes, they do. Not quite the same, but almost. And Lucifer's not married to all those cows, is he? Well, a man doesn't have to be married to a woman, either. Uncle Joel—my pa—

he must have done it with that Suzanne, before he was married to Aunt Jessie."

"He couldn't do it afterward, could he? When he was already married to someone else?"

Laurie hesitated. He wasn't at all certain on that point. "The thing is, see, they didn't want to admit I was illegitimate. That's a disgrace, sort of, because you aren't supposed to do it with people you aren't married to. But they cared about me, at least Uncle Joel did, so he took me to raise, only they didn't tell anybody I was really his son. That's why I'm his favorite," Laurie finished triumphantly.

Tristan didn't argue the point of favoritism. It had always been obvious to him that Pa more often took Laurie with him to interesting places, and that he let Laurie do things whenever he wanted. Pa never accused Mama of babying Laurie, the way he said she did with Tris. It was disconcerting, though, when Laurie now added, "I wonder who your pa is."

Tris scowled. "He's Pa, naturally. You trying to say I'm that thing, that illegitimate, too? I read in the front of the Bible the same as you did. And it says I was born to Jessie and Joel Shand, the spring after they got married."

"You don't look anything like Uncle Joel, the way I do," Laurie said.

Tristan's scowl deepened. "I look like Mama. It doesn't prove anything, who you look like, or don't look like. You can look like either your ma or your pa, or like neither one of 'em."

"Well, maybe, but if you *do* look like someone, it's more'n likely that's your own pa. Come on, let's go swimming," Laurie said. He leaped to his feet to lead the way to the dam on the creek which served the dual purpose of saving water for irrigation and being a swimming hole.

Laurie led the way in most things. He was nearly a year older, and would always be the sturdier of the two, though Tris was able to keep up with him in height from that summer when they were ten and eleven.

The age difference was just enough to give Laurie the edge in a physical contest of any kind. They were always scuffling and wrestling, and almost always Tris came out second best, which made Jessie more than annoyed, especially if they did it in the house. Joel just laughed and said it was good for both of them, though Jessie privately doubted that it was good for Tris to be beaten so much of the time.

Not that he seemed to mind it unduly. With boys who

weren't a year older, like the Allen and Curtis kids, Tris held his own all right.

Tris knew that his mother usually blamed Laurie when the two of them got into trouble, and he didn't bother to tell her any different. Quite often it *was* Laurie's idea to begin with, whatever the escapade, but though Laurie had exciting ideas, Tris had more imagination and frequently topped Laurie's original plan with something better.

It was when they began to include Rosalie in some of their exploits that Jessie tried to put her foot down. "It's nothing for a girl to be doing," Jessie would say. But Rosalie wasn't to be left at home sitting with Miss Smythe, stitching at something, when the boys were having adventures. And secretly, remembering how she'd always wanted adventures of her own, Jessie would sympathize a little, and weaken when Joel laughed about that, too.

"Hell, yes, let her learn to swim," he'd declared. "One of these days there're going to be irrigation ditches all over this country, as well as the rivers and the creeks, and a female's as likely to fall in as a male is. More, in fact," he said, grinning, as he watched his daughter trying to balance as she walked over a board laid between two sawhorses in the yard, while the boys taunted her from the sidelines.

It seemed to the children that Joel was obsessed with the idea of irrigation ditches. He would propound his ideas to anyone who came within reach, and if there was no one else, he told the family, though they'd heard it often enough before.

"It's the only thing that makes any sense," he would say, sometimes hitting the table with his fist for emphasis. "There's never any rain from May to September, and if we had ditches out there carrying water—and God knows there's plenty of water available when the snow melts in the mountains—we could grow anything. Anything! Just like you do in the garden, Jessie, only acres and acres of vegetables instead of a little plot like that one."

Laurie and Tris, after a summer of hauling bucket after bucket of water from the creek for Jessie's trees and also for the garden, went Joel one better. They put his theories into practice.

"Why don't we dig a ditch ourselves," Laurie said, "and pour the water in this end, and let it run down into the garden? We can make it so it goes between the rows, and save a lot of walking back and forth and a lot of lifting; we'll only have to lift it from the waterwheel into the top of the ditch."

Tris considered. "Won't it all soak into the ground? When I pour it around the trees, it sinks right in before I can get back with another bucketful."

"Sure, some of it will, but not all of it. Plenty will stay on top and run down into the garden. Let's try it."

Joel watched their efforts in amusement, with the comment to Jessie, "They're working harder to dig that ditch than they would if they carried the water in the first place."

He was impressed when he saw it in action, however. For the water flowed down the ditch into the garden, and by a series of little earthen dams, which Rosalie was happy to build and tear down for them (to Miss Smythe's dismay at the condition of her clothes), they were able to send the life-giving water wherever they wanted it, through the entire garden. And once the system was set up, there was far less work than there had been before, leaving the boys with time to do something more interesting.

Joel praised them lavishly, until they all glowed with this unaccustomed adult approval. "That's exactly the idea, get the water everywhere it's needed. If they built a few more dams on the rivers, held back the water when it's coming down so heavy in the spring, and then let it out through the summer when it was needed, we could water the whole damned state. Everybody says it's too expensive, and it is, for individuals to do, for more than a garden plot like this. But if everybody got together, if the state took a hand and got it started, it would work, just the way this thing does that the kids built. In the long run it wouldn't be expensive at all, because we could grow so much of so many things that the sale of the produce would pay for the ditches. If they can build flumes for the mines, why can't they see the advantage in building irrigation ditches?"

"The gold is more valuable than the grain," Jessie said mildly. "So that makes it more worthwhile to carry the water for a few miles to wash the ore for the gold."

"But that's just it, don't you see? The gold *isn't* more valuable! Oh, sure, a nugget the size of my hand is worth more than an acre of wheat, maybe. But there's only so much gold in the ground, and they're coming to the end of it, while the wheat can be planted over and over, forever. In the long run, the things the land can be made to produce will be worth far more than the gold, only people are too stupid to see it."

Except for Joel, nobody thought very seriously about irrigation ditches, once the little one had been built that freed the boys from one of their most onerous summer chores.

The heat that often sent Jessie to her bed with a wet cloth over her head, the shades drawn to keep out every glimmer of sun, was something that bothered the children very little. They had, after all, been born to it and grown up in it. They were brown and firm, even Rosalie, though Jessie fought to keep a hat on her to shade her face, and tried to keep her indoors during the hottest part of the day. They liked the sun on their skins—as much of it bare as possible—though even Joel was perturbed enough to blister them when they were caught swimming naked behind the dam with Rosalie as innocent of clothes as the boys.

"We saw her when she was a baby," Laurie argued, but Joel's mouth for once didn't curve into a grin at his words.

"She's almost eight years old now, and has to be learning about being a lady. Ladies don't appear before their brothers and their cousins with nothing on."

Rosalie's exquisite face was upturned with dismay, and tears filled the dark eyes so like Jessie's. "But Pa! I get just as hot as they do, and I can swim as good as Tris, too!"

Joel had never been able to deny her anything; the heart melted within him when her lower lip quivered that way. "Well, you can still swim, but you have to wear clothes. All of you," he clarified. "Now get into your pants, you two, and Rosie will have to wear clothes, too."

"All of them?" she demanded, staring in disgust at the heap of petticoats and undergarments she had left atop her dress and stockings. "I'll drown for sure, Pa, with all that weight on me."

"If you aren't a good enough swimmer to stay afloat with a few pounds of clothes on, then you better stay out of the water," Joel said, and strode away down the hill, leaving them staring at each other in disgust.

"Huh!" Laurie said, as soon as Joel was out of hearing range. "I don't know what all the fuss is about. She hasn't even got anything to see, for God's sake!"

"No," Tris agreed, but he was looking at his sister's slim, tanned body. "What does it feel like, not to have all your parts, Rosie?"

"I have all the parts I need," Rosalie said, dragging on her garments with difficulty, since she was still wet and the cloth stuck to her skin. "I think it's just silly that I have to wear all this stuff! And Miss Smythe will have a fit when I get it wet." She paused, brightening. "Maybe I can just wear everything but the dress. The rest will dry in a few minutes when we're finished swimming, and I'll put the dress over it, and she'll never know. And I won't show any more than if I wore everything, will I?"

Laurie gazed at her through sleepy lids. "The easiest thing, Tris," he said cruelly, "would be to just go swimming by ourselves, like we used to. Then we could go naked. We only have to wear pants when *she's* with us."

Tris pulled a red cotton handkerchief out of his pocket and laid it atop the dam, anchored with a stone. "We could use this as a signal that we're swimming naked, so you couldn't come up, Rosie."

For a moment she stood there, tears filling her eyes, the lower lip trembling again. "You're mean," she said in a small voice.

It was Tris who relented. "Well, we won't do it all the time, will we, Laurie? On the hottest days, we'll wear pants, so you can swim with us. Don't cry, Rosie."

Tris never liked to see his sister cry, though he often went along with Laurie's teasing. She didn't always cry when they tormented her, however.

One day, when Laurie had performed an amputation upon her favorite doll, Rosalie went into a rage and struck him with a rock that cut him above the eye and left him with a scar near his left eyebrow. When he got older, he rather liked it; it made girls ask how he'd come by it, and he made up a long, involved, and totally fictitious tale about it, far more to his credit than the truth.

On rarer occasions, it was Tris who felt the weight of her wrath. When he invaded her dollhouse with his lead soldiers, "raping and pillaging," as he put it, Rosalie emptied a pitcher of water over his head to make him stop, and then complained to Joel when his retaliation included a live mouse in her bed. Not that she was afraid of mice, for she caught and played with little wild things the same as the boys; but she objected to finding it between her sheets, as did Miss Smythe.

Though they liked Miss Smythe, they all three banded together to torment the poor woman at times. After a few rather drastic things like filling her chamberpot with chicken blood and an episode in which the governess drank wine that she thought was grape juice so that she had to retire to her room at midday and all lessons were canceled until next

328

morning—neither of which struck Jessie as amusing and had brought down swift punishment upon them—they stuck to less hilarious but still entertaining diversions such as foxtails in her stockings and jumping out at her from behind doors, to make her shriek.

After one such episode, Jessie came to the end of her patience. "I think," she told Joel in a tone that brooked no argument, "that it's time the boys went to school."

"To school?" He echoed the words, looking up from the paper he was perusing. "But the nearest one's in Knight's Ferry."

"All right. We'll send them to Knight's Ferry. They're too much for Miss Smythe. The poor woman was nearly hysterical today after they brought that dead rabbit up and put it in her rocking chair, and she thought they'd killed her kitten. They need a firm hand, Joel, and you're not around enough to administer it in the proper places."

And so, to their vast delight and Rosalie's further dismay, the boys were enrolled in the school in town. For the first time they had other boys to play with on a regular basis. Both were bright, though Laurie tended to try to get away with more fun and less work than Tristan did. They had both had their own horses since they were old enough to ride them, and getting to school was no problem. They had strict orders about the daily journey; they were to cross the Stanislaus nowhere except over the covered bridge, they were to go straight to school, and come straight home.

In spite of those restrictions, they managed to enjoy the change immensely. It was rare that the weather was too inclement for the daily ride. There was almost never any snow, and they were quite accustomed to rain.

Rosalie was understandably desolate without the boys. Lessons became boring; nothing was much fun any more. After a week of these dreary days, she crawled up onto Joel's lap and put her arms around his neck and stared into his eyes. "Pa, I'm lonesome. Why can't I go to school, too?"

"Because," he said, kissing the small nose upturned to him, "you're a girl, and you're too little."

Having expected this response, Rosie was ready with the next step. "Then why can't I have someone come and have lessons with me? Miss Smythe is used to teaching three, and she gets just as much money for one, doesn't she? Wouldn't it be cheaper to have someone else to teach?"

He suppressed a smile at this example of feminine logic.

"And where do you propose we find another student? Bring in old Katie, the milk cow? Or Tweeny and the rest of the hens?"

Rosalie's giggle had won her father over to many favors. "Oh, Pa, you know they can't learn to read and write! But," she sobered at once, "what about Teresa Dolores? Why couldn't she come and stay with us, and study with me?"

Joel opened his mouth before he had any ready excuse, and was amazed to hear Jessie say from across the room, "I wonder if that might not be a good idea, Joel? She's growing up there with no one to play with but those ignorant little Mexican children. She scarcely speaks English, either, and it might be good for her to study with Rosalie. Maybe we should ask Bonifasia about it."

"You expect someone to bring her all the way over here every day?" Joel demanded. "Even in the bad weather?"

"No, of course not. She could come and stay through the week. Or even, to begin with, just a few days a week. At least Rosalie wouldn't be alone *all* the time."

And so that change was made, too. At first Teresa Dolores was shy in this house so different from her own, where she had previously only visited and had usually stuck like a burr to her mother's knee. At first she came only for a day; Luis was there to take her home that evening, and she scarcely said two words.

However, she had been as deprived of companionship as Rosalie now was, and within a week she was willing to stay overnight. Within a month, she was living with the Shands except for weekend visits to her own home, though Bonifasia sometimes rode over with Luis for a midweek visit. The child had had practically no English when she arrived; after two months, except for the retention of the Spanish way of phrasing things, Teresa Dolores spoke the new language as if she'd been born to it.

The two little girls might have been sisters. Both had dark curls and brown eyes, and they became inseparable. When the boys teased, Rosalie was there to champion the younger girl.

Rosalie wasn't Teresa's only champion. Once when Tris came upon the child backed into a corner, her eyes wide, lips parted helplessly while Laurie threatened her with a fat spider, one of the poison ones that could make a man's arm swell to twice its normal size, Tris took a firm stand.

"Cut it out, Laurie. Leave her alone," he said in a voice modeled on Joel's authoritative tones.

Laurie didn't bother to look at him. He was enjoying the expression on Teresa's face, one of sheer horror that the creature known as a black widow would, indeed, be dumped on her. "Mind your own business," Laurie said, and moved the jar containing the spider a little closer so that Teresa now had her head pressed firmly against the wall behind her.

A moment later, Laurie let out a yowl of pain and protest as a broom handle crashed down on his wrist. The jar fell and broke, the spider scurried away, and Laurie rubbed at the reddened place where the broom handle had landed. "What'd you do that for?" he asked, more astonished than angry. "It took me more than an hour to find that spider."

"I told you," Tristan said. "Leave her alone."

From that moment on, Teresa Dolores adored Tristan. She would follow his movements with her big velvety eyes, a worshipful expression on her face, until Laurie noticed it and began to make fun of them both.

"She's making calf eyes at you, Tris. She's in love with you!"

Tris tried to ignore this, wishing fervently that Teresa would turn her attentions elsewhere.

"You can marry her when you grow up," Laurie persisted. "And I'll marry Rosalie. She's the prettiest."

Rosalie, happening on the scene, stared at him with a maturity beyond her ten years. "I'd rather marry a goat," she said, lip curling with a controlled contempt. "There's a mean streak in you, Laurie. Tris teases, but you're *mean*. Even an Indian squaw, used to *savages,* wouldn't marry *you.*"

For once Laurie was silenced, the other three, however briefly, aligned against him.

It was after that that Tris noticed a change in the way Laurie fought him when they tussled. It would begin as it always had, with the scuffling over some minor thing, usually in fun. Yet before it had ended, Laurie was fighting in earnest, trying to hurt.

Tris was lighter, less well coordinated, and he invariably got the worst of it. More than once he had to grab for a handkerchief to staunch the flow from a bleeding nose or cut lip.

Yet, for the most part, they remained companions, brothers in all but name. None of the adults in the household seemed to notice an increased intensity in Laurie's actions;

331

Jessie would reprimand them both if the wrestling match took place inside, and Joel would only grin if he saw them going at it out of doors. Tris felt quite desperate, sometimes, that his father always saw him bested; his muscles simply weren't developed enough to overcome Laurie's superior strength.

Once he mentioned it to Jessie, standing as he often did leaning against the kitchen table while she rolled out pie crust or cut biscuits or kneaded bread. "I wish Laurie wasn't older than me. He always can wrestle harder."

Jessie gave him a glance so filled with love that for a moment he forgot about Laurie. Her smile enveloped him in a blanket of affection. "You'll catch up to him one day, Tris. You're tall for your age now, as tall as Laurie. When you're both men, you'll probably be taller. Then you'll be a match for him."

"Really? Do you think so, really *taller?*"

"Yes, I think so. Fetch me some more firewood, will you, dear?"

And he'd gone off for the wood, basking in the new idea that someday he'd be bigger, taller, stronger than Laurie. And then he'd show him, Tristan thought, as pleased as if it had already happened.

38

The household never suffered or lacked for anything, but times were hard for a few years. If it wasn't drought, it was taxes. Even Joel railed against the taxes, and Luis found them desperately difficult to deal with. His riches lay in his fields and his cattle, but fields dried up, and when the water was gone, the cattle starved or died of thirst. Some of them were driven up into the mountains, where his men found it impossible to protect them from rustlers, but at least they had a better chance to survive there than on the barren hills.

He might have entrusted his young niece to one of his men for the trips to and from Rancho Sañudo, but he seldom did. When he came, Luis often stayed long enough to visit with Jessie and drink a cup of her tea, and perhaps to eat whatever was freshly baked. He was, Luis confessed with a smile, becoming addicted to gringo foods, when they came out of Jessie's kitchen.

They stood one day on the front porch, watching the two little girls who raced to meet Joel as he rode toward them, and Luis's voice was soft, serious. "It is a wonderful thing you do for our little Teresa," he said. "She is much changed since she has been coming here. Not only in her studies, but in her personality. She has gained confidence in herself; she is braver, and she laughs more. It is good to see a child laugh."

"She has improved, hasn't she?" Jessie's gaze rested upon the two of them, shouting with laughter as Joel pulled them up before him on the big horse, their skirts flying, faces open and happy. "She's very good for Rosalie, too, you know. They've become so close, and Rosie loves her like a sister."

"Your Rosalie is a beautiful little girl," Luis said. "Almost as beautiful as her mother."

And then, when Jessie looked at him, startled, he smiled, a smile meant only for her.

"You don't think I come over here two or three times a week simply because of Teresa, do you? I come at least as much because you are here, Jessie."

Flustered, not knowing what to say, Jessie said nothing, though her heartbeat quickened. She was, for heaven's sake, thirty-two years old, practically middle-aged, and married for nearly thirteen years.

When next Luis spoke, his tone was lighter, though his words were not. "If you ever tire of that handsome lout, or he ever mistreats you, don't forget that I am only a short ride away. If you ever need me—" The tone became more jocular as Joel rode to the porch and allowed the laughing little girls to slide down before he dismounted. "Ah, here they are, the entire noisy crew! I wonder where you find the patience to put up with them, señora!"

The moment had passed, leaving Jessie feeling oddly pleased and slightly disturbed that Luis had spoken to her in such a way.

Another day, when he and Joel had been closeted in the parlor for an hour discussing taxes and ways to raise the cash

333

to pay them, Luis paused at leavetaking to regard her with a rueful smile.

"I hope you do not think less of me, Jessie, because it is so difficult for me to cope with these gringo ways. Learning to read and write the American language was not too difficult, but understanding the gringo mind and customs is considerably more so. For so many years my people lived on these lands in prosperity and peace with one another; now I fear I am one of a dying breed. There is no longer any place for such as I in California, and since it is my homeland, I have no place to run to. Even if it were in my nature to run, which it is not." He grinned at her, recalling the way they had met. "The Indians have been driven off the best lands, up into the hills, away to far places, and I fear that it is to be the same with people like me. The gringo laws will one day deprive me of all I hold dear."

Jessie didn't know what to say in response to this. She felt she should reassure him, somehow, yet so much of what he said was true.

"At the time I suggested a partnership with your *esposo* I thought it would be largely to my own benefit, to protect my lands by having them under an American title. This has proved to be true, to some extent. No one has attempted to take my lands, by either legal or illegal means, since the alliance was made known. But this matter of taxes, of great sums of money to be raised in cash at a time when my cattle are worth fifty cents a head—is this a plot against such as I? Joel insists that I must rid myself of the responsibility for all my workers, but how can I do this? Where would they go? What would they do? Who would care for them? They are like children, *my* children, used to my providing for their needs. It would be like sending Teresa Dolores off on her own, to dismiss them. There is no other place for them to find work, no one else who will see to their welfare. Yet it is true that it grows increasingly difficult to provide for them as I have always done."

Then his smile flashed. "But I break the code of the gentleman, burdening a lovely lady with problems which fall into the realm of the man to solve. I only want you to think well of me, Jessie. I could not bear it if you did not."

"I'll always think well of you, Luis," she told him sincerely.

Yet she was troubled by this conversation, and she did not repeat any of it to Joel.

* * *

Although Joel made it a point not to discuss financial matters, at least not distressing ones, before the children, it was inevitable that the boys, at least, should be aware of the problem of taxes. Every man who came to the place, and an increasing number of them came to Joel not to only pay on their loans but for advice, talked taxes and hard times. There were those who thought the taxes had been imposed initially in part to finish off the Mexican land-grant holders, for they had so long lived a life of luxury without the curtailing effect of taxation that they did not know how to change. But the laws and levies hurt the Americans, too, particularly during the years when neither crops nor livestock did well.

For once it was Tristan who came up with the brilliant idea, and Laurie who enthusiastically seized upon it.

It was only by chance that Tris found the map in the back of a drawer in his father's desk. He was looking for a list Joel had sent him for, and he found that, and stared down at what lay underneath. He took the list to Joel, then returned to examine the hand-drawn map in mounting excitement.

"It shows how to find Uncle Collie's mine," he told Laurie as they lay on their stomachs to go over it in Laurie's room. "Look, the directions are very clear, aren't they? What if nobody else ever found it? What if the gold is still there?"

"It's been a long time," Laurie said, though he, too, felt the thrill of discovery, of anticipation. "Almost ten years. Anybody could have found it by now."

"But what if they didn't?" Tris had a lean face beneath the sun-bleached hair, and lively, expressive dark eyes. "What if it's still there? I bet if we found Uncle Collie's gold, it would pay the taxes for a hundred years."

"You might be right," Laurie admitted. "Since the fire wiped out Big Oak Flat, the mining's just about come to an end, except for a few stray prospectors who haven't given up. What do you want to do? Go up there and look for it?"

Tris hadn't quite dared put that into words, but as soon as Laurie did, it seemed feasible. "Why not?" he asked.

They did not, of course, tell their parents what they intended to do. They suspected, and rightly so, that not even Joel would approve such an expedition on their own. Yet they were, after all, twelve and thirteen years old, practically grown up.

"It'll take a while," Tristan mused. "It would be best if we had a couple of weeks, just in case. Maybe we could tell them

335

we're going to be staying somewhere they'd think was all right, so they wouldn't worry."

"Like where?" Laurie wanted to know.

"Well, last fall Pa took us hunting. We camped out for three days and we each shot a deer. You think they'd let us go camping on our own? If they thought it was on Rancho Sañudo land, they'd think that was safe, wouldn't they?"

"For two weeks? They wouldn't agree to that unless they thought there was somebody else with us. Maybe Pedro, if they thought Pedro was with us . . ."

"Luis will never let Pedro go with us for two weeks," Tris said.

"No, I know that. But we could *say* he was going. Maybe we could even get him to go, for a couple of days, and then we'd all pretend to come home, and we'd go back up there."

"You want to tell Pedro we're hunting for Uncle Collie's mine?"

"No, no, stupid, just tell Pedro we're going after deer, and then when we get one, have him take it back to the ranch, and we'll say we're coming on down as soon as we get one more to bring home, or something like that. And he'll think we've gone on home, and everybody else will think we're still up there with Pedro."

It was a brilliant scheme. At the last minute, Tris decided that someone else should know the truth, and he told Rosalie.

"Mama'll have a fit when she finds out the truth," Rosalie pointed out. "Even Pa may get angry and take the hide off you both when you get back."

"I'll bet he doesn't. Not if we find the gold," Tris said. "You're not to tell anyone, see. Not unless we don't come back in two weeks."

"And what'll that mean, if you don't come back by then?" Rosalie asked. "That some Indian has scalped you, or a claim jumper has murdered you for the gold, or you've both drowned in the Stanislaus? What good'll it do to tell them then, after you're dead?"

"We won't be dead, silly. We'll be back by then. I'm just telling you as a precaution, in case."

"In case what?"

Tristan shrugged. "Just in case. You're smart, Rosie. Use your own judgment. Only don't tell anybody until we've had time to find the gold."

Laurie carried the map. Occasionally, after they'd left the Stanislaus and climbed up the arroyo, they'd stop to spread the map out and study it.

The sun was hot, and the hills were quiet. Very quiet, except for the crunch of dry grass under their feet and the small sounds of the grasshoppers they stirred up as they passed. Once they heard another sound, one they recognized, and they paused, holding their breaths, until they spotted the rattler.

They edged away from the rock where the thing had lifted its head, both sweating more profusely, and they didn't talk as much as they went on. Rattlers could be deadly. Tris felt to make sure he still had his pocketknife, wondering if he'd have the courage to cut into his own flesh in the X-shaped mark he'd once seen his father make on a worker's leg, and then to suck out the poison and spit it out without swallowing any of it.

They saw no more snakes. Nothing moved in the vast expanse of drying hills except a hawk that circled overhead in the cloudless sky. At noon they stopped to eat a few strips of jerky beside a stream that was so shallow that they could hardly scoop anything out of it for a drink. Laurie looked at the trickle of water and scowled.

"It doesn't look like the place Collie described. What if we have the wrong creek, Tris? The one on his map was a lot bigger than this."

"He made the map in the winter," Tris reminded. "All the creeks are bigger then. If this is the right one, we should come to a big dead oak, right over the next hill."

Laurie's scowl held. "There's dead oaks all over the place, for God's sake."

"Yeah, but this one is a great big one." Although he knew it by heart, Tris consulted the map again. "Look, he drew a picture of it. It's got thick low limbs, and there's a big rock under it, to the east."

"In ten years it could have fallen over, or burned up in a fire, or anything."

"Yeah, but what if it's still there? We'll know it's the right canyon, won't we? That we're getting close."

They lay on their stomachs in the warm dusty grass, putting their mouths into the water for a final drink, then continued on their way, seldom talking now. Tris felt as if they were a hundred miles from home, a hundred miles from anybody, though it had taken them only a day and a half to get here, once they'd left Pedro at the eastern edge of Rancho Sañudo.

They came over the hill, and there it was. Just as Collie had drawn it on the map. The big spreading dead oak tree. Tris strode toward it, his flagging energy renewed, and cried out.

"There's the rock! See, just like the map!"

"We found it," Laurie said, incredulous, eyes shining. "Goddamn, Tris, we actually found it!"

Two days later, they stood stripped to the waist, greasy with sweat, hair hanging limply in their eyes, and Laurie swore with all the curses he'd ever heard.

"It's changed," he said furiously. "This is the right place, but the goddamned water has come down here and moved the rocks all around."

"Yeah." Tris straightened and rubbed at his aching back. "It was a flood that year, remember. He made the map just a little while before he was drowned. It was funny, wasn't it, because he was so young, but it was almost like he knew he wasn't going to come back here, and he made the map for Pa. And made his will and everything."

Laurie didn't care about any of that. All he cared about was the gold, and where was it? How could they tell, in this great jumble of rocks that had been shifted by waters impossible to imagine now, with only this little trickle going through the floor of the canyon?

He did remember, though, what it had been like. The familiar Stanislaus had reached an incredible depth in front of their home place, and he remembered the terror of falling into it, of swallowing muddy water, of choking and hurting. He'd been pretty little, but he remembered it. He'd always felt that Aunt Jessie blamed him for Collie's death, though she'd never said so.

If the river had been that deep and wild, this little stream would have been swollen, too. There could have been enough water here to move the rocks. Only where did they look now?

"It's here, somewhere," Tris said. "I know it is. I can feel it, Laurie. It's here."

They went back to their painstaking search, moving the rocks that were small enough so that their combined strengths could do it. They tore their fingernails and left bloody smears on the hot rocks. Once Tris fell and slashed open a gash in his left arm. It scared him a little, until the bleeding stopped.

Then he looked at Laurie and grinned crookedly. "I've got a scar to tell lies about now, too."

"Yeah." Laurie returned the grin. "Except for you're fair, and I'm dark, we could be twins."

They laughed and returned to their task.

And then, on the eighth day since they'd parted company with Pedro, there it was. On the creekbed, glinting in the sunlight through the clear water.

Tris stared at it, his heart suddenly hammering so that his chest hurt. They'd both seen fool's gold before, the tiny flakes so often mistaken for the real thing. Maybe that's all this was, fool's gold.

Only it wasn't. They were sure of it.

"There's more under that rock," Laurie said, when they had captured as much of the stuff as they could. They'd both gone panning for gold with Joel, just for fun, and they'd found it in small amounts before. What they laid out on the large flat boulder looked like quite a bit, but it wasn't all of what was there. "We have to move that rock, Tris."

Move it. With what? All their straining didn't shift it at all.

"It would roll downhill," Laurie speculated, "if we could just get it started. If we could get on that side, and pry it up. A branch or something."

They returned to the dead oak and brought back a fallen limb, but they knew before they began that it wouldn't be enough. The wood was old and rotten; it broke without having the slightest effect on the rock they were sure covered their fortune.

They stood panting, frustrated, staring at the offending rock. "I know what Ma would do," Tris said, brushing back a sweat-soaked lock of hair.

"What?" Laurie asked, without much hope.

"She'd say a prayer. For God to help."

Laurie looked at him. "Sure. That ought to do it, all right. A prayer and a big enough shove, and we'll move it."

"Well, what have we got to lose?" Tris asked. "A crowbar might do it, though I'm not sure we could put enough weight on it to make it work. You got any better suggestion?"

Laurie laughed abruptly. "All right. Let's try your ma's way. Let's say a prayer, and push it like hell."

They stood uphill of the massive rock, placing their hands on its side, and bracing their feet.

"You say the prayer," Laurie suggested. "He's more likely to listen to you, maybe."

They were laughing, yet Tris was serious, too. He closed his eyes. "Please, God, help us move this big old rock so we can get our gold out from under it. Thank you, God."

They counted to three, and pushed with all their strength, and Tris muttered again, "Please, God!"

The earth shuddered beneath them, so that they nearly lost their footing on the smaller rocks, and they felt the big rock moving under their hands. Only a little pushing, it only took a little, and then the boulder plunged away from them so that both boys went sprawling on their hands and knees in the shallow stream. Laurie chipped a tooth on a projecting rock and swore. Tris scraped a forearm so that it stung like crazy, and he'd reopened the gash which was not entirely healed.

For a minute or so they didn't move, while the sand and pebbles trickled down into the stream from both banks with a rattling sound. When that stopped, it was so silent all they could hear was each other's labored breathing, and the faint gurgle of the water wetting their knees.

Tris drew in a long breath. "It worked! He did it, God moved the rock for us!"

"It was an earthquake," Laurie said, sounding shaken, a hand at his mouth. "Just an ordinary earthquake."

They'd felt lots of them, some hard enough to shake plates off a shelf, some just a rolling of the ground that didn't even open a crack anywhere except one time when it had split the little dam above the house and they'd worked beside Joel for two days to repair it.

"Who you think makes earthquakes, stupid?" Tris asked, eyes shining. "Look, Laurie. Look."

He stuck his hand into the water and lifted the nugget, opening his palm so that Laurie could see it.

"Rosalie, how could you?" Jessie demanded, resisting the urge to shake her daughter. "Why didn't you tell us?"

Rosalie shrugged slim shoulders. "Tris would never tell me anything again if I tattled on him. Besides, Mama, they're back safe. They brought that gold, and then Pa and Uncle Luis went up there and got the rest of it, and we're practically rich now, Pa said. So what difference does it make? Laurie and Tris both came back safe."

"They might not have," Jessie said, still feeling sick even

though it was all over. "Anything might have happened to them up there, and we didn't even know where they were."

"Nothing happened, Mama," Rosalie said. "Except they found the claim. Uncle Collie's diggings. Pa would never even have gone and looked."

Joel would have been furious, too, if they hadn't found the gold. As it was, he could hardly take a strap to two boys who had solved not only his present problems but a good many future ones.

"It was Collie's claim," he reminded them. "You can't become millionaires overnight on Collie's money."

"We'll get part of it, won't we?" Laurie asked.

"Yes. We'll figure it out, what's fair. You and Tris will each have a share, because you worked for it. We'll put it in the bank until you're old enough to make sensible use of it. The rest of it will be split between me, as Collie's heir, and Teresa Dolores, as Collie's daughter. Part of her share will take care of the Rancho Sañudo taxes, and her Uncle Luis will decide about the rest of it."

"We're rich, aren't we, Pa?" Tris asked. "It's a lot of money, isn't it?"

"It's a lot of money," Joel agreed, and his smile warmed Tris as he had never felt warmed before. And then, to cap it off, Joel reached out and ruffled Tris's hair in a gesture of affection. "It's a good job, son," he said. Tris carried that memory inside him for a long time.

39

A two-and-a-half-year drought was broken in the winter of 1871, in a deluge that again swelled the Stanislaus and surrounding rivers to flood stage. There was less damage this time, however; the bridge held, most of the new buildings in Knight's Ferry were also spared, and only a few foolish souls who had built along the river bottom learned their lesson the hard way.

It was a wet, cold winter, and illness claimed a number of victims. The boys had colds, so Jessie kept them out of school for most of January, and Teresa Dolores stayed at home, too. It was a great relief when things returned to normal, for having three active children confined indoors for a month was enough to drive Jessie out of her mind, she said.

The first day of February, Sarah Groves succumbed to pneumonia.

The funeral service was held beside the grave dug on the hillside above the town. Alice and Harry Kelly stood with their four children, Alice bulging again with the child soon to be born. There were friends there, old ones like the Allens and the Shands from the wagon-train days, new ones from the town. Though Sarah had not been the kind of woman who inspired warm friendships, she had been respected; and almost everyone liked Mamie and would have showed their support of her regardless of what they thought of her mother.

Mamie stood a little apart from the family group, willing herself not to think about her mother in the pine box over which the words were being read from the Bible. If she thought about Sarah, she would cry, and though she supposed it was expected of her, she did not want to cry.

She felt drained, dry, exhausted. Life was not easy for any woman, yet Alice, for all her three miscarriages and the loss of one child soon after birth, did have a husband and a family. She felt this loss, too, of course, but she had someone to go home to when it was over.

Mamie had dreamed of a family. She looked across the sodden earth to where the rain dripped off the brim of Daniel Porter's hat. She might have married Dan any time in these past six years, she thought, yet there was no comfort in the realization. He'd asked her several times, and she knew he was a good man. He'd probably ask her again, now that she was alone.

Yet she wasn't in love with Daniel. She'd tried to be in love with him, God knew she had, but all she could feel was liking and respect. Was that enough? Should she have forgotten the past, given up any idea of romantic love, and settled for a decent man who'd have earned their living so she didn't have to sweat in that bakery six days a week, so that she could at least have had children?

She glanced at Alice and saw the two girls leaning against

their mother as Alice stood with an arm about each of them, the younger one with her thumb in her mouth. And the boys, though still so young, were straight and tall beside their father. Good-looking, healthy children, they were, those that had survived.

I might have had children, Mamie thought. It was late in the day for her, now, but not *too* late. Other women had children when they were past thirty. Yet when her attention again drifted to Daniel, she knew she couldn't do it. She couldn't marry him and spend the rest of her life with a man who stirred nothing the way Collin Aubin had done. She couldn't sleep in his bed at night, submit to his caresses, even to have the babies she longed for.

As soon as the brief service was over she walked quickly down the hill, pretending she didn't hear Harry Kelly's call after her, inviting her to join them at home for a meal brought in by neighbors.

What would they think of her, not joining the others? Well, she'd never made many decisions on the basis of what the townspeople thought, and she wouldn't now. The time she'd sent Collie away because of the scandal that would have touched her family was the last time she'd worried that much about what anybody thought of her. Her mother was gone now, nothing could hurt *her,* and she thought Alice and Harry were strong enough to stand against the forces that might batter their family. If only she could find some strength, some meaning, for her own life.

Mamie let herself into the bakery, the oven cold today, the CLOSED sign in the front window. She walked through the place, running a finger through a trace of flour on the big table where she worked every day. Would she go on by herself, rising every morning long before dawn, mixing and kneading the bread, selling it to earn her living, for the rest of her life? How long would that be? Her mother had died at forty-nine. Would she live that long, or longer? So many years, yet, to be alone.

For a moment she wavered, imagining what it would be like to turn back into the family living quarters and find Daniel there, and then she renewed the decision she had made years earlier.

She'd rather be alone than tied to someone she didn't truly love. She went into the tiny kitchen and made herself a cup of tea and sat there, thinking, wishing, eventually reconciling herself to what was to be.

It wasn't until four months later that anything happened to rouse Mamie from that dreary resignation.

Not that she was depressed or depressing to the casual eye. She continued to make her bread and pies and cakes; she sold them with a smile and a friendly word to each of her customers who came in. It was only inside herself that Mamie felt the shriveling process, the drying up of all her vital juices. On the surface she was as she had always been, without a trace of gray in her hair, no stoop, no wrinkles, no sign of aging, though she scrutinized her image in the mirror, expecting what she dreaded.

The late-April day had been a glorious one, with the sun warm against the windows so that the bakery had overheated by late afternoon. She'd propped the door open for ventilation, though that meant that flies came in and she'd had to cover her baked goods to protect them.

Such a lovely day. Mamie thought about walking up to talk to her sister, then decided against it. Alice would be busy with supper and her brood was such a noisy one they wouldn't be able to carry on a conversation of the sort she craved. Jessie would be better, if she didn't live so far away. Jessie had someone who would take the children into another room, and Jessie would be a good listener, a good friend.

A good listener, Mamie mused. What did she want Jessie to listen to? No, she didn't want to unburden herself of her problems, which, after all, were common enough. She needed help in the bakery but didn't earn enough to enable her to hire anyone, so she lived very simply, unable to save anything. Sometimes it frightened her, thinking what might happen when she was too old to work these long hours and earn her own keep. Still, she had plenty of youthful years left before that became a problem; maybe she'd be lucky, Mamie thought with wry humor, and be taken off with pneumonia as Ma had been, during one of the wet winters.

No, she wouldn't go to Alice's, and she wouldn't try to get to Jessie's, either. Instead she'd eat her supper and then walk out along the river where it was peaceful and quiet. The sound of the water, when it wasn't in flood and sweeping everything in its path down toward its junction with the San Joaquin, had a soothing quality. She would simply sit and try not to think of anything at all, and let the music of the Stanislaus ease away her weariness, her worries about the future. And then she'd return home as soon as it was dark, and go to bed.

She had washed up and removed her apron, and was heading for the front door to lock it when it opened, and a man came in.

He was a stranger, dressed in the kind of clothes the miners wore, the jean trousers and plaid flannel shirt, and the big hat that didn't quite conceal dark blond hair. He was roughly bearded, and there was a black patch over one eye.

Youngish, she thought; early thirties, and then was inwardly amused at herself. There had been a time, in her mind, when thirty was a milestone of middle age.

"I'm sorry," she told him. "I'm about to close, and I've sold out everything. I'll have more tomorrow."

For a moment the man looked at her with his one eye, and then he said quietly, "Mamie?"

She didn't know him, although there was, perhaps, something hauntingly familiar about the voice—perhaps she'd known him a long time ago, before the voice grew so deep?

"I'm Mamie Groves, yes," she said, reserved, waiting for him to explain that they had met in the distant past, or that they had some mutual acquaintance.

"You've hardly changed at all," the man said, and suddenly terror swept through her so that she lifted a hand to her throat, as if an obstruction there prevented her breathing.

The voice, the voice she surely remembered, she thought, and felt giddy, faint. It could not be, it could not.

Yet, looking into that one good eye, a bright blue eye, Mamie felt her numbed lips shaping a name.

"Collie?"

He was dead, she thought frantically, Collie had been dead for ten years. And even as she thought that, the mouth softened, broadened into a smile, a rather sad smile.

"I call myself Cole Aarons now," he said.

He caught her before she slid to her knees. Supporting her, he led her to a chair behind the wide counter.

"You were drowned in the big flood," she said, fighting for consciousness, cursing the damnable stays that restricted her breathing at a time when she needed to inhale deeply and could not. "Swept downriver. They searched for you . . . for days. No trace."

"Put your head down on your knees," he instructed, and she felt the warmth of his hand on her back as he knelt beside

345

her, a hand that he didn't remove as she gulped and sucked in air and gradually fought back the vertigo.

After a time she lifted her head and stared into the face, so different from the one she remembered. He was older, browner, his hair and beard were darker, and there was that terrible patch—yet the remaining eye was blue, and the shape of the mouth—she felt her own mouth trembling, like the hands knotted together in her lap.

"It's been ten years," she said, almost inaudible. "Ten years of grieving."

He was near enough to kiss, but she felt no urge to kiss him. She felt, in fact, almost dead inside, though there was something that fluttered with life, buried beneath the shock, a life that was so threatening she was afraid to let it surface.

He reached for her hand, and though his touch was searing, she was too weak to draw away. He stroked her palm with his thumb. "You're not wearing a wedding ring."

"No." Could he even hear her whispered response?

"You never married. You must have had chances, lots of them. But you didn't marry."

This time she didn't try to answer. Her throat closed, aching with unshed tears that she could not explain.

"Mamie, I know this was an awful thing to do to you, but I had to know. I had to find out if you were still here, still well, still . . . single."

What did it matter? she wondered. He had a wife and a child only a few miles away. She didn't put that into words, either. Why had he done this? Anguish swelled inside of her, an anguish she had thought long since dulled by time, a reopened wound that seemed even worse than the ones she had endured before, first when Collie married Bonifasia, last when he had supposedly drowned during the flood.

For a moment she did not hear his words, and he sensed that and halted, still kneeling beside her, still holding her hand.

He began again. "Mamie, I never intended to hurt you. Before God, I didn't. Can you listen to me now? Can you understand what I'm saying?"

She could not speak. Neither could she conceal her agony as she stared at him through the curtain of tears.

"I told you how I felt, what a mistake it was to have married Bonifasia," Collie said, his voice so low that had she been less than scant inches from him she would never have heard it. "I hoped you'd go away with me and start over somewhere else, but I understood the reasons why you couldn't go. Only I think now maybe it's different. Your mother is gone, so you can't disgrace her, and I'm—" He paused, and his voice grew a little stronger. "I'm a man named Cole Aarons. I have been for a long time. And there's no reason you shouldn't marry Cole Aarons and move away from this place. Nobody but you ever has to know I once had another name."

Mamie blinked to clear her eyes, though the improvement was momentary. Her throat worked, yet no sound issued from it, and his fingers curled protectively around her hand. A warm, strong hand, it was, and callused as befitted a man who worked at manual labor. A hand that sent rolling shock-waves through her, as disturbing as the earthquakes that occasionally wakened her at night or held her breathless, waiting for the roof to fall, while she worked in the bakery during the days.

Yet nothing serious ever came of the earthquakes, and nothing could come of this, either, she thought, except renewed suffering on her part. He was still married to Bonifasia.

"Collie Aubin died," the young man said, leaning closer to her, his hand more insistent in its pressure. "In the flood. He was swept away downstream, and he died. Officially. Forever."

Her lips trembled so that she lifted her free hand to press against them; still she said nothing.

"Listen," he said quietly. "Only listen. Judge me, then, but first listen to me."

She did, for she could hardly do anything else.

"I thought I was gone when the water swept me out from the bank after Joel grabbed Laurie away from me. I knew I'd saved the boy, and if it hadn't been for that tree that came down the river and struck me in the head, I might have made it to the shore then. Only it hit me, the root system of a huge tree, and it damaged my eye. I was blinded, and being swept away from shore, and I don't even remember reaching out for the tree and hanging on, but that's what I did. It carried me a long way downstream; my arm was entangled in the roots even after I lost consciousness, I guess, and it held my head above water most of the time, so I didn't drown. Only I was battered senseless. Literally senseless, Mamie."

She waited, not wanting to have this picture painted for her so vividly, unable to rise and walk away from him, seeing

347

it as she had seen it in her mind's eye before, only this time there were authentic details.

"The tree finally wedged in some rocks at the side of the river, and there's no way of knowing how long I was there. I don't remember any of it. An elderly couple came along and found me—Ed and Nora Whitlock. They were on their way to Oregon Territory; they were bitterly disappointed in the San Joaquin Valley, and they wanted something more like what they were used to, in Minnesota." A faint smile touched the lips revealed in the midst of darkened blond beard. "Trees, they said, and water, but not floods. They had a wagon, two dogs, and a cat, and damn little else except for a bag of corn-meal and one of beans. Ed was seventy. Nora wouldn't let anyone talk about how old she was." There was affection in his tone that she recognized through her own inner turbulence, an affection he perhaps did not even realize he conveyed.

"They thought I was dead. One of the dogs found me, actually. A little mongrel named Tippy; he barked and barked and wouldn't come back to where they were, so they finally investigated, and found me wedged between the roots of that oak. One eye was gouged out," he said with no appreciable emotion, "and at first they didn't think I was breathing. Because the dogs made such a fuss, they hauled me ashore and took a closer look. I had a broken collarbone and a welt on my head that they figured accounted for the fact I didn't know who I was, when I finally came around. And my left foot was smashed up."

He shifted position, reestablishing the grip on her hand. "I didn't know for six years, Mamie. I didn't remember anything, not the flood, not where I came from, not even my name. I was wearing a belt buckle with the initials C. A. on it, so after a week or two, when they decided I was going to live after all, Nora gave me a name. Cole Aarons. And that's who I've been ever since. Who I'll go on being for the rest of my life."

She forced air into tortured lungs so that she could speak. "But Joel and Clifford went looking for you! So did Luis Sañudo! They didn't find anyone who'd seen you, or heard about you!"

"They must have come after Ed and Nora loaded me into their wagon and moved on. They camped on the north side of the river for a week or two, and they talked to some people, but nobody knew who I was. There were plenty of bodies to be identified when the waters went down. I don't know how hard they tried to find where I came from. They didn't read or write, so they didn't see any newspapers, when those finally came out. And mostly, I think, I was a young man, and they'd recently lost their only son, so maybe they didn't try very hard to find out where I belonged. They took a liking to me, and since I was helpless as a baby for quite a while, Nora more or less adopted me. I don't think they really wanted to find where I came from, after they discovered I didn't even know who I was."

"You said—you didn't know for six years."

"Yes. And it's been ten. By the time things began to come back to me, I was a long way from here. The Whitlocks carried me with them to Oregon, because I was in no shape to turn loose on my own. It's a long way to Oregon, a hard way. There're plenty of trails running east and west, but nobody's made any good ones going north and south, yet. It was a rough trail, and I was in a lot of pain. I don't remember half of it. But after we got to Oregon I began to heal, and except for not having one eye, and for a foot that hurts sometimes in bad weather, I got better. Except that I still didn't remember anything about what happened to me before the flood, until poor old Ed felled a tree and it didn't fall quite right. He yelled, and I tried to get out of the way. I wasn't fast enough, and it shaved the side of my head. Same place I got hit the first time. It knocked me out, and he thought he'd killed me.

"Well, he hadn't. And when I woke up that time I had a sort of hazy memory of being in the water, in the flood— *before* I lost my eye—and gradually, over the next few months, the memories kept coming back. Until I remembered who I was, where I came from."

Her lips were so numb she could barely make herself understood. "But why...after all this time? You came back, after so long..."

"Because I remembered you, that's why. I remembered how much I loved you, Mamie." There was no doubting the sincerity in his voice. "I thought about you a lot, for a long time. How you'd turned me down, and how I had nothing to come back here for. Everybody thought I was dead, and I figured it was better to leave it that way. What use was I to anybody here? Bonifasia didn't want to live with me, she'd thought me dead for years. My daughter's growing up without ever having known me, so it wouldn't matter to her, either.

349

I'd signed everything over to Joel before I left, so there weren't any loose ends. Except you."

The night was very quiet. Somewhere down the street a mother called for a child to come inside; other than that, the silence pressed in on them, suffocating, oppressive, though silence had never bothered Mamie before.

"Nothing has changed with me," she said finally. "Except that Mama's gone. Alice and her family are still here. My friends, the people whose respect I appreciate."

"But I'm not Collin Aubin any more. I walked into the general store, and then into the saloon, and saw men I could have called by name, and none of them knew me. Joel and Jessie might, if I spent any time with them. But maybe not, if I was careful what I said. The thing is, I thought about you for a long time, and two months ago, when Ed died—Nora passed away year before last—I was all alone, and I knew I didn't want to stay that way. I'm mining in the Blue Mountains, and I like the life. Our cabin—Ed and Nora's cabin— is mine now. It's not fancy, just a good sturdy house. It's in a little valley, high up in the hills. It snows in the winter, pretty deep sometimes. The summers are warm, not hot like the ones here, and the smell of trees is something I never get enough of. I got neighbors, three-four miles away. Nancy and Hawk Rogers. What I'm saying, Mamie, is I still want you very much. Everybody here thinks I'm dead and buried, and I have no ties left to any of them. I don't intend to tell any of them I'm here, still alive. In the eyes of the law I'm a man named Cole Aarons, and there's no record anywhere I've ever been married to anybody. I know you're a religious person, like Jessie; you have high moral standards, and I respect that. We're not Mormons, like those people she lived with, but they were God-fearing, religious folks too, and they took more than one wife. I don't want more than one, I only want you. Bonifasia was never really a wife to me, nor I a husband to her, and she's happy as a widow, I know she is. Who would we be hurting, Mamie, if we took comfort in each other for the years we have left? If you married Cole Aarons and moved to the Blue Mountains of Oregon, and we had a family of our own? Legitimate kids, Mamie. Nobody would ever say different."

He looked into her face, his own pleading as much as his words had done. Waiting.

The picture was as clear in her mind as if she'd already seen it. A cabin with smoke curling from the chimney, surrounded by fragrant pine and balsam and fir instead of all these ugly oaks, a crystal stream meandering down the hillside behind the cabin. A garden plot, and children playing in the meadow, picking wildflowers.

Her children. The children she had long since given up hope of having.

"They'd know," she said feebly. "If they ever saw you and talked with you, Jessie and Joel would know, and Alice and Harry. They all knew you too well. I couldn't go away without inviting them to my wedding. Without telling them anything."

Hope flickered in his smile, gone almost before she'd seen it. He grasped both her hands and squeezed them. "No, they wouldn't. They're not looking for me back. I'll get some stuff to make my hair a little darker, walnut stain, maybe, and I'll walk with a limp instead of trying to walk straight, and I won't talk much. My voice is changed, anyway, I think. It's deeper and quite different. You can tell them we met some time ago, that I've been mining up in the Sierras, and now we're going to travel to Oregon, where I came from before. All I'd have to see them would be one time, at the wedding, if we do it right. I won't give myself away in one meeting."

Mamie's eyes brimmed over, and then she was in his arms, their lips wet with her tears; she clung to him, murmuring his name, "Collie! Collie!"

"Cole," he told her. "From now on, it has to be Cole."

"Cole," Mamie repeated obediently, and lifted her face from his soaked shirtfront for a long, deep kiss that scorched her very soul.

She didn't know if he was right, if his identity could be successfully concealed. She only knew that it was the last chance she would ever have, and she had to grasp it.

"When did this all happen?" Jessie had demanded excitedly. "When did she meet him? Where?"

Alice, busy with her growing brood of children, shrugged as she brushed her older daughter's hair. "She never mentioned him to me at all, until she announced they were to be married on Sunday afternoon. I guess he came into the shop and bought bread several months ago, and they were taken with each other. And then when he came down out of the hills again and proposed marriage, it didn't take her long to make up her mind. She's getting on to thirty-one years old, and I sure thought as we all did that she'd die a spinster, so I suppose she couldn't turn him down."

Jessie's excitement dimmed. "But she *does* care for him, doesn't she?"

"Oh, yes. No doubt about that. She's wildly happy. I didn't mean to imply that she was taking him simply because he *asked*. After all, if she'd wanted to marry just anybody, Daniel Porter was after her for several years, until he gave up and married Molly Coombs. Mamie could have had Daniel, and he was a decent enough fellow. No, I think she's in love with this one, though I'm not sure what it is she sees in him. Great straggling beard, he has, and only one eye—of course, he keeps a patch over it so that you don't have to look at an empty socket, but—Barbara, hold *still!* I'm amazed that he ever proposed. He doesn't say two words at a time, that I've heard. Just nods and smiles once in a while, says yes and no when you ask him something. But Mamie's ecstatic. You won't be disappointed about that."

Jessie was not. For Mamie glowed. Her cheeks were pink, her eyes were bright, and no one would have taken her for thirty years old the afternoon she stood up with Cole Aarons before the preacher. She had had little time to prepare, but she'd made her wedding dress herself, and she'd sold off the bakery to a young man who'd saved enough gold dust to get into something that was "warmer in the winter," as he put it, than mining.

Mamie's belongings were all done up in bundles ready to be carried on a pack horse, for since there were few roads north to Oregon and none of them very good ones, they would not try to take a wagon. Her husband had recollections of one such jolting journey and would not do it that way again.

So eager were the newlyweds to be off on their honeymoon that even the celebration was to be cut short. Mamie had done her own wedding cake—at last, after everyone had given up hope of the need for one—and there was real champagne to drink with it. Most of the guests would have stayed on for hours, enjoying the refreshments and the fellowship of friends, but the bride and groom were ready to leave within an hour of the time they'd tied the knot.

Jessie went back into the little rooms behind the bakery for the last time, to help Mamie change from her wedding dress (to be folded and kept from now on for best) into something more suitable for traveling. Mamie was so nervous she kept dropping things, and her fingers were not up to the intricacies of small buttons, so Jessie did them for her.

When at last Mamie was ready to go, they faced each other for what both assumed to be the last time.

"Write to me," Mamie begged. "Alice will mean well, but with all those children she'll never get around to it more than once or twice a year. Write to me, Jessie, tell me about everybody."

"I will." Jessie smiled into her friend's face, then impulsively hugged her and kissed her on the cheek. "And you write, too. You've been like a sister to me, Mamie. I can't tell you how happy I am that *you're* happy. You know," she said, growing thoughtful as she stepped away from Mamie, "I couldn't help thinking, as you were cutting the cake together a little while ago, that there is something about your Cole that reminds me of Collie, though I couldn't exactly say what it was."

Mamie's face went still and perhaps a trifle pale, and Jessie was immediately contrite. "Oh, Mamie, have I distressed you, reminding you? It was so long ago, I thought the pain would have eased by now! But then it's never gone entirely, is it, when we've loved someone? Just because they're gone, we don't forget them. But you do love Cole, don't you?"

The warm color came back into Mamie's face. "Yes, I do love him, very much."

"I knew you did. I could tell by the way you look at him. And the way he looks at you, for that matter. Goodbye, Mamie dear, and God bless you both."

A few minutes later, as the newly married couple rode out of town to the shouted well-wishes of friends and family, Jessie thought again that there was some quality about Cole Aarons that reminded her of Collie, though it continued to elude her. What an odd coincidence, she realized, that even his initials were the same as Collie's had been.

And then she dismissed the thought, and turned back to Joel, who was pressing her to load up the children and head for home, and she gave no more consideration, ever, to the similarity of the man Mamie had married to the one she had once loved.

40

Laurie and Rosalie were totally uninterested in the visitors who came to the house to talk politics and ways and means to influence the men who made the laws in the state of California.

Tristan was fascinated.

"It's not that I like the men, mostly," he said. "But what they say is interesting. It's going to effect all of us, because they're talking about things that are going to be laws, and they'll set the taxes, and even if these men aren't elected officials, they're in power."

That was the one thing the men had in common: they manipulated, and they controlled. When Jessie learned of some of these dealings, of buying and selling candidates, of making deals—I'll get you this vote, if you get me that one— she was uncomfortable, and she worried about the legality of what they did.

When Jessie voiced her doubts about Joel's new acquaintances, he justified the relationships succinctly. "The only way we're ever going to get an irrigation system built is to enlist the help of men like these. They're the ones who have the power."

And irrigation was Joel's dream, the dream that would ensure success not only for himself but for the children who came after him.

Tris simply studied what he read and heard. The entire machinery of government, both local and statewide, engrossed him. What he learned worked in him like an overabundance of yeast in dough, filling him, expanding him.

"Someday," he told Rosalie seriously, "I'm going to be one of the men who make the decisions."

After one such remark, at which Laurie jeered, Tris didn't talk to him any more about his own aspirations, though he continued to discuss men and issues. He was, after all, used to Laurie's good-natured ridicule, but there was no point in exposing his vulnerabilities for Laurie's entertainment.

Tristan was used to playing second fiddle to Laurie's first. Nearly a year older, Laurie had always been of a more aggressive nature, and was also, Tris thought, better-looking as well as stronger.

Jessie had been right about the height; in fact, when they were sixteen and seventeen, Laurie had reached his full growth and Tris was still growing, eventually standing almost a head taller than the older boy. There was some gratification in this, but not as much as he'd have liked, because Laurie was still heavier, and could still best him, most of the time, in a wrestling match.

"For heaven's sake," Jessie would say crossly, "aren't you old enough to begin to behave like grownups? All this tussling, upsetting things. Be careful of the lamp, Laurie!"

If Joel had backed her up, the scuffling matches would have been relegated to the outdoors. His attitude continued, however, to reflect the opinion that young men must try their muscles and that the brotherly competitions were healthy. Jessie didn't share that opinion, yet she no longer championed Tris when she felt he was being treated unfairly, because it only made Tris feel worse when his father accused her of coddling him. She didn't do that at all, Jessie knew. She only wanted Joel and Laurie to be fair, and often they were not. To his credit, Tris didn't complain, but there were times when Jessie fully understood the meaning of the phrase "to feel one's blood boil" in indignation.

By the time they both became interested in girls, Laurie was ahead in that department as well. Tris watched him with silent envy. Laurie might not be the tallest, but he was the best-looking with his dark hair and eyes, the most muscular, and the most glib-tongued. He held any female entranced with tales of his exploits—some real, many imaginary—and approached them with a confidence that Tristan simply could not gain.

Rosalie knew, with very little being said, how her brother felt.

"The girls who fall for Laurie's tales are the silly ones," she told Tris. "When they really get to know him, the way we do, they won't think he's so wonderful."

Tris grinned ruefully, brushing back a lock of fair hair that, because it did not curl like Laurie's darker locks, was continually falling forward over his face. "They're always the pretty ones, though, who gather around him."

Rosalie sniffed. "They deserve what they'll get, if they believe him," she predicted.

Teresa Dolores avoided Laurie as if he had the plague. Since she spent a good deal of her time in the Shand household, it was impossible to avoid him altogether. And when, the year she was fourteen, Bonifasia died of an ailment Annie could not cure, one that made her last week an excruciatingly painful one, Teresa Dolores moved all her belongings over to the Shand household, to live there permanently.

Luis had discussed it at some length with Jessie, when she made the suggestion.

"I'll miss her very much," he confessed. There was a trace of silver at his dark temples now, which gave him a romantically dashing air. "A household without females is...not a home at all." His smile was wistful. "But it would be selfish of me to keep Teresita with me, to provide a few hours of companionship in the evenings when I can sit down with her, when she could be part of a family like yours."

And then his smile broadened. "Besides, this way it gives me an excuse to visit you frequently, which might otherwise arouse...talk...if I came as often as I'd like."

Jessie pretended not to catch the innuendo there. Over the years Luis had made many such statements, and though he often came when he had every reason to think he would not find Joel at home, he had never made any inappropriate move in Jessie's direction; they visited with an open door in the parlor, with various servants and the young people moving freely about. Sometimes Jessie felt a spark of disappointment that Joel felt no jealousy over the visits of a man who admired his wife.

Once, after an evening when she'd drunk more than her customary single glass of wine at one of the dinners for Joel's business friends, she asked him with a touch of asperity, "Don't you notice when I spend the entire evening with Luis, in the library?"

Joel, also mellowed by considerably more wine than his wife had imbibed, grinned as he watched her disrobe for bed. "Luis is a gentleman. Those Mexicans sweet-talk a female as naturally as they ride a horse. It's bred into them from the cradle. And you had more fun talking about books with Luis than you'd have had listening to a discussion of who'll make the best next governor, didn't you?"

"Luis isn't Mexican, he's a Spaniard," Jessie corrected crossly.

Joel shrugged. It was immaterial. "He doesn't fit in with the others. It's fine with me if you entertain him elsewhere. I don't want to hurt his feelings, but he hasn't much to contribute to the kind of discussion we had tonight. He's not interested in donating money to gringo political candidates, though he'll benefit as much as I will if we get our own men into office. Come on to bed, love, and I'll show you what a real man does when he cares about a woman."

A small frown crept over her features. "I'm spotting again, I'm afraid. You'd better not count on me to go with you to Stockton next week, the way we'd planned."

He was immediately solicitous. "Why didn't you tell me you were expecting again? Come on to bed, we can hold each other, anyway, can't we?"

Why hadn't she told him? Jessie lay awake in the dark after Joel's regular breathing assured her that he was asleep. Because, she thought sadly, it happened so often. She knew she would never again have a child grow to new life within her. She didn't even remember any more how many times it had happened, that she had suspected she was pregnant, and then, within a month or two, the bloody flow had resumed and she knew that another baby had died almost before it had begun.

Joel was always tender and loving when she went through one of those episodes. True to her promise, Jessie didn't try to bargain again with God for the safe delivery of another child, though sometimes it was all she could do to conceal her heartache at the sight of an infant in another woman's arms.

Tonight she couldn't go to sleep. And it was not only the loss of yet another child. It was Joel, Joel who sometimes went for weeks without making love to her. She knew that it was upsetting to him, too, when she conceived yet could not carry a baby; it was for that reason that he tried to restrain his own urges so that he would not put her through this so often. Was it fair to Joel, this enforced celibacy, limited though it was?

No, it wasn't fair. It wasn't fair to her, either, yet nothing about life was fair, was it? She remembered her mother, married of economic necessity to a man she did not love, a man who provided for her but showed her no affection. A man who had taken a younger, prettier woman for a second wife while Viola still lived.

No, nothing was fair, but she was luckier than her mother had been. Joel loved her, and she loved him, and she did have a family—four of them now, with Teresa Dolores. At last Jessie curled warmly against Joel, and slept.

It bothered Joel far more than Jessie realized that he could not make love to his wife without the risk of making her pregnant, and thereby subjecting her to yet another miscarriage. Sometimes, lying beside her in the dark, wanting her so badly that he ached with the wanting, he cursed her God who had allowed such a situation to occur.

His choices, other than inflicting suffering on his wife with maddening regularity, were celibacy and seeking out other women.

For a long time, except for that one incident with Clara Ridback, Joel chose self-denial. It wasn't easy. He was young, healthy, virile, and he'd become accustomed to a normal sex life. Sleeping in the same bed with Jessie, touching her, trying to limit himself to no more than caresses and kisses until his need—and hers, too—was so overpowering that no human being could have withstood it, tore him apart emotionally.

He took to staying downstairs until he thought Jessie would have fallen asleep, so that he wouldn't have to tempt either of them past resisting by touching her. He realized that Jessie was sometimes hurt by this, that she felt his ardor, and perhaps his love, was cooling, but which was worse? To hurt her feelings or her body?

The first time after Clara that he turned to another female was on a trip to Stockton. That was far enough away from home so that he didn't much worry that any word would get back to Jessie. He'd gone for a load of supplies, and spent the night, and he'd drunk too much in one of the saloons where the voices were loud and the lights were bright, and there were girls who made it plain that they were available.

That first one's name was Myrtle; he remembered her name though he had forgotten her face. She wasn't a girl, at all. She was older than Jessie, and between the guilt he felt and the whiskey he'd consumed, the experience was less than a success.

His need was somewhat diminished, however, so that he didn't feel compelled to approach his wife for almost a week and a half. He tried to show Jessie, during the day, that he loved her. Smiles, kisses, intimate pats, and the words, too.

358

"I love you, Jess. You're the most beautiful woman I ever knew."

True, and sincere, every bit of it. During the day there were other people around and he couldn't sweep her off to bed, the way he had when they were first married. And if kissing her aroused him, as it often did, he could go out and work off his frustration in the fields or the barnyard or the corrals, until the worst of the sensations had subsided.

There were whores in Knight's Ferry, but he was afraid of them. The town was too small, and everybody knew him. He didn't want word of his indiscretions to get back to Jessie.

So, during those early years after Rosalie's birth, Joel restricted himself to quick liaisons as far from home as he could get. Since he was a farmer and had few excuses to leave his own land, that wasn't nearly often enough to keep him comfortable. Yet he knew that any sort of intimacy with a female of Jessie's acquaintance would be very dangerous, and he resisted that as long as he could.

Having Miss Smythe in the house became torture. She was not a beauty, like Jessie, but she was a pleasant person, and her figure was excellent under those drab garments she wore. Joel swore and tried not to look at the woman. She was alone, and he suspected she'd have married almost any man who'd ask her, only none had.

After a time, Miss Smythe began to look at him in a way that told him, making him alternately scorching hot and icy cold, that she might be amenable to his advances, should he care to make them. She, too, must have her unsatisfied needs, and she couldn't help being aware that Jessie was forever miscarrying, spending several days in her bed, drenching dozens of rags in blood that must be soaked out and the rags prepared for the next using. The governess was intelligent enough to see that Joel needed a sexual outlet besides his wife.

Once or twice Joel was on the verge of suggesting to Jessie that they replace the governess. He never voiced the idea, because he knew that Jessie was quite happy with the woman, the children were somewhere between liking her and tolerating her, and if Miss Smythe left, there would only be some other female to teach the girls, someone who might tempt him even more than Miss Smythe did. Joel despaired of a solution.

Part of his tension was pitted against the problems involved in the politics to which he was drawn with a fierce interest. His primary thought had been for irrigation ditches, a series of them that would water the entire valley, and only by banding together with other men whose dreams matched his own could this ever be accomplished.

Once he'd met these other men, however, he found that there were many other issues of interest as well. There were mayors and city councilmen to be elected, then representatives and senators.

He even, for a brief time, dreamed of running for political office himself.

The dream was short-lived. Frank Renton, a man of vast resources and one who enjoyed pulling strings behind the scenes, initially greeted Joel's tentative suggestion with enthusiasm. A few weeks later, however, he drew Joel to one side and spoke gravely.

"I'm afraid it's out of the question, Joe. There are too many prissy old women who won't vote for a man who's illegitimate."

He was not, of course, referring to women, but to men influenced by their wives, who did not yet have the right to vote, and it was a good thing they didn't, in the opinion of Joel's entire circle. Women had their uses, but selecting government leaders was not one of them.

Joel had gone first flaming red and then chalky. His curse was a vehement one.

"I'm sorry, Joe. I really am. Even in this frontier country people set standards, and when you get someone like old Babcock and his wife against you, it's harder than hell. Babcock may not have won the mayor's job, but he's still got money and influence. And you musta done something to get his wife against you, and that old biddy has money in the family behind her, too."

"I don't have to lie down and die because Louise Babcock says so," Joel ground out.

"Hell, no! Everybody knows she's an old bitch. But they control a lot of property, are owed a lot of money, and can influence too many voters."

"How do we know it's more than *we* can influence, without even trying?" Joel demanded.

"We don't. But we know they got enough so it would make it damned hard to get past them, and the group just don't think we want to sink a lot of money into a campaign for a man with a big black mark against him to start with. You don't want to do it either, Joe. You don't want to drag your family through a dirty campaign. You got a nice wife, nice family. And you don't need the job, for God's sake. You got a good spread here, plenty of work to do, make a comfortable living. With the kind of contribution you can make, you can control things from behind the scenes as well as you could in the capitol."

Though most of that was true, Joel was hurt and angry. "You've known me long enough to know better than to ask me to knuckle under to the likes of the Babcocks, Frank."

Renton, a big portly man some years older than Joel, sighed. "I didn't want to throw this in, Joe, but you're making me do it. The fact your ma wasn't married to your pa is only part of it. There's been talk for years, ever since that Ridback woman died. Quiet talk, so far. But you try to run for office and it's going to come out into the parlors. Louise Babcock told me some women saw you there, in Ridback's shop. And practically everybody knew why the woman had that outside stairway, back there in the dark where a man could break his neck getting in and out. Hell, Joe, there ain't a man in the county really gives a damn about a thing like that. But the womenfolk do, and your wife has to live with the womenfolk, same as all their husbands have to. You don't want to put her through that. Be a lot worse on her than you being talked about because you're illegitimate. I reckon she knew *that* when she married you, didn't she? But my guess is she don't know about anything else, and you don't want her to."

Joel stared at the man in almost blind rage. Once, he thought bitterly, only once he'd touched that bitch of a woman who'd enticed him upstairs and into her bed. Was this what she'd had in mind, to punish him for not being one of her regulars? Leaving him that goddamned money and property, just for spite? Knowing what everybody'd think about it? How much guilt was a man supposed to suffer for one brief lapse?

Frank Renton was watching him, guessing at what went on behind the angry features. He sighed again, and clinched the matter. "It wasn't only Clara Ridback, Joe. There's the other ones. A man can't keep things like that a secret forever, and there's enough people know about the woman over at La Grange, and that girl up past—"

"All right!" Joel interrupted savagely. "You've made your point. Forget it. Forget it."

He, of course, was unable to forget it. A hatred for the Babcocks ate at him, and along with it ran a trickle of fear. The women had meant nothing to him, nothing more than

361

a necessary physical relief, but would Jessie believe that, if they told her? Yes, he thought in his saner moments, she would, because she'd understand why he'd sought release elsewhere, but it would hurt her so badly. She felt guilty enough now that she couldn't love him as freely as they both wanted, and it was no more her fault that she conceived and miscarried babies than it was his that he craved relief from his own pressures.

For a time, deprived so quickly of his dream, afraid for Jessie if any of those bitches told her anything to upset her, Joel struggled with his problems alone. He didn't go into town, and he found himself being grateful that the couple currently inhabiting the little house where he and Jessie had started out were elderly and the woman so fat and ugly that the most desperate man would not have glanced in her direction.

And then the ugly old woman died, and her despondent husband shot himself, and the Wallaces came.

The little house had been enlarged over the years, so that it would now shelter a family rather than only a couple. It was painted whenever the big house was painted, so that it had a solid, respectable look. It served for whatever man Joel currently hired to help him on a regular year-round basis, and he hired Hal Wallace before he saw Hal's wife.

Hal was in his early forties, a stringy, tough individual with a knowledge of farming and a laconic manner. Joel expected a plump wife edging into middle age.

He saw Mary Ann Wallace the day they moved into the little house. Joel wasn't there when the wagon with their belongings arrived, but Jessie sent him out with a pot of stew for their first supper, and he knocked on the frame of the open door and then felt his mouth go dry when the woman came toward him with a smile.

Mary Ann was at least fifteen years younger than her husband, and she was pretty. Very pretty, he amended, seeing the rich cloud of hair—not pale, like Jessie's, but a flaming blond with red highlights when she stepped outside into the afternoon sun. Her eyes were blue and thickly lashed, and her waist was so tiny he thought a man could snap it in two with his bare hands.

She was dressed in everyday clothes, for the tasks of moving and settling in, and it was a warm day; she'd loosened the neck of the cotton gown. Her throat, pale ivory, rose from the blue-and-white-checked gingham, and he caught a tantalizing glimpse of the beginning of the separation between her breasts.

If it hadn't been two weeks since he'd slept with Jessie— well, he *slept* with her every night, but he hadn't touched her in that long—maybe she wouldn't have aroused him so quickly and so completely.

He felt as young as Laurie, as gauche as a schoolboy.

"Mrs. Wallace. My wife sent out some stew for your supper."

"Why, how kind of her! Thank you, Mr. Shand." Mary Ann had a crooked tooth, much like his own, which he'd always hated. On a female, it was oddly appealing. "This is a nice house. I'm sure we're going to be very happy here."

"I hope so," he told her, sounding quite normal. "If you need anything, let us know. Tell Hal we'll start at six in the morning."

The smile widened. "Thank you. I'll tell him. He's always up early, he says it's the best time of the day."

He glanced past her into the little house. "You don't have a family, do you, Mrs. Wallace?"

She shook her head, and the thick blond hair swirled and shimmered. "No. We've never been so blessed, unluckily."

"You're young," Joel heard himself saying. "You still have time."

A perceptible shadow crossed her face, though she murmured, "Yes, maybe there's still time."

He left her then, his errand completed, but he couldn't get her out of his mind. Jesus, if he'd thought it was difficult watching Miss Smythe with her ordinary looks, what was it going to be like having this little beauty living just across the creek?

He'd have to stay away from her, Joel told himself, and for a while he believed he could do it.

41

If Mary Ann Wallace had been happily married, satisfied in her relationship with her husband, Joel might have succeeded in doing what he'd always sworn to do: stay away from any woman in Jessie's circle of acquaintances. Mary Ann didn't work in the big house, as some of the other wives had done, but she loved making a garden, and she spent a good part of her day outside, where Joel couldn't help passing her or at least viewing her from a distance. She dug and planted and hoed and watered, and hung out her laundry, and took walks for exercise.

Any man would have watched her with appreciation, because she was young and lovely and lively. She wasn't forward, nor was she particularly bashful; she was simply friendly and knew her place, which was to say that she didn't expect Jessie to treat her as a social equal.

Jessie treated everybody as if they were human beings, however. While she was too busy with her own concerns to take Mary Ann to her bosom, she was friendly right back, and told Joel that she liked her and that, if Mrs. Sullivan ever left, she'd like to have Mary Ann working in the kitchen, if she'd agree to it.

Joel hoped fervently that Mrs. Sullivan would stay forever, at the same time fantasizing about Mary Ann moving around in the kitchen while he ate his breakfast, that tempting behind within inches of him. Pouring his coffee, bending over the table to give him a glimpse of those perfect breasts.

"I don't think Hal wants his wife to work in the house," was all he said, and Jessie nodded.

"More than likely. Well, it would be up to them to decide, and Mrs. Sullivan is still here, so it doesn't matter, does it?"

He stayed away from the little house where his new hired man lived. If he had a message to send over there, he sent one of the boys. He tried to give Hal his instructions the day before, so that he had no excuse to approach Hal's wife.

If he hadn't learned Hal's secret, he thought he would have gone on keeping things under control, staying away from Mary Ann. Only he *did* learn about Hal.

He didn't remember how the subject came up in the first place, because although they often worked side by side for many hours a day, Hal was not much of a talker. But one day, perhaps because each of them had needs he could not fulfill and talking might make it easier, Hal confessed that he was not really a husband to Mary Ann.

Joel stumbled over the grain bag he was lifting, and in spite of himself felt an upsurge of excitement.

"I shoulda known I was too old for her," Hal said. "Forty when we was married two years ago. She's only twenty-five. She don't blame me for it, never said a thing when I couldn't make it like a man. But I reckon a woman has needs, too, of her own, even if she don't talk about it."

Joel moistened his lips and rested the grain bag on the edge of the manger. "Forty-two's not old. And I guess it's something that happens to everybody, once in a while."

Hal shook his head. "It ain't just once in a while. Last six months, it's all the time. I can't do it at all no more. It ain't fair to Mary Ann, but it don't look like I'm ever going to be able to do it again. She says she won't leave me because of it, but she's a pretty little thing. Too young to live with a man like me. She might change her mind, one of these days." Hal forked hay into the manger, then leaned on the pitchfork. "It might've made a difference if we'd had a baby or two, but we never did, even before I...just couldn't. She wanted babies, guess most women do, don't they? When we didn't have none, she talked to one of them doctors up to Stockton. He said it was probably because she had a bad fall once, when she was younger. Hurt her pretty bad. He said that might be why she didn't never get in the family way. If she ain't got a whole man, it would've been nice if she'd had a family, anyway, but that wasn't the way it worked out."

The words were branded into Joel's mind. *A woman has needs of her own.* He knew that was true. Why else had Clara Ridback lured him into her bedroom, if not to satisfy her own needs? And Jessie, Jessie didn't say much when he didn't go near her, but he knew Jessie had plenty of inner fire. Before Rosalie was born, before every act of love became the forerunner of another of those goddamned miscarriages, her passion had matched his own.

He remembered the morning she'd slid into bed with him and waked him from a sound sleep, after helping Annie deliver Belle Snow's baby, and for the first time initiated lovemaking on her own. She wanted him then, and she probably wanted him a lot more often now, though she didn't add to his frustrations by saying so.

He'd heard there was something the whores used to prevent conception, but he didn't know what it could be. He wasn't even sure it was true, that conception could be prevented. It wasn't the kind of thing he could go around asking about, even if he'd known anyone to ask. Annie didn't know, or she'd have told Jessie, and that old drunk of a doctor who came through periodically didn't know, either. He was the only one Joel had approached on the subject. Either the old man was as ignorant as Joel, or he was too drunk to remember. At any rate, he hadn't been able to offer any sensible advice other than abstinence.

Christ, Joel thought, a man could only abstain so long. He was nearly forty himself. What if he got like Hal Wallace? What if he couldn't do it with Jessie, and not with anybody else, either? What if he couldn't ever make love to a woman again?

Certainly there had been no sign, so far, that his sexual powers were on the wane. Quite the contrary, he was in a state of heat most of the time. But Hal had been like that once, too. And now it was over for him.

He didn't want it to make a difference, that Mary Ann's needs, whatever they might be, were unfulfilled. But it did.

He would never take advantage of a woman who didn't want him, Joel thought. Not like Luis Sañudo, who, he knew, used several of the Mexican women who lived in the workers' quarters a distance from the hacienda. Luis had not married —he said frankly that there was no woman of good family for him to marry since so many of his countrymen had fled before the gringo invasion in the late '40s and '50s—but that didn't mean he didn't have the male's normal appetites. Not for a moment did Joel believe that Luis failed to satisfy those urges. Luis's attitude toward women was that they were delightful and entertaining. And Joel doubted very much that he asked permission of those women on his estate before entering their beds. Not, he admitted, that they were likely to object, for was not Luis *el patrón*, the giver of all good gifts, the one who kept them from being turned out of their homes to starve?

The whole business preyed upon Joel. One afternoon he left Hal in a distant field and returned to the house with the intention of riding into Knight's Ferry to see if there was any word on the new plow he'd ordered.

Jessie was in bed for the second day, bleeding again. He looked in on her, bent for the gentle kiss that went with the wan smile.

"Damn it," he said. "I wish there was some way to stop this from happening to you, Jess."

Her fingers traced the outline of his jaw. "Darling, it isn't your fault. It isn't mine, either. It just happens, to lots of women. I'll be up and around within a few days. Don't worry."

He straightened. "I don't care about the other women. I care about you." He made a snorting sound. "I remember telling you that your precious God doesn't punish people by killing people they love, but sometimes I wonder what I've done, bad enough to make you suffer this way."

"Oh, Joel! I'm used to it. The cramping is almost gone. Maybe I'll even come down to supper tonight. What are you doing inside this time of day?"

"I'm going into town to see about that plow. It should have been in a week ago, and I'll be damned if I'm going to plow another acre with an old one. Hal's trying to fix it again, but it's plain wore out. You want anything from town?"

Jessie considered. "I wish Mamie was still there, baking bread and cakes. Mrs. Sullivan is fine with bread, but she has a heavy hand with cakes. The boys are so disappointed when there's no cake."

"I'll stop by the new bakery and see what they have," Joel offered.

"And the post office, Joel. Maybe there'll be another letter from Mamie or Zadie. Mamie sounded so happy in that first note."

"All right. I'll look for mail. Don't worry about coming downstairs for supper. Why don't I bring mine up here and eat with you, and let Miss Smythe handle everybody else? Incidentally, how long are we going to continue to keep her on? The girls aren't going to need her much longer, are they?"

"Oh, yes, I should think so!" Jessie raised herself on her elbows to look earnestly into his face. "There are still plenty of things she can teach them. I want them to have as good an education as the boys. It'll be an advantage when it's time

367

to marry, Joel. Girls from good families learn about all kinds of things. I'd teach them more myself, about running a house," she said, a small frown creasing her brow, "if I weren't busy with so many other things."

If she weren't constantly miscarrying, Joel thought. "All right. I guess that means a few more years, then."

"She hasn't anywhere else to go," Jessie reminded. "No family to turn to, if she leaves us."

He didn't argue the point, though on his way downstairs he reflected that Jessie and Luis would have made a good pair. Give board and room to all the family retainers, no matter how old and useless they got, whether they could earn their keep or not. He'd never been able to persuade Luis to turn off any of his people, and they were draining his resources to the breaking point. He wasn't willing to give up any of his own extravagances, either.

To begin with, it had been an advantage to Joel to tie the two ranches together; now, Luis was the one who benefited the most. Without Joel's management and financial assistance, Luis would have lost everything he owned by this time. Not entirely because of all those peons, of course, but they certainly contributed to the problems. It was a damned good thing Luis wasn't convinced they had to live the same way *he* did, having the best of everything. Well, there was nothing wrong with living well, if you could afford it. Only Luis couldn't be made to understand that he could no longer afford to live like a king.

Joel walked out through the back door, speaking to Mrs. Sullivan, who was taking her afternoon rest in the rocker with her feet up. She always spent an hour or so that way in midafternoon.

There was no one else around. The boys had gone to Knight's Ferry for the day, and the girls were busy upstairs making new dresses for some party or the other, under the governess's supervision.

The yard was quiet when he opened the door and stepped onto the porch; he stood for a moment, smelling the aroma of freshly turned earth and the blossoms on Jessie's fruit trees, a pink-and-white border that encircled the house. Beyond the trees, in the dimness within the barn, he saw movement, and he squinted against the sun. A sprigged muslin dress—the skirt caught the sun as the wearer passed through an area where the sunlight came through a window in the loft—and then the flash of exposed petticoat ruffles as the woman climbed the ladder to the level where they stored the hay.

A warmth spread through him. Mary Ann. It had to be Mary Ann. Joel went down the steps and walked across the yard, oblivious of the garden Jessie had recently planted, of the trickle of water through the irrigation ditch that still served the garden after all these years.

He was a large man, but he moved gracefully and quietly. A glance at the naked hills reassured him that Hal Wallace was still beyond the nearer ones, working with the old plow. He stood in the doorway of the barn, inhaling the odors of hay and cows and manure, all so familiar that they scarcely registered.

There was another scent, too, one too light to compete for long with the others: soap, the kind Mary Ann used to wash her hair, a scented soap Hal had bought her in town for a present a few weeks ago.

What was Mary Ann doing in the loft? There was nothing up there but loose hay, and not much of that, since the horses and the few cows they kept for milking had been turned out to pasture several weeks ago.

There was always a scattering of hay on the barn floor, hay that muffled his footsteps. He reached the ladder, eyes now adjusting to the diminished light, and he began to climb.

Mary Ann knelt in the hay a few yards away, unaware that she was observed. Even in shadow her hair was a glorious color, though the reddish highlights weren't so apparent. Her lips curled in a smile, and she cuddled a small furry creature against her breast and spoke to it, soothingly.

"Don't be afraid of me, I won't hurt you. Oh, you're a darling thing . . ."

Joel had reached the top of the ladder and stepped off onto the loft floor. Mary Ann whirled, still kneeling, with wide, startled eyes.

"Oh, Mr. Shand! I didn't hear you coming!" She rose and showed him what she held. "Old Molly's had kittens. I've been looking for them for days, and I finally found them. There are five. This is the prettiest."

She came toward him, unself-conscious, attention more on the kitten than on the man, until she stood only a few feet away and lifted her head. "Could I have one of them, do you suppose? This one? I've wanted a cat for ever so long."

"Take whichever one you want," Joel said. His voice sounded odd in his own ears. He could smell the soap, and the distinctive woman-scent of her. He'd never noticed before that she had a sprinkling of freckles across her nose; afterward he would think wryly that she could have been cross-eyed and he probably wouldn't have done things any differently.

Gradually his tension seeped through to her. She drew a deep breath that lifted her breasts, and held it. Her lips were parted, showing the crooked tooth; he imagined he could feel her breath when she finally exhaled.

Surely it was there in the pretty face, the same yearning he felt himself? Or did he only imagine what he wanted to be there?

He spoke very softly. "Put the kitten down."

She obeyed without question, bending to set the squirming creature at her feet, not looking after it when it scampered back to the hole in the hay with its siblings.

Joel reached for her, and Mary Ann did not draw away. He drew her into his arms, felt the rapid heartbeat under the softness of her breasts, the yielding of the mouth that opened under his.

He would never have touched her if she'd given any sign that she did not want him. Taking a woman by force was not in his nature.

But this woman was as love-starved as he was. A hot sweetness raced through his veins, blotting out everything except his need, as Joel eased her onto the hay.

She did not struggle against him. Indeed, it was her own hands that reached for the buttons of her bodice, exposing the loveliness he had known was there.

Neither of them said a word. She was young and pretty and eager, as eager as he. Months, Hal had said, since he'd been a husband to her, and only with intermittent success for some time before that.

Hal was impotent, and Jessie's health was fragile and endangered by lovemaking. There was nothing wrong with either Mary Ann or Joel, and they took each other lustily, greedily.

Afterward, Mary Ann redid the buttons and looked at him almost apologetically as he sprawled beside her in the hay. "Hal's a good man," she said softly. "He took me in when my folks died, married me. He's a good husband, except for..."

Joel pushed himself to a sitting position. He didn't want to talk about Jessie, but he had to make his position clear from the start. "I love my wife, only her health isn't good. I would never want anything to hurt her."

She considered that, then nodded. "Nor would I hurt Hal, if I could help it."

She was so close he could see the specks of deeper color in her blue eyes. Her mouth looked so soft. Joel suddenly leaned toward her, resting a hand on hers before she could finish the buttons. "Not yet," he said, and took her backward onto the hay, covering her mouth once more with his own, feeling desire rising again already.

There would be guilt. He knew that, and accepted it. He accepted the risk, too, that Jessie might someday find out, though he planned that she would not.

He'd sworn to himself that he would never take a woman within Jessie's world of acquaintances, and he'd broken that vow. He had to do it, Joel thought, and he couldn't stop now. Whatever happened, he couldn't go back, couldn't pretend this hadn't occurred.

Mary Ann moaned with pleasure beneath him, and he forgot everything but the female flesh that gave him such pleasure, such release.

They were not in love with each other. Neither of them ever mentioned the word. They were discreet, they were careful, and the hours they spent together in the haymow made all the rest of their lives so much easier.

Hal Wallace felt better that his pretty young wife seemed to be adjusting to a rather lonely life in the country with good humor and good spirits. Maybe, he thought, a female didn't need the same as a man did, after all.

And Jessie noted a gratifying change in Joel, subtle though it was. He was happier, he smiled more; she thought he must have had some sort of success in the political world that he was not yet willing to discuss with her.

He found other ways than the conventional ones to satisfy her physical needs. When he told her, softly in the darkness, what he wanted to do, she was first shocked, then fearful. But this was her own beloved Joel, after all, and he wanted only to love her without making her pregnant. The least she could do was try what he wanted her to try.

She cried, that first time, not because she was upset by these things she had not imagined men and women did together, but because she once more felt so close to him, as if the love they bore each other was an overpowering thing as it had been when they were first married. She felt as joyous as a bride—no, more so than a bride, because she was not frightened in the way that a bride is apprehensive about her wedding night. This was Joel, and he loved her, and she loved him.

Jessie, too, began to laugh more, and to sing as she went about the house. Who would have thought a couple well past thirty could be so happy? she wondered, and did not question the source of that happiness.

42

Joel was not the only one who noticed how attractive Mary Ann was.

Laurie, at nearly eighteen, thought himself a grown man. So far he hadn't found a way to prove it. He knew plenty of girls, all well supervised and gently reared. They had met his overtures with disgust, dismay, or, at best, amused rejection. He'd managed to kiss a few of them; none had allowed him to go any further than that.

Had he dared, he'd have tried to get Teresa Dolores alone for an hour. Though she had not grown as tall as Rosalie, and she had not her cousin's confidence and outgoing personality, Teresa Dolores was an exquisitely pretty girl even at the age of fourteen. Her dark hair was caught and held back with a ribbon that usually matched her frock, and he had never seen a tinier waist.

Once he'd tested the water, so to speak, by playing up to her a bit. Only the silly baby was intimidated by him, for some reason, and she'd been standing there saying nothing, just looking scared, when Tristan came upon them.

Tris hadn't even asked what was going on. He'd simply surveyed the scene and said brusquely, "Leave her alone, Laurie. Ma's looking for you, Teresa. Something about going to town. She's in the kitchen."

Teresa Dolores fled in obvious relief, and Tris had lingered for a moment longer to give Laurie a decidedly unfriendly look. "I mean it, Laurie. Don't bother her."

Laurie laughed it off. "She's such an infant. She's terrified to talk to a man. Except for you, of course." His mouth twisted in malicious amusement. "She's been sweet on you ever since she came here, but I think it's because you're safe. You know, not really like a man at all."

For once Tris didn't redden or squirm under Laurie's verbal attack. "Just remember what I told you," he said, and there was a note in his voice that gave Laurie pause.

If he did ever corner the little chit, she'd be easy picking, Laurie thought. But afterward she'd cry, and probably if Tris or Rosalie saw her, they'd induce her to tell anything that had happened. He wasn't afraid of either of them, of course. Neither of them could hurt him in any way. If they carried the tale to Joel, however, that was a different matter. Laurie knew if he touched the girl, Joel would beat him senseless. Joel hadn't punished him in years, since he'd taken a belt to him over an incident that had resulted in burning off a couple acres of ripening wheat because Laurie'd been careless.

And then Mary Ann came to live in the little house beyond the creek. Any male would look at Mary Ann, even Tris, though he was unobtrusive about it. And she was married to a man damn near old enough to be her father, Laurie thought. How much pleasure would a young woman get from going to bed with Hal Wallace?

It was a long time after the Wallaces arrived before Laurie found an opportunity to be alone with Mary Ann. For the most part, Joel felt that the boys should work a full twelve-hour day along with him and Hal, once they were out of school. That left only Sundays, when everybody was around and a fellow couldn't even scratch an itch without being observed.

The day before Nellie Allen's wedding on a Saturday night in late June, Laurie's hopes rose. Everybody would be going to that, and they wouldn't be home until late. And he knew that Hal Wallace had been sent to Sacramento with the wagon to bring back harvesting equipment Joel had ordered from Chicago.

Laurie had coveted that task, since he'd never seen the train that now climbed Donner Summit and plunged down the other side to cross Nevada and connect with the eastern cities as Joel had long ago predicted that it would.

Joel squashed his hopes on that score the moment Laurie mentioned wanting to go. His appraisal was curt. "If you think I'm going to turn you loose in the city overnight you're out of your mind. The last time I sent you to Knight's Ferry for feed you raced the wagon and damn near wrecked it, not to mention what you did to the horses. No, Hal can go."

All right, Laurie thought when he heard about the wedding. This would be even better. Everyone would be gone, except for himself and Mary Ann.

He had to pretend that he was going to the wedding with the others, of course. Not to go would rouse all kinds of suspicion, since he always leaped at an opportunity to attend any kind of social function. It was his primary source of contact with females of any age, other than those in his own household. After the wedding there would be the customary dancing, drinking, and eating...plus the socializing that would, the girls all hoped, lead to their own weddings.

He waited until half an hour before the rest of the family was to leave on Saturday afternoon, then stretched out on his bed with an arm over his eyes to wait until someone arrived to remind him that it was time to go.

It was Rosalie who came, knocked lightly, and poked her head around the edge of the door. Rosalie was nearly fifteen, and though rather taller than Laurie liked in a girl, she was slim and vibrantly lovely, today in a rose-colored silk dress that molded small breasts and waist. She was wearing the pearls she'd talked Joel out of for Christmas last year—Rosie never had any difficulty getting anything she wanted from her father—and Laurie studied her with the objectivity of a brother. Rosie certainly wouldn't have any trouble finding a husband when the time came.

"Laurie? We're ready. Why are you lying down?"

"I must have eaten something that didn't agree with me," Laurie muttered, trying to make his voice sound sick. "I just threw up, and I feel a little better now, but I don't think I'm up to a whole evening of carousing. Tell Aunt Jessie I'm going to stay home."

True to form, Rosalie didn't accept his explanation and let it go at that. "What did you eat?" she asked.

"How do I know? All I know is I just puked, and I feel rotten." The vulgarity was intentional, in the hope that it would drive her away.

"You didn't eat anything the rest of us didn't eat, did you?"

"For crissake, Rosie, I don't know! I feel terrible, I just

374

want to lie here and wait until it goes away, and I'm not up to any buggy ride or wedding or anything else. Go away and leave me alone."

"Mama thinks you're going with us."

"Well, I'm not. You want to see where I puked, if you don't believe me?"

Rosalie's mouth flattened. "No, thank you." She turned and went away, heels tapping on the stairs, and Laurie smiled. He didn't get up. He knew better than that; Jessie would undoubtedly come up to feel his forehead before she left him.

She did, expressing mild concern. Mild, because she suspected that it was more likely something he'd drunk than something he'd eaten. He didn't have a fever, and he was neither cold nor clammy to the touch.

"Well, Mrs. Sullivan won't be here to fix you any supper," she told him, "if you decide after a while that you're hungry. She's going with us."

"I don't think I'll be hungry for a long time. If I am, I'll fix something for myself," Laurie told her, wishing to God she'd quit fussing and *go*.

He waited for a full hour after the buggy had disappeared from sight out his bedroom window. He didn't dare move earlier than that for fear one of those stupid females had forgotten her gloves or her earrings or some other fool thing, and would insist on returning for them.

After the hour had elapsed, he felt safe enough. Joel would refuse to return for anything once he'd gone more than a few miles, even for Rosalie. He spoiled Rosalie absurdly, in Laurie's opinion.

His mind was not on Rosalie as he went down the stairs and out the back door. The pulses quickened within him as he crossed the yard, made his way beyond the row of fruit trees, along the well-trodden path, and approached the little house.

He'd lived there, once, though he didn't remember it. He hadn't been inside it in years. He stood for a moment before he lifted his hand to knock, feeling the late-afternoon sun on his back, hearing the leaves whispering on the trees behind him. And something else...did he hear something else?

Laurie spun, scanning the open space between the little house and the creek where the willows Jessie had planted years ago now provided a sixty-foot screen for the big house beyond.

375

There was no one there. He knew there couldn't be; they'd all gone to Nellie Allen's wedding. He turned back and rapped sharply on the door in front of him.

Mary Ann was wearing brown calico with tiny red flowers in it, and a red ribbon in her hair, which was not loose today but secured in a bun at the back of her neck. It didn't make her look less appealing, however.

She wiped her hands on her apron . . . floury hands, Laurie noted. "Yes?" she said, puzzled. "I thought everyone had already gone to the wedding," she said, glancing behind him as if expecting the others to be with him.

Laurie allowed her a lazy smile, though inside he was taut and struggling to control a tremor. "I didn't go. I thought I'd rather stay home and keep you company, since Hal's gone."

Her face shifted from bewilderment to reserved hostility. "You've wasted your evening, then, I'm afraid. I don't need any company."

"Sure you do," Laurie told her. He put out a foot so that she couldn't close the door in his face, for her hand was on the edge of it. "A pretty young woman like you. A man as old as Hal can't be all you want out of life."

"Whatever I want," Mary Ann said, softly yet clearly, "it isn't a little boy like you."

Anger snapped his head back as if she'd slapped him. Heat suffused his face, and he moved closer to her, blocking the doorway with his body now so that she stepped back from him. "I can show you whether I'm a little boy or a man," he told her. "I've seen how you look at me, at any man comes around, besides old Hal. You need something more than him."

"I think you'd better go," Mary Ann said. She seemed calm, though a telltale pulse pounded at the exposed base of her throat. "I'd hate to have to tell Mr. Shand you had annoyed me."

"Why don't you just try what I have to offer?" Laurie asked, mortified when he squeaked a little. "You don't have to tell Uncle Joe anything. He'd understand how a young woman with an old man could want somebody else."

"I asked you to go," Mary Ann said, and tried to push against him with the door. "I haven't looked at you or anyone else in an improper manner, and I'm not interested in anything you have to offer, Mr. Laurie. Get out of my house."

She was so close he could see how her pupils had dilated in the deep blue eyes, could see the crooked tooth as in her agitation she breathed open-mouthed, could see the rise and fall of perfect breasts under the dark calico.

Laurie reached for her, fingers closing around her arm so that she cried out.

And then Laurie felt himself spun around by a force that, for a moment, he feared was Joel's. He was slammed against the wall of the house and punched in the mouth so that he tasted blood.

"Damn you!" Tris said between clenched teeth. "I ought to beat the hell out of you! How dare you try something like this?"

It was only Tris. Tris, whom he'd beaten hundreds of times over the years. Laurie's fright subsided, and he managed a grin through bloodied lips.

"Mind your own business, Tris. I'm just talking to Mary Ann."

Tris was livid with rage. "Rosie said you were up to something. I had to lie, the same as you did, to be left behind, to pretend we'd gotten into something together that made us both sick. Rosie convinced Ma we just had upset stomachs and it was safe to leave us behind, but she said you were up to some deviltry. I never thought it would be something like this, forcing yourself on a helpless woman."

Laurie's grin was distorted as his lips pulled back in a grimace that showed his teeth as if he were a wild animal. "I told you, Tris. It's none of your business. Go home."

For answer, Tris struck out again with a fist that slapped Laurie flat against the wall, followed by another blow to the midsection that knocked the wind out of him.

"All right," Laurie said, feeling his lips swell against his teeth, "you asked for it, my friend."

They had fought many times, but never like this. This time they were in earnest, each trying to hurt the other. Tristan drew strength from an inner desperation; he had to stop Laurie from doing this thing, the thing he'd contemplated with other girls at other times.

They rolled on the ground, flailing at each other, cursing, each vying to put a knee into his opponent's groin, gouging, pounding. Laurie rolled with Tris and managed to smash his head against the doorstep, so that for a moment the younger youth seemed stunned; Laurie thought he'd won, as he expected to win.

It wasn't over, however. Before Laurie could rise, Tris recovered enough to reach out for his half brother's shirtfront and draw him back, and then deliver a solid blow to the chin that made Laurie's eyes glaze as he slid sideways.

Tris hit him again for good measure before he shoved him to one side and got to his own feet, chest heaving painfully. Mary Ann stood in the doorway, one hand covering her mouth, her eyes wide.

When Laurie groaned and attempted to rise, Tris delivered the *coup de grace*. He brought his knee under Laurie's chin, hard, and flipped him backward, eyes rolling up; the maneuver staggered Tris, but he steadied himself and gazed down at the one he'd never whipped before.

"I think he's... unconscious," Mary Ann said, her voice sounding faintly in Tris's ears.

"Good. It's too bad I didn't kill him," Tris panted. "He didn't hurt you, did he?"

Mary Ann slid up her sleeve and examined the bruises forming there where Laurie had gripped her arm. "No. Nothing serious, anyway." She offered him a tremulous smile. "Thank you, Mr. Tristan. I hope you aren't seriously hurt."

He was still breathing with an effort, but he didn't think he was injured, though Laurie had landed some solid blows and there would undoubtedly be bruises.

"You're going to have a black eye, I think," Mary Ann told him. "Come inside and sit down, and I'll put a cold cloth on it."

He felt strange, entering her house, but the way the blood was pounding in his head he thought it might be wise to sit for a few minutes. He stepped over Laurie's legs, glancing at the cut lip, the swelling under one eye, the bloody knuckles. Well, it would be Laurie's problem to explain his cuts and abrasions. He could tell the family anything he wanted.

Tris sat on the wooden chair while Mary Ann ministered to him. There were more sore places than he'd realized at first, and he guessed he'd have to think up some excuses of his own. He had no intention of telling anybody why he and Laurie had fought; if Mary Ann wanted to make a complaint to Pa, that was her business, though he guessed she wouldn't want to.

Her fingers were deft and light, and he felt giddy yet increasingly triumphant. He'd licked Laurie, by God. For once he hadn't had to take the beating himself, and Laurie had been fighting his damnedest.

"That's the best I can do," Mary Ann said at last. "Except maybe... a glass of whiskey? Hal has a bottle."

It wasn't as good as what Joel kept in the study; it burned all the way down and it was all he could do not to choke on it, but after he stood up and made his way to the door he began to feel better for it.

He gave Mary Ann a crooked grin, because his mouth was swelling, too; one side of it didn't move right. "I guess I ought to haul him away, so he won't bother you again when he comes to."

Mary Ann scrutinized the fallen would-be lover, who only now had begun to stir. "I don't think he will."

"Lock your door, anyway," Tris advised.

Laurie twitched, and moved his head to one side, opened his eyes long enough to groan, then closed them again.

Tris bent to haul the other youth to his feet, where Laurie stumbled and would have gone down again if Tris hadn't balanced and held him. "Come on, let's go home," he said.

At the creek, instead of using the little bridge that enabled one to cross even during flood season without getting wet, Tris thrust Laurie forward onto his knees—a simple enough matter, since Laurie was walking only with assistance—and stuck his head into the water.

Laurie came up gasping and shoved against the restraining hands. "All right! That's enough! Let go!"

Tris obeyed, watching with an enigmatic face while Laurie finally rose under his own power and staggered on across the shallow stream. When Tris followed, Laurie turned a bruised and puffy face toward him.

"I wasn't going to hurt her, Tris. I wasn't going to *force* her, for crissake. If you'd left us alone, I'd have talked her into it."

Tris didn't argue the point. "Just stay away from her from now on," he said in a new, flat, yet authoritative tone Laurie had never heard from him.

"You think maybe she'll reward you for coming to her rescue, is that it?" Laurie attempted a grin. "She sure as hell needs somebody besides that old man she's married to."

Tris's face was troubled. "There's something about you, Laurie. Something that makes me feel kind of sick, deep inside. As if you don't really ever think of anything but yourself—what *you* want, what *you* need. And even when you don't actually intend to harm anybody, you seem to enjoy scaring them. Showing them you can hurt them, if you want to."

Laurie held up a protesting hand. "Hell, I don't want to

hurt anybody. And I'm no more selfish than anybody else, far as I can see. *You* don't have to prove anything to anybody. You got a ma and a pa, a real family, not just somebody that took you in. I've never been part of the Shands, not really. Your ma bends over backwards to be fair to me, but she never wanted me around. And Uncle Joe, maybe he cares, but not enough to admit to anybody that he's my father."

"You don't know for sure about that."

"The hell I don't. I know it as sure as I'm standing here. God, my head hurts! What did you hit me with?"

Tris refused to be drawn into a camaraderie he didn't feel. "Everything I had. And I'll do it again, Laurie, if I ever hear of you scaring some poor female that way."

They stopped just outside the row of fruit trees that encircled the house grounds. Laurie's eye was swelling shut, and no one had cleaned him up, the way Mary Ann had done with Tris, so he looked considerably the worse for wear.

For a long moment they stared at each other, these two young men who had grown up together in the same household, who had wrestled and run and played and fought, and the realization formed within them both.

They would never again wrestle or fight in fun. They had grown up, and they didn't really like each other very much.

Tris inhaled deeply, exhaled, and without a word turned and strode toward the house. After a few seconds, Laurie followed, moving quickly to catch up.

"What are you going to tell Aunt Jessie? About the way we look?"

Tris slogged straight ahead, his eyes on the distant horizon. "Nothing," he said.

"She's going to ask questions about why we're both so battered."

"Tell her anything you like. I'm not going to tell her anything," Tris said.

And he never did.

43

Jessie was appalled at the condition of the two of them. "Obviously they had a terrible fight," she told Joel. "And they won't talk about it."

Joel shrugged. "They're neither of them seriously injured, so forget it, Jess. Leave them alone. They're men now, not boys."

"But what could have caused them to fight so...so *ferociously?*"

"Almost anything." He grinned a little. "A girl, maybe. They're old enough to be interested in girls. Forget it, Jessie."

He didn't give the same order to Rosalie, because Rosalie didn't discuss the matter with him. She did ask her brother, point-blank, what had happened.

Usually she and Tris talked openly together. This time, Tris gave her a moody glance and busied himself rearranging the books on the shelf beside his bed.

"You can see what happened. We hit each other a few times."

Rosalie sidled around so that she could more fully see his face. "He looks as if you took after him with a club. You beat him this time, didn't you, Tris?"

Something flickered in her brother's face, and a reluctant grin responded to hers. "I knocked him out," Tris admitted.

"For what? What did he do?"

"There are some things, Rosie, a man doesn't need to talk about."

Undeterred, Rosalie speculated. "He stayed behind for some reason, and it wasn't because he was sick to his stomach, any more than you were. What did he do? Lie in wait for Mary Ann? She was the only one left on the place. Did you rescue Mary Ann?"

This was a new Tris, one who didn't deign to answer if he

didn't want to. After a moment, coming to her own conclusions, Rosalie pulled him down and stood on her tiptoes so that she could brush a kiss across his cheek.

"I'm glad you beat him," she said, and left him with mingled emotions. When he was very small, he'd thought growing up would solve all his problems.

He suspected now that growing up was going to be just the start of them.

They were reconciled eventually, at least on the surface. They talked, rode together, they went into town looking for excitement. They still swam in the summer and rode a canoe together down the Stanislaus, shooting through the rapids in a dangerous sort of sport that left them both exhilarated and gratified at having cheated fate of the opportunity to smash them against the rocks.

. There were girls in town, and Laurie discovered a few who would allow him at least small liberties without his having to intimidate them into it. Laurie could be completely charming when he chose, and most of the time he worked at it, though it was disconcerting to glance over the shoulder of an entranced young lady at a dance and find Rosalie's sardonic gaze upon him, or Tris's enigmatic one.

In time Laurie learned that well-brought-up young ladies had neither the inclination nor the opportunity for more than kisses and hand-holding. There were, he discovered, other places a man could go for further favors, not all of them having to be paid for.

Once Laurie invited Tris to join him at a discreetly run sporting house. A spot of color appeared in each of Tris's cheeks, and he shook his head. "No, thanks," he refused, and Laurie didn't urge him.

While Laurie did not again approach Mary Ann Wallace, he continued to watch her. The way she moved, so light and quick and with such lithe grace, was impossible to ignore. It was no more than that to Laurie, the observation of a pretty woman. But after a time he realized that there was a pattern to her wanderings.

There was also a pattern to Joel's movements. And that pattern meshed with Mary Ann's.

At first Laurie didn't believe the evidence unfolding before him. Uncle Joe, and his hired man's wife?

No one could live in the same house with Jessie and Joel and doubt their genuine affection for each other. Would Joe risk the happiness the two of them had for a tumble in the hay with a hired man's wife, even if she was a proper beauty?

Laurie had grown up with the fact of Jessie's frequent withdrawals into her own room, where she was waited upon by whatever female was in charge at the time. He'd seen some of the bloody rags that were carried out of the room and left soaking in the shed until they could be laundered. At first he'd assumed that this was the result of the regular monthly bleeding women did, and then he'd realized the truth, that Aunt Jessie suffered periodic miscarriages.

"Amazing what you can find out," he blithely related to Tris, "if you listen at keyholes once in a while."

He'd succeeded in embarrassing Tristan, which always amused him.

Was that it? he wondered now. Joe loved his wife, but he hated to put her through a miscarriage so often, so he found his own outlet somewhere else?

Once the idea came into his mind, Laurie was obsessed by it. He didn't mention it to Tristan this time—there were lots of things he didn't talk to Tris about any more—until he was certain.

"They meet out in the barn," he finally revealed with relish. "She was too good for me"—it still stung that Mary Ann had considered him a little boy—"but she's not too good for Uncle Joe. They go up in the hayloft, when Hal's miles away, and Aunt Jessie's gone to town or is taking a nap or something. He has her skirts up over her head before he's all the way up the ladder."

Tris did not flush this time. He went white and struck out with a fist before Laurie realized his intention. Laurie backed away, nursing a bruised lip, sputtering.

"Hey! Damn it, Tris, don't be so handy with your fists! I'm not making it up. They're up there right now. I saw them."

"You're a liar," Tris said, but there was a lack of conviction in his tone, because Laurie didn't look as if he were lying.

"No, I'm not. I've suspected them for weeks, and I've been watching them. Her, in particular, because she's easier to keep track of. So I went out there today, when I heard Uncle Joe giving Hal his orders, and I knew Aunt Jessie was going to visit Ginny Allen for the day. I sat in the shadows, over there behind the grain barrels, and just waited until she came in. I didn't even hear her at first. It's lucky I didn't sneeze or something, sitting there in that dusty corner. It wasn't until she started climbing the ladder that I knew she was there. She went into the hayloft, and I didn't hear a sound out of her, and then about five minutes later, Uncle Joe came in. He glanced around, right toward me, only his eyes weren't used to the shadows and he didn't see me, or he'd have picked up some tool or something and left, no doubt. He didn't call out to her. In fact I never heard either of them say a word, but he climbed that ladder and I heard them *then,* all right."

Laurie grinned. "Even if you didn't know anything at all, you'd guess what they were doing. You don't believe me, Tris, you sit behind that back window and look out through the curtains, and you'll see them both leave. One at a time, of course."

Tris felt sick and betrayed, and the loathing was as much for Laurie as for his father. If it was true, and the way Laurie looked he supposed it had to be, why had Laurie had to prove it? Why had he had to tell Tris?

They were on the back steps, where Tris had been reading a book in the afternoon shade. He'd seen his father enter the barn; he hadn't seen Mary Ann. Maybe she'd gone in the back door, away from the house. The door that Joel had had put into the old barn only a month or so ago, saying that it would make it handier than having to circle the barn every time he wanted anything from there.

He couldn't think of anything to say. He wanted to smash in Laurie's face, wanted to pound him into the dirt at the foot of the steps, wanted to throttle his father, too. How could he do such a thing?

The door behind them opened and Rosalie came out, eating an apricot and catching the juice in her handkerchief. She didn't notice the expressions on their faces, but pushed against Tris with the edge of the door.

"Would you mind letting me through?"

Tris shifted so that she could pass, not speaking to her, his gaze fixed on Laurie. She lifted her skirts as she went down the steps, revealing trim ankles. Tris's fury boiled up, filling him to overflowing, as he saw Laurie looking at Rosalie's ankles.

She walked off toward the grassy area near the willows along the creek, joining Teresa Dolores there on a blanket spread in the shade. They were well out of earshot.

"Wonder what Miss High and Mighty Rosalie would think of her pa, tumbling Mary Ann in the hay?" Laurie speculated, and once more found his shirtfront in Tristan's grasp; he was jerked around with a violence that telegraphed Tris's turbulent emotions. "Hey, cut it out! I'm not going to tell her, for God's sake!"

"You'd better not," Tris said softly, through his teeth, "or I'll kill you, Laurie. Rosie, or Ma, or Teresa Dolores, or anybody else. You ever breathe a word of this to anybody, so it ever gets back to any of them, and I swear I'll kill you."

For a moment they stood face to face, and then Tris released the shirt and shoved Laurie backward.

Tris had never been a violent person. He'd never even been especially forceful. But Laurie read conviction and determination in Tris's face today. His mouth twisted in a grimace intended to be a smile.

"Hell, Tris, I don't intend to tell anybody," he said. He turned and walked away, and after a few minutes Tris sat back down and picked up his book and pretended to read. Pretended, because his eyes blurred and he didn't even remember what the book was about, and it didn't matter because he couldn't see the printing anyway.

Jessie did not hear any gossip about Joel and Mary Ann, because there was none. Years earlier she'd been uneasy about Joel's legacy from Clara Ridback. The woman wouldn't have simply signed over all her wealth to a man without some reason, and Jessie had known there was talk then. How could there fail to be?

On a conscious level, Jessie accepted Joel's denial of any knowledge of Clara's reasoning except for spite and jealousy. In the back of her mind, however, Jessie suppressed the horrid little suspicion that tried, from time to time, to arise.

What would she do if she discovered that Joel had lied to her? That there had been something between him and Clara?

The woman was, after all, dead and buried. And she knew Joel loved her. Would she throw away what they had together, make not only themselves but the children miserable, because Joel might have succumbed to temptation during that pregnancy when Jessie had been out of bounds for him?

It would hurt her terribly to learn that Joel had been unfaithful, Jessie knew. And so she refused to consider the matter, swept it out of mind whenever the idea tried to surface, and told herself that no matter what Joel had done in the past, it need not tarnish the future.

Yet Jessie knew Joel very well. And that summer of 1875, while things went on around her as usual, she began to suspect him again.

The signs were so small that at first they were easy to ignore. After the Wallaces came, it had begun. That was when he'd given up making love to her in the usual way, and introduced her to intimacies she'd never imagined, ways in which each of them could fill the needs of the other without risking another doomed pregnancy.

Why had he chosen now, instead of years ago when the problem was at its peak, to seek this solution? And having sought it so belatedly, was this in itself enough to keep him as contented as he clearly was?

Or had it something to do with that pretty girl out there who was Hal Wallace's wife?

It would have been relatively easy to find out for certain. Yet Jessie did nothing, asked no questions, and prayed that if Joel was having an affair with Mary Ann Wallace, nobody would feel duty-bound to tell her.

As long as she didn't *know,* she could pretend that nothing was happening at all, and that was the only way Jessie herself could survive.

44

Rosalie was seventeen that spring of 1877, and a lovelier girl would have been hard to find. Jessie began to talk of possible suitors, and it became a family joke that no one was good enough for Rosie, according to Joel. He found fault with everyone anyone mentioned; Laurie and Tris brought up the most unlikely people as candidates, just to see what Joel would find wrong with them.

Jessie laughed along with the others, but when they were alone she admonished him gently. "Joel, the girl needs a husband, and soon. You have to be realistic about her choosing one. It's unlikely we're going to find a rich, handsome, saintly man that she'll care to fall in love with."

"There's no hurry, is there? You were nineteen when we got married."

"That was because we couldn't manage it any sooner, remember? I was in love with you from, oh, when I wasn't much more than thirteen! And my stepfather didn't think you were good enough—don't you see, some of those young men you despise will probably be good husbands, when the time comes."

It was a subject which Joel alone could not view with any sense of humor. He stared at her in exasperation. "Jessie, if you think I'm going to turn my daughter over to an idiot like Bob Salwell, or a fop like Whitney Paulus . . ."

Jessie touched his arm gently. "Of course not. All I'm saying is that you're going to have to let her marry *somebody*, and she's headstrong enough to expect she'll have something to do with the choosing. She should be allowed to meet and learn something about a variety of different young men. If you could only restrain yourself from expressing an opinion of every man who's mentioned, a *negative* opinion, she would calm down, too, and be much more sensible about the matter. If you say the man is shiftless, or stupid, or homely, she feels compelled to defend him, even if she secretly agrees with you. Don't you remember how Rosie's always sided with the underdog? How she's always rescued strays? She's doing it now with young men. If everyone would leave her alone, let her look them over and pick what she wants, she has *sense,* Joel. She'll choose a good man, if she isn't pressured so much that she does something only to prove that she can do it herself."

"She'd damned well better choose a good man," Joel said, "because I'm not going to let her marry anybody who isn't."

The hilarity over Rosalie's admirers grew. Laurie and Tris were no longer much intimidated by Joel, and they dared to make fun of him. There were admirers aplenty, for there wasn't a prettier girl in the county than Rosalie Shand, nor a more vivacious one.

Rosalie herself had considerably more sense of humor over the matter than her father did, but sometimes the boys roused her to a fever pitch of irritation. Even the young men she rather liked were held up to ridicule, and as Jessie had perceived, she felt compelled to protest the boys' assessment of her suitors' physical and mental attributes. Even Tris, who was not ordinarily unkind to her, would grin and point out that if she married Bob Salwell she could expect to have to buy a new pair of slippers every time she went to a dance, because he would ruin a pair, stepping on them, each time.

Rosalie, who had become quite provoked the previous evening for precisely that reason, could not help pointing out that there was a good deal more to a marriage than dancing occasionally, only to have Laurie roll his eyes and nudge Tris with an elbow.

"Shall we tell her what else there is?" Laurie asked, and Jessie put an end to the matter with a softly delivered, firmly stated, "That's enough, boys."

It was a warm evening in late April, and the rest of the family was already at the table, when Joel came home late and cross, taking his seat with a violence that sent small shockwaves rippling away from him.

Laurie and Tris, engaged in their customary banter only moments earlier, exchanged a glance of mutual agreement to cease and desist, at least for the time being.

Teresa Dolores, always rather timid, shrank into her chair and ate cautiously, as if someone might suddenly challenge her right to the food on her plate. Only Rosalie and Jessie continued to eat in a normal fashion.

Joel allowed himself to be served rare roast beef, a mound of potatoes with gravy, and an assortment of vegetables, then waited for the new serving girl to leave the room before he spoke.

"Laurie, have you been along the lower boundary lately?"

Startled, Laurie cast an apprehensive glance at Tris, who could only lift his eyebrows in an equal puzzlement. "No, sir. Not in a week or two, I guess."

"A week or two?" Joel's glance made him feel as if he'd been speared and was now held motionless against the back of his chair with the spear through his throat. "Sure it hasn't been more like a *month* or two?"

Not having any idea what Joel was getting at, Laurie squirmed slightly. "Well, I'm not sure, Uncle Joe. Maybe it's been a month since I rode all the way around the west end."

"Tris?"

Tris didn't squirm, but he was no more comfortable under Joel's scrutiny than Laurie was. "I think it's been three or four weeks. You set us to building fence back on the..."

"I know what I set you to doing. I also told you, years ago, to ride the perimeter of the entire ranch at least every couple of weeks, didn't I? Just to check things over?"

"Is something wrong?" Tris asked. "We were just busy, Pa,

and there's nothing down there. There aren't even any cattle, so we didn't see that it mattered, going down there to look at nothing."

"No?" Joel asked, indictment in his tone. "Well, there's something to look at there now. Right on the riverbank, in plain sight, if you'd gone within two miles of it."

The silence drew out while Joel buttered his bread—he liked Jessie's sweet butter and he usually had the butter as thick as the bread—and then Tris gathered the courage to put the question Joel was waiting for.

"What did we miss that we should have seen, Pa?"

"A house," Joel said succinctly, and waited for the impact of that to wash through them all before he added details. "A goddamned squatter's built a shack, and he's taken long enough over it to do a good solid job. Right there in the hollow between our place and John Curtis's."

A frown formed on Jessie's face. "That isn't our land, is it, Joel? Isn't that where those people—what was their name, Ferrill—had a cabin that burned six or eight years ago?"

"The cabin burned, and Ferrill pulled up stakes and left. And if Laurie and Tris had ridden the borders the way they were supposed to, we'd have stopped this squatter before he skinned his first log. I always intended to fence it in along with our own; we've been using it for graze land ever since Ferrill disappeared. We had cattle in there up to six weeks ago."

Rosalie leaned forward so as to see her father better. "But if it wasn't fenced, and we don't actually have a deed to the land, it's no say-so of ours, is it, Pa?"

"It's some of *my* say-so," Joel informed her, attacking his plate as if it were the audacious squatter. "He wasn't around so I could tell him to get the hell off, but I'll do it the next time I get back there."

"But if he has built a cabin—"

"Cabins can get burned down," Joel said, "the same as the last one did."

The way he said that made them all withdraw a little, wondering. Had the burning of Ferrill's cabin been an accident, as everyone assumed at the time, or was there something more ominous in Joel's turn of phrase?

None of them, not even Jessie, could quite bring herself to put another question, and they finished their meal in silence.

* * *

Most of the time Rosalie invited Teresa Dolores along when she went for a walk or a ride. This morning she did not. The other girl was reading in her room, and Rosalie walked quietly past the open door, down the stairs, and out to the stable.

She didn't need anyone to saddle her horse; she'd been doing it herself for years. She saw no one except Mary Ann Wallace, who was starting out for a walk in the opposite direction from the one Rosalie intended to take. That was just as well, because anyone divining her intention would have stopped her.

It wasn't often that anyone prevented Rosalie from doing what she wanted to do. She rode southwest, following the course of the Stanislaus, enjoying the spring sun on her back and the fresh, sweet fragrance of plowed earth and grasslands.

The house was there, as Joel had said it was. Only today smoke rose from the chimney, so the squatter was at home.

Joel hadn't described the man, of course, so there was no reason for Rosalie to assume that he was young, except that he'd put up his cabin very quickly; that suggested youthful strength and stamina. She urged the horse forward, riding down the slope into the depression which protected the cabin from view on either side, approving what she saw.

It wasn't a shack, not like some she'd seen. It was a sturdily built log house, with a garden patch already planted behind it, and a man was building a corral. He was planning to stay. On a line strung between the cabin and a tall corral post several items of underwear were drying. Male apparel, not female, Rosie noted.

He *was* young, she could tell that by the way he moved even before she was close enough to make out anything more about him. He turned and watched her approach, and Rosalie saw with pleasure that he was tall and wide through the shoulders, and that he moved gracefully as he came toward her.

He was blond and bearded and wore rough garments such as the miners used to wear, or the farmers. His hands were large and well shaped; Rosalie felt a tremor go through her as she looked at his hands.

"Morning," he said, and his voice was deep and melodious.

"Good morning. I'm Rosalie Shand. I live over there." She gestured behind her, and the man nodded.

"Sam Shute," he introduced himself. She watched his ap-

390

praisal, saw approval in his eyes and then the softening of his mouth; he reached up his arms to help her dismount. "You're the first company I've had since I got settled in," he told her.

Rosalie allowed him to lift her down, feeling an odd sort of tingling sensation she'd never experienced before, an excitement that heightened her senses. She smelled horse and fresh grass and man-scent, the sweat of a laborer, and it was all good.

"Not quite the first visitor, I think," Rosalie told him. Though she was a tall girl, Sam Shute was a head taller; another point in his favor, she thought, though she had not yet admitted to herself quite what the points were destined to do. "My father was here yesterday."

"I was gone yesterday. Went over to the county seat, took all day."

His eyebrows glinted with golden hairs in the sunlight, and he wore his plaid shirt open at the neck, revealing more of the fine gold hairs on his chest. He had a wide, mobile mouth which revealed good teeth. He was older than she was by quite a bit. Thirty, maybe, Rosalie thought. That wasn't a point against him, however. She was used to young men in their early twenties, and most of them were rather juvenile. Including Laurie and Tris.

He had lifted her so easily, as if she were a child. Yet she saw with a quiet satisfaction that he wasn't regarding her as a child at all.

She gave him the smallest of smiles, watching his eyes, because that was where his initial reaction would be; she'd already learned that. After his eyes, he'd let it show in the rest of his face, if he wanted to.

"My father considers this to be his land," she told him.

This time the eyes revealed nothing. They were blue, a peculiar light shade she'd never seen before, and the lashes were so fair that from a distance it would appear he didn't have any.

"Your father's mistaken," Sam Shute told her, and turned back to the corral fence he was building.

"He's very upset that you've built a cabin here."

He gave her a look at that, a slow, measuring look that saw beyond the fresh-faced young girl with the dark hair escaping its ribbon, and the worn but obviously expensive riding habit and boots. "So what do you want me to do? Tear

391

it down and move it? After I've recorded my deed at the courthouse?"

She caught her lower lip in her teeth and held it. "Did you pay anyone for the land?"

"Well, Miss Rosalie Shand, it ain't exactly any of your business, as I see it, but I'll tell you. I heard the fella lived here before had his place burn down, and he just up and left. All I had to pay was a recording fee to the county clerk. And that makes it legal."

He lifted a skinned lodgepole pine into position and secured it in the notch formed by crossed poles. It was a long pole, a heavy one, and his muscular arms handled it easily. Rosalie stared at his bared arms beneath the rolled-up shirt-sleeves, and swallowed, suddenly imagining what it would be like to have those arms around her.

She made no reply to his statement, and the pale blue eyes swung again in her direction when he'd finished with the pole. "You come to tell me your pa's going to run me off my own land?"

She swallowed again. "I don't know. I know he's angry about you being here."

He bent for another pole, adjusted the end of it, and suddenly gave her a blinding smile. "How about you, Rosalie Shand? You angry about me being here?"

She felt as if she were suffocating, as if her stays were too tight to allow for ordinary breath. Dear God, she'd never seen a smile like that one before!

"No," she said slowly, "I'm not angry. I just came out to see . . . what you were like, I guess."

The grin held. "And now you've seen me, eh? My coffee should have boiled by now. You want a cup?"

She seldom drank coffee at home, but she heard her own voice saying, "Thank you, I'd love some." And she found herself walking beside this blond-bearded giant, who shortened his steps so that she could keep up, and crossing the dooryard where a dozen hens clucked and scratched, and entering his house.

For a moment she visualized her mother's shocked face—no well-brought-up female would walk, unchaperoned, into a stranger's cabin—and then she forgot what Jessie or Joel would have thought of the matter and let the impressions, the sensations, overwhelm her.

Sam Shute seemed even bigger inside the house than he had outside. He was not awkward, however; he moved deftly, getting down cups from an open shelf, placing them on the handmade table. "All I got is tin," he said, without a trace of apology. "Watch your mouth; it's hot."

On the rare occasions that she had coffee at home, she diluted it with thick cream and sugar. Neither appeared to be available here, so she sat across from him at the small table and cautiously sipped from the tin cup. And while she drank, she looked around at his home.

It was new enough so that it still smelled good, of freshly cut pine. Only one room, and that simply furnished: the table and two chairs, and a third chair in the making before the fireplace where he did his cooking. A few shelves on the walls held basic supplies; pegs on one wall made a hanging place for his extra clothes. The bed, unmade, boasted a colorful quilt and no sheets, just the feather tick.

There were no amenities like rugs or pictures. No books or lamps, only a candle stub or two, and the fireplace. Her attention was caught by the fireplace; it dominated the room, a magnificent one of gray rock with a greenish tinge, including one stone that had what appeared to be a fossilized bas-relief of a large maple leaf, right in the center of the chimney at eye level.

"Did you build the fireplace yourself?" she asked. The coffee was really too hot to drink without scalding her tongue.

"I built everything myself. Hauled the rock from up near Jamestown. Hand-picked every piece. You like it?"

"It's lovely," she said.

"Eventually I'll build on a lean-to kitchen, on that side, and a bedroom on the back, and this'll just be the sitting room. I got my garden in, and when I find me a bargain, I'll buy a cow."

"Pa says nobody can make a living on fifty acres."

"Maybe your pa and I got different ideas about what constitutes a living," the man said. There was something about his voice that delighted and puzzled her, and she couldn't quite make out what it was.

"Where are you from?" she asked, and then flushed a little. "I'm sorry, I guess that's impertinent, isn't it? Mama says one doesn't ask personal questions."

He drank deeply of the steaming bitter coffee, and she wondered that he had a throat left.

"Your mama's a lady, no doubt. Ladies worry about other people's feelings." He didn't quite drop the g's off the end of his words, but he came close. "I'm from Georgia, and I ain't running from anything, if that's what you're worried about. Except a country where I got no place any more. All the family I had died in the war, and I came damn near it, and there wasn't anything to go back to. So I thought I'd try me a little of that California everybody kept talking about like it was the promised land."

"My folks came out from Michigan, a long time ago. Before the war. In covered wagons." Curiosity impelled more questions. "Did you come on the train?"

"Trains cost money. No, I rode me a good old horse, the only thing I still had when the Yankees got through with us. Took me quite a while to get here. I saw a lot of places I knew I didn't want to stay. I ain't quite made up my mind about this one, yet, but I think maybe this is it. I like this place."

She was uncomfortable with that, because if her father wanted him off the land, he had all sorts of influence and power this young man didn't have. She tested the coffee again, wondered if she could bear the bitterness of it even when it had cooled enough to be safely drunk, and knowing that she'd drink it to the dregs if that gave her an excuse for staying here, talking to Sam Shute.

The grin was back, lazy, speculative. "Yes, I think maybe the neighbors here are prettier than any I've come across so far."

That was all that happened, on that first visit. They talked, and Rosalie drank strong coffee she didn't want, and felt the sensations shuddering through her. This was the man, she kept thinking. This was the one she wanted.

And she was convinced, although Sam Shute said nothing that even Joel could have objected to, that he felt the same way.

45

Jessie knew, the moment her daughter came home.

It was in Rosalie's eyes, in the curve of her lips, in the breathless quality of the speech that she tried to keep ordinary and normal.

Rosalie had fallen in love.

Something softened and warmed within Jessie, remembering her own girlhood. A century ago, it seemed now. It had happened to her the same way, quickly, sweeping her along on that irresistible tide of mingled joy and pain. Perhaps love was always that way, even when there were no things like stepfathers, religious fanatics, and prohibitions against seeing one's beloved.

Jessie's courtship had been more agony than happiness; she'd been nearly forced into a loveless marriage more than once, and she'd been told in no uncertain terms that she'd never be allowed to marry Joel Shand.

She had thought Joel dead, while she carried his child though not his name. She had been brutally raped, and lost that child, and pressured into a marriage with an unfortunate young man who would never be a husband to her in a physical sense, poor Ben whom she had not loved. And then, perhaps the ultimate tragedy of all, she had found Joel while she was yet married to Ben, when she could not possibly have then taken the man she really loved.

It would be different with Rosalie, Jessie thought. Though Joel was being absurdly critical of possible suitors, he would come around. Rosie need not go through the things her mother had suffered, to have her love.

Jessie felt her lips curving in a smile to match Rosalie's unconscious one. "You're looking very pretty today," she said, and watched the dreamy eyes come to a focus upon her, and the smile widen.

"Thank you, Mama. Oh, Mama!" Rosalie hugged Jessie, then stepped back, only this time the happiness did not flower but drooped with the corners of her mouth. "Mama, I've met the most marvelous man, only Pa isn't going to like him."

Jessie's heart sank. "Why? Who is he? Where did you meet him?"

Rosalie swallowed hard. "His name is Sam Shute, and he fought in the war and lost all his family, and he came west looking for something better than what he had left in Georgia. He's the one who built the cabin on that little strip of land between our place and Curtis's."

"Oh, Rosie! Oh, darling!" Jessie felt as if she stood in the midst of shattered dreams, as real as bricks fallen around her.

"He has title to the land, Mama. He went into the courthouse and recorded it. Why does Pa feel he has to have that land, when he has so many hundreds of acres already?"

"How did you meet him?" Jessie asked, her lips feeling wooden.

"I just rode out there to look at his cabin, and it's not a shack, at all. It's every bit as nice as the little house Pa built across the creek, when you were first married. He isn't hurting anything. All Pa ever used that land for was grazing a few head of cattle, and he won't even miss it if Sam fences it in."

The name came so naturally to her lips; and she'd only met him this morning? "Your father will be unhappy about the way you met him, riding out and introducing yourself," Jessie said slowly.

"I know, but what could I have done that Pa would have approved? He acts as if I don't have a brain in my head, and as if I didn't have sense enough to choose a man of my own!"

"He loves you, darling. That's all it is. He wants to protect you, to keep you the little girl you've been for so long."

"I'm not a little girl any more," Rosalie said, her breast rising and falling rapidly in her agitation. "And I don't want to be protected. I want to choose my own husband. Can't you talk to him, convince him that I have a right to choose for myself?"

Jessie moistened her lips. "I'll certainly try," she agreed, not expressing the little hope she had that she would be successful. Joel resented this man before he'd even seen him, and though it was true the land Sam Shute was squatting on was insignificant in terms of the acreage Joel already held, she knew he wanted it in a way out of proportion to its value.

With no verbal agreement between them at all, Jessie and Rosalie knew they would not breathe a word about Sam Shute to Joel, not until they'd figured out some sort of strategy.

Luckily Joel became involved at that point in something that took precedence over a mere squatter. As always, he was extremely busy at this time of year with planting. Hal Wallace and the other men he hired needed supervising. And the matter of removing the squatter was too important to entrust it to the boys; it would have to wait until Joel could handle it personally.

A few days earlier Joel had been introduced to a man whose name he had been hearing for some time, a man whose reputation was impressive, both because of his wealth and because of the power he wielded behind the political scene in Sacramento. J. Murphy Kendrick had recently had a magnificent house built, high on the hill overlooking Knight's Ferry and the river, because his wife had decided she wanted to live in a town—though not a city like Sacramento—instead of on the ranch which had brought them prosperity.

Murphy, as he was known, was as indulgent with his family as he was cold-blooded about everything else he did. He smoked expensively fragrant cigars, scattering ash with a complete disregard for carpets or upholstery; he was corpulent and going bald at fifty, but though he was neither tall nor imposing, he exuded confidence and authority.

He knows damned well he's got it made, and he's in control, Joel thought, not without admiration. It was gratifying, when they were introduced, to learn that Murphy Kendrick had heard of *him,* too.

"Hear you're moving on up in the world," Kendrick said, with a smile that touched only his lips, broadening them in a grin so wide that most people didn't notice his eyes. "You're a man to deal with."

Joel remained noncommittal on that score; that first evening, he mostly listened to Murphy Kendrick and observed him, and unobtrusively surveyed the Kendrick mansion.

A mansion it was, with roughly three times the floor space of Joel's own substantial home. Where the Shand house was comfortably elegant—after all, four children had grown up in it, and though Jessie occasionally refurbished the parlors,

397

she felt young people should feel free to *live* in their home—the Kendrick place was ostentatiously opulent.

Murphy betrayed his origins more than he realized when he pointed out chandeliers, carpets, paintings and works of art: everything was imported, everything was expensive, and in case his guests didn't realize that, he told them.

His wife, Myra, was a strikingly pretty woman some ten years younger than her husband. Her rich chestnut hair was elaborately dressed, and her gown of dark blue watered silk was in the latest fashion; the diamonds and pearls she wore gave her an air of elegance that suggested her own beginnings had been at a higher level than Murphy's. She was quiet, smiling, hospitable.

"I hear you got two boys," Murphy said to Joel during a lull in the more lively conversation.

"A son and an adopted son. Laurie's a sort of cousin, actually, but he's been raised as our own," Joel said.

"I heard about them. Good-looking young fellas. And pretty girls, too, eh?"

"Yes. Rosalie and Teresa Dolores. Teresa was the daughter of my cousin. When her mother died, we took her in as company for Rosie."

Murphy nodded and flicked ash a foot away from the nearest ashtray. "Nice thing, having youngsters around. We only had the one daughter, but she's a real beauty, Melissa is. Bit headstrong, maybe, but what woman worth her salt isn't, eh? Have to see that she meets your boys. Might get something going there. Ah, here's Horace. Let's go talk to him about the governor's plans, shall we?"

It was part of the riveting aura about Kendrick, his friendship with the governor and various senators and representatives. He was on a first-name basis with most of them, and Joel did not doubt in the slightest that he was able to influence their thinking and their legislation.

As they walked across Kendrick's Persian rug toward the group of men before the fireplace, Murphy suggested casually, "Maybe we can get our families together for dinner one night real soon. I'll speak to Myra about a date, all right?"

"I'd like that," Joel said, and felt a stirring of excitement. If this man took him under his wing, Joel would be moving into the true inner circle of politics in the state of California, which was precisely what he wanted.

The invitation to dinner was accepted, only to meet with more resistance at home than Joel had anticipated.

"I have another engagement that evening," Laurie said at once.

"Postpone it," Joel suggested. "This man is important."

Laurie's jaw took on a stubborn jut. "So is this, Uncle Joe. A young lady I've been trying to make an engagement with for months. I can meet Mr. Kendrick some other time, can't I? I'm not the one interested in a political career, anyway. Tris is. Take Tris. They'll never miss me."

Tris demurred as well. "I'm not interested in sitting around all evening listening to some fellow tell how he bought this senator and that mayor. That's not my idea of politics."

"No? Well, I guarantee you, son, that that's how a good deal of politics is handled. Who you know means a lot."

"Not to me, it doesn't. I'd really rather stay home, Pa. I'm not a good mixer, and I won't say two words all evening."

"You don't have to. You can learn a lot more by listening. I want you to go, Tris, especially if Laurie can't be there. Murphy especially asked to meet my family."

Rosalie said nothing in front of her father (and Teresa Dolores never protested any decision of anyone else's) but in private she was disgruntled. "Do I have to go, Mama? I can't imagine anything more boring than sitting around listening to Daddy and Mr. Kendrick talk politics!"

Though Rosalie had not said so, Jessie knew she had ridden out again that morning to see the man who had taken up residence on that sliver of land between their own and Curtis's. Fear for her daughter was like a small wild bird trapped in her chest, fluttering frantically, yet Jessie was outwardly calm.

"I think you'd better go with us, Rosie. If there's a battle coming up over this young man, the less friction we stir up ahead of time the better." Her smile flickered. "Your father's authorized new dresses for all of us for the Kendrick dinner. There won't be time to make them ourselves, but we could go into town and see what Miss Hampton has, and probably have time to do our own alterations."

Usually the prospect of a new gown was enticing. Today Rosalie's expression did not lighten, though she nodded in resignation. It seemed a terrible waste of time, now that the moments had become so precious. Still, her mother had indicated an intention to be on her side in any battle that did arise, and Rosalie was young enough to hope in the face of insuperable odds.

399

"Let's go see about the dresses, then," she said. "I'll call Teresa Dolores, shall I?"

The dinner that was so important to Joel was not an unqualified success. Joel had thought it was to be an intimate family affair, with only the Shands and the Kendricks; instead, he found that Myra Kendrick's idea of a "small dinner party" was twenty-two people.

It wasn't that he didn't have an opportunity to talk to J. Murphy Kendrick, for he was seated close enough to him so that by leaning out to speak around Jessie he could manage to convey at least part of what he wanted Kendrick to know. And he was in an excellent position to listen when Kendrick spoke. But there were other people also maneuvering for Murphy's ear before and after the meal, leaving Joel frustrated in his hope for a truly private conversation.

Nothing really important was going to be discussed in front of twenty-two people. On the other hand, Joel was widening the wedge of acquaintanceship, and that was valuable in itself. He'd been around enough to know that men of Murphy Kendrick's type didn't bother with anyone they didn't expect to find valuable. Well, that was all right. Joel wasn't above manipulating Kendrick, if he could.

Rosalie, as she'd expected, was bored to distraction. She cared not a whit who was in the governor's seat, nor in any of the lesser positions in the capital. Most of the guests were older men and their wives; there were two younger males who gazed at her with interest, though neither of them appealed to her in the slightest. Neither of them was Sam Shute.

She had dreamed of falling in love, but never quite like this. She had not expected it to be instantaneous nor so devastatingly deep and complete. From the moment she'd seen Sam, she had wanted him; when she was with him, she was deliriously happy. When she was not, she looked forward only to their next meeting and cared little what happened in between except that it should get over with so she could go on to what was important.

She knew that she looked quite lovely in her soft rose silk gown with a lower neckline that Mama usually allowed; this was a ready-made dress and there had been no practical way to alter the neckline short of filling in with another fabric that would not have matched and would have appeared just what it was: a block to anyone's view of her emerging bosom. In the end, Jessie had decided that it would call less attention to Rosalie's breasts if they left the dress unadorned, and if Sam Shute had been there to see her, Rosie would have been supremely happy.

As it was, she responded in monosyllables to the young men seated beside her, and dreamed about riding out in the morning to see Sam again.

Tris was the only one, aside from Joel, who was not bored through an interminable evening, and this was not because he found the talk out of the ordinary, though some of it was of interest to him.

The object of Tris's attention was Melissa Kendrick, J. Murphy's only child.

Melissa was just past seventeen, as fresh-faced and sweet as anyone could ask, though there was something about her mouth that suggested she was not always as passive and amenable to her father's wishes as she appeared tonight. Her hair was a rich chestnut brown, naturally curly and swept up to make her appear taller than she really was. Her complexion, contrasted with Rosalie's sun-tinted apricot shade, was like cream with the tinge of a newly opening pink rose. Her figure was superb.

She wore a coral-colored gown that bared her throat and displayed her bosom and tiny waist, and there was a diamond circlet on one slim wrist. Her eyes were her most stunning feature, being an unusual shade of dark gray with, in some lights, a greenish cast; they were thickly lashed and she used them effectively.

She smiled at Tris when they were introduced, the same way that she smiled at all the rest of them; Tris barely had the wit to acknowledge any of the other introductions.

She was the most beautiful girl he'd ever seen. He wanted to touch her, wanted to get her off in a corner somewhere and talk to her, wanted to do anything to get better acquainted with her.

He'd watched Laurie often enough; why couldn't he just do it, the way Laurie did? Walk up to a girl and start talking? Smile, let her know he liked her and thought she was pretty?

Only he didn't have the expertise. Laurie's words, coming out of *his* mouth, would only make Tris sound ludicrous; he knew it. He couldn't even smile at her without feeling a fool. A girl like this had been smiled at, and sweet-talked, by experts. He could tell that just by looking at her.

She was used to these fancy dinners, engaging in conversation with all these important people, wearing diamonds on her wrist and in her ears. What would it take in a man to earn her interest?

Whatever it would be, Tris was wretchedly sure he didn't have it. He wasn't seated next to her at the table, a mixed blessing. He didn't have to talk to her, to pretend to a sophistication he didn't have. On the other hand, he could look at her across the silver bowl of yellow roses, and dream.

Was that all he'd ever be able to do? Dream about a girl like this?

It was a relief when the meal was over. Tris scarcely registered what he ate. He drank two glasses of wine, wishing that alcohol worked on him the way it did on Laurie, making him bolder and wittier. All it would do to him, if he drank enough to notice it, was make him sick.

Mrs. Kendrick, flashing her diamonds, fluttered about rounding up the women so they could retire to make their polite conversation while the men talked business.

J. Murphy Kendrick had already lighted one of his expensive cigars and was wafting its aroma about the room. "I have an excellent brandy, gentlemen. Shall we leave the ladies to their recipes and talk about the next election?"

Tris stood uncertainly, as did the other two young men. He was wishing by now that he hadn't had the second glass of wine; he had an appalling sensation of being about to say something totally stupid, disgracing both himself and his father. The safest policy, no doubt, would be simply to say nothing at all. That way they might all think him a fool, but he wouldn't prove it for them.

And then Melissa Kendrick said, "Mama, may I take the young people to the game room? I think it might be a more pleasant way to pass the evening than listening to Daddy's plans to elect a new senator."

Myra flashed her daughter a smile, and for a moment Tris saw where the girl came by her beauty. "Of course, dear. Have a nice evening, all of you."

She turned away, and Melissa spoke to the hesitating group. "Do any of you play billiards? Or will I have to teach you?"

She had an oddly low-pitched voice with an intriguing husky quality. Tris felt as if he'd been stung when she suddenly put a hand on his arm and smiled up into his face.

"The billiard table is Daddy's toy, really, but he needed someone to challenge him, so he taught me. Do you play?"

"No, I'm afraid not," Tris said, strangled and short of breath.

"Then I'll show you how," Melissa promised, and began to walk along the wide corridor into the interior of the house, allowing the others to follow, still holding his arm.

She wore some light scent that made him feel giddy. Or was it only her presence, her touch? There was the sleeve of his shirt and also his coat between his arm and her fingers, yet he could feel the warmth of them as if they somehow injected a stimulant into his veins.

The game room was huge; in addition to a billiard table there was a piano and a small table for cards or chess. The other two men, both a little older than Tris, were reintroduced, since they'd all forgotten names. Stuart Linnington was a skinny fellow with an excellently cut suit and a prominent Adam's apple that betrayed his nervousness when he kept swallowing. He made Tris feel just a trifle better about his own insecurity. The other guest, Melvin Hodges, was a stocky individual with a heavy beard; he had cut himself while shaving and had several bits of sticking plaster on his chin plus a drop of blood on his shirt collar. Tris thought that ought to make him feel better, too, but with Melissa so close to him, it was hard to think.

Rosalie took one look at Tris and recognized a fellow sufferer in the throes of passion beyond his ability to cope. She smiled then at Linnington and Hodges and suggested that they play chess.

"Such a lovely set, isn't it? I'm not very good, and neither is Teresa Dolores, but maybe you'd take pity on a couple of amateurs and not beat us too quickly? Or, since we are four, should we make it cards so that we can all play at the same time?"

Both their adversaries took on a glazed look. Tris had seen it happen before, when Rosalie smiled at anyone over the age of twelve. They moved as a group to the table with the chessboard inlaid in its top, leaving him with Melissa. Why did this kind of thing come so much easier to females than it did to men? he wondered, and loosened his collar.

The evening was more or less a blur when he thought back on it. He'd known nothing about billiards. Melissa did, and she played with an artless expertise and instructed him in such an open, friendly way that he couldn't feel embarrassed to be taught anything by a girl as he might otherwise have done.

He couldn't have cared less about the billiards, but he'd have learned to grow a tail and hang from a tree if it would have kept him in Melissa's presence. And when, at the end of the evening, she had put out her hand to shake his, Tris had to force himself to let go after the required few seconds of contact.

The ride home was a quiet one except for Joel's occasional comments on the men he had spoken with tonight. In the back of the buggy, Rosalie dreamed of a blond giant who would, very soon, kiss her. She expected to swoon when it happened, and wondered if he'd try to loosen her stays when she did so. It almost made her swoon now, to think about it.

Tris was totally silent, sunk in a euphoric haze, remembering how Melissa Kendrick's dark lashes looked against creamy cheeks, and how soft her hand had been, and the way the corners of her mouth turned up when she smiled. She had dimples, too. He imagined kissing her cheek where a dimple was, and then working over to her mouth, and then—he broke out in a gentle sweat—moving down to the hollow at the base of her throat. And while he was kissing her *there,* he would be...

God! It made him dizzy to think about it. He was grateful that neither Rosalie or Teresa Dolores had anything to say to him, because he wanted to stay lost in his dream of this exciting girl. Was it possible to fall in love at first sight, after all? Not the attraction that Laurie felt with any pretty girl, but real love?

He didn't even know they'd reached home until Joel asked him to unhitch the buggy and put the horses away.

46

Jessie looked at her daughter with troubled eyes. "Rosalie, this isn't the way to do it. A lady shouldn't be riding off to visit with a man, unchaperoned."

There was a defiant tilt to Rosalie's head. "Shall I invite him home for dinner, then? To meet Pa?"

Had Sam Shute not built his cabin on what Joel considered to be rightfully his land, that was exactly what Jessie would have suggested. Under these circumstances, however, it would be the height of folly.

Yet she could not allow a potentially scandalous situation to develop any further than it already had. Jessie visibly drew herself together. "No," she said quietly. "Not yet. I think I'll ride out there with you today and meet this young man."

Rosalie was torn between elation and uncertainty. She felt quite comfortable with Sam, for all that she'd seen him only four times. She could talk to him when they were alone. She wasn't sure she could say a single natural word with an audience, and she didn't know how he'd react to the additional company, either.

On the other hand, her mother's championship of her would be a major step in winning over Joel. Her parents seldom openly disagreed over anything, and when they did it was most often Joel who had the last word—except in a few isolated instances where Jessie felt strongly enough to fight.

One look at her mother's face now convinced Rosalie that Jessie was the most valuable asset she could have, if she could be won over completely to the cause. And that would only happen if she liked Sam, too.

Although her lips trembled, Rosalie managed a smile. "Thank you, Mama."

They didn't talk much as they rode out across the familiar

hills. Rosalie had never known anything else, and she didn't think about the hills at all, only about the man who would be there in his cabin, expecting her. She hadn't agreed to come, he hadn't asked her, but he'd be expecting her, all the same.

Jessie tried not to think about the stranger, not yet. No matter what she thought of him, she didn't know how in heaven's name she was going to persuade Joel to Rosie's need. She kept her mind on her surroundings, instead. She hated these hills, even though they were spring-green now, not sere and brown.

After all these years, Jessie still longed for green pine forests and sparkling blue waters, for Beaver Island. She didn't know what had happened there since she'd left; after King Strang was assassinated, the island seldom if ever made the news, certainly not with any story that carried as far as California. The beaches would still be there, the little cove where she'd been swimming naked when Joel came upon her, unaware.

It gave her courage, remembering. Because Joel had not been one of the Saints, he had not been an acceptable suitor, and they'd struggled through years of heartaches before they'd finally been able to marry.

If Rosie really loved this young man, she'd help them find a way to be together.

They rode into the clearing at midmorning and found Sam fixing a wheel on a farm wagon. He straightened and waited for them, giving Rosalie a slow smile, reaching up for her in a way that bespoke a certain intimacy in spite of their brief acquaintanceship. She was lifted down, set lightly on her feet, and then he turned to assist Jessie.

He was strong, Jessie observed, the way Joel had always been strong, with the strength of a man who works in the outdoors, with his back and his arms and sturdy legs. He held her easily, as if she were a child.

Jessie looked into his face and liked what she saw. Older than Rosie, though not too old. Intelligent eyes, lips that seemed on the verge of smiling even when he was serious.

Sam in turn scrutinized the lady in the dark riding habit. Glorious hair, so pale and fine, especially with those big dark eyes. Rosie had her mother's eyes, he saw, but she must have gotten her dark curls from the ogre father still lurking in the background.

"This is my mother," Rosalie said, sounding a trifle breathless. "Mama, Sam Shute."

"Pleased to meet you, ma'am." He gestured with a large thumb toward the cabin behind him. "Can I offer you a cup of tea? Or coffee?"

Rosalie laughed. "He makes terrible coffee, Mama. I recommend the tea."

"The tea, then," Jessie agreed, smiling.

They stayed half an hour. Jessie took in his home without being obtrusive about her inspection. She talked without probing too deeply into the young man's background. He had come of a good family in the South, a family decimated and impoverished by the war. He knew he was being inspected, and he was good-natured about it. When the time came to go, he took Jessie's hand, and said he was happy he'd met her.

Rosalie could hardly wait until they topped the nearest hill before she turned to her mother and demanded, "Didn't you like him, Mama?"

"Yes. He seems very nice. A lot like your father when he was younger," Jessie told her.

Disbelief made Rosalie's jaw sag. "Like Pa? Mama, he's nothing like Pa at all!"

Amusement, tinged with sadness, touched Jessie's mouth. "Oh, yes, he is. Young and strong and determined to succeed in spite of great odds. He seems a good man, Rosalie."

"Will you talk to Pa, then?"

Jessie's silence was more eloquent than words would have been, and Rosalie's heart sank before her mother finally said, "I'll have to think what's best, darling. I wish he hadn't built a cabin on that particular section of land, but since he did . . . well, let's hope your father is too busy elsewhere to bother Mr. Shute for a time, and give us a chance to think of something. And Rosalie, I do think you'd better stop riding out here alone."

Rebellion formed before Jessie's eyes. "Mama, don't ask that of me. You don't know what it's like, to want so badly to be with someone, and be told you can't."

"Don't I?" Mist obscured Jessie's vision for a minute or two. She hadn't accepted the restrictions put upon her, all those years ago, and she doubted that Rosie would accept the ones proposed now. Jessie had deceived her family to be with Joel; she had needed him so desperately.

And now she was nearly forty years old, though her mirror

did not yet seem to reflect that incredible age, and Joel was changed a great deal, and she didn't know how to approach him in this matter, how to win him over.

"I only want to protect you, darling," she said finally, and Rosalie tossed her head so that her thick dark hair caught the breeze and curled in tendrils around her face.

"I can take care of myself, Mama," she said with confidence, and Jessie prayed that it was so.

"Tell them, if anyone asks, that I had a headache and I've gone to bed," Rosalie instructed her cousin.

Teresa Dolores stared at her in horror. "But what if Aunt Jessie comes in to check on you?"

"I'll make a roll of pillows in my bed, and you can assure her I'm sleeping, and that I'm not sick enough to need any attention, just sleep."

"Rosie, you know I'm not a good liar."

Rosie's grin flashed. "All it takes is practice."

"But they'll kill me if they find out I've lied to them!" The younger girl's voice rose in distress, and Rosie quieted her with a quick hug.

"Don't let them find out, then. Or if they do, I'll tell them I threatened you, that it wasn't your fault."

"Rosie, your father will be furious."

"I think that's probably an understatement," Rosalie agreed. "So I'll tell the first lie, that I've got a light headache and don't think I want anything to eat, and then you can bring me up a bowl of soup or something, later on, and pour it in the slop jar and bring the bowl back downstairs, and that'll satisfy them. You don't have to say anything, just carry the tray past Mama so she doesn't think I'm starving."

Teresa Dolores did not want to do it, but she knew Rosalie. The girl would do what she chose, and what she chose was to ride out after dark to see Sam Shute, since she'd been prevented for three days from riding out to see him during the mornings.

It did not seem possible to Rosalie, riding through the darkness along the river bluff, that Sam could have become so important to her in such a short time. She worried about what he'd think when she hadn't returned since the visit with her mother, and she prayed that Pa would continue to be engrossed in whatever he was all wound up in with J. Murphy Kendrick, and leave Sam alone. Pa hadn't even talked to Sam yet. He didn't know Sam had legal title to the land. When he learned that a deed had been recorded, surely he'd have to back off and leave Sam alone. And eventually he'd get used to Sam's being there. She only hoped that wouldn't take him too long. She'd have told Joel herself, about the recording of a deed, if that wouldn't have meant having to explain how she came by the information.

Riding alone at night didn't bother her. There was nothing here that she was afraid of. It was not like the gold-rush days, when there had been men wandering the countryside who had no roots, no ties, no responsibilities; the people she was likely to encounter now were all permanent residents. They knew her father, and they respected and possibly feared his influence and power. They wouldn't bother her.

She met no one anyway. There was a moment, when she crested the hill, that Rosalie was afraid Sam wasn't there because she couldn't see a light in the window of his cabin. And then she smelled woodsmoke, and her heart soared as she kneed the horse on down the trail.

She slid off the mare and looped the reins around the post near Sam's front door. Was he gone, after all? He must have heard the horse, yet he hadn't come to the door.

For a moment she stood there and heard not a sound except the deep-throated bullfrogs in the little pond behind the cabin. She rapped on the door and called out, "Sam?"

When there was no response, Rosalie lifted the latch and peered inside. "Sam? Are you there?"

On the hearth the fire crackled as if someone had added logs recently. The aroma of stew wafted toward her on the steam from the kettle swung over the flames.

He wouldn't be far away, with his supper still cooking, would he?

Rosalie stepped inside, leaving the door ajar behind her. She hadn't come all this way only to turn around and go back without seeing him.

The evening was cool, and she advanced toward the fire, sniffed, and reached for the hot pad to lift the cover over the kettle; there was a wooden spoon on the table, and she stirred the meat and vegetables, squinting to see them in the dimness, tasting the concoction. He must have candles somewhere...yes, there they were on the mantel.

She had lighted the second one, adding to the light from the fireplace, when the door creaked as it swung inward.

Rosalie spun, heart in her throat suddenly hammering.

409

She had been so eager to see him, and now that he was here her conviction of his welcome wavered. What if he hadn't missed her at all? What if he resented her walking into his house?

"I tasted your stew," she said inanely. "It needs salt."

Sam came into the room, his head almost scraping the rafters, and closed the door behind him. "It's on the table there, behind you."

She made no move toward the salt. "I couldn't come before. Mama kept thinking up things to do to keep me busy at home."

"She doesn't know you're here now," Sam said, a statement of fact. "She's a lady. She's brought you up to be one, too. She must have told you it's dangerous to visit a man alone, at night."

He'd been doing late chores, she guessed. His shirtsleeves were rolled up to reveal brawny forearms covered with fine hair that glinted golden in the candlelight as he came toward her. He emanated the odor of horse, which was a familiar smell and not an unpleasant one.

Her chest felt congested; her throat was closing, so that she had to swallow hard in order to breathe. "Is it? Dangerous?"

He had, up to now, not touched her except to lift her down from the horse, or to help her to mount. Tonight, Rosalie thought, feeling slightly giddy, he was going to touch her in another way. Mama would be upset, and Pa would be outraged enough to shoot someone, but she stood there and waited for him, this man she wanted so badly that her body had ached with the longing ever since she'd first met him.

Sam reached her and bent his head, cupping her face with his big hands. The suffocating sensation became paralysis, spreading through her as she closed her eyes. Her legs would have given way under her if she hadn't reached out for him, steadying herself with her hands against his chest.

The kiss began as a gentle, chaste thing, the sort of kiss one would give to a child. Not releasing her face, Sam asked softly, "How old are you, Rosalie Shand?"

"Seventeen and a half. I'll be eighteen in September." She opened her eyes, looking into the pale blue ones so close to her. "I'm not a baby, Sam. I'm grown up."

For a moment there was hesitation in his face, and then he kissed her again.

This time there was nothing chaste about it. He drew her

into his arms, hard, and captured her mouth in a kiss that barely escaped brutality in its passion.

Rosalie sagged against him, not knowing exactly how to convey to him her own rising passion, which was so new to her.

"Are you really grown up?" Sam asked, and then, after searching her face and seemingly finding the answer, he suddenly scooped her up and carried her back across the room to the bed.

She hadn't really anticipated going this far, this fast, but her bones seemed to have taken on the consistency of young willow boughs, bending at the slightest touch, unable to bear their own weight without drooping.

His breath was warm on her throat, his hands working with buttons, tugging at garments. I'm going to faint, she thought, but she did not faint; instead she floated in a delicious lethargy that robbed her of all volition. How clever he was, kissing her, stroking her, keeping her in that euphoric state while he got her and himself out of their clothes.

And then the petticoats slid over the edge of the bed, and Sam bent over her, his bronzed body glinting with the golden hairs where the candlelight touched him. He was smiling, and she knew he liked the way she looked, the way she felt to his touch.

"If you're not grown up," he told her softly, "you will be. Very soon now."

Rosalie lifted her arms to slide them around his neck. The voice, so far away in the back of her mind, warned her that this was, indeed, dangerous, but she didn't care.

As his callused hand slid down the curve of her waist and hip, drawing her closer to him, she knew it would be worth it.

47

Joel was gratified at the interest Tris suddenly took in the political situation. He'd always talked politics to the family, and Tris had been more interested in the issues than any of the others, though they'd all listened politely. Now, Tris was actively enthusiastic about going with his father to various meetings, talking to the men, listening to the plans.

It didn't dawn on Joel that the drawing card, especially to the meetings held at J. Murphy Kendrick's house, was not all political.

The evenings when neither of the Kendrick females was in evidence were bitterly disappointing to Tris. When he got to see Melissa, he was in a state resembling drunkenness, except that after that first time he never again drank more than one glass of wine all evening.

He couldn't tell if she was glad to see him, too: Melissa was polite to all her father's friends, friendly to the younger men who flocked around her. That sweet, husky voice sent shivers up his spine, and he suspected miserably that it did the same for all the others, and that Melissa would have acted the same way if he'd had buck teeth and pimples.

Still, she did invite him into the game room several times, to play billiards. Was that because she liked him, or simply because she wanted an opponent for the game?

The urge to touch her was so overwhelming that Tris sometimes felt sick with it. When they accidentally touched hands, the electric shockwaves that swept through him made him forget whatever he was supposed to be doing. It was a good thing, he supposed, that they were almost never alone, because he'd probably do something foolish, and alienate her forever by some unintentional impropriety.

Dances were a favorite entertainment in the county, and were often held on Saturday nights at various ranches where barns could be cleared out to make space for the dancing. Jessie and Joel were both good dancers, and all the children had learned the steps at an early age. It was one of the few things Tris felt reasonably adept at; he'd had to practice with Rosalie and Teresa Dolores as partners, and since he wasn't the least bit nervous with either of them, he had relaxed and finally come to enjoy it.

He wanted to ask Melissa to a dance, but so far he hadn't gotten up the courage. What if she said no? Would he ever dare ask her to anything again? Probably she didn't feel she knew him that well yet. And her father—Tris got cold, thinking about J. Murphy Kendrick. He didn't really like the man very much, didn't trust him, and didn't want anything from him, as Joel apparently did.

Except his daughter.

One evening the Shands were leaving the Kendrick home after a dreary evening during which Tris had listened with increasing boredom to an argument about the use of the San Joaquin Ditch, originally built to carry water to the gold diggings, which had now been exhausted. At the moment he didn't care if they irrigated farmland with it or drowned themselves in it; he kept praying that Melissa would magically appear before it was time to leave the house.

She did. She came down the stairs, her chestnut curls tied back with a blue ribbon that matched her dress, raising her skirts enough so that he glimpsed slim ankles.

She paused halfway down, one hand resting gracefully on the polished railing. "I'm sorry, Daddy, I thought your guests had gone. Mama is having such a coughing spell, she asks that you bring up a small glass of brandy for her."

"I'll be there directly," Murphy agreed, then turned to shake hands with each of his half-dozen guests. Tris, who had no inclination to shake hands with the man, hung back, looking toward Melissa. After a moment, she continued on down the stairs until she was close enough to speak to Tris unobtrusively.

"I didn't realize you were here, Tristan. Daddy didn't mention you were coming, too." Her smile revealed both dimples. "I hope you weren't as bored as I was tonight. This whole week has been boring, as a matter of fact. I haven't been out of the house. We'll all be going to the dance at the Satterbys' tomorrow night, though, and that will be fun. Will you be there, by any chance?"

Tris, who had had no intention of going to the Satterbys'

dance, responded with alacrity. "Yes, I think Mama and the girls were intending to go, so probably we all will." *He* certainly would, whether the others did or not. This small measure of encouragement imbued him with a burst of daring. "Will you save the first dance for me, then?"

The dimples deepened. "I'd love to. Oh, Mama's calling! Goodnight, Tris!"

She was gone, scampering back up the curving stairway before he could echo her farewell. Dazed at his good fortune, Tris turned to find his hand enveloped in Murphy's powerful grip, and heard himself muttering, "Thank you, sir. Goodnight."

On the way out he nearly ran into the post beside the steps, collecting his wits just in time to avoid making a complete ass of himself; he glanced quickly around and didn't think anyone had noticed.

Oh, God, how he loved that girl, Tris thought, and didn't know whether he was more joyful or miserable because of it.

At the last minute, Laurie decided to join the others at the dance. He'd been planning something else with a group of male friends, but his horse had thrown a shoe and was showing a bit of lameness.

"I don't think I'd better ride him for a few days. Is there room in the buggy for me, if I go with the rest of you?" Laurie asked.

"Of course," Jessie assured him. She felt better about Laurie these days; he and Tris seemed to have stopped competing and sniping verbally at each other, which had bothered her for so long.

She was not unaware that something was happening to Tris. At first she thought he'd simply taken a genuine interest in the things that mattered to Joel, and that pleased her. They had never been as close as she'd have liked; Joel seemed to have reserved his primary affection for Laurie, who was so active and so much more like Joel himself.

After a short time, however, she realized that though Tris was concerned and knowledgeable about irrigation ditches and what was going on at the county seat—which had been moved to the growing town of Modesto several years earlier—there was more to the change in him than that.

Tris, Jessie thought with growing delight, had fallen in love.

Though she couldn't bring the matter up directly, she did make a discreet inquiry of Rosalie.

"Well, the only girl he's seen anything of, as far as I know, is Melissa Kendrick," Rosalie said. "Do you think he's sweet on her?"

"I think he's sweet on someone."

"Then it's probably Melissa," Rosalie's mouth twisted wryly. "At least that's a match Pa would approve, wouldn't he?"

Jessie had not asked about Rosalie's progress, if any, with Sam Shute. She was, to be truthful, afraid to. There was a glow about her daughter that meant only one thing, and if she knew for certain that Rosie was still riding out to see the man (when in heaven's name was she managing it?) she would have felt compelled to do something about it. If she didn't know, Joel wouldn't be able to blame her for not telling him about it.

That happiness in Rosalie's face was alarming in a way. Jessie wished her well, and thought it quite possible that Sam's intentions were honorable, but it worried her that the girl was sneaking off to see him. She hoped to God Rosalie was remembering what she'd been taught, and that she was mature enough to handle a man of thirty. It was a little different from the crushes she'd had on boys her own age. Quite different, actually.

She thought that if she asked, point-blank, what the relationship was, Rosie would tell her. Yet she didn't dare to know, not yet. She hadn't thought of any way to bring Joel around, and only thanked God Joel had been so taken up with this Kendrick man, who he thought might advance his own plans for government financing of an irrigation system, that he hadn't had time to do anything about the man he considered to be a squatter on land that was morally if not legally his own.

Jessie looked forward to the dance that Saturday night for several reasons. She still loved to dance as much as she ever had, and so did Joel; if he were dancing, he wouldn't be doing anything outrageous about Sam Shute. The Kendricks were going to attend; she'd know, Jessie thought, as soon as she saw Tris and Melissa together, if the girl was the one Tris had fallen in love with.

Jessie wasn't particularly fond of J. Murphy Kendrick, either, but she liked his wife and thought his daughter a charming girl. Joel would indeed be mightily pleased if Tris and Melissa made a match of it, and such a family connection might defuse Joel's temper on other matters.

She came downstairs in midafternoon, ready to leave for the hour's ride to the Satterby ranch, to find the boys in desultory conversation in the parlor, slicked up and in their best.

"The girls will be down in a few minutes," she said, looking in on them. "Where's your father, Tris?"

"I saw him heading for the barn about half an hour ago. I suppose he's doing some last-minute chore."

"Well, the last minute is about up," Jessie pointed out. "Run out and call him, will you? We want to get there early enough to sit down with everyone else for supper. Laurie, see if Mrs. Sullivan has the supper baskets packed, will you?"

She saw them exchange a look that she couldn't interpret, an odd, guarded look. They rose, however, to do her bidding. Jessie watched them go, hoping they weren't at cross purposes again. She hated it when they quarreled. Yet it hadn't seemed like that at all; it was more as if they shared some secret they did not want to reveal to her.

Rosalie's voice floated down the staircase, calling Jessie in that direction. "Mama, will you help? Teresa Dolores just tripped on her skirt and tore out the hem!"

Jessie climbed the stairs, her own skirts lifted well above the hazard level. "Why doesn't she change dresses? Wear the yellow one, maybe."

"She wants to wear this one, and she does look so lovely in it, Mama. If we both work on it, we can rehem it in only a few minutes," Rosalie said.

Jessie stood in the doorway, unable to repress a smile of pride in them both. Teresa Dolores wore white taffeta, a dress that had once been Bonifasia's and had recently been remodeled to fit her; it had a wide pink sash and an artificial pink silk rose at the shoulder, and she did look exquisite. Rosalie knelt at Teresa's feet with her mouth full of pins, busy turning up the hem so that it could be restitched. Without looking around, she spoke through the pins.

"Would you get another needle, Mama? I dropped the one I had, and I can't find it."

Jessie murmured agreement, and moved toward the back of the house, to the room that had been Miss Smythe's until the governess had taken another position two years earlier. Now it served as a sewing room.

She found the needle and had turned to retrace her steps

when she saw, through the back window, Mary Ann Wallace emerging from the barn.

Jessie paused, well back from the window, because there was something furtive in the way that Mary Ann looked over toward the big house.

Fortunately she did not glance toward the upper story, or she might have seen that she was observed through the sheer curtains. And had she not looked so—so guilty—Jessie might well have paid no attention to her at all.

There was no reason why Mary Ann should not have been in the barn. Hal might have sent her to fetch a tool or a bit of harness to repair, or she might have come for feed for the chickens. Only in that case, why would she have acted as if she were afraid of being noticed leaving the barn?

Jessie hesitated, watching the young woman until she disappeared behind the row of fruit trees. And then, just as she would have shrugged in puzzlement and gone on back to the girls, Jessie saw Joel come out of the barn in long strides, heading for the house. And he lifted his head for a quick survey of the house, including the window where she stood.

Jessie froze. Instinct told her not to move at all, that she was probably not visible behind the thin material of the curtains.

Joel and Mary Ann, together in the barn?

Something formed, tight and painful, in her chest. And then she walked quickly away from the window, down the hall to the room where Rosalie was coping with the hem, and handed her the needle. "I have to run downstairs a minute," she said, and was gone before Rosalie could protest that it would take twice as long to redo the hem by herself.

Tris and Laurie were in the front entryway, each carrying a basket from which rose the aroma of fried chicken and fresh bread. They paused to look up at her.

"I brought the buggy around in front," Laurie said. "Are the girls nearly ready?"

"In a few minutes. Tris, did you speak to your father?"

"I called him. He's coming right in."

"What was he doing?"

"Looking at that springing heifer, I guess. He thinks she'll calve tonight or tomorrow."

"Oh. Did you go into the barn, too?"

Was there something, an uneasiness, an apprehension, in his face? Or did she imagine it?

"No, I just went to the door and yelled. Told him it was

417

time to get ready. He said he'd be right in. You aren't going without a shawl, are you, Ma?"

"No. No, I forgot it. Oh, Joel, there you are. Are you ready to go?"

"Just have to get my coat," Joel told her. He looked as he always did, not flustered or guilty or like a man who had been interrupted by his son while he was making love to his hired man's wife.

Jessie turned to climb the stairs ahead of him, unwilling to look into his face, not wanting to read the truth if it was in his eyes. My God, how could she think such a thing? And if she thought it, how could she maintain an even tone of voice, keep her face so rigidly under control?

It could not be true, Jessie prayed. It could not.

Yet it took all her self-possession not to turn and scream at him, for everyone to hear, *Are you sleeping with her? Tell me, damn you, tell me the truth!*

"I have the hem finished, Mama," Rosalie called. "Come on, Teresa, let's go."

There was enough other conversation so that it wasn't too obvious that Jessie was unusually quiet when they'd all climbed into the buggy. Joel clucked to the horses and they were off, the girls chattering and joking with Laurie and Tris, both of whom were in unusually high spirits.

It was an evening that would remain forever etched in their memories, for a variety of reasons.

A large number of people came to the dance, bringing their picnic baskets and their dancing shoes. First there was supper, set out on long tables made from planks laid across sawhorses: baked beans and vegetables and salads from the spring gardens—the one good thing Jessie conceded about the California climate was that one could have strawberries in December and lettuce and peas in May—and hot breads and cakes and pies and cobblers that necessitated digesting some of the food before anyone felt like dancing.

The Kendricks were late, and Tris had begun to steel himself for the disappointment of their nonarrival before they came, just as a hundred people were sitting down to eat.

To his intense disappointment, there was no space for them with the Shands, and they sat far down the table. Melissa had seen him and waggled her fingers at him, however, so his spirits began to rise again.

Sam Shute was there.

He, too, sat far apart from the Shands; it was only when

the music began he crossed boldly to where Rosalie stood with Teresa Dolores, watching the musicians tune up, and said, "Will you dance with me, Miss Shand?"

His voice had a carrying quality, and Joel turned to look at him. It was not until later in the evening, however, that he questioned his wife. "Who's that big fellow with Rosie? This is the fourth time he's danced with her so far, and he acts as if he knows her."

Jessie made her tone offhand. "No doubt she'll introduce him sooner or later. Have you noticed the romance in our midst?"

"Romance?" Joel looked down at her, frowning. "What are you talking about?"

"Tris and Melissa Kendrick. Didn't you count how many dances *they've* had together?"

The frown cleared as Joel's eyes scanned the crowd, finding the pair he sought and noting the way they were laughing together, like old friends. "Do you think there's something there? With Tris and Melissa?"

"He's been acting as if he were in love," Jessie said. "And he's certainly very happy to be with her now, wouldn't you say?"

She had, for the moment, diverted his attention from Rosalie, though that could not last for long.

"Well," Joel said, "the boy's got good taste, I'll say that for him."

Jessie murmured agreement, and turned to John Curtis, who came to claim her for the next dance. She tried very hard to relax and enjoy the dancing as she usually did, and could not. She felt wooden, clumsy, and deep inside, she churned with anger and pain.

That look she had intercepted between the boys earlier in the day, had it been an acknowledgment between them that Joel was in the barn with Mary Ann? Had this been going on for years, as some small voice had long ago warned her before she managed to put it down? Were the boys protecting her from this hurt, knowing Joel was unfaithful to her? How long had they known? How had they found out? And how hurt had *they* been, to realize Joel had feet of clay?

Long before the evening was over Jessie was totally convinced that she had correctly interpreted what she had seen. There were so many clues, long suppressed in her conscious mind, all of them dating back to the time the Wallaces had moved into the little house beyond the creek, when Joel had

419

initiated her into another sort of intimacy that could not result in her pregnancy.

And she, fool that she was, had taken it for granted that he was subduing his own natural passions in order to protect her from the resulting miscarriages.

Had she not been so engrossed in her own inner turmoil, in the effort of making small talk with various neighbors and dancing partners, in pretending that she was having a good time, Jessie would have seen that Rosalie was spending too much time with Sam Shute, and that the happiness on her face was too clear to pass unnoticed. She would have warned the girl, so that Joel, at least, did not see.

Even Teresa Dolores was having an especially good time tonight, for beside her at the table had been a young man who looked vaguely familiar, who had struck up a conversation almost at once and who made no bones about the fact that he found her charming.

"You don't remember me, do you?" he asked, smiling.

Teresa Dolores studied the strong face topped by a shock of brown and unruly hair, and blue eyes that *did* strike a chord, though she could not remember where she'd seen them before. "I'm sorry. Have you . . . have you *grown* a good deal since I last saw you?"

The amusement exploded into a chuckle that did something to her nerve ends, a something both disturbing and intriguing.

"About a foot and a half, I guess, if I correctly remember when it was we last met. It was two and a half years ago, before I went east to go to school. I'm Brad Mismer, remember, Tris's friend?"

"Oh, yes, of course! But you—" She stared at him in disbelief. "You were no taller than I!"

He groaned good-naturedly. "Don't I know it! The smallest boy in school, and they never let me forget it. Ma kept saying there were no midgets in our family, and I'd eventually get to be a reasonable height, but I didn't believe her. I was miserable about my size for years. I'm still no giant, like that fellow that's dancing with Rosalie, but at least I can look another man in the eye without getting a crick in my neck. You've gotten even prettier, Teresa, than I remembered."

Teresa, who had also suffered the indignity of being smaller than other people, at least all of those in the Shand household, was suddenly glad that she had not grown as tall as her cousins. She liked Brad's open, friendly face and his easy manner. "Have you come home to stay?"

"Oh, yes. I'm going into business with my father and my brother Paul. We have a feed business in Modesto; Pa moved there from Knight's Ferry when the business slowed down so much after they moved the county seat. You'd like living in town, Teresa. There are so many exciting things to do. Maybe one day soon you'd like to attend the theater there with me. Our whole family goes," he added quickly, "so you'd be well chaperoned."

"I should love to go to the theater," Teresa Dolores assured him.

And she, too, was so busy elsewhere that she did not notice that Rosalie was attracting unwanted attention.

She should have known better, of course. Rosalie recognized, after the fact, that she hadn't handled it right. Her intention, upon learning that Sam was at the dance, was to manage an ordinary introduction to her father, and let him like Sam a little before he found out that he was the squatter on the land adjoining Joel's and that Rosalie was in love with him.

Retaining a small measure of common sense, she did avoid dancing every dance with Sam, though he was all she wanted. She *was* in love with him, she had no doubts about that at all, and he'd said he loved her, too. Her initiation into the pleasures of lovemaking had intensified, not diminished, her certainty about her feelings. And it was such sheer joy to be with him that she was not as cautious as she should have been.

By the time she got around to bringing him over to meet her parents, Joel had already observed too many dances, too much laughter, and the proprietary air each of them displayed toward the other without even realizing it.

Joel spoke civilly enough, yet as soon as the couple had returned to join a circle of young dancers, he moved in on Jessie. "How did they meet? Who introduced them to each other?"

"What does it matter?" Jessie asked, striving to sound as if it really didn't. "They are attracted to each other. Remember what it was like, when you and I began to fall in love, and almost nobody found it appropriate?"

Joel refused to see the parallel. "What do you know about him?"

421

"Almost nothing other than what she just told us. He came from Georgia, lost his family and property in the war, and came west for the same reasons as all the rest of us—to find a new home, a new fortune."

"Doesn't look like he's found much of a fortune yet. And he's too old for her."

"Oh, Joel, plenty of couples are ten or twelve years apart in age! The important thing is that they care for each other, and only they can decide that."

"Fortune hunter, that's most likely what he is. He'd heard Rosie's from a good family, a family with money. Not like the Kendricks, maybe, but better than what he's used to."

"You can't know anything of the sort about the man, just from looking at him," Jessie said with a touch of asperity. "He has the good taste to prefer *our* daughter, after all, which speaks well for him."

A moment later she was whirled away by old Silas Wofford, who was surprisingly agile for a man of his advanced years. When she told him so, Silas chuckled: "Good for a man to get married again, even at my age. Gets the juices all flowing again, eh?"

Jessie's own juices were flowing, although there was a corrosive quality about them. She had, she thought, known all along that it was too good to be true that anyone of Joel's virility could be content with less than wholehearted love-making. She had allowed herself to be duped, to remain blind to what was going on.

Now the blinders were off, and she had to do something. Suspecting was bad enough; *knowing* was agonizing. She could not go on the way she had been doing, pretending to a happiness that was no more than a facade, not when her husband was unfaithful to her.

Halfway through the evening, Tris wound up a polka with Melissa in his arms, breathless and seemingly enjoying himself, when suddenly he was tapped on the shoulder. He knew, even before he turned, that what he'd dreaded and tried to avoid was finally happening.

"Well, no wonder you haven't wanted to go anywhere with me lately," Laurie said. "If I'd had such a lovely lady under wraps, I wouldn't have settled for lesser company, either."

Melissa waited, smiling, for the introduction Tris was forced to make. "My cousin, Laurie Shand. We've been raised

422

as brothers, actually," Tris said, and wondered if he sounded as reluctant as he felt. Damn Laurie, why couldn't he have stayed away? He had all the girls he needed. Why couldn't he leave Tris alone with the only one who mattered to him?

That wasn't Laurie's way, of course. As soon as he saw an attractive girl, he had to try to ingratiate himself with her. Just as he was doing now, Tris thought in despair, hearing the pleasantries roll off Laurie's tongue in the easy manner that Tris despaired of ever achieving.

"May I have the next dance, Miss Kendrick? Or may I presume on Tris's acquaintanceship and call you Melissa?"

Tris watched them twirl away as the fiddlers struck up the music again, feeling bereft. Not this time, please God, not this time, he thought, and almost groaned aloud when he saw Melissa's sweet upturned face, laughing at whatever Laurie had said to her.

If he hurts her, I'll kill him.

The thought stabbed at him, and he knew it was true, literally true. Yet Laurie could be so charming, and if Melissa was charmed, what could Tris do?

He didn't seek another partner but stood on the sidelines, watching, waiting for the dance to end so that he could reclaim her. And even then, he knew, he would not feel a renewal of the happiness he and Melissa had shared for the first few hours of the evening. Laurie had spoiled it, as Laurie usually spoiled everything.

48

It was nearly two a.m. when they reached home, all of them so tired that little talking had been done. Rosalie, not having overheard the exchange of words between her parents, hoped that Pa was coming around, that he'd found Sam an acceptable young man at least on the surface of things. Teresa Dolores was sunk in romantic dreams; when she dozed off occasionally during the ride, Brad Mismer kissed her, and when the buggy jolted over a rut in the road and wakened her, she wanted only to fall back into slumber.

In the back seat, Laurie leaned across Teresa to say in a low voice, "My God, Tris, where did you find her? She's stunning! And that voice! I've never heard anything so seductive in my life, and I'd swear she doesn't even realize it!"

Tris stiffened. If Laurie made one of his suggestive remarks, anything intended to cheapen Melissa, Tris would hit him in the mouth, right here in the buggy with the whole family looking on.

"She's the kind of girl a man looks for all his life, until he's lucky enough to find her," Laurie mused, and the timbre of his voice relayed nothing derogatory, nothing sensual, nothing at all that Tris could reasonably object to, except that Laurie, too, found Melissa delightful.

Tris made no response, and when Laurie asked earnestly, "You haven't proposed to her or anything, have you?" Tris wasn't sure he could form a reply.

"Of course not. I only met her a few weeks ago."

"And you didn't mention her? I'd have come home raving about her! Those eyelashes, did you ever see such eyelashes? And that skin, and dimples—I always thought dimples were sort of babyish, before, but on Melissa...she's exquisite, Tris."

Miserable, although Melissa had said goodbye in the same way that she customarily did and squeezed his hand when he took hers, Tris had to agree. "Yes, she's...very lovely."

They straggled up the stairs, each engrossed in his own dreams or apprehensions. Jessie left a lamp burning on the landing for Joel, who had to put the horses away, and let herself into the room she had shared with him for so many years. Half her lifetime, Jessie thought, or close to it. She'd loved Joel passionately, and been secure in her belief that he loved her as well. That love was the very fabric of her life; while she adored the children, she knew now that they were all grown that she had loved Joel more. It was he who would be with her until the end of whatever life remained to her, as the young people went their own ways and created new lives with other people.

Yet Joel was unfaithful.

Tears prickled in her eyes, and resolutely Jessie fought them back. Not yet, she thought, she could not indulge in the release of tears. How she had managed to get through this evening, in front of a hundred other people, she did not know, because she felt as if there was a physical tear in her own flesh, a bleeding wound that she could not reach to ease it.

The room was the same as it had always been: the big bed, the carpet that had come from the orient, the handsome cherrywood desk where she wrote letters to Zadie and Mamie, the chair where she sometimes sat before the fire to read, the massive armoire where her gowns were a far cry from those she had worn as a member of King Strang's Mormon band.

She had a fine house, an elegant wardrobe, and in the box atop the massive dresser were the jewels Joel had promised her—a string of pearls, and even diamonds.

Were the jewels for her, or for Joel's own gratification? He urged her to wear them at the dinners when they entertained, or were entertained by, those wealthy and powerful men he wanted to impress.

Jessie turned away from the jewelry box. The gems meant nothing to her. Nothing at all. She wondered in despair if there was anything left to her that had meaning in the face of what she'd discovered this afternoon.

She heard the door close downstairs when Joel entered the house, and her heartbeat quickened until it was a painful force in her chest. What was she going to say to him? What was she going to do?

Her fingers were as inept over her buttons as they had been on her wedding night, Jessie thought. That night she had looked forward with joyful anticipation to lying in Joel's arms. And now, what did she look forward to now?

Was it her fault? Had she driven him to the arms of another woman because of the inadequacy of her own body to carry a child to term? Should she have continued to conceive and miscarry indefinitely, all those small babies with no chance to live, in order to keep Joel faithful to her? Some of the times when she had miscarried she had bled so profusely that she had been frightened that she would die of it. For a moment now, she almost wished she had. Dying could surely not be any more painful than this. If she had lost Joel, she was not certain she wanted to live on without him.

He must have paused in the library for a drink, because it was some time before she heard him climbing the stairs. The young people had settled down for the night, apparently; there were no sounds at all when she opened the door and

looked down the hallway, nor were there lights under any o
the doors.

She turned back quickly before Joel should see her ther
in their own doorway; she was in bed when he entered th
room, which was lighted only by an oil lamp, turned low.

"You asleep, Jess?" he asked softly.

"No. Not yet." Did her voice sound as strange to him a
it did to her?

He sat on the edge of the bed, his back to her, and begar
to take off his shoes. She could smell the brandy he'd im
bibed. Though Jessie never drank anything more than ar
occasional glass of wine, she wished that she, too, had hac
the fortification of the brandy.

"You think Tris really likes that Kendrick girl?" Joe
asked, setting his shoes aside and unbuttoning his shirt.

"I don't know," Jessie muttered. She didn't want to tall
about Tris and Melissa; she didn't even want to think abou
them.

"Wouldn't surprise me. She's a lovely little thing, isn'
she? And her old man is rich and influential, as much so a
anybody in California outside of the governor."

"I hardly think Tris would be swayed by what her fathe
is," Jessie said, amazed that Joel had so little perception o
the way his son's mind worked.

"Maybe not. Still, even Tris would have to admit it woul
be an advantageous marriage, if she'd have him. Looks to m
like she could have her choice of just about anybody. I wisl
to God Rosalie wasn't so headstrong. I don't like the look o
that Shute fellow; there's an insolence about him tha
bothers me."

Jessie quite desperately did not want to get into a discus
sion about the children tonight, yet she could not allow thi
to pass unchallenged. "Joel, that young man is so much lik
you were when I met you that it's incredible. He's not in
solent, he simply thinks he's as good as anyone else is, even i
he's not rich. Where would you be if you hadn't had confi
dence in your own worth, if you hadn't determined to mak
something of yourself against all odds?"

Joel twisted on the edge of the bed, bringing up one kne
as he swiveled to look at her in astonishment. "Like *me*
Jessie, you're out of your mind! I have nothing whatever ir
common with Sam Shute!"

Jessie raised herself on one elbow to look at him, unawar
of the picture she made in the lamplight with her pale hai

426

streaming loose over her shoulders and down her back. "Joel, for the love of God, leave Rosalie alone. She's intelligent enough to make her own decision about the man—about any man—if you leave her alone. But if you pressure her by criticizing him, you'll only drive her into his arms. You've never denied her anything, all her life, even when I didn't agree with you and felt she shouldn't have something, or do something. You've spoiled her so that if she didn't have a basic sweet nature and a native intelligence, she would have been totally ruined by this time. And now, after years of allowing her to think that she had the right to make her own decisions and to have what she wants, she's come to the biggest thing she's ever wanted, and you're proposing to put your foot down and deny him to her! If you do that, you'll only make her more determined to have him. And this is all premature, anyway. We don't know that he wants her—"

"He wants her," Joel interrupted grimly. "I saw the way he looked at her."

"—or, for certain, that she wants him. She'll find out, if we leave her alone and don't push her."

"She's too young to know what she'd be getting into," Joel said gruffly. He turned around, peeling off his shirt, then rose to step out of his trousers. "She doesn't know what it would be like, living in poverty, doing all her own housework without help, having babies in some damned shack—"

"I did all my own housework," Jessie reminded, "for a good long time. And had one baby in a shabby room back in Westport, and another in the little house when it wasn't much more than a shack, before we moved into this place. Rosie's young and strong and healthy, and if we let her make her own choice about a husband, she'll manage as well as I did."

As if he hadn't heard her words, Joel said slowly, "I'll ask around about that fellow, see what anybody knows about him. Too bad John Curtis went home early. I'd have asked him. John keeps track of people who move into this area. Maybe next week I can find time to ride over and see him."

A thrill of pure terror coursed through her. Quite possibly John already knew who Sam was, since he'd built his cabin between John's land and their own. More likely, though, he didn't, or he'd have mentioned it tonight. Yet if Joel rode to Curtis's, he'd go past the little house, and very likely see Sam Shute there, and then what?

"I don't want to talk about it any more tonight," Jessie

427

said, with as much firmness as she could muster. "Please pu
out the lamp and come to bed, Joel. It's very late."

He blew into the lamp chimney, and the bed creaked a
he slid in beside her. He sighed deeply, and Jessie though
that he would turn his back to her and fall asleep before sh
could say anything else to him, as he often did.

She turned toward him, pulses racing, and stretched ou
a hand. For a matter of seconds it rested on his belly, an
then she moved it in an unmistakable quest, so that she fel
his immediate response.

"Jess? I thought you were sleepy."

She could not reply in words—she did not feel capable o
speech at all—but she pressed against him, and when h
rolled readily toward her, met him with a kiss. It was a kis
of extraordinary intensity, an intensity born of her fear an
desperation, though of course Joel could not know that.

He was drowsily gratified, however, and drew her into hi
arms with a low chuckle. "For an old lady of nearly forty
sweetheart, you still have a lot of fire."

He would have met her need in the ways he had employe
for several years now, the ways that could not possibly mak
her pregnant, but Jessie would have none of that. She wa
like a tigress, moving against him, nails digging into hi
flesh, limbs entwined with his. "No, no, not that way! Joel
make love to me the way we used to! Really make love t
me!"

She felt his hesitancy, though she felt his rising need, too
"Honey, you haven't had one of those goddamned miscar
riages in a long time, and..."

"I haven't even had a normal monthly show in tw
months," Jessie said, although in actuality there had bee
some spotting. "I'm getting to the age where it will probabl
all stop soon, anyway. Eva Curtis has, and she's only a fe
years older than I am. Joel, make love to me."

There was no way he could resist, not with her mouth an
her hands and her still supple body teasing, stimulating
compelling him. It had been so long since they'd come to
gether this way, and they both climaxed more quickly tha
they'd have liked. Joel was already regretting his impetuosit
as he fell back, sated yet feeling guilty.

The rising moon reached into the room and sent a wid
band of light across the middle of the bed. Jessie sat up, an
the pale glow lit up her hair as if it were silver-gilt when sh
turned her face toward her husband.

"Was it as good for you as it was for me, Joel?"

He groaned. "Oh, God, Jess, maybe I'm getting too old for such passion," he told her, laughter in his voice. "I'd forgotten how exciting it could be, and how good. I love you, Jess, even more than I did when I married you. You're more beautiful now than you were then..."

She leaned forward, into the shadow, striving to see his face in the reflected glow. "Was it as good with me as it was with *her?*"

He sucked in a deep breath and forgot to breathe further. For long seconds she thought he would not answer. His eyes were wide open, she could tell that. "What are you talking about?" he asked finally, but the hollow ring in his voice confirmed what she knew to be true.

"I'm talking about Mary Ann," Jessie said, very softly. The pain was back in her chest; indeed, it spread throughout her body so that she wondered if it was possible to die of it.

Joel did not speak, and she thought wildly that if he denied it she would strike him, pound him until he either stopped her or allowed himself to be bloodied.

She had never heard his voice the way it was when he next spoke, and she hoped to a merciful God that she never would again. It was heavy with grief and shame.

"How long have you known?"

"Since this afternoon," Jessie said. "I suspected a little when the Wallaces first came here, but I didn't want to believe it, and I managed to convince myself there was nothing to it. Only it's been going on for years, hasn't it? It wasn't enough for you, the things you felt you could do with me, and you had to have her, as well."

To his credit, Joel didn't attempt to justify his actions. He didn't put any of the blame on Jessie, for her physical inadequacies, nor remind her that he had needs she hadn't been able to meet.

His voice was unsteady, though she knew he made a tremendous effort not to lose control of it altogether. "Jess. I have never loved anyone but you, and I never will. I'm sorry I hurt you. I never intended that. I love you more than anything in the world."

The tears, so long restrained, began to slide down her cheeks, glistening where the moonlight touched them. She made no sound. It was only when she crumpled forward over her knees that Joel reached for her, drew her into a tender embrace, and held her close while the anguish burst within

429

her. She wept, and was not sure if all the tears were hers, or if Joel shared them.

His murmured endearments, his gentle touch, at last soothed her, and Jessie lay spent in his arms. If she had asked him, at this moment, whether or not there had been anyone besides Mary Ann, he would have told the truth. If she had demanded to know what had taken place between her husband and Clara Ridback, he would have disclosed that as well.

Yet did she really want to know? Would it not add to her suffering to learn that there had been, not one, but a series of women? And what did it matter, now, since she would not allow it to happen again?

Jessie did not ask. She made no attempt to extract a promise of fidelity from this point on. Joel made no voluntary promise, nor did he ask for forgiveness. But when the storm of emotion was past, they slept in each other's arms. There was a renewed closeness between them, and Jessie prayed that it would last.

49

Laurie was in love.

Totally, gloriously in love.

He could talk of nothing but Melissa Kendrick. Had he spoken in the lighthearted way that he had often discussed young females of his acquaintance, Tris would have had an excuse to pulverize him. Laurie did not.

"You must not have any red blood in your veins, Tris," he joked, oblivious of the pain he inflicted. "How did you manage not to fall in love with her the minute you saw her?"

As it would only have been humiliating to confess that that was exactly what he had done, Tris kept still. He endured Laurie's chatter, endured Laurie's company on the rides to and from the Kendrick mansion, and hardest of all, watched in misery when Laurie and Melissa were together.

Not that she was any nicer to Laurie than she was to Tris. She was happy, smiling, and cordial; it didn't matter whether it was Tris or Laurie who opposed her at the billiard table, or walked with her through the Kendrick gardens or along the river. At a dance, she laughed as they squabbled over her favors, as if it were all a game instead of deadly serious.

Jessie watched in dismay, seeing her son grow morose and silent. Laurie had had so many girls. Why did he have to want this one, too? The only girl Tris had ever seriously looked at? Had she been able to think of anything to further Tris's cause, Jessie would have done so, but what was there to do? Both young men were free to court her, and the decision would eventually be Melissa's.

She worried too about Rosalie. The girl had to be slipping out after dark to visit Sam Shute; a perceptive mother could not fail to see, simply by looking at the child, that she was in love, and that she was building her hopes for a happy resolution to the situation.

No, Jessie amended, Rosalie was not a child. Only seventeen, yet a woman grown. A woman with a woman's desires and needs, and she believed that Sam Shute would fill those needs.

Jessie could, of course, have put a stop to any nocturnal excursions. She had a strong compulsion to do so, simply to protect Rosie. Yet she remembered so clearly what it had been like when she was Rosie's age.

Tully Ritter, her stepfather, had forbidden her to associate with Joel. Jessie had loved Joel so much, and she'd gone to elaborate lengths to see him. She had lied, at least by omission, about where she went and what she did. And if Tully had attempted to restrain her physically, Jessie knew that she would have struggled to the utmost of her ability to escape from him, to be with Joel.

She prayed that Sam Shute was the kind of man that Rosalie thought he was, that he was trustworthy, that he loved the girl. Jessie's own judgment was that he was an honorable man; his callused hands indicated his willingness to work, and if he loved Rosie, what more could anyone ask?

Except that Joel did ask more, of course. Somehow she must convince him that they must let Rosalie choose her own pathway. Perhaps, she thought, the renewed lovemaking of their own would mellow him, somehow, allow her to persuade him.

She had not known what was to be done about Mary Ann. Having her out there in the little house, available to Joel should he feel the need for her, tempting him, perhaps even rousing guilt within him if he simply stopped seeing her, was intolerable. Jessie thought about walking over there, during a quiet afternoon when no one else was around, and talking to Mary Ann. Telling her that it was over, everything the younger woman had had with Joel. Telling her to go away.

Yet Mary Ann was married to Hal Wallace, and Mary Ann would not go away unless her husband went as well. Jessie could not quite bring herself to request of Joel that he deprive the man of his livelihood by dismissing him.

And then, only two days after Jessie and Joel had returned to normal lovemaking, the problem was resolved by a higher power than Jessie's.

Joel came in from the fields in midmorning, striding so purposefully that Jessie, observing from the back porch, knew at once something was wrong.

He called out for Tris and Laurie as he neared the house, then came on toward her after the boys had appeared and been given an order that sent them scurrying for a horse and wagon.

"What is it?" Jessie asked, and then felt guilt at the relief his answer brought.

"It's Hal. He collapsed; he's dead. His heart, I suppose. The boys will bring the body in. Do you think the news might come easier from you than from me, for Mary Ann?"

Hal was dead. Which meant that as soon as he'd been buried there would be no reason for his wife—his widow—to remain in the little house across the creek.

"Of course," Jessie said swiftly, moving down the steps. The guilt subsided, overwhelmed by compassion. Jessie knew what it felt like to lose a loved one, and even though she did not think the Wallaces had been deeply in love in the sense that she herself had loved, it would be a shock, nevertheless. Mary Ann would have to shift for herself now.

Not that that should prove any long-term problem, Jessie decided a few minutes later. She stood in the middle of the living room which seemed so small, now, filled with Mary Ann's things, and watched the younger woman push back her heavy honey-colored hair with both hands, hands that trembled only a little.

"He'd been having pain in his chest, I think," Mary Ann said. "In the night, several times."

She was a lovely young woman, Jessie realized. No wonder Joel had been tempted beyond endurance. Even all these years after the gold rush that had brought thousands of hopeful men rushing west, there was still a shortage of women, especially young and pretty ones. Mary Ann would find another man with no difficulty.

"I'm very sorry," Jessie told her, and oddly enough it was true. Although she wanted this woman gone, and her husband's death was the surest way of achieving that, she could sympathize. "What will you do? Do you have anyone to go to?"

Mary Ann swallowed and turned away to pour the tea she had been brewing, though once she poured it she seemed to forget it was there. The cups sat on the table between them, untouched, topped by rising curls of steam.

"I've a friend in Stockton. Grace Rhoades. Her husband has a small shop, and they have young children. I don't know how I'll get there, though."

"I'm sure my husband will arrange for the boys to take you," Jessie offered.

And then she was free of the house, almost free of Mary Ann, and she didn't quite dare thank God that Hal Wallace had died, though she thought about it. God could read her thoughts, of course, and might one day chastise her for them, but a person couldn't help what she thought, could she?

Jessie walked back to the house with the sun warm on her face, unable to suppress the bubbles of relief within her. It would be so much better once all the details were taken care of. She made a mental note to remind Joel to give the girl a little money, in addition to whatever was owing to Hal, to help her establish herself elsewhere. Not very much, not enough so that it would appear that Joel was paying off an ex-mistress, only a sum that any concerned employer might pay out to provide for a helpless female until she could make plans to support herself.

Yes, Jessie thought, what Mary Ann needs now, mostly, is kindness, and she cannot expect me to provide that. It will be best if she goes to her friend, and God forgive me for wishing it to be quickly.

The man hired to take Hal's place was young, awkward, and newly wedded to an angular and just as awkward young woman; Jessie took one look at Bess Jones and decided that no one but a man as homely as Bill Jones would ever look at her twice. And then she was immediately ashamed of herself, because the Joneses were a nice young couple, eager to please, and they could hardly help their looks.

Joel was certainly giving Jessie no reason to think that he was looking at any other woman. He stayed close to home, except for working in his own vast fields; when there were errands to be run in town, he sent the boys when he could. It was only for those political meetings that he dressed up and rode away, and he persuaded Jessie to go with him when the meetings were at the Kendrick place, where Myra Kendrick graciously entertained the wives of her husband's cronies while the men talked.

Tris and Laurie were both eager to join the party as well when such an excursion took place, though Tris was quiet and subdued. Jessie watched him in sorrow, guessing at the things he did not put into words. Poor Tris! All his life he'd been overshadowed by the older boy, and now, in a matter that was really important, it seemed that he would be trailing Laurie again.

It was not Tris she was most concerned about, however, but Rosalie. Rosalie with love shining out of her eyes, reflected in her up-curving lips, in the happiness radiating from her in every word, every gesture.

How could Joel not notice?

Yet it seemed that he did not. He was too busy teaching Bill Jones what he wanted him to do, too busy with the work that must be done. Too busy, as yet, to ride over and talk to John Curtis, to see Sam Shute at his offending small cabin. Jessie prayed for a miracle.

Once more, it appeared that God was not listening.

Jessie was in the backyard, taking clothes off the line, when she heard him coming. She turned, watching the figure draw nearer, guessing from the way he used the horse that he was in a hurry, or angry. And he came from the south, from the direction of Sam Shute's cabin.

She forgot to take the next pin out of the sheets. There was no need for her to handle the laundry, of course; there was a hired girl as well as Mrs. Sullivan, the cook and housekeeper. But Jessie liked hanging out wet clothes in the warm sunshine, and liked even more taking them down, warm and fragrant, a few hours later.

434

She heard a horse from the opposite direction and swiveled her head. Laurie, who had ridden off early this morning on some unexplained errand, was heading back at a gallop.

She forgot about Laurie. It was Joel who alarmed her, swinging down from the saddle, heading for the barn in long strides that revealed his anger as clearly as anything could have done. Jessie left the sheets in the basket, hurrying toward the door where her husband had disappeared into the barn.

"Joel?"

He swung toward her, tight-lipped, eyes blazing. "Where's Rosalie?"

Her instinct was to retreat before his fury, though she resisted it. "She and Teresa Dolores have gone riding. They took a picnic lunch with them, hours ago. Joel, what's wrong?"

"A picnic? And she's even dragging poor Teresa along to cover up for her?"

"What are you talking about?" Jessie asked, but her voice was hollow because there could be only one thing.

"I'm talking about Sam Shute. Did you know he's the one who built a shack on our south boundary?"

"He owns the land," Jessie said automatically. "He's recorded it, Joel. The land does not belong to us, and it's none of our business."

"So you knew all that, did you, and didn't think to tell me? What else do you know, Jess?"

It had been a bad tactical error. It was too late to worry about that, however. She watched him gathering odds and ends that were meaningless to her, though she was tensely aware that his movements were urgent, even violent.

"She's in love with him, Joel. Leave her alone. Leave *him* alone. If you really care about Rosalie, let them be. Let them decide for themselves what they want to do."

She might have been talking to a brick wall, she thought in rising alarm, for gradually it dawned on her what he was assembling. "What are you doing? Joel, you're not going to burn him out! It's his land, his house, he has a right to be there!"

He paused for a moment in the act of filling a lantern with coal oil. His mouth was flat and ugly. "Does he have a right to have our daughter there, in his bed?"

Jessie's mouth went slack, while the constriction in her chest became a painful pressure that interfered with her breathing. "Oh, Joel, no!"

"She wasn't in it when I got there, and he wasn't there, either, or I'd have killed him on the spot." His tone reminded her, briefly, of the way he had once talked about Richard Aubin, the father who had refused to acknowledge him. Yet this was worse, Jessie thought, because he meant it about killing a man. "She'd been there. She apparently dressed in a hurry, because she forgot an item or two."

Jessie wondered if the giddiness she felt was the precursor of an actual fainting spell; she was so sick, so dizzy. Yet she could not escape the horror that way. She had to find some way to stop Joel in whatever it was he planned to do.

"Any man who respects a woman doesn't take her into his bed and use her, and that's what Shute's done," Joel said grimly. "Oh, I won't kill him. Don't worry, they won't hang me for *that,* not unless I catch up with him *with Rosie,* and even a jury in town wouldn't begrudge me the satisfaction of putting an end to *that.* Taking advantage of my innocent young daughter."

Her hand went out to close on his wrist, so that he was stayed for a few seconds from putting incendiary materials into the saddlebag draped over the stanchions. She felt her fingernails bite through the skin before Joel jerked loose and continued his methodical packing of the oil and matches and a coil of rope. Rope? For what? she wondered, suddenly drenched in icy perspiration. For fuses, maybe, but no, if he intended to pour oil around the cabin and set it afire, there would be no need for fuses to carry the flames. Not to hang Sam Shute, she begged silently. Not to take the law into his own hands, especially when he was wrong. Oh, God, he *was* wrong, wasn't he?

"Joel," she said, willing her words to get through to him. "We can't know the entire truth of whatever has happened, not without talking to Rosalie. If she went to him, she went willingly. The same as I did, when I first came to you. For the love of heaven, don't you even remember what it was like for us?"

Her next words scalded her tongue, words she had never thought to say, yet words that must be said now. "I slept with you, Joel, before we married. You gave me your mother's wedding ring, and we pretended we were married, but we were not. In the eyes of God, in the eyes of my family and the world, you took me in sin, Joel! Because we loved each other, because they wouldn't let us get married, and we needed each other! Were you *using me,* as you say he's using

Rosie? Or did you love me as much as I loved you? Why can't you give them the benefit of the doubt, that they're as much in love as we were?"

It was an impassioned speech, and it won her nothing. Jessie stared up into his face, as unyielding as if chiseled from one of those granite monoliths that had blocked their passage through the Sierra. He didn't even bother to answer her.

Laurie rode into the yard behind them, scattering chickens squawking in every direction, and slid to the ground, looping the reins over the nearest post. He didn't seem to notice the tension between them.

"Uncle Joel? I brought you a message from Murphy Kendrick; he wants to see you right away. Where did that horse come from? The black stallion in the big corral?"

"Stay away from him. He's not broken, and he's dangerous." Joel closed the saddlebags and swung them over an arm, facing the doorway. "Kendrick will have to wait. I've got some other business to take care of first."

Laurie glanced at Jessie, dismissed her. "Is it our horse? He's the most beautiful stallion I've ever seen! Where did you get him?"

"I bought him," Joel said, striding into the yard. His horse, hard-ridden and needing a rubdown, raised a head at Joel's approach, allowing the saddlebags to be put into place. "And he's *my* horse, Laurie. I don't want any of the rest of you near him, not until he's ready."

Laurie swiveled to follow Joel's movements, then reached into his pocket and brought out a folded paper. "Here, Murphy sent you this. It's important, I think, Uncle Joel. He wants everybody at his house as soon as they can make it. Something to do with that Klauser who's talking about building another mill upstream from the ferry."

Joel paused, finally drawn out of his preoccupation with the problem of Sam Shute. He scowled. "I thought that was settled. Klauser couldn't get the financial backing he needed, not after we put out the word we don't want another mill on the river."

"Well, he's got it now, from somewhere. You better read this before you go anywhere else, because he told me to send you back as soon as you could make it."

Joel accepted the missive, still frowning. "I don't have to jump because Murphy Kendrick says so," he said, but the frown deepened as he read. He swore, and stuffed the paper into his pocket, and Jessie's hope leaped. Would he respond to Kendrick's summons before he did whatever he planned to do about Sam Shute?

"You're going, aren't you?" Laurie pressed. "I told Melissa I'd be back, and I don't especially want to face up to old Murphy if you aren't there, too."

"I'll go," Joel said, and Jessie, her bones melting with relief, put a hand against the barn to support herself. "It won't matter in the long run. I can take care of that bastard later. In fact, after he goes to bed maybe I'll be lucky enough to burn down his goddamned shack with him still in it."

Laurie's eyes widened, and this time his gaze lingered on Jessie, as if he might better read in her face than in Joel's what was going on. "Who? You going to put a torch to somebody's shack?" When there was no reply from either of them, he moistened his lips and guessed. "That Shute fellow? *His* shack? You going to burn it, Uncle Joel?"

"Keep your mouth shut," Joel told him, and vaulted into the saddle. "Come on, if you're going with me."

He did not bid Jessie goodbye, nor even look in her direction. Laurie scrambled back into the saddle and kneed his mount to catch up with Joel, who rode as if eager to finish his business with Murphy and then to get on to more important matters.

Jessie stood in the sunny barnyard looking after them. She'd forgotten the basket of laundry. She'd had a reprieve, at least until Joel had been to Kendrick's and back, but she was under no illusions that by then her husband's angry determination would have faded.

What should she do?

She could ride out to Sam's cabin, of course, though since Joel had not found him there, she had no assurance of finding him, either. She could leave a note warning of what Joel intended. But what good would that do? It wasn't likely that Sam Shute would simply step aside and allow his home to be incinerated. No, more likely he'd be waiting with that rifle, and they'd carry Joel home draped across the back of his horse—

Dear God, what was she doing, standing here imagining the worst, when there might be a way to prevent disaster?

She began to move toward the house, slowly, ignoring the chickens clucking around her in expectation of a handful of corn. She must think, and fast, because her time was limited, and she had to stop him. To save Sam Shute, to protect Ros-

438

alie, and to keep Joel himself from doing something that might shatter their family forever.

She went up the back steps and heard Tris's voice in the kitchen, bantering with Mrs. Sullivan over eating her fresh baked cookies.

"You're worse'n you were as a little tad," Mrs. Sullivan said. "Then you'd settle for one cookie at a time."

"And another one I'd snitch when your back was turned," Tris admitted. "But that's because you make such good cookies, Mrs. Sullivan."

Tris? If she told Tris, he'd help her, she thought. And then at once Jessie realized that this was not the answer. Tris was too used to knuckling under to Joel; he might be a man grown, in size, and he would certainly side with Jessie in this matter, but he had not the authority to stop his father from doing something he'd set his mind on. And if she tried, pitting son against father, it would be only one more area in which Tristan would fail.

She would have risked that, if she'd seriously thought there was any chance she and Tristan could win over Joel's strength. Since there was not, what did she do, then?

Jessie opened the door and went into the house, a wordless prayer running through her mind. Please, God, let this one be answered, she thought.

50

"Where's Rosalie?" Jessie demanded of the slight girl who turned toward the door as she entered the parlor.

Teresa Dolores jumped, startled, for she had not known Jessie was in the house. Indecision played across her face, the face of one unaccustomed to deceit. Her dark eyes rolled upward toward the ceiling, as if to perceive whether or not her cousin was up there in her own room.

"She...I don't think she's feeling well," Teresa Dolores offered hesitantly, and Jessie wanted to shake her.

"Did she tell you to say that? That she was ill? Where is she? Don't tell me she's home if she's not, because I intend to go and look."

The color faded out of the girl's cheeks, and her eyes were wide and frightened. She made no attempt at replying.

"Teresa, this is a matter of life and death." Jessie spoke in a low, compelling tone that carried conviction. "Tell me where she is, what she's doing. She's with Sam Shute, isn't she? Where? At his cabin, or somewhere else?"

Teresa swallowed convulsively, her fingers entwined in the silver cross that hung on a matching chain between her small breasts. Her mouth was open, and she made a gasping sound as she sought escape from this trap in which Rosalie had placed her.

"Your Uncle Joel came from his cabin only a little while ago," Jessie said, sounding as grim as she felt. "He found something of Rosalie's there, enough to convince him she and Sam Shute were..." She hesitated, then decided it was a time for brutality, if that was what it would take to elicit the information she needed. "...sleeping together," she finished, and saw poor Teresa first flame bright pink, then turn chalky and reach for a chairback for support. "Can you imagine what he intends to do about that? For God's sake, Teresa, tell me where they are!"

Teresa Dolores gasped again, then blurted out the terrible words. "I don't know! I swear, Aunt Jessie, I don't know where they went! On a picnic, perhaps along the river, perhaps up in the hills—I honestly don't know! Rosie said if I didn't know I couldn't...tell."

"And you were to come home and convince the rest of us that she was lying down upstairs with a headache? Teresa, how could you be so foolish!"

Even as she heard her own words Jessie knew they were unfair. Rosalie had always manipulated the younger girl, simply because she was a stronger personality. And now the two of them were in open conflict—well, it would be open as soon as Joel caught up with his daughter—and there was no point in blaming Teresa Dolores.

Better to blame herself, Jessie thought bitterly. Because she'd known Rosalie was slipping out of the house to meet Shute, and she'd turned a blind eye to it, hoping it would all come right in the end.

Well, it hadn't come right. It couldn't be more wrong.

If Joel burned down Sam's cabin, it would eventually be replaced. But given the mood Joel was in, she wasn't at all sure he wasn't sincere in his expressed desire to burn the place with Sam Shute in it, and at the moment she even feared for Rosalie. Oh, he wouldn't do her permanent physical injury, but he might well do something that would have the same crippling effect in the long run, the way Tully Ritter had once tried to do to Jessie.

For a moment Jessie stared helplessly into the girl's tortured face. Teresa couldn't help her. Tris couldn't help her. And she couldn't stop Joel alone.

For a matter of seconds Jessie trembled inwardly. It was possible that during his ride to see J. Murphy Kendrick Joel's temper would cool, but it certainly wasn't something she could count on. He might even, she feared, enlist help in running Sam Shute off that little piece of land, out of the county.

She remembered Joel's reaction to reading in the newspaper about a vigilante group punishing a man who had seduced two young girls. Though there were indications that the girls had been reasonably cooperative and had certainly not been raped, the men who had banded together with the girl's father, a prominent businessman in Modesto, had shown no mercy. They had taken the law into their own hands for this desecration of young womanhood, and had hanged the perpetrator from the nearest tree.

"Damned easterners come out here and violate Californian codes, they deserve what they get," had been Joel's comment.

If he mentioned to his friends that Sam Shute had not only had the effrontery to build on a section of land Joel had been using to graze his own cattle but had then seduced Joel's daughter, would they band together in another impromptu vigilante group to swoop down on the unsuspecting man? It wouldn't matter in the slightest that Sam had legal rights to the land, not after the deed was done. And if they came in an anonymous horde, perhaps even masked as those earlier vigilantes had been, who would identify any of them? Who would testify against them?

No one, Jessie thought sickly, unless by some terrible mischance she was unable to find Rosalie, and Rosalie was *there*. That would not stop the night riders, of course; while they would not harm the girl, they would not consider what it could do to her mind to watch her lover burned alive within

his cabin, or left kicking on the sturdy branch of a nearb
oak.

The image was so vivid that Jessie fought against th
vomitus that rose in her throat. She drew a shuddering breatl
and tried to speak calmly and rationally.

"Teresa, I only pray that no one dies because of Rosalie'
foolishness. If you know where she is, I beg you to ride to he
and tell her to return home at once, and to warn Sam Shut
that he'd be well advised to head for the hills for a few day
until the worst of Joel's anger subsides. I don't suppose he'l
do it, but at least he'll be forewarned. Tell him that if h
truly cares about Rosalie, and wishes to stay alive for he
sake, if not his own, to let them burn his cabin and not com
back, at least until the furor dies down a bit."

Teresa stood rigid with hopeless terror. "I don't know
where they are, I swear it, Aunt Jessie!"

"Well, maybe you'd better ride out and see if they're wher
you left them, or if you can pick up a trail to them." Sh
hesitated, seeing that the girl was in such a state of frigh
that she was probably beyond being able to act. "Take Tri
with you," she decided. "He's a good tracker. He may be abl
to pick up their trail from wherever you left them. You ca
explain the situation to him, tell him his father's gone t
answer a summons from Kendrick, but he'll certainly be bacl
after dark, and under no circumstances must Rosalie and Mr
Shute be at that cabin when he comes. Do you understan
that? No matter what anyone has to do to keep them away!

Teresa looked as if she would collapse in a pathetic littl
heap, tears springing to her eyes at this unwanted respon
sibility, a responsibility entirely too heavy for her.

"Maybe if you find them and explain to Rosie, she'll b
able to persuade Mr. Shute to take her elsewhere," Jessi
said, not believing it herself. She had been entirely seriou
about the similarities between Shute and Joel, and she knev
she would never have been able to dissuade Joel from ar
action he felt compelled to take, no matter how dangerous i
was.

A memory touched her, a flickering recollection of th
hours she had huddled beside a windowless opening in th
top floor of an unfinished house on Beaver Island, on th
night Joel had gone to infiltrate the Gentiles who had planne
a massacre of King Strang's people; the fear she had felt, fo
him and for all the Strangites, and how he had brushed asid
her anxiety about the dangers to himself and had strode o

442

into the midst of those who would have killed him in an instant had they recognized him as a spy.

She had not been able to talk sense to Joel then, and she was even less likely to be able to do it now.

Jessie swallowed the painful lump in her throat, and turned toward the door, giving Teresa Dolores a small push ahead of her. "Go on, hurry. There's no time to be lost." She knew now what she had to do. "I'm going for Luis. Maybe he can stop what Joel's planning to do. I don't know anyone else who can. Go, Teresa."

The girl fled, and Jessie heard Tristan's voice, at first light and then gruff, heard Teresa's tearful response, and prayed the child would have the control to convey to him what must be conveyed. Jessie didn't want to take any more time to do it herself.

She couldn't ride in these clothes, and ride she must, as if her life depended upon it. No, not her life, but Sam Shute's, and possibly Rosie's. She knew how she would have felt if Tully Ritter had taken such drastic steps to eliminate Joel Shand as a suitor, and she thought that if Joel succeeded in killing the man, or seriously harming him in any way, it might well be more than Rosie could deal with. Quite apart from what happened to Shute, Jessie could not allow her daughter to be destroyed.

The ride to Casa Sañudo had never seemed longer. The sun was low behind her when Jessie at last slid from the saddle and relinquished the reins to a young Mexican boy; it would be full dark before she could return, and Joel and whomever he enlisted to aid him might well reach home before her.

All the way over, riding the greenly carpeted hills, heedless of any damage her horse might do through the fields of young grain, Jessie had prayed. Prayed that Teresa Dolores and Tris would find Rosalie and Shute; prayed that the lovers would, by some miracle, be sensible enough to remove themselves from the battleground until the skirmish was over, or at least until more troops arrived.

Now, when Luis did not meet her on his own doorstep, she added another prayer. Please, God, let him be home!

He was not. The housekeeper invited her in, smiling face sobering at Jessie's obvious agitation. "He is out somewhere, señora. Riding in the hills, with the men and the cattle. I will send someone for him pronto."

"Yes," Jessie agreed. "Please, and tell them it's urgent that I see him at once! A matter of life and death."

"Life and death," the woman agreed. "Please, señora, make yourself comfortable in there, by the fire, and I will send a girl with something to eat and drink. Manuel shall go for el patrón."

The woman disappeared, and Jessie made her way toward the library, where the fire was welcome in the chill of the big house. There must be servants somewhere, off in the kitchens at least, but the place felt empty and cold. She stretched out her hands to the blaze, working the stiffness out of her muscles, for she was unused to hard, fast riding and now it seemed that she ached all over.

Dear God, let Luis come at once! She had no way of knowing how long Joel would be detained in town, and it was entirely possible that if he explained the situation to Murphy Kendrick the man would set aside any business that was not extremely pressing, and organize a vigilante group of his own. She could not suppress her imagination, could not help picturing the men galloping toward Shute's cabin, waving torches that would be used to set off the shingled roof. She could even see Shute's powerful figure standing in the doorway as the cabin blazed around him, probably with a rifle that he would be firing at any of the men he could bring within his sights.

"Señora."

Jessie spun, her skirts swirling dangerously close to the fire.

"I have brought food, and tea. I remember that the señora likes tea."

"Thank you," Jessie said, trying for a smile she could not quite manage. "Nothing to eat, thank you, but yes, I'd like the tea."

"Manuel believes that el patrón is on his way in now; he will meet him to assure that he comes quickly." The woman's eyes were bright with curiosity, yet she asked no questions. "Please be comfortable, señora, and rest until he comes."

Rest. Yes, she needed rest, but how could she? When her heart hammered in her chest, when fear turned her icy, when she did not know what would happen?

At the sound of Luis's steps on the tiled floor of the passageway, Jessie put down her cup and raced toward the doorway. She nearly collided with him there, and for a moment his arms came around her in a steadying embrace before he stepped back to see into her face.

"Jessie! What is it?"

"Oh, Luis, thank God you've come home! I need your help, and at once! Please, come with me, and I'll explain as we ride!"

He did not move. "It would be better, I think, if I know before we start what it is we ride to, *querida*." The endearment slipped out so naturally that neither of them took note of it. "I have the feeling that I should be prepared for whatever it is, and preparations must be made before we ride."

It spilled out of her then, in words that she struggled to keep coherent. Her daughter's involvement with a man Joel had taken a dislike to, the cabin built on land Joel had intended to claim for his own, and then finding proof that Rosalie had been there with Sam Shute.

It was almost unthinkable to relate the story to this man who was not really a member of the family, yet she knew she must, for all that the words were reluctant to leave her tongue.

"He found—garments—of Rosalie's. She had obviously..." Jessie sought for a way to say it so that it would not sound so bad, and did not find it, so brought the matter out in bald and ugly terms. "She had been in bed with him. Joel is furious, of course, and—"

"Any father would be furious," Luis agreed, and the steely glint in his eyes was disconcerting. "A man of honor does not do this with a gently bred female."

"What is this thing men have," Jessie cried out, "that makes them want to protect a woman from every man but themselves? For the love of God, don't take Joel's side in this! I need your help, Luis! I need someone capable of stopping Joel from doing whatever terrible thing he intends to do! He said if he's lucky he'll burn down Shute's cabin with him in it, and I think he's planning to do just that! If he hadn't been called to Kendrick's for something important, he'd be doing it right now!"

"You don't feel that your husband has a right to protect the honor of his family, of his daughter?"

"I don't defend my daughter for sleeping with someone she's not married to," Jessie said swiftly, "but a great many women have done that, and a great many men, and it's not an offense for which they should be murdered. It will be

445

murder in the eyes of the law, Luis, and I don't want Joel charged with murder!"

"It is most unlikely that any jury would so convict him, under the circumstances," Luis pointed out, and Jessie wanted to pound on his chest to make him understand.

This was not going at all the way she had imagined it. Luis was no white knight charging to her rescue; from his expression and his tone of voice, it would be no wonder if he joined the vigilantes.

"That isn't the point! He would still have a murder on his conscience, and when he comes to his senses he'll realize that it's the wrong way to handle this! And it will destroy Rosalie, she loves the man! Besides that," she marshaled her final argument in desperation because there was no yielding in his face, "Sam Shute isn't going to stand there and let them burn his house, with or without an attempt to kill him, too! He has a rifle, I saw it, and he's going to kill somebody if he can! Joel will be right up front, and what if Sam shoots him? I can't take that chance, Luis, I have to stop it! Only I can't do it alone, I need help! Just come and keep Joel—and anyone else he brings back from town with him—from doing some dreadful thing that we'll have to live with and be sorry about for the rest of our lives! Come so that Sam doesn't kill Joel to protect his property!"

She had not intended to cry. Indeed, the tears that gathered and began to spill over were of rage, a rage directed as much at Luis now as at Joel, more than they were of fear.

Yet it was the tears that swayed him.

"All right. All right, *querida,* do not weep. I will see if I can stop the carnage, though I do not guarantee that I can do what you ask. Your husband is filled with righteous indignation over the dishonor done his daughter, and like any father feels that he must be avenged. However, it is true that sometimes vengeance is a bittersweet thing, and that it might be best if it is stopped short of murder. I think, if there is the possibility that some of Kendrick's friends may accompany Joel, that it would be wise to take some of my men with me."

Jessie sagged in relief, the tears welling anew. "Thank you, Luis. I'll never forget this, never."

And then, without having the least idea how it happened, Jessie was in his arms. Perhaps he had reached for her, to comfort her; perhaps she had leaned into him for simple physical support.

All she knew was that suddenly Luis was cradling her

446

against his shoulder, murmuring endearments, stroking her head. "Ah, *amada*, there is no time for this now. Come, dry your eyes, and I will call out some of my men to ride with us."

Even in her own agitated state, Jessie heard the ragged emotion in Luis's voice. The touch had meant something to him, too much, she realized in a burst of clarity. Luis's sympathies were with Joel, but he was willing to do what she asked for *her* sake.

Because he loved her.

He left her there before the fire, shivering with something that was not cold. She had known for years that Luis was strongly attracted to her; there had been times when she had been uneasy, uncomfortable, because of it. Yet she'd never faced the matter squarely, as she was doing now.

She had nothing to offer Luis. Nothing, Jessie thought numbly, except the friendship she had always offered him. If he came with her now, would he expect something more than that in the future?

No, of course not. He knew that she loved Joel. Her love for Joel was one of the reasons she was here. And Luis was a man of honor.

There was a constraint between them that had not been there earlier as they went out into the dusk. Luis had betrayed more than he'd intended, and he knew that she was fully aware of it.

A dozen men, shadowy figures on horseback, hovered at a respectful distance as Luis put her into the saddle, then mounted his own horse. "Come," he said over his shoulder, and they began to move.

Jessie forgot, for a time, those moments in Luis's embrace. She must concentrate on only one thing, and she must not hold up these men who might be able to prevent the disintegration of her entire family. She rode with grim determination, ignoring the discomfort of the too-fast pace, continuing her prayers that they would not arrive too late.

51

They clattered into the yard in full darkness, finding their way from the road by the lights that shone from the windows facing the river. Mrs. Sullivan came to the front door, her ample figure nearly filling the lighted rectangle, wiping her hands on her apron.

"Lord save us, who is it now? Oh, Miss Jessie, praise the Lord! I'd begun to think the entire world's gone mad! Miss Teresa crying her eyes out and not saying a blessed word except how it's her fault, and Miss Rosalie nowhere to be found, and then Mr. Joel coming in with all those men—"

Jessie's heart sank under the barrage of words.

"—and asking for Mr. Tris, and him not here, neither, though he showed up right after the others had left, and he's gone again now—and everybody in such a tearing hurry— what is it, ma'am?" Mrs. Sullivan peered through the darkness at the men and horses. "Is it Señor Sañudo with you? Why won't nobody tell me what's going on?"

Jessie did not dismount. She was freezing; she'd left here in afternoon warmth without thought of a wrap, and now it was dark and the temperature had dropped twenty degrees, yet she did not dare run inside for a cloak.

"How many men were there with Joel, Mrs. Sullivan?"

"Oh, dozen or more. They didn't come inside, except for Mr. Joel and Mr. Laurie, so I didn't count 'em."

"How long have they been gone?" Luis asked, leaning forward so that his saddle creaked under his shifting weight.

"Oh, no more'n a quarter of an hour, I should say. Mr. Tris has been gone maybe ten minutes or less. Can't say as I looked at a clock. Miss Jessie, aren't you going to come inside?"

"Yes," Luis said at once, "stay here, Jessie. We'll take care of it."

"No," Jessie objected, just as firmly. "I'm going with you. I can't wait here crying with Teresa Dolores, wondering what's happening. Come on, they have a fifteen-minute head start on us. There's no time to waste."

She wheeled her horse, and was gratified that Luis made no further protest. Hooves thundered over the ground as the small band headed toward the cliff road, and Sam Shute's small cabin.

They had spent the day in the hills, first riding, then walking. Walking was better, Rosalie thought, because then they could hold hands. They could stop to look out over the panoramic valley below with its greening fields and scattered chimneys etching smoke against the sky. And when they stopped, Sam would take her in his arms and kiss her, his big hands gentle yet compelling, warming her with his smile as well as with his own body heat.

She had not dared pack a lunch at home for fear of comment—Mrs. Sullivan would have known at once that such a quantity was intended for more than two young girls—and so Sam had brought it; a simple yet filling meal of his own cornbread and cold venison and a dried-apple pie Rosalie had baked at his place the previous day.

She felt at home in Sam's cabin. She felt comfortable and beloved in Sam's presence. The urge to touch him was strong, so that she did not resist it for long at a time.

They returned to the cabin at dusk. The sun was blooded on the western horizon, casting a pinkish light over everything, and Rosalie felt a surge of love for this land in which she'd been born and grown up, a love intensified by what she now felt for this man beside her.

As Rosalie slid off her mare into Sam's arms, he held her for a kiss. And then he said, in the most sober tone he'd used all day, "What are we going to do about us, Rosalie Shand?"

Her breath was suspended. "What do you want to do about us, Sam?"

"I want to marry you," Sam told her. "Only I don't get the idea that your pa is going to cotton to that idea. Will your mama back us up?"

The happiness that had risen in bubbles, like champagne in her blood, began to dissipate a little, too soon. "Yes. Only I don't know if even she can win him over, if he's dug in his heels. Not right away, I mean. He's awfully particular on my behalf; he doesn't think anybody's good enough for me."

449

"They aren't," Sam admitted. "Not even me. But that doesn't stop me wanting you."

Rosalie's smile flashed. "He's always given me whatever I wanted, except for allowing me to swim naked with my brothers after I was about eight years old; it was just a matter of waiting him out and letting him see my woeful face from time to time. He never could resist that, or tears. I try to save tears for a last resort."

He regarded her with speculation. "Is that what you intend to use to manipulate me, too?"

"I don't know. I hadn't decided, yet." Rosalie's mouth curled at the corners, provocatively. "I'll have to see what works, I suppose."

"Honesty and anger, probably. I never liked the artifice my own mama used on my pa—she could turn on the tears the way you'd open a window for fresh air, and turn them off when her purpose was served. I'd rather see you fight for what you want than shed false tears."

"I'm like Mama in that, I think. Sometimes she cries when she's furiously angry and nothing else she does is helping matters. If I cry, it won't be to manipulate you, Sam. It will be because I'm hurt, or because I'm so angry I can't help crying in rage."

"Well, let's leave that to investigate later. For right now, I think we'd better plan to go to your father and tell him we want to get married."

Rosalie shivered, all amusement gone. "He may react violently, Sam. He's so . . . so old-fashioned, so prudish, where I'm concerned. It might help to tell Mama first, and let her tell him."

"That isn't the way I want to do it. I suspect he'd think me less a man if I didn't walk up to him and tell him, face to face, that I want you. We can tell her at the same time; she already knows anyway, I'd bet. We'd better do it soon, Rosie. Maybe we should go over and tell him yet tonight."

"Oh, no, Sam, not tonight! Today has been such a perfect day, I don't want anything to spoil it!"

He bent to kiss her again, on the nose, this time. "It was perfect for me, too. The only thing that would be more perfect would be to know you're my wife, and that you wouldn't have to go home tonight at all. Come on, it's getting cold. Let's build up the fire and see if those beans we left in the kettle are ready to eat. Then we'll decide what we're going to do."

The savory aroma of ham and beans permeated the cabin

when they entered, and though the fire had dwindled to no more than a few glowing coals there was retained warmth, too, that was welcome. While Sam poked the fire into renewed life, Rosalie lit a pair of candles to set upon the table, and was reaching for plates from the open-fronted shelves when Sam spoke sharply.

"Somebody's been here."

Rosalie spun, heart lurching within her. "How do you know?"

"You dropped this on the bed." He lifted a wispy petticoat she'd left off deliberately, which was now draped over the back of a chair. "I remember seeing it there, on the bed. And your scarf—" His gaze had ranged the room and fixed upon the bit of scarlet silk she had worn at her throat when she came. "It was on the floor, beside the door. I noticed that, too, and meant to pick it up, and then you called me and I forgot it—"

Rosalie, ravenous only moments earlier, felt sick at her stomach. "Who?" she wondered aloud.

"Somebody who took note of your things," Sam said. "They didn't take them, but they picked them up and then dropped them again. Maybe somebody who recognized the scarf, anyway."

Not Pa, Rosalie prayed numbly. Please, not Pa.

A moment later, they heard the hoofbeats of the night riders.

Jessie heard Luis grunt when they topped the next-to-the-last slope, and she knew at once why. There was a faint luminosity beyond that final hill, a glow that could only come from fire.

Oh, God, not too late! she begged, and dug her heels into the horse's flanks, urging him over the crest of the hill at a full gallop. A dozen riders were silhouetted against the flames, but to her intense relief it was not the cabin that blazed, only the haystack beyond it. Even as Luis and his band thundered toward the hellish scene, however, one of the night riders threw a burning stick that landed on the threshold of the small house.

Jessie cried out in protest, and saw Sam Shute, in the doorway, pick up the stick and hurl it back with a bellowed defiance. It was only too clear that the newcomers had arrived barely in the nick of time if they were to stop a total conflagration, and Jessie was by no means sure they could do it.

451

She rode with Luis and his men right into the thick of the night riders, wishing she had a gun or even a whip, to lash out at the masked faces round her.

They had not expected company; several of them wheeled and retreated at once, to hover uncertainly on the edges of activity. Joel, however, easily recognizable because of both his size and his horse, did not retreat at all. He jerked off the bandanna that had covered his face and yelled toward Luis, "Get out of here! This is none of your business, Luis!"

"It's mine," Jessie cried, and forced her own mount between two others whose riders had simply come to a halt between her and Joel. Fortunately they did not try to prevent her passage, and within seconds she was knee to knee with her husband, white face blazing almost as hotly as the haystack. "Stop it, Joel! Stop this at once!"

He was as furious with her as he was with Sam Shute. "Go home where you belong! Luis, get her the hell out of here!"

"You have reason to be angry, my friend," Luis told him in a carrying voice, "but this is a time to reconsider the matter, before you have done something which can never be undone. Your wife does not want you to become a murderer, and she is right. There are other means to deal with transgressors."

Joel's words were savage. "He seduced my daughter, and no court is going to convict me of murder. Damn it to hell, get out of my way! Fire the house, men!" The last was a bellow that carried clearly to the others over the sounds of restless horses and the crackle of burning hay, which was rapidly being consumed.

Jessie cast a frightened glance toward the house and saw that this time Sam Shute held his rifle in a position to fire it, and that there was a shadowy figure behind him in the open doorway.

Her throat constricted in panic. "Joel, Rosalie's in there! Tell them to stop! Joel, for the love of God!"

She wasn't sure he even heard her. "He can't shoot us all at once," Joel yelled, waving an arm to bring his men in closer again. "Fire the goddamned house! Run him out of there!"

Sam fired. The bullet spat into the ground before them, and the horses reared, backing, so that Jessie struggled with all her strength to control her own animal. Sam's howl lifted the hair off the back of her neck, and she dared to turn her head as the mare came down once more on all four feet.

"I'll kill the first man reaches for a gun or a torch," Sam declared. "You damned Yankees burned one house out from under me, but you'll pay as much as I do if you set fire to this one!"

Again a shot ripped the night, but this time it wasn't Sam's, nor Joel's. It was Luis.

"Señores! That was only to gain your attention, but the next shot will be on behalf of law and order! I did not come here to witness a murder, nor to countenance one! I suggest that you all go home, unless you intend to take on me and my men in addition to Señor Shute!"

Jessie did not know how she continued to breathe, for her chest ached as badly as her arms did after pulling so hard on the reins, and she was dizzy from sheer fright. Luis rose in the saddle, as always an imposing figure with his silver-embroidered hat and vest, so that all could see him. There was still enough light from the dying fire and two remaining torches to show the strong planes of a determined face, cold and set.

Jessie did not doubt that he intended to shoot anyone who moved to throw one of those torches, or to reach for a weapon. Even Joel, she thought in an icy paralysis. Luis would shoot Joel, though not to kill him.

There was a muttering throughout the ranks of the masked men. They had tied concealing bandannas over their faces, but a man's horse was as easily identified as its rider, and there was no disguising the horses. Coming here to run off this interloper, as a favor to Joel Shand, had seemed a lark to most of them. They had Shand's assurance that no one would ever see them, and they hadn't anticipated *killing* anybody, just burning the fellow's cabin and his barn.

Caught up in a frenzy of excitement, they might have gone along with Joel once they got there, had not this horde of Mexicans—and Joel's own wife—shown up to interfere.

The arrival of outsiders, witnesses, put an entirely different light on the matter. It was one thing for Shand to avenge his daughter's dishonor; it would be quite another if they were hauled into a courtroom and asked for an accounting of their actions, identified by Mrs. Shand and that Sañudo fellow. Everyone knew Luis Sañudo by reputation; he was, as his own people put it, one tough *hombre*.

Not a man there doubted that Luis would shoot to kill. He

had, after all, dispatched several different bands of brigands in the past, for which deaths no penalties had been imposed by the authorities. And behind him, silent yet with rifles at the ready, were a dozen men to match their own numbers.

For a moment there were no sounds but the whinny of a horse and a strangled cough. And then one of Joel's followers wheeled his horse and galloped off into the night; within seconds, the others followed, so that except for a single torch burning on the ground and the few scarlet embers in the haystack, they were left in darkness.

Sam Shute still stood in his doorway, lighted from behind by candle glow, with Rosalie beside him, clinging to his arm, her face white and terrified. Slowly, now, he lowered his rifle, then set it aside. His voice was clear and strong; if he, too, had been terrified, it did not show in his voice.

"We were coming tonight to tell you we wanted to be married," he said. "I intended no dishonor to your daughter, Mr. Shand."

Beside her, Jessie heard Luis clear his throat. "I do not think we are needed here any longer." And then, when Joel swore, Luis added, "I believe you will eventually forgive my interference, *amigo*. And even if you do not, I will have done what my conscience dictated that I do. *Buenas noches, señor y señora.*"

Jessie saw his face, not smiling, just before the torch on the ground flickered and went out. She reached for his sleeve, only brushing it with her fingertips as he wheeled away. "Thank you, Luis! Thank you!"

"*De nada, señora,*" he responded, and then he was gone, leaving Joel and Jessie and one other figure, a rider who eased his mount forward and spoke before Jessie realized who he was.

"Tris is out there somewhere," Laurie said, "on foot. His horse went into a hole at full gallop and broke a leg, and I didn't wait for him. I'd better go find him now, though. I'll see you at home."

Joel did not reply, and Jessie could not, either. She was glad Tris hadn't arrived to see the dreadful scene his father had created, the ugliness of it. She scarcely was aware of Laurie's departure; she ached all over, trembled with weariness, and knew that it was not yet time to allow herself the release of tears.

Her voice wavered in spite of her best efforts. "Rosalie, I think you'd better come home with us now."

Rosalie had had a few minutes to gather her own resources, and her words were loud in the night stillness. "I don't care if I never go home again, Mama. I belong here with Sam. I'm going to marry him, no matter what anyone says. And if Pa hates him enough to try again to burn him out, he'll have to burn me out, too."

"You'll do as you're told," Joel said harshly, his anger thwarted yet undiminished. "You can't marry anyone without my permission, and you don't have it. If I have to keep you locked in your room for the next year, I'll—"

"No," Jessie interrupted, cutting through the tirade, "she won't be locked up. And no more burnings will take place, either. Come home, Rosie. You don't belong here yet. If there is to be a wedding, it will be a civilized one, at our own house, in the midst of your family."

"Jessie, mind your place! This is my decision, and I won't have my daughter married to a good-for-nothing Confederate bastard—"

"Rosalie's my daughter as much as she's yours," Jessie reminded, and though there was no longer any heat in the words they were strong and firm. "I intend that she stay my daughter, and she and her husband will always be welcome in my house."

"It's my house, too," Joel reminded her grimly. "And if she marries that damned Confederate—"

"The war's over and done; which side he was on has nothiing to do with this—"

"Neither of them will be welcome in my house, ever," Joel finished, unable to temper his emotion.

Explosive words trembled on Jessie's lips; it was almost more than she could do to hold them back. Not now, she thought, not when Joel was in this mood. Wait until he was more receptive to reason. She swallowed hard and turned again to Rosalie.

"Come home now, Rosie. Mr. Shute can come over tomorrow, and we'll talk about it then."

For seconds Rosalie stood there, unmoved and unmoving, and Jessie was afraid they might have lost the girl forever. And then Sam put a hand on Rosalie's shoulder and nudged her forward.

"Go with your mama, girl." He stepped into the night, lifting his face to Jessie's. "If Rosie's half the woman her mama is," he said, "I'll be a lucky man, ma'am."

"You'll be along tomorrow," Jessie said, and it was not a question. "Around noon, perhaps?"

"Noon would suit me fine," Sam Shute told her gravely.

She knew he stood there, watching, as Rosalie mounted her own horse, which had been turned into the corral and needed calming before it would allow anyone near it. She could not see Joel's face now, for the only remaining light was inside Sam's cabin. As they rode away Jessie felt no triumph. She was a quaking jelly inside, for though she had prevented one catastrophe, there was no sign that all the family problems were solved.

They rode silently through the night, Joel ahead of the others, unspeaking. Rosalie put enough space between herself and her mother so that Jessie could not communicate with her, which was perhaps just as well; Jessie didn't know what to say that would not make matters worse than they already were.

Half a mile from Sam Shute's cabin, they encountered Tristan and Laurie.

Joel thundered on past, ignoring them, but Rosalie and Jessie reined in at the sound of voices and the horses whinnied a greeting; Rosalie's mount shied and danced sideways, until Tris reached up for the bridle and spoke a few soothing words.

"She smells the blood," he said, and even in her present state Jessie heard the pain in his voice. "I had to shoot him. He'd broken a leg."

He'd had the gelding since he was a young boy. Jessie leaned forward in the darkness, although she could see no better at closer range, and put a hand on her son's shoulder. "Oh, Tris, I'm sorry, darling."

"I'm sorry, too. I didn't get there in time to do anybody any good. Rosie, you all right?"

"Yes," Rosalie said shortly.

"Good. Don't wait for us, Ma. Go on ahead. We're going to have to ride double on Dusty, and we're really too heavy for him, so we'll go slow and I'll walk part of the way."

Laurie's voice came out of the blackness. "Maybe the smart thing would be for me to ride home and bring back another horse. Did you see that stallion Uncle Joel has in the corral? Magnificent beast, big black powerful creature—"

"You were told to stay away from that horse," Jessie said, sounding sharp. "Here, take my mare, Tris. Rosalie's can carry the two of us."

It was so decided, though Jessie sensed Rosalie's unvoiced

sentment. She doesn't want to be close to me, to anyone,
ght now, Jessie thought. Yet after Tris had boosted her up
hind her daughter, Rosalie made no protest but urged the
rse on toward home.

Rosalie's body was warm and pliant against her own, and
ssie felt an overwhelming surge of love and compassion as
e put her arms around Rosie's waist. She was so young, so
grant, and so in love that she would defend her relationship
th Sam fiercely even to the point of foolishness.

Yet perhaps, Jessie prayed, she had opened a way for Ros-
e's eventual happiness, after the worst of this episode had
d down.

52

If everyone else had spent as restless a night as she had,
ssie thought wearily, none of them was in the best condition
discuss anything.

Her eyes burned and she felt as if she'd walked for miles,
climbed a high hill that left her short of breath and dry-
outhed in fatigue. Had she been a drinking person, she
uld have fortified herself for the upcoming ordeal; in a way
e envied Joel, for that was precisely what he was doing.
e'd never seen him pour brandy in the morning before,
ich he did as they awaited the arrival of the principals in
e matter.

Rosalie had not yet come downstairs, though she was or-
narily up early. Teresa Dolores appeared at the breakfast
ble, eyes downcast and lids swollen from yesterday's weep-
g. She drank only a cup of coffee and picked at the hotcakes
rs. Sullivan brought to her.

Joel had eaten his customary hearty meal across the table
m her, but he'd scarcely spoken to Jessie since they'd
rted in anger at the site of the near-massacre.

He had reached home ahead of the others, and he'd pre-

tended to be asleep when Jessie slipped into bed beside him.
That was all right; she didn't know what to say to him anyway.

Mrs. Sullivan did not quite understand what was taking place. She asked no questions, however, instead plying them all with maple syrup for their hotcakes, refilling coffee cups, fluttering about the kitchen in a manner revealing her agitation at this lack of harmony in her family.

Once Joel had finished and gone outside, Jessie forced herself to clean up her plate, though the food was making her queasy. She wondered if it would be safer to throw up now or chance doing it later, in the midst of the discussion yet to come.

They would sit in the parlor, she decided, and went there to make the place ready, to be sure that everything was dusted and that there was a fire, for though the day promised sunny warmth, the house itself was chill.

Or maybe it was only within herself, Jessie thought. She felt so cold, and so frightened, because what she said and did after Sam Shute got here, might be the most important thing she would ever be called upon to do. Important to Rosalie's happiness, and important to her own.

The Bible lay on its own stand, and Jessie hesitated beside it, then opened its heavy leather cover to turn the pages slowly until she came to the ones where the family statistics were written in her own fine hand.

Tears blurred her vision so that she could not read, but she didn't have to see to know what was there.

It was her mother's Bible, and it chronicled the lives of the members of her family from the time of her parents' wedding. Marriages, births, deaths, all compressed onto two pages.

Her mother, her father, and her sister Audra, all gone. Jessie was nearly as old now as her mother had been when she died. But Rosalie was young, and Rosalie deserved her own chance at happiness.

Jessie blinked away the moisture and saw the written names. Joel and Jessie, married so long ago. What happened to them, the people she and Joel had been all those years back?

She didn't feel changed, in many ways, yet Joel had changed so much from the boy she remembered. He had always harbored hostility toward the man who sired him, but he'd been a good son to Leona Shand; he'd cared for her to the best of his ability, and grieved when she was gone. He'd

458

ved Jessie so passionately, had promised her everything
at his rich and hateful grandmother had had—and he'd
livered on that, hadn't he? This big house, a reasonable
nount of prestige, though there were still those who did not
d the Joel Shands socially acceptable because of his ille-
timate birth.

That continued to hurt him, she knew. He had never told
r that he'd wanted to run for public office and that he'd
en persuaded not to so humiliate himself, but Jessie knew.
ere had been small signs, a few unguarded words. That
ntinued to rankle, too.

Perhaps a person never escaped the scars that were in-
cted at an early age. Perhaps there was always hurt, of one
nd or another, for almost everybody, as they went through
e.

Tris and Laurie, she thought, loving the same girl. Rosalie,
anting a man her father could not accept. Joel, loving his
fe but unable to settle for what she could give him, the
fe who could not bear more children but who conceived so
adily that her life had been for years a series of bloody
scarriages. He had loved her, she was sure of that, but
ere had been so much pain mingled with the loving.

Her whispered words hung in the silent room. "Why, God?
hy does living have to hurt so much?"

There was, of course, no answer. She closed the Bible and
oved to straighten the cushions on the settee and to put
other stick on the fire.

She was as ready as she could be, and she was not ready
all. Not ready for a further confrontation with her husband,
no had become a man driven by his own inner compulsions
d conflicts, whose needs and desires she knew herself to
inadequate to fill. The Joel she had fallen in love with
nen she was a girl would never have become a night rider,
igilante, willing to burn down a man's house and the man
th it because of a personal grudge.

Rosalie had been foolish, both in going to Sam Shute and
being careless enough to leave her belongings so that her
her would know she had slept with the man. But it was
e sort of foolishness women are prone to when they fall in
re. There had been no malice in it, no true wickedness.

Burning a man's house, and not caring if the man was
stroyed as well, was evil. Yet if she had not arrived in time,
she had not persuaded Luis to back her up with a dozen

men, Joel might very well have accomplished that terrib[l]
thing.

She had lived with Joel, and loved him, for twenty year[s].
Yet she felt that she did not know him at all.

She turned toward the doorway when she heard his step[s]
and he came into the room still in his work clothes, not prepared to receive a visitor.

The words rose in her throat, *Aren't you going to change[?]*
And then Jessie stifled them. No, this was a deliberate thing.
His clothing denoted his contempt for Sam Shute, and bringing up the matter now would only give them one more thing
to disagree on.

His face was ugly. His gaze slid to the clock on the mantel
which showed a quarter of twelve.

"I think it's time we talked about this, Jessie," he said.

She refrained from pointing out that she'd have been
happy to discuss the situation anytime since midnight la[st]
night. "I think so, too," she agreed. "Mr. Shute will be her[e]
soon."

"I don't want Rosalie to marry him," Joel said. There wa[s]
aggressiveness in his voice and in his stance, feet wide[ly]
planted on the best carpet. "He's not good enough for he[r]
and she'll get over him, eventually."

"The way I got over you?" Jessie asked. Her heart wa[s]
leaping in her chest, and again she resisted the urge to d[o]
what came naturally, to press her hands over the spot wher[e]
the pounding threatened her ability to breathe. "Joel, pleas[e.]
Please, think just of Rosie. Think of what she wants an[d]
needs."

"She doesn't need to be married to a man like Sam Shut[e.]
Someday she'll thank us, that we didn't let her do it."

"I don't think so," Jessie purposely pitched her voice lo[w,]
partly so as not to announce all their business to Mrs. Su[l]-
livan in the kitchen, and partly as a matter of control, becaus[e]
if she allowed her voice to rise, she was afraid she would star[t]
to scream. "We've all joked about it, Joel, the way you haven['t]
considered anyone worthy of Rosie, but it hasn't really bee[n]
amusing. It's been tragic. There's nothing wrong with Sa[m]
Shute, nor with Rosie for wanting him. It's you who's wron[g,]
who won't see that they are adults and that they have a righ[t]
to the same happiness that you and I sought for so long befo[re]
we were able to marry. It's almost as if—"

Jessie stopped, appalled at what she had been about t[o]
say.

Joel's scowl deepened. "As if what? Go ahead, Jessie, this ems to be the day for clearing the air. As if what?"

She moistened her lips and spoke in an even lower voice, if she'd suddenly lost the strength to project the words cross the room. "As if you were jealous of the attentions any an pays your daughter. As if you want to keep her all for urself, forever."

Heat suffused his face, rising from the open neck of his old irt, flooding his countenance with angry color. "That's a tten thing to say, Jessie."

"Yes," she agreed slowly. "It sounds terrible. But I think 's true, Joel. It isn't Rosie's happiness you're thinking about, 's your own. I know you love her, but I don't think it's a ealthy kind of love. It's almost...incestuous."

For a moment she thought he would strike her. The color as gone now, and he was deathly white beneath the tanned kin. "I've never hit you, Jessie, but by God, I'm thinking out it this minute."

She didn't move except to steady herself on the little table at held the Bible. "Will it make you feel any better to do at? I don't mean you've ever touched Rosie in...in a carnal ay, or that you ever would, but you're nearly insane with alousy at the thought that another man might do so."

"He already has! I found the goddamned evidence plain ough—Rosie's scarf, she was the woman who was there, d there'd sure as hell been a woman in his bed!"

"If she was there, she went willingly. The same as I went you, Joel, when you begged me to. You gave me your other's wedding ring, but it didn't really mean anything; e were committing a sin just as surely as Rosie and Sam ve done, and my stepfather would have killed you and rhaps me, as well, if he'd known. And he had no love for e at all! For the love of God, Joel, think! If you really care out her, let her do what she wants to do!"

In the ensuing silence, while his eyes blazed at her in what emed almost hatred, Jessie heard her own breathing and s, raspy and ragged. And then Joel drew in a deep breath d turned on his heel to leave her there.

"Joel." She let the words rise now, to make sure he heard he began to walk away. "Wait. Wait."

He paused, though his expression was hardly one to en- urage her further attempts.

"Joel," she said, and now there was a quaver in her voice, intensity that made her throat ache. "There have been

very few times that I have pitted myself against you, or trul;
crossed you, but in this thing I must. If you destroy Rosalie
you'll destroy me, and perhaps yourself, too. You'll certainl;
destroy *us*, and everything we've ever had together will b
gone. Because if you deprive her of this, the most importan
thing she's ever wanted, you're going to split this family wide
apart." Her mouth was dry, her chest hurt, and she went on

Her hand slid over the cover of the Bible and stopped. "]
you do this, Joel, I swear on this Holy Bible that I will neve
be a wife to you again, in any sense of the word."

The terrible words were out, hanging almost palpably i
the air between them. For a moment she thought they ha
been in vain, for Joel stared at her as if he wanted to throttl
her.

And then she saw realization work its way through him
conviction that this last desperate threat was not an empt;
one. He knew the store she set on the Bible; he knew sh
would never have carelessly sworn anything on it.

His wide mouth twisted in a grimace that could have beei
scorn, or pain. "Blackmail, Jessie?"

"Call it anything you like. I only know that I cannot bea
for you to continue on this terrible path. I cannot love you
or be your wife if you persist in your determination to destro;
our daughter. It will destroy us all."

He did not reply, but his answer was there in the fain
relenting of his frown, in the barely perceptible tremor in hi
lips. He turned and walked away, and she knew that she ha
won.

She was close to collapsing. She was soaked in cold sweat
she could smell the acrid tang of it on her skin, and she wa
trembling. She lifted her hand from the Bible and allowe
herself, now that it was over, the luxury of pressing agains
the tumult in her chest.

She'd have to wash and change her clothes, she thought
before Sam Shute arrived. She couldn't greet a guest lik
this, smelling as if she'd spent the night with a herd of goats

She met Rosalie in the passageway, coming from th
kitchen. When had the girl come down? Jessie hadn't hear
or seen her pass. Had she overheard the words between he
parents?

Rosalie was pale, though there was a spot of color in eac
cheek. She reached for Jessie's hand, not seeming to notic
that it was both cold and damp with perspiration.

"Mama? Did you talk him into it? He just brushed by me

nd stalked out of the house, but he said...I asked if Sam
as here yet, and he said...that you could take care of it,
alking to Sam and me."

Her face was so hopeful, so dear. Jessie wanted to cry,
hough she could not have said exactly why. She squeezed
Rosie's hand.

"Yes, I'll talk to you. Isn't that a rider coming now? Take
him into the parlor, by the fire, and offer him a glass of your
ather's brandy, if he wants it. I must change my dress, I'll
e down in a few minutes."

Joy rose and overflowed in Rosalie's choked cry. She
ropped her mother's hand and hugged her, instead. "Oh,
Mama, thank you! Thank you!"

She broke away then, and sped to the front door to greet
er lover. Jessie heard their voices behind her as she climbed
he stairs, young, happy voices.

Rosalie would have her Sam, thought Jessie. She wondered
vhat she herself would have, if her own marriage would ever
again be what it once had been. But if she'd had it to do over,
he knew she would do the same thing.

By the time she joined the young people in the parlor ten
minutes later, she had composed herself, at least outwardly.
Only inside was she still hurt, confused, and frightened. For
he had gambled with her own life, and she still didn't know,
on that score, whether she'd won or lost.

53

The wedding was to be held the first of June.

If there were those who knew that the bride and groom
had anticipated their marriage lines by a month or so, the
Shands heard no murmur of their disapproval. Perhaps, Jessie hoped, the men who had been involved in the vigilante
action were sufficiently ashamed of themselves, or leery of
legal repercussions, so that they would remain silent.

Though Joel continued to share her bed, he did not turn to Jessie in the darkness. She could not quite bring herself to stretch out a hand to touch him, unbidden, because his rejection then would be worse than the way he ignored her now.

Not that he maintained a sullen silence, after that first day. He sat across the table from her and made the customary dinner-time conversation. As usual he read aloud to the family bits from the various newspapers he subscribed to. He made the necessary decisions pertaining to the upcoming celebration, the ones the women hadn't already made, such as the quantity and variety of beverages to be made available for the guests, and the construction of a bower to be decorated with flowers where the ceremony would take place.

Rosie was so radiant that it would have been easy to overlook the lack of joy in Tristan's face. Jessie saw, and bled for him, but there was nothing she could do. If only Laurie didn't feel the need to talk about Melissa Kendrick so much, if only he would constrain some of that enthusiasm about the girl when Tris was around!

On the eve of the wedding, Tris looked up from morose contemplation of a newspaper he did not even see to find Laurie standing in his doorway, obviously on his way out.

"New coat?" Tris asked, trying to sound normal.

"Yes, I picked it up this afternoon. Handsome, isn't it? I thought I'd ought to look my best tonight." His grin flashed. "Melissa's too sensible a girl to be influenced by a man's clothes, but when he's about to propose, a fellow wants to feel top-drawer."

Tris swallowed audibly before he could stop himself. He hoped he'd not revealed his shock at Laurie's words, though why he should feel shock he didn't know. Laurie had talked about nothing and no one but Melissa from the night he'd met her, so it shouldn't come as a surprise that he intended to ask her to marry him.

He ought to be saying something, but he couldn't for the life of him think of anything that wouldn't reveal his own anguish.

"Well, wish me luck," Laurie requested, after some seconds of silence had passed. "If she says yes, and you're still awake when I come home, what do you say we celebrate with some of that brandy Uncle Joel keeps locked in his desk?"

Luckily Laurie didn't seem to require a reply. Tris listened

464

o him running down the stairs, then struck a fist on the arm of his chair.

Damn him! Damn him to hell! Laurie had always had the best of everything, had taken it by force if he couldn't get it by guile, and at this moment Tristan hated him.

How would he stand it if Laurie married Melissa and brought her here to live?

He wouldn't do that, of course. Laurie had some money of his own, his share of the gold they'd found on Collie's claim, so he could support a wife even without a continuing share of the ranch income. He could afford a modest home of his own. Or maybe J. Murphy Kendrick would give his only daughter a house for a wedding present, to be certain she had as good as she was used to.

Would Melissa accept Laurie? Tris's head hurt, thinking about it. She'd never shown partiality to any of the young men who swarmed around her, but since Laurie was the most aggressive of the bunch, he'd most often been the one to dance with her, or bring her supper or punch at a party.

Why hadn't Tris proposed to her himself?

Because he'd been so sure she would turn him down, of course, and the thought of it nearly killed him. Then he'd know, once and for all, that she didn't care any more about *him* than she did about that pimply-faced young assistant of her father's, a young man recently hired to write Murphy's letters for him. She'd never said anything unkind about the young man, whose name was Thomas Bittenwort, but there had been an amused twinkle in her eye a few times when the unfortunate youth had virtually swooned over her. Melissa could do a great deal better than Thomas, even if she didn't have a rich and powerful father.

Like Laurie, he supposed. Laurie was good-looking, and quick-witted, and though he wasn't rich yet, he undoubtedly would be. He had some money in the bank, and because he worked the ranch he shared those earnings the same as Tristan did.

In his despair, thinking about Laurie proposing to Melissa—down on his knee? or standing over her—well, Laurie wasn't all that tall, but he was taller than Melissa, though she didn't have to crane her neck to look into his face when they talked, the way she did with Tris. What female wants to marry a man who'll give her a permanent crick in her neck? he wondered, despair deepening. Tristan knew that he'd never be able to eat a mouthful.

He hadn't replaced his own horse yet, but he had to escape the house and the company of those females planning his sister's wedding. He'd break down and cry right in front of them, he supposed.

He timed it so that only Mrs. Sullivan was in the kitchen when he passed through it. Mrs. Sullivan wouldn't argue about whether or not he would eat with the family. She stared after him, shaking her head, for she knew a heartsick young man when she saw one. Pity that Kendrick girl hadn't taken to him, the way he'd obviously been taken with her, the cook thought. She'd known both boys a long time, and while she liked them both, she thought there were plenty of other girls for Laurie to choose from, and only one that Tris had ever wanted.

Tris let the back door slam behind him and went down the steps. The weather promised to be perfect for Rosalie's wedding tomorrow. It would take place outdoors in the gardens where the roses and fruit trees (the latter unfortunately past the blooming stage, but still lushly green) would provide the ideal backdrop.

Sweet Christ, he thought, how would he endure it? Standing there watching the two of them, Rosalie and Sam Shute, with love and trust shining out of their faces, while he himself bled to death inside!

Nobody was going anywhere tonight, so it didn't matter which horse he took, he thought sourly. Laurie's was the only one missing, and of course there were a few utility horses, available to anyone.

The magnificent stallion Joel had bought a few months ago was in the near corral; Joel spent nearly all his spare time working with it, and it had gentled considerably, though Joel had cautioned them all away from the animal. It nickered now and thrust its head over the top rail, but Tris didn't have anything to feed it.

"Sorry, fella," he muttered.

He chose his mother's mare, a sweet-natured beast she called Daisy, and wished he had nerve enough to take the stallion. He didn't want some obedient creature he'd have to be careful with; he'd have welcomed a power struggle with the stallion, welcomed having to use his muscles and his wits to keep the horse from unseating him.

He rode for hours, out across the hills turning summer-brown. Acres and acres of land, and someday at least half of it would be his, but he knew he didn't want it. He understood

466

hat farming was the future of California, but he didn't want o farm. He could do more for farming if he could win a seat n the legislature, if he could do something to influence the construction of irrigation ditches and equitable tax laws for armers, and promote more railroads to take California products east to wider markets.

He knew that Joel would assist him financially if he sought public office. But he didn't want his father's help either. He wanted to gain his goals in his own way; he didn't want Joel to be able to smile and tell his cronies, like Melissa's father, that *he* had put his son into the legislature.

What he really wanted most, regardless of what happened to him elsewhere, was Melissa. And probably right this minute Laurie was asking her to marry him.

The pictures rose in his mind as he stared sightlessly out across the broad valley of the San Joaquin. Laurie and Melissa, smiling into each other's faces. Laurie, kissing her, kissing that soft, sweet mouth after which Tris had hungered for so long. Laurie, putting his arms around the girl, drawing those marvelous breasts against himself. Laurie, exploring that slender yet rounded body—the curving hips, the enticing belly, the secret places that even in imagination made Tristan wet with sweat, thinking about them.

Fatigue and darkness finally drove Tris home. There were lights in the house, but he saw no one when he entered through the kitchen. Food odors lingered, and he saw that the wedding cake, four tiers high, was completely decorated except for the real roses that would adorn its top, to be picked at the last minute, just before the guests arrived.

He wasn't hungry. He'd have liked a stiff shot of his father's brandy. He wasn't a drinker, though, and on an empty stomach such a drink would be disastrous. He would have welcomed oblivion, only he knew from sad experience that that wasn't what he'd get; he'd get sick, and throw up all over the place, and he'd still be able to think about Laurie and Melissa. God, would he have to endure this pain for the rest of his life, thinking about Laurie and Melissa?

His mother and the girls were in the back parlor; he could hear their voices, and he eased past the open doorway quietly, so they wouldn't notice him. There was no sign of Joel, for which he was grateful. His father would know from his face that he was miserable, but Joel wouldn't have any sympathy. His attitude would be the same as Laurie's, that a man didn't deserve any better in life than he was willing to take, to wrest away from someone else if that was the only way to get it.

Only Melissa wasn't an object, she was a woman with a mind of her own. A woman who could have any man she wanted. Even Rosie had managed that. Though Tris didn't see what was so special about Sam Shute, he liked him all right, and he wished his sister happiness. She'd had the courage to fight for Sam, and in the face of Joel's opposition, that had taken some courage.

What was it they had, Rosie and Laurie, that had been left out of himself? There had been a time when he'd almost have given his soul for Joel's approval, which both of the others had had all their lives. Now, he told himself, he didn't care what Joel thought. Damned if he'd grovel at Joel's feet for his approval or his attention.

He was in his room, lying in the darkness with hot, dry eyes, when he heard Laurie come home.

Tris didn't move.

It had to be Laurie's horse, because everyone else in the family had come up and gone to bed hours ago.

He waited, imagining his cousin—his half-brother—taking the saddle off the horse, rubbing it down, turning it into the corral. He had cramps in his stomach and wanted to roll over, to curl up and ease the misery, but he didn't move. The discomfort moved into his chest, affecting his breathing, and still he lay flat, hands beneath his head, waiting.

The footsteps were light on the stairs, then paused outside his own open doorway. Tris forced himself to breathe, though he couldn't do it normally. And then Laurie turned away, toward his own room, and Tris spoke quickly.

"That you, Laurie?" He couldn't let Laurie go to bed without learning, for certain, how bad the news was.

"Yeah. I thought you were asleep. God, how can you breathe in here? Why don't you open a window? It's really warm. I'm glad the wedding is early tomorrow, or we'd all wilt before it got started. Once the eating and drinking and dancing start, it won't matter so much."

"I hadn't noticed," Tris said, and it was true, though suddenly his room seemed stifling. "Open the window, why don't you?"

The wood squeaked a protest as he raised the sash, and then Laurie came back to stand beside the bed. He didn't need a light to know where the furniture was; the room was as familiar to him as his own. Tris caught the scent of brandy.

"Smells like you're already celebrating," Tris said, and wondered if he sounded as strangled to Laurie as he did to himself.

"What? Oh, the brandy. Something new—or I guess it's old—that J. Murphy had tonight. No, I'm not celebrating, you mean about Melissa? Hell, I didn't get two words alone with her tonight, though I tried like the very devil. The house was full of people, and her mother kept asking her to do things, and every time I'd think maybe we could have a private word or two, somebody would interrupt. How can you propose to a girl that way?"

Tris felt as if his body were collapsing inward on itself. Not relief, that would be unfounded, but at least...at least it hadn't happened, yet. Melissa hadn't said yes.

"I wish I'd taken you along," Laurie said. "You could have helped me, kept everybody away from us for a few minutes, long enough for me to ask her. Well, hell, the Kendricks will be here for the wedding tomorrow, and maybe that will seem more romantic, anyway. Being proposed to at a friend's wedding, I mean. Listen, Tris, I shouldn't have any trouble getting her alone tomorrow, since we'll have all day, but if I give you a signal, will you intercept whoever's keeping us from talking in private? Or stand guard if I manage to get her alone for a few minutes? In the barn or somewhere?"

In the soft summer darkness, Tristan went rigid. It was all he could do to keep from leaping up and throttling Laurie, actually putting his hands around Laurie's throat and squeezing the life out of him. His rage was so great that he shook with it; it even made the bed creak beneath him.

He came to a sitting position, hands balled into fists. A vision of Laurie and Melissa in the barn, in the hay—even though he knew perfectly well that wasn't what Laurie intended—blurred inside his head in a reddish haze.

"I'll just raise my eyebrow, the way we used to signal each other when we were kids," Laurie said, and Tristan wondered how it was possible that his own emotion was not palpable, that Laurie did not *feel* it. "We had some good times together, didn't we?" The timbre of his voice changed. "We haven't seen eye to eye on everything, but we've been brothers, Tris, whether the world knew it or not. I guess what I've always wanted more than anything else was for...him...to admit he was my father, not my uncle. Even if he only admitted it to *me*, and kept the secret from everybody else. Sometimes

469

I've almost hated you, because he's acknowledged you all along."

Tris never knew where his voice came from; he'd been convinced he could not speak. "You've always been his favorite, though. It was always you he took with him, you he admired because you were daring and wild. Even when he dressed you down, anybody could tell he was proud of you."

"Well, I hope he'll be prouder yet when I tell him Melissa's agreed to marry me. He wants family connections with the Kendricks. My God, is the clock striking three? I'd better get to bed, or I won't be fit to propose to anybody tomorrow, with the damned wedding set for eleven. See you in the morning, Tris."

Laurie was in the hallway before Tristan could bring himself to speak again.

"You're on your own tomorrow, Laurie. Don't ask me to help you do...anything."

Laurie's chuckle reached him through the night stillness.

"Jealous, Tris? Well, I don't blame you. I would be, too, if she chose you over me. Goodnight, Tris."

This time it truly was impossible to respond. Tris tasted blood and realized he'd bitten his lip. He rose and walked to the window, drinking in the fresh, cool air, unable to see anything outside, yet equally unable to blot out the pictures that formed and reformed in his mind.

He was still there at the window at dawn, and he wondered how he would ever get through the coming day.

54

Everyone agreed that the wedding was beautiful.

Rosalie was radiant and smiling in white silk and lace; Sam wore a store-bought suit and had polished his boots. They made a handsome couple.

If the father of the bride was unusually reserved, he was

generous enough with his liquor, which flowed freely. And the tables set out with food, in addition to the wedding cake, drew the guests into conviviality that made the gardens buzz with talk and laughter, covering the lack of enthusiasm Joel displayed.

Joel was not the only one with a sober face. Tris watched the festivities from the sidelines, making no attempt to mingle with lifetime friends, until the Kendricks arrived.

Melissa greeted him with her customary lively smile; she wore her chestnut curls caught back with a green ribbon that matched her pale green summer dress. The bodice was form-fitting and the vee at the throat was low enough to afford a tantalizing hint of cleavage between small, perfect breasts. The styles of the day were designed more to conceal than to reveal a woman's figure—Tris especially abhorred the bustles that all fashion-conscious women adopted—but nothing could have disguised Melissa's beauty.

Her hand rested lightly on his arm, sending shockwaves through him that Tris strove to cover. "Tris, there you are! Why didn't you come with Laurie last night? We had a whole houseful of people. I'd told him to bring you."

"He neglected to mention that I was invited," Tris said. Over her shining head, he summoned a smile for the benefit of her parents. "Good to see you, Mrs. Kendrick. Mr. Kendrick."

Myra Kendrick was beruffled, beflounced, and bustled in pale mauve, with a parasol to match. She returned his smile with warmth. "You know you're always welcome at our house, Tristan, whether you have a specific invitation or not. Oh, Jessie! My, how smart you look! The bride will have difficulty competing with a mama who looks so young and so lovely!"

The two women moved off, chattering, leaving Tris with Murphy and Melissa, whose hand was still disconcertingly on his sleeve. Murphy had taken out a cigar and lighted it; now he squinted at Tristan through the aromatic haze.

"Something came up today that put me in mind of you, young fellow," he said, with that joviality that never quite seemed to touch his eyes.

"Oh? What was that, sir?" Tristan found himself wishing desperately that Melissa would stop touching him, yet fearing that it was for the last time and therefore wishing it could go on forever.

"Saunders, on the *Sacramento Union*, told me he's looking for a very bright young man to cover the political scene up there. It occurred to me—well, actually, it occurred to my daughter—" he gave Melissa a fatuous smile—"that you might be interested. She tells me you write very well. You certainly are articulate when you speak, when you can be persuaded to speak at all. If you're interested in a career in California politics, this might be a way to enter the scene, get acquainted, learn a few things. Meet the right people, though you have some of the important ones right here at home." He winked, and Tristan knew he referred to himself, and to Joel. "I told him I'd have a word with you about it. If I recommend you, the job's as good as yours. What do you say?"

Tristan felt his jaw slackening. What did he say? Such an idea had never occurred to him, though it had an immediate appeal. Except for the fact that Melissa had suggested it, that he take a position in Sacramento. The capital was a hell of a long way away, and he'd hardly ever have occasion to return to Stanislaus County. Well, if she was marrying Laurie, of course, that wouldn't matter much, would it?

"You write so beautifully, Tris," Melissa said earnestly. "More beautifully than one needs to, I think, to do newspaper writing. At least I never read anything in the papers as beautiful as that story you wrote for me about..." She suddenly recollected that the story in question was in the mode of a popular romantic novel, and perhaps best not detailed before her father. She laughed and squeezed his arm. "What do you think? Living in Sacramento would be exciting, wouldn't it?"

Nowhere would be exciting without her, Tristan thought. Yet if she belonged to someone else, what difference did it make where he was? Better at a distance than where he could see her and know she was forever beyond his reach.

"It sounds very exciting. Both Sacramento and working on a newspaper, covering political activities. I'd...I'd like to talk to Mr. Saunders about it, sir."

"Good! Good!" Murphy scattered ash over the lawn, which had been assiduously watered this past month so that it would remain green at least long enough for the wedding. "Ha, I believe the ceremony is about to begin. Shall we join the others?"

Laurie was coming toward them, grinning a welcome. "I've staked out a place for us, right close to the bower. I want you to appreciate, Melissa, the way we stuck flowers all over the confounded thing, Tris and I."

"It's lovely," Melissa opined, and without taking her left,

nd of Tris's arm, put the right one on Laurie's. "Let's all nd together, shall we?"

Tris never knew how he got through the ceremony; he uldn't have been more in a turmoil if the wedding had been s own. He had a glimpse of his sister's face as she turned kiss her groom, and he felt a pang of envy. She was in love, d she could show it, and the love was returned. What more uld a person ask in this life?

He ate cake, and drank champagne, and watched Melissa. e was so exquisitely beautiful, he thought. So innocent. aurie didn't deserve a girl like Melissa. For that matter, obably he didn't either, but that was cold comfort.

There was music now, two violins, a mouth harp, and a itar; a few people were dancing, though most would reserve at activity until later in the afternoon, after it began to ol off a little.

"Tris!"

He turned at her voice, looking down at her. "I'm sorry, d you say something?"

"I asked if you'd agreed with Daddy just because . . . well, ecause he's Daddy. I know he's overpowering to most people, ut you don't have to agree to something just because he puts at the idea. If you don't really want to go to Sacramento to ork on the *Union*, why, he won't care. He admires people ho stand up to him when they don't agree with him."

"No. I mean, no, I didn't agree just because it was his idea. think I'd like to go to Sacramento. It might be just what I eed to start moving in the right direction."

Laurie looked at him quizzically. "J. Murphy offer you a b, Tris?"

"Sort of. He told me of one. Look, I'm going to get out of his mob. Ma won't notice if I'm here or not, and Rosie won't ither."

"Good idea. Let's all go. Melissa wants to see that new tallion Uncle Joe bought; let's show it to her, all right?"

Tris didn't want to go anywhere with the two of them. Yet vhen she reached for his hand, at the same time she also ook Laurie's, smiling so happily that way, what else could e do?

"I've cornered the two best-looking men at the entire wed-ling," she declared, bouncing a little as she walked. "Includ-ng even the groom, though he is attractive, isn't he?"

They strolled beyond the row of fruit trees and toward the barn. The stallion was in an area by himself, apart from the

other horses in the small training corral; Melissa rested h
chin on the top rail and exclaimed in pleasure at the sig]
of him.

"He's magnificent! What do you call him?"

"Pa hasn't called him much of anything but swear word
yet," Tris said. "The Mexicans where Pa got him called hi
Diablo Negro."

Melissa, too, had grown up in the San Joaquin Valley. Sl
knew some basic Spanish. "Black Devil," she translate
softly, eyes fixed on the stallion. "He's like satin. Beautiful

The animal stood in the middle of the small enclosur
shying a little as they took places along the fence.

"He's not used to females in party dresses," Laurie o
served. "Just stand still, and he'll get used to you. Tho
fluttering ribbons are spooking him."

Melissa obediently froze into position. "What must it I
like to ride such an animal? He looks as if he could ru
forever."

"He injured a man on the Benton ranch," Laurie told he
"They were going to shoot him, but Uncle Joel said he'd tal
him and gentle him. He has the makings of a fine horse, al
there aren't many big ones like him. Uncle Joel needs a b
animal to carry him all day."

"He doesn't seem very tame yet," Melissa said. "See tl
way his nostrils are flaring. He doesn't like us being here.

"It's probably the ribbons. Here, let me tuck them in
your sleeves," Laurie said, and in a proprietary way proceede
to do so. "There, see, he's calmer now. I'll bet I could walk
there and ride him, right this minute."

At first Tris thought Laurie was joking, until he mov
toward the gate. Then, as it dawned on him that Laurie a
tually meant to enter the corral, he spoke in alarm.

"Don't be a fool, Laurie! You know Pa hasn't had time
work with him enough yet. Pa's had a saddle on him, but l
hasn't ridden him so far! Stay out of there!"

He ought to have known that accusing Laurie of being
fool, after he'd had considerable champagne and in front
the girl he planned to marry, was a mistake. Because Laur
gave them both an impudent grin and let himself into tl
arena, securing the gate behind him. "Watch," he said jau
tily.

Diablo snorted, tossing his spectacular head so that tl
black mane swirled and fell back into place. And he pawe

e ground once with a powerful hoof, leaving an indentation
the dry earth.

Truly apprehensive now, Tris kept his voice level so as not
further agitate the horse. "Get out of there, Laurie. Come
, before you get him mad. Even Pa hàsn't tried to ride him
t, and he won't like it if you do it."

Laurie was facing Diablo, inching forward, hands slightly
ised. "Steady, boy, steady. I won't hurt you. Just stay right
ere, boy, and don't tremble that way, I'm a friend."

Tris glanced around, wishing that his father would sud-
nly come through the row of trees and put a stop to this.
urie had always enjoyed showing off, particularly for young
males, but this went beyond a prank. Not only would Joel
 infuriated if anyone interfered with his training of the
rse, but the animal was dangerous.

There was no sign of Joel, though, nor of anyone else.
rough the row of trees that effectively screened the scene
m the wedding guests, he caught glimpses of ladies' bright
 pastel-colored gowns, and heard the music and laughter,
t no one could see the barnyard or the trio at the corral.

"Laurie, damn it, come out of there, or I'll come in after
u."

Laurie turned his head, still grinning, and waved a de-
ecatory hand. "Don't worry, I can handle this! He's going
 let me walk right up to him if you don't keep making a
ss and spook him again."

In that instant while his gaze left the horse, Diablo's nos-
ls flared wide, and his lips drew back to expose vicious
eth. And he charged.

Head down, almost serpentine in his grace and speed,
ablo closed the distance between himself and the intruder.
ere was a sturdy post within the enclosure, placed so that
man could dodge behind it where the horse could not go,
t Laurie was on the opposite side of the paddock from that
fety feature.

Melissa cried out, her voice drowned in Tristan's louder
out of warning. "Look out, Laurie!"

Laurie spun as the stallion reared on his hind legs and
me down with his front hooves, slashing at this creature
 regarded as an enemy. Diablo screamed, a high, shrill
und, terrified and terrifying as his forefeet carried the man
 the ground. The horse reared again and again, pounding,
ushing, grinding this enemy into the dirt.

475

Melissa clung to the fence rail to keep from falling, h
eyes wide in horror, forgetting to breathe.

Tristan sprang for the coiled rope over the gate post ar
went over the fence without pausing to open the gate itsel
He yelled, and struck at the stallion with the rope, trying
force him backward.

He was drenched in acrid sweat, and he feared that at ar
moment those lethal hooves would strike him, yet he conti
ued to flail at the animal with the rope, the rope Diablo kne
and hated. Tris bellowed and attacked, and the horse at la
retreated to stand trembling and flecked with froth again
the far side of the corral.

Behind him there were running feet, men's voices. Th
horse's scream had carried over the music and the laughte
which had now fallen silent. Tris didn't dare look back; h
wasn't certain that Diablo would not charge again. "Get La
rie! Somebody get him out of here!"

He heard his father's voice amidst the other voices, hea
the creak as the gate swung open and at last dared to tu
when Sam Shute came running with a pitchfork to hold th
stallion at bay.

Laurie lay on the ground, his blood soaking the pale pov
dery earth in ugly dark stains, unmoving. Joel had reache
him and knelt in his best suit, heedless of blood and dust,
gather his son into his arms.

Tris knew by the way Laurie's head lolled backward th
his neck was broken.

His own breath still came in painful gasps. He retreate
and Sam with him, and Tris saw his father's face.

He would never forget it as long as he lived.

Would Joel feel such agony had it been Tris instead
Laurie who lay dead in his arms?

Yes, of course he would, Tris thought dully. He would fe
the same about any of us.

Melissa still clung to the fence, so pale that Tris was a
tonished she had not fainted. She reached for him with finge
that dug into his flesh and sagged against him when his arn
automatically encircled her. "Oh, God, Tris! Oh . . ." The tea
came then, and he held her and watched his father cross th
farmyard as the subdued wedding guests, mouths slack an
eyes glazed in the horror if it, melted out of his way. Tr
saw Jessie pushing through the crowd, apprehensive but n
yet understanding what had happened, and Rosalie, eye

arching the crowd for her new husband, her relief palpable hen she saw that he, at least, was safe.

Joel carried Laurie's broken body into the house and laid im on one of the brocade sofas in the parlor. Those who llowed could trace his passage by the bright blood that :ained Jessie's floors and carpets.

Jessie rushed to Joel's side, crying out to him, resting a and on his shoulder as he knelt beside the dead son, but she aw that Joel did not hear her, did not know she was there. Ie doubled over in anguish so great that she feared he might ie of it, and she could offer him no comfort at all.

Tris had handed Melissa over to her father, scarcely know- g when he let her go. He stood in the doorway of the parlor, eling that it must somehow be a nightmare from which hey would all awaken, yet knowing at the same time that ; was real.

Laurie was dead. *He would never propose to Melissa now*. he realization flicked at him like the tip of a whip, yet there as no satisfaction in it, only sorrow for Melissa, sorrow for is father and all the rest of them.

His mother turned and saw him, eyes filling with tears, nd Tristan moved to hold her. They stood together for a long ime, neither of them speaking, watching Joel, hurting more or him than for themselves.

Eventually the wedding guests went home. John and Eva Curtis remained behind, and it was John who finally got Joel o let loose of his son's lifeless body, to sit down and allow hem to do what had to be done.

The Kendricks were gone by the time Tristan emerged rom the house. Almost everyone was gone. The lawn was a ness with dropped food and some broken glasses; the punch n the bowl had grown warm, the flowers in the wedding ower had wilted into limp, pathetic remnants; the food, uneaten, was covered with flies and ants as it dried out.

"Tris..."

He turned his head with great effort—any movement at all seemed to be painful, as if during those moments in the corral he had exerted all his strength with every muscle— and saw Rosalie and Sam.

"He's dead," Tristan said dully. "I couldn't move fast enough to save him."

Rosalie swallowed. Sam's arm was around her, and she leaned into him. "I know. It wasn't your fault, Tris. He had no business in the corral. But it was always Laurie's way,

wasn't it, to do the dangerous thing? To tempt fate? Tri
what shall we do?"

He stared at her, uncomprehending. "There's not muc
you can do. Mrs. Curtis is...is preparing him for...buria
We tried to get Ma to take a dose of laudanum and lie dowi
but she refuses to leave Pa, so they're both just sitting there

Her tongue curled out to moisten her lips. "I mean, abou
us. Sam and me. We...we were going to go home, to Sam
cabin, when everything was over, but I don't think I ough
to leave Mama now, do you?"

"I doubt if there's anything you can do for her, but mayb
it would be better if you stayed here tonight." It dawned o
him, at last, that this was his sister's wedding night, wha
should have been such a happy time for her. "Why don't yo
ask her? Tell her you'll stay if she needs you."

But Jessie was stronger than that. She kissed her daughte
gently on the cheek and then stretched up to kiss her nev
son-in-law as well.

"You don't need to stay for my sake, darlings. Eva is—
she faltered, then regained control of her voice. "Eva's doin
what needs to be done, and I'll stay with your father. The tw
of you can go on home; it will be easier for you."

Rosalie would gladly have done as her mother suggested-
she had been stricken at the sight of her father's face, age
a dozen years in as many minutes—for Joel did not seem t
know she was there, and while it could not be the weddin
night she had anticipated, she longed for quiet and seclusio
and the comfort of Sam's embrace.

Sam, however, spoke with firmness. "We'll stay here to
night, in Rosalie's room. Until after the burying. Then we'
go home. We'll be here, if you need us."

Jessie's lips quavered in a parody of a smile. "Thank yo
Sam. All right, then. Excuse me, I must get back to Joel."

The wedding day was over. Tomorrow they would hav
the funeral.

55

Jessie had known the loss of father, mother, sister, child. She had thought herself wild with grief. Yet she did not think she had ever suffered as she watched Joel suffer now.

He had refused laudanum or even whiskey, and he did not sleep before his son was laid to final rest. No one slept very much, judging by the way they looked when they came down to a breakfast that no one tasted.

Teresa Dolores, though she had not really liked Laurie, was red-eyed from weeping; her tender heart told her what the others were feeling, and she cried for them. At the gravesite on the hill behind the house, she clung to her Uncle Luis and was grateful that he was there, for each of them needed someone. Tris supported his mother, who in turn remained close to her husband although he seemed completely unaware of her. Rosalie had her Sam.

The Kendricks were there, though staying back from the family with other mourners from town and the surrounding ranches. Melissa wore a veil, so it was impossible to judge from her face how personally she was affected.

After the words had been said and the mound of raw earth replaced over the coffin, as they walked down the hill toward the house where the neighbors had brought in food for yet another meal that no one really wanted, J. Murphy Kendrick approached Tristan unobtrusively.

"Dreadful thing," he muttered under his breath. "Yet life is for the living, eh? It goes on, whether you want it to or not."

Tris made no response, and Murphy cleared his throat before he continued. "What do you want to do about that job, boy? Saunders needs someone right away. I told him you'd talk to him today, actually; he's staying with the Colliers in Modesto, but he'll be heading back to Sacramento tomorrow.

I don't think he can hold the position for you, not for long anyway. You up to riding over there this afternoon and discussing it with him?"

Jessie, walking ahead and overhearing, paused to look back. "What is this, Tris? A job?"

"Mr. Kendrick's recommended me for a position on the *Sacramento Union*," Tris said uncomfortably. It seemed unfeeling to be thinking of such a matter when Laurie was scarcely cold. "I can't leave now, though, sir. Not right away. There'll be all kinds of things to do, decisions to make, and Pa . . . Pa can't make them, just yet."

"A writing job?" Jessie said. Her hand rested on his arm briefly, lightly, yet with firmness. "Take it, if you want it, Tris. Your father will be all right. He wouldn't want to deprive you of an opportunity to do something you want to do. Go, darling, talk to your Mr. Saunders. And if he wants you in Sacramento tomorrow, go with him."

Tris hesitated, looking into her face. He'd like nothing better than to go, but could he leave her with all this?

"Go," Jessie urged, and smiled a little in encouragement, and he felt as if something had snapped inside his chest, some band that had constricted his heart.

"All right," Tris said. "I'll talk to him this afternoon."

The house would have been lonesome without Rosalie and Tristan in any circumstances. With Laurie gone forever, and Joel morose and silent, it was hell.

Jessie, too, felt Laurie's loss, though she had a moment or two of guilty relief that it had not been Tris's mangled body Joel had carried out of the corral. Immediately after the funeral service, Joel had returned to the house for a rifle, and he'd killed Diablo. He never mentioned the animal again, and he didn't say much about anything else, either. Not for a long time.

He rose at the customary hour every day, and went out into his fields. He cared for his stock, harvested wheat and corn, and continued to attend the planning sessions at Kendricks'. He slept in the same bed with Jessie, and he did not talk to her. He didn't make love to her.

She waited patiently, knowing that the loss had been much greater to him than it was to the rest of them, praying that he would heal and resume his life as best he could, but Joel had withdrawn to some secret place to which he did not admit anyone else, not even Jessie.

She tried everything she knew to draw him back into the mainstream of life. She read him the letter from Mamie, sounding contented and happy in her life in the Blue Mountains in Oregon, expecting her second child. A girl this time, they had decided, since they already had a boy.

"I'm so glad for her," Jessie said. "Do you suppose we could ever visit Mamie and Cole, and Zadie and her family? I would dearly love to see them all again."

Joel stared at her with apathetic dark eyes. "It's five or six hundred miles, Jessie. And even now there aren't any decent roads to speak of."

"But they got there! It must be possible! Joel, will you think about it? It would be good for us to get away for a while, and so wonderful to see them all. We wouldn't have to go on horseback. We could take a ship from San Francisco, and then one of those steamers up the Columbia. You have good men to look after things here."

He had no response to that. He didn't refuse, he didn't agree. He simply slid away from her, back into his own private hell.

A month after Laurie's death, Jessie first put her concern into words. Luis was there; he had been there frequently, sometimes dropping in unexpectedly, sometimes at Jessie's invitation, because the dinner table was less noticeably silent when he was there to lead the conversation in the absence of any attempt on Joel's part to do it.

They had been talking about Teresa Dolores and her growing attachment to Brad Mismer, and Luis had reluctantly agreed that young Mismer's background was impeccable and that he might be allowed to call upon Teresa.

"I suppose he's no worse than any of the rest of them," Luis said, and Jessie's lips twisted in a rueful smile.

"Now you sound like Joel. As if nobody is good enough for her."

"Nobody is," Luis retorted, and then he, too, had to smile. "But I suppose some lout will have her, all the same, and she prefers that it be this Mismer fellow. She will be well chaperoned, of course, if he calls upon her."

"Of course." Jessie remembered how poorly she'd managed that with her own daughter, but Teresa Dolores was not the headstrong girl that Rosalie was. "I said some terrible things to Joel, after that night at Sam's place. I accused him of wanting to keep Rosie all to himself, of being jealous of any of her men."

481

Luis allowed an expressive eyebrow to rise. "That must have set well with him."

"Oh, yes! He was so furious that I thought for a moment he was going to hit me. It was true, though. He had no valid objections to Sam except that he would take Rosie away from us. From Joel. I suppose it's the way of doting fathers—or uncles—to want to protect their little girls, long after they've become women. I only wish..."

Her voice trailed off and Luis regarded her perceptively. "You wish... what, *amiga?*"

"That Joel and I had become fully reconciled, after that terrible night, before... before Laurie was killed."

Something shifted in his face and the dark eyes changed, too, as if he would conceal his thoughts from her by sheer willpower. "You are not, then, reconciled now?"

"It's impossible to tell what we are, because he doesn't talk to me." She didn't add that he didn't touch her, either, which bothered her even more. "Is it natural, Luis, for him to grieve so long, so bitterly? Everyone loses children, parents, people they love. We all grieve, and to some extent we go on grieving forever. It still brings tears to my eyes when I allow myself to think of Joella Viola, the baby I lost over twenty years ago. But I don't shut out everyone else because of it. I don't let the sorrow consume me, as Joel is doing. I don't think I did, even then, when it happened. I knew that I had to go on living and make the best of things. Joel isn't even trying to make the best of anything, and it's as if the rest of us are of no importance to him, compared to Laurie."

"He also feels he lost his daughter, to this man he dislikes, at the same time. And you, as his wife, challenged him in a way he has never before been challenged—and won your point. He allowed Rosalie to marry the man, but his pride and his authority were damaged, and this is not easy for a man to accept."

His eyes were keen, and Jessie flushed, glad he could not possibly know how she had brought the pressure against Joel. It had been the most potent threat she could think of, that she would never again be a wife to him in any sense of the word if he did not allow Rosalie to marry Sam. She had sworn on the Bible, and she had meant what she said, and Joel knew it. He had capitulated, because he did not want to lose her forever.

Yet he had shown her no affection since. He did not make love to her, and last night on her first tentative attempt to

each him, when she had stretched out a hand in the darkness
and laid it on his chest, Joel had ignored it until he finally
turned his back to her and went to sleep, leaving her eyes
prickling with tears.

"I'm afraid for him, Luis," she said softly. "It's not right,
not normal grief he experiences. And I don't know how to
bring him out of it."

His face had a wooden look. "As his wife, you have ways
no one else can use to reach him. You're too much a woman
not to know those ways."

She stared at him with blurred vision. "He doesn't want
me that way. I don't think he wants me at all."

Luis stood very still. He had never spoken to her more
softly. "*Querida,* you ask me for help, for advice, and though
you and Joel are both good friends of long standing and I
have always considered myself to be an honorable man, the
only thing that comes to my mind now is to plead my own
cause."

For a few seconds she didn't credit her senses as to his
meaning. Across the hall, in the dining room, she heard Mrs.
Sullivan laying out silver on the table, and somewhere overhead a door closed loudly. She sought Luis's gaze as if to
extract understanding through those hooded dark eyes.

"I have been in love with you for many years," Luis said,
and now there could be no doubt about it. The words were
spoken in a near whisper that barely reached her, yet there
was a throbbing intensity in them that stirred her in spite
of herself. "Ever since that day when you came down the
bank and rescued me, a stranger, from men who intended to
kill me and throw my body into the river. I thought you were
the bravest, most beautiful woman I had ever met, and the
more I knew of you, the deeper that impression became. Perhaps I should be pleading the cause of my friend Joel, urging
patience and tenderness. Instead, my impulse is to draw you
into my arms and kiss you, the way I have dreamed of kissing
you, *amada mia,* for so long."

She had never anticipated any such thing as this from
Luis. Oh, she'd known he was attracted to her, of course he'd
made that obvious, but it had been a *friendship,* she thought
wildly, not a romantic attachment, not an affair.

She found herself swept into an unfamiliar embrace,
strong arms holding her, stranger's mouth upon her own. For
the space of seconds she knew panic, that Mrs. Sullivan would
for some reason step to the doorway to consult with her about

483

something, or that Joel would come in from outside, or that Teresa Dolores would come downstairs and pass by the room and glance in.

And then pure physical sensation blotted out such concerns. Because Luis's was a lover's kiss, gentle yet with a controlled passion, it stirred her in its compulsion as she had not been stirred in a long time. Her love-starved body responded with leaping pulses and heat that spread like flames through a stand of dry grass, igniting everything in its path.

It was a miracle that she heard the small sound, that it penetrated her consciousness enough to allow her to draw back in time. When Joel spoke to the housekeeper, only a few yards away, Jessie felt as if her entire body had been scorched.

"I won't be in for supper," Joel said. "I'm going to ride over to Modesto. You can tell my wife it'll be late when I get back."

"Yes, sir. She's visiting with Señor Sañudo, Mr. Joel. Did you know he was here?"

"I saw his horse," Joel said shortly. "I don't feel like talking to anybody, Mrs. Sullivan."

Jessie heard his footsteps crossing the dining room—had he made the same sounds coming in, and she'd not noticed?—and then on toward the kitchen.

What if he'd come in here, instead?

The thought made her tremble with the chill of it. Dear God, she must have lost her senses entirely to have allowed Luis to kiss her, to hold her in that way!

"I think," she said now, quickly before she should lose her nerve, "that it would be best if you didn't stay for dinner, after all, Luis."

He dropped his hands to his sides. "Whatever you say, *querida*. If I have offended you, I apologize. But there is nothing insulting about a man desiring a woman, is that not so? And having gone thus far, I must take one more step. I must tell you that I will have you on any terms, my Jessie. If you offer me marriage, after a divorce from Joel, or a discreet relationship while maintaining the pretense of a continuing marriage to Joel, the choice is yours. I am not a novice in the art of romantic intrigue, and I offer you total protection from any hint of scandal. I will go now, as you suggest. But all you have to do is send me word—any message that contains the name of a color will do—and I will come at once. *Por Dios*, let the message come soon, *mi amada*."

He lifted her hand to his mouth and kissed it, then stared

deeply into her eyes before at last turning to walk out of the room.

Jessie stood there, in the same parlor where she had spoken so harshly to Joel—where she had threatened him with ending their marriage if he did not accede to her demands regarding Rosalie and Sam—and shook as if with the ague.

Inadvertently, her hand rested on the same Bible to steady herself; Jessie jerked away as if from a hot stove.

Good God, she thought, dazed, what was happening to her?

She was flooded with guilt, for she had allowed Luis to embrace her, to say words he had no right to say, that she had no right to listen to.

Yet, during those few moments in his arms, she had felt passion and a life that had withered and died within her these past few weeks. She had welcomed Luis's kiss, had allowed her lips to part beneath his, and she had a dreadful suspicion that if the house had been empty, if she had been assured that no one would know, she might have been guilty of the worst thing a Christian woman could succumb to.

Adultery.

She stared across the room, into the gilt-framed mirror that showed only her pale face, dark eyes wide under the coronet of flaxen braids. Even as she watched, a bright spot of color appeared in each cheek.

Would she really have allowed Luis to make love to her, if it had been "safe" to do it?

No, Jessie thought numbly, of course not.

Yet her body still tingled, still yearned for a caress, ached for the release that only a loving man could provide. She had never wanted that man to be anyone but Joel, until today.

Instinct had told her, even before she reasoned it out, that Luis must not stay for dinner. Must not be in the house alone with her, while Joel was gone.

Because Luis was dangerous. He had invited her to become his mistress, and, God help her, she was tempted.

Not a novice in the art of romantic intrigue, he'd said. Well, what did she expect? That he would have lived out his life in celibacy? Of course there had been women, and no doubt some of them had been married to someone else.

It didn't hurt to think of Luis with other women, not the way it had hurt with Joel. Because she loved Joel, and she didn't love Luis, did she?

How could she contemplate—even knowing she would never do it—making love with Luis, if she didn't love him?

He was a friend, the brother she'd never had, Jessie thought. And then, because she was an honest person, she amended that thought. No, she'd never thought of Luis as a brother. A friend, yes. Could a woman have a man for a friend, with no sexual overtones at all?

She'd known for years that Luis was attracted to her, hadn't she? Beyond the ordinary attraction of good friends, if she were honest enough to admit it. He'd brought her books, flowers, all those trees out there in her precious orchard had come from Luis—these were all things a man would give to a woman he loved. Not just because she'd saved his life, but because he saw her as a desirable woman.

She should have told him at once, Jessie thought now, as the color faded from her face leaving it chalky in the mirrored reflection, that it was impossible. She was not the kind of woman who could indulge in an affair with her husband's friend. She was incapable of "romantic intrigue," of scheming and planning, lying and deceiving. She would never be able to look into her own face in that mirror again if she deliberately stepped into an adulterous role.

Yet her body continued to ache with the need Luis had aroused. Well, no, to be truthful the need had already been there, building night by night as she'd lain beside Joel, who neither spoke to her nor touched her.

She remembered how that had happened before. When she was only a girl, when she'd thought Joel dead, when the need had been overwhelming, she'd contemplated seducing poor Ben, believing that the only reason he didn't approach her was his consideration for her grief over the loss of the man she'd loved and giving her a recovery time after the birth of Joella Viola. She hadn't loved Ben, she'd known she could never love him, but she had needed the physical relief of lovemaking; her loins had cried out for it.

As they did now.

The answer could not be an illicit affair with Luis. No, Jessie firmed the resolution in her mind, she could never degrade herself in that manner.

Yet it was a long time before the desire Luis had aroused began to subside. A long time, and Joel was not there, and she did not know if Joel would ever again love her the way she needed to be loved.

What would she do, if Joel never loved her again?

56

Jessie woke in the predawn darkness, hearing the small sounds of movement in the room. It was not yet light enough for her to make out where Joel was, but she knew before she put out a hand to his side of the bed that he was up, dressing.

There had been a time when she'd have asked softly, "Joel? What are you doing?"

She could no longer do that. Though they shared a bed and a daily life, they were strangers. She could not demand of a stranger why he was going out so early.

He always rose early, of course. He was a farmer, he worked in one of the hottest valleys in the world, and he rose to take advantage of the morning coolness.

Yet this was too early. In late summer the dawn came by four or four-thirty, and it was still black night. Even as she listened, she heard the clock on the landing strike out the half hour. Three-thirty? she wondered.

She sensed rather than saw Joel cross the room, near enough to the bed so that she could have reached out and touched him. The door eased open, then closed quietly behind him.

Jessie sat up.

Sleep was gone. She was still tired, because she'd slept badly this night, as she'd been doing ever since Laurie's death. Sometimes she was assailed by guilt, because she'd been grateful that it was not Tris who had died. Sometimes she grieved for him, for the little boy he'd been, for the fact that she had not been able to love Laurie the way she had loved her own children, though she had tried.

Was that why Joel didn't talk to her now? Did he blame her for not being able to love Laurie as he had?

The windows were open to allow the house to cool as much

as possible, and she heard the door close below as Joel left the house.

Without conscious thought, Jessie was out of bed and at the window, though she could see nothing. What was he doing? There was no work he could do in the dark, and he carried no lantern.

Would he ride out over the hills, seeking the solace of solitude as she herself was wont to do? She leaned against the windowsill, listening, and heard only the minute chirping of crickets or other small insects.

There were no sounds from the barn or the corrals. Surely she'd hear if he rode a horse out. She heard nothing at all.

On impulse, Jessie turned from the window and groped for her own clothes. She could not have said why she had to know where Joel went and what he did. She moved swiftly, buttoning her everyday dress, fastening her shoes, then letting herself out into the pitch blackness of the upper hallway.

Behind one of the doors Teresa Dolores slept. There was no one else on this floor, and the house had an empty feeling to it. Jessie needed no lamp to light her way; she'd walked these passageways, descended the stairs, so often that she could do it in her sleep.

Yesterday had been hot, and today promised more of the same; the house retained the heat, in spite of opened windows and a faint breeze to waft in the night air.

When she stepped onto the back porch, however, Jessie shivered a little and considered returning to the house for a shawl. The first faint touch of light outlined the mountains to the east, though the shadows were still deep around her.

Jessie stood listening and heard nothing. Where had Joel gone?

And then she saw him, his dark clothes setting him apart from the stubble in the wheatfield behind the barn.

The graveyard, Jessie thought. He was going to Laurie's grave.

She almost went back into the house then. But she was wide awake; she didn't think she could fall asleep again, and Joel was up there alone with his anguish.

There was no reason to assume that he would be any more receptive to her sympathy now than he'd been all along. Jessie set out after him anyway.

They could not go on forever the way they were now, she thought. She ached for Joel, longed to comfort him, but her

488

mary concern—yes, admit it—was for herself. Because
: couldn't live out whatever was left of her life in this way.
f she didn't win Joel back, she was afraid she would,
ntually, turn to Luis, and the idea terrified her.

he made her way along the path, surprised to find that
vas a path; Joel must have been up here very often to
e worn such a trail through the field. She was grateful for it,
ause walking through a cut-over grainfield could be haz-
ous; she didn't want to step into a hole and twist an ankle.
'here was a faint pink in the sky over the Sierra now, and
could see better. Well enough to tell that Joel had reached
destination, the small plot fenced in wrought-iron to keep
predators.

Ie didn't hear her until she was within a dozen yards of
1. He was on his knees on the ground, and he turned his
d, not rising, as she approached.

Joel—" She said his name, and then could find no further
·ds. Why hadn't she planned what she would say to him?
Ie looked up at her from his old man's face, and she put
a hand to his shoulder.

Joel, let me help. Share it with me," she said then, and
a surge of wild, sweet joy when he lifted his own hand
·lace it over hers. It was the first time he had voluntarily
ched her since the night riders had gathered to fire Sam's
in.

I always intended to tell him, someday," Joel said in a
·e thick with emotion. "That he was my son."

essie's throat closed.

And then, without any warning, it was too late. Now I
. never tell him anything. Not that he was my son, not that
ved him."

he forced herself to speak. "Joel, he knew. Knew that you
·d him. How could he not know, when you favored him in
:rything, even over Tris and Rosie? And I suspect he knew
ut the other, too. I used to see him looking at himself in
mirror, then looking at you. Even if he only suspected
n, he knows now, Joel. He's with God, and he knows all
things nobody was able to say in his life. Believe that,
I stop punishing yourself for something Laurie would
·er have blamed you for."

he didn't know if he heard, or understood, or not. His
d remained over hers, resting on his shoulder. "I hated
hard Aubin. Long before I knew what my father's name
·, I hated him. Hated him for allowing me to be illegiti-

489

mate, for allowing Ma and me to suffer and struggle the wa
we had to do. I knew you didn't want to take Laurie whe
he was a baby, but I couldn't abandon him the way Aubi
abandoned me. Only I never quite had the courage to te
him, that he was really my son."

"I didn't want him, to begin with," Jessie said truthfull
And then, perhaps a shade less honest, she added, "But
came to love Laurie as if he were my own. He grew up su
rounded by love, Joel, not the way you did. He's never bee
a social outcast, he never knew poverty, or neglect. He wasn'
unhappy or deprived. If there is any guilt left over, it's i
your own head. Laurie wouldn't have blamed you for any
thing. And God doesn't, either. Joel, I know you've never ha
the faith in God that I have, and I'd give my soul to share i
with you now. The faith to ask God to forgive you for whateve
your shortcomings have been, and then to believe that He'
absolved you of them, and to go on with living without guilt."

His mouth twisted. "Maybe that's easier for you to believe
Jessie. You don't have any guilt."

"Oh, Joel! Oh, dear God, that isn't true! I have so man
things to feel guilty about—" In a burst of candor, she knel
beside him, drawing his hand with her own so that both reste
on his knee, looking earnestly into his face. "Don't you thin
I've felt guilty, for years, about loving you before we wer
married? About having your baby, after I thought you'd died
About resisting taking Laurie, because he was your son an
Suzanne's, not mine, and I resented him? It was hard for m
to love him, I admit it, because he wasn't mine, because m
baby had died! Joel, everybody has something to feel guilt
about! I'm no more a saint than anyone else!"

At last she seemed to be getting through to him. He wa
listening, which was more than he'd done in weeks. He wa
touching her, allowing her to touch him; their hands ha
instinctively clasped together, and that gave her courage.

"Darling, I know how you felt about Laurie. I know how
much it hurts to lose him. It always hurts to lose someone
you love. Only you're taking a load of guilt onto yourself, as
if you'd done something deliberately to hurt Laurie, and you
never did that. You're making it hurt worse by blaming your-
self, and Laurie never blamed you for anything. I know he
didn't, because he was too transparent to have concealed re-
sentment when he had any. Wherever he is now, he knows,
and he forgives you for not telling him what you thought you

d plenty of time to say. Remember what Laurie was like,
l, and you'll know that's true."

He swallowed. "You really believe that, don't you, Jess?
at Laurie's gone to heaven, to something better than he
d on earth, the way Ma used to say we'd all do?"

"Yes. Yes, I believe it." Please, God, she prayed, let him
ieve it, too. Don't let him go on suffering this way.

For the first time in all their years together, in the gray
ht of a summer dawn, Jessie saw tears in his eyes. He had
 cried when Laurie died, and he did not break down now,
 suddenly he reached for her, and Jessie was in his arms.
The barrier between them was broken, their emotions
oding over it; they clung together, kneeling there beside
 raw grave, and the flood included words, too.

"I lost Rosie, and I felt I'd as good as lost you, and then
urie—I couldn't bear it, Jess! I couldn't!"

"You haven't lost Rosie, Joel. She still loves you very
ch. She needs you—not in the same way she needs Sam,
 very much, because you're her father! You still have a
ce in her life."

"The way you looked at me that day, when you said you'd
er be a wife to me again. You meant it, I could tell you
, and as furious as I was with you, I couldn't do that. I
ldn't walk away from you forever, not after you swore on
 Bible. I kept seeing your face in my sleep, the hatred in
ur eyes."

"It wasn't hatred, it was determination, to be fair to Ros-
 and to all the rest of us. I couldn't let you hurt her, the
y Tully Ritter tried to hurt me. I love you, but I love Rosie,
—"

t poured out of them, over them, releasing the tensions
 the misunderstandings, healing the wounds. Oh, Jessie
w they weren't all healed, and there would always be
rs. But walking down the hill together as the rooster first
wed, arm in arm, she felt safer and happier than she'd
n in a long time.

Hours later, when Joel had eaten a hearty breakfast and
e off to the fields, Jessie sat at the desk in the small study
 penned a message to be carried to Casa Sañudo when
esa Dolores rode over that afternoon.

The note was not sealed, and Jessie had not indicated that
vas a private or personal message, so the girl glanced at
efore she put it on her uncle's desk to await his return.

Dear Luis:
There will be no colors in my life, now or
ever, but I thank you.

As ever,
Jessie.

What a peculiar note, Teresa Dolores thought. It didn't
make any sense, and that wasn't like Aunt Jessie. She
shrugged, and walked out into the sunny courtyard, the note
forgotten.

She would tell Tío Luis that Brad Mismer had requested
permission to call upon him, to ask for her hand in marriage.
And she wanted to be very certain that when he did, Luis
would say yes. A smile curled her lips.

She had learned long ago, as a little girl, how to get what
she wanted from Luis. She wouldn't fail to succeed now, in
the first thing that was really important.

She heard her uncle coming, and walked back inside in
time to observe him when Luis picked up the small folded
paper from his desk.

The room was dim, as were all the rooms in this house
designed to filter out the terrible summer heat, so perhaps
it was imagination that made it seem that a spasm of anguish
passed over his face.

There was nothing in the note to upset him, and certainly
he seemed quite normal when she spoke his name, and he
turned.

"Ah, Teresa Dolores! Manuela said you were here."

Yes, quite normal, she thought.

"Come into the *patio,* if you please. I have something serious to talk about," she begged, lifting liquid dark eyes to
his, the smile lighting her pretty face. "This is a good time
to talk, isn't it?"

Again for split seconds, she thought she saw something
there in his impassive face. And then he smiled, too.

"Of course. What do you want to talk about?"

57

Sacramento was the most exciting place Tristan had ever
[be]en.

He liked Jim Saunders, the man he would report to on the
[Sa]cramento Union; he liked the people he met, both on the
[pa]per and in the legislature. Many of these men he knew
[al]ready, because they had been visitors at the Kendrick place;
[th]e others he'd read about and knew by reputation, the men
[wh]o ran this state, who made its laws, who would control
[Ca]lifornia's destiny.

He found a room at a price he could afford—he'd decided
[no]t to touch any of his share of the ranch earnings or the
[m]oney banked from Uncle Collie's claim, if he could help it—
[an]d though it was cramped compared to his room at home,
[he] wouldn't be in it much, so that didn't seem important.

He'd visited cities before, but he'd never lived in one. There
[we]re so many people, so much going on, that he didn't even
[ge]t around to writing home for the first two weeks he was
[th]ere. He felt guilty about that, because he knew that with
[on]ly Teresa Dolores left, his parents must be lonely. Only
[th]ere simply wasn't time to do everything, and he was eager
[to] learn his job and do it to the satisfaction of Jim Saunders.

Jim was a man of middle years, nondescript as to looks
[bu]t with a sharp, inquiring mind. He knew everyone, and
[th]ough he liked the way Tris wrote, he edited in a savage
[fa]shion that at first took Tris aback.

"You have to be careful what you say in print about a man
[li]ke Robles," Jim told him. His pencil made slashes on Tris's
[co]py. "Here, write it this way, and you don't leave the paper
[op]en to a libel suit. See?"

It took a while to understand it all. Tris was fascinated.
[H]e wasn't defensive about the changes made in his work, and
[th]e first time he read one of his own articles, with a by-line,

493

in a paper that would go out to his own home and to thos
of his acquaintances in Stanislaus County, he was so buoye
with pride that he bought an extra copy of the paper and sei
it to Melissa, just in case she didn't read her father's copy.

He had not written to Melissa up to this point, and h
didn't write much now. His note was brief and relativel
impersonal—after all, what could you say to a girl you love(
who didn't know you were alive, who would have marrie
your brother/cousin if he'd lived?

Still, he couldn't bear losing touch with her altogethe
and she *had* been the one to recommend him for this positior

The day he received a reply from Melissa he knew h
hadn't even begun to stop loving her. Just the sight of he
handwriting made his stomach tie into a knot.

> Dear Tris;
> Congratulations! I knew you would make
> a wonderful reporter! I have cut out your
> story and put it in a frame, under glass, to
> preserve it for posterity. How does that
> sound?

It was a bright, chatty note, with news about a party she'(
attended, a new gown Daddy had allowed her to buy, thei)
mutual friends.

The sort of letter one would get from a sister, Tris thought
Well, he couldn't think of Melissa as a sister, but he wouldn')
allow himself to attach undue importance to the fact tha:
she'd written back so quickly.

He would, he decided, wait at least a week before he responded.

Jessie wrote once a week, regardless of his own writing
schedule; she, too, was a purveyor of news about family and
friends. She mentioned having seen Melissa at a tea, and said
she'd asked about him.

In mid-November, there was a line in one of Melissa's
letters that brought him up short.

> You are coming for Christmas, aren't you,
> Tris? Your mama told us at church Sunday
> that you'd decided not to come for Thanks-
> giving, to everyone's great regret. But you
> *must* come for Christmas! Daddy says
> everybody leaves Sacramento—from the

legislature, I mean—to go home then, anyway, so there won't be any news of that kind for you to cover. And it wouldn't be Christmas without you, for either your family or for me. Daddy has said we may have a big party—a ball, really, with a small orchestra, and I'm to have a new dress—yes, *another* one! It's red velvet, and the most beautiful thing I've ever worn; Miss Kerns is cutting it out now. Please, say you're coming, and that you'll dance the first dance with me, and the last one?

had consciously avoided thinking about Christmas. Only months after Laurie's death, what would the family celebration be like? They'd always had such fun, at Christmas.

He'd thought it might be easier just to stay here, in his room, and pretend it was only another day when he didn't have to work. Well, he could work, all right. There was a piece he was doing about the changes being wrought in the valley since the establishment of the railroads.

She wanted him to come to her Christmas ball.

There was no way he could resist anything that Melissa wanted, he thought, even though it would probably be painful, even more painful than going home to a house without Laurie.

There had been times when he'd actually hated Laurie, but mostly he remembered the good times. The riding out by themselves, hunting, playing games, swimming in the river the ditches, finding Uncle Collie's gold. They'd been competitors in almost everything, and usually Laurie had been the winner, but Tris missed him. He dreaded the thought of looking out of his own bedroom door into the room across the hall, knowing nobody slept there any more.

If he was going home, he'd have to find a present for Melissa. He looked for weeks before he found it, a garnet pendant on a gold chain which the clerk assured him would be just the thing for a young lady wearing a red velvet dress.

He shopped for the others, as well, and arrived home four days before Christmas, laden with colorful packages and bracing himself for a subdued holiday if that was the way it turned out.

Everybody was making an obvious effort to keep it from being subdued. Jessie and Rosie and Teresa Dolores had decorated a gigantic tree, brought down from the hills by one o the hired men.

"Teresa did the top branches, and I did the lower ones, Rosalie told him with a grin, patting her bulging abdomer "They wouldn't let me climb the ladder."

He was mildly embarrassed by her pregnancy. "Nobod told me you were expecting."

"About the first of April," Rosalie said complacently. "San says it's a girl. You've gained a little weight, too, haven' you? You aren't quite as skinny as I remember."

"You're looking great, even if you are fat." It was true He'd never seen his sister looking so lovely; her color wa high and there was a fullness, roundness, that enhance her customary beauty.

She punched him in the ribs. "It's not fat, it's baby, idiot Listen, Tris." She grew solemn. "Don't talk about Lauri much, all right, when Pa's around? Ma does it, but he alway looks so . . . so sad, and then it takes a while to get him bacl to normal; it seems cruel to keep reminding him."

"Maybe Ma figures that talking about Laurie helps hin to get used to it. So he *can* think about him without it hurtin; so much. I think maybe you have to let it hurt first, befor it begins to heal," Tris said.

He was rescued from that anticipated but unwelcome turi of conversation when his cousin entered the room carrying a big bowl of fruit. "My gosh, is that Teresa Dolores? I haven' even been gone six months, and she's all grown up and beautiful!"

The girl's smile was livelier than he remembered, and she seemed less shy. "Will you come home for my wedding, Tris? In February?"

"Wedding! To who? Whom? Hey, you aren't *that* grown-up yet, are you?"

"Brad and I are getting married February sixth. Please be there, Tris. It means so much to me, to have the whole family present."

Everyone except Laurie. The thought hit them all simultaneously, and then Rosalie cried, "Sam! Sam, come and put the star on the top of the tree! Teresa Dolores couldn't reach it!"

There were other such moments, of course. It was impossible for them to avoid all mention of Laurie, and even when they didn't they thought of him frequently. He had, after all, been a part of every Christmas celebration they'd ever had.

It was when Jessie, in a nearly natural way, had reminded them of the time when the boys were eight and nine, and Laurie had nearly set the tree afire with the candles, that Tris observed his father and decided that Jessie's method was better than Rosalie's. Joel smiled, a little, and if there was hurt behind the smile, why, there was a good memory, too. If they didn't allow the good memories to surface once in a while, they'd be deprived of something important to them all as a family.

He watched Sam and Rosalie together, and knew his sister had chosen wisely. They were happy, anybody could see that. And Brad Mismer came over, his pride in Teresa Dolores shining out of his eyes with every glance.

Everybody paired off except me, Tris thought.

He was home two days before the Kendricks' ball, and though he thought of Melissa almost constantly, he didn't ride over to see her ahead of time. He was afraid to. Afraid that she'd treat him like a brother, when he wanted so much more. Afraid she'd be kind to him, when what he wanted was passionate response to his own turbulent emotion.

The rest of the family stayed home the night of the ball; Rosalie, visibly pregnant, would remain more or less in seclusion within her family until she had given birth. And the others didn't feel like dancing, at least not in public. Not yet.

So Tris rode over alone, and found the party in full swing. There must have been over a hundred people present, he thought, making his way past a cluster of guests at the doorway. A servant took his coat—mercifully dry, for once, because the day had been a fine one—and discreetly suggested that if Mr. Tristan would like to retire to the study, Miss Melissa would join him there directly.

Tris was moderately alarmed at this. Melissa herself must have issued such an order, something she'd never done before. Why wasn't she greeting him out here, along with everyone else?

There was a fire in the study, and several lighted lamps. There were deep, comfortable chairs, which Tris ignored. The last thing he could do was sit down.

Instead, he paced, imagining the meeting to take place any minute now. He'd brought the garnet pendant, in a velvet-lined box in his coat pocket, but suddenly he had doubts about it. Would Murphy consider it inappropriate for a relative stranger to give his daughter a gift of jewelry? Or would he be contemptuous of such a modest gift, which did not compare to the rubies and diamonds with which he adorned his own wife?

"Tris!"

She came into the room, pausing long enough to close the door behind her, and he felt as if he were falling into a bottomless pit. My God, how could he not have remembered how exquisite she was?

She came toward him, smiling, her throat and shoulders rising in creamy perfection from the low-cut bodice of her deep red velvet gown. She wore no jewelry with it; she didn't need it, not with that skin and those thick-lashed eyes.

"I was afraid you wouldn't make it," she said. "You're late." There was no censure in the words, only pleasure that he'd finally arrived. "I told Calders to bring you in here, because..."

The smile faded away as she looked up at him. Always with a crick in her neck, he thought again, because he was so damned tall he towered over practically everybody.

"Why did you? Have me come in here? Won't people think it's...peculiar?"

"Nobody will know about it. They're all dancing and milling around like sheep out there, and nobody knows if I'm here or where. I..."

Her welcome had been warm; now she was suddenly diffident. "It's been so long, Tris. I wanted to be sure...you were the same as I remembered."

"I'm the same. Tall and skinny and awkward, just the way I've always been."

"You're not awkward, nor skinny, but I can't deny the tall. I wish now I'd asked you to come some other time, not for the ball...then we wouldn't have to go back out there and be sociable to a lot of people who don't mean anything to us. I want to sit here before the fire and talk and talk...."

And yet, inexplicably, they couldn't talk, after all. They looked at each other, and a constraint between them grew. Finally Tristan brought out the silver-wrapped box and thrust it at her.

"I brought you something. Merry Christmas, Melissa."

She unwrapped it with eagerness, exclaiming when the bauble was displayed in its velvet bed. "Oh, Tris, it's lovely! And it goes with my gown! Put it on for me, please!"

She spun to allow him to fasten the chain at the back of her neck, which he did with fumbling fingers. And then she urned swiftly back to him and rose on her toes. "Come here, end down," she said, and kissed him.

He had dreamed of kissing her from the first time he'd een her. The mere brushing of lips that Melissa initiated as so chaste, however, and that wasn't the kind of kiss he'd een thinking about. So innocent—yet it kindled a fire that as out of hand before he knew it had been lighted.

He drew her into his arms, and this time the kiss was of is making; a deep kiss that left them both stunned and aken. He was horrified that he'd gone too far, too fast, that e'd overstepped propriety and that if her father knew it lurphy would personally throw him down the front steps.

A voice in the passageway carried clearly through the osed door. "Calders, have you seen Miss Melissa?" Myra endrick asked.

"I will look for her, ma'am," Calders said in a respectful oice. "Shall I send her to you, Mrs. Kendrick?"

"No, that's not necessary. I only wanted to be certain that e greeted the rest of our guests and that nothing was rong."

"It's possible that she's retired to repair her gown, ma'am. believe she did step on the hem, coming downstairs. I will ll her you are concerned, ma'am."

"Thank you, Calders." They heard Myra's heels on the arquet floor, and then there was a faint tap on the study oor.

"I'll be right there, Calders," Melissa said quickly. Her mile flickered toward Tris. "I think it's our dance, isn't it?"

The evening was a blur of music, laughter, voices, women bright gowns, men in evening dress. He'd never even ought of evening dress; he was the only man there in an dinary business suit. He felt a fool, but he was too over- owered by a stronger emotion to worry too much about his othes.

She had kissed him back. Melissa had kissed him back.

They had no further opportunity for private conversation. elissa was much in demand as a dancing partner, and after e first waltz Tris was forced either to observe from the delines or find other partners. There was no one else he anted to dance with, of course, but he thought he'd better o it anyway.

When it was time to go in to supper, where an impressive llation had been set out on the long tables to be eaten buffet-style, Melissa materialized at his elbow. "Quick, tell them I've already promised to eat with you," she said. "Didn't I?"

The three persistent suitors behind her clamored for attention, and Tris waved them away. "Sorry, fellows. She's promised to me for supper. I asked her first."

"How the hell could you ask her first when *I* asked her before you ever got here?" one of them demanded, though there was good humor in the words. After all, a girl like Melissa had more invitations than she could possibly accept.

They had to eat in full view of the assembled company, of course. Tris tried to send messages with his eyes, and had no idea whether or not she was intercepting them and correctly interpreting them.

It was nearly time to leave, he thought in desperation, and he didn't know how she felt. How could he go away, not knowing what she had meant by returning his kiss?

"Will you ride with me tomorrow?" he asked. "Early?"

Her dimples appeared. "How early? It's going to be two before you get to bed."

"I don't care if I go to bed at all. Will you? Say at seven?"

"Seven," she echoed, and for a moment he didn't know whether she was agreeing or not. "I'd better bring something to eat, hadn't I? The servants won't be cooking for anyone early tomorrow, not when they've been kept up late with the party tonight."

"Seven," Tris confirmed, and felt his spirits rise. He could say that now, knowing it would only be a matter of hours before he was with her again.

58

December in the San Joaquin Valley could be a beautiful
me of year. The day before Christmas was one of those
rfect days, balmy and clear. They rode upriver, along the
anislaus, picnicking on a promontory rock overlooking the
ater.

"It's an odd assortment," Melissa confessed. "I didn't take
me to fix anything special, with all the leftovers from last
ght. Here, would you like a deviled egg? Or would you
efer a salmon pâté? Or a lemon tart with meringue?"

Tris didn't reach for any of the offered tidbits. "Melissa,
n no good at this business. I don't know what to say to you,
cept what's uppermost in my mind."

She carefully lowered the lemon tart onto the tablecloth
at had covered the picnic basket. "All right. What's on your
ind?"

He sucked in air and took the plunge, feeling as if he were
ing over the edge of the rock on which they sat, diving
wn into the boiling water below. If he didn't break his neck,
might be the most exciting risk he'd ever taken.

"Will you marry me?"

For the space of seconds her face didn't change. She was
close to him that he could count her thick dark lashes,
uld see the moisture on her parted lips.

And then she said, without a hint of coquettishness,
Vhen?"

They were married in March. Melissa would have married
m at once, run away with him to Sacramento, if he hadn't
tained a modicum of common sense totally at odds with his
sires.

"I don't want you to be sorry about anything," he told her.
want you to have the kind of wedding you want to have."

Melissa had made a moue of amused regret. "It'll be the kind Mama and Daddy want, more likely. Still, I don't mind. If Daddy wants to put on a show for us, why, let's let him." The moue became a gamine grin. "Think of all the wedding gifts we'll have to start our own household with, if they give us a big formal wedding."

Myra was consulted, assured them she was delighted, and that she would need at least two months to prepare.

"Two months! Mama, why do we need two months?"

Myra told her.

J. Murphy grunted his approval and pounded Tris on the back. "Welcome into the family, boy. You're going to go far, maybe even become governor of California if you play your cards right."

"I don't want him to buy me into anything," Tris told Melissa later. "I don't mind having an influential and wealthy father-in-law, as long as he doesn't try to manipulate me."

"Daddy manipulates everybody," Melissa said cheerfully. "But we're smart enough to outwit him, aren't we?"

Jessie and Joel were extremely pleased. They liked Melissa, and Joel's immediate thought was for the connection with Murphy Kendrick. Besides, it was obvious to them both that Tristan was deeply in love with the girl.

One wedding in February, one in March, and her house would be empty, Jessie thought. Only Joel and herself. She suggested, casually so that Sam would not feel she was intruding upon a province that should have been his and Rosalie's alone, that it would be a good idea if Rosie moved back home before the baby was due.

"Just to be on the safe side," she said. "And that way we can all take care of her during the delivery, and until she's well enough to manage with the baby alone. Maybe I can talk Annie into coming out and being on hand, as well. She doesn't deliver babies very often any more, but she's the best midwife I know of. She'll keep both of them safe."

"I guess she'd feel better, being here with her mama when it's time," Sam admitted. "All right, whatever you say. I didn't reckon on delivering a baby all by myself, anyway."

A grandchild, Jessie thought. She was going to have a grandchild. The idea filled her with great joy. She had not been able to bear all the children she had yearned for, but Rosalie was young and healthy. There would be more babies, and Jessie knew she would love them as she had loved her own.

Tris thanked Murphy Kendrick for his offer of a honeymoon in San Francisco, and declined. "I can't take the time to go, for one thing," he said. "And I'd rather start our married life paying my own way. So no thanks, sir."

Murphy was not insulted. He nodded approval. "Stand on your own two feet. Good way to do, boy," he said.

During the two months that gowns and undergarments must be made, invitations written out and sent, plans made for the most lavish wedding Knight's Ferry had ever seen, Tris, too, had been busy.

The job took up most of his time, and he attacked it with renewed enthusiasm. When he wasn't working, he found a rental house and managed to get it minimally furnished, drawing on the money from Collie's gold mine for the essentials, leaving the rest for Melissa to do.

"You want to go to a hotel, for our wedding night?" he asked her. "I can afford that much, I guess. A hotel, and a bottle of champagne."

Melissa laughed. "It's a morning wedding. I insisted on that. I wish we could just go home to our house, but it's too far, isn't it? So we can stay in a hotel in Stockton, maybe, the first night, and then go home."

"There won't be any servants there. And it's pretty sparsely furnished," Tris warned.

"There's a bed, isn't there?" Her cheeks were pink, but her eyes were bright and happy. "That should be enough, to begin with, at least."

She admitted later that she was scarcely aware of the house when they arrived there.

Tris had been a little nervous about it, because it was a modest rented house with only two bedrooms, one small parlor, and a kitchen, a far cry from the house where Melissa lived with her parents.

Yet she had married him, and come there to the little house only a few miles from the Capitol building, and she came to him as he'd imagined she would. Slim, beautiful, innocent and a little timid, but not too much.

That first night together, in the hotel in Stockton, their marriage was not consummated. They both were exhausted, and though it was late at night there was drunken revelry in the adjoining room, followed by a silence that made Melissa whisper nervously, "The walls are so thin! If we can hear someone cough or snore, they'll hear us, too. Oh, darling Tris, would it be awful for you if we waited to have our real wedding night in our own house?"

His disappointment was brief. There would be many years ahead of them; he convinced himself that one more night wasn't that important, and he, too, was worn out. They were asleep in each other's arms within moments of crawling into bed.

The following morning, refreshed and happy, they went on to Sacramento.

She cried out when he entered her, and then, before he had time to react with concern to the pain he was inflicting, she wrapped her arms securely around him and drew him closer until he climaxed and lay shuddering against her wonderful body.

"Was it too awful?" he asked when he'd rolled to one side and could look into her face in the moonlight.

"It gets better when you've practiced a little," Melissa told him. "Rosie said so."

"You talked to Rosie about it?"

"Don't sound so horrified. Did you imagine that women don't talk about it, the same as men do? Oh, Tris, we're going to have a good life together, I know we are. I hope I get pregnant right away, the same as Rosie did. I want a boy one who looks just like you."

"It's early to be worrying about that, isn't it?" Tris teased. He couldn't get enough of touching her, sliding a hand over her flat belly and mounded breasts. He wondered if she could be persuaded to make love in the daytime, so he could really see her. "Melissa, will you tell me something, honestly?"

He hadn't intended to ask her. He knew he'd be better off not knowing, if she gave the wrong answer. Yet the compulsion was irresistible; he had to know.

"What?" Melissa asked. She was running her finger through his hair, making sure he didn't move too far away from her.

"Did you know Laurie was going to propose to you, that day...the day he was killed? I was along to keep everyone else out of the way, so he could ask you. Would you have accepted him, if he'd had time to ask you?"

For the space of half a dozen heartbeats, Melissa did not reply, and he almost shouted at her not to tell him after all before she spoke.

"Oh, Tris! How could you think I would have ever married

504

urie? I fell in love with you the first time I saw you, only never really paid any attention to me! You didn't ask me do anything with you, you didn't give me any sign! At first en Laurie started coming around I thought it would mean see more of you, but you came less often, not more, after t. I thought if I encouraged him it might make you jealous, d *that* might drive you into acting, but that didn't work, her. And when Laurie died, and you went away and hardly ote to me at all—well, I'd thought you liked me a little, ly then I wasn't sure you liked me at all except the way i liked Teresa Dolores and Rosie . . ."

His choked cry was incredulous. "You mean you cared all e time, the same as I did?"

"I tried to show you that I did, every way I knew—at least ery way a decent woman is supposed to show it."

Iris buried his face in her hair, dark upon the pillow.

"Oh, God! If you knew what I went through, thinking you re in love with Laurie as much as he was in love with you!"

"Don't let's talk about Laurie. It was terrible, what hap- ned to him, but he has nothing to do with you and me, is."

His lips slid from her ear to her throat. "Well, there's one ing we don't have to worry about any more. Whether or not ybody thinks you're a decent woman. Show me, Melissa. ow me what you'd have done to convince me you loved me, you hadn't been worried about that."

In the moonlight, Melissa smiled.

Epilogue—1904

The house had a solid, substantial look to it, as if it had rown there on the bluff overlooking the river, surrounded y its gardens and the orchard that was the pride of Stan- laus County. In April the trees were in blossom, sending rifts of pink and white petals drifting across the lawns.

It had been a fine warm day, promising perfect weather for tomorrow's celebration. Michael had taken off his coat and it lay in front of him, across the horse's back; he debated putting it back on before he reached the house, then decided against propriety in favor of comfort. That wouldn't matter in this house.

He loved both sets of grandparents, and they'd all been good to him—hell, they'd spoiled him rotten all his life, both the Kendricks and the Shands—but it was these grandparents, his father's parents, that he was the closest to. And it was here, on this land, on these vast acres, that he would work out his destiny.

The idea amused him. Grandpa had been a farmer, and then Pa became a senator, and Michael had trained in the law and passed the bar, but what he'd always really wanted would soon come true. The third generation would revert to the soil. Michael would become a farmer, too. An educated farmer. Maybe he'd practice a little law on the side, because he rather enjoyed that, too, but it was the land that drew him.

There was a lot of land now. Far more than there had been when Grandpa set up here in that little shack back in '57. There was still a faded sign, on the road over the hills, proclaiming that part of the property was Rancho Sañudo, though the Sañudos were all gone now.

Michael barely remembered Luis Sañudo, though there was a portrait of him hanging in Cousin Teresa's house; a bold, handsome man, Luis had been. Michael didn't know the particulars of how the two ranches had been tied together even before Cousin Teresa's mother had married Grandpa's cousin Collin. (His cousin Gracienne had whispered to him once that Collie had actually been Grandpa's half brother, though he didn't know how she'd have found that out, if none of the rest of the family knew it.)

Anyway, when Luis Sañudo had been killed in an unfortunate hunting accident twenty or so years ago, when Michael wasn't even old enough to go to school yet, the properties had merged completely. It was now one big spread, not quite enough to equal El Rancho del Rio de Estanislao's acres, but impressive enough for all that. All Michael had to do was mention that his grandfather was the rancher Joel Shand, and respectful ears pricked up around him.

Not that he felt any need to impress anyone with the fact.

time Michael would have his own accomplishments, and
was confident that they, too, would be impressive.

he sinking sun lighted the windows of the big house in
osy glow as he trotted toward it. One day, maybe, his own
ily would live in that house, though he wasn't sure about
t. Maybe his wife—when he had one—would want a fan-
r place of her own, not a house that had stood here for fifty
rs or so. For himself, Michael liked this house; it was
etly elegant, rather than ostentatious like Grandpa Ken-
ck's place, and it was comfortable, well-lived-in. A place
aise a herd of young ones.

lis own pa had grown up here. Tristan came for family
herings, as he would come tomorrow, and he was at ease
t at home, but Michael had the impression that he was a
happier in their own house in Sacramento.

here had been a major estrangement between Tristan
l Joel Shand some years ago, which had lasted until Mi-
el was about twelve. He'd never clearly understood it at
time, though there were enough clues so that he even-
lly figured out most of it.

Vhen Pa first ran for office, Grandpa Shand and Grandpa
ndrick had conspired—and probably paid somebody, or
eral somebodies—to assure that he won. When Pa found
that some of the votes that carried him into the political
na had been the result of their money rather than his own
suasiveness, he'd been furious. And then when some im-
tant bill came up—Michael didn't remember which one,
it had something to do with irrigation-system construc-
1—and Tristan didn't vote the way Grandpa Shand
nted him to vote, there had been a big fight. Not a physical
it, but a verbal one, laden with emotion, and not even
ma and Grandma Jessie had been able to calm them down.
Ie'd heard Grandma Jessie say they both wanted the same
ults, and it was only in the manner of obtaining them that
y differed, but since both men were incredibly stubborn,
y had disrupted the family peace for years.

Vlama rolled her eyes when the subject came up, even yet.
till, that was in the past, now. The Shands, father and
, were civil to each other these days, even if they weren't
ecially affectionate. Michael thought it was a shame, be-
se they were both fine men, only a little different in their
look about things.

here was Grandma Jessie on the porch now, shading her
s against the pink light from the sun sinking behind the

507

mountains of the Coast Range to the west. Trying to figure out who he was, no doubt.

Michael grinned. She'd recognize him shortly. She might be going to be sixty years old tomorrow, but Grandma Jessie's eyesight and her hearing were as sharp as they'd ever been. She didn't miss a thing. He lifted an arm to wave, and she waved back.

He called her Grandma Shand, so as not to set her apart from his other grandparents, but privately he always thought of her as Grandma Jessie. If he had a favorite among them, Jessie was the one. And that was funny, in a way, because she'd spoiled him less than the others. Oh, she'd always made it plain she loved him, and she was generous with birthday and Christmas gifts, but she had never let him get away with things, the way the Kendricks and Grandpa Shand did. He remembered one time when he was seven, and he'd run away down to the Stanislaus against her express orders. Jessie had switched his bare legs with a willow frond, all the way home. He could still recall the sting of it.

From this distance, riding into the front yard, Michael would have taken Jessie for a much younger woman. She'd always had pale, fair hair, and it was only up close that you could tell there was a lot of white mixed in with it now. She was still slim, she stood straight and tall, almost regal in bearing, and the only time she used spectacles was for reading or sewing.

She turned, now, to speak to someone behind her as Joel appeared in the doorway. "It's Michael," she said, and her voice was as clear and as youthful as a girl's.

If I could find a girl like Grandma Jessie, Michael thought just before he reached the front steps, I'd grab her in a minute. Only I'm not sure there are any like her any more.

Joel walked to the front of the porch, hands in his trouser pockets. He was a big man, tall, but with no paunch such as Grandpa Kendrick had. There were streaks of gray in the dark hair, and the weathered face was lined, yet Joel Shand gave the impression of vigor rather than age. His face split in a grin that belied the almost surly tone of his voice.

"You never could keep track of time, boy. The party ain't until tomorrow."

"I know when the party is. I came early to get a few minutes alone with my best girl," Michael said. He dismounted, looped the reins over the hitching post, and came up the steps

508

gather Jessie into his arms and give her a sound kiss on mouth. "Happy birthday, Grandma."

Joel surveyed him critically. "Instead of kissing my girl, y don't you have one of your own? When you going to get rried?"

"When I find a girl as good as yours," Michael said easily. ere were chairs on the porch, and he dropped his jacket o one of them. "Here, Grandma, I brought you something."

"You don't want me to wait until tomorrow to open it, ng with the others?" Jessie said smiling up at him.

"No, this isn't a birthday present. I'll save that for the ty. This is something I came across on my way back from ston, and I thought you might like to have it. It's little, little to put on your walls, I guess, but it sounded like the y you used to talk about it, when we were small."

The package was indeed a small one, only six inches are. Jessie ripped off the tissue paper and then drew in eep breath as she held the painting to the fading light.

"It's the lighthouse on Beaver Island," Michael said un-essarily. "I met this fellow who'd spent his summer there, l painted a number of pictures. He had some bigger ones, I couldn't carry them on the train. In fact," he said without int of apology, "I couldn't afford them. But I thought you'd ybe like this."

Jessie's dark eyes shimmered with moisture. "I love it. ank you, Michael. It's beautiful."

Joel maneuvered around to look, too, and put out a thick wn finger. "That's where I used to stack split wood, right re beside the dock, so when the boats came in to refuel it ald be handy. I'd pretend to have to rest, or get a drink of ter, when Jessie came along, so we could talk without body realizing we were doing it. I wasn't supposed to talk er."

His mind shifted back to his former topic. "Be plenty of s here tomorrow. Pick one out, boy, and get on with it. 're wasting some of the best years of your life. Twenty- years old, aren't you? I was married and had a family by time I was your age."

Michael groaned. "I suppose Aunt Teresa and Aunt Rosalie joining Mama, trying to find me a girl? I'll find my own, nks."

"Of course. Any man wants to pick his own. I'm just telling not to be so damned fussy. No sense overlooking the ales right under your nose, just because your ma or your

aunts point 'em out to you. We had nothing but females i
this family for so long, all those girls of Rosie's and Teresa'
so get a girl with lots of brothers. Maybe she'll be able
produce a boy or two on the family name. You don't want
be the last of the Shands."

"Dorothy says she's never going to marry," Michael sai
wickedly. "She'll stay a Shand until she dies at ninety, sti
bossing everybody around the way she does now," he said
his younger sister.

Joel snorted. "Huh! Rosie didn't reckon she was going
get married, either, when she was twelve. And then sh
couldn't hardly wait until she was in long petticoats to g
and do it."

"And it worked out beautifully, didn't it?" Jessie aske
holding the painting against her bosom. "What would yo
have done all these years, without Sam for a son-in-law?"

"Reckon I'd've managed," Joel said, but there was no a
imosity in the words. "Come on in, boy. You didn't come fixir
to stay yet, I guess, unless you're going to get by with what
in your saddlebags?"

"I'm having the rest of my stuff shipped. I'm going hom
to Sacramento when my folks go, to wind up a few thing
and then I'll be back. First of March at the latest. Ready
be a farmer, Grandpa."

Joel snorted again. "There's a lot to learn before you'll I
a real farmer."

"All right. That's what you're going to teach me, isn't i
Who the devil is that? I thought nobody but me would I
here this early."

Feminine laughter drifted out through one of the ope
windows from the parlor.

"House is already full of females," Joel said. "Seven gran
daughters, I got, and it takes all but one of 'em—and Doroth
would be here too, if she could—to decorate the house for
birthday party. Plus they brought some friends with 'er
They don't stand still long enough to count, but I think there
eleven of 'em in there."

"Eleven!" Michael braced himself. "Well, all right, let
get on with it. I might as well meet them, save me the troub
tomorrow."

He put an arm around Jessie's shoulder and hugged he
"How long you and Grandpa been married now? Over for
years, isn't it? Forty-one? Well, I tell you, you point out a gi